1634:
THE RAM
REBELLION

Baen Books by Eric Flint

Ring of Fire series:
1632 by Eric Flint
1633 by Eric Flint & David Weber
Ring of Fire ed. by Eric Flint
1634: The Galileo Affair by Eric Flint & Andrew Dennis
Grantville Gazette, ed. by Eric Flint
Grantville Gazette II, ed. by Eric Flint
1634: The Ram Rebellion by Eric Flint with Virginia DeMarce et al.
1635: Cannon Law by Eric Flint & Andrew Dennis (forthcoming)
Grantville Gazette III ed. by Eric Flint (forthcoming)

Joe's World series:
The Philosophical Strangler
Forward the Mage (with Richard Roach)

Mother of Demons

The Shadow of the Lion (with Mercedes Lackey & Dave Freer)
This Rough Magic (with Mercedes Lackey & Dave Freer)

The Wizard of Karres (with Mercedes Lackey & Dave Freer)

Rats, Bats & Vats (with Dave Freer)
The Rats, the Bats and the Ugly (with Dave Freer, forthcoming)

Pyramid Scheme (with Dave Freer)

Crown of Slaves (with David Weber)

Boundary (with Ryk E. Spoor)

The Belisarius series, with David Drake:
An Oblique Approach
In the Heart of Darkness
Destiny's Shield
Fortune's Stroke
The Tide of Victory
The Dance of Time

The General series, with David Drake:
The Tyrant

1634:
THE RAM REBELLION

ERIC FLINT
with Virginia DeMarce

1634: The Ram Rebellion

This is a work of fiction. All the characters and events portrayed in this book are fictional, and any resemblance to real people or incidents is purely coincidental.

A Baen Books Original

Baen Publishing Enterprises
P.O. Box 1403
Riverdale, NY 10471
www.baen.com

ISBN 10: 1-4165-2060-0
ISBN 13: 978-1-4165-2060-7

Cover art by Tom Kidd

First printing, May 2006

Distributed by Simon & Schuster
1230 Avenue of the Americas
New York, NY 10020

Library of Congress Cataloging-in-Publication Data

Flint, Eric.
  1634 : the Ram rebellion / Eric Flint with Virginia DeMarce.
    p. cm.
"A Baen Books original."
 ISBN 1-4165-2060-0
1. Thirty Years' War, 1618-1648—Fiction. 2. Germany—History—1618-1648—Fiction. 3. Americans—Germany—Fiction. 4. West Virginia—Fiction. I. DeMarce, Virginia Easley, 1940- II. Title.

PS3556.L548A6184   2006
813'.54—dc22

                                                              2006005327

10 9 8 7 6 5 4 3 2 1

Printed in the United States of America

Map of the
United States of Europe

As of March, 1634

CAST OF CHARACTERS

German Nobleman and Officials

Bayreuth, Christian: Margrave of Brandenburg-Bayreuth, ally of Gustavus Adolphus

Bimbach, Fuchs von: *Freiherr,* estates both near Bayreuth (headquarters and Schloss there) and near Gerolzhofen; leader of the opposition to the NUS administration in Franconia and to the Ram Rebellion

Dantz, Adrian von: Pomeranian captain in Swedish army stationed in Grantville

Faber: Bamberg city councilman

Seifert: Head of Bamberg city council

Felder, Bruno: Commander of the Swedish garrison in Suhl

Hesse-Kassel, Wilhelm V: Duke of Hesse-Kassel, ally of Gustavus Adolphus

Krausold, Johann Friedrich: Saxe-Weimar treasury official sent to Würzburg with the auditors; informant for Wilhelm Wettin

Lenz, Polykarp: Adviser to Freiherr Fuchs von Bimbach

Wettin, Wilhelm: Formerly Wilhelm, Duke of Saxe-Weimar; leader of the opposition party

Members of the Ram movement

Ableidinger, Constantin: School teacher in Frankenwinheim, organizer of the Ram Rebellion

Blumroder, Ruben: Gun manufacturer in Suhl

Jost, Gerhardt: *Jaeger;* associate of Constantin Ableidinger in the Ram movement

Kronacher, Else: Printer's widow in Bamberg; the "ewe" of the Ram Rebellion

Kronacher, Martha:	Daughter of Else Kronacher
Neideckerin, Judith:	Mistress of Freiherr Fuchs von Bimbach
Neideckerin, "die Alte":	Boardinghouse keeper in Bamberg; widow, mother of Judith Neideckerin
Vulpius, Kaethe:	Wife of Rudolph Vulpius
Vulpius, Rudolph:	Mayor of Frankenwinheim

Officials of the New United States

Bellamy, Arnold:	Deputy, then Secretary of the NUS Department of International Affairs after Ed Piazza becomes President of the NUS
Carstairs, Liz (Thornton):	Chief of Staff for Mike Stearns 1632; later for Ed Piazza; president of Grantville LDS Relief Society and secretary of the League of Women Voters
Hatfield, Anse:	Warrant officer in TacRail; NUS military representative to Suhl
Junker, Egidius "Eddie":	Law student at the University of Jena; later assistant to Noelle Murphy
Murphy, Noelle:	Grantville tax official; special envoy and general troubleshooter for Mike Stearns and Ed Piazza in Franconia
Stearns, Rebecca "Becky":	Wife of Mike Stearns; national security advisor 1631; senator in the NUS (New United States) 1632; daughter of Balthasar Abrabanel
Stearns, Michael "Mike":	Head of RoF Emergency Committee; later President of NUS; later prime minister of USE
Piazza, Ed:	Secretary of the NUS Department of International Affairs; succeeds Mike Stearns as President of the NUS in autumn 1633
Rau, Jochen:	Corporal, NUS TacRail unit, assigned

	to Suhl with Anse Hatfield
Riddle, Veleda:	Founder and President of Grantville League of Women Voters; mother of NUS Chief Justice Charles (Chuck) Riddle
Swisher, Jamie Lee:	Staff member, NUS Department of International Affairs
Sybolt, Red:	UMWA organizer, working in Bohemia as one of Mike Stearns' unofficial troubleshooters

NUS officials in Franconia, headquartered in Würzburg

Salatto, Steve:	Chief civilian administrator in Franconia, headquartered in Würzburg; married to Anita Masaniello
Blackwell, Scott:	Chief military administrator in Franconia, headquartered in Würzburg
Haun, John Frederic "Johnnie F.":	Head of NUS "Hearts and Minds" team in Franconia, headquartered in Würzburg
Masaniello, Anita:	NUS official in Würzburg, married to Steve Salatto
Meyfarth, Johann Matthaeus:	Lutheran pastor, poet, diplomat; chief of staff for Steve Salatto in Franconia; founder of a new Lutheran congregation in Bamberg
Petrini, David:	NUS economic liaison in Franconia, headquartered in Würzburg
Weckherlin, Georg Rodolf:	Poet and diplomat, originally from Wuerttemberg; previously stationed in England; succeeds Johann Matthaus Meyfarth as chief of staff for Steve Salatto in Franconia, stationed at Würzburg
Wendell, Saunders:	Deputy to Steve Salatto in Franconia, stationed in Würzburg

NUS staff in Bamberg

Hawker, Stewart:	Head of NUS "Hearts and Minds" team in Bamberg
Jackson, Wade:	UMWA official in NUS administration in Bamberg
Kacere, Jane "Janie":	NUS real estate specialist in Bamberg
Kacere, John Christopher:	NUS economic liaison in Bamberg, married to Janie Kacere
Marcantonio, Vincent:	NUS head civilian administrator in Bamberg
Miller, Walter "Walt":	NUS military in Bamberg, dealing with Forchheim fortress, assigned to the Special Commission on Religious Freedom in Franconia
Priest, Cliff:	Captain, NUS head military administrator in Bamberg
Trelli. Matthew "Matt":	NUS military in Bamberg, dealing with Kronach fortress, assigned to the Special Commission on Religious Freedom in Franconia

NUS staff in Fulda

Beattie, Orville:	Head of NUS "Hearts and Minds" team in Fulda
Jenkins, Wesley:	NUS head civilian administrator in Fulda
Utt. Derek:	NUS military administrator in Fulda

Auditors assigned to Franconia

Fodor, Willa:	NUS auditor in Franconia, mother of Lynelle Calagna
McIntire, Estelle:	NUS auditor in Franconia
Utt, Maydene:	NUS auditor in Franconia

Special Commission on Freedom of Religion

Calagna, Lynelle (Fodor):	Wife of Paul Calagna; daughter of Cyril and Willa Fodor
Calagna, Paul:	Member of the Special Commission
Early, Mark:	NUS military in Fulda, assigned to the Special Commission
Ellis, Reece:	Member of the Special Commission
Longhi, Philip:	Member of the Special Commission

Members of LDS (Mormon) Church active in Franconia

Carstairs, Howard:	LDS member in Grantville; husband of Liz (Thornton) Carstairs
Thornton, Willard:	LDS missionary in Franconia
Thornton, Emma (Davidson):	High school English teacher in Grantville, wife of Willard Thornton
Faerber, Lydia:	Wife, later widow of Councilman Faerber in Bamberg; convert to LDS church

NOTE ON TERMINOLOGY:

"Ewegenia": Depending on time and place, can be either the head of Veleda Riddle turned into a sheep as the symbol of the Franconian League of Women Voters or the name assigned to Else Kronacher as the "ewe" of the Ram Rebellion

Table of Contents

Preface

ERIC FLINT

This is something of an oddball volume, so it's perhaps fitting that it has an oddball history. Many of the stories contained herein first saw life as stories intended to be published in the electronic magazine devoted to the 1632 series, the *Grantville Gazette*. (Of which, seven volumes are now published, and the first two in a paper edition as well.)

As I watched these stories being written, however—originally with no overarching framework—it occurred to me that, willy-nilly, the writers were in fact shaping the way in which the revolution begun by the Ring of Fire was starting to have an impact on central Germany.

Once I realized that, this volume was born. I had long intended to write a companion volume to *1632, 1633* and *1634: The Baltic War*, that would depict the same events covered in those novels but with a focus that you might call closer to ground level. (*1632* and *1633* are already in print. David Weber and I are now close to finishing *1634: The Baltic War*.)

It's in the nature of fictional narrative that an author tends, whether he agrees with the Great Man theory of history or not—and I happen to despise it—to write stories that focus on "great heroes." It's simply hard to avoid that, given the dramatic imperatives of story-telling.

But such stories give a skewed view of the way human events unfold. People in their great numbers are creators of their own history, not simply the passive material from which history is shaped. The purpose of this book, more than any other, is to depict that in the form of fiction.

It's an oddball volume, as I said, something of cross between a traditional anthology and a novel. There are many different stories in these pages, written by many different authors. At the same time, all the stories share not only a common setting but a common story arch and a common plot thread—as obscure as that may seem to the reader in the first two parts of the book.

Virginia DeMarce and I provided that, partly in stories we wrote separately, but especially in the short novel we co-authored that concludes the volume and shares the same title: *The Ram Rebellion*. All the separate threads that are first introduced in Parts I and II begin to come together in Part III, and reach their final culmination in Part IV.

So what to call it? I don't know, to be honest. Let's just settle for "a 1632 book," and I hope you enjoy it.

Part I: Recipes for Revolution

The hand of the Lord came upon me, and he brought me out by the spirit of the Lord and set me down in the middle of a valley; it was full of bones. He led me all around them; there were very many lying in the valley, and they were very dry. He said to me, "Mortal, can these bones live?" I answered, "O Lord GOD, you know."

Ezekiel 37:1-3

Cookbooks

Eric Flint

June, 1631

After Melissa Mailey ushered Mike Stearns into her living room and took a seat on an armchair facing him, she lifted her eyebrows. The expression on her face was one that Mike still remembered from years earlier, when he'd been a high school student and Melissa had been the most notorious teacher in the high school.

Which she still was, for that matter.

For the adult population of Grantville, Melissa's notoriety stemmed from her radical political opinions. For her students, however, that notoriety had an entirely different basis. Whatever flamboyantly egalitarian views Ms. Mailey entertained regarding society as a whole, there was not a shred of evidence for them in her classrooms.

The students who thought she was basically okay—Mike himself had been one of them—called her either *The Schoolmarm from Hell* or *Melissa the Hun*. Behind her back, of course. The terms used by other students went downhill from there. Very rapidly downhill, in many cases.

Granted, all of her students would admit that she was fair. But *fair* is not actually a virtue admired in a schoolteacher, by her students, especially when it was almost impossible to slide anything by her.

Merciful, yes; *easy-going*, yes; *absentminded*, best of all.

Fair, no.

As one of Mike's schoolmates had grumbled to him at the time, "Who cares if she's 'fair'?" The boy pointed an accusing finger at the book open before him on the cafeteria table. "So she's making all of us read this crap, equally and with no favoritism. Gee, ain't that great?"

Mike grimaced. The volume in question was Dante's *Inferno*, a book he had soon come to detest himself. Ms. Mailey's notions of "suitable reading" for teenagers bore no relationship at all to what teenagers thought themselves.

" 'Fair,' " his friend continued remorselessly, the accusing finger still rigid. "Sure she is. Just like Satan himself, in this miserable book."

The expression on Melissa's face today was the same one Mike remembered from years before. The aloof, questioning eyebrow-lift with which she greeted a student who approached her with a problem after class. A facial gesture which, somehow, managed to combine three different propositions:

One. You wish?

Two. Yes, I will be glad to help you.

Three. You will almost certainly wish I hadn't.

"You've got the oddest look on your face, Mike," Melissa said, bringing him back to the moment. "What's up?"

He smiled, a bit sheepishly. "Just remembering . . . Ah, never mind. I need your advice."

"Yes?"

That was point one. Fearlessly, Mike plowed on.

"It's fine and dandy for me to give a fancy public speech about launching the American revolution ahead of schedule, now that our town is stranded in seventeenth-century Europe. I even got elected head of the emergency committee, because of it, thanks to you. But now, ah . . ."

"You've got to put your money where your mouth is. And you don't really know where to start, other than with some fine generalities—very vague, very politicianlike—about freedom and equality." She leaned forward in her chair, lacing her long fingers together. "Yes, I understand. I'll be glad to give you whatever advice I can."

Point two, coming like the tides. Paralyzed for a moment, Mike studied her fingers. Very elegant and aristocratic fingers, they were.

Absurdly so, really, for a woman with her political attitudes.

"Ah. Yes. I was thinking maybe . . ."

But Melissa was already shaking her head. Another characteristic Mike remembered. Melissa Mailey was no more likely to let a student frame their own question than she was to provide them with an answer they wanted.

"Start with the land problem," she said firmly. "It stands right at the center of any revolution that shatters the old regime and ushers in democracy and the industrial revolution. That was true even in our own American revolution, though most people don't realize it."

He couldn't think of anything better to say than he had as a teenager. "Huh?"

She smiled. Very coolly, as he remembered her doing. "Mike, it's complicated. Land tenure is always complicated, especially in societies with a feudal background—and there's nothing dumber than trying to carry through a revolution based on misconceptions. For instance, you're probably assuming that seventeenth century German farmers are a bunch of serfs toiling on land owned by the aristocracy. So the simplest way to solve their problem is to expropriate the land from the great nobles and turn it over to the peasants."

He emitted the familiar response he remembered from high school. "Uh. Well. Yeah."

That firm, detestable headshake.

"Not in the least. That's true in eastern Europe, if I remember correctly, but it's not true here. Mind you, my memory of the details of German social history in the early modern period is a little vague, now. I haven't studied the subject since college, because it's not something we teach in this high school. Or any high school in America, so far as I know. But I remember enough to tell you that land relations in Germany in this day and age are a tangled mare's nest. If we approach it the wrong way, we're just as likely to infuriate the farmers as the nobility, which is the last thing we want to do."

She rose, moved over to one of the bookcases in the living room, and deftly plucked out two of the volumes there. "I've still got some of the relevant books, fortunately, and I've been refreshing my memory these past few days."

Then, as Mike feared she would, she came over and handed one of them to him.

Blessedly, the more slender volume.

"Start with this one. It's Barraclough's *The Origins of Modern Germany* and it's still—for my money, anyway—the best general history on the subject, even though it was written half a century ago."

Quickly, and as surreptitiously as possible, he flipped to the end of the book.

Not surreptitiously enough, of course.

"Oh, grow up," she said. "It's not even five hundred pages long. You can read it in a few days. What's so funny?"

Despite himself, Mike had started chuckling.

"Dante's *Inferno* was shorter than this, and you gave us a month to read that one."

"You were a callow youth, then. Besides, it was in *terza rima* and this is simple prose. So stop whining. Now . . ."

A moment later, the other book—the great, fat, monstrous tome— was deposited firmly in his lap. It was all he could do not to groan.

"Then read this one."

The size of the thing would have been bad enough. The title— *Economic History of Europe*, for the love of God—made it even worse.

"For Pete's sake, Mike, it's just a book. Stop hefting it as if I were asking you to lift weights."

"Be easier," he muttered. "What'd they print it on? Depleted uranium?"

She returned to her seat. "Make fancy speeches, get elected the big shot, pay the price. No pain, no gain. And if you think that book looks like a bitch, wait'll you—we, I should say—run into the real world."

And that, too, he remembered. Such an oddly contradictory woman.

"Isn't that word politically incorrect?"

"Sure is. Ain't life a bitch?"

She was grinning, now, nothing cool about it.

Walking back to his house—listing, some, from the weight of the books tucked under his arm—Mike started muttering to himself.

"Point three. I almost certainly wish I hadn't."

The worst of it, of course, was that it wasn't true, and Mike knew it. In the times coming, the books would look like a piece of cake, compared to the real world.

It's complicated . . . coming from Melissa Mailey . . .

"Damn," he muttered. "Can't we just dump some tea leaves in a harbor somewhere, storm a famous prison or two, and be done with it?"

Birdie's Farm

GORG HUFF AND PAULA GOODLETT

Part I

June, 1631

"Birdie" Newhouse stood on his back porch and looked over his farm. Looked over, in fact, what was left of his farm. The farm was a little chunk of Appalachian valley, which was abruptly cut off by a German granite wall. The farm had been about half again as big before the Ring of Fire, but even then it hadn't been big enough to make a real living.

Out to one side of the remainder of the farm, there was a little bit of field that you could plow, if you were real careful about the contouring. Most of his farm, though, consisted of skinny trees holding on to the hillside for dear life. A dry creek ran through the middle of the property. The creek was going to stay dry, unfortunately. The German land on the other side of the cliff tilted the wrong way to feed the creek.

Birdie's eyes lost some of their worry as he again noticed the wellhead for the natural gas well on his land. He was more thankful every day that he had gone ahead and converted his equipment to work on natural gas. Willie Ray Hudson had made that suggestion several years ago. Birdie was glad he had listened.

Birdie had everything a man needed to make a real farm. There was a tractor, a plow, the works. He even had some livestock, chickens and a couple of hogs.

Buy much to his disgust, Birdie simply didn't have enough land. Even worse, the little bit of land that the Ring of Fire had left him was mortgaged to the Grantville Bank. There was plenty of land on the other side of the cliff created by the Ring of Fire, including a village about a mile beyond it. It wasn't much of a village, according to Birdie's sons Haskell and Trent, who'd been patrolling the area with the UMWA guys. But they said the land was good.

"Birdie," his wife called, interrupting his thoughts, "staring at that wall won't undo the Ring of Fire. Come inside. It's time for dinner."

"Be right in, Mary Lee," Birdie answered, all the while thinking, *There's land on the other side of the Ring Wall, if only I can get it.*

"What do you think Mr. Walker will say?" Mary Lee asked as he was sitting down to dinner. When she was worried about something she couldn't just leave it alone, she had to talk about whatever it was.

"Don't know. Coleman's a decent enough sort but he's still a banker. The Ring of Fire took a third of our land. From where he's sitting, that means we have two-thirds the collateral for our loan. On the other hand, there's a fair bit of property that the bank is gonna get, chunks of land where the owners were outside the ring. Anyway, I think he'd rather extend the loan if he can see his way clear to do it. Maybe he'll give us six months to work something out."

"And what will we have in six months that we don't have now?"

"Well, I've been giving that some thought while I was staring at that damn wall. Maybe, just maybe, I have a solution." He then refused to say another word on the matter, much to Mary Lee's dismay. Birdie loved teasing her like that. It still worked, even after almost thirty years.

Birdie had an appointment with Coleman Walker, but didn't get to talk to him. Coleman was busy trying to set up some kind of money changing business for the Emergency Committee. Instead, Edgar came out to meet him, and escorted him to an office, chattering all the way.

"You know, Mr. Newhouse," Edgar said, "here at the bank, we know that the farmers are going to be really important to the success of Grantville. There's been a lot of talk about that. The Emergency Committee got involved and asked, well, demanded, to tell the truth about it, that the bank put a hiatus on calling in any farm loans for at least a year. Mr. Walker agreed to it, right smartly, too."

Birdie thought that was something of a miracle, all by itself. Getting Coleman Walker to agree to anything "right smartly" hadn't ever happened in Birdie's experience.

"Don't get me wrong, Edgar," Birdie responded, "Coleman's always been a good sort. But, there's got to be a catch in there, somewhere. Spit it out."

"I don't know all the details, Mr. Newhouse. Mr. Walker talked to Mike and Willie Ray, as well as J. D. Richards and some other teachers from the tech school. It seems that the problem, well, one of the problems, is the stock of seeds we have here. We don't have enough improved crop seeds. And there's something about hybrid seeds not breeding true. And even if they did, there still isn't enough."

Edgar's explanation wasn't any too clear, but Birdie got the gist of it. Willie Ray might have to ask the farmers to do things that weren't that profitable in the short run. Things like building up seed stock. Birdie, like many farmers, bought seed every year, instead of saving his own. Saving your own seed hadn't made much sense up-time.

"What it boils down to, is the bank is going to cut all the farmers some slack. Considering the circumstances, what with the Ring of Fire and all, we're giving you a year to get caught up."

Birdie was pretty sure that Edgar wasn't telling him everything. Bankers always acted like it was their own money you were asking them for.

"Suppose I need some more money? Bank gonna be good for that? There's a lot that needs doing, and it ain't getting done for nothing."

"We might loan you more money, Mr. Newhouse. If Willie Ray agrees that what you need it for is important to the town, it's more than likely that you'll get what you need."

All this support came as a bit of a surprise to Birdie. Grantville had never been farming country. The hills were just too steep and the valleys too narrow. The focus had always been on industry of some sort, natural gas, coal mines, even the toilet factory. Just before the Ring of Fire, a fiber optics plant was being built. Farmers had never been a big part of the local economy.

*   *   *

"Poor bastards," Willie Ray remarked when he and Birdie reached Birdie's tractor. Willie Ray had been introducing Birdie to the local farmers. The introduction had been accomplished with gestures, for the most part, with a few badly accented words of German thrown in here and there.

"What happened to them?" Birdie asked.

"From what I gather, Sundremda, that's this little village here, used to have fifteen farming families plus a few folks who had houses and gardens in the village but weren't farmers. There was a blacksmith, a carpenter, and the like. This last year has been rough though. Now there are six farming families and four of those families are part-time farmers. *Halbbauer* the Germans call 'em. 'Half farmers,' that would be in English."

Birdie knew what that was like. He regularly had to work odd jobs to keep the farm going.

"They also lost a bunch of their livestock," Willie Ray continued, "which made getting in this year's crop just about impossible. Some of it was lost to the mercenaries that hit the place a few months back, and some to Remda, a little town that way, a ways, where they ran when the village got hit.

"Ernst, that fella you shook hands with, called it theft when I was out here before with Miss Abrabanel to translate. From what I understand the folk in Remda are saying they took the stock for rent and fines. Then, some bug came up about the same time, and quite a few folks died. So everyone's blaming everyone else and there are law suits goin' both ways. Meanwhile, the folks in Remda seem to figure possession is nine points of the law, so they're holdin' the stock till everything's settled. I'm guessing they're also holdin' the oxen to force the Sundremda villagers to settle their way."

"You clear on what's needed?" Willie Ray asked when he had finished his explanation.

Birdie nodded. He and Willie Ray had walked the fields with Ernst and defined what was needed where. Willie Ray headed back to town and Birdie got to work harvesting and thinking. His farm was just over the Ring Wall, less than a mile away. If he could cut some sort of gap in the Ring Wall this would be the perfect farm for him. He didn't want to put anyone out of their homes but it looked like they needed him as much as he needed the land. Maybe he could buy this place or most of it anyway. Once he got done here he'd go see if Willie Ray would support him with the bank.

July, 1631

Willie Ray had agreed that buying a farm outside the Ring of Fire and near Birdie's place, what was left of it, was a good idea. However; he didn't know much of anything about how Birdie would go about buying a farm here. Birdie had talked to Mackay, who had recommended one of his troops who spoke English and German and knew a bit about farming.

Danny McTavish was willing enough to act as translator and guide, for a fair payment. Fair payment, in McTavish's eyes, was five one-liter plastic soda bottles, complete with their lids, and a gutting knife. Birdie threw dinner into the deal, so they could eat while they talked over the plan. Birdie liked McTavish, anyway. The scruffy Scot sure could use some dental work, but he spoke German and knew the area fairly well.

"Won't work, what you're saying," McTavish said. "You won't be able to buy a farm for the working. Farmers around here are mostly tenants. They don't own their farms the way you up-timers do."

"I didn't really expect them to," Birdie answered. "I was just glad to find out that things aren't as bad as I thought they would be. I never paid much attention to history, back in school. I figured that just because they didn't own their farms, there was no reason I couldn't buy one though."

"You understand, I'm no expert." Danny tugged his goatee, apparently to help organize his thoughts. "You don't exactly buy land here, at least not to use it yourself. What you do is rent a piece of a farming village. Along with the rent you pay, you get some specific rights, all of them written down proper, in the contract. You get a house, or the right to build a house. You get the right to gather or cut a given amount of firewood, and to pasture so many head of cattle or sheep or whatever. It's all specified in the contract. Finally, you get a strip of field to plant.

"Mostly you lease a piece of land for ninety-nine years or three generations, whichever comes first. Now, you don't always go to the laird for this. The laird might have sold off some part, or all of the rents. When that's happened, and I'm told it happens most of the time, there might be a whole bunch of different people, and each one of them owns a part of the rent."

"What does the lord own after he's sold the rents?" Birdie asked "Mining rights?"

"Mining rights belong to the ruler. The laird never had those. Timber rights, probably. Maybe hunting rights. It could be. It depends on how he sold the rents. Sometimes, a laird would even give the rents to someone, like as a dowry or for the support of a relative. Sometimes, all that's left to the laird is the right to control who cuts down how much of the forest. Or, other times, he might have nothing much. It could just be a leftover from when the 'von Somewheres' really were lairds with rights and duties to the folk under them. Back when only a 'von Somewhere' could own land and owning land meant you were a noble. Maybe back then you couldn't sell your land and still have 'von' in front of your name." Danny shrugged. "The truth is I don't know why it's that way. But, I've talked to a lot of farmers since I came here with Captain Mackay, and that seems to be the way it is."

"Do we have to track down everyone that owns a part of the rent if we want to rent a farm in one of the villages around here?"

"If lots of people own a piece of the rent, they generally hire someone to handle the rental. You have to deal with who ever that is, and it's usually a lawyer. The Germanies are a lawyer's paradise."

"What about just going to the guy that owns the land and buying it?" Mary Lee asked.

Danny was shaking his head. "Even if he hasn't sold the rents, the village is probably rented. If you bought the land, you would be the new laird, but the rent contracts would still be there. You couldn't use the land yourself. All you could do is collect the rents. If he's sold the rents, I don't think you'd be buying more than a piece of paper, or maybe hunting rights. If you want to farm, you pretty much have to rent a farm in a village. Then, after you got the rent worked out with the landlord, you have to be approved by the *Gemeinde*."

"The Ge . . . Gem . . . the what?" Birdie asked.

"The *Gemeinde*," Danny explained, pronouncing the word carefully. "All the people who rent land in a village get together to decide what to do and when to do it. I've heard Mr. Hudson say it's sort of a village co-op. Everyone plows, plants, and reaps together, and your 'strip' is your share of the profits. They're usually a bit careful, the

Gemeinde, about who they let rent the farms. Can't really blame them for it, I suppose. You wouldn't want to share the load with someone who wouldn't pull their share, now would you?

"The *Gemeinde* has a right to refuse someone if they can find a reason for it. Usually, they use 'moral turpitude' of some sort. Mostly, the only people they allow to buy in to a village are someone they know, relatives or friends of people that already lived there. What with the war, and all that sort of thing, people are being a bit less particular about who they take on, lately. You'd have to have the animals to plow your fields, and you'd have to have the start-up money."

Come to think of it, the farmers around here are a bit more independent than I would have guessed, Birdie thought. *Kind of interdependent, too.* He sat quietly and considered all this new information for a while and tried to apply it to what he already knew. The farmers in the area had turned out to be different from what he would have expected from his vague memories of high school history classes. They were a lot more like American farmers than the downtrodden serfs he'd thought they'd be, in most ways. The one big difference, which McTavish had just explained, was that seventeenth-century German farmers worked and thought in collective terms, where up-time American farmers were used to operating as individuals.

That meant . . .

Sundremda had about two thousand acres of land but only about three hundred and fifty or so acres were cropland. The rest of the land was forest for firewood and building needs, a carp pond and more grazing land than the village really needed.

The important thing, though, was that Sundremda was missing most of its tenant farmers. So, maybe he could buy the place, or at least buy that part of it that wasn't rented to anyone. Maybe he could buy the rents, and pay himself. He might even be able to get some of the fallow fields as cropland. If he could arrange it, he would have over two hundred acres, maybe even three hundred acres. He would also have grazing rights, rights to a big share of the wood in the forest, as well as rights to the fish in the little pond the village had set up.

Birdie didn't want to just rent his tractor, or his services, he wanted to buy into the village. By preference, he wanted to own his own land. If he couldn't do that, he'd try to buy the rents. At a minimum, he wanted to have a fair say in what got planted where and when. He wanted a vote in how things went down. Now, if he could just figure a way to do it.

*   *   *

"Mary Lee!" Birdie yelled. "Where are you, woman?"

A muffled "Down here" led Birdie to the basement steps, where he heard Mary Lee clattering around. He descended, carefully. The light never had been that great down here.

"What are you doing?" he asked, when he saw Mary Lee was counting things, then writing something on a tablet of paper.

"Taking an inventory."

"Taking an inventory of what? And why? This stuff has been around for years. It's mostly junk."

Mary Lee looked up from her counting with an annoyed expression on her face. "Junk like that old tractor of yours? Junk like those plastic bottles that are bringing about fifteen dollars each? There's no such thing as junk anymore, Birdie, in case you haven't noticed. Even rusty nails are better than no nails at all. There's no telling what we've got in this basement, not to mention what's in the attic. If stuff like plastic soda bottles can bring in that much money, we might get rich from this room. If you don't want to help me here, go do your own inventory."

Mary Lee had been a bit testy lately, to Birdie's way of thinking. Still, she might have a point. He left her to her business and went to do his own inventory.

Birdie came up with a fair amount of stuff with his inventory. He had more than some of his fellow up-time farmers, but not as much as others. There was quite a lot of junk that simply hadn't been worth the cost of repairing up-time, but turned out to be irreplaceable down-time.

With the help of Willie Ray and Danny McTavish, Birdie was able to gauge the down-time value of his stuff pretty well. It was a little frightening, in a way, the number of things that had a value ten or even a hundred times what it had been before. It really gave Birdie an appreciation of mass production. Mary Lee was right about the plastic coke bottles he had given Danny. They were selling for five to fifteen bucks apiece and the knife would sell for about a hundred bucks.

The real money was in the machinery, though. Birdie had two tractors, one that worked, and one that didn't. The one that didn't work wouldn't have been worth repairing up-time. It was over fifty years old and had been sitting in one of his sheds for the last twenty of those years. Now, though, if the engine could be repaired, it was worth the cost of repair and more. Each of his tractors was worth as much as his truncated farm.

There was also the family car, which used gasoline, the farm truck that used natural gas from his well, and two junk cars. Birdie still didn't know exactly what Mary Lee had found in the house. They had lived in this house for over twenty years, raised two children here, and rarely threw anything away. That was about standard, for a West Virginia farm.

Ernst Bachmeier looked at the men before him. The two up-timers he recognized. One was Willie Ray, who had bought the village's crops while the crops were still in the field, and the other was Birdie, who had come out with his tractor and harvested those crops. The Scottish mercenary who was doing the translating made Ernst nervous.

Nervous or not, Ernst dragged his mind back to what the Scot was saying. "Herr Newhouse is a farmer, but a part of his farm was left up-time by the Ring of Fire. He has the tools and equipment to support a farm much larger than he has now, and the skills of an up-time farmer. What he doesn't have is the land to farm, or the knowledge of local conditions."

"With his tractor he would be a great help, and the village needs more people, but we don't have the houses rebuilt," Ernst replied.

"His house is less than two miles from here. He says he can cut a way through the Ring Wall that will let him bring the tractor and other equipment back and forth." There was a short discussion between the Scot and the up-timers, and then the Scot continued. "He does want to build a house in the village, and he wants to make something called a 'septic system,' so that he can have indoor plumbing, but that need not be done this year."

"In that case, it would be very good if he leased a farm in the village. I just wish we could find four more farmers to do the same." Ernst was a bit concerned about getting all the land rented.

"Well, actually, what he would like to do if he can is buy the land rather than rent it. Who owns the village?"

"Until January, the owner was Ludwig von Gleichen-Tonna, the count of Gleichen, but he died without issue and the ownership is in question. Herr Junker is running things because he holds the *Lehen* on the village. He got the *Lehen* from his mother. She was the illegitimate daughter of an uncle of Anna Agnes of Hohenlohe-Weikersheim, who was married to the brother of the count of Gleichen. Anna Agnes of Hohenlohe-Weikersheim is also the niece of William the Silent."

Birdie wondered who William the Silent was. Someone important, obviously.

Ernst was tempted by gossip and yielded to temptation. "They say Lady Anna Agnes bought her cousin a marriage using the leases on Sundremda and some other villages. Herr Junker's mama, she was high strung."

Ernst wasn't really sure about these people from the future buying his village. True, the up-timers had been fair, so far, but how would they treat the villagers if they owned the village? Would they have any need for tenants?

He decided to evade the problem, for the moment. "I really don't know who you would see about buying part of the village."

The soldier talked again to the up-timers then asked about buying the leases.

"That would be Herr Junker, but I doubt he would sell. He sets great store by the villages. They were his mama's dowry."

The soldier didn't bother to consult before asking: "Is he the one to see about renting the parts of the village that aren't rented now as well?"

"Yes. But, I have a question. We do more than plow, sew, and reap. Does Herr Newhouse have tools and machines that will do the other work the village needs?"

There was more discussion back and forth between the Scot and the up-timers.

"Some of it, yes," the Scot finally said. "For the rest, he believes the village could support more nonfarming families to help with the other work. Also, the Ring of Fire means that many things that would have to have been made locally can now be bought in Grantville. Brooms and such things could be bought, instead of being made here. Also, people can be hired as needed from Grantville."

Ernst considered that for a while then nodded. "He should talk to Herr Junker then."

More discussion took place. Then with a wink: "He also wanted to find out the rents. Herr Newhouse prefers not to bargain blind."

Ernst wasn't supposed to be in charge and he knew it. Mercenaries had hit the village a few weeks before the Ring of Fire and he had been sent off to Remda, while others had tried to delay the mercenaries. The delay had worked, but at a high cost. Most of the delaying force was dead. The village had been burned to the ground, and any animal they had been unable to evacuate or hide had either been butchered or taken by the mercenaries. Two days after their victory, the mercenaries had left, and the survivors had returned soon after that.

Ernst was convinced that the sickness that had afflicted the survivors was a result of their stay in Remda. During the next two weeks, disease had killed almost half the survivors.

Ernst had the village's contracts with Herr Junker and the records of who was owed what. He knew about The Battle of the Crapper and believed it would be good to be connected to people who could defend the village. Still, Ernst was a bit nervous about the up-timers. He did show them the record books and helped to explain what each clause meant, but he didn't tell them everything. For instance, he didn't mention what Herr Junker had said about offering new tenants a break on the rent. The break would only be good for a few years, just to help the tenants to get started.

"Claus Junker is a good *Lehen* holder. He is knowledgeable and reasonable about the rent, but he is stuffy. His mother was of noble blood even if she was born on the wrong side of the blanket. He expects to be treated like a von Somewhere. We humor him, and he treats us well."

The Scot laughed. "That could be a problem. These up-timers have enough trouble treating a real noble like a noble. I don't know how they'd do with someone who just thinks he's a noble." Then the Scot turned to the up-timers to explain his comment.

"I don't suppose you could explain what '*Lehen*' means, can you?" Birdie asked McTavish.

"Nah," McTavish answered. "It's not always the same thing. Sometimes the holder of the *Lehen* has the right to collect rents, but the laird has the right to do all the bossing around of the folk. Other times, the holder of the *Lehen* does all the bossing. Sometimes the laird still lives in the district, and can put a stop to problems. Sometimes, he only comes to hunt. 'Tis verra confusing."

"Are you saying that I could rent this farm, and some joker could still come and tell me how to do my business?"

"I'm not sure. Might be." McTavish grinned. "Reckon it'll be fun finding out, won't it?"

*   *   *

"They have no concept of their place in the world." Claus Junker complained again.

His wife Clara, though in basic agreement, had heard it all before.

With the up-timers' proven knowledge and ability, they should have been acting like nobility. Instead, they permitted the marriage of a camp follower to one of their young men. That support was a slap in the face for all the nobility.

Claus felt this slap especially keenly because he wasn't quite noble. His mother had been of noble blood but his father was no more than a wealthy merchant. His parents hadn't had a very happy marriage. His father had married because that's what his family wanted. His mother had felt that she was being married beneath her station and had virtually been forced by her family to accept the marriage. It hadn't taken long before both had become convinced that each had gotten the worst of the deal. The result was that Claus' mother had focused on her pedigree, clouded as it was, and impressed her son with his rank and the noble blood of his ancestry. He had been her pet, and had not gotten along with his father.

Clara had known all this for years. She was the daughter of another wealthy property owner. Her marriage to Claus, while more romantic than his parents' marriage had been, had still had a significant mercantile component.

Sometimes Clara felt that Claus' emotions got in the way of his normal good sense. Areas like his unreasonable rejection of certain offers from certain up-timers. Not to mention the way he objected when she ventured to offer an opinion on his business ventures. Clara had been raised to be the wife of a man of business like her father and brother, the social half of the equation and a help in business matters. Claus was all right with the social part but less comfortable than her family with the business part.

She manipulated Claus subtly, which didn't come naturally to her. Still, she had had a lot of practice over the years. "Yes, Husband, but we must still deal with them, like it or not. They have the force of arms to coerce our compliance. Besides, they don't seem to have the subtlety of nobles. With care, these up-timers should be easy enough to manipulate to our profit."

"And how, my dear wife, do we profit by the loss of our lands? The

Ring of Fire took land that had been in my mother's family for over a hundred years and replaced it with this West Virginia. The Ring of Fire left people that will not recognize my claim or pay my rents. How does that profit us? Now, to add insult to injury, this Newhouse person calmly informs me that he would like the rest of Sundremda to add to what he's already living on."

"All these things haven't been decided, not yet. The up-timers talked about reasonable compensation when they met with the council," Clara answered. "Besides, it's all the more reason to do business with them. Doing business offers the opportunity to regain at least a part of what we have lost. If we refuse to talk to them or deal with them, how can we persuade them that our claims are truly just?" *This isn't going very well,* Clara thought as she spoke.

The paper Claus was waving about as he talked was the problem. The paper contained an offer to buy both the land and rents for five farming plots in the village of Sundremda. Herr Newhouse wanted to gain clear title to the land if he could. He offered what Clara considered a fair price for it. If that wasn't possible he wanted to buy, for less money, the rents for the same five farming plots. Failing that, in turn, he offered to rent the five plots for a lot less money.

It was clear that Mr. Newhouse wanted to actually farm the land, whether as owner, *Lehen* holder or tenant. The offer was for far more land than would normally be used by a single farming family, and it included provisions to treat the "tractor" as a replacement for several teams of horses. How did one judge the value of a tractor? If tractors were as good as the reports suggested, perhaps it *could* replace several teams of horses.

The offer was a godsend for the Junker family. The village farms would be fully rented and that would be a windfall. The Junkers had expected to lose most of the rent this year and probably next year as well. This farmer, Mr. Newhouse, had done his homework. He was offering what the other farmers in the village paid, maybe a little less, but that was understandable, given the circumstances.

Claus' problem with the offer was that it came from Mr. Newhouse. Mr. Newhouse's farm within the Ring of Fire was on land that would have been part of Sundremda, if the Ring of Fire had not happened. To Claus, it seemed the Ring of Fire had deposited squatters. Worse, they were squatters who then refused to pay his lawfully due rent. The fact that the land that was there now was worth considerably more than the bit of forest that had been there before only made it worse.

"Very well, then. We will see if we can profit from these rich up-timers." As Claus sat down and began to write, Clara shook her head and retreated. You could only push Claus so far before he snapped back hard. At least he would respond, and perhaps he was even accepting the offer.

The letter to the lawyer representing Birdie Newhouse was polite enough.

"Please inform Herr Newhouse that there is no one available at this time from whom he could purchase the property in question. Further, I will not consider the sale of the rents in question because they are an inheritance from my noble mother and have great sentimental value. Finally, the Ring of Fire has caused an unfortunate loss in revenues by removing lands owned by my family for generations. Herr Newhouse is now living on some of that land. Due to this loss, I will be forced to charge higher rents to new tenants than had previously been my policy. Surely, with the greater efficiencies of his mechanical arts, he can afford these higher rents."

The letter went on to suggest a rent four times as high as Birdie's original offer.

The letter came at a bad time. Birdie was having some problems of his own. The old tractor was high on the repair list because farming equipment came right after military needs, but that didn't change the cost of the repairs. The tractor was going to have to be taken completely apart and several parts would have to be especially machined before the tractor would work again. The tractor would also need to be converted to the use of natural gas. The cost of repairing the old tractor left Birdie stuck between a rock and a hard place.

If he had the old tractor fixed and then sold it to the grange Willie Ray was setting up, he might break even on the deal. To make any profit from selling a tractor, he was going to have to sell the newer tractor. Birdie would have to sell the tractor with the enclosed cab, heat, air conditioning, tape deck, and more horse power. Birdie loved that tractor.

So, when the lawyer from Badenburg brought Claus Junker's counter offer, Birdie was quick to suggest that Claus Junker depart to have intimate relations with an aquatic avian that quacks. This, in the cruder form that Birdie used, was Birdie's favorite expletive phrase, and was also the main reason he was called Birdie. Well, his given name, Larkin, might have had something to do with it, too.

After refusing Junker's counteroffer, Birdie then proceeded to go looking for better deals. The news was not great. It turned out that buying land mostly amounted to buying it three times. First, you had to buy the land, then you had to buy any *Lehen* that existed on the rents, and finally you wound up buying out the contracts with the tenant farmers. This didn't just mean three price tags. It meant getting lots of people to agree. All the people involved knew that one holdout could blow the deal. It took lots of money or lots of clout or both. Birdie imagined that it was something like putting together a big real-estate deal up-time. Just renting he could do. He could lease four or five sections and end up with about the same amount of land to farm, but those sections were spread out among two or three villages. Birdie wasn't the only up-time farmer looking for land.

When the few farmers in the area realized that they needed to grow more than hay for their horses or corn for moonshine, and especially after Willie Ray—*that duckfucker*—had gone around pointing out the benefits of renting land, most of them started looking for better land to farm outside the Ring of Fire.

"Larkin Newhouse, if you slam one more cabinet door, I'm going to throw this frying pan at you!" Mary Lee snapped. "Yes, I know you're mad, the whole world knows it. They can hear you slamming doors all the way to Paris. Knock it off."

Birdie started to say something, then thought better of it. It was kind of hard to make Mary Lee mad, but it could be done. Right now, after discovering that both daughters-in-law and all five grandchildren were going to have to move in, Mary Lee was a bit short-tempered herself. Love all the grandkids or not, it would make for a crowded household. Birdie knew it would be an adjustment, but rents in Grantville had skyrocketed. The boys, Heather, and Karin needed their help.

"I'm sorry, Mary Lee. I'm just . . . well; I don't know what I am, anymore. What a mess this is."

Mary Lee's face softened a bit at his apology. "I know. I really do," she said. "But tearing the cabinets off the walls isn't going to help. Go outside and kick something if you have to, go build something, anything. Just get out of the house and quit driving me crazy, will you?"

As Birdie complied with her "request," Mary Lee heard a soft snicker. McTavish had shown up again this morning, looking like a lost pup. You almost had to invite someone who looked that sad to breakfast, didn't you?

"It's a hard thing, Missus, a hard thing, to want something so bad and not be able to do it."

"True, Mr. McTavish, very true. And it's just about time to see if something can be done. I'm going to need your help. Are you free tomorrow?" Mary Lee asked.

"Might be. For a small consideration."

"And just what kind of 'small consideration' did you have in mind, Mr. McTavish?"

"It's a bit fond I am, of your cooking, Missus. There's a plan you have, and I'm thinking I know what it is. We'll be going to Badenburg, will we not? I'll be helping you and I'll be keeping my mouth shut about it, if you like. That is, I'll do it in exchange for an open invitation to your table, whenever it is that I'm here."

Mary Lee decided it was time to take matters into her own hands. Men had a tendency to get, well, masculine. They stood on their pride and kept things from getting done. The next day, she told Birdie that she had some shopping to do. This was literally true, since she was shopping. She just didn't mention that she was shopping for land and doing it in Badenburg. She took Danny with her to translate, and caught the bus into Grantville. There she hired transport to Badenburg, and went to see Mrs. Junker.

"You'll be wanting to act the lady with this one, Missus," McTavish suggested. "You'll be needing to treat me as they treat their own servants."

When he explained what that meant, Mary just shrugged and went along with his suggestion. She wasn't going to the Junkers to convert them to civilized behavior, after all. She was going to see them to get the best price she could on land. Mary Lee had no particular objection to painting her belly button blue, if that's what it took.

She wore a calf-length paisley skirt, along with high-top boots, and a faux-silk blouse which was actually made of irreplaceable Dacron. The Dacron probably made the blouse cost more than silk. In the time since the Ring of Fire, Mary Lee had learned that patterned cloth was either not to be had, or expensive as all get out. She had picked her outfit carefully. She also wore her fanciest wrist watch. In short, her outfit screamed *status*.

Mary Lee and Danny waited in the front room for about fifteen minutes before Mrs. Junker arrived, obviously wearing her best outfit. She introduced herself as "Clara Kunze, Frau Junker." Danny translated.

Conversation was slow and stilted at first, especially with the delays for translation.

"It is a lovely fabric you are wearing, Frau Newhouse," Clara remarked. "Very colorful."

"This old thing?" Mary responded. "I'm afraid I've had it for ages. It's just so practical to wear here. I find that some of the up-time clothing causes comments here in Badenburg. I don't care for public notice."

"Do you come to Badenburg often? I understood that you have a house to keep. Perhaps you have servants who take care of these things for you?"

"Oh, servants aren't really necessary. The machines we have, many of them make housekeeping much simpler."

The women continued to speak of clothing and furnishings, of servants and laborsaving devices. Each woman was getting a feel for the other, and gradually getting used to the translation time. Eventually, Clara said, "I understand that it's not your fault, but the event that you call the Ring of Fire took much of our lands. Isn't it reasonable for us to expect some compensation?"

"Perhaps that is true. But suppose we were to claim the part of our property that extended out beyond the Ring of Fire? I can show you on a map just how far our land extended. Would that be reasonable? Do you think we should have a claim to your land? Before the Ring of Fire I could step out my door and walk onto land that was mine, but now that land is yours.

"We've lost a whole world. All our friends and relations that were beyond the Ring of Fire are gone, along with all our properties outside the Ring of Fire. I sympathize with your loss. I really do. But I think the best compromise, the fairest thing, is to leave it the way God set it."

Mary could see that Clara didn't much care for her counter claim. "God?"

"I think so. I know we couldn't have done it. I guess it could be a natural thing that we don't understand, but to my mind, that still means God did it, or at least allowed it."

The conversation shifted back to safer topics for a while. "I have heard of a thing I do not understand. Perhaps you could enlighten me," Clara said. "What is this thing called a microwave oven?"

"It's another of those labor saving devices, like the washing machine. You can use a microwave to quickly warm food, even to cook it, if you wish. I never really use mine much. I use it to heat cups of water for tea, mostly. They are very convenient, though, for a lot of people."

"And this ice cream I hear of, it is made how?"

"It's a mixture of cream, milk, eggs, sugar and flavorings, perhaps chocolate or strawberries. They are mixed together and frozen. It's quite delicious. My favorite was always butter pecan. Perhaps I'll be able to introduce you to ice cream, someday."

After a time Mary brought up the leasing of farms in Sundremda, or possibly not in Sundremda. Clara suggested that Grantville and its new dollars might cause inflation. "It's new money; how are we to know if it will be worth anything next year?"

Mary had no better answer for that than Clara had had for Mary's point. "I'm not saying you have to take payment in U.S. money. It's what we have, but we can go to the bank and change it."

By the end of their chat, the women had the basics of an agreement worked out. Now, the only trouble would be selling that agreement to their respective husbands.

Neither husband was thrilled with the compromise worked out by their wives.

"I do not trust them, Clara," Claus said, in a worried tone. "They tried to take advantage of you. It is not proper for married women to be involved in matters of business. That is what you have husbands for."

Claus knew Clara was familiar with business, but there was a proper way of doing things. The up-timers didn't seem to respect tradition or custom at all. They seemed to have no standards or morals. It would have been different if Clara had been a widow. Widows had to manage their business affairs. Somehow that thought didn't make him one bit more comfortable with the situation.

"We merely spoke, Claus," Clara answered calmly. "It is true, is it not, that the rents will be welcome? When Frau Newhouse suggested this, I agreed to speak to you, but I did not make an agreement further than that."

"You offered him how much?" Birdie grumped. "Are you out of your mind?" Birdie didn't like the compromise because he felt Mary Lee had been taken to the cleaners. In a way, she had been, but, on the other hand, by up-time standards the rent was actually low.

"Not yet, but I'm going to be. Between you stomping around,

grumbling and griping, and having seven more people in this house," Mary grumped back, "I'll be out of my mind within the month. Do it or don't do it, whichever you want. But I warn you, something has to change, or I'm going to go screaming off into the sunset someday."

In any case the ladies had put a deal on the table. It was a deal that their husbands could live with. Of course, the husbands had to stir the pot a bit. They almost managed to dump the deal a couple of times before they had everything worked out to their satisfaction.

Rent would be paid in local down-time currency at Claus' insistence. There was a provision to adjust the rent based on the average price of half a dozen products. Birdie Newhouse would gain the right to farm two hundred and eighty acres. Fifty of those acres lay fallow this year. He would also have the right to build a house and was allowed to cut sufficient wood to build a two-story farmhouse, a barn and a silo. In addition, he had rights to a certain number of cords of firewood each year. He had the rights to a certain number of animals of varying types, so many fish from the pond each year, and so on. It was all very detailed and specific.

The first year's rent and proof that he had the wherewithal to plow the fields and so on would be required. It had taken a demonstration to convince Junker to count his tractor. His tractor could plow all of the village's fields in less than a week. That was part of the problem. The whole darn village of Sundremda was a single smallish farm by up-time standards. In fact, it was a smallish farm with quite a bit too much pasture in place of crop-producing fields. There was also a lot of forest, to produce the firewood the village needed. It wasn't like West Virginia, where the trees were holding the hillside in place and you couldn't plow anyway with your tractor riding forty-five degrees off plumb. That sort of plowing was plumb dangerous.

If you judged the deal by the contracts of the other Sundremda farmers, the rent Birdie paid should have been worth three hundred and thirty acres, six houses, four times as much firewood as allowed, as well as pasturage for twice as many animals, and twice as many fish.

If Birdie had been a down-time farmer, working with down-time tools, he would have had to hire so many people to help get the crop in that there would be no way he could have paid the rent. If he had been a down-time farmer with refurbished nineteenth-century gear, it would still have been a tough go. As it was, he had a working tractor with several attachments. Birdie's biggest problem was that he would have preferred to have more cropland. He would still be supplementing his income by renting out his tractor to the other farmers in Sundremda, as well as to other local villages.

"I can't believe the rents they're getting," Edgar Zanewicz commented, with a shake of his head.

"Are the evil landlords ripping off the peasants again?" Marlon Pridmore was sipping a cup of the thin soup that had inadequately replaced coffee, while the two loan officers took a break.

"Nope, just the opposite. Birdie Newhouse was just in here wondering about how he was gonna pay the rent on that farming village he's trying to rent from some fella in Badenburg. Turns out he'll be paying less than half of what renting the same sort of farm would cost up-time. And that's with us lowballing the dollar to get it accepted."

"Maybe it's the difference in labor costs? Or productivity?"

"I don't know. It must be something."

They hadn't heard Mr. Walker come in, but they heard him close the door to the break room.

"Quietly, gentlemen." He held a finger to his lips "Shhh! And yes, it is because of differences in labor costs and productivity. Mostly the labor costs, I'll admit. When someone rents a piece of land, the rent has to come out of what's left over after the people working the land have produced enough for their living expenses. Even if those people wear rags and live on the edge of starvation, they still have living expenses. If ten or twenty acres have to provide for a family of four, there's going to be less left to pay the rent than there is if two hundred acres are providing for the same four people.

"You can only get so many bushels of wheat from an acre of land, no matter how many people are working it. After the wheat is sold, and the expenses are paid, including the living expenses, any money that's left over is profit for either the farmer or the landlord. The farming villages are really just farms that need a whole village to farm them, so those farms need to support a whole village rather than a family. When that many people are being supported by one farm, it means that there's less money available to pay the rent."

"Fine, but what's the big secret?" Edgar asked.

"Mostly, the secret is how high up-time rents were. Also, to an extent, just how much less labor is needed by up-time farming methods. All that extra profit can go to several places. It can go to the local landlords to make them richer, it can go to our farmers, or it can go towards bringing down the price of a loaf of bread. I would prefer that those profits go toward bringing down the price of bread. After that I'd like to see them in the pockets of farmers. Making a bunch of down-time landlords rich is right at the bottom of my priority list. I'd be really happy if those landlords didn't realize just how much more the land is worth when it needs fewer people to work it. At the very least, I'd rather they didn't realize it until after they've signed some of these three generation or ninety-nine year contracts. So would Willie Ray, the Mayor, Huddy Colburn, and Thurman Jennings. So, don't go mouthing off about what I've just told you, understand?"

"So, dear, what's the verdict?" Mary Lee asked, with hope in her voice.

"Good news and bad news, just like always," Birdie answered. "Good news is we can pay down the bank loan and get caught up on that. We'll have enough to live on, and pay his damned rent, too, the duckfucker."

"Larkin," Mary Lee responded, this time with a warning in her voice. She never had cared for that particular use of the language.

"Sorry, ma'am." Birdie grinned. He just loved to set her off. "Problem is we've got to cut the slot in that cliff. It's going to cost a bundle. Between that and a few other things that just have to be done, there's not going to be enough left to build a house this winter. Sorry, hon. I know you really wanted it."

Mary Lee's face fell for a moment, but then she shrugged and put the best face on it that she could. "Oh, well, I guess I'm starting to get used to it. I do kind of miss the days when it was just you and me around the place, though. We'll build another house when we can."

Between the sale of the newer tractor and his pay for helping to bring in this year's crop from Sundremda, Birdie would have enough money to pay down the bank loan, pay the first year's rent, have enough to live on, and still be able to make some improvements. Building a house where the mercenaries had burned an old one down would have to wait.

"Fire in the hole!" screamed Johan Jorgen. There was a boom and a bit more of the rock that made up the ring wall was loosened. The explosion didn't cause the ring wall to blow out, or send rocks flying around, at least not much. The wall was simply fractured into smaller pieces which made it easier to move.

"How long are we going to have to look at that pile of rocks?" Mary Lee asked.

"It's gonna take a good long while to get it all moved to Sundremda, even if it's only a couple of miles away," Birdie answered. "There's a mason who's going to come to the village, just because of all this rock. He'll do all the work of making the stone ready for floors and half walls."

"There's an awful lot of it, isn't there?"

"Yep," Birdie agreed, "It ought to make good building material. It's here, it's free, and it's ours. Might as well use it."

Most of those pieces would be shifted to Sundremda. The shifting would happen over the next several months, by means of Birdie's truck, and later the pieces would be used as construction material. The wall had to be removed, anyway, since they had to make a gap for the tractor. Birdie felt that they might as well use the remnants of the wall for something.

There was months of hard labor ahead of them, but Birdie was in a good mood. He was finally getting something done, and he finally had a real farm to look forward to.

Scrambled Eggs

Eric Flint

"Mike Stearns, how in the world did you manage to attend college?" Melissa demanded.

"I didn't graduate," he pointed out, defensively.

"You didn't flunk out the first semester, either. God knows how." Accusingly, her long, elegant forefinger tapped the tome lying on Mike's desk. "You *still* haven't finished it?"

"It's boring," he whined. "Why can't this guy write like Barracuda? That book was pretty good."

"Barra-*clough*. And 'this guy' is actually a pretty good writer himself, for an historian. But Cipolla edited this volume, he didn't write it." In a slightly milder tone of voice, she added: "Academic anthologies are heavier going than single-author books, I'll admit. There's still no excuse for not having finished it."

Mike slouched in his chair, feeling like a seventeen-year-old again. Which meant, under the circumstances, resentful.

"You're not my schoolmarm any more," he pouted. "And I'm not a kid."

"Yes, that's true. On both counts." Ignoring the lack of an invitation,

31

she sat in the chair facing him in his office. "What you are is the leader of a beleaguered new tiny little nation, which is depending on you for its salvation. And I'm one of your advisers. Which means you don't even have the excuse of being a seventeen-year-old twit."

Mike seized the armrests of his chair in a firm grip—he was a very strong man—and glared fiercely out the window.

Then . . .

Said nothing.

"Well, that's good," Melissa continued. "At least you've stopped whimpering. For a moment there, I thought I was going to have to wipe your chin."

A scowl was added to the glare. "Do you know what your students used to call you?"

"*Used* to call me? Don't be insulting. They're still calling me those things, unless I'm slipping. Lessee . . ."

She began counting off on her fingers. " 'Schoolmarm from Hell' and 'Melissa the Hun' have usually been the terms used by the better-brought-up students. From there, manners fly south for the winter. 'The Bitch from Below' has always been popular, of course. The alliteration's pretty irresistible. But I think my personal favorite is 'She-Creature from the Black Lagoon,' although it never made a lot of sense to me. Is there a lagoon anywhere in West Virginia?"

A wince got added to the glare and the scowl. "Well . . . that one's pretty low. A couple of guys in school—never mind who—came up with it one night when they were sneaking some drinks out by the water treatment plant."

Melissa burst into laughter.

Mike couldn't help but grin. "Like I said, low. All right, Melissa. I'll finish the damn thing. But—!" He levered himself upright in the chair. "I will also tell you this. We're not going to find any answers in those books."

"Well, of course not. But they do help frame the questions."

A grunt was as much as Mike would allow in the way of acknowledgement. Not because he disagreed with Melissa, but simply because he really, really, really detested that damn book. Reading a collection of scholarly articles on the economic history of Europe made watching paint dry seem like a form of wild entertainment.

"We'll get our answers in practice, by getting our hands dirty," he stated firmly, feeling a bit pompous as he did so.

"Oh, how charmingly pompous," said Melissa.

Mike winced again. "Well, yeah. But it's still true."

"Of course it is. I've learned a lot just watching the merry-go-round Birdie Newhouse is on. I'd be laughing my head off, except I feel sorry for Mary Lee."

"Ain't that the truth?" he chuckled. "I like Birdie well enough, but he can be a real pain the butt when he decides to be a pain in the butt. Fortunately, it all seems to be working out okay."

"For the moment," Melissa cautioned. "Don't get your hopes up."

"Do you *ever* order eggs sunny-side up?"

"Don't be ridiculous. Eggs are scrambled, Mike. Eggs are always scrambled."

Birdie's Village

GORG HUFF AND PAULA GOODLETT

December, 1631

Things had changed in the last half year. "The Slot," a cut in the Ring Wall twenty-five feet wide, had been made with some expensive explosives and a lot of back-breaking work. Ernst had turned out what was left of the village to help. The summer harvest was in and the winter crop planted. Birdie and his tractor had done most of that work. There were changes Birdie wanted to make in crop choices and rotation. Most of the changes would have to wait till spring.

This winter, Birdie and the villagers were rebuilding Sundremda. The use of the tractor and truck had sped construction phenomenally. Most of the increase in speed was due to getting the building materials where they were needed faster. The equipment let Sundremda recover much more quickly than it would have otherwise. Birdie's involvement also meant that the village could support some extra nonfarming families.

Sundremda had been on the small side of average for a farming village. This meant that Sundremda had less than a larger village would have had in the way of support industries. With Birdie around, though, the village could afford a few more people who were not devoted to farming. Now, there was a new smith. A cooper, a brewer and a mason were moving in and setting up shop. Mostly these people selected Sundremda because rents were cheaper than they were inside the Ring of Fire. The various inhabitants were a pretty standard village comple-ment, except for the mason.

Most villages this size wouldn't be able to attract a mason, because there wouldn't usually be enough work to keep him busy. The mason was finishing stone from the Slot to use in half walls and flooring for buildings and paving for the village square. Later, when work in Sundremda dried up, he would be able to continue his trade, thanks to the transportation available to him in Grantville. His products could be easily transported by Birdie's truck.

Mary Lee's new house kept getting pushed back on the list of things that needed building, mostly at Birdie's insistence. The Newhouse clan already had a house, crowded though it was. Birdie wanted to wait till everything was ready before building the new house in Sundremda. And he took the heat from Mary Lee because when he built the house he wanted to do it right.

Birdie's hogs had been moved to the village and were under the care of Ernst's son. Birdie was convinced that the darned pigs were learning German faster than he was. The chickens were still at the old place. It seemed as though the Newhouse clan lived with one foot inside the Ring of Fire and the other outside. For that matter, so did the people of Sundremda.

Sundremda wasn't really flat until you compared it with the chunk of West Virginia delivered by the Ring of Fire. The village itself sat on a rise that the villagers called a hill. Well, Birdie would call it a hill, too, if he had never seen a West Virginia hill. Every day Birdie took his tractor to Sundremda, and every day he waved at Greta, Ernst's wife, who was headed in the other direction. Greta drove his truck and carried most of the village kids and a few of the women to Birdie's place inside the Ring of Fire.

The village kids loved TV, children's movies, and videotaped car-toons. The cartoons were teaching them such important English phrases as *What's up, doc?*, *Let's get dangerous,* and *Th-th-th-that's all, Folks!* Barney, the disgusting dinosaur, was as popular in this universe as the last, much to Birdie's annoyance. *Sesame Street* tapes were hard to come by, but the few that were found were copied and passed around.

While the kids watched TV, and did lessons, the village women used the food processor, gas range, microwave, and other up-time kitchen gear to cook dinner for the village. It was an assembly line process. There were almost a hundred people in Sundremda now. Using the up-time appliances bought time and freed up extra labor for the village as it got ready for winter.

Birdie had started taking his paper and heading out early to avoid the noise. All those women and children in one place could make quite a racket. Once he got to Sundremda, he joined Ernst and the other farmers sitting around Ernst's new kitchen table. There, they would read the morning papers and plan the day's work.

This morning's paper had a synopsis of an article written for the "Street." The article dealt with how the Federal Reserve system worked, and how it had been implemented in Grantville. It touched on how debased many down-time currencies were. The article also discussed the relationship of goods and services, and money supply, and the effect of not having enough of either.

The article had focused on how conservative the bank of Grantville was. It read like a complaint, but in truth, the article was a sales pitch for up-timer money. It was a good sales pitch, and very persuasive. Birdie was persuaded that Claus Junker just might have fooled himself by insisting on getting the rent in down-time currency. The thought made a good start to the day.

Relations with his down-time landlord had not started well and they had gone downhill ever since. Claus didn't like most of Birdie's improvements and didn't like the influence Birdie was gaining with the other tenants. Birdie didn't like the way Claus treated some tenants better than he treated others. Claus seemed to prefer the tenants that were good at sucking up. Their relations were particularly headed downhill since Birdie had learned that Herr Junker was giving the other new renters, down-timers only, a break on the rent.

Oddly enough, elections were just finished and were still coming up. The elections for delegates to the constitutional convention had ended and the Fourth of July Party had won. The convention was in the process of editing the Fourth of July Party's platform into an actual Constitution. Most of the editing was just so the convention could say that they had actually had a hand in writing the Constitution. Meanwhile, elections for the first Congress and President had already been scheduled.

"This means that we can vote in the next election?" Greta asked Ernst. Ernst was a bit unsure and looked to Birdie for an answer.

"Don't know." Birdie shook his head. "If people have lived inside the Ring of Fire for three months they just have to register; then they can vote. Sundremda ain't inside the Ring of Fire, though."

It was a Saturday afternoon and they were gathered in Ernst's new house. This house was similar to his previous home but still different. This house didn't have indoor plumbing but it was designed to accommodate it. Before the indoor plumbing could be added, Ernst would need to install a septic tank and leach field.

The delay of the installation was partly a matter of expense and partly a matter of timing. He was waiting till spring when the ground thawed. The plumbing still needed to be installed before planting, but he needed to see if they had enough money to install it. This left the house with a bathroom but no bathtub or toilet. At the moment, there was just a covered hole in the floor that had a buried clay pipe leading outside. Birdie and Ernst had also worked out how electricity would be added when it became available.

All this gave the house an odd, half-finished look. That half-finished look was common to the new buildings in Sundremda.

"I have been following the election discussions. This is an important right. To vote is also a responsibility of proper citizens. We should vote," Greta insisted pedantically. Greta could do pedantic better than just about anyone Birdie knew.

Birdie looked at Greta for a moment. He knew that the outcome of this election was pretty much a forgone conclusion. On the other hand, Greta was right. Voting was even more important now than it had been up-time.

"Yes. Yes, it is, but I don't know how we'd go about it." Birdie had sort of fallen into the role of village leader. Partly it was because he was an up-timer and partly because he owned his own land even if he rented land in the village.

"Well, don't you think we ought to find out?" Mary Lee asked, utterly unimpressed by Birdie's newfound status.

"We have discussed this in the village. We all agreed that we wish to be citizens of the New United States. We approve of the Bill of Rights," Greta concluded with certainty.

Liz Carstairs looked at the petition with a sort of bemused incomprehension. The first line read, "A petition to be annexed by

Marion County, New United States." The document went on to give the reasoning behind the request. Sundremda wasn't an independent town but rather a village that was part of a county that no longer existed. Since the death of count Gleichen, who died without heirs, his county had ceased to exist. Legal authority over the territory had gone back to Ferdinand II, the Holy Roman Emperor. Actual ownership of the land was, in this case, a function of legal authority over it. If Ferdinand II continued as the government then he owned the land. If he didn't, then who ever was the government owned the land. In effect the village of Sundremda was public land with a permanent *Lehen* on it.

Ferdinand II's claim was impractical since Ferdinand II didn't actually control this part of the Germanies. Accepting the emperor's authority wouldn't really be in the best interests of the New U.S., either. For the emperor to own land butting up against the Ring of Fire was a bad idea. The document also pointed out that six of the signers were already citizens of Marion County. Even though the signers didn't actually live in Sundremda, they were still legal renters since they were members of Birdie's family.

The document also pointed out that Marion County was the closest county to Sundremda. It gave assurance that the people of Sundremda would abide by the laws of Marion county and the New U.S. Then, the document went on to provide the dimensions of the territory and even included a map. Finally it was signed by every person living in the village of Sundremda, not just all the adult males or even just all the adults. Apparently every person in the village signed the petition, including one three-year-old, who signed with a hand print. The signers gave their name, age, and gender. The signers included, of course, Birdie and Mary Newhouse, their two sons and two daughters-in-law. Apparently, the Newhouse babies hadn't signed on the dotted line.

This petition was going to have to go to Mike. While attitudes toward the Holy Roman Empire were not favorable inside the Ring of Fire, the fact remained that Grantville wasn't actually at war with the Empire, officially. True, Grantville had protected a town from Tilly's mercenaries. Grantville had also protected another town from mercenaries who no longer worked for anyone but themselves. Grantville had cooperated with troops employed by the king of Sweden in doing that protecting, but there wasn't a state of war between the still forming New United States and the Holy Roman Empire.

If the New U.S. approved this petition, a state of war with the Holy Roman Empire would exist. Annexing another country's territory is pretty much universally a *casus belli*, even when the folks who actually live there ask to be annexed.

On the other hand, there might be two or three mental defectives who actually thought Grantville wouldn't be at war with the HRE before long, but not more than that. Besides, Grantville had already offered to admit several cities to the New U.S. As soon as one of those cities accepted admission, it would mean the effective annexation of that city.

As it turned out the people of Sundremda didn't get to vote in that first election. President Stearns had tabled the matter till after the first elections, and then had presented the petition to Congress. Congress had accepted the petition and several others like it. This set at least one precedent of acquisition of territory by the New U.S. So, the people of Sundremda would be able to vote in the next election.

Egidius "Eddie" Junker shook his head, but only after he left his father's office. Eddie liked the up-timers. It was a point of considerable tension between him and his father. They didn't talk about it much. Neither one wanted a breach in their relationship.

"Michel, please have Shadow saddled. Father wants me to visit Sundremda again."

Eddie had picked up the up-time habit of being polite to servants, but not where his father could hear. Eddie was a charming young man, and an excellent rider. He had been a student at Jena when the Ring of Fire happened. He had first encountered Grantville on one of his monthly trips home. The battle of Jena had strengthened his admiration for the up-timers. Eddie was rather less concerned over his ancestry than his father. Nor did he see any reason to be constantly checking on Herr Newhouse.

The ride to Sundremda was pleasant and easy, even if the road from Badenburg wasn't improved all the way. Eddie had known the villagers of Sundremda all his life. He remembered well what the village had looked like before the raid and after. This new village looked like it was going to be a much more prosperous place, when it was finished. The villagers seemed to be leaving quite a bit unfinished till they had everything ready. They had carted, or rather "trucked," a lot of stone from the gap to the village and had a mason finishing stone for floors and the bottom half of walls. Most of the houses had places where the stone floors weren't installed yet. The snows had slowed the work, mostly limiting it to what could be done from inside.

Herr Newhouse was friendly enough, considering the circumstances. "How's school?"

"Confusing, Herr Newhouse. Everyone is trying to figure out what the Ring of Fire means. Especially in the college of theology, but all of us do the same, really. Every time I go back I get questioned on everything. My father wishes to know what this petition for annexation is about."

"You can tell your . . ." Herr Newhouse visibly caught himself. "Never mind, boy, it's not your fault. The petition is just what it sounds like. The village wants to be part of the New U.S. We didn't ask your father about it because we know he's opposed to Badenburg joining the New U.S. Besides, he doesn't live here. We didn't ask Ferdy Hapsburg to sign either."

Ferdy Hapsburg? Ferdinand II, the Holy Roman Emperor? Sometimes up-timers made Eddie nervous. He changed the subject. "How are things here?"

"We're doing all right. Got most of the stone up from the slot and the mason is cutting and finishing it. Everything is a bit crowded this winter but we'll have plenty of stone for our needs come spring. I understand the kids at the high school have some sort of concrete project going so it looks like there will be mortar, too. Talked to Mrs. O'Keefe and she figures she can fit us in once the ground thaws. So we should be putting in a bunch of septic systems come spring."

They discussed the village for some time. Eddie then went home to report to his father and escaped back to Jena as soon as he could.

Spring planting was a little different. Birdie had never really gotten to know Tom Stone. He hadn't really wanted to get to know him. There was a very basic difference between them: Birdie was a solid upstanding hillbilly and Stoner was a hippie freak. Now, Birdie was consulting with Tom Stone on the planting of a new crop.

"This is not a crop I'd ever have dreamed I'd be planting," Birdie remarked. "Never in a million years."

Stoner grinned. "Don't feel lonesome, man. It's the last thing I'd have dreamed of, too. Ten full acres of prime Colombian, and it's planted right out in the open. Man, what a sight that's going to be."

Stoner, in his laid-back way, explained the details of planting to get the best, meaning the most powerful, product. His knowledge of agriculture in general and marijuana in particular was pretty impressive. Aside from breeding for the active ingredient, you also had to plant the marijuana farther apart to get a potent plant. So the number of plants per acre went down when you were planting for dope instead of hemp.

"We're going to need it," Stoner explained. "It's the best locally grown painkiller we have. I'd grow it all, myself, if I could. Just so I could donate it to the hospital."

"Man's gotta make a living, Stoner. I'm growing it for the lowest price I can manage," Birdie explained. "Best I can do."

After much argument, the Sundremda *Gemeinde* had decided that most of this year's crop would be beans and wheat. It would be down-time beans and wheat, at that. Birdie had wanted to plant sweet corn but there wasn't enough seed to go around.

The population of Grantville was getting up to around fifteen thousand and Badenburg had over seven thousand. The population was going up. Consequently Sundremda was switching from growing flax to producing food.

Neither Birdie nor the other farmers in Sundremda were sure that this was the best plan. As the population increased, the need for both food and flax was going up. Flax might have brought in more profit.

"Ernst, the real problem with growing flax is the spinning," Birdie argued. "We can send wheat to Grantville, get it milled real quick, and then the flour can be made into bread when it's needed. Flax will have to be spun into thread and no one has come up with a spinning machine yet. That's the bottleneck."

The down-timers had spinning wheels, but even with spinning wheels, turning flax into thread was a lot of work. Birdie wasn't sure how long reinventing a spinning machine was going to take, but from what the newspapers said, it wasn't going to happen this year.

"The price for flax in the field is going to go down, I think," Birdie continued. "It will have to be shipped to towns and villages all over the place, spun into thread, and then the thread will have to be shipped somewhere else to be woven into cloth."

Spinning was the seventeenth-century version of flipping burgers at McDonald's, except it didn't pay as well, was harder work, and had less opportunity for advancement.

Grantville was the land of opportunity. The spinners would be looking for better ways to make a living and a lot of them would find those better ways. The way Birdie figured it, the increase in demand for cloth was not going to be reflected in an increased price of flax until the spinning bottleneck was fixed.

"Someone will build a spinning machine," Ernst disagreed. "So many people who can build so many things, surely someone will figure out a way to get more flax spun."

"Yep, but it ain't gonna happen soon. And until it does, all it means is more spinners. Spinners who are going to demand, and get, better pay. That's going to mean less money per acre for the raw flax."

Ah, the simple farmer's life. Birdie thought *Predicting market trends a year in advance, and then hoping like hell the weather doesn't screw you over.*

"LaDonna, have you finished all those tax assessments?" Deborah Trout asked, as she breezed into the office. "We need to get the notices sent, even though I dread the reactions we're going to get from the public."

"It's not going to be pretty, that's for sure," LaDonna agreed. "Strange, isn't it? All those years back up-time, and everyone complained about their taxes. Wait until everyone sees the new valuations. We're going to be in hot water with everyone we know. They're going to completely flip out."

"We did tell everyone," Cary Marshall pointed out. "It's been on television, and there have been articles in the newspapers."

"True, absolutely true," Deborah agreed. "And you know as well as I do that the new rate is still going to come as a shock to half the town. People just don't really pay attention until they get the bill. Anyway, we've got about a week of peace and quiet before the frenzy starts, so let's get some work done while we can."

Deborah turned to head back to her own office, but stopped when Noelle Murphy cleared her throat. Noelle always made that sound when she had a question. It was usually a good question, but Deborah had begun to dread that sound. Noelle tended to complicate things unnecessarily, to Deborah's way of thinking.

"Umm, Deborah, I don't know where to send these notices," Noelle began. "There's no owner of record for these properties."

"What properties, Noelle?"

"It's that village, what's its name, Sundremda, I think. The people don't own the property, they just rent it. The guy who has the *Lehen*, well, near as I can tell, holding the *Lehen* isn't the same as owning the property. And, I don't really think that Ferdinand II is going to pay taxes on it, either, since we sort of took it away from him. So, who pays the property taxes on Sundremda?"

Deborah worked through Noelle's logic and sighed. "That's all we need, another complication. I guess Marion County owns Sundremda now that we've annexed it. And the county doesn't pay taxes to itself, does it? So, the county is responsible for yet another piece of property that doesn't bring in any revenue. Crap!"

"Claus, what has happened?" Clara asked. "What is it?"

Claus Junker sat in his home office, devastated. "Pomeroy is dead. The only one of these up-timers I could tolerate, and he is dead in an accident."

It looked to Clara like the news of Guffy Pomeroy's death had hit Claus hard. Claus didn't know that many up-timers, and mostly didn't like the ones he did know. Claus been opposed to joining the New U.S. and believed that his own was the single voice of sanity on the council. Now, the one up-timer that he had liked and trusted was dead.

"The microwave project, it is dead, also. The paper says that Pomeroy was a charlatan and there is no hope for a microwave projector, not for years!" Claus stormed. "And I used funds . . . funds from the town to finance this project, and it will not happen."

Clara felt her stomach clench with fear. "Town funds, Claus? How could you? You never should have trusted that man with so much. Can we pay it back? Before we are disgraced?"

Claus rose from his desk in a rage. He stomped around the room, shouting and swearing. "No, Clara, no, we can't pay it back! This Ring of Fire, it is the work of the devil! Act of God, people say, therefore the rents due me are void. Even the pastor, that Pastor Schultheiss, is preaching that this Ring of Fire was an act of God!" Claus shouted. "The only good thing that came out of the Ring of Fire was Pomeroy. And now, now, I am told that he was a thief, and he has ruined us! There is no hope, they claim, no possible way to create a microwave projector, not for years!"

Claus was becoming incoherent. He continued to rant and shout, at times towering over Clara, at other times stamping around the room. He shouted that all around him people were getting rich from the up-timer's knowledge, and getting above themselves. The riffraff were thrilled with the Ring of Fire, the up-timers, their inventions and their

Committees of Correspondence. Even people that should know better were fawning on the up-timers.

Then the real reason for his rage began to come out. Clara knew as well as Claus that Endres Ritter was just waiting for an excuse to go over the books and accuse Claus of theft. Before the Ring of Fire, a member of the council would have been protected from such an accusation. It wasn't all that unusual, after all. Using city funds for personal advantage was standard practice. As long as the city got its money back it was no problem. Even when something went wrong, there was a slap on the wrist and a lot of looking the other way. Back then, the council wanted to avoid the scandal. But now there was the Ring of Fire and new rules.

The Ritter and Junker families had been feuding so long that most people didn't remember why. Ritter would raise the accusation no matter the scandal to the council. He would raise the up-time cry "freedom of information." Never mind the fact that the Ritter family had done the same thing a few years ago and made a small fortune at the city's expense. That was then; this was now.

Clara Junker was terrified. She left the office as soon as she could get away. Claus had been ready to actually hit her. She was sure of it. Claus had never threatened her with violence before. He was gruff and often sarcastic but not violent, not to those of his own class.

Clara was less involved than she would have preferred in the financial decision-making for the Junker family. She knew that Claus had mostly done a good job. He'd been willing to listen if she was careful how she approached him, at least until the Ring of Fire.

After the Ring of Fire, things at home had gone downhill. Every change the up-timers proposed caused Claus to become more insistent on keeping things the way they were before. Claus became less inclined to listen to her and more insistent that she had no business interfering.

Clara knew that they weren't really worse off than before the Ring of Fire, depending on how much Claus had spent on that microwave business. Clara was beginning to suspect that he had spent much more than she had thought. Still, as everyone around them seemed to be getting richer, it felt like they were worse off. She wished her son Egidius would get home. She didn't want to have to turn to her brother, Franz.

Egidius came into Claus' office while he was going over the books looking desperately for any readily convertible assets.

"Father, what is this I hear?" he asked, insisting on becoming part of the disaster. "What has happened?"

Claus had always tried to keep his son away from the darker aspects of doing business. Yes, everyone did things like using town funds in backing private ventures, and his heir would eventually have to learn that, but not yet.

"It is only a temporary problem," Claus blustered. "I have only to raise some money and it will be overcome. We have assets, after all." The Junker family owned several townhouses in Badenburg, and owned the rents on the village of Sundremda, along with the rents on two other villages that were farther from the Ring of Fire. The family had interests in several trading ventures. Together these things brought in quite a bit of money annually. Unfortunately, most of them were tied up in ways that made it hard to get quick cash out of them.

Claus finally gave in to his son's persistent questions and dogged determination to get to the heart of the problem. When Claus disclosed the amount of money he had invested in the microwave project, Egidius was clearly appalled. That was the hardest thing to take, the disappointment in his son's eyes. Claus gave up and waved Egidius to the accounts and retreated. He felt driven to run from his office by the look in his son's eyes.

Eddie Junker was left alone in his father's office. Since the Ring of Fire there had been quite a bit of talk about the financial innovations the Americans were introducing. At Jena, in the college of law, there was a lot of talk about civil rights, and the concept of equality before the law, but a lot about the up-timer business law and practices. Many of the students would never actually practice law. Like Eddie, they were there to learn enough to be able to deal with the lawyers in their employ, or their family's employ. For them, especially, the focus was increasingly on business law and practices.

There were no colleges of business or economics at Jena, but there was talk of starting one. At least, a college for economics was being discussed. A college of business was considered, well, too plebian. Economics, though, that was a proper theoretical field of study. Determining the GNP might actually be as esoteric as determining the number of angels that can dance on the head of a pin and be useful at the same time.

Eddie's favorite professors were those who were pushing hardest for a college of economics. One of the professors had even been heard to say that a college of business might not be all bad. The notion of treating those necessary matters of business as a science appealed to the professor.

The notion appealed to Eddie, too, especially now. Written there, neat and tidy, in his fathers' books was a tale of disaster waiting to happen. Every ready source of quick funds had already been tapped. The village rents would come due in the fall, too late to help. And even if hadn't been too late, the rents weren't enough.

The Junkers were going to have to sell something. But, selling things meant finding a buyer. There was enough talk in town about his father's failed investment that everyone knew they were in need of quick cash. That would force the prices down. The Junker family would be bargaining from a position of weakness.

"I've been over the books and father's notes," Eddie told his mother. "From what I can tell, this man Pomeroy actually did try to make a microwave. I wish he hadn't. It would have cost less. We do have assets to sell, but we won't be getting a good price for them. By now, everyone knows that father was invested in the microwave project. Everyone will know that we need the money.

"There is one bit of good news. Land prices in and round the Ring of Fire have been going up drastically. The rents are set and we cannot raise them. But, if we can broker a deal where the villagers of Sundremda get the *Lehen* and buy the land from Marion County at the same time, the price will be higher. Owning the land with clear title would make it worth more."

His mother frowned. "Frau Newhouse has told me several times how much she and her husband would like to have clear title to the farm. From what I understand, the government of Marion County doesn't really know what to do with the land. It seems that the county cannot collect taxes on the property, because the county owns the property. It cannot tax itself; there would be no point."

"That makes sense," Eddie said. "They do things one way and we do them another. Trying to make the two ways fit together can't be an easy task."

"You go to Grantville and find out what Marion County would want for their title to the land. I will go see Frau Newhouse and see what the villagers would be willing to pay for clear title."

"Excuse me? You could perhaps direct me?" Deborah looked up to see an attractive young German man standing at her office door.

Poor guy, he looked like he was completely lost.

"I'll be happy to, Herr . . . ?"

"Junker, but call me Eddie, please. Could you perhaps tell me who I would see about property? I have some questions, but so far, three people have sent me to four different places. I have been unable to get an answer."

"Well, ah, Eddie, I guess you've found the right person, at last. At least, I hope I'll be able to answer your question," Deborah answered. "I'm afraid that government agencies, even our government agencies, tend to make finding an answer harder than it has to be, unfortunately. What is your question?"

"*Mein*, ah, my father owns the *Lehen*, the rents for the village of Sundremda. It is possible that he may wish to sell this. But, with all the new laws, the new government, we are not sure how to go about this, anymore," Eddie answered. "Do you know anything about this?"

Deborah remembered the name Junker. This must be the son of the man who had funded Guffy Pomeroy. No wonder he wanted to sell something, from what she had heard Pomeroy had taken him to the cleaners. *Poor man.*

"You've definitely come to the right place, sir. Please sit down, and we'll discuss what to do. I can even tell you why there was so much confusion."

As Eddie Junker took a seat in front of the desk, Deborah began speaking, "You see, before the Ring of Fire there was Grantville. Grantville was a town inside Marion County. Marion County was inside the state of West Virginia and the state of West Virginia was inside the United States of America."

"Back up-time, we had a lot of governments, I'm afraid. We had the town government, the county government, the state government and then the United States government. When the Ring of Fire happened, the only government that came back was that of Grantville, the town."

"When we started rebuilding government functions, we started with the New United States. At the very beginning, the New United States and what was left of West Virginia and Marion County were all the same size. Now, though, the New U.S. has more states but West Virginia and Marion County are still the same territory. West Virginia and Marion County still exist legally but don't exactly have their own governments."

"So, for all practical purposes the state that includes the Ring of

Fire area and now includes Sundremda and some other villages is the same territory as Marion County. That makes Marion County the owner of the property, because the folks in Sundremda asked to be annexed by Marion County."

The young man was clearly baffled by the explanation but trying gamely to follow along.

"Never mind, you've found the right office."

The knock on the front door made Mary Lee want to scream. For the first time in three weeks, she actually had her own house to herself. The quiet and privacy were so welcome that she very nearly didn't answer the door. When the knock came again, though, she got worried that there might be an emergency of some sort. It seemed that emergencies happened every time she had ten minutes of quiet.

Mary Lee pulled the door open with a certain amount of force, prepared to glare at the person who was invading her limited privacy. Her visitor's identity caused her to start in surprise.

"Frau Junker, oh . . . I'm afraid I wasn't expecting you."

Clara smiled politely, "I regret that I did not inform you, so that you might prepare, Frau Newhouse. Do you think that you and I might talk?"

Caught at a disadvantage, flustered and out of sorts in general, Mary Lee sighed internally as she wondered what this visit could be about. "Please, come in. Would you care for a cold drink? I have some tea, chamomile, in the fridge."

"A cold drink, Frau Newhouse? How unusual. Yes, I should like very much to have a cold drink. It is perhaps an imposition, and I regret if it is, but may I see this 'fridge,' did you call it? I have not yet had the opportunity to view the inside of an up-time house."

"Certainly, Frau Junker. I would be pleased to show you around, if you like. Please excuse the disorder. I'm afraid that my grandchildren tend to destroy the place if you don't watch them every second of every minute of every day. The fridge is in the kitchen. This way, please."

As they entered the spacious kitchen, a room that Mary Lee had spent a lot of time and effort making just right, Mary Lee watched her unexpected guest's face. Mary Lee was proud of this kitchen. It was her favorite room, one she was very pleased with. She hoped that Frau Junker wouldn't turn her nose up at her efforts.

It was a great relief when Clara smiled as she gazed around the room. Mary Lee began to relax a bit, and lose some of her irritation.

"It is very lovely, Frau Newhouse. I would never have considered this possible. So bright and colorful. Such light. It does not look like any kitchen I have ever seen."

"I'm pleased you like it, Frau Junker. It's my favorite room. We spend most of our time here, Birdie and I, when we have the opportunity. I've always felt that the kitchen was the heart of the home, and I tried to make this one reflect that feeling. Please, have a seat, here at the table."

As Clara sat down, Mary Lee retrieved her best glassware from the cupboard, filled the glasses with ice and poured the pale yellow tea into the glasses. Returning to the table, she set a glass down in front of Clara and took a seat across the table. Clara's face didn't reveal much, but Mary Lee felt that the woman was worried about something.

When Clara still remained quiet after a few sips of tea, Mary Lee decided she might as well just jump in. "You had something you wanted to speak to me about?"

"Yes, well . . . yes," Clara hesitated. "Last year, your husband offered to purchase the *Lehen* for the farm in Sundremda. I wondered if perhaps he would still wish to do so."

Mary Lee knew about Guffy Pomeroy and his swindle. She had even heard that Claus Junker had been involved in some way. As she looked closer at Clara she realized that Clara was a very worried woman. *Damn it,* she thought, *there's a lot of trouble brewing for her, I can tell. And I like her. I liked her from the first.*

"What Birdie wants, Frau Junker, is clear title to his own land. He wants to be able to farm, without interference, without being checked up on, and to be free to do his best at it. Yes, I'm sure he would want to buy the *Lehen*. I imagine that most of the villagers want the same thing."

"Each to buy their own land, each to be free, Frau Newhouse?" Clara asked.

"You might as well call me Mary Lee. We're not a very formal people, as you may have noticed. Yes, that's exactly what they want. Is your husband willing to sell it all?"

"I am Clara, then, Marilee, *und* yes, he is willing."

Mary Lee noticed that Clara's carefully pronounced English, apparently something she had learned in the last year, was beginning to slip. She suddenly realized the truth.

"He doesn't know about this visit does he, Clara?"

Clara started at the directness of the question. It was clearly unexpected. She flushed a bit, and looked away from Mary Lee for a few moments. Finally, composure regained, she looked directly into Mary Lee's eyes.

"No. No, he does not. I prefer that he never learns of it."

Mary Lee understood completely. She hadn't had to deal with this kind of attitude herself, Birdie being the type of man he was, but she had watched many wives deal with it. Slip in the back way, offer hesitant suggestions, and never show your own good sense.

"He won't hear it from me, Clara, or anyone else I know. In fact, Birdie is playing cards this evening and won't be home for several hours. The girls and the grandkids shouldn't be back for a good while, either. So," she said, as she rose and went to a cupboard, "You and I are going to have a nice long talk and work this out."

Mary Lee moved to the freezer and pulled out her very last can of frozen limeade, "First, though, I think we could use something a little more relaxing than this tea. I don't suppose you've ever heard of a frozen margarita, have you?"

"Horace, we sort of have a problem," Deborah Trout said, as she entered the room for the meeting that was due to start in a few minutes. "We're basically the county seat now, aren't we?"

"Well, I suppose so," Horace Bolender answered. "Considering the number of problems that keep landing on my desk, I suppose we must be. What is it this time, running out of paper?"

"Don't I just wish? Maybe if we ran out, I wouldn't have so much of it to shuffle around. The problem is a little more serious than that, though. You know I never meant to become the tax assessor, right? And, I never really wanted much to do with organizing the finances for anything as big as Grantville is becoming, either. But, since I'm stuck with it, I want to do it right."

"Completely understandable, Deborah. So what is the problem, exactly?"

"Money. When *isn't* the problem money? Do you realize that Grantville now owns Sundremda? It was crown land. Now that we're the government, it's county land. We need money to run things, but we can't exactly tax ourselves, now can we? I can assess all the taxes I want, but a property that has no owner isn't going to pay anything into the coffers, is it? We can't sell it either. Well, we could, but, who to? It's surrounded by a bunch of contractual obligations that seriously limit what the owner can do with it. About the only people who would have any interest would be the tenants or the *Lehen* holder. Sundremda isn't the only place like that, either. Half a dozen other villages have petitioned to become a part of Marion County.

Horace thought for a few moments, and then looked at Deborah with a grin. "You wouldn't have come here complaining if you didn't have a solution worked out. What do you think we should do?"

"Well, somehow or other, we need to sell off some of this stuff. To do that, we need clear title or at least clearer title. We need to either buy the *Lehen* or sell the land to the *Lehen* holder or the renters. We won't get full price, but we'd at least get something, and taxes, eventually."

"I'm pretty sure that Birdie Newhouse wants to own the land outright. He's been complaining to Willie Ray about the restrictions on usage," Horace remarked. "Tell you what; you come up with what you want to do. Write out proposals for it and I'll see what Mayor Dreeson and Senator Abrabanel have to say. Congress has decided that they can act for Marion County in this sort of situation."

Deborah looked at Horace with a bit of fire in her eyes. Damn it, life had gotten so complicated lately, ever since they had a real government with a constitution, instead of the emergency committee.

"Father, you must be realistic. It is the only way," Egidius insisted. "There is nothing else we can sell that will bring in the amount of money that the *Lehen* will bring in. Not without taking a much greater loss."

Claus stared at his son in disbelief. "You wish me to sell your heritage? What comes to you from William the Silent and the counts of Gleichen? Why should I agree to this, this travesty?" Claus knew the reason, but the knowledge was burning a hole in his guts. He didn't want this. He had been doing everything he could to avoid it for months, long before Pomeroy had died.

Egidius was looking at him with concern. "Perhaps, Father, you do not fully understand what has happened here. I know what you did was customary. It was done the way things had always been done. But it was against the law even before the Ring of Fire. Now, with the Committees of Correspondence and Herr Ritter's connections to them, there will be no looking the other way. You have diverted public funds to private use. It is a crime with criminal penalties. If we do not replace the money, and do it very soon, you could be sent to prison. Do you think I would see you in prison for the rents on a village? Not only the disgrace, not only the lessening of our family's position, is at stake here. You can be criminally charged and go to prison. Do you wish that to happen?"

Claus felt as though he had been slapped in the face. What he had done had been done by others for centuries. Now, he, a man of wealth and position, had no more protections. From the time the Ring of Fire had happened the world had been changing faster and faster. He had tried, with every means he could find, to prevent the life he knew from being swept away. He had failed, although he hadn't realized how badly until just now. His son, the child for whom he had lived, worked and dreamed, had adjusted to the changes, but he had not. He still did not want this new world. He hated it, wanted it to go away.

Yet, here was this young man. Where had he come from, this tall and strong man of business? It was just a week ago that he had been laughing as he sat his first pony.

"Very well, my son, if we must, then we must. I will sell the *Lehen* of Sundremda, and I will sell it to that Newhouse person and the villagers," he answered. "But the price! I know the market. It is worth twice that."

"Yes, Papa, I know. But not to us, not for years. The rents are set. We could not change anything without buying the renters out, then buying the property from Marion County."

Mary Lee had talked to Birdie and Ernst Bachmeier after Clara's visit. While Birdie had been in no mood to do any favors for Claus Junker, Ernst was thrilled at the prospect. The lines of status were much more severe in the seventeenth century. Owning property, actually owning it, meant you were a person of considerable status. Not a peasant, not someone's tenant, your own man. Nor did Ernst bear Claus Junker any ill will. He had always been a fair and decent *Lehen* holder, understanding if the crops had been bad. Yes, Herr Junker had been harder to deal with since Birdie had leased his farm, but Ernst felt that the difficulties were partly Birdie's fault.

There had been phone calls from the Newhouse residence to the government to try to figure out who had the authority to sell the property. Now that there was a government other than the emergency committee, Deborah Trout was apparently the person to see. Deborah had already been approached by Eddie Junker. There then followed quite a bit of back and forth, working out the various ends of the deal. The Junkers needed cash up front, Marion County wanted some of the land both for public right of way and some to sell. The village would lose almost a thousand acres. Birdie would have to give up some of his land as a right of way, which would put a public road right across his original property.

Ernst and Birdie called a meeting of the village to talk about the proposal. They discussed the pros and cons. The pros were that agreeing to the proposal would give the villagers more control over how the village was run and greater status in the eyes of most down-timers. The cons, well, there was only one con, a big one. If the village agreed to the proposal it would probably cost them more money. Their mortgage payments would run about fifteen percent over their rents. Also, part of the village property, much of the forest and some of the pasture would no longer be part of their village.

People were concerned, and rightly so, about the consequences to the village and the *Gemeinde*. If Birdie owned his own land why should he use his tractor to help with the plowing of the rest? What about the people in the village who didn't own farms, the people who had been helping the farmers as part of their rent? Who would be responsible for what part of the obligations set out in their rental agreement?

There would need to be some sort of an agreement, or rather, several agreements. One agreement must be made for all of the villagers, and another agreement must be made for the farmers of the *Gemeinde*. It was a very long meeting, and quite loud.

Eventually, most of the villagers agreed that the prospect of actually owning their own land, even if they had to pay the bank, was just too attractive to let pass. Only two families refused.

The mason refused because he wasn't sure how long he would be living in Sundremda. He hoped that he could continue to work in Sundremda and sell his stone work using transportation provided by Grantville. But he couldn't be sure and was unwilling to take on such a debt.

Surprisingly, there was one farming family that disapproved of the whole business. Friedrich Schultz stood up and began speaking, after everyone else had reached agreement.

"I will not be a party to this, I will not. How do we know that this bank will be as reasonable as Herr Junker if the crops fail? How do we know that this man will truly use the tractor for the good of the village, no matter what he promises?"

Birdie stood up to answer, offended that someone would question his integrity. "My word is my bond. I always keep my promises because it is the only honorable way to be. I will sign another agreement if necessary, if it will make you happy."

"This entire plan, it is unnatural. We are not meant to be gentry. We are farmers, good honest farmers. Why should we do this? We have always been tenants to Herr Junker and his family. He has held the *Lehen* for many years and has been good to us. I cannot believe that he would agree to this."

At this point, Eddie Junker, who attended the meeting in lieu of his father, stood to answer Friedrich. "My father feels that this is a good plan. You will be free of obligations to him, free to farm as you wish. It is a good plan that benefits us all."

Friedrich shook his head. "I am disappointed in Herr Junker. My contract is for ninety-nine years and I am the second generation. I have my contract and I will work my farm according to the terms of that contract. I cannot be removed from my farm as long as I pay my rent. I will pay the rent, but I will not, absolutely not be a party to this insanity."

Birdie sat through that little speech dumbfounded. Birdie had always figured that Friedrich was just a suck up. Thought he was too afraid of Junker to answer back. Birdie was amazed to realize that the guy actually believed that his proper place was as someone else's tenant. Birdie couldn't understand how anyone could actually feel that way.

Friedrich was trying to queer the whole deal for everyone because he was terrified of owning his own property. He almost managed it, too. Before the deal could go through an agreement must be reached. Agreement took a couple of extra days of negotiations and no one was especially happy with the result.

Friedrich was unhappy because he didn't want the mayor of the village as his landlord. And Birdie was unhappy because he was afraid he was going to be stuck as mayor and have to deal with the duckfucker on a regular basis.

Twenty-four loan applications, twenty-two of them using the land they wanted to buy as the collateral for the loan. All of them were from down-timers with no, or very little, credit history. Larkin Newhouse's application, the twenty-third, used the land in Sundremda plus his equity in the farm inside the Ring of Fire as collateral. The villagers of Sundremda wanted to buy their village and wanted the bank to loan them the money to do it. It was not unexpected. The twenty-fourth application was from the township of Sundremda, requesting funds to buy two public buildings and one farm.

September, 1632

Ernst Bachmeier leaned against the fence post and mused. The fall of 1632 had given him no answers as to whether wheat or flax was the better cash crop. He suspected that if they'd planted dandelions then dandelions would have sold amazingly well. The lousy weather had almost been compensated for by the addition of lime to the soil. The crops were good, very good, even though Birdie claimed they were only passable by up-time standards. There was something called an "industrial revolution" getting started in and around the Ring of Fire and labor was increasingly hard to come by. But, the goods! Oh, the goods that came out of Grantville. A bed with springs in it!

Ernst once again found himself looking over the land. The land that would be his someday, his alone. The land that he would pass down to his children, someday, hopefully in the far future. Ah, such a future.

Bacon

ERIC FLINT

"All right, I finished it," said Mike Stearns, the moment he strode into Melissa Mailey's office. Triumphantly, he dropped the *Economic History of Europe* onto her desk. The tome landed with a resounding thump.

Mike stooped and peered at the legs of the desk. "Pretty well built. I thought it might collapse."

"Well, now that you've finished that one, I'm sure—"

"Not a chance, Melissa!" He held up his hands and crossed his two forefingers, as if warding off a vampire. "Besides, I don't need to. Birdie Newhouse—bless him—has shown us the way. In practice, by getting his hands dirty, just like I predicted."

Melissa frowned, almost fiercely. "Mike, be serious! You can't solve the tangled land tenure relations of seventeenth-century Germany by simply *buying* the land. Even if everyone was willing to sell, we couldn't possibly afford it. King Midas couldn't afford it."

Mike shook his head. "I'm not talking about that. Tactics come, tactics go. What matters is what Birdie *did*, not how he did it. Birdie and Mary Lee both. They got in there and mixed it up with the people on the ground, and took it from there. That's what we need—only organized. Something like a cross between the OSS of World War II days, Willie Ray's grangers, and—and—I dunno. Maybe the Peace Corps. Whatever. We'll figure it out as we go."

Melissa laced her fingers together and stared at him.

"You're nuts," she proclaimed, after a few seconds. "On the other hand, it *is* a charming idea. Like the poet said, in beauty there is truth. You'd need the right people to carry it out, though—and *not* somebody like Harry Lefferts."

Mike chuckled. "Can't you just see Harry as an agrarian organizer?" His voice took on a slightly thicker hillbilly accent. " 'Let's all get together, boys. Or I'll shoot you dead.' "

Melissa grimaced. "That's not really funny, Mike."

"Sure it is. But I agree, Harry's not the right type. You got any suggestions?"

Melissa's eyes narrowed, as they did when she was chewing on a problem.

"Well . . . There's somebody I think we could at least raise the idea with. Deborah Trout."

It was Mike's turn to frown. "Len's wife? She's always struck me as pretty straitlaced."

"Well, not her personally. She's in her fifties now, anyway. A bit long in the tooth to be gallivanting around the German countryside. But she's got someone in her office that I think she'd be willing—delighted, actually—to part company with."

"Who?"

"Noelle Murphy."

Mike's frown was now as fierce as Melissa's had been earlier. "I thought she wanted to be a *nun*. I can't say I know her at all, but I always got the sense that she's as straitlaced as they come. I can't really see her . . . why are you grinning at me like that?"

"Because the idea's charming in its own right. Don't forgot that Noelle's a bastard, too—or do you really think that idiot Francis fathered her? Pat Murphy's bastard, at that."

Mike rolled his eyes. "Melissa, if there is any single person in Grantville who can be described as 'not playing with a full deck' more than Pat Murphy . . ."

Melissa clucked her tongue reprovingly. She did that extraordinarily well. "Thou shalt not visit the sins of the mother on the daughter. The follies, neither. This much I can tell you, because she was a student of mine—Noelle's smart as a whip, and there's a lot more going on under the surface than it looks. As for the religious business, she's never actually decided to become a nun, so far as I know. And what difference does it make anyway? We're not asking her to play Mata Hari, are we?"

Mike rubbed his chin. "Well, no. But . . ."

Melissa rose from her desk. "Come on. Let's at least raise the idea with Deborah and see what she thinks."

Deborah Trout was enthusiastic. As Mike had darkly suspected.

"Noelle would be perfect! How soon can she clear her desk out?"

"What I thought," he muttered under his breath. Then, loudly enough to be heard:

"Oh, not any time soon. For the moment, she'll appear to be staying on the job. Undercover, you might call it."

"Oh." It was almost comical, the way Deborah's face fell.

On their way back, Mike grumbled to Melissa. "This is a screwy idea. The only reason Deborah likes it is so she can get rid of Noelle."

"You're right," agreed Melissa serenely. "But look at it this way, Mike. How would you characterize Deborah Trout?"

Naturally, she didn't wait for an answer. "I'd characterize her as follows: earnest, efficient, serious, dedicated, hard-working bureaucrat."

"Um. Yeah, okay."

"And she's ecstatic at the idea of getting rid of Noelle."

Mike started to brighten up. "Mind you," he cautioned, "there's a place and a need for levelheaded public officials."

"Oh, sure. But not where you'd be sending Noelle."

There was still a problem. "Uh, Melissa, I admit I don't know the girl—sorry, young woman—as well as you do. But I get the distinct impression that Noelle *thinks* of herself as, well—"

"An earnest, efficient, serious, dedicated, hard-working bureaucrat, with strong religious convictions that are leaning her toward joining a religious order. But don't forget she's also a bastard. Trust me on this one, Mike."

They walked on a little further. Melissa added:

"The next thing we need is a symbol of some kind."

Mike shook his head. "Stick to what you know, Melissa. No way you can gimmick a symbol that means anything. You just have to wait until something emerges on its own."

"From where?"

He shrugged his shoulders. "Who knows? Maybe the meatpacking industry."

"Huh?"

"Bacon. To go with your scrambled eggs."

Part II: Enter the Ram

Then he said to me, "Prophesy to these bones, and say to them: O dry bones, hear the word of the Lord. Thus says the Lord GOD to these bones: I will cause breath to enter you, and you shall live. I will lay sinews on you, and will cause flesh to come upon you, and cover you with skin, and put breath in you, and you shall live; and you shall know that I am the Lord."

Ezekiel 37:4-6

The Merino Problem

PAULA GOODLETT

"It's ironic," Flo Richards said to herself, as she sipped the last of her coffee. "I may just be the only person in Grantville who gained time, instead of losing it."

J.D. had gone to work and Flo had the house to herself for a few more hours, until the Sprugs arrived. She and J.D. had met them yesterday and agreed that they should move in. The house was certainly big enough, and with the four girls gone it was sort of lonesome. Johan, Anna, and all six children would barely make a dent in the space. It would be nice to have company.

Flo intended to enjoy the quiet time. She hadn't had much of it over the years. Four daughters, the farm, J.D., all these had used up most of her time. Now, it looked like she just might have the time to do some things she had always wanted to do.

"Who would have thought," she mused, "that J.D.'s membership in the Seed Savers Exchange would turn out to be so important."

Flo agreed with the aim of the Exchange, to preserve genetic diversity in crops by growing and exchanging the seeds of endangered domesticated species. What she had disagreed with was the fact that she had done most of the work of growing, saving and exchanging of those seeds. J.D. was busy teaching during the week and the girls had been busy with school and their own activities. J.D. had helped, of course, when he'd had time. Otherwise, Flo thought, he'd have wound up wearing those heirloom veggies.

Now, the organization people were calling "The Grange" was in charge of those same heirloom plants. The members of the Grange had recently realized that the seeds from the hybrid plants common on farms and in gardens up-time wouldn't produce the same plants in the next generation. Flo and J.D.'s stock of nonhybrid seeds had gained hugely in value.

Flo smirked. J.D. had tried for years to convince them, but very few up-timers would listen. It was easier to go to the store and buy seed every year. There were times she'd have liked to do it herself.

It was nice that J.D. had been vindicated. It had raised his status in the eyes of the local farmers and led to his being appointed as one of Willie Ray's assistants. Who knew where that could lead?

Flo had been thrilled to turn the stock of seeds over to the Grange. Let someone else take charge of that project. She wouldn't be stuck in the kitchen, canning all the produce this year, either. The lack of new canning lids in town was worrying, but she could reuse some old ones. Some of them would seal properly. Other methods of preservation were possible, also. Flo was sure they'd make it through the winter. Most of her crops, planted before the Ring of Fire, would be dedicated to seed for next year.

She did think Willie Ray was getting a bit high-handed, though. True, Flo would admit that he had a lot on his platter and she was glad she didn't have his responsibilities. Still, she resented Willie Ray treating her like "Little Bo Peep" when she tried to talk to him about a better ram.

The Grange, Willie Ray, and J.D. were all focused on food production. Flo understood that this and the war were priorities. She hadn't been able to get any of them to listen to her concerns about the sheep, though. "I need an ally. Maybe Johan will listen. He seemed to be interested when we spoke yesterday."

Flo stood up, and rinsed her coffee cup. "I don't think I'll mention that last few cans of Folgers to anyone," she murmured slyly. J.D. could be a little overgenerous on occasion. Flo would just keep that guilty little secret to herself.

*   *   *

It was about 2:00 PM before Johan, Anna and the kids arrived. Flo showed them to their rooms. She was pretty surprised when the entire family seemed prepared to move into the single room she had intended for Johan and Anna alone. After some effort, she finally convinced them to take two more bedrooms, one for the boys and one for the girls. There were two bathrooms up there, and two more bedrooms. Flo had originally intended for the family to use all the rooms, but they seemed dead set against it.

Melissa Mailey had been right, Flo thought, as she and Johan walked toward the sheep pasture. The privacy standards of seventeenth-century Germans were certainly different from those of the up-timers. She was glad their bedroom was on the first floor. The Sprugs could deal with the kids' squabbles and she and J.D. wouldn't even need to know about it.

Johan was leading the ram. Flo looked at it again and sighed. She was sure it was a good enough ram for this time and place. She was also sure she didn't want the scraggly thing anywhere near her Merinos.

Time for a small demonstration, she decided.

Johan had some English. Flo's German was limited, even though she was trying to improve it. She still hadn't been able to explain the problem clearly. After coaxing one of the ewes to come near, Flo undid the ties of the coat that protected the precious wool. She watched as Johan's face changed from confusion over the sheep coat to curiosity and then to sheer pleasure as he buried his hands in the luxurious wool.

"Do you see what I mean now, Johan? These are the only type C Delaine Merinos in the world. I'm not going to breed them to just any ram that's available. Compared to these sheep, that ram of yours might as well be a brillo pad with legs. You can see the difference in the wool.

"Merino sheep were used to improve the wool of nearly every breed of sheep in the world. There's no reason we can't improve the sheep of Germany in the here and now, but my rams are too young to breed successfully. Spain has around three million Merino sheep. We need a better ram, one with some Merino blood. Do you understand now?"

Johan was smiling as he stood up. "Yes, Flo, I understand better now. We need a better ram; we must find a way to make them understand. We must not waste this chance. I help. We will convince Willie Ray. Must have better ram, must."

Flo smiled. Finally, an ally. With Johan's help and experience, maybe she could finally get a breeding program to improve the wool breeds, as well as the meat breeds.

"Fine, Johan, fine. I'm really glad to hear that. We'll work on it together. Now, since you enjoyed that wool so much, let's go look at the rabbits."

"Rabbits? Vermin. Must get rid of, before they damage crops." Johan appeared to be ready to go on a rabbit hunt that very moment.

"Not these rabbits, Johan. They're not your average pest. Though I'm not sure how much use they are, to tell the truth. Come see."

As they walked to the bunny barn, Flo continued to explain. "These are English angora rabbits, Johan. They couldn't possibly survive in the wild. Their own wool would cause their deaths."

"Rabbits do not grow wool, Flo."

Flo grinned as they approached the first cage. "These rabbits do grow wool, Johan. They take a good bit of work, but their wool is very warm and soft. Take a look."

Johan stood in stunned surprise as Flo took one of the does from her cage. The rabbit was covered with long, soft hair, which could be gently plucked from the rabbit without harm. As Flo demonstrated the technique, she continued to watch Johan's face.

"So tell me, Johan," she asked, "do you think there's a market for this, too?"

"Flo," said Anna, "I have question."

"Sure, Anna, what's up?" asked Flo as she watched Anna sit down. It was the first time Anna had ever sat in her presence without an invitation.

Flo had begun to wonder if Anna would ever get over the tendency to treat her as the lady of the manor. The constant deference had made Flo really uncomfortable for the first week or so. Finally, in desperation, she'd let Anna in on her secret vice, the hidden stash of Folgers coffee. That had sent Anna into fits of giggles and had seemed to even the ground between them. Anna had relaxed around Flo and had been opening up ever since.

"I have sister, Flo. Is married to Wilhelm Schmidt, five *Kinder*. Are in camp still. Is hard, so many *Kinder*. Maybe come here with us? All will work, und boys be help with sheep. Johan not want to ask, but Ilsa wants home again. We all work, Flo, und, und . . ."

Anna's English had failed her, but Flo had the gist of it now.

"You don't think five more kids will be too crowded, Anna?"

"*Nein, nein.* Is big beds, much, much room. We be fine. I want Ilsa close, und you and Johan keep boys busy. Truly, Flo, is goot." Anna seemed very concerned that Flo might object, but as long as Anna was happy, Flo could be happy.

"Anna, it's fine. As long as you don't mind the crowding, I don't mind them moving in. You already have the house in wonderful shape. I can't imagine what the two of you will accomplish when Ilsa gets here."

Anna was a wonder, as far as Flo was concerned. Six kid, ages ranging from about fourteen to the baby, who looked to be about six months old, and all the kids toed the line far, far better than the average up-time child. Anna and Johan's discipline seemed a bit harsh to Flo, but she wasn't going to interfere. The kids would be starting school when it resumed; time enough for the up-time kids to try to ruin them then.

"How is search for ram going, Flo?" Anna was concerned because Johan was concerned. Flo knew that Johan and Anna had discussed the sheep project in detail. Anna, after a demonstration of the difference in wool softness, followed by a visit to Flo's angora bunnies, had joined in enthusiastically. "Will we use Brillo, after all?"

Flo grinned at that question. Her undiplomatic remark had resulted in the nickname. Johan had proved to be a good-humored sort. He'd later asked what a brillo pad was. After a demonstration of a brillo pad, he'd laughed uproariously. They'd all been calling the poor ram "Brillo" ever since.

Even J.D. had joined in the search for a ram, although with some reluctance. Flo had caught him giving her some thoughtful looks lately. Johan's support had made a difference in J.D.'s attitude toward the sheep.

"Flo, Flo, are you in there?" Anna asked, grinning herself.

Flo jerked back to reality and smiled over at Anna. "Sorry, Anna, I got lost in my thoughts again." She laughed. "We'll use Brillo if we have to. He's certainly a strong, hardy critter. If the Ring of Fire has thrown the sheep out of cycle, it will be good to have him around. Whatever we can do to spread the Merino strain will help. I'd still rather have a ram with some Merino blood, just for the wool quality. We still have some time before fall. Maybe someone will make it through the armies, yet."

"Well, we all have things to do," Anna said, "I'm going to clean the attics today. I will leave you to your own work. You will use the telephone, und call for Ilsa und Wilhelm? Today, Flo?"

"Yes, Anna, I'll call right now. They'll probably be here in a few hours. Do you need any help?" Flo always asked, and Anna always refused, just as she did today. Flo had begun to think that she just got in Anna's way. She'd decided to stand aside and let Anna go at it. The woman was amazing. If those bozos down at the 250 Club had any idea what they were missing, Flo mused, they'd be standing in line, begging for German houseguests.

Flo called the administrators of the refugee camp and arranged for Wilhelm, Ilsa and their kids to be given the news and started on their way out to the farm. The administrators were very careful to get the right relations these days. A few mix-ups had caused them to get the original village name, before they asked for people by name. The names Johan and Anna were as common here as the names John and Ann had been up-time. No one wanted any more confusion.

"Well, a few more people won't make that much difference here. I wonder what Wilhelm and Ilsa went through, getting to Grantville?"

The German population had amazing resilience. The war rolled over them, they grabbed what they could and started over. The war rolled over them again, and they started over again. When they reached Grantville, and were convinced of their relative safety, they dug in with a vengeance, determined to succeed and prosper. While many families had arrived with little more than the clothes on their backs, others had saved the most astounding things. A few chickens here, a ram or an ox there, a few family heirlooms, a few coins sewn into a child's frock. They'd saved anything they could.

It was almost as amazing to Flo as the weird things that had value now. Who would have thought that things like jelly jars, coffee cans with plastic lids, even old mayo jars, could be so valuable?

Flo shook her head in wonder. She'd heard her parents' rhyme—

> Use it up, wear it out
> Make it do or do without

—so many times as a child that frugality was ingrained in her nature. She had washed and saved any container with a lid just from force of habit. There was a shelved area of the basement where she'd stored box after box of jelly glasses, mayo jars, canning jars, coffee cans, and whatever else she felt might be useful someday. J.D. had teased her about her saving ways for years. Flo hadn't listened. She'd continued to save things. Old clothes, cloth diapers, plastic pants, baby bottles, sheets, towels—if it wasn't in the basement, it was in a cedar chest or a box in the attic.

Anna's excitement when she'd started cleaning the basement was contagious. Knowing her own limitations in the art of bargaining, Flo let Johan or Anna handle that part. If a German noble wanted a set of Flintstone jelly glasses to serve wine in, that was fine with Flo. Johan and Anna would make sure he paid very well for the privilege.

Johan had been a bit insulted when Flo had suggested watching the shearing video. "I know how to shear a sheep, Flo," he'd objected. "Do you think I know nothing?"

"Johan, I'm sure you've sheared plenty of sheep in your lifetime. Have you ever done it with electric shears?" Flo had asked.

The mention of electric anything was a conversation stopper. His interest piqued, Johan joined Flo in front of the TV to view the video of New Zealand shepherds and shearers at work. They viewed it three times before he was confident of his ability to adapt.

Flo and Johan arrived at the shearing shed together. Johan checked the shears, turning them on and off until he was comfortable with the sound.

None of Flo's ewes was especially rambunctious. They'd been sheared before, after all. Even so, Flo chose an especially mellow ewe for Johan's first attempt at electric shearing.

Johan had paid serious attention to the video, Flo noticed. After a couple of nervous false starts, he began rolling the fleece off the ewe as though he'd been doing it all his life. Which he had, of course, now that Flo thought about it. The electric shears just made it go faster.

A couple of small nicks, easily treated, a check for foot rot, hoof trimming and worming and the ewe bounced away. Johan had very few problems, even with the unfamiliar shears, and they were finished very soon. Flo had sorted the fleeces as Johan had sheared. Even in coats, there was some dirt involved in the process and the heavy lanolin in the fleece made Flo feel greasy.

"Johan, we've both got things to do. If I don't get a shower, I won't be responsible for my temper."

"*Ja*, Flo. I will check that *meine Kinder* have finished their work.

Sheep, they seem well." Johan seemed eager to get on with his other work.

"We'll have to come up with a way to clean that fleece. I'll think about it. Maybe the old wash boiler. My grandmother used to use it, along with that old wringer Anna found in the basement. I'll need to check the rollers. I don't remember if they were rubber or wood. It may come in handy. Never thought I'd have to use it. I just kept it, like that old glass churn my mother used to use. Sentimental value, then. Much more practical value now." Flo grinned as she walked away. "Anyway, I can't think when I feel like an oil slick. See you in a while."

Standing in the shower, under the pounding hot water, Flo gave in to the depression she'd been feeling all day. The delay in shearing the sheep had been caused by her last few weeks with Jennifer, before Jen had returned to school for the summer semester.

She knew she was lucky to have kept three of her children, but she missed Jen so much. She was Flo's youngest, and the closest to her. The other girls had their own families and their own lives. Jen was still Flo's. She'd encouraged her to buy the sheep, because she knew Flo needed something to care for. Flo missed her so much.

Flo forced herself to turn her thoughts away. Jen had always been self-sufficient. She would manage and succeed, even without Flo and J.D. Flo held that thought as she began drying off.

As she dressed, Flo noticed how soft her skin felt. She still had shampoo, bought on sale and stored, but there hadn't been a good sale on bath soap. Her stock was low on that commodity. They were saving the gentle soaps for the babies, to keep them from skin irritations. The Ring of Fire had put paid to her usual practice of stocking up on soap.

"Wait a minute, soft skin, lye soap, lanolin—that's the difference! The lanolin in the sheep fleece. We can't just destroy it. There has to be a way to recover it and use it. Soap, lotion, didn't I read something somewhere about surgery? I've got to do some research. Soap making, lotions, what else?" Flo threw her clothes on, ready to start another project.

She stopped and finished buttoning her shirt. "I'd better not go running out of here half dressed. The Schmidts could be here any minute. Coffee. I need coffee. I always think better with coffee."

Naturally, they would get there while she was in the shower. In the middle of the day, yet! A little embarrassed, Flo extended her hand to greet Wilhelm and Ilsa Schmidt.

"We are pleased to be here," said Wilhelm. "I know Johan und Anna well. We work well together. You will be pleased."

"I'm happy to have all of you," said Flo. "It may get a bit crowded, but we'll manage. Wilhelm, Johan, I know you have things to talk about. Johan and I discussed our plans earlier, so I'll let him explain. Ilsa, Anna, let's go up and get the rooms arranged to suit you."

As the three women and the children went upstairs, Flo heard Anna and Ilsa speaking rapid-fire German. Too rapid for her to understand, but apparently the room arrangement was settled before they hit the top step. Anna began directing traffic and Flo noticed that the boys were at one end of the hall and the girls at the other. Both sets of parents were in the middle. They were going to have to have a talk about what could and could not go down a toilet, she thought. Two bathrooms and fifteen people could be a nightmare on the septic system. She didn't even want to think about what could happen when the toilet tissue ran out.

"Fifteen people," she muttered to herself, "eleven of them children, me and J.D. Feeding this crew isn't going to be a picnic either. It's a good thing I did all that canning last year. And that sale on hamburger. Boy, am I glad I took advantage of that one. We need to do an inventory and some planning. Tonight, though, I wonder if this crew has ever had spaghetti? It's easy for a crowd."

Wrapped up in thoughts, plans and concerns, Flo left Anna and Ilsa to their arrangements and went down to the freezer. Spaghetti sauce for seventeen people would still take a lot of hamburger.

The spaghetti, salad and bread seemed to be a hit. At any rate, there wasn't going to be a leftover problem in the Richards-Sprug-Schmidt household.

For once, being a packrat had paid off. Everyone had a few changes of clothes, although underwear was limited. The females had at least one pair of jeans or overalls for heavy work, although Anna and Ilsa appeared to prefer skirts. They'd get over that eventually, Flo thought. You couldn't get her back into skirts with an act of Congress.

Clean-up proceeded rapidly. Older children helped the younger, everyone washed their own dishes and placed them in the drying racks. Flo had cooked, so she cleaned the pots and pans, and wiped down the counter and table. It looked like a system that would work.

The children, after a long, exciting day, were drooping in their chairs. All but the four oldest were sent up to bed, with orders to wash up and brush their teeth. The adults and near-adults sat up to discuss their plans for the following days.

"J.D., tomorrow is Sunday. I'll be going to church. What are your plans?" Flo asked. It was an old arrangement. Flo attended the Methodist church when she could, averaging once or twice a month. J.D. did what J.D did. They'd found that arguing was not productive.

"I'm driving in around ten AM to see Mike and Willie Ray. If we're careful, there's no reason that everyone can't fit into the truck and the truck bed. I know you don't like kids in the truck bed, but Johan and Wilhelm can keep them in line. I'll go slow. Will that suit everyone? We can meet around four in the afternoon and ride back home together."

"Sounds like a pretty good plan to me, J.D. It'll get everyone into town in time for the various services. Is it okay with the rest of you?" Flo asked the Sprugs and Schmidts.

With everyone in agreement, and everyone tired and yawning, they all retired to their rooms and slept.

"How does anybody wake up that energetic without coffee, especially at the crack of dark?" Flo wondered aloud, trying to hide a yawn.

The Sprugs and Schmidts were up, dressed, breakfasted and had the chores done before she had her eyes open good. "I sometimes think we up-timers are soft, especially on a morning like this."

Flo had decided that it was time to introduce Anna and Ilsa to crock pots. Deciding on chili and corn bread for supper, she'd thawed more hamburger and was showing them how to set up the crock pots when Anna handed her a cup.

Taking a sip, her eyes widened. Coffee. Blessed, life-reviving coffee. Anna had apparently decided that Flo would need a cup or two and had made a pot for her.

Anna grinned, "I don't know why you like that stuff, but I know you do. You will need to be awake. So, I made you a pot. We will not tell. Is our secret."

"Not much of one, Flo. Do you think I could scrounge a cup?" asked J.D. from behind her.

Jumping, Flo turned around. "You devil, you knew all along, didn't you?" she asked.

"The way you pack-rat? Of course I knew." He said, "I just figured it made you happy to have that stash, so I let it alone. Don't worry. I'm not going to give it away. I have enough to handle without you going through caffeine withdrawal on top of it. Besides, I need a cup now and then, myself." J.D. moved over to the coffee pot and poured himself a mug. "More people than you know have a little stash of this or that. It makes them feel better and does no real harm. If it were antibiotics, it would be a different story."

They arrived in town in good time for services. Everyone dispersed to their preferred church or meeting place, after making plans to meet that afternoon.

Flo felt peaceful as she sat through the service. It was so quiet and calm. She gazed around her and saw Irene Washaw and her son, Mac, with his family. She'd thought Mac had been in Charleston. How did they wind up on this side of the Ring of Fire?

After services, Flo approached Irene. "Irene, how wonderful that you have Mac and his family with you."

"Oh, I know, Flo. I feel so lucky," Irene bubbled. "They'd come in for Starr's birthday and were planning to leave that day. It's just wonderful for me that the Ring of Fire didn't happen an hour later."

Choking up and trying to hide it, Flo agreed and greeted Mac and his wife. Excusing herself, she headed for the restroom but was stopped by Mary Ellen Jones.

"Oh, Flo, I'm glad I caught you. I wanted to ask you about some yarn . . . Why, Flo, what's wrong?" Mary Ellen guided Flo to a private area. "What's happened, and why are you crying?"

"I'm sorry, Mary Ellen. Seeing Irene and Mac and hearing how happy she is to have him with her. If the damn Ring of Fire had just happened one week earlier, I'd still have Jen. I miss her so much. The other girls are busy with their families, and I don't even see them at church. They've moved to their husbands' churches. I could just kick myself sometimes. If I'd just been more insistent that the family come to church, maybe they'd be here today. I married J.D. knowing I couldn't change his mind, but maybe if I'd just tried harder . . . I miss all the kids, but Jen . . ."

Flo shuddered to a stop. "Sorry, Mary Ellen, you have your own set of problems. Didn't mean to go to pieces on you. I just wish . . . Maybe if Jen had just gone for the two year degree, like Noelle Murphy did. Maybe she'd still be here. And I hate that I feel that way, really I do. Surely, Jen is better off back up-time. She must be."

Mary Ellen smiled. "Flo, regrets are a part of life and we can't undo the past, however much we'd like to. You did your best. You have most of your family, J.D., your health, and I even hear that Willie Ray speaks well of your sheep project. The past is the past. Leave it there and move forward. I know you've done your best, and so do you. You just have to keep going."

Flo had gotten herself under control by now. "I know, Mary Ellen, I really do. Things aren't as bad as they could be. I'll be okay. You go minister to someone who needs it more than I do. Temporary weakness. I can overcome it."

"I know, Flo. You're a strong, vital woman with years ahead of you. How am I going to get good wool yarn for Simon's socks if you don't raise those Merino sheep? I want real knitting yarn, not the tiny, fine stuff they make here. Let me know when you have a few skeins ready. I need it. His socks are wearing out."

Mary Ellen began to move away. "Oh, Flo, if anyone has an extra can of coffee, let them know I'm in the market for it, will you?"

It was so good to speak her own language and be understood. Resorting to gestures and mime could be very wearing. Anna Sprug was very happy to have her sister, brother-in-law, and their children with her in this strange place. Now she could just talk, and not have to act out her words.

"These people, they are very rich, aren't they?" Ilsa commented.

"Not only are they very rich, they are so rich that they are foolish with their wealth. Did you see how much meat Flo thought we needed? I liked the 'corn bread' well enough, but that 'chili' . . . what was that stuff? Too much meat, too much something else. I'm in for another night of listening to Johan groaning about his stomach every two minutes, just wait and see. Your Wilhelm, he will be the same."

"Do you eat like that all the time, here? I thought the food at the camp wasn't so bad, although there was still a lot of meat. And, I'm still not sure it's safe to drink so much water. I'd really rather have some thin soup for the children to drink. I know the Americans say the water is safe, but it makes me nervous to drink so much of it." Ilsa really didn't want to complain, but she did have some concerns.

"We will have thin soup tomorrow. I used that wonderful 'crock pot' to start some. I think Flo said that if you set it on 'lo' it could cook all night and be ready in the morning. We will see." Anna seemed a bit triumphant, to have succeeded at such a basic task. "There is only a small piece of bacon and a few vegetables in it, with some salt and thyme. I hope Flo doesn't notice it. She uses too much of everything. That 'spice rack' of hers has stuff I've never heard of. She really ought to be saving it, not using it every day."

"Why do you suppose she has so many of these 'crock pots,' Anna?" Ilsa asked. "How could she and J.D. need so much food? There are only two of them."

"Flo said something about 'Christmas presents' from her daughters and I think she said something about them not paying attention to her interests. She seemed unhappy about this."

Anna seemed a bit confused about "Christmas presents." Ilsa certainly was.

"I don't think she had ever used them. All but one were still in boxes. Don't misunderstand me, Ilsa. Life is very strange here, but it is also very good. Flo is a generous, kindhearted woman. Her J.D. is a good man. Flo is very insistent that we are not servants here. She says we are partners.

"If we are to be real partners, then we must help them. Flo knows nothing of bargaining and has no idea how to feed so many people. All Americans eat so much rich food. And, they all have so many things. Have you ever seen so many clothes? And they're all so soft!"

"The clothes are soft, Anna, but I don't feel very proper wearing those 'jeans.' They are so tight and so immodest. And, they make everyone look like a hired worker. I don't like that very much."

"Don't worry, Ilsa. Flo just doesn't understand. We are not young girls, to enjoy showing ourselves so. We just need to go slow and get used to this. It is very hard, sometimes. Still, we have bread for the morning. We have those wonderful double ovens and we have the 'crock pots.'

"Flo does not wake up well, unless she has her coffee. We will make her some, and she will be so busy enjoying it that she won't notice the soup. I'll make bread to bake and then show you the rest of the house. Just wait until you see the basement, Ilsa. There's a room there, with nothing but shelf after shelf of what Flo calls old junk. There are containers that mice can't get into. 'Canning jars,' Flo calls them. They have metal lids. And there are 'coffee cans' that have another kind of lid. It's amazing that Flo doesn't understand the value of these things.

"Ilsa, you are going to help me, aren't you?" Anna asked. "We have to take care of Flo and J.D. They're like children in so many ways."

*   *   *

"No, Mr. Canaro, I'm not going to sell any of my sheep. I'm in the market to buy more, not to sell what I have. When you have some to sell me, please call again."

Flo hung up the phone, a bit bemused.

Relieved of domestic and farm responsibilities by the Sprug and Schmidt clans, she had turned her energies toward acquiring more sheep and trying to find the ram she needed. Some of the local 4H members had been willing to sell their project sheep.

"I just wish they'd take money," Flo muttered. "That little Rambouillet ewe cost me a whole three pound can of coffee. And J.D. just snickered, and said I should have expected a small town to know what I had stashed away. Smart aleck."

Johan came in grinning. "Flo, another sheep coming. I think it is another wether."

"You know the policy, Johan. We'll buy it for its wool, but a wether can't breed. Not more than one pound of coffee for a wether, and only if we can use the wool. If it's another Suffolk or Hampshire, we don't need it. When I think of the wool genes going to waste in the wethers we've bought, I could just bang my head against a wall."

"*Ja*, is just easier for *Kinder* to raise wether or ewe. Rams, they are harder to handle. But, we have some ewes, you know. They will work in program. Little rams, they put on weight. Maybe only one year with Brillo." Johan went out again to deal with whatever teenager had shown up.

Flo was happy to leave the bargaining to Johan. She knew she was too softhearted with the kids. They were all tired from the walk and Flo hated to disappoint them. She bought any ewe, regardless of breed, intending to improve the wool quality in the coming generations. "Those Suffolks and Hampshires were always intended for meat. The kids knew they shouldn't make pets of them and get too attached." Flo held herself firmly in place. "If I go out there, the teary eyes will get to me again. I'll just stay here till it's over."

Flo hadn't been very successful at becoming a hard-hearted businesswoman. It took a lot of effort to turn someone down. She was learning, though, and the coffee stash had come in handy. As supplies had dwindled, coffee was more and more in demand. Flo saw no reason not to use it as a trade item. Nor the rest of the little luxuries stashed in her freezer. These days, a bag of chocolate chips was worth its weight in gold. It was small things, like chocolate chips, candy bars, and cheese puffs, that people missed most.

Herr Oswald Ulman had risen to new heights in his shouting. Farley Utt was trying to do the right thing here. He knew this wasn't going to be easy, but Maggie was twenty and he loved her. It wasn't the end of the world to marry a little sooner than they'd planned. If the old man would just stop the hollering, maybe they could get this settled.

With a last, thundering shout, Herr Ulman slammed out of the door. Maggie, in tears, turned to Farley.

"What's wrong, Maggie? He didn't call you any bad names, did he?" Farley asked, worried sick. "Did you make him understand? And I don't understand why he keeps calling me an Arminian. I've told him a dozen times that I'm an American and a Methodist. It's not like I'm an atheist or something."

"Papa says that all Americans are too easy with religion. They do not believe as he does. He does not like this. He will not listen and he will not understand. He says I must leave, now, and I must never come back. He says you will be killed in the war and I must not be a beggar. I am allowed to pack my things. We must leave, soon."

"Do you mean he's disowned you?" Farley was outraged at what he felt was an overreaction. "Why the old jerk, I ought to . . ."

"No, *mein* Farley, it will do no good. We will go. Do you still want me, now I am not a woman of wealth?" Maggie looked up at Farley, concern in her eyes.

"Of course, I still want you. No matter what, I'll always want you. We'll go to Grantville and find our own place. Mom and Dad will be happy for us, you'll see. We'll get by, and when the war is over I'll find another way to make a living. We don't need your father, or his property. I never wanted to farm, anyhow."

"Good," said Margaretha Ulman, soon to be Maggie Utt. "We must hurry. Papa will be back with the sheep soon."

As Maggie turned away, Farley thought, panicked, *Sheep! What sheep?*

An hour or so later, as he struggled to keep the stubborn, stupid, ornery sheep headed in the right direction, Farley decided the old man had done it on purpose, just so he could laugh at him. They'd show him. Somehow, all seven of these rotten, stinking animals were going to make it to Grantville. Maggie and he were going to get married, and someday that old coot would regret this. Farley just really dreaded what the lieutenant was going to say when he saw the sheep.

"Sure, Mary Ellen, I'll see you then." Flo hung up the phone and went to find Anna or Ilsa.

She found them checking on one of the crock pots.

"Anna, Mary Ellen is coming out with J.D. when he comes home, along with two other folks. I'm not sure who, but we'll need three extra plates at the table tonight, if we can manage."

"Sure, Flo, we just add another jar of potatoes to stew." Anna and Ilsa started giggling again.

I wonder why the two of them are forever giggling about those new potatoes I canned? Flo thought, as she headed for the pantry. When she'd told Anna that J.D. loved new potatoes and green beans, you'd have thought she'd said something dirty. Flo did have to admit that they were better at stretching supplies than anyone she'd ever heard of.

Flo cooked, now and then, whenever she and J.D. felt the need for a roast or some other meat dish. Most of the time, however, the meals were soup, soup and more soup. "And don't forget, bread, bread and more bread," Flo grumbled. They had taken to baking their own bread, as it meant fewer trips to town and ovens were already here. *Still,* Flo continued musing, *That "duenne suppe" stuff and a slice of bread just isn't a substitute for a pot of coffee with bacon, eggs and toast. Guess we'll all have to get used to it, though.*

Chores were done and everyone had cleaned up from the day's work. They were all waiting for J.D. and Mary Ellen to arrive. Some of the younger children had already been fed and were being prepared for bed by Anna and Ilsa.

Johan and Wilhelm were taking this opportunity to discuss possibilities for expansion. "Will need more space someday, Flo. Even with Brillo, will be good increase in sheep next year. Should prepare for it." Wilhelm was an ambitious man.

"I know, Wilhelm, I know. We'll look into it. Right now, I'd like to know what's keeping J.D. and Mary Ellen . . . Never mind, I think I hear the truck now."

J.D. pulled the truck up in front of the garage. *What's he doing with a stock trailer?* Flo wondered. *And isn't that Farley Utt? What's he doing here? I thought he was off with the army.*

Mary Ellen was smiling as she brought forward a pretty brunette. "Flo, I'd like you to meet Margaretha . . ."

"Maggie. I will be Maggie in my new life, please," the young woman interrupted.

"Very well. Flo, I'd like you to meet Maggie Utt. She and Farley were married this afternoon. I thought of you when Maggie told me her story. Gary and Maylene have a full house already, anyway."

"I have a fairly full house, myself, Mary Ellen. Why would you think of me? I know Farley from church, but . . ."

Flo looked up as J.D. shouted her name.

"Because of these, Flo." Mary Ellen was grinning from ear to ear as she pointed at the trailer. "They're Maggie's dowry. She's been dis-inherited, but her father gave her these."

The ewes, which appeared to be at least three-quarters Merino, weren't interested in trying the ramp yet. But the ram, the beautiful, heavily fleeced, mature ram, stalked down the ramp as though he knew exactly why he was here. He was there to breed.

Flo glared at the rabbits. Then she glared at Johan. By now Johan knew that it wasn't really directed at him. At least he hoped it wasn't. He had talked to J.D. about it. Flo took a great deal on herself and got upset when she made mistakes. All of the people around all the time wasn't helping. She was concerned about the welfare of Johan's family and the other down-timers, and afraid she might make a mistake. Plus, she was almost out of that vile coffee stuff she liked so much.

"Okay," she asked, "how many?"

"Twenty-five." Johan said. Last night three of the does had litters of baby rabbits. The others were pregnant. More of that marvelous angora hair. They were going to get so rich.

"Okay," she said, "each of the does has had an average of eight babies, right?"

Johan nodded cautiously. There had been something in Flo's tone. Like she was trying not to yell.

"So in the next couple of weeks we've got a lot of baby rabbits coming. Half of which will be female, or a bit more. We had forty does from the last cycle. Plus the ten mothers. Fifty does. Average of eight babies. Every three months or so . . . that's a lot of new rabbits in three months . . . half of them female . . . plus what we started with . . . that gives us about two hundred breeding does . . . Is that right?" Flo looked up at Johan. How did she seem so big? She was only five foot one.

"Two hundred and fifty," Johan said. "Then one thousand two hundred and fifty at the next cycle. Very good ratio." He pronounced the word carefully. "Rabbits are very good return on investment. But it won't happen that way." He added regretfully. "We use separate cages to limit the breeding." Then he grinned. "No Brillo rabbits to break into the does' cages."

Flo wasn't so sure. "I don't know. Some of those bucks are mean."

"Meat." Johan's voice was flat.

"They're not exactly bred for meat," she pointed out.

"Hardly matters," Johan said. His blond hair fell over his eyes as he shook his head. "Meat is meat. We want only the best. Best wool. Easiest to manage."

Flo swallowed the bile. "Fine, Johan," she said. "We'll breed the best, and keep the rest in separate cages." Johan could tell that Flo didn't like it either. He hated giving up the fur they could produce. They were a resource he hated to lose, but the feed situation, not to mention the space situation, was going to get out of hand real soon. Johan wished there were some way to spread the load.

"You'll like her," Mary Lee Newhouse said. "She's about as down-to-earth as anyone ever was." They were walking up Flo Richards' long drive. "See?" Mary Lee flipped her hand, indicating the farm. "She's got her stuff together."

Clara Kunze, or Kunzin as the Germans would say, the wife of Herr Junker from Badenburg who had sold the *Lehen* on a farm to Mary Lee's husband, looked at her. She lifted a pale eyebrow. "This friend of yours, Flo? She's the one who claims that her wool is better than any wool in Thuringia? Why should I believe that?"

"Because it is." Mary Lee said. "I've known Flo for years. Went to school with her." Had been there for the infamous cheerleader episode. Had cheered Flo on, for that matter. Quietly, of course. Grantville was a small town. It didn't do to make more enemies than you had to.

"Flo," Mary Lee said, "will have an answer for your widows." She hoped. There were widows in Sundremda and she knew from Clara that there were others. Every village had them; more now, because of the war. They made their living, what living they had, by spinning wool. Flo knew about wool; maybe she would have an idea.

Mary Lee knew that wasn't all of it. Clara was worried about a number of things. Only one of them was the plight of the widows in the villages her husband held *Lehen* on. Mary Lee wasn't real fond of the stuck-up Claus Junker but she at least respected the fact that he wouldn't put a widow or orphan out, rent or no rent. Still, if those women could make a fairly decent living, it would help. Clara had made it very clear that what she didn't want was another Guffy Pomeroy. They'd reached the porch. She rang the bell and hoped.

She rang the bell again, when Flo didn't answer.

"I know she's here," Mary Lee muttered. "I checked with J.D."

After the second ring, Flo pulled the door open. "Oh," she said. "It's you, Mary Lee. Come on in."

Flo waved them in. She looked . . . well, while Mary Lee hated the term, Flo looked stressed out. "What's wrong?" she asked.

"C'mon to the kitchen," Flo said. Grumpily. A glance told Mary Lee that Clara was not pleased with this lack of manners. Clara was pretty down-to-earth as upper-class town women went, but even the best of them didn't care for being ignored or treated rudely.

Mary Lee and Clara followed. "Flo," Mary Lee said, "do you want to tell me what's wrong?"

Flo's bangs fell over her eyes as she looked fierce. "I," Flo said, "am sick of this place. The problems. Trying to deal with it. All of a sudden, I've got too many rabbits and not enough angora. I've got a ram that doesn't have wool, he's got steel wool. And he keeps getting loose. I'm afraid he's going to get to Jen's Merinos, that . . . thing." Flo's face was flushed. "And not only that . . ." She gestured around the room . . . "I'm having to cut back on coffee."

"Oops." Mary Lee stifled a grin. Flo had been hooked on coffee since she was about eight years old. "That bad, huh?"

Flo glared at her. "You can laugh." Then she looked at Clara. "Sorry," she said, then blushed a bit. "I've forgotten my manners. May I offer you something to drink?"

Clara Kunze, who clearly recognized a woman on the edge, grinned at her. "I don't suppose you have any of Mary Lee's frozen limeade about the house, do you?"

Flo grinned. "Who, me?" she asked innocently. "Me?"

Mary Lee gave Flo her own glare. "Tootsie, I saw that sale at Costco, didn't I?"

Flo blushed. "Jeez, Mary Lee," she said. "You'll give away all my secrets, won't you?"

"Only if you've run out of tequila." Mary Lee grinned. "Of course, we can always do daiquiris, can't we?"

"Tell me about these rabbits," Clara said sympathetically. "Are they getting into your garden?" Mary Lee could tell that Clara was feeling her way and she was thankful for it. She had gone to some trouble to arrange the meeting and Flo had almost blown it in coffee withdrawal.

Flo laughed. "No. Not that kind of rabbit. These are angora rabbits. They have marvelously soft hair; you spin it with wool." Then, seeing Clara's expression. "It's true. Here, I'll show you." She fetched a scarf made from merino wool and angora hair.

Clara felt the scarf. She rubbed it on her cheek, while Flo explained about plucking the fur from the rabbits and the other steps in making the incredibly soft, warm scarf.

"It's like a warm cloud on a sunny day," Clara said enthusiastically.

Flo smiled "What a nice way of putting it. The problem is it takes a lot of rabbits. Feeding them and housing them; the bucks have to be kept in separate cages or they fight. We don't have enough room." She turned the blender on, and waited for the margaritas. While they were blending, she salted the rims of three glasses. After pouring the frozen concoction into the glasses she set one each in front of Mary Lee and Clara, then slumped into a chair. "We have angora rabbits and can make angora yarn but not enough." Flo sighed "They're rabbits. They breed like rabbits but keeping them cared for is labor intensive and we don't have the labor. Keeping the colors separated is going to get kind of dicey, too."

Clara looked up from stroking the scarf. "Flo," she said, a bit dreamily, then took a drink from her glass. "My son Egidius, just yesterday, was telling me about a marvelous invention. A franchise, he called it. I understand your keeping this to yourself. It is very valuable but there are poor women in all our villages. They need work. Can't something be worked out?"

"Huh." Flo was confused. "I'm not keeping it to myself. At least I didn't mean to. I'm not real sure what a franchise is. Not in detail." She shrugged. "And I don't really want to know, to tell the truth. If it's like the franchises up-time, well, anybody who owned one got inspected and had people coming around making sure they were doing what they were supposed to. I don't have the time, or the inclination." She stared into her glass. "Mostly, I bought the rabbits and sheep to try and coax Jen to come live in Grantville when she graduated. Probably silly of me, but I'm a mom, you know. Now . . ." Flo drained her glass. "Now I'll never see her again. Every time I see one of her friends, like Noelle, I choke up. Yeah, the rabbits are probably going to be a moneymaker, but that wasn't what I had in mind." She stood and gathered the ingredients for another batch of margaritas.

Clara was staring at Flo in surprise. "Then you would not object to selling the rabbits?"

"No." Flo shook her head. She didn't seem to notice Clara's sudden intensity but Mary Lee did.

"Not all of the village women would be able to pay in advance," Mary Lee said.

"We can work something out," Flo assured her. The sound of the blender stopped conversation for a minute or so. "I'm not trying to keep the damn things secret," Flo said. "I could sell them on spec." At Clara's look, she explained. "Sell them to people who would take care of them, then pay me what they owed later. Jeez, Clara. The sheep are enough to keep me busy. The rabbits—well, they're rabbits. I've already got too many." Flo prepared another set of glasses and served the drinks.

"Mary Lee, did your church do the Heifer Project? You know, where you donate animals?"

"I've heard about it," Mary Lee said, after she'd licked a bit of salt from the rim of her glass. "I always thought it was a good idea."

Flo reached for a pad of paper and made a note. "I don't think anyone has started one here. I'll get in touch with Mary Ellen at my church." She pointed at Mary Lee. "You get in touch with your pastor, too. And Clara can get in touch with people she knows."

"Heifer project?" Clara was clearly wondering what they were talking about.

"It was a program we had back up-time," Mary Lee explained. "Someone would donate a female animal to a family in need of food. In return, that family agreed to donate female offspring to another family, and then that family would do the same. Of course, it'll be a bit different with the rabbits."

"That's what we'll do, then," Flo said. "Sell what we can . . . say twenty dollars for a breeding pair. Give people a break. If they can't pay right away, we'll go for some interest, but not much. Donate the critters, if we have to. Johan will just have to suck it up."

Clara grinned at her. "Your husband?"

"Nah," Flo said. "My partner, I guess. He deals with the farm and the animals. And I think he's gotten a little too fond of the idea of getting rich off all this wool." She frowned. "There's no way we can keep up with as many animals as he wants us to. But the angora hair is pretty valuable, so we'll just do what you said. Sell them cheap, donate others. That way the hair gets harvested, the spinners make some money and we all have nice, soft clothes."

"Hear, hear," Mary Lee said, raising her glass.

Flo and Clara grinned. "Hear, hear," they echoed, touching their glasses to hers.

"It's going to take a while, I imagine, before it really gets going, Flo," Mary Lee warned. "Months, I bet.

"Piffle," Flo said, waving her fingers. "It will get done, sooner or later. Just a matter of getting organized, just like always. We can do it. Now . . ." Flo sighed. "If we could just get some coffee imported before I have to hurt someone."

Mary Lee just about snorted the margarita up her nose.

"J.D. if you make one more smart-ass remark, I'm going to throw this damn soup stuff at you."

J.D. looked at Flo, seeming a bit startled. Flo rarely cursed.

"I know I'm going to run out. I know everyone is. I don't need you to remind me of that every stinking morning of the world. If you say 'you're going to have to give it up sooner or later' one more time, you will regret it." Flo had a headache. "Just shut up, will you?"

J.D. apparently decided that discretion really was the better part of valor and murmured, "Yes, dear." As he rose from the table, Flo could see him hiding a smirk.

Jerk, she thought. *Mr. I-can-take-it-or-leave-it jerk.*

After J.D. had driven away, Flo headed outside. "Anna, I'm going for a walk. I need to get out for a while."

"*Ja*, Flo. We take care of things." Even Anna had started walking on eggshells around Flo these days.

Flo stepped out into the warm morning and headed down the drive. It was the noncoffee days that were making life difficult. Her coffee stash had been devastated by the purchase of sheep. Only a couple of teenagers had been willing to take money for their sheep. The others had held out for coffee. Now, Flo was trying to ration herself. It wasn't easy.

"Damn sheep. Damn wethers. Damn rotten, bargaining brats. Damn it all, I have got to get hold of my temper."

Flo had gotten used to soup nearly every day. She could live with the inconvenience of not having a car. There wasn't even a decent sale to get to anyway. She'd even stopped listening for the phone on Sunday evenings, when Jen used to call.

Coffee was her only real vice. And Flo really, really missed coffee.

"Be honest, at least with yourself, Flo," she chastised herself. "Two or three pots of coffee a day, honestly. A coffeeholic, that's what you are. Don't you feel silly? Don't you hate being controlled by a craving?"

The headache was subsiding to a dull throb. Flo walked around a curve, and came to a sudden halt. *Damn it, he's loose again!*

"You have to be the single most stubborn, stupid creature on the face of the planet, you know," she said in the sweetest tone she could manage. Brillo had gotten loose so many times that they'd had to put a collar on him, so they'd have something to grab. "You're going to be hit by a truck, you know. And then we're going to turn your pathetic fleece into a rug, just so I can walk on it every day."

Flo had her suspicions about Brillo. Breeding season was nearer every day. Brillo seemed determined to participate.

"Not going to happen, you scraggly so-and-so. Not going to happen." Flo reached for the collar, and the infuriating creature moved away. Twice more, she nearly had him.

Finally giving up, Flo turned to go back and get help. As she walked, she continued to mutter. "Don't know why he just won't stay put. Has to get out, has to cause trouble. Can't just stay in the pasture, has to get in the garden. Clover isn't good enough. Has to have weeds. Weeds. Chicory weed. *Chicory!*"

Breaking into a run, Flo started shouting as she reached the barn. "Johan, Johan! That damn Brillo is loose again! And we need a couple of shovels!"

"Roasted and ground, my rear end." Flo was getting irritated. She'd been experimenting for two days. Cleaning the roots and putting them in the oven didn't work. The roots wouldn't dry. Now she was chopping the chicory roots as finely as she could.

"If they did it in the civil war, I can do it now, Ilsa. I'm going to keep trying. It won't be coffee, but I can mix it with what's left. It will stretch the supply. I might make it through the winter without hitting a certain smart aleck, if I can figure this out."

It took a week of experiments, but Flo finally discovered that if she dried the roots thoroughly she could grind them. Then she could roast the ground roots. Now it was time to try a pot of chicory coffee.

"Let's try it with one scoop of coffee and one scoop of chicory, Anna. Then we'll see what happens." Flo was jittering with excitement.

The smell of coffee drifted around the kitchen. It was a different scent than usual, richer somehow. Flo took a cup from the cupboard and stood near the coffeemaker, enjoying the aroma.

When the coffeemaker beeped, she poured a cup full and sat at the table. She sniffed. "Unusual, but good."

Taking a sip, she stopped to savor the taste. "Not quite the same." Another sip. "I can live with it."

Yet another sip. "I think, ladies, I may last out the winter, after all."

"Umm . . . Johan, do you think he's going to hurt himself doing that?" Flo asked. "Throwing himself against the fence that way looks like it would hurt pretty badly. He shook the corner post, that time."

"He will be okay, Flo. He is just mad. He can smell time to breed. We only keep him just in case. One more year, maybe. If good lambs and no rams die, I will see if someone wants him. Maybe Grange can use him." Johan was not sentimental about his stock.

"It's kind of a shame, Johan. He's a really hardy sheep." They started to walk away. "That wool, though, it's awful. In a way, I wish we could use him. It's silly to be sentimental, but he was our only hope for a while."

"Will be useless, probably, Flo. Only need few rams. Need many ewes."

The next morning, Flo was ready to personally castrate the Ram From Hell. The fence was down and Brillo had been found wandering through the breeding flock. There was no way to tell which ram had impregnated which ewe. They'd have to wait for spring.

"Flo, we've got to do something."

Flo and J.D. were getting ready for bed. J.D.'s tone caused Flo to look up quickly. J.D. was usually a relaxed, casual sort of person. He rarely sounded upset, no matter what happened.

"What's the problem, J.D.?"

"It's Mother, Flo. I've had Price Ellis, Charlotte Green and Hope Underwood on the phone today. They insist that Mother has to be convinced to leave Prichard's. It's getting pretty crowded and they've got a lot of people with real problems now. Mother doesn't need to be there. Her only problem is the arthritis. She's taking up space they could really use. What are we going to do?" J.D.'s voice cracked from stress.

"We had the same kind of day, J.D. In my case it was Mary Jo,

Claudette and Joellen. They must all be using the same list. They all know we've tried to move her in with us for two years, now. It's Lena who objects. Every time I visit her she says the same thing. No."

"I know. I talked to Wallace today. The 'Adopt-an-Elder' people are calling him, too. They interrupted meetings all over town today. We've got to get Mother to see reason, Flo," J.D. said. "We could give her my den. It's closest to the bathroom."

"Heavens, J.D. You're going to give up the boys' club?" Flo exclaimed in mock surprise. "Will wonders never cease?"

"You're a real smart aleck, when you want to be, aren't you, woman?" J.D. smiled. "I'll be happy to give up the den, now that I don't have to listen to you and the girls talk. How could any man sit and listen to five women talk about that kind of stuff? You could make a statue blush."

Trying to keep from snickering, Flo said, "Okay, big fella. You and Wallace bring her bedroom and living room furniture here. In fact, empty her storage unit. Clyde probably needs the space. We'll get the room ready, and make it as private as we can. Then I'll tackle Lena."

Lena Richards was a strong, independent woman. After being widowed at thirty-one, she had raised two strong, decisive, competent men. She didn't want to give up her own independence, but she refused to "be a burden" to her sons. At seventy-five, when housekeeping had become more than she could deal with, Lena had sold her house. She had used the proceeds, as well as her savings and Social Security payments, to continue living as she chose.

Prichard's hadn't been a nursing care facility prior to the Ring of Fire. Now, due to the war, it had become more and more crowded and had truly needy patients. Lena with her sharp mind, sharper tongue, and ability to get around with a walker, didn't need that kind of care.

"So, that's the situation." Flo had finished her explanation to Anna, Ilsa and Maggie. "What do you think?"

"We should get busy. Lena should *kom heim* und be with family. Ilsa, we get to see the 'secret room.' What treasures we will find, eh?" Anna laughed.

"Oh, *ja*, Anna. Flo, is full of gold und silver, yes?" Ilsa grinned.

The "boys' club" had become another standing joke in the household. Anna and Ilsa were appalled at the idea of a room in a private home dedicated to avoiding family. That was, after all, what taverns were for. The one time all the men had tried to sneak away, Anna had called in the troops. With ten of the eleven children lining the walls and staring, the men had given up and returned to the living room. In truth, they were all usually too tired to spend time talking when they could be sleeping.

The den had yielded very few secrets. Old papers and catalogs were just about the extent of the treasure. J.D.'s desk had been moved to the bedroom, along with a few boxes of odds and ends.

"Where can we put this ugly old thing, Anna?" Flo wondered aloud. "It's really an awful old chair."

Catching a flicker of Anna's *Oh, you rich Americans* look, Flo said: "Come on, Anna, it's not a throne. It's just an old fake-leather recliner. It takes up too much space. There must be dozens in Grantville. Lena won't want it in her room."

"Is good of J.D. to give room to mama, yes? J.D. should not have to lose favorite chair. Is sturdy. Where can we put it?"

"You do have a point." Flo admitted. "I suppose it can go back in the living room. I warn you, Anna, anyone who sits in it will fall asleep. J.D. used to nap in front of the television. Just wait until you hear the snores."

The room was finally ready. Lena's furniture had been arranged to provide both a sleeping and sitting area. Her books and pictures were placed on the built-in shelving of the former library. There was even a door that opened onto the porch, where Lena could enjoy good weather.

"Well, ladies, we've done the best we can. It looks just fine." Flo commented. "Tomorrow, I'll ride to town with J.D. It's time to bring Lena home."

Fortified with a pot of chicory-laced coffee, Flo felt ready to tackle Lena. Riding into town with J.D. had given them a brief time alone. While killing a few hours until Lena would be ready for visitors, Flo had visited with friends and walked the length of Main Street. The changes in the once dying town were amazing. It was wonderful to see all the activity and people.

After she reached Prichard's, Flo stopped in to see Price Ellis. She told him her plans and received his quick agreement.

"I'm going to try again, Price. You know I've tried before. There's no guarantee that she'll agree this time, either. If she doesn't, I expect you to get Hope and her crew off of J.D.'s back. They can call me, but they've got to leave him alone. J.D. has enough to worry about. Agreed?" Flo asked.

"Agreed, Flo. They are a little overzealous, aren't they?" Price nodded. "Hope even came to see Lena. Maybe that will help. Lena just doesn't need skilled nursing care. I'm sure she'll be happier out at your place."

I hope Lena isn't angry about Hope's visit, Flo thought as she walked toward Lena's room. *A mad Lena isn't going to make this any easier.*

"Good morning, Lena," she said as she entered the room after knocking.

"I'm not going, Florence. I know why you're here, and I'm not going." Lena definitely had her back up. No one ever used the name "Florence" unless they were trying to irritate Flo.

"Hope Underwood was here yesterday." Lena continued. "She had me walk up and down the hall and look into all the rooms. So don't try that one either."

"Lena, would you just stop being so stubborn? Honestly, if you don't want to be a burden, come home with me. Hope and her merry crew of nags are driving the town crazy. They've got J.D. and Wallace all upset. They're burning up the phone lines."

"I'm not giving them the satisfaction, Flo. No one has any business butting in. They've been after me for a week now. I'm sick of it and I told her so."

"I can just imagine that conversation. I'd have liked to have seen it. Still, Lena, it's not just the space issue. We could use your knowledge out at the house. You lived through the Depression and you went through the rationing of the war years. With so many people out there, one more isn't going to be a problem. Besides, I'd like to be able to speak English to someone. Having to learn German, eat soup every day and put up with the coffee shortage is getting on my nerves." Flo laughed, "Come on, Lena. The German women have eleven kids between them. You like kids.

"Besides," Flo continued, "the only good thing about the Ring of Fire is that so many people have rediscovered the importance of family. We need you. I miss Jen, the girls are busy, and Mom has her own concerns. I'm outnumbered and overwhelmed. You wouldn't believe the mess I made, trying to add lanolin to a batch of soap. Come out and join the circus. Help me keep my sanity."

Lena and Flo had always gotten along well. Hearing the description of an average day had Lena laughing with Flo.

"You really do need me, don't you, Flo?" Lena said. "I can't imagine how you've stood it. Eleven kids, five or six other adults, a husband and a lunatic ram. Are you sure you don't want to just move in here with me?"

"There are days, Lena, when I feel like I could run away. Still, though, Grantville is home. Even Grantville in 1631 Germany is still home. We can't go back to West Virginia, so we'll have to do our best with what we've got. So, are you coming or not?"

"Oh, I'm coming, Flo. I'm coming. I've got to see the Ram From Hell, if nothing else. He's getting famous, you know?"

The Brillo Legends

Bad, Baaaad, Brillo

Paula Goodlett

J.D. came in the door laughing like a maniac. Flo looked up to see him waving a rough-looking piece of paper at her.

"What's so funny?" Flo asked. "I haven't heard you laugh like that in a while."

J.D., gasping for breath, handed Flo the sheet of paper. "Remember when you saw Cora Ennis the other day? It seems someone overheard you telling her about that ram and his exploits. This was making the rounds all over town today. You and that miserable excuse for a ram are famous!"

Flo looked down at the sheet, saw the drawing and read the first few lines. The further she read, the more she blushed. "Oh, no, please, no. Tell me this is a joke, J.D. Please let this be a joke."

The top of the sheet had two drawings. One was of a ram with beautiful wool. The other, well, the wool wasn't beautiful. The title was:

B-A-A-A-D, B-A-A-A-D BRILLO

91

*   *   *

Flo was pretty sure that no ram in history came with that kind of equipment.

Just who does this fur-ball think he is? Brillo thought. *Those wimmen are mine. I'm the one who's been here. I'm the one they've all been making up to. I'm the one they cuddled up to after the shearing. I'm the one who put up with all the hormone surges. What makes him think he can strut in here and take over?*

Of all the people in the Richards-Sprug-Schmidt-Utt household, only one was unhappy. *In fact, I'm not just unhappy,* thought Brillo. *I'm well and truly, to the bottom of my heart, PISSED OFF!!!*

"Umm . . . Johan, do think he's going to hurt himself doing that?" Flo asked. "Throwing himself against the fence that way looks like it would hurt pretty badly. He actually shook the corner post that time."

"He vill be okay, Flo. He is yust mad. He can smell zat ze breeding season has begun. Ve do not need him, now. I vill zee if zomeone vants him. If not, I vill check vit ze Grange, to zee if zey need him."

"Gee, Johan, I kind of hate to get rid of him. He was our only hope for a while. I know it's silly to be sentimental, but he's really not awful . . ." Flo's voice trailed away, as she and Johan turned to walk away.

Wool, wool, that's all they think about. What about stamina? What about vigor? That hair-ball over there would fall over dead before he could walk half the distance I could. There's nothing to him but hair. Brillo knew what was coming. He was being deposed.

First they'll see if anyone wants me, then they'll send me away. Worst of all they might turn me into . . . NOOOOOOO! I'd rather go to the butcher! Brillo continued to ram the weak spot of the fence.

Hours later, in the dark of night, the fence finally gave up. Brillo stomped away.

I'm getting' some before I leave. He was determined. *I'm gettin' some and then I'm headin' north. North to where a sheep can live free. North where they can't take my wool, my wimmen or my lambs.*

Spying one of the furry ewes away from the flock, Brillo bounded over and satisfied himself.

"Thank you, ma'am," he baaed as he sauntered away. "Very nice of you, I'm sure."

As he stalked farther away, Brillo began to get sleepy. Blearily, he looked at the sky. "Which way is north?" he wondered.

When Brillo Met Annie

Stanley Leghorn

Brillo jerked to full wakefulness. Something was making the ewes nervous and they were bleating and moving away from the back of the fence. Brillo shouldered his way through the shifting crowd and looked, listened and smelled. It was the smell that told him what had upset his ladies.

Stupid yapper. If he's in here I'll smack him into the back of the house, I swear I will! No one bothers my wimmen but ME!

The canine was not in the pen, but traveling past it on the way towards the woods with something in its jaws. Flo had described Brillo's many faults: Destructive, greedy, Destructive, pigheaded, Destructive, sneaky, Destructive, arrogant, and did she mention Destructive? The one thing she had, grudgingly, praised him for was being a good family ram. And having the tremendous personal courage that job required.

Brillo slammed into a part of the fence he had tested earlier for just such an event. The section pulled up out of the ground and Brillo squirmed under, leaving a bunch of scruffy fur behind. *Da lady don't like my fleece anywho,* he thought as he swiftly set off in pursuit. As he got closer, he was surprised to hear a soft feminine voice berating the canine: "Put me DOWN! I do not taste good and you are ripping me! Stop this before you get in more trouble!" But he wasn' so surprised that he failed to lower his head and go to ram speed as he got close.

"Ooh, *now* you are going to get it!" exclaimed the voice. The small canine, little more than a cub, looked over his shoulder and yelped in fright. The warning was enough for him to get *mostly* out of the way. But mostly is not the same as all, and Brillo shifted his attack as much as possible to make it as much as possible. The result was a glancing blow to the tail, which sent the pup flying. When the pup landed, he leapt to his feet with a yip of pain and saw Brillo turning around for another pass.

His mother had told him that discretion was the better part of valor in a failed attack such as this one, and he became rapidly discreet, all the way to the woods, yipping in pain each time his hind legs hit the ground.

Brillo slowed as he saw his victim in full flight, and stopped near where he had hit the pup. "Snort! Don' come back, ya stoopid yapper!"

Brillo was about to head back to the pen when the voice said, "Thank you ever so much for saving me, Brillo!" Brillo quickly looked around but could see no one. "Who dat?"

"My name is Annie, I belong to Johan's daughters." Brillo peered down at the ground. There indeed was the doll he had seen before, when the daughters had been out playing near the pen. "How come you never talked afore?" asked Brillo.

"It is part of the Guild rules, we have to listen to people and children, but we can talk to animals," replied Annie, who was mournfully holding her left leg in her arms.

"Stoopid hooman rules, humph! Well, I gotta get back te my wimmen. They don' feel safe witout me."

"Oh, please, do not leave me out here in the field! Please, *please* take me back to the house where I can be found!"

"Why? I gots family te watch and take care of."

"I know, but it will only take a few minutes for you to run me over there. You run so fast, I bet you could go it in less time than it takes to squirm back into the pen. Besides, a good deed is its own reward."

Brillo puffed himself up with pride. "Yah, I will take ya." Leaning over, he grabbed the doll in his mouth, growling about the horrible doggy aftertaste. Quickly he went to the back porch and tossed the doll onto it.

"Satisfied?" Getting no answer, Brillo repeated, "I said sat—"

Brillo stood like a sheep in a headlight. Only in this case it was a flood light. He heard the door open.

"You *monster*! Johan, tomorrow we have mutton! This is the last straw! Ripping up your daughter's doll!"

Johan and J.D. were scanning the woods edge. Johan bent over to pick up the doll and his nose flared open. Brillo had an easily identified scent. As did dog. "Where is the wolf now, eh?"

Flo's husband was scanning the woods edge with the sight on his rifle. Brillo looked towards the woods and snorted. He pawed the ground, gave a tossing motion with his horns and sneered.

"J.D., did you see that?" quavered Flo.

"See what, honey?" He lowered the rifle, and said, "Johan, I don't see anything now, it must have run off."

"But, but, but . . ." Flo stuttered to a halt.

"You all right?" asked her husband.

"I need to get back to bed. Johan, take that creature back to the pen and see that he *stays* there!"

"All right. Come on Brillo, back to your post." Fortunately, Flo could not see the grin on Johan's face as he firmly guided Brillo home.

A good deed is it own reward, huh? snorted Brillo . . .

Local Woman Goes Buggy

Paula Goodlett

"Flo, have you seen this one?" J.D. asked, while hiding a smirk. "It seems you've made the news again."

Flo, irritated beyond endurance, read the broadsheet J.D. handed her. The title, under the usual graphic drawing, read:

LOCAL WOMAN GOES BUGGY

An interested observer reports that Mrs. J.D. Richards appears to be having a nervous breakdown. As evidence, we present the following letter, purported to have come from the desk of the person in question:

Dear Mary,

Brillo is NOT my silly ram. Brillo is my business partner Johan's silly ram. And he's not silly. If he was silly he wouldn't be a problem. The problem is he's SMART, and he's out to get me. Everybody seems to think he's just a poor misunderstood dumb animal, but they are WRONG. He is the devil in sheep's clothing. He takes every opportunity to get at me, and when I try to point out his behavior, he stands there all innocence. But I know what he's really like. If he wasn't such a hero to everyone else he'd have been dinner ages ago.

With thanks,
Flo Richards

Flo finished reading, stunned. "J.D., I've never said that to anyone. I didn't write this letter!" she wailed. "What am I going to do? The whole town is going to believe this, just like they believe that stupid sheep killed a wolf."

"There, there, dear," J.D. answered. "No one is really going to believe that you're crazy. I've lived with you since 1967. I'd know if you were really crazy."

"I'm not crazy. Really, I'm not." Flo began to babble. "I don't think he's out to get me. He's just a sheep. I know a sheep doesn't have that much brains. He couldn't have planned this. Someone is out to get me, I just know it. Who is it? Why are they doing this?"

J.D. put his arms around Flo and patted her back. "I know, darling, I know."

No, No, Brillo!

Virginia DeMarce

"We could do it, Mrs. Nelson," Trissie Harris coaxed. "I know that you have the booklets for *No, No, Nanette!*"

"We are not," Iona Nelson said firmly to the class, "going to enliven the organizational meeting for the League of Women Voters with a Brillo skit. We are going to sing our entry for the national anthem contest, and that is *all* we are going to do." She was using her best schoolteacher voice.

"But," Trissie protested, "some of them are sooo cute. Grandpa made up the one about Charlie."

Against her better judgment, Iona found herself asking, "What one about Charlie?"

"Charlie was in the original." Trissie's grin made it plain that she was going to cherish this day for a long time. She rarely got to solo in the middle school chorus:

> "Get Wild Root Cream Oil, Brillo!
> It's full of lanolin.
> Get Wild Root Cream Oil, Brillo!
> It keeps your wool in trim.
> Get Wild Root Cream Oil, Brillo!
> Don't chase the ewes away.
> Get Wild Root Cream Oil, Brillo!
> It'll really make your day.
> But wait just a minute, Brillo!
> Wild Root just isn't in.
> You don't need Wild Root, Brillo!
> Your fleece has lanolin."

Trissie opened her mouth for another line; then looked around the classroom, said, "I don't think I'd better sing the last verse right now," and sat down with a plop. The rest of the class laughed loud enough that Iona suspected that they had already heard it.

She was saved from having to comment by the bell.

"Okay," Flo said to J.D. "I can believe that Dex Harris made a bawdy ballad to the tune of the Wild Root Cream Oil commercial. I really can. I can even believe that he taught it to Trissie. But no way do I believe that he wrote the rest of those. I know the guy, J.D. I've known him all my life. There's no way that he spends his spare time reading collections of American short stories."

"Look, Flo," J.D. said. "This could be like the story about the monster. The one that every time the guy chopped one head off, it grew a couple more. If people get the idea that the stories really upset you, they're likely to do more of them. Just to get your goat. Or your sheep."

He fled in mock terror. It was definitely mock, because he knew perfectly well that no matter how upset Flo was, she wasn't upset enough to dump a cup of rare and valuable hot coffee over his head.

Flo stared glumly at the table. No, there was no reason why any of the Harrises would be out to get her. Dex had just written that as a joke. But, "Local Woman Goes Buggy?"

That one had meanness to it.

The kind of meanness that only kids had. On the back of an old envelope, not bothering to sharpen the pencil first, she started making a list of everyone in Grantville who had gone to grade school and high school with her. Annotated.

"I don't think that you're really stopping to think about it, Mom," Amy said impatiently. "You were right the first time, when you said that the 'Buggy' one isn't like the others. Even if you figure that one out, the person who wrote it won't be the person who wrote the rest of them."

"Get to the point," Kerry said.

"She will," commented Missy as she buttered another piece of rye bread. "It's just that by the time she gets there, the rest of us will have written the Great American Novel, built our own greenhouses to grow citrus fruit in our back yards, opened up home businesses, and sent off expeditions to start colonies back in America. Just thinking about all the stuff people think we ought to do since we came back in time makes me tired before I've even gotten breakfast."

Flo wondered when her daughters, who were rapidly approaching thirty, were going to start talking to one another like they weren't still squabbling about who got the bathroom first. *I love them, I really do*, she assured herself. *I love them all. I love the grandkids that I have. I love*, she paused and looked at Kerry, *the grandkid that it looks like I'm going to have any minute now. I'll love the grandkids I'm almost certain to have next year or the year after, if somebody doesn't reinvent the pill.*

Kerry's David was in school, which reduced the noise level somewhat. Amy's David and Missy's Mike were still small enough to corral in a playpen, but since it was the same playpen and Mike had recently bopped David on the head with a toy Brillo, both were squalling in the background. Amy's Kayla and Missy's Caitlin had both been in moods all morning that would have driven the author of "sugar and spice" to take it all back. Little girls appeared to be made of sour pickles and tabasco sauce.

But Amy was not distracted. "Look, except for the Buggy story, they're all Peter Rabbit stories."

"Amy," said Missy. "Get to the point."

Amy, sad to say, stuck her tongue out at her sisters.

Flo mentally gave herself one more black mark for Abysmal Failures in Maternal Training.

"The Peter Rabbit stories aren't about the guy who had the garden, Whatzisname. Mr. Whatzisname is just there in the background, for scenery. That's where Mom is in all the others. They're about the animal. So he's a stupid ram, so what? She's only there in the background trying to keep him in his pen, or away from the ewes, or not appreciating how brave and clever he is, or something. The stories are about him. Some of them don't even mention Mom at all. Except the 'Buggy' one. That's about Mom."

Kerry thought a minute. "You're right. I hate to say it, but you're right. And some of them do have to be guys. It must have been a guy who wrote 'Bad, Baaad, Brillo!' But 'Buggy' was written by a female. It's just nasty."

Amy wasn't finished. She just ignored Kerry and kept going. "So live with the rest of them. You think that Beatrix Potter didn't laugh all the way to the bank. He isn't what you wanted out of this sheep project, but he's what you got. So make the most of it, Mom."

Flo sighed. "All right. But I still want to find out who wrote that one."

"Who are your candidates?" Kerry asked.

"I thought there had to be two things. First, she didn't like me. I had a bunch in that column. Second, she has to be here—not off in the oil field with her husband like Lelah Johnson—Kidwell that was. And willing to do it—that lets out Charmaine Dwyer—Elkins that was—because she's actually turned into a nice person, much as I sort of hate to say so."

"Someday," Missy said, glancing at the envelope Flo had brought along to the Richards girls' brunch and kaffeeklatsch, "I think that I really want to hear the stories about what went on in Grantville when you were in grade school and high school, that you ended up with so many people in your 'enemies' column."

Flo glared at her.

"The candidates left are Stella Pilcher—Burroughs that was. But she doesn't have the gumption. She just whines."

Flo realized that her daughters were looking shocked. "Well, she does. Always did. I didn't like her. Still don't. And it showed, back then. Now I just avoid her."

Flo looked down into her cup of coffee before she went on. "And Idalee Jackson—Mitchell that was. And I think that it's Idalee. She's the scheduler for the Grange meetings. Most people would have had to show up at the paper and leave that thing and someone would have remembered it. She drops stuff off all the time, meeting notices and the like. If it was just on the bottom of things she left in their 'incoming' box, on a different kind of paper, nobody would ever know."

"Mom," Kerry asked rather cautiously, "what did you do to her?"

"Before the final game at the state basketball tournament, I carefully glued lots of little pieces of straw inside her flippy cheerleader skirt. Just with little bitty dots of library paste. First, they pricked her bottom and itched her. Then, when the cheerleaders really got going, they started to fall out, right in front of the crowd."

"Mom!" The horror was unanimous.

"That was junior year. I had caught her trying to put the moves on your father. I had him staked out, already. And, face it, as a husband, he's been a lot better deal than Butler Jackson. But she didn't have to marry him."

"Mom!"

"Well, she didn't. Everybody assumed that she did when they got married, because they couldn't imagine why else she took him, but it was twenty-two months before Wade was born. I guess she was just starting to be afraid of being an old maid." Flo paused. "I'm not saying for sure that she did it, and I'm not going out and accuse her. But just sort of pinning it down makes me feel better inside. Idalee does hold grudges—and she's smart enough."

Flo came to a decision. "As for the rest of them—Amy's right. I think I'll just laugh along with everybody else."

"We can do it," Trissie insisted. "We only need to snitch one copy of the booklet. So Michelle can play."

Ashley Walsh and Liz Russo looked at her doubtfully.

"The only other person who'll need to know at all will be Michelle. Grownups think that kids can't do *anything* without someone to tell them how. We can do this ourselves. Honestly we can."

"And with Michelle Matowski at the piano." Mrs. Nelson finished the introduction and moved to the director's post.

The girls' chorus finished their presentation to polite applause from the League of Women Voters. (Iona had been quite right in saying that the tune was almost impossible to sing, even if it was very popular.) The girls filed out of the front of the room.

Except . . . three of them didn't. Liz Russo slipped off in the other direction and hid behind the piano. Trissie Harris and Ashley Walsh stayed on the little stage, reached into their pockets, and each brought out a pair of fuzzy white earmuffs.

Flo's heart sank.

At the piano, Michelle segued into, "Tea for Two." Brillo and the ewe started to sing, "A ram for me, an ewe for you." Between every verse, Michelle switched tunes and from behind the piano came Liz Russo's high soprano admonishing, "No, No, Brillo!"

Flo laughed.

Brillo and the Blue Problem

Rick Boatright

Brillo looked up and noticed that the child had left the gate unlatched. *YES!* he thought. *This time I'll get my wimmen, and I'll head north, where a sheep can be a sheep.*

This time for sure.

Brillo began butting the gate, and quickly realized that it was more useful to butt it at the latch end. Heading for the ewes' field, he looked over to the house where no one was yet up.

You know, he thought, *every time I get myself some of my wimmen, I fall asleep before I can get out of here.*

This sudden rush of realization set Brillo on a new mental path. How to stay awake? What was the magic of waking? Then, suddenly, he realized. It was the Blue Cup. Each morning, Flo came out and drank from the Blue Cup and said that she was waking up.

That was the magic. It was the *blueness* of it. He looked around. Blue . . . Blue . . . Blue. It was certain that no one was going to bring *him* a blue cup. No, that was reserved only for the yoomans.

Blue. Suddenly, his eyes lit on the flowerbed. Pansies were blue. Weren't they?

Anyway, Brillo had figured it out. The secret to staying awake, and getting away to the north was finding the magic blue substance. Brillo was determined to eat every blue thing he could find. No matter how many trys it took, he *would* go north with his wimmen.

Cindabrillo

Paula Goodlett

"Got another one, Flo." J.D. grinned.

"Oh, good," Flo answered. "I thought it might be about time for a new one."

Unknown to Flo, who was interested in the latest Brillo broadsheet, J.D.'s face fell. Her new attitude had him confused. She'd griped and groaned about those broadsheets for weeks. It had been fun to watch. Where was the fun in seeing her not react?

Oblivious to J.D.'s disappointment, Flo continued to read: CINDABRILLO

Brillo walked around the enclosure, muttering to himself. "Work, work, work. It's all I ever do. The other rams, they get all the bennies. Me, I just work and work and work. Can't have any wimmen without a fight. 'Course, I like to fight. Can't have any blue. The Flo lady is *still* mad at me about those jeans. How was I supposed to know? No rest for me. No, no goodies for Brillo."

"So, would you like to change all that, my fine ram?" a voice asked from the darkness.

"Whozat?" Brillo exclaimed.

A shining blue light appeared before his eyes. A little too shining, if the truth be told. Brillo, a bit dazzled, shook his head and blinked.

"Ya wanna tone it down a bit?" he asked.

"Umm, sorry, my friend. The lights are on a separate control, hang on a min . . . there, is that better?" the voice asked.

Blinking a bit, Brillo looked toward where the light had appeared. It was much less bright now.

"Yuh. Better. Who're you?" he asked.

"Why, Brillo, I'm the fairy god ewe. Haven't you heard about me?" the voice answered.

Peering at the light, Brillo was able to discern a rather shapely form inside it. Quite a shapely form, if you were a ram. Things got a bit slobbery for a moment, until Brillo managed to regain his dignity.

"Fairy god ewe? Never heard of you. And, I'm sort of busy right now. Wimmen to guard, lambs to protect, that sort of thing. Whaddaya want?"

"I want to help you, Brillo. It's what fairy god ewes are for, after all. I can give you a beautiful fleece. I can make you king of the rams. The real question is, what do you want?"

"Wanna be ram. Wanna have wimmen. Wanna have lambs. Wanna eat. S'what sheep do, y'know. Got all that."

"Brillo, listen carefully. I can make you one of the pretty rams. I can make the Flo lady like you. You can have all the wim . . . women you want. You can be king of the rams, with my help."

"Don' wanna be pretty. Useless, they are. Can't fight, can't protect. Run like rabbits. Don' wanna be king. Too much paperwork. Why do?"

"Do it because you'd have the respect of the yoo . . . humans, Brillo. Do it because you're the best ram ever. I can make it happen, with a wave of my wand," the shape answered. "Just ask, and I'll do it. Tomorrow morning, the Flo lady will come out and be happy to see you."

"Flo lady already happy to see me. Me here, wimmen here, lambs here. She don't like to say, but she happy. Only want one thing."

"Well, I really want to give such a wonderful ram something," the shape answered. "What do you want most of all?"

"Don wanna say out loud. Come closer."

"I don't think so, buddy. I don't think I trust you that much. I said I'm a fairy god ewe, not that I'm stupid."

"Aw, come on. Won' do nuttin'. Just don' wanna say out loud," Brillo said, with his best imitation of injured feelings. *Here, fishy, fishy,* he thought.

"Well, okay. I'll come closer and you can whisper in my ear," the shapely ewe answered as she moved closer. "Just don't get any ideas, buster."

Brillo waited patiently as the nervous ewe moved within his range. Finally, after a lot of skittering around, there she was. Brillo quickly reached over and grabbed the glowing wand, crunched it up, and swallowed.

"Oh, no!" screamed the fairy god ewe, as her magic fell away. "You've turned me into a real ewe, you lousy . . ."

Brillo turned his now faintly glowing eyes upon her and grinned evilly. Very evilly. "Yup. Now, about that wish, honeybunch . . ."

"It's got to be an up-timer. Got to be. It's the 'Here, Fishy, Fishy' line. Remember, I bought you one of those tee-shirts once. The one with the trout on it. And the one that said "I fish because the voices in my head tell me to."

J.D. grinned. "You did. Didn't they both go in the pile of stuff we gave away for the refugees?"

"Darn, yes, they did," Flo answered. "I guess those jokes wouldn't take much explaining, would they? Wonder if I'll ever know who's doing these?"

"Doesn't really matter, does it?" J.D. asked.

"Oh, I suppose not. It's just unsatisfied curiosity, I guess. I'd just like to know."

The Ransom of Brillo

Paula Goodlett

"What the . . ." Flo started to exclaim, then noticed J.D.'s grin. "What's so funny, so early, J.D.?"

"Somebody left this on the porch last night, Flo." J.D. snickered as he handed Flo another broadsheet.

"Oh, no. Please not another one." Flo moaned. "I just can't deal with another one of those things. That ram may be a big part of the business, but those stories are beginning to be an embarrassment. Nothing on earth could walk with that, that . . . kind of equipment"

"Whoever's doing it has kind of settled down on that part. The 'equipment' isn't any bigger this time. The story, though, now that is really funny."

"Did he save the world for democracy again? Beat up a wolf? Tear the seat out of my jeans? What now?"

"Here, silly. Just read the darn thing."

The broadsheet had the usual heading of a pretty ram and a not-so pretty ram. Flo didn't even want to look at the not-so pretty ram. The story read:

THE RANSOM OF BRILLO
(Names have been changed to protect the guilty)

These yoomuns is gonna regret this, Brillo thought. *They is really, really gonna regret this.*

Brillo was trudging along between two young men who had placed a rope around his neck and forced him to desert his harem. He was not a happy camper.

Brillo suddenly stopped, planted his feet and jerked his head. As the ropes loosened he began to run, only to be jerked to a halt. "And just where do you think you're going, buster?" one of the men asked. "We know your tricks, and we're ready for them. Just be a nice little sheep and everything will be okay."

Nice little sheep! How dare they? Brillo thought. *I'm gonna show them 'nice.' Come a little closer, yoomun, come a little closer.*

As one of the overconfident young men got a bit too close, Brillo used his left horn to snag his trousers and jerk him off his feet. When the man was down, Brillo followed up with a "nice" little trample across his belly.

"Get up, you idiot," the other man yelled. "I can't hold him alone."

No you can't, can you? I'll show you yoomuns, Brillo thought. He continued to jerk and rear and buck and generally make life miserable for his captors until he was exhausted. *Damn rope,* he thought. *Just you wait.*

The men continued on their way, pulling the ram, or sometimes being pulled by the ram, until they reached a camp. They tied Brillo to a convenient tree and sat down to eat and rest. They kept a wary eye on the ram, although it looked like he might settle down.

"So, Bill, you can stay here with the ram, and I'll go drop off the ransom note. I'll bet that Richards woman will pay a lot to have him back," one man said.

"Bob, why don't you stay with the ram, and I'll go to town. He's already given me rope burns and a bruised stomach. Are you sure this is a good idea?" the other asked.

"Sure it is. I don't know why so many people like this critter, but he's real popular in town. She ought to be happy to pay to have him back. He's tied up, real secure. Just make sure no one sees you. I'll be back later, Bill."

Bob got up and headed towards town, to deliver his note, and have a few beers at the Gardens. He wanted to listen for rumors about the ram-napping. Besides, he just wanted a beer.

Bill, meanwhile, was nervously watching Brillo. He really wasn't sure about Bob's latest get-rich-quick scheme. Besides, Miz Richards was a nice lady. It seemed wrong to pick on her. And, the ram was kind of, well, different. He seemed a lot smarter than the usual sheep.

Bill sat for a while, and eventually drifted off into sleep.

A rank odor woke him after what he thought was only a few moments. As he started awake, he hit his head against a rough surface. Eventually, by wiping his eyes with his sleeve, he saw the wrong end of Brillo in front of his face. As he began to try to stand, Brillo settled down on his chest. And stayed there. And stayed there. Bill was sort of a scrawny type, and didn't have the strength to move the ram. Only one arm was free, the other was under the ram.

Bill began yelling and screaming, but the ram just stayed where he was. And stayed. And stayed. Bill's voice began to hoarsen. He gave up the screaming and just lay still. Maybe the ram would move soon.

Brillo was enjoying his stay at the camp. *No wimmen,* he thought. *But I can find wimmen. Maybe we can head north.*

Bob walked back into camp, after a long walk, and a few too many beers. The sight he saw made him think he'd had a lot too many beers. Here was Bill, trapped under the sheep, bawling and choking, and generally carrying on like a girl.

"Honest to Pete, Bill," he yelled. "I can't leave you alone for a minute."

Bob kept making the choking sounds as Bill walked closer. As Bill reached for the ram's handy collar, the ram turned his head quickly and a horn caught him right in the privates.

Bob fell to the ground and screamed, and choked, and generally carried on like a girl.

The sound of men laughing gradually came to the notice of Bob and Bill. They looked up from their individual pains to see Johan Sprug and Wilhelm Schmidt standing over them.

"Tell me, young man," Sprug began, "Just how much money will you give me to take the ram home? Or would you rather I left him with you?"

Bob and Bill both reached into their pockets and emptied them. Sprug picked up their money, grabbed the ram's collar and headed home, leaving Bob and Bill to moan as long as they needed to.

*   *   *

Flo finished reading the broadsheet in a fit of giggles. Whoever was writing these stories did have quite a good sense of humor. She looked over at J.D. with mirth in her eyes.

"Funny thing, Flo. I went outside this morning and found Brillo out again."

"That's not funny, J.D. That darn ram is going to get himself killed eventually. He's become a big part of the business, and I can't afford to lose him. I think he knows it, too."

"Now, Flo, he's just a sheep." J.D. snickered. "He doesn't have enough brain to know much beyond eat, breed, eat, breed. You really shouldn't humanize him so much."

"Yeah, right. I know what I know. He's the devil in sheep's clothing, that's what he is. Anyway, what's the funny part?"

"He had a bag tied around his neck. Here you go."

Flo opened the small blue bag's drawstring neck and found a few coins inside along with a note.

"Dear Mrs. Richards," she read. "I've made a lot of money telling these stories. Felt like it was time to share."

The Brillo Letters

VIRGINIA DEMARCE, PAULA GOODLETT, KERRYN OFFORD AND LAURA RUNKLE

Dear Flo,

I've been reading in the paper about your problems with your silly ram.

I still have the original 4-H patterns for making wrist pincushions stuffed with wool that has lanolin in it. These were used back in the 1930s and 1940s, when pins and needles were just steel rather than stainless steel. The lanolin keeps them from rusting.

The wool inside these doesn't have to be smooth or fine or long-fibered. It just has to be there.

If you want a copy of the instructions, just come by the Fabrics and Textile shop one of these days when you're in town. I'll put them on the shelf underneath the cash register and tell all the girls they are there.

Your Friend,
Mary Ellen Shaver

*   *   *

Dear Mary Ellen,

Thank you very much for your suggestion. I'll be making a trip to town in a day or so and will be very happy to have the use of your pattern.

I imagine you're talking about those silly broadsheets, instead of the *Grantville Times* or the *Daily News*. I must say that I do not approve of their content. Suggesting that a silly ram could save the world for democracy, beat up a wolf, and so forth is clearly ludicrous. Brillo is just a sheep, after all. I won't even address the issue of the drawings.

If you should happen to hear anything about who may be writing those outrageous stories, I'd appreciate being informed. I fully intend to take whatever measures necessary to stop this travesty.

Again, thank you for your suggestion. I'm looking forward to seeing the pattern and evaluating its usefulness.

Your friend,

Flo Richards

Dear Flo,

I don't know whether your ram can make the world safe for democracy.

But Veleda Riddle has decided that Grantville needs a chapter of the League of Women Voters. It was that pile of offal down by the slaughterhouse that the garbage guys didn't haul away Friday a week ago that made her decide we need one.

We didn't have one up-time, so she'll sort of be inventing the way she wants it to work instead of just copying the one that used to be. She's put your ram (head only) on the stationery, along with the motto, "Might as well be hung for a sheep as for a lamb."

When Veleda gets going, smart people get out of her way.

Your friend,

Mary Ellen Shaver

*   *   *

Dear Mary Ellen,

I'll be writing Veleda to volunteer my services, such as they are. I'll be happy to help with the League of Women Voters. I have to agree, some things need to be fixed around here.

Please let me know if there's anything else I can do.

Your friend,

Flo Richards

Dear Veleda,

Mary Ellen Shaver tells me that you're planning to start a chapter of the League of Women Voters here in Grantville. I just wanted to let you know that I'll be happy to help.

Please let me know if I can assist in any way. I certainly agree that some things need to be fixed around here. I do wonder, though, if the ram's head logo on your stationery is absolutely necessary. Wouldn't an eagle or hawk be more expressive of the organization's goals?

Your friend,

Flo Richards

Dear Flo,

Thanks so much for your offer to help. The next meeting is Thursday the 17th at 1:00 PM at the public library. The topic is horse manure.

I would really like to keep the ram on the stationery. The Air Force already has taken falcons and eagles. It is only the head (I do remember the furor about President Clinton and the bison on the Department of the Interior seal), and he has such a belligerent expression. When my grandmother used to leave the house to give the city council a piece of her mind, she always said as she went out the door, "Might as well be hung for a sheep as for a lamb."

Think about garbage collection. It will help keep your mind off your troubles.

Your friend,

Veleda Riddle

*   *   *

Dear Veleda,

I'll be happy to attend the meeting as scheduled.

Regarding the letterhead, well, it's your project, so I'll agree with your plan. I can't say that I really care for this ram motif that seems to have consumed the area. I just don't understand how sheep could have acquired such a reputation. They're fairly stupid animals, after all.

I'm a bit anxious to do something about the horse manure problem, myself. Maybe it should be collected and composted, rather than left lying on the streets. Perhaps we could require the type of collection bags horses wore in New Orleans, back up-time. J.D. and I were there on our second honeymoon, and it really seemed odd to see horses wearing those odd looking bags under their tails. Of course, those horses were pulling those romantic carriages. At any rate, something must be done.

Troubles? I don't have any troubles. Do appreciate the thought, but life's just fine here.

Let me know if you need anything.

Your friend,

Flo Richards

Dear Flo,

We're all looking forward to seeing you at the meeting.

The city council was feeling so pleased with itself for closing the main streets to vehicular traffic during the day. But they have to open them for deliveries at night, of course, or all the stores would go out of business. So come start of business the next day, there it is—making outdoor Grantville smell all rustic. And, if anyone steps in it, making indoor Grantville smell all rustic for the rest of the day. Not to mention what the rural roads look like, and the streets in Deborah!

The garbage guys say there's no real market for it. Or, at least, that there's some market, but not enough in Grantville itself, so that it doesn't pay enough to cover the costs of collection and transportation out to the farms. Sort of like recycling used to be.

Your friend,

Veleda Riddle

*   *   *

Dear Flo,

I hear you're planning on doing something about the horse manure problem. May I suggest a money-making idea? I'm not yet sure where the best location would be for a composting operation, but I know that as a gardener, I would pay for manure composted with straw.

I know someone from one of those new chemical firms was also stopping by to see if he could get my chicken manure for a nitrate farm. Have they stopped by asking about sheep manure?

Anyway, the gardens need good compost. I might even buy some if it were delivered. The nitrate farms need good manure, too, and might even pick it up, free of charge.

Your friend,

Fran Genucci

P.S. Are the Methodist ladies planning on hosting the Catholic ladies this month, or is that second Saturday of next month?

Dear Flo,

I, along with my class, have been watching the stories about your ram and I may have a suggestion for a use for the wool that doesn't meet the standards for clothing. Our Junior ROTC class has a problem in finding cleaning supplies for our target rifles. Wool-tipped swabs are perfect for putting a final coat of oil on the bore of a larger bore rifle. Obvious the quality of the wool is of little matter as long as the fibers are of a reasonable length.

A number of the younger children are sending you their drawings of Brillo in another package, but I did not want my letter to get lost in the shuffle.

P. Henry Johnson

Grantville Middle School

Dear Veleda,

I agree completely about the rustic smell. Enough is enough. Market or no market, expensive or not, Something Must Be Done.

Fran Genucci seems to think a composting operation is the answer. I simply don't have the time or the space for this operation.

Perhaps the kids involved with the 4-H club might like to get involved with this. They've certainly done a good job of salvaging plants.

I know it wouldn't be popular, but have you considered a "pooper scooper" law? I'm sure most of the ladies of the town would vote for it. If we got enough signatures, surely the city council would listen. I don't care how big a pooper scooper would have to be, the amount of manure on the streets and roads is getting completely out of hand.

I'll see you at the meeting.

Your friend,

Flo Richards

Dear Fran,

According to Veleda, the garbage guys don't feel there is any profit to be made from a composting operation. Like you, I feel that there is some profit potential there.

Unfortunately, I just don't have the time or space to run this type of operation. I suggested to Veleda that we might try and interest the 4-H Club.

I believe that the second Saturday of next month is when the Methodist ladies host the luncheon for the Catholic ladies. I could be wrong about that, and will check with Mary Ellen Jones to be sure.

You are coming to the League of Women Voters meeting, aren't you? See you there.

Your friend,

Flo Richards

Dear Mr. Johnson,

The drawings were adorable. Please let the children know that I really appreciate them.

I would be perfectly willing to provide the Junior ROTC class with some of the lower quality wool. Please let me know just how much you need. We don't have a huge amount of the lower quality wool, but I'm pleased to find another use for it. The pincushions are proving to be rather popular.

I do hope that the children will be able to make the swabs themselves. I'm afraid that things are pretty busy just at the moment so we won't be able to make the swabs.

I would appreciate a receipt for the wool. Taxes, you know.

Please let me know if there is anything else I can do.

Regards,

Flo Richards

*   *   *

Dear Flo,

Someone suggested horse diapers. I saw some of those bags on horses when Tom took me to Philadelphia to see the Liberty Bell.

Those are just a very few horses, though—for historical carriage rides. Here in Grantville, we've got thousands of horses it seems like, every day. It looks like we're going to keep on having them.

We can keep the idea in reserve, but I'm also afraid that just making the bags would take more cloth than we have right now. We pretty well need most of it to put clothes on people. The Ecumenical Emergency Refugee Relief Committee is bound to think that people are more important than prettifying the scenery.

Not to mention what the men are likely to say! I know what Tom said when I mentioned it to him at dinner!

Maybe at the meeting we can have one of those brainstorming sessions where everyone comes up with ideas and then we weed them out gradually.

Would one of those scraper things that the guys are using to scoop up creek gravel to surface the roads work as a giant pooper-scooper, do you suppose?

Your friend,
Veleda Riddle

Dear Veleda,

I do suppose the cloth shortage will end someday. I'd certainly like for it to be soon. My jeans are wearing out, and you know me, I just hate to have to pay those kinds of prices at the tailor's. Perhaps the canvas people will be able to develop those bag things someday. Are they really called horse diapers? I giggle every time I think those words.

J.D. did do one of his snort noises when I mentioned them. Men! No imagination. Can't live with them and there's no resale value. Sigh.

I do wish someone were able to use Fran's composting idea. We're already composting here on the farm, but it's the rabbit waste. It's amazing how much waste such small critters can produce.

I really don't see why one of the scraper thingies wouldn't work. The trick will be getting one of them released for the work, I expect. Still, streets full of horse poop are not a good thing.

Well, I see I have yet another snooty noble type coming up the drive. Wonder if this one will do that "stare past me and demand" thing like the last one? I'm really getting tired of this dress-up and suck-up thing. And, I still don't understand this fascination with that rotten ram.

See you at the meeting.

Your friend,

Flo Richards

Dear Flo,

I asked Hannelore Heinzerling, and she agreed on three things—first on the luncheon date. She also agreed that it would be a good thing to be members of a League of Women Voters, and she asked about childcare plans for the meetings. I told her that I had no idea what the plans were, but that I'd be happy for Kathi to volunteer as a sitter. I told Kathi that it was her civic duty, and now she has gotten Anne Penzey to help her. Mina Matz wanted to help, but Kathi told her that since she's eighteen now, she should come to the meeting.

Did you know an idea would grow like this?

Finally, Hannelore thinks it's a shame that no one is making money off all of the horse manure. "It should be good for something beyond flies," is what she said. I really think that we could get one of those guys from the back hills interested in using it for a nitrogen farm for stuff that goes "boom." As for a place to put the manure, is the meeting at the library? Could Christy Penzey use all those land maps to help us figure out if there's even a place in the ring of Fire that would be safe to compost that much manure without endangering the water downstream?

Your frustrated friend,

Fran Genucci

P.S. Thank you so much for entertaining us with that ram of yours. Which of your partners writes those stories? Is it Herr Sprug? He seems so quiet.

Dear Fran,

It is amazing, isn't it? Once I finally convinced Anna Sprug, Ilsa Schmidt and Maggie Utt, that, YES, they really can vote and have a say in the world, they dug right in. So, they and Lena and I will all be at the meeting. We do plan to leave the children at home, under Ursula's supervision. There's just so many kids around this house, I don't feel it would be right to overload the baby-sitters that way.

Veleda and I have been discussing the manure problem. I certainly agree that it ought to be good for something. How about you talk to one of those guys you mentioned and see what he says? We're thinking that we might be able to at least get the stuff in question scraped off the roads with one of those scraper thingies. Surely if we get enough signatures and raise enough of a stink, the city council will listen. Have you spoken to Christy? It would be good if she could come to the meeting. That way, she could report to everyone at one time.

That reminds me, Veleda said there's a meeting, but I'm not sure where it is. Guess we better find out, hadn't we?

Fran, I have no idea who is writing those stories. It's making me crazy. It wasn't so bad when they just talked about the devil in sheep's clothing, but that last one! I'm seriously ticked off about it. The very idea that I'm going buggy! I do not think the ram is smarter than I am. Honestly! I really don't think it could be Johan Sprug, unless he's hiding a much better understanding of English than I think he has. Although, there are translators, now that I think about it. Hmmm. I assure you, when I find out who's doing this, I will do something. Maybe I can put whoever it is in the pen with Brillo.

Of course, with my luck, the rotten ram will make nice.

Speaking of frustrated!

Your friend,

Flo Richards

Dear Veleda,

Thanks so much for the notification concerning the League of Women Voters meeting. Since it's during the day, I'll be sending the boys in my classes at the high school to the other section, and bringing all the girls from both American History sections. I'm getting Sarah Beth Cochran to bring her girls, too. We don't want to fall into the trap that happened up-time of getting this looked on as a project of busybodies who all fall into the category of, "The Old Gray Mare, She Ain't What She Used To Be!"

Even though most of us are, except for a few of the younger gals like Flo and Fran.

I do think that Sarah Beth and I can make a contribution to the manure discussion. Oliver and I keep five horses, you know, and have been riding to school with Sarah Beth since they hired us all to teach. Unless you work with animals, you don't realize just how big a manure pile just cleaning out the stables for five horses makes.

If we take the manure off the streets of Grantville, where are we going to put it? It will have to be somewhere that won't leach into the water supply, you know.

Should we ask Iona Nelson to bring the girls' choral group from the middle school? I know that we're keeping the "Star Spangled Banner" for the RoF anthem, but the contest for the N.U.S. anthem is going strong. Iona has picked a tune written by a man who's still alive. Melchior Franck, from down in Coburg. The original words are by Johann Matthaeus Meyfarth and it's called, "Jerusalem, *Du Hochgebaute Stadt.*" She says that it fits the tradition properly, because it's just as hard to sing as the "Banner."

The middle school students are working on writing lyrics in English and German. They can give us a sample before they take it to the competition at the fairgrounds.

Yours,

Ardelle Edgerton

Dear Flo,

Well, I just talked to Veleda. She had the meeting scheduled for the public library, but she expected about twenty-five people.

She's moved it to the council room at city hall. Even that's going to be tight quarters. But the girls' choral group from the middle school will just come in, sing, and then go help with the baby-sitting.

The newest Brillo story is really cute.

Ciao,

Fran

Dear Veleda,

I announced the organizational meeting for the League of Women Voters when the Baptist ladies met on Wednesday. We have voted to provide refreshments.

It will be a memorable occasion for everyone.

Do you remember that flash flood in March before the RoF? That was the day before the Grantville Baptist ladies were to host the association for the District Women's Missionary Society. It hadn't been rescheduled yet. So we've been hoarding the supplies (it's not as if anybody was going to starve without them, really) until something came up that was worth using them for.

So we have five gallons of canned black cherries, and plenty of black cherry flavor Jell-O mix, and several cases of Coca Cola, and goodness knows we can get plenty of cottage cheese here down-time. Claudette will drop a note to Fred Swisher to put in a special order for us with the dairy that's supplying USE Steel and they'll send us three kegs the day before the LWV meeting, when the commuter bus returns.

So the Grantville Chapter of the League of Women Voters will be seen into existence by the very last black-cherry-and-Coca-Cola-and-cottage-cheese Jell-O salad in the world. If that doesn't make all our new immigrant voters sit up and start working for a world that can provide the ingredients again, we don't know what it will take.

We'll bring the serving dishes, too. We never did get rid of them when people started using paper plates. We just stored them.

Flo Richards picked up a copy of the old 4-H wrist pincushion pattern. I'll wait three days. If she hasn't decided to use it, then I'll just ask her for some of the wool she doesn't like. Karen can pay her something for it, and it's the kind of thing that Fabrics and Textiles can probably sell.

Yours,

Mary Ellen Shaver

Dear Fran,

Just got your note about the League of Women Voters meeting. Are we even sure the council room at city hall will be big enough? From the response I'm getting from the ladies I've seen lately, I don't think "voter apathy" is going to be a problem around here. I remember being so frustrated when people wouldn't vote in the up-time elections, don't you? The down-timers I've spoken to are thrilled to be able to contribute to the common good.

Yes, I agree that the ransom of Brillo story is cute. It's one of the reasons I don't think Johan Sprug can be the culprit. Where would he get time to read old short stories? The poor man works from sunup to sundown.

At any rate, I'll find whoever is doing this someday.

Have you heard of any possible nominations for officers of the League? Surely, Veleda will be president, as well she should be. But, who is going to be willing to be secretary and publish notes of the meetings?

Looking forward to seeing everyone,

Your friend,

Flo Richards

*   *   *

Dear Flo,

Gosh, I hadn't gotten as far as thinking about nominations. I'll have to think about secretary, but what about Jeannie May Glazer for treasurer? She never says anything, but she's a real good bookkeeper.

Yours,

Fran

Dear Mary Ellen,

I really appreciate the old 4-H pincushion pattern. We've made a few and found that they sell very well.

To be honest, as much as I'm enjoying using my own new pincushion, we don't really have the capacity to produce very many. All these kids, the sheep, the rabbits, and so forth have all of us stretched to the limit already.

I wonder if your shop wouldn't be a better place to make and sell these pincushions. I can provide the untreated wool, if you'd like. What with unauthorized breeding going on around here, there's a fair bit of less-than-perfect wool to go around. The latest lamb crop had a certain number of crossbreeds that I didn't expect.

Do let me know.

Your friend,

Flo Richards

Dear Flo,

What a generous offer. I took it to Karen and she'll be getting in touch about the business part—about whether you want to be paid for the wool up-front or want a percentage of the sales on the wrist pincushions. It won't be lots of money, because in addition to the wool, there's the cloth (luckily we can make these out of very small scraps) and the labor.

She's having most of these smaller pieces that we sell as "notions" made by the women in refugee housing. Lots of them used to do spinning part-time in their homes, but of course they lost their spinning wheels when they were burned out or whatever. She pays them the equivalent of minimum wage, which is apparently more than the people they did spinning for ever paid them.

Karen's looked into buying more spinning wheels and setting up a shop, but those things are expensive! The refugees say that after the bed and kettles, they were the most valuable thing the average woman owned.

See you at city hall!

Your friend,

Mary Ellen Shaver

Dear Veleda,

I really had to let you know that the response to a League of Women Voters is tremendous. I know you've moved the meeting location to city hall, but I'm not sure that will be big enough. The local women I've spoken to seem to be very taken with the idea.

I've heard that the Baptist ladies are going to provide refreshments. I'm so looking forward to something besides soup. Just a little bit of up-time treats will do so much for my morale.

J.D., in his usually grumbly way, mentioned that street cleaning could be done as a community service by a certain element of the population. Especially those who use community services by winding up in jail on Friday and Saturday nights. It does seem like it might be a deterrent for some of the less staid members of the population.

Of course, scooping it up is one thing. Where we're going to put it is another. Have you heard anything from Christie Penzey yet? We certainly don't want to contaminate the ground water. I've noticed that animals produce a surprising amount of waste product.

Looking forward to the meeting.

Your friend,

Flo Richards

Dear Veleda,

Wednesday, Mary Ellen Shaver announced to the Baptist Ladies that you're organizing a League of Women Voters. We think that this is wonderful. I don't know what you're thinking of tackling first, but somebody really ought to do something about the horse manure on the streets!

Of course we're all hoping for a wild success, but if a lot of people come, space could get to be a problem. I hope that you don't think that I'm butting in, but I talked to Archie and he is going to invite you to meet in the cafeteria here at the middle school. That will give you more space and the Baptist ladies can put the Jell-O salad in the refrig-erators.

I also mentioned it to John, of course. The VOA is willing to make free announcements as a public service, if you would be so kind as to send him a paragraph.

If you're still looking for nominations, I suggest Liz Carstairs for secretary. I realize that she's Mike Stearns's personal assitant, but you know what they say. "If you want to get something done, ask a busy person."

Your friend,
Carole Ann Grover

Dear Veleda,
The Presbyterian ladies are very excited to hear about the League of Women Voters project.

We talked about it this week and Beryl Lawler is willing to write up a piece for the *Grantville Times* and then cover the meeting. Because of the society column, you know, she has a lot of contact with the down-time families—my goodness! Have you ever seen so many birth announcements and weddings in Grantville for as long as you can remember? And sometimes in that order, I'm sorry to say!

But, anyway. Beryl will be glad to do it. Please drop her a note when you finally know where it will be held.

Your friend,
Inez McDow

Dear Mary Ellen,
Well, Karen and I got the wool thing all worked out, so I'm including this note with the first batch. I think it's enough to get you started.

Have you noticed the huge response to the idea of the League of Women Voters? It's growing by leaps and bounds, and we haven't had the meeting yet! Speaking of the meeting, I've heard that it's going to be at the middle school cafeteria, instead of at city hall. Do hope we can get the location settled soon. I don't know about you, but I can hardly wait for a taste of that Jell-O salad.

Fran and I both think that Jeannie May Glazer should be nominated treasurer, and of course Veleda should be a shoo-in for the post of president, since it was her idea in the first place.

See you soon,
Flo

*   *   *

Dear Jewell,

I just wanted to thank you again for the wonderful idea of selling Master Mix as a fundraiser for the Home Ec programs. (I know, it's domestic science, and I'm sorry to offend you, but I just can't call it anything beyond Home Ec.)

Anyway, that Polish wheat really does make a difference. My biscuits are lighter than they've been since I ran out of Martha White flour. Thank you so much. And it's going to such a good cause. I'm glad that you are reworking one of the model kitchens to have an icebox, a cast-iron stove, and a pump. Now that some of those new houses are equipped with these items, it really does help to have the students practice on them.

Lolly told me that this year for the joint eighth-grade science and home ec unit, you covered proteins. She was so proud of students learning to measure gluten content in flour by the water-method. I didn't tell her that I learned that method from my grandmother, who had to leave school before she got through sixth grade. She also told me that in the animal protein area, you showed the difference between animal proteins by making gelatin, and then by making meringue and marshmallows. I understand that the chicken and honey taste of the marshmallows was not nearly as bad as it sounds.

Would you be able to donate some marshmallows to the League of Women Voters Luncheon? It's hard to have Jell-O-and-cottage-cheese salad without marshmallows. I'm sure that Mary Ellen Shaver would appreciate some. I do hope the next meeting will be an evening meeting. One o'clock is right at the start of nap time for the children I'm watching.

Your Friend,
Miriam Aossey

My Dear Mrs. Riddle,

May I have the privilege of informing you that Mr. Agustino Nobili has told Mrs. Vivian Nobili and Mrs. Isabella Nobili that the League of Women Voters is a radical socialist organization.

With my most sincere compliments and best wishes for your further prosperity,

Hannelore (Mrs. Gus) Heinzerling

*   *   *

My Dear Mrs. Heinzerling,

My husband has known Tino Nobili since he was a boy. Tino thought that the John Birch Society was dangerously liberal.

With best wishes,

Veleda (Mrs. Thomas) Riddle

Dear Linda,

Just out of curiosity, where did Hannelore Heinzerling learn to write English?

Veleda

Dear Veleda,

So you got one too? I think she's using an 1883 "epistolary manual" that she found in the rectory. She even uses the style when she leaves me notes about what hymns the priests want me to practice for Sunday.

The book has all sorts of forms. The writer just has to drop a couple of nouns and verbs into the blanks.

Linda

A Night at the Ballet

KERRYN OFFORD

Hi, my name is Elizabeth Matowski, but everyone calls me Bitty. It's short for itty-bitty. Just like me. I'm what my loving son Joseph calls "vertically challenged." Only the family knows about the Itty-Bitty, but they aren't telling. I have compromising childhood and baby photographs, and they know I'm prepared to use them. I was born several weeks early. Family legend has it I came out running, and haven't slowed down yet.

Apparently, way back when I was five, Mom and Dad left my big brother Joe baby-sitting while they went out. Needless to say, this didn't go down well with a sixteen-year-old male. His girl friend of the moment wanted to go to a ballet recital in Fairmont, and they ended up dragging me along. Joe claims I was a real pain in the butt, but they finally got me quieted down and concentrating on the performance while they did what teenagers do. I was hooked.

For the next few years, until he enlisted, Joe happily transported me three times a week to after-school ballet lessons in Fairmont. I think Dad paying for the gas and his girlfriend living in Fairmont had a lot to do with his attitude.

From that first exposure to the dance, I progressed through the grades, even being a professional for a few years. I met and married Harvey. Then, just as I was starting to realize I would never be a prima ballerina, and was destined to a career stuck in the *corps de ballet*, I found out I was pregnant with Joel. I took the pregnancy as a sign. It was time to leave professional dancing and move back to Grantville to be near Harvey's and my families.

Harvey soon found a job through the family. Meanwhile, I hunted for a position as a dance teacher, finally hooking up with a good school in Fairmont. I taught there right up until the Ring of Fire, some twenty-one years.

Early on, Harvey converted a shed into a studio where I could practice. Needless to say, I taught all four of my children to dance. Staci and Melanie, as girls, had no trouble sticking to dance. Joel, and Joseph, my baby, being males, came under intense peer pressure to quit such unmanly activities, especially as they entered their teens. But they had been caught young and were able to resist. Both boys were comfortable in the company of girls, a benefit of years of exposure to girls in dance classes. This translated into social confidence around the opposite sex at a time when their peers were interested in girls, but lacked confidence around them. I played on this to suggest that peer pressure to quit was mostly envy.

The Ring of Fire was a shocker, a really traumatic event. Those first few months were lost in the struggle to survive. Everyone had to help, doing "important" things. There wasn't time for formal ballet lessons, nor the spare resources to pay. However, we, my family, all went religiously into the studio every day to do the exercises. Even Harvey joined in. I think it was one thing that kept us sane during that period. As the year progressed things gradually became easier. The starvation we had all feared didn't occur. There was sufficient food for everyone, and nobody who was able to work, and did so, went hungry.

As we went into 1632, GV Biogas and Methane Corporation, a new start-up business, drew me from the pool of available workers. Don't ask me what it is they do. All I do is shuffle paper all day. Needless to say, I still had an itch to dance. So I looked into the prospects of teaching dance at the school. I needed something, anything that would get me back to my first love.

I lucked out when Sherrilyn Maddox, the PE teacher at the high school, arranged for me to teach a couple of classes after work, "Ballet for Beginners" targeting children, and "Dance for Fitness" for adults. Initially I found a lot of my adult students were down-time females coming in for the dance classes, hoping to make themselves more attractive to up-time males. However, over time I started to collect a number of down-time males. Soon I was in that most enviable position of all for ballet teachers. I had as many males as females.

The students paid the school a small fee to attend my classes, and in turn the school paid my assistant instructors and me a flat hourly rate. I noticed that my dutiful sons, Joel and Joseph, had no qualms about unmanly activities when there was money to be had.

This took us through that year. The only blot on the otherwise pleasant landscape was when a horde of horrid horsemen attacked the town and school. There were anguished moments when we first heard about the school being attacked, but they were soon alleviated when we heard that all students were alive and well.

Because of the massive amount of construction going on and the call of the military, not all students could attend regular lessons. That meant most of my students were unable to progress as quickly as I would have liked. The lack of progress meant that for only the second time since I was five, I missed a live performance of *Nutcracker*.

Quite frankly, I lacked the competent company needed to put on a performance. We did put on a recital made up of various parts from several ballets for students' families though. There were a few simple pieces for the youngsters and the less experienced adults. However, the pièce de résistance was a new ballet that I wrote and choreographed. It was based on the stories circulating about Flo Richards and Brillo, her "favorite" ram.

Part of the fun was that Flo was ambushed. We managed to get her to the recital without revealing the content of the principal performance. Nothing was actually said, but everyone there had heard about the antics of Brillo and his harem of ewes. The whole performance was greeted with howls of laughter, with Flo joining in.

We grabbed and held the audience from the beginning when our "Flo" stood between Brillo and her ewes, protecting them from the horrible nasty underbred Ram, while the ewes looked at Brillo with interest. The attention held right through to the last scene where Flo, brandishing a big knife, gives Brillo a verbal warning after finding him asleep in the same paddock as the ewes.

Carl Schockley danced Brillo. He was an out-of-towner in

Grantville, part of the construction crew building a new high-tech factory of some sort. He first came to my notice a few months before the Ring of Fire, when he turned up at the dance school in Fairmont asking about classes to maintain condition. When my son Joel, who was originally cast as Brillo, was called away for military maneuvers shortly before the recital I had been desperate. Then Melanie, my youngest girl, casually mentioned having seen Carl on a Kelly Construction building site.

Carl was magnificent as Brillo. First in his solo where he showed angst at the new ram Flo had purchased and determination to get to his harem, and then in the set of *pas de deux* with the four ewes. He became one with the music. He was Brillo. A critical eye could see he lacked practice. However, his *Coupè Jetè en Tourants* grabbed the audience. Such *èlèvation* as he danced around the stage, leaning back in the turns so that he was almost horizontal to the floor. It was obvious to me that sometime in the past he had fallen into the hands of someone trained in the Russian School of ballet.

For the four separate *pas de deux* he gave the girls the confidence to excel. They knew they could trust him to support them and that he would be there when they needed him. The girls danced better than I had ever seen them dance before. All four managed to spend some time *en pointe*, and the audience loved it. They gave a standing ovation, calling back the cast to acknowledge the applause.

And that's when I realized something was up. There were more people in the audience than expected. There was one group at the back who absolutely screamed money, lots of money. It was something about their clothes and the way they carried themselves. As the cast did their final bows and retired to do their cool-down exercises, I turned and made my way to meet these interlopers, greeting parents and their families as I walked down the hall, accepting compliments on the performance as I passed.

Helene Gundelfinger, a young widow who came to the "Dance for Fitness" class, was with them. She hurried over as I approached. In class I had noticed the respectful way other down-timers always treated Helene. I refused to ask questions, but my eldest daughter Staci was soon able to inform me that Frau Gundelfinger was very well connected locally. Not only had she married a very successful merchant, she was also very friendly with the local nobility. She had been the governess of the duke and duchess of Saxe-Altenburg's only child for several years before leaving to marry. It seemed I was about to meet some of her local connections.

Helene dragged me up to three of the most expensively dressed people I had ever seen. Then she made the introductions. "Duke Johann Philipp, Duchess Elisabeth, Duchess Elisabeth Sofie, may I present Frau Matowski, the *maîtresse de ballet*? Frau Matowski, His Grace and his family wish to talk to you of this ballet."

"Thank you Helene," Duke Johann Philipp said. "Frau Matowski, my wife and I wish to compliment you on such a magnificent performance. Frau Gundelfinger has related to us the story of 'Brillo,' and we were able to fully enjoy the finale. We were wondering if you would be able to put on a private performance of *Bad, Bad Brillo* for our guests on Twelfth Night, January the sixth?"

"Well, it will depend a bit on the availability of our dancers. All of them have day jobs. As it is, Brillo was supposed to have been danced by my eldest son, but he was called away by the army. We were lucky to have such a competent understudy . . ." I was about to talk money when I felt my hand being squeezed. Following the hand that held mine I found myself looking into the eyes of Helene Gundelfinger. Her expression and the faint shake of her head caused me to hold back the words. "Anyway, if Your Grace were to let me have some more details, we will see if it will be possible to accommodate you. You do realize that we will need a space bigger than the stage you can see?"

"Yes Frau Matowski," His Grace replied smiling, "we have put on little entertainments before. I am sure we have enough space."

"Father."

I looked at the young woman tugging aggressively at the duke's jacket, and stifled a smile at the picture they made as I waited to see what his daughter wanted.

"Now, Elisabeth Sofie, stop pulling at my coat. You'll ruin the hang, and you know how much that upsets Matthias." Holding his daughter's hands in his left hand he brushed at his wrinkled coat with the palm of his right hand before turning back to me. "Frau Matowski, my daughter here wishes that I ask about dance lessons. It seems she wishes to learn to dance like Brillo's ewes."

I had to smile at Elisabeth Sofie. There had been similar requests after performances before. It was the *en pointe* that did it. The girls saw a ballerina *en pointe* and immediately wanted to dance on their toes. "Your Grace?" I queried, hoping I had the style of address correct.

It seemed strange calling a child "Your Grace."

"Yes, Frau Matowski."

"Your Grace, what you have just seen are dancers with years of experience dancing *en pointe*. It is not as it may appear. They are not dancing on their toes. The human toe can't support the weight of a body. I don't want you trying. What they have is specially made shoes that make it look as if they are dancing on their toes. I don't let girls who haven't finished growing dance *en pointe*, because it can cause considerable damage to their developing feet. Also, it takes years to develop the muscles needed to support a dancer's body *en pointe*. Are you still interested in learning to dance?"

"But Frau Matowski, I am almost fourteen, and I can dance. I have been taught to dance by the best teachers for many years. I want to learn to dance like them." With that she pointed back up the hall, towards the four girls still in their white ewe outfits, circulating with the other students.

"Well, the classes are open to anybody. They start again in just two weeks. Can you come to this hall after school Monday, Wednesday and Friday?"

"Two weeks! Can't I start immediately? Can't you give me private lessons? Please."

I looked to the duke and his wife for direction. All I got was two pairs of grinning eyes. Apparently they were accustomed to their daughter's behavior and were watching to see how I handled her. "Well, I have a small studio attached to my home where a few of my students and my family and I train to maintain condition. If Your Graces wish, I am willing to add your daughter to the class." Looking up to see His Grace's gracefully nodding head in acceptance, I asked, "You don't mind your daughter wearing the training clothes? Or being exposed to similarly dressed males?"

"The clothes are necessary for the activity. As long as she does not walk around the streets dressed like that—" the duke pointed to the four ewes "—then I have no problem. As for practicing in the presence of men, other than your family, I believe a Herr Carl Schockley is the only other male member of your practice group?"

I was bemused by his knowledge of my arrangements, but after I nodded that yes, Carl was the only other male, all was revealed. "Helene has vouched for him. So, if you will please make arrangements with Helene, Elisabeth Sofie will turn up when and where you request. Thank you for your time Frau Matowski. Dear, Elisabeth Sofie, come, it is time we left."

As the ducal party left the school hall I sighed with relief. An amused Helene Gundelfinger looked on. "It's all right for you," I said, detecting the smile. "You're obviously used to dealing with nobles. That's the closest I've ever been to one. I didn't make any mistakes, did I?"

"No, Bitty, you didn't make any mistakes. It was good of you to talk to Elisabeth Sofie as you did. Still, I expect she will be trying to dance on her toes."

"They all do. I remember rushing home from watching my first live performance, and trying to stand on my toes. The warning was meant more for her parents, so they know what to watch out for. But what do I call the girl when she turns up to class?"

"As her teacher you may call her Elisabeth Sofie; it will be a symbol of your authority. I will accompany Her Grace and her servants to the first session to introduce her and see that she is settled. Thereafter, only her servants will accompany her."

"Servants? As in, more than one?"

"Surely. Her Grace is a young lady of good blood from a wealthy family. The family cannot afford to take risks. There must be no suggestion of impropriety, or her marriage prospects will be damaged. She must be accompanied by her maid, at least one footman, and of course, her coachman."

"Coachman?"

"But of course. You can't expect Her Grace to ride or take the common coach. It would be unsuitable."

"But what am I going to do with all her servants while I teach?"

"They will wait. The coachman will return at the appointed time to collect her; however, Her Grace's maid must be with her at all times. The footmen may be left anywhere convenient. They are used to waiting. Now, as payment for you allowing the duchess to join your private classes, I suggested a couple of gulden a week. However, my friend Carl Schockley pointed out that the other students didn't pay more than a token, and that maybe the equivalent of about ten dollars a session would be acceptable?"

I thought about that. Nearly two hundred dollars a week for adding Duchess Elisabeth Sofie to the private classes would have been useful. However, it would have stunk of taking advantage of someone just because her family had money. On the other hand, ten dollars a session was more than what students paid to take my normal classes at the school. "Ten dollars a session will be more than sufficient. It is more than the school charges for a student to come to my other classes, but with a much smaller class I will be able to give her more individual attention."

"Good, that is settled. Now, the duke and his family are spending this Christmas in their castle just outside Saalfeld. It is about an hour's drive by carriage from Grantville to their home. I understand you will want a full rehearsal. Will it be possible for the servants and younger children to watch?"

"If they don't mind seeing mistakes." Then I paused, hearing Helene's words rebounding in my head. "Castle? They live in an honest to God castle?" At Helene's nod I snorted as I swallowed a laugh. No wonder the duke was confident they would have enough room. Then another thought hit me. Horrified at the possibility, I looked to Helene. "The floor isn't stone is it? Because that's impossible."

"No, Bitty, the floor isn't stone. The castle is not the fortress you imagine, but rather a comfortable home. The floors are wood."

I relaxed with a sigh of relief. Then I queried Helene, "That just leaves remuneration. How much can we expect to charge for the performance? I assume the duke is expecting to pay?"

"Oh, His Grace expects to pay your people for the performance. How does twenty thousand of your dollars sound?"

"Twenty thousand dollars?"

Helene's eyebrows went up and a pensive look crossed her face. "It is not enough? Carl suggested that it would be sufficient, but if you require more, His Grace might be willing to go a little higher."

"Oh, no, it's quite sufficient. Really. It's just I can't imagine paying twenty thousand dollars for an entertainment that lasts less than an hour." My brain was frantically trying to find an anchor point. *Twenty thousand dollars?* Of course, if I'd had time to think about it—which I didn't, not then—it really wasn't as absurd as it sounded. When you figured the start-up costs of getting a ballet company going, the hours and hours of training, all the rest of it, running a ballet on a professional basis was *expensive.* But I was still thinking like an amateur, someone who was basically doing it for the love of the art, and to be offered out of the blue *twenty thousand dollars*—

"Bitty, you don't realize how important this performance will be. It will be unique, the first public performance of *en pointe* ballet. Today doesn't count. It was just a school recital. Nobody of importance was in the audience. You must realize who is going to be at this entertainment. The duke and his wife wish to impress some very important guests. Twenty thousand dollars for the chance to really impress his guests is, how you say, 'peanuts.' Some Twelfth Night entertainments have cost more than ten times the amount. Come. Let us join the others at supper. You can ask the other members of the cast if they are able to attend."

As Helene fed her arm through mine and we walked towards the supper tables, I considered what problems I might have getting a cast together for the private performance. Then I shook my head for wasting my time. For a share of twenty thousand dollars, they were all going to find a way to be available.

The girls had charged through, taking the showers first, so Joseph and Carl continued to cool down in the warm-up room. Joseph looked at the man stretching out beside him. About thirty, Carl had been dragged into the Christmas recital when Joseph's brother Joel had become caught up in training operations with the army. He claimed to have been in the old United States Army back up-time, yet he was a skilled dancer. "Carl, why did you stick with dancing?"

"How do you mean?"

"Well, you said you were regular army since you were eighteen. I was just wondering why you stuck with ballet?"

"You can blame my sister for that. Dad was career Air Force, and often wasn't around. Mom was a Thai war bride. She didn't really get along with the other service wives, so she saved on childcare by dragging me along when she took Chatrasuda to her classes. You could say I was caught young."

"Yeah. I'm in much the same boat. With Mom teaching, there was no escaping it. But what about when you were in the army? Wasn't it hard doing . . . I mean, what did the other guys think?"

"What did the other guys think of me doing such an unmanly thing as ballet?" Carl grinned before continuing. "I didn't tell them, and by the time any of them found out, they also knew I was regularly scoring the maximum three-hundred on the fitness test. It's pretty hard to question the masculinity of someone who is outperforming you on the fitness test."

"Well, why have you stuck with ballet? For a professional soldier, surely something more martial would be more suitable?"

"Why have I stuck with ballet?" Carl's eyes lost a little focus, as if he was looking in at himself in some other time and place. "Because you can lose yourself in the dance, become one with the music and forget everything but the flow of the dance. You can forget all your troubles for the duration of the performance." With a gentle shake of his head Carl looked back at Joseph, his eyes regaining their focus, a wry grin on his face. "That's getting a bit deep and intense, isn't it? Just take it that ballet offers me more than any martial art. It gives me better balance, control, flexibility, and stamina than most black belts I've seen. And you meet a better class of people."

"What do you mean, 'a better class of people'?"

"Look at your average group of martial artists. Most of them are males, and overly aggressive ones at that. Compare that with ballet. It's the complete opposite. It's mainly females, they are in it for the love of the dance, and unlike in martial arts, they usually don't come with boyfriend attached."

"Hey, guys, the showers are free. Hurry up, or all the food will be gone."

Carl and Joseph turned to see the girls, all dressed up for a party, at the door. "Then you should have let us go first. You could all do with missing a meal or two," called out Carl.

"We heard that!" they chorused back.

With Joseph joining him on the way to the showers Carl called back over his shoulder: "You were supposed to. Remember who it was who had to lift you."

Four heads turned accusing faces to stare at Carl. "Are you suggesting that we are fat?" an anonymous voice hissed.

Pushing Joseph ahead of him into the shower room, Carl looked back through the door, "Perish the thought. A true gentleman would never suggest that a lady was fat." He quickly shut the door behind him before the girls could answer.

Duke Johann Philipp's carriages and a wagon arrived early in the afternoon on the sixth. They soon had us all aboard and safely on our way to his castle outside Saalfeld. The trip was uneventful, but I did worry a bit when I realized this was the same trip Elisabeth Sofie must have been making three times a week to attend class. I could now understand why her maid and at least one footman always accompanied her. I wouldn't want my fourteen-year-old traveling these roads alone in winter.

We arrived after an uneventful trip. Carl and a couple of the girls actually slept right through it, rough road and all. Me, I rubbernecked the whole way. It was the first time I had been outside Grantville since the Ring of Fire, and was my first sight of Germany. I didn't want to miss any of it. Just over an hour after setting out the convoy entered the duke's Saalfeld estate. The coachmen drove around to the tradesmen's entrance, where servants assisted us from the carriages and unloaded the wagon.

Once in the castle the dancers hurried off to change into training clothes and start warming up. That left me to direct the servants and Harvey's stage crew as they set up the scenery in the large room set aside for the performance. When planning the performance I had feared that there might be problems with lighting, the duke's residence not having electricity. However, Helene had allayed those fears, informing me that the duke had been able to hire a couple of generators, as well as a couple of televisions and video players over the Christmas season. With generators we didn't have to worry about batteries, and we could really go to town on the sound system. We could also have some real lights to illuminate the dancers.

With the scenery set up, I examined the setting. There would be some problems keeping the spotlights on the dancers. The room, not having been designed with modern theatrical lighting in mind, had no handy places to hang lights, or to put the spotlights and their operators, but we should be able to project the general effect desired.

While Harvey led his work crew setting up the sound system and connecting the lights, I walked around the floor with Joseph, Carl and the girls. Carefully we plotted the dance movements, using chalk to make discreet marks on the floor. We checked that the spotlight crews could point their lights where we wanted them.

Elisabeth Sofie and a couple of other children slipped into the room, and for the next hour it seemed as if I was forever tripping over them. They were rescued from a particularly hideous fate when they were called away. I directed a servant to guard the door in an effort to keep them out until we were ready to cope with visitors.

Finally we were ready for a run-through. Humming the beat, I had Joseph, and then Carl run through their solos. Then I had Carl dance with each of the girls. We had to make slight changes because of the size and shape of the performance area, but we were ready for a full rehearsal to music. I asked Carl to let the servants know we were ready for them, and the room quickly filled with servants of all ages and some of the children of the duke's guests and their governesses. With an audience of almost a hundred people waiting eagerly, Harvey started the generator and brought it up to speed. The lights were turned on, and then I started the music.

From the first notes the audience was spellbound. Brillo made his entry to cheers, and Carl played up to the audience. Joseph, as the young upstart Merino ram did well. He was greeted with hisses in true pantomime villain fashion, making me wonder what videos the people had been watching. However, his leaps and pirouettes grabbed the audience. There was many an *oh* and an *ah* as they watched. I couldn't wait to see how they responded to Carl in his solo. The fact that Carl was half-Asian in appearance—something which was very exotic in Europe of the time—would make him somewhat fascinating to the audience anyway, I thought. Add onto that his tremendous talent and skill . . . If they thought my baby was impressive, Carl was going to blow them away.

I was right. He had been practicing hard since the school recital for this performance, and it showed. The hesitation and momentary stumbling I had seen in that earlier performance were gone. He was moving faster, and leaping higher, with great sureness and confidence, seeming to hang in the air at times. The audience was so appreciative we had to stop the music until the applause quieted before going into the sequence of *pas de deux*. But finally the audience let the performance continue.

The girls danced well. They weren't giving their all; they were saving something for the evening performance. However, they put on a good show. There were gasps and applause at each gravity-defying lift, but it was the girls dancing *en pointe* that really stole the show. The sense of wonder I could see on many of the faces in the audience was a reward in itself.

As the last strains of music faded the audience burst into spontaneous applause. Young servants presented each of the girls with small bouquets as they took their bows. It had been a good rehearsal. Nothing drastic had gone wrong. Occasionally the spotlights had lost the dancers, but hopefully they should be better in the evening.

After the rehearsal we were led to a side room where a light supper had been set out. As everyone ate, the dancers sparingly, Harvey and the rest of his crew with gusto, we discussed the rehearsal. Nobody had any complaints or suggestions. We were as ready as we could be.

It would be several hours before we were called upon to perform. We were an after dinner entertainment for the duke and his guests. So our little troupe passed the time as best they could. Harvey and his crew checked and rechecked the generator, lights, and sound system, talking amongst themselves. Most of the dancers huddled in a group talking, or sat and read. Everybody tried to get some rest, with varying degrees of success. Carl shuffled off into a corner, wrapped himself in his sleeping bag, and was out like a light, much to the envy of the others.

Finally, around ten o'clock, the duke's majordomo came to the supper room to tell us the guests would soon be ready for our performance. A couple of the girls slipped over to Carl, ready to prod him awake, but he was moving before they could get to him. Seeing his grin, and the way he poked his tongue out at them, I was sure that there was something I was missing. Seeing the look on the girl's faces, I had the distinct impression that they had intended to be less than gentle wakening him. Joseph had also been watching. He seemed amused by what had happened. There didn't appear to be any malice involved, but I made a mental note to ask my son what it was all about.

The cast quickly got into costume and helped each other apply their stage makeup. They pulled on loose coverings before starting their warm-up exercises. With ten minutes to go they stripped to their costumes and wrapped themselves in blankets. Meanwhile, Harvey and his crew started up the generator and tested the lights and sound. We were ready to start.

While we had been waiting in the other room, servants had been busy arranging extra seating and candelabra. Just before the guests started entering the room the extra candles were lit. When the last guest was seated, His Grace's majordomo gave the signal to begin. With that, I gave a brief introduction of the piece to be performed before starting the music.

It was, even if I do say so myself, a brilliant performance. Nothing went noticeably wrong. The spotlights tracked the dancers, never losing them like they had in rehearsal. Nobody stumbled or missed a beat. Joseph rose to the occasion, as did the whole cast. Carl was his usual dynamic self, and the girls were graceful and beautiful. It was some of the best dancing I had seen outside of a professional performance. Come to think of it, this was a professional performance, and I felt they had all earned their pay. Topping this performance would take some doing.

As the music died and the cast took their bows to the applause of the audience, I took my first good look at the guests. I was tempted to cut and run. Other than the Swishers and Pierces from Grantville, I only knew the duke and his family, and Helene.

As yet another duke and duchess complimented me on the performance, Harvey and Carl joined me. At last, someone to lean on. I latched onto my husband, a little afraid that he might leave me to the wolves. Fortunately Carl came to the rescue, his German being much better than mine. With Carl interpreting when necessary, I was able to talk about the performance they had just seen and about ballet in general.

Talking with the guests I started to realize how much they had appreciated the performance, and how interested in modern ballet they were. Several of them asked when I would be putting on a full-length ballet, something like the ones they had been watching on video. I was flabbergasted. I hadn't thought there would be the demand, and said so. The response was surprising. Apparently the guests, especially the males, were accustomed to performing "ballets" as part of the normal run of entertainments, but nothing like what they had seen on the videos.

I stuttered a little before collecting myself. I ran through some of the problems. Mainly those had to do with the size of the pool of trained dancers, and a need to be able to pay them so they could spend the time training, but also the cost of costumes, and a need for somewhere to practice and to perform.

That's when Helene broke in. She had been quietly listening while I laid out the obstacles I saw. "So, the problem is money?" she asked. It was a brazen question, but it did cut to the crux of the matter. Given enough money I could recruit and train students to perform, but where to get that money?

"Ballet doesn't make a good investment," I said. She just shook her head and waved a hand indicating the guests. She smiled and said, "Ballet might not provide a good monetary return to investors, but for some, there are things mere money can't buy. For the merchants amongst us, there is value in advertising."

Then she dragged me off to talk money and just what it would take for me to create a ballet company capable of putting on performances just like those on the videos.

I spent that weekend worrying. The duke's bank draft for twenty thousand dollars was burning a hole in my pocket. I kept on touching it to make sure it was still there. I pulled it out constantly, tracing a finger over the strong handwriting, and all those magnificent zeros. It was more money than I had ever held in my hands before, and I couldn't bank it until Monday.

My loving son Joseph didn't help matters when he suggested dramatically that I should think of all the interest I was missing. I worried about that until I spent a few moments on a calculator. Then I stopped worrying and started hunting. It came to less than five dollars a day at the on-call rates, and I meant to make it all up out of his hide for scaring me like that.

As for what I was going to do with the money, we had all agreed on the distribution of the money when we agreed to put on the performance. Ten thousand would cover expenses, plus wages for everyone involved, leaving the other ten thousand to put towards a professional ballet company.

Come Monday, I asked for time off work to go to the bank. The boss, Linda Jane, was a bit unbelieving, until I showed her the check. Then she dragged me straight to the bank herself. On the way back to work she asked me what I was going to do with the money. Her interest faded a bit when I told her how I was going to try to create a ballet company, but she managed to ask a few pertinent questions. Like, would I still be working full time for her, and did I have enough dancers to form a company. Unfortunately, I didn't have any answers.

Over the weekend I'd spent the time I wasn't worrying about the bank draft thinking about starting a dance company. The first question I asked myself was: did I really want to start and lead a company? That was a no-brainer. Of course I did! All I needed was some trained dancers, and a supply of money. The latter would help ensure I had plenty of people willing to train.

So I had to think about the problems. The big one was the makeup of the potential company. There were eight girls who had been dancing *en pointe* in the recital. There should have been nine, but Glenna Sue Haggerty's mother insisted that she was needed to help around the house, and she had been forced to miss the recital. There were about a dozen other girls coming to classes who could develop into real performers, given a little time, and regular lessons.

Then there was the girl I considered the jewel in the crown of my up-coming students. Cathy McNally had been taking dance with me since the first grade. Much to her mother's distress, she just about lived to dance. At eleven going on twelve she was still growing, and I wouldn't let her near *pointe* shoes. However, her ability was such that her performance really didn't seem to miss it. When she started performing *en pointe*, well, up-time I would have said, "the sky's the limit."

I'm pretty sure she could have won a scholarship to one of the best schools, maybe even Juilliard. She had real potential and, with the support of her parents, the world would have been hers for the taking.

So I had a good core of girls. The real problem was guys. I had two leading men, Carl and my eldest son Joel. But the army owned Joel, while Carl was heavily involved in the local construction industry. It was unlikely that I could ever be sure of having one of them, let alone both of them. The next best males were my son Joseph and my nephew Mike Matowski. Both were coming along well, Joseph being the better dancer, something to do with training every day with me, Joel, and the girls.

However, neither was strong enough to lift any of the older girls. At least the girls weren't confident they could lift and hold them. That lack of confidence was important. It meant the girls would be constantly on guard. There might be easier ways to ruin a performance, but at least I could avoid that one. I'd have to restrict them to working with the schoolgirls while they worked on their strength and technique. Although I didn't think I'd phrase it quite that way.

So, where did that leave me? Up the creek without a paddle. I had a useful core of girls. The real problem was reliable males. An oxymoron if ever there was one. My two most capable males had commitments that meant they might not be available when I needed them, and the only alternative male dancers needed time to develop. Maybe next year, if they trained regularly, and the damned army didn't grab them.

It was with a heavy heart that I made my way to dance class after work. Without at least one male lead I couldn't have a company, at least not one capable of putting on performances for paying customers. As I entered the room set aside for the dance class I passed a gaze over who was there. My eldest daughter Staci, and two of the other senior dancers, Casey Stevenson and Marcie Haggerty, were busy supervising the children's warm-up. I was surprised to see Marcie's half-sister there. Laurie Haggerty had been very forceful just before Christmas about how she didn't want her Glenna Sue wasting her time on ballet, and had put every obstacle possible in the way of her training.

All was revealed when the Marcie came up to me. "Miz Bitty, you better watch out. Glenna Sue's mother is on the warpath. She doesn't think it is right that neither her Cameron nor Glenna Sue were included in the private performance of *Bad, Bad Brillo*."

I can't say I was totally surprised. It was a complete turnaround from Laurie's position leading up to the recital. Then she had insisted that Glenna Sue was needed at home and couldn't be spared for rehearsals for the recital performance of *Bad, Bad Brillo*. However, the envelope in my pocket was probably the reason for the about face. In it were bank checks made out to the cast and crew. Glenna Sue's share, if Laurie had allowed her to perform as the ewe she was originally cast as, would have been worth about eight hundred dollars.

"Your stepmother's heard about the payments for the performers?" I asked Marcie.

She nodded her head, a wry smile on her face. "Saturday night Jonathan Fortney was at the City Hall Coffee House talking about what he was going to do with his share."

I sighed over that. It was a good bet Cora Ennis, the proprietor, was aware that Laurie had pulled Glenna Sue out of the cast for *Bad, Bad Brillo*. No doubt she had heard and passed on the tidbit. She had probably done so deliberately, with relish, and maybe a bit of malice. There was little love lost between them.

"How do you feel about the performers getting paid?" I asked.

"It's the luck of the draw. I didn't audition for one of the parts. Nobody thought of the piece as anything more than a bit of fun. Certainly nobody thought those people would pay for a private performance. The guys earned the fee. The money would have been nice. Maybe next time." Grinning, Marcie asked, "There is going to be a next time, isn't there?"

I told her that I expected there would be similar evenings spread through the year. I wasn't ready to tell everyone about my dream of putting on a performance of *Nutcracker*. Currently only my family knew how much the last two years without a performance had affected me. I had spent part of the Christmas break watching my collection of *Nutcracker* videos, but they knew it wasn't the same as being there.

After that I was caught up in teaching the class. Every time I looked at a student I found myself examining them, looking to see if they had what it takes to perform. I was reassured with what I saw. There were a number of promising up-time boys and girls who had been taking lessons for a number of years, and some who had only been coming since I started teaching after the Ring of Fire.

What really interested me, though, was the number of down-time students who were doing well. Not only were there girls, there were guys, and some of the guys were in their late teens. For some reason, the down-timers didn't have a problem with guys and dancing. It was similar in the advanced class. There was one guy about the same age as my youngest boy, Mathias Steinbach. I had high hopes of him. He had been coming for about a year now, and his suppleness had improved considerably. If I could keep him, he would make a great foil for Joseph in another couple of years.

The long-term prospects were good. All I needed was a few good men to hold everything together until the youngsters were ready.

After class I hunted for my few good men. I had checks for three of them. Joel I just wanted to talk to about his military commitments. Eventually I traced them to the gym. Through the windows in the door I could see them. Joel was running Carl, his cousin Mark, and his baby brother through some dance sword-fighting moves he had learned while he was at college.

Joel was directing Joseph and Mark, with Carl watching, when I tried to sneak in. Carl turned almost immediately. Seeing me, he waved me over. Apparently Joel, hearing from Joseph that I wanted to put on *Nutcracker*, had suggested that the fight scene between the Nutcracker and the Mouse King should be a real swashbuckling affair, and had been teaching the others the basics of performance fighting.

Joel was pretty sure he would be based in Grantville for a while. He was being trained to be an officer and here and now, an ability to dance was, if not essential, very desirable. He was sure he would be able to continue training and maybe even drag along a few of his fellow officer trainees. Unfortunately, he wasn't sure where the army would be sending him when he was commissioned.

Carl, on the other hand, could tell me he would be working just outside the Ring of Fire on a major building contract. With a bit of effort, and the cooperation of his fellow directors from Kelly Construction, he was sure he could, barring an act of God, continue training and, outside of the summer period, be available for any performances.

Over the next few days it seemed as if I was forever dodging questions from parents about why their child hadn't been involved in the *Bad, Bad Brillo* production. The worst of the offenders were those who had been against their sons and daughters being involved in dance in the first place. Fortunately, the real ballet mothers understood just how unexpected the request for a private performance had been. That didn't stop more than a few of them dropping hints about how much their sons or daughters would love to perform if something similar was offered though.

It soon got to the point that I called a meeting of students and parents to discuss where I thought ballet was going here and now. One of the first things I told the assembled horde was that profits from the private production were going towards providing *pointe* shoes, and the development of improved *pointe* shoes. This went down well with all the girls and their parents. Most of them had firsthand experience of the bloodied torture devices called *pointe* shoes, or they had seen the damage.

I then described how I wanted to put on a full performance of *Nutcracker* next Christmas. There was a mixed rendering of *ohs* and *ahs* from the crowd. Some had, like me, missed the annual performance and were happy that it was coming back. Others made it obvious that they didn't want to wait that long. Many of the dancers just wanted to perform, but others were thinking about the money. They asked if there was any chance of me putting on performances for a paying audience like the private performance of *Bad, Bad Brillo*.

I was honest. I said that I was in discussion on that very thing, but I needed to have something other than *Bad, Bad Brillo* to offer. Maybe a few selected acts from well-known ballets, but casts had to be small. Also, I warned them that I didn't think future payments would be anything like the Twelfth Night performance. That performance had been the first performance of *en pointe* before a noble audience. One of the teachers suggested that we could put on inexpensive performances in the high school's auditorium. Say ten dollars for adults and five dollars a head for children to see a full-length production or a selection of scenes from famous ballets. We talked about that. Would we be able to fill the auditorium's seven hundred and fifty seats? How much would it cost to hire the auditorium? And would we cover our costs?

Then Deanna Matowski, ballet mother, piano accompanist, and programming planner for the radio station made a suggestion. What about getting an advertiser to sponsor the production of performance videos to be aired on the television as part of an arts program? Payments probably wouldn't be very large until we could prove the economic benefits, but if we shot the performances before a live audience in the high school auditorium, maybe the advertiser would meet the production costs, and the ballet company could take the gate.

The idea had promise. It would give the dancers something to work towards, and would generate revenue, something that would be essential if we wanted to hold onto performers. The only problem would be getting sponsors willing to do a deal. Maybe Helene Gundelfinger knew someone who would be interested in sponsoring some performances. I made a mental note to contact her.

One of the parents asked if Harvey had videotaped the *Bad, Bad Brillo* performance. Well, of course he had. That's why I kept him around. He recorded all my school recitals, and had been doing so for years. It was suggested that maybe I could offer the video to the television for public broadcast, sort of checking out the market before looking for sponsors.

I promised to review the video and then try to make contact with the television people. Staci piped up that the person to see was Janice Ambler, one of the O'Keefe clan. She then offered to arrange a meeting for sometime in the next couple of days. With everyone attending to the conversation I could only agree to the appointment being made, but I resolved to have words with Staci about putting her mother into an awkward position.

A couple of days later I was able to talk to Janice Ambler about broadcasting the video of *Bad, Bad Brillo*. She asked if I would introduce it, maybe even rope Brillo's owner, Flo Richards, into joining me in the studio to talk about Brillo. Maybe even bring the real Brillo into the studio, or failing that, get some footage of Brillo. I told Janice about the epitaph that Flo added when talking about Brillo. Somehow I didn't think "the Ram from Hell" should be brought into the studio. She agreed that maybe it might be better to film Brillo in his natural environment, and suggested that I arrange a time with Flo, and she would send some of the kids working on the television station round with one of the school video cameras.

That Saturday I found myself face to face with Brillo, the Ram from Hell. He didn't look that bad. He was fairly solid, with an impressive set of horns. Of course his wool was nowhere near as fine or luxurious as the Merino ram everyone in the ballet called "Young Upstart," but I could see no reason for the "Ram from Hell" label.

The students set up the camera and started taping Flo as she described her first meeting with Brillo, and of course, the event that I had made into a small ballet. All the time she was talking, Brillo postured, showing off his lines, just like a Mister Universe contestant. I'd heard about animals responding to being the center of attention before, but this was the first time I'd seen it firsthand.

There was a dangerous moment when the camera crew moved over for some shots of the Merino ram. Brillo objected to sharing the limelight. The young upstart was aware of Brillo's objection and scampered as far away from him as he could. The pretender routed, Brillo looked back at the camera crew, as if to ask, *why do you want to waste your time with him, when you can pay attention to me?*

The reporter with the camera crew asked Flo why she called Brillo the Ram from Hell. She was a little lost for words. I think she wanted to proclaim "because he is." However, except for chasing off the other ram, something one expects when males are competing for the limelight, Brillo had been a perfect angel. He even went so far as to eat from the reporter's hand and rubbed affectionately against her.

In an attempt to show Brillo's true colors, Flo walked right up to him. I'm sure she fully expected him to try to attack her, just like she had told me he normally did. Even her down-timer partner, Johan, could see the humor of the situation when Brillo let her walk right up to him. He even let her put a hand round one of his horns. Flo gave me a beseeching look, a real *this-isn't-normal* type look.

I think Flo must have been distracted, because she let Brillo get her between him and a wooden fence. Then he started to lean on her. The students thought it was cute, but Flo was well and truly caught. She couldn't lash out at Brillo like she desperately wanted to, not while they were filming. She had to just grin and bear it.

Eventually the television crew had enough material. They discussed how to edit it for the program going out later next week, asking both Flo and me what we thought. Personally, I thought that as soon as they were out of sight, Johan better get in there between Flo and Brillo, before they went after each other.

Thursday night Flo and I dutifully made our way to the recording studio of the television station. I talked about ballet in general. About how we hoped to put on a few performances, including a Christmas performance of *Nutcracker*, and where I saw ballet in the near future. I talked a little about the ballet the viewers were about to see, *Bad, Bad Brillo*, explaining how it had been the first ballet performed in this universe with dancers dancing *en pointe*. I carefully didn't mention that I was pretty sure it was also the first public performance using female dancers. That was something nobody needed to know.

The presenter then introduced Flo. She was wearing a merino-angora blend knitted sweater and passed around a selection of wool and angora products as she talked about her farm and what she was trying to do. The presenter was impressed with the feel of the garments, and asked about them. Flo explained that it was because of the fineness of the fiber. She also commented that her merino wool was probably the finest available in the world, being the product of over three hundred years of selective breeding. Finally, she related her side of the story of *Bad, Bad Brillo*. While she was talking, the viewers were shown the recently shot footage of Brillo at his sickeningly sweetest.

With Flo's introduction over, it was time to show the ballet. It was the footage shot at the recital that was broadcast. Harvey was an old hand at recording ballet recitals, and he had done his usual good job, catching the spirit of the story and the glory of the dancers. At the conclusion of the ballet the presenter, with a grin on her face, thanked us for our time.

Finally, at last, the torture was over. Both Flo and I staggered out into the fresh air. We giggled together like schoolgirls as we discussed what we thought of our performance.

The television program on the *Bad, Bad Brillo* ballet went over well with the audience. Certainly a lot of people turned up at Flo's place wanting to have a look at Brillo. He was turning into a real little moneymaker for Flo and her partner. Although I was a little surprised at just how big the interest in Brillo was. I mean, why would anybody be interested in the actions of a ram? But Brillo, and the stories attached to him, had caught the public imagination. He was a fad, just like the hula-hoop and Rubik's cube, and who were Flo and I to ignore a fad? We had no idea just how long the Brillo fad would last, so sought to "make hay while the sun shines."

The positive audience response to that first show resulted in me being invited back to do a weekly *Night at the Ballet* program. In each show I introduced a ballet and talked a little about the story line and the history of the story. Then they played the video of that night's ballet. Once a month, rather than show a ballet from my stock, I showed a compilation of the company performing scenes from ballets or, I'm a little embarrassed to say, performances from the continuing adventures of Brillo.

Brillo was becoming a bit of an industry all of his own. Flo, acting with advice from my son, Joel, who was happy to put some of what he learned at college to good use, was now selling Brillo branded merchandise. The first thing Joel had done on the Monday after the Brillo story was broadcast was to drag Flo into town to register her claim to the Brillo brand. It wasn't a moment too soon, as others were soon trying to jump on the Brillo bandwagon.

Soon there were Brillo short stories by Lena Richards, Flo's mother-in-law, and even a comic strip; author anonymous. There were products either featuring Brillo, like the Brillo soft toys, or claiming an association with Brillo. Of the latter, the one that most concerned me was the new Brillo dishwashing pad. Having licensed the use of Brillo's image, the manufacturer was willing to sponsor the production of ballets of the continuing adventures of Brillo for the public and for the television. It was tacky, but it paid.

So we had our first sponsor. The sponsorship payment barely covered the cost of producing and recording each performance, leaving only a pittance to distribute amongst the small cast involved in each episode. We could make a small income charging people to come and watch the performances being recorded, but the few dollars a head we were charging didn't really compensate the efforts of the performers.

However, we had a foot in the door. With the evidence of how the Brillo connection helped the manufacturer of the Brillo pads we started to get a few more inquiries from people willing to sponsor us, if they could somehow tie in their product. The most promising of these was a fabric merchant who wanted to show off his brilliantly colored fabrics. Not only would he provide fabric for costumes at cost, but also he didn't require the company to perform Brillo-oriented shows.

There was, of course, a price to be paid. His daughter was one of my students, and he expected that she be given important roles in every performance he sponsored. I don't know what I would have done if she hadn't been able to hold a place on her own merit. I like to think I would have stuck to my guns, but money is money. Fortunately, not only could she twist her father round her little finger, she was actually a good dancer, and one who was fully aware she still had a lot to learn.

Fräulein Catharina Matzinger was fully prepared to use her power as her father's daughter to push for the plum roles, but she had caught the bug. She wanted to be a prima ballerina, and my company was the only game in town. To achieve her dream, the company had to flourish. I managed to persuade her not to always push for the good roles.

All it took was a few long drawn-out discussions on where I saw the company going, if it stayed solvent and continued to draw an audience, to get her to see reason. Convincing her mother and father took a little longer. In the end I let Catharina introduce them to her new dancing friend and competitor for some of the plum roles, Duchess

Elisabeth Sofie. Somehow, that friendship seemed to negate most of their objections.

Gradually, as the months rolled on, my little ballet company grew in size, confidence, and ability. The company started to perform monthly ballet days in the hall at the middle school. There was an early matinee for children, where the younger students could perform simple ballets and simplified versions of the continuing adventures of Brillo, and there were evening performances where the senior dancers could show their paces.

Just before the second anniversary of the Ring of Fire we put on an evening of selected excerpts at the high school auditorium. I had carefully gone through my collection of ballet videos looking for scenes we could perform. Sorting out what was and wasn't possible brought home to everyone how dependent we were on Carl and Joel. It was going to be a couple of years before we could develop our upcoming male talent into anything like their combination of technical ability, strength, graceful dynamism, and, well, to cut to the chase, showmanship.

The evening was a technical success, and we even made a tiny profit. The audience was appreciative of the girls as they danced *en pointe*, and then Carl and Joel astonished them with their grace and strength as they performed, and when they lifted the girls, the seemingly effortless lifts drew loud applause. Now, if we could just pay the dancers a living wage, we would be set.

It was as we entered summer that my troubles started. First, there was the second anniversary of the Ring of Fire. It was an emotionally charged time, with people remembering family they had lost forever on that fateful day. A lot of people were feeling particularly vulnerable on the anniversary.

The next problem was the male leads. First, as he had warned, other commitments ate into the time Carl could devote to the company. Then delayed spring fever hit my eldest son. He was suddenly very serious about Alice Abodeely, one of my senior *en pointe* dancers. I think this might have been another effect of the emotionally charged anniversary of the Ring of Fire, but it made for some really good performances. Unfortunately, the romance and intimacy Joel put into his dances with Alice didn't carry over to the other girls, and his performances with them became as stilted as when he danced with his sisters. The performances were technically proficient, but they lacked any spark.

Coming into June, I posted the proposed cast for *Nutcracker*, and quickly ducked for cover. The male lead, Carl or Joel, was not a problem, my son Joseph as the Nutcracker and Nephew, again, no problem. It was the female roles that had mothers up in arms. It was bad enough I bracketed Joel's girlfriend and my eldest daughter for the female lead. But when I put twelve year old Cathy McNally down as Clara, the second female lead, it was too much for some of the mothers.

Again Laurie Haggerty was to the forefront. She demanded to know why her Glenna Sue wasn't playing Clara. She pointed out vigorously that her Glenna Sue could dance *en pointe*, unlike Cathy, who was still limited to *demi-pointe*. Before I could point out that Glenna Sue was needed for other roles the rest of the combative mothers waded in.

There were squabbles over whether their sons or daughters were to play mice or soldiers, who got which part in the Land of the Sweets dances, who got to wear what color costume in the party scenes and what order they appeared on stage. Even pettier was the squabble over what color doll the girls were to be given in the party scene.

Calm was only restored when Elisabeth Sofie asked what the problem was. Every mother knew just who Elisabeth Sofie was. In fact, she was a prime reason why some of the mothers were making such a fuss. They wanted their daughters, and in some cases, their sons, to be on the same side as the duchess.

I put my foot down and said that the leads and Sweets dances were nonnegotiable. I indicated that assignments for the party and fight scenes could be negotiated, but that if I couldn't get the right numbers for each group, I would resort to random assignment. Which I'm sad to say, is what I ended up doing. Colored tokens were put into a couple of socks and everyone drew one to determine what color they would wear in the party scene, and drew again to determine whether they played the fight scene as either a mouse or a soldier.

Not everybody was happy with what they drew, so there was some trading of roles. It ended almost amicably, at least among the children. The mothers . . . well, if the children hadn't been avidly watching, blood would have been spilled.

Of course I hadn't put up all the roles, just those I intended to fill from my students. I was looking for a few parents to volunteer as party guests and either soldiers or mice, and for a few "props" for the *en pointe* dances in the Waltz of the Flowers. Joel and Duchess Elisabeth Sofie between them delivered a number of down-timers either training as officers or known to Elisabeth Sofie's family who were not only willing to participate, but could actually dance. Not ballet of course, but they could move in time to music without tripping over themselves or their partners. Additionally, they knew the current courtly dances, which I was assured would fit nicely for the party scene. That was one less problem. With a number of men and even some women who knew the steps, the party scene should be a lot easier to produce than I had originally expected.

The icing on the cake was when a group of East Europeans came knocking on my door. They had seen the broadcast of *Nutcracker* and heard my appeal for people able and willing to put on a Russian-type dance for our production. They demonstrated one of their folk dances. It was impressive, very athletic, and reminiscent of what we consider "Cossack" dancing. With a little work it could be modified to fit the music. Then the women showed me their festival costumes. They were beautiful, such embroidery, and so much of it. Well, needless to say, that filled the Russian dance slot.

So I now had a cast. With roles allocated, the dancers settled to learning their parts. Meanwhile I got busy arranging costumes and sets. The first step was to announce on the television and radio that we were interested in any clothes people might want to donate. The call got a good response. Not only did we have people willing to give us some of their surplus cloth, clothes and stockings, but also some of the older women offered to help make and embellish the costumes.

Amongst the clothes we were given were quite a few colorful bridesmaids' outfits. The sheer fabrics and vivid colors were perfect for costumes. Most of them had been sitting in their plastic wrappers since their one and only outing, having been buried deep in the darkest recesses of the bridesmaids' closets, and their owners were only too happy to sacrifice them to a good cause.

Shoes, and more importantly, *pointe* shoes, had been solved over a year earlier. My uncle Mark had owned a local shoe shop for years. He had done a lot of shoe and boot repairs while he had the shop, and when he sold out, he spent his retirement repairing and making boots and shoes in his workshop. Of course I had taken advantage of the connection, and Uncle Mark had made and repaired dance shoes for my students and me for years. He hadn't made *pointe* shoes of course, just the common dance slipper.

When I started teaching dance again after the Ring of Fire I asked him about making *pointe* shoes. He tried, he really did try, but they were little better than the torture devices I had worn when I was performing. They were better than nothing, but not by much.

Fortunately, Uncle Mark and Auntie Mary had taken in a refugee family. Either someone was thinking when they made the allocation, or God was watching. Hans Bauer and his son were shoemakers. The family had been on the run from marauding mercenaries when they stumbled into Granville with all their worldly goods and the tools of their trade piled into a handcart.

Not only did Hans and his son Jacob adapt easily to the up-time machines in Uncle Mark's workshop, but also Jacob was a bit of an innovator. He worked out a way to make a *pointe* shoe that lasted longer than the classical shoe, and gave the foot more support. They weren't as good as the latest up-time *pointe* shoes, but they were much better than the torture devices I had danced in.

As we hit late September, things threatened to go to hell in a hand basket. There had been a major naval battle that had sunk most of the Dutch fleet, and we were now at war with France, Spain, Denmark and England. Nobody seemed to know what it all meant, but there were rumors of an upcoming battle raging through the town.

I was starting to worry what this could mean for my elder son Joel, so I made arrangements to visit the newlyweds. After their marriage in August, Joel and Alice had moved in with Casey Stevenson. There was no way Joel and Alice could afford to buy a house on their salaries, and renting their own place would have been crippling.

But anyway, there I was, walking down the road to visit Alice, when what did I see coming out the drive? That damn son of mine was actually riding a *horse*. The fool, didn't he realize what damage he was doing? I just about sprinted after him, but first things first. Alice was expecting me, so I would see Alice first. Joel could wait.

It got worse. At the door, one of Alice's friends, Noelle Murphy, literally dragged me into the house and frog marched me through to the lounge, where she pushed me towards the emotional mess that was my daughter-in-law before making her escape.

Alice was bitterly denouncing the army as the tears ran down her face. I had just missed Joel, she explained between sobs. He had just been around to tell her they were sending him to Fulda until further notice. This was a disaster. My worst nightmare was coming true. I'd been banking on having Joel available for the *Nutcracker* performance. Carl had been even less available than expected, often going missing for weeks at a time. Now it looked like I was going to lose Joel as well.

As Alice cried in my arms, I pondered the options. Either I rewrote the production without an *en pointe* Sugar Plum Fairy, or I bit the bullet, and ran my nephew Joe Calagna, as the Sugar Plum Fairy's Cavalier. Either way, the dual parts of Soldier Doll and Mouse King would have to be redistributed.

Neither option was attractive. I really needed to have an *en pointe* dancer as the female lead. But to do that I needed someone strong enough to support, lift, and carry her. The trouble was there was only one male left in the company with sufficient technical ability who could lift Staci or Alice. And he made a statue look dynamic. Well, okay, my nephew, Joe isn't really that bad. He could make the lifts look effortless, but I couldn't hang a performance on his ability, not like I could Joel or Carl. I was just about in tears myself as I pondered what to do.

As if that wasn't enough, I received a letter from Magdeburg, from Her Ladyship herself. Mrs. Admiral Simpson had apparently heard that I was planning on putting on a full-length performance of *Nutcracker*. Mary Simpson was suggesting that wouldn't it be nice if, instead of only the one performance, I was to put on a short season in the high school auditorium. No more than a weekend's worth of performances of course. She had already talked to any number of important people in Magdeburg, and they were all indicating a desire to see a live performance of a modern ballet.

I was horrified. I had heard that Mike Stearns had helped Tom Simpson's parents be socially rehabilitated. It appeared that the rumors were true. There was little doubt that with Mike's support, that if her ladyship put her mind to it, important people would be coming to Grantville to watch the performance of *Nutcracker*. I had met her type often enough before. Once started on their course they were unstoppable.

Now it seemed that my fledgling company had better be able to put on a short season of ballet, or else life wouldn't be worth living. As I said, I've met her type before. If you deliver what they want and expect, they can't do enough for you. Fail to deliver to their expectations, and watch out. Nothing is more dangerous than a Society Matron who feels you have made her lose face amongst her contemporaries.

The postscript asking me to get in touch if I needed any help made me laugh. Need help? Of course I needed help. There was a world of difference between the friendly performance I had planned and what her ladyship wanted. There was no way I could put on the performances she wanted without Joel or Carl. Maybe she could use her influence to get Joel's deployment deferred or postponed? And what about the expense? Who was going to pay for everything? And what about my performers?

It was one thing to plan a single performance among friends. However, to perform in front of the people Mary Simpson was proposing to bring to watch, I really needed the dancers to train more intensely. Still, they couldn't live on air. They had to earn a living. There was no way they could afford to increase the number of hours they spent training, not unless they were reasonably compensated for their time.

The first indication that someone was listening to my prayers appeared on my doorstep a few days after the battle at Wismar. In the days since I sent that desperate reply back to Mary Simpson there had been no order canceling Joel's posting to Fulda, so I was desperate for some good news. And there he stood, waiting to come in for the regular practice session, as if he had never been away. I retaliated of course, pushing him throughout the session, trying to make him suffer as I had suffered for all those sessions he had missed. Carl didn't turn a hair.

He also didn't explain where he had been or what he had been doing. That didn't matter, because he assured me that he would be available up until after the performances. I picked up on that. He seemed to have heard that instead of just the one performance originally planned, we were now going to be putting on a season of four performances. A smug smile and a tapping of his nose with his forefinger were all the answer I got.

Anyway, the girls were pleased to see him, especially Staci. She hadn't been looking forward to performing the lead with her cousin, Joe. For that matter, Joe just about fell on Carl as well. He hadn't been that enthusiastic about dancing the male lead himself. The class started to bubble. With Carl confirmed as the male lead there was a new confidence amongst the company.

I was deeply immersed in guiding the dancers through the Waltz of the Flowers when the music stopped suddenly. My first look was towards Deanna at the piano. She was looking towards the back of the hall. My eyes followed her gaze. There were visitors. After indicating to the class to take a breather I made my way to the group standing at the door. I had recognized Mary Simpson with that first glance, now I looked at her companions. There was nobody I recognized.

They were, judging by their style of dress, down-timers, and important ones at that. They were richly dressed, one of them really richly. I had thought that Duke Johann and his wife had been expensively dressed that first time I met them, but one of the ladies took conspicuous consumption to new levels. Acres of fine lace on top of a colorful batik style dyed silk overdress, with fine silk embroidery, in all the latest colors from Lothlorien Farbenwerk, and yes, gold and silver wire embroidery as well.

I quickly looked to where Elisabeth Sofie's guardian usually sat, to see if she knew any of them. Apparently she did. The new Countess Emelie of Schwarzburg-Rudolstadt was already on her feet and moving rapidly towards the visitors. Even as I snatched up my woolen cardigan and struggled to put it on she was sinking into a curtsey that would have put most of my students to shame.

As Countess Emelie rose and exchanged hugs with the most distinguished of the ladies I took my rapidly diminishing courage in my hands. I took a deep breath, straightened my back, and walked towards them, doing my best to glide gracefully along the floor. Anything to distract their attention from the tatty training sweats I was wearing.

With the down-time ladies clustered around Countess Emelie, I approached her ladyship, Mrs. Mary Simpson. "Who is the young lady?" she asked, nodding her head towards Countess Emelie.

"Countess Emelie, Count Ludwig Guenther of Schwarzburg-Rudolstadt's child bride. She's staying close to Grantville for educational reasons. She's also acting as guardian to her cousin Elisabeth Sofie. That's why she's here now. She's waiting for class to finish."

"Elisabeth Sofie?" Mary asked, obviously not sure who the young lady was.

I quickly searched the class. No, Elisabeth Sofie wasn't around. She had probably already gone to shower and change. "The daughter of Duke Johan Philipp of Saxe-Altenburg. Really, I should have been more careful and said Duchess Elisabeth Sofie, but one of the perks of being her teacher is I can drop the title," I replied smiling. "So, what can I do for you, Mrs. Simpson?"

"Mary, dear. Please call me Mary. I'm sure we're going to be the best of friends, and friends should be on first name terms."

Swallowing a bit, mainly because I didn't see us ever being close friends, I invited her to call me Bitty. "Er, Mary, how can I help you?" I asked.

"My guests and I have come to Grantville for other reasons, but we would like to see how the performance is shaping up. Could you show them something from the ballet you are working on?"

"Well, we were going through the Waltz of the Flowers. I was just going to have them run through the dance when you arrived. It's about seven minutes long, if you have the time."

"Thank you, Bitty. I'm sure my companions would just love to see how the ballet is progressing. Come, I'll introduce you to them."

By the time we arrived at the group of down-time ladies Countess Emelie was chatting away with a younger woman. She turned when I arrived and smiled while she let Mary make the introductions.

"Your Grace, may I present Elizabeth Matowski, the *maîtresse de ballet*. Elizabeth, Her Grace, Dorothea Sophia of Saxe-Altenburg, abbess of Quedlinburg."

I sank into my very best, thank you audience, curtsey, front foot fully turned out, left leg sliding back as I sank down gracefully before bowing the torso forward. I thought about that Saxe-Altenburg bit. Did that make her some kind of relative to our Elisabeth Sofie? Was she here to check up on her? As I lifted my head up I caught a smile from Her Grace.

"Brillo?" she asked, pointing to the Ram's head logo on the breast of my cardigan, a wide grin creasing her face.

As I rose to my feet I admitted that yes, it was indeed Brillo. The abbess nodded her head. "The princess, she is much enamoured with Brillo. She was very impressed by him." She looked at the young woman talking to Countess Emelie. "Isn't that right, Kunigunde? The princess really enjoyed her visit to see Brillo."

"Yes, Your Grace." The young woman turned to face me, her face alight with remembered humor. "The princess is very impressed with the heroic Brillo. She has been buying anything associated with him she can find."

Starting with Kunigunde, the abbess introduced me to the other visitors. "Frau Matowski, this young lady is Kunigunde Juliane of Anhalt-Dessau, she is here with her *Tante* Eleonore, the duchess of Saxe-Weimar to visit her cousin, Emelie."

"That's Mrs. Eleonore Dorothea Wettin, Dorothea. Remember, Wilhelm has surrendered the title so he could stand for the Commons."

"Puh, rubbish. Just like a man, letting his duchy be slid out from under him. There is no need for you to forgo your title. You are not involving yourself in politics."

The abbess turned to me and continued, "This is, as you just heard, Mrs. Eleonore Dorothea Wettin." The abbess finished the introduction with a significant snort, indicating, I'm sure, her opinion of Wilhelm and his activities. As she passed from Mrs. Wettin, the abbess then introduced Madame Conspicuous Consumption. "And this is Sophia Hedwig of Brunswick-Wolfenbuttel, countess of Nassau-Diez. She is, as are the rest of us, visiting Grantville to see the sights, also to find out more about this ballet you are to put on for us."

I curtsied for the last time, then looked at the visitors. They were all looking hopefully at the men and women at the other end of the practice room. Taking the subtle hint, I asked them to wait just a moment while I asked the dancers to start.

Once amongst the dancers I quickly told them who the visitors were, and that they wanted to see how the ballet was progressing. I directed the dancers to their starting places while Deanna got ready to start the CD player, then I returned to my guests. I arrived back beside Mary and the abbess to the sound of the first notes of the Waltz of the Flowers. My guests watched in silence, their eyes not leaving the dancers for the whole seven-minute performance.

As the last notes died, I started forward to talk to the dancers. There were a few things I had noticed that needed work and I had forgotten about my guests. Seeing that the dance was over they started to applaud. The girls fortunately knew how to respond. They turned to face their audience and sank into deep, thank you audience curtsies. The men, all of them down-timers, seemed to have adopted the ballet style, and just bowed their heads, keeping an arm out to support their partner.

I hung back with Mary as the down-time ladies surged forward to talk to the dancers. I was feeling a bit smug. Not only had the dance gone well, but the look on the faces of the male dancers filled me with hope. This evening was becoming a very good retention tool. Dance with the Grantville Ballet Company and meet important people. There were going to be a few families who were going to be really impressed by the names that their menfolk dropped when they got home. Maybe, just maybe, I wouldn't have to replace any of this group of down-time dancers. It had been a bit of a pain over the months with the level of turnover I had been suffering among the male dancers. I just about turned around and hugged Mary there and then.

Eventually the ladies returned. They had other places to go. Other places to be. As I walked them to the door Mary asked if I had recordings of any of the company's performances they could borrow. "Especially anything concerning Brillo," commented a smiling Kunigunde. "The princess has been told that she can see *Bad, Bad Brillo* and the continuing adventures of Brillo on 'video.'"

"Yes," said Mary, "Mrs. Richards said you had copies of all your performances. If we could borrow them for the princess, especially any of the Brillo performances, you would have our hearty thanks." That last was greeted by sounds of agreement from the ladies. Apparently this princess of theirs really liked Brillo. Well, Flo would be happy about that.

As I shut the door on my departing guests a thought struck me. *Princess?* What princess? I called out to the dancers, asking if any of them knew who the princess was. There were some stunned looks shot my way. "The princess Kristina Vasa," the men chorused.

At my bewildered look they tried again. "King Gustavus Adolphus' daughter and heir," a couple of the men said. I started nodding my head at that. I knew who Gustavus Adolphus was, of course. I'd even seen him when he passed through Grantville last year. It was nice to know his last name, though.

"Elisabeth Matowski to see the princess. I come bearing gifts." I repeated to the strange woman who answered the door. The first time had been for the large down-timer that I assumed was a servant or something. I showed the contents of my basket to her. She touched the boxed videos.

"You are the *maîtresse de ballet*?" At my nod she continued, pointing to the videos. "These are the 'videos' of the Brillo ballets?" Again I nodded. She burst into a smile, her face lighting up. Reaching out she guided me in. "The princess, she will be very happy to see you. Please, I am Lady Ulrike, come in, come in, follow me."

After shooing off the servant, Lady Ulrike led me to a large room set up as a television room. Elisabeth Sofie and her cousin Countess Emelie were already seated there chatting with a much younger girl. They all turned round when Lady Ulrike knocked on the open door. All three jumped to their feet. Elisabeth Sofie and Countess Emelie smiled at me and all three dipped their heads in token bows.

The little girl looked at me. Elisabeth Sofie whispered something in her ear. She tilted her head to one side as she continued to look at me with a growing smile lighting up her face. Lady Ulrike started the introductions "Your Highness, Elizabeth Matowski, the *maîtresse de ballet*. Frau Elizabeth, Her Highness, Princess Kristina. Kristina, Frau Matowski has brought you some 'videos.' What do you say?"

The princess gave me a sweet curtsey before approaching. She was wearing one of Flo's finest quality sweaters. It was one of the special Brillo pattern range, with the horned head of Brillo blazoned prominently across the front. There were also other signs of the Brillo merchandising machine in the house, the ceramic cup, the branded back pack, the branded cap.

There were even some of the new ceramic figurines being produced by Melba Sue Freeman and her collection of artists. Not just Brillo, but also some of the new range of ballet dancers. I smiled at that. There was a good chance the school might be getting yet another student, or at least a new patron.

"They are Brillo videos? Oh, thank you, Frau Matowski!" It was all she could do not to clap her hands in joy, she seemed so happy.

"Here you are, Your Highness. Please be careful with them. They are the only copies I have." Kristina was too polite to actually snatch the basket from my hands, but it was a close run thing.

"Would you like some refreshments, Frau Matowski?" She was totally the graceful hostess, but I was pretty sure that she would prefer I didn't accept the invitation. There was no sign of impatience or anything, but the message was clearly there. She had her videos and now she wanted to watch them.

"Thank you for the offer, Highness, but I have to get back to work. Perhaps after you have seen the performances we can get together and talk about them." She smiled, her arms wrapped around the basket of videos. Then with a small curtsey she returned to Elisabeth Sofie and Countess Emelie. I waved to them as I turned and followed Lady Ulrike.

"She really should have followed you to the door. What are manners coming to?" I turned my head to look at Lady Ulrike. She was slowly shaking her head at the lack of manners being displayed by her charge. "Thank you, Frau Matowski, for bringing the videos. The princess will take good care of them. Both Duchess Elisabeth Sofie and Countess Emelie know how to use the 'video player' so that should present no problems."

Just as we made the door I could hear clearly the opening notes of the "William Tell Overture." I turned to Lady Ulrike and took her hand in mine and gripped it lightly. "I hope you do not come to hate me for bringing the videos. I think you are going to get very tired of that piece of music." With a shake of her head and a smile, she waved me on my way.

I bumped into Mary Simpson and her loyal lieutenants a few times over the next few days. They dropped into rehearsals to keep me up to date on progress, and what a lot of progress there was. Mary's Mafia, as I had come to think of her gang of women, had gone though town like a miniature tornado. A bank account was arranged so I could pay expenses and wages. Cloth was arriving for costumes. Artisans were building props and backdrops. Even the programs had been sent off to the printer. They were going to print color pictures of the dancers in the program, at least for the first night and collectors' program. There was some serious money being spent on this first season of ballet.

As far as I was concerned, the most important thing Mary achieved was getting the high school auditorium for five days around the New Year, Wednesday through to Sunday night. Hopefully this would give us sufficient time to set up scenery and lights, and run a couple of dress and lighting rehearsals. I was thankful for her intervention. There was no way I could have persuaded the powers-that-be to give me full access to the auditorium for that period of time. Not with the demand for the facility being what it was.

The dancers moved into the auditorium on Wednesday, straight after morning training. Crews under the control of Mary's lieutenants had been moving the scenery and backdrops into place before we arrived. While the technicians set up the props and scenery according to my plans, I chased up the lighting technicians, hoping to get the lights set up quickly so we could have a lighting rehearsal.

Meg and Deanna Matowski, a couple of my cousins by marriage, led the ballet mothers as they checked out the changing facilities. Their reports weren't promising. When we had used the auditorium for the Gala night we never had more than a dozen performers on stage at a time, and most hadn't needed to change costume. Suddenly we had over forty performers trying to change, fix make-up, or stay warm and limber in an area not designed for that number of performers. It was going to be a madhouse.

"Bitty, there's no way my Glenna Sue is getting changed in those rooms. The only separation between the boys and girls is a few blankets hung over a wire. It's not good enough. I demand that my daughter be given a proper changing room," came a voice from behind me. It wasn't actually bellowing, but it was close. That could only be the Ballet Mother from Hell, Laurie Haggerty. I turned around. Right the first time.

"Laurie, there are *no* changing rooms. There is that tiny Green room, or the showers. Otherwise the only other space is the couple of classrooms we have managed to grab. Believe me, I would love to be able to give your Glenna Sue a proper place to change and put on makeup. But we have to go with what we have."

"Well, can't you at least have the boys in one room and the girls in the other?"

"Sorry Laurie, but it's easier if rooms are allocated by role, the Mice in one room, the Soldiers in the other. Party guests in one room, Land of the Sweets dancers in the other. Otherwise we'd never keep track of the performers."

"Well, it's not good enough!" Having had the last word, Laurie went off in a huff.

She was right. It wasn't good enough. However, it was the best we had. If someone ever built a proper theater for the performing arts it would be nice if they could actually build one that catered to the needs of the performer. Maybe, but I wasn't going to hold my breath.

I'd danced in too many less than ideal facilities in the past to think catering for the performers actually rated as important to the designers and people funding them. The problem was all those special features performers would love to have are hidden from the audience. Out of sight, out of mind.

The punters like to see what they are getting for their money. So what if there is only one shower for all of the performers, and it runs out of hot water too quickly. The audience doesn't care.

Thursday morning the sun still hadn't shown itself as I made my way to the high school auditorium. We were about to have some real fun, a morning of general rehearsals on the stage, followed in the afternoon by a full dress rehearsal before visiting officials and media.

I just love performing to the powers-that-be and the media. They sit just there. You know you have to put on a good performance, but there is no feedback. Politicians and critics, as a rule, make a lousy audience, hardly raising a cheer or applauding. If they weren't so important to the continued well-being of the company I would have banned them. However, Mary Simpson had arranged for them to attend. So attend they would.

To make best use of our limited time the company worked out in one of the classrooms that had been set up with temporary barres while various scenes were practiced on the stage. People were coming and going between the changing rooms as costumes were checked out, and students practiced quick changes of costume. Those playing soldiers would be worst. At least the mice didn't need a lot of makeup.

We had to run through the scenes several times before the lighting technicians learned what and when to illuminate. The *pas de deux* between my two pairings of leads were real fun. I had let Carl talk me into trying to recreate the scene from the Covent Garden version of *Nutcracker* where Nureyev, as the prince, first appears just after the fight with the Mouse King. It looked like it might work. First Cathy McNally as Clara was lit, then Joseph as the Nutcracker, standing in the back corner of the stage, arms raised as the spotlight is suddenly turned on.

It took three tries, but eventually the lighting technician worked out where to point the spotlight. It lacked a little of the dramatic impact of the original, but then, Joseph was no Nureyev. Other than that, it was mainly a matter of getting the technicians used to tracking the performers. They just weren't used to tracking people moving with the speed of my dancers, but by carefully making notes of where the performer should be at what point in the music they finally started to keep the spotlight on the soloists.

Then we tried the full dress rehearsal with the audience of politicians and media. Anything that could go wrong did. Fortunately, there was nothing the audience could pick up on. First, there were logjams as the party guests poured off stage to change for the fight scene. It threatened to degenerate into an all-out brawl. There was considerable pushing and shoving. Some of the children were whacked around the ankles with out of control hobbyhorses, and a couple of the girls retaliated with their dolls. A couple of the dolls lost heads and limbs. One of the ballet mothers picked up the pieces and chased after the girls. Hopefully repairs would be possible.

Then the Christmas tree refused to grow. There was supposed to be an Alice in Wonderland type effect, with Clara shrinking to the same size as the mice and toy soldiers. But the tree refused to move. Oh well, I doubt any of that audience would notice.

Then we moved into the fight between the soldiers and the mice. It was flowing nicely. Carl and Joseph were making a real production of the fight between the Mouse King and Nutcracker. And then one of the children, trying to "die" theatrically, tripped and fell heavily. The young boy was in tears as he marched from the stage at the end of the scene. I managed to give him a cuddle and compliment him on staying in character until he was off stage before he was led away for attention by one of the small army of stage mothers. Hopefully he would be ready to come back for the final scene. I made a note to use what happened as a warning to the others.

The performance seemed to be going well. The mass *en pointe* dances went without a hitch. The Sweet dances all went well, and the lighting technicians were even able to follow Carl at his most dynamic. Finally the rehearsal came to an end. We even got some applause from the audience. Most of it was from family of the cast who had been invited in to watch. The politicians and media representatives were embarrassed into giving nominal polite applause. Not like the princess. She was almost bouncing in her seat. It was probably only Lady Ulrike's heavy hand that was holding her in place. The cast bowed and curtseyed to the audience before the curtain closed for the last time. I quickly got changed from my costume so I could go out and talk to politicians and media.

Friday morning. The end of the beginning, or the beginning of the end, I didn't know which it was going to be. Tonight we put on our premiere performance, according to Mary Simpson, to a full house. The future of my ballet company could live or die on tonight's performance.

Everybody who had any claim to being anybody, who wasn't otherwise detained or required for military service, was going to be there. Half of the blue bloods from Magdeburg had already invaded Grantville. Most were staying in the houses of friends and acquaintances who had homes in the area. Duchess Elisabeth Sofie's mother and father were back for the performance and had opened their Saalfeld house to guests. Count Ludwig, Emelie's husband, was in attendance. The sudden influx of people and their money was pushing up demand and local prices for accommodation.

On the merchandising front, Melba Sue and her team of ceramic

artists were working overtime, and were still unable to meet demand for their range of ballet and Brillo figurines. Other artists were pumping out paintings of the performers, and hanging in pride of place in the auditorium foyer was a large oil painting of Carl and Staci as Cavalier and Sugar Plum Fairy in a scene from the ballet.

Meanwhile, I had heard that Flo was being run into the ground with demand for Brillo merchandise. There was even a story going around that someone had offered some obscene amount to buy Brillo. The fact that he was still on Flo's farm was, as far as I was concerned, proof positive that there was no truth in that story.

Before class started I did a check for injuries. Franz Sprug, the boy who hurt himself yesterday, was a little bruised and tender, but otherwise okay. Nobody else admitted to carrying an injury. That was expected. Not only were the performers going to get paid for this short season, but tonight would be a historic occasion. Nobody wanted to miss it.

My son Joseph played up a little, pretending to have developed a limp, but a whack on the back of the head with a thrown *pointe* shoe soon had him scampering away. I couldn't be too hard on him. His fooling around had broken the ice and people were visibly relaxing.

For the next four hours I worked everyone into the ground. We were all sweating heavily, and some of the dancers were starting to droop when I called an end to rehearsal. I was happy with how everything was going. I sent everyone out to clean up, eat, drink, and get as much rest as they could before the evening premiere. They had about five hours before the curtain went up.

***

"Where the hell is Carl?" I was just about in a panic. The auditorium was starting to fill up and I couldn't see him anywhere. Looking around I found Casey. "Casey, have you seen Carl? I've looked everywhere."

She pointed to a lump off in one corner of the Green room. He was sleeping. Again! How could he sleep at a time like this? I stamped my way over to him. A head poked out of the sleeping bag as I got close. "Is it time to start?"

"Yes," I just about roared. How dare he be so relaxed when I was so on edge? I watched as he slipped out of his sleeping bag, and bundled it into a corner. He then had the nerve to turn round and smile at me. "Warm up; you don't want your muscles getting cold, not with how the soldier doll dance is supposed to end," I said in a relatively

controlled voice, all things considered.

I was just turning away when a stifled chuckle stopped me dead. I turned and glared at Carl as he stretched out on the floor, warming up. I was severely tempted to kick him. Just then I felt a certain fellow feeling for Flo when Brillo was being unusually agreeable.

Amber Higham, the knowledgeable expert Mary Simpson had dug up to serve as theater manager for the ballet season, waved me over to look at the audience from behind the curtain. The seats were filling rapidly. There was a central roped off area that was filling up with dignitaries, and I'm sure, the princess. There couldn't be that many young girls who might be seated in the VIP area. Around the roped off area, the more expensive seats were rapidly filling. Amber had told me how much she was charging for those seats. I'd been horrified. Then she told me the latest scalper's price. Ouch. It looked like someone was making money out of my show.

Looking at the rest of the audience I felt that Catharina Matzinger's father would be happy. It looked like half the audience was fitted out in clothes made from his fancy new colored cloth, and the women didn't look too drab either. With their batik silk gowns topped with fancy shawls made by Flo's ladies, they made a pretty picture.

Receiving a signal from somewhere in the auditorium Amber pulled me back to the performers. It was time to start. A quick survey of the technicians brought a forest of up-raised thumbs. We were ready to go. "Places" I called. With the stage set for the opening scene, and the party guests ready in the wings, I took one final calming look around. In just under two hours the performance would be over. I could hold together that long. From my position on the wings I signaled Deanna to start the music.

The curtain opened to the street scene. Snow was falling as guests started arriving for the party. Then, as Count Drosselmeyer passed into the house, the walls of the house pulled away, opening the drawing room to the audience. Doctor Stalbaum, his wife, Franz, the son, and Clara, the hero of the story, are greeting guests as they enter the drawing room. Then the children of the guests come in. They are seated on the floor for a puppet show. I don't know if the audience really paid much attention to the puppet show, but it showed the Mouse King turning Count Drosselmeyer's nephew into a nutcracker.

After the puppet show it was time to carry on the dancing dolls. First there was Carl as the soldier. He was good. The full splits he fell

into at the end of his little performance drew a few sympathetic groans from the audience. But there was little chance of Carl hurting himself. He would have practiced it a few times before coming on, and if he wasn't comfortable with it, he would have left that bit out. It's visually effective how his legs just slide out from under him, but if he hurt himself it would have killed the evening's performance there and then.

Next was Staci as the dancing doll. She spent only moments *en pointe*; if you weren't watching carefully you could miss it or mistake it for *demi-pointe*. Mark Matowski, yet another nephew, livened things up a bit as the Clown doll. Then it was time for the children to collect their gifts. Hobby horses for the boys, dolls for the girls. Except that Clara was given a nutcracker doll. The one used in the puppet show. The Nutcracker was subtly dressed in a Mackay plaid. The boys danced riding their hobby horses while the girls danced carrying their dolls. Nobody got tripped up or stumbled, and nobody got belted with a doll. All in all it went better than expected. Finally they were off stage and it was time for Cathy's solo.

As Clara, Cathy danced for her nutcracker. She was adorable. She could only have done better if she was dancing *en pointe*. However, that was three or four years off. But she was doing really well even restricted to *demi-pointe*. I was so enthralled watching her that Harvey had to shake me to attract my attention. It was almost time for us to go on. There had been howls at home when I identified who would be the grandparents. There had been more howls, of laughter this time, at my husband's reaction. But he was a good sport. Besides, we all knew he could do the part justice. He had performed it often enough in the past. The dance received the desired laughs from the audience as Harvey gloried in his bumbling grandfather act. Then we were off stage.

There was pandemonium with dancers dashing to and from the changing rooms. The mice were already lining up as they finished changing, ready for the next scene. Cathy McNally slipped onto the darkened stage. Going over to the Christmas tree to check on her nutcracker, she cradled it in her arms she lay down. As the clock struck midnight, the mouse dancers started to appear. They even managed to appear one by one, at their designated place, in time to the striking of the hour. They were chucking around the toys from under the tree as Cathy awoke. She was without her nutcracker. She fought off the mice as she searched for her nutcracker.

Meanwhile the wall flats were withdrawn into the wings, giving the impression the room was growing. This time, thankfully, the Christmas tree grew on schedule. Then the soldiers, led by Joseph as the Nutcracker, appeared to fight the mice led by Carl's Mouse King. There was much leaping and jumping, and the ringing of steel as they fought with swords. I had protested about using steel blades, but both Carl and Joseph had insisted that the audience wouldn't be impressed with the sound of wooden swords. While they fought, the mice seemed to be winning.

Almost unobserved at the back of the stage, Cathy took a rifle from above the fireplace and took aim. There was a gunshot, and Carl's Mouse King took a long time dying. As the mice carried their fallen king from the field, the soldiers formed up and marched off leaving Cathy alone on stage.

That was the first bottleneck safely navigated. I could safely stand in the wings and admire Joseph in his Mackay plaid dance with Cathy. I wondered if any of the audience had picked up on the play on current events, with Cathy as sharpshooter Julie Sims and Joseph as Julie's Scotsman Alex Mackay, but I was too entranced with what I was watching to really care. I'd be sure to find out after the performance anyway.

As Joseph and Cathy's *pas de deux* came to an end snow started to fall. It was time for the first *en pointe* dance, just as soon as the audience stopped applauding the *pas de deux*. Eventually they let Joseph and Cathy leave the stage.

I could see the stage manager as she signaled the girls she was restarting the music. On they went in their startlingly white, calf length skirts. I just purred with contentment. It had been too long since I last saw a live performance, and this one was going well. As the Dance of the Snowflakes drew to an end, the lights slowly faded out. Then the curtain fell. It was the end of the first act.

As dancers madly dashed for the changing rooms and stage hands moved scenery and props, I leaned back into Harvey. He held my hands and gave me a cuddle. "It's going well, girl, it's going well. Only the second act to go." I snuggled into Harvey as we waited for the warning bell to call back the audience.

"They love it, Bitty. They love it." I reluctantly withdrew from Harvey's embrace to see who was pulling on my arm. It was Amber Higham, the theater manager. "I snuck out to the foyer to listen in on the guests as they discussed what they had seen. They all seemed to be impressed, and they haven't even seen the *Grand Pas de Deux* yet. I think we have a winner."

Then, I heard her mutter to herself, "I wonder if we can increase the price for the remaining performances?" Harvey and I left her mumbling as we moved off to see how the dancers were coping.

The second act opened to the young lovers, Joseph and Cathy as Nutcracker and Clara, being greeted by Staci as the Sugar Plum Fairy and Carl as her cavalier. Joseph related how he vanquished the Mouse King in a mimelogue, while behind him Cathy shook her head and mimed that it was she who killed the Mouse King with a single shot. That drew a trickle of laughter from the audience. Then the four journeyed by boat to the Land of the Sweets, yet another mechanical contrivance, which actually worked.

Then it was time for the upcoming performers to strut their stuff in the character dances. First off the blocks were Mathias Steinbach and Michelle Matowski, Deanna's daughter. They had the Spanish or Chocolate dance. Their costumes were brilliant, a real credit to the dyer's art and Tom Stone's chemistry.

Mathias and Michelle were followed by five girls in pseudo-Arabic harem clothes performing the Arabian or Coffee dance. The guys had all been in favor of copying the outfits from the Covent Garden version of Nutcracker, but I wasn't prepared to put thinly clad girls with bare midriffs on the stage.

Next came Mike Song and none other than Duchess Elisabeth Sofie and our friendly cloth merchant's daughter, Catharina Matzinger, to do a Chinese Fan dance. It should have been just one couple, but which girl do you leave out? I'd crumbled and put in both of them. It was only for a bit over a minute and they would both glory in being given such an important part.

They departed to be replaced by my find of Eastern Folk dancers. We had agreed on a modified version of their dance that fitted the music. It was extremely athletic, but glorious to watch. The audience appreciated the upbeat tempo of their dance as well. The *pas de trios* followed. Two of my best down-timer girls, Richelle Kubiak and Ursula Sprug, with, I'm sad to say, my nephew, Joe Calagna. Fortunately the male can get away with being little more than a prop for the girls to hang onto and dance around. A good male dancer helps. It's not that Joe is a poor dancer. Technically he's quite good. He just seems to lack that certain something that lifts a performance above the ordinary.

I was almost shaking with excitement. Everything was going so well! Nothing had gone wrong, the dancers were excelling, and the audience was responding. There was just the Waltz of the Flowers to go before the *Grand Pas de Deux*. The couples came on. All those willing down-time males who could dance had been a real windfall. I leaned back into Harvey and watched and appreciated what I was seeing. The brilliant colors of their costumes glistened as the girls danced. This was the second *en pointe* dance and the audience loved it. You could sense their excitement at what they were seeing as the dancers worked their magic.

Now it was time for the *Grand Pas de Deux*, the Cavalier and Sugar Plum Fairy in their great romantic dance. If Thursday's rehearsal had been steamy, this was too hot to handle. Every look spoke volumes, every touch shouted of the feelings between them. I licked my lips, spellbound, as they danced. They finished to absolute silence. You could have heard a pin drop. Then the audience exploded in a sea of applause. I snuggled into Harvey as I took a peek at the audience. They were starting to stand as they applauded.

Eventually Carl and Staci escaped from the stage and the music restarted. It was time for the penultimate scene. With all the Sweets and the Waltz of the Flowers couples performing short sequences, and the two lead couples each performing a short *pas de deux*.

As the scene ended, the lights dimmed. For a moment there was total darkness. Then a glimmer of light was illuminating Cathy, asleep in a chair. Gradually the lights increased. The party guests started circulating again. Cathy looked around for her nutcracker, but it was nowhere to be seen. Then Count Drosselmeyer appeared with Joseph as his nephew. Joseph was dressed as the nutcracker prince, but without the plaid. He had in his arms a nutcracker, just like the one Cathy had lost. As Cathy accepted the replacement nutcracker and wrapped her arms around it, the lights faded out, and the curtain fell for the last time.

In return for the horrendous price the audience had paid to attend the premiere performance, they were all invited to attend a "meet the cast" dinner and cocktail party in the school cafeteria. When I had first heard what Mary intended and where, I laughed. Who would attend a dry cocktail party? But Mary had surprised us all. Somehow she managed to persuade the powers-that-be to allow the serving of alcohol on school grounds. That really brought home to me how socially powerful Mary was becoming.

As the cast entered the cafeteria we were split up by Mary's Mafia and guided to various tables. Looking around I could see that there was a definite hierarchy. The more important the guests at a table, the more important the cast members they were allocated. Harvey and I were at the head table with Mary and her senior lieutenants. Carl and Staci were seated at the table beside us.

The dinner was magnificent. I didn't know the school caterers could prepare so many up-time delicacies. The pièce de résistance was the marvelous mountain of cream puffs with a spun sugar web covering them. There was enough for everyone to get a cream puff and whipped cream.

There was also the down-under sweet, the Pavlova, a meringue dessert smothered in whipped cream and preserved berries. Carl had talked about the dessert when the idea of this dinner first came up. He had a recipe he had picked up in Australia just before the Ring of Fire. And as the dessert was originally created to celebrate the tour of New Zealand and Australia by the celebrated Russian ballerina Anna Pavlova, he had suggested that serving it tonight would be a fitting celebration of the coming of modern ballet to down-time Germany.

After dinner the cast walked around meeting as many people as possible. Harvey and I were taking a moment to ourselves as we looked on at the guests and sipped our wine. I stifled a giggle as I looked at my wineglass. Harvey examined his glass and smiled back. We were both sipping wine out of peanut butter glasses. Something I had thought we left behind years ago. Apparently up-time peanut butter glasses, especially those with characters printed on them, were considered amongst the ultimate status symbols. So the guests had to be served from peanut butter classes. How Mary had managed to dig up sufficient to serve everyone I didn't want to know.

Speaking of the devil, there was Mary Simpson heading my way. I saluted her with my wineglass.

"A brilliant performance, Bitty. Please pass my compliments to the cast. Everyone I have spoken to has been most impressed." As she paused for breath Mary gave me a social kiss. Then she dropped her bombshell. "A couple of my guests asked about performances in Magdeburg. I said that you would be able to put on a season of *Swan Lake* in the summer."

My jaw dropped.

Mary, a little concerned, continued, "That won't be a problem, will it?"

I was astounded at the naiveté of her question. Putting on a performance in Magdeburg would be hard enough. *Swan Lake!* That was pushing impossible.

"Mary!" I wailed. "Magdeburg? Where would we perform? Surely there is no suitable theater?"

Mary didn't even bat an eyelid. She just waved her hands casually. "Didn't some ballet company put on a performance in Red Square in Moscow once?"

I had to nod. Yes, the Kirov Ballet had put on such a performance.

"If the Russians can do it I'm sure your people will have no trouble." Having established that my objections were of no importance, Mary went off on a tangent. "Wouldn't it be marvelous to hold the performance in Hans Richter Square? Think of it, the people of Magdeburg watching a performance by your company in the shadow of the monument to the Hero of Wismar."

I thought about it. The whole idea reeked of cheap theater. Also, I could see nothing but problems. The Kirov Ballet had at least limited themselves to selected scenes and used a bare stage. A production of *Swan Lake*, on the other hand, would be a logistical nightmare.

I could see that ideas were zipping through Mary's mind, some to be accepted, others rejected. It was a pity I couldn't listen in on the process and give an opinion before her flights of fancy committed my company to something we couldn't deliver.

"Maybe we could schedule it to coincide with the unveiling of the Hans Richter memorial? No. That wouldn't work. It would be better with a ballet featuring a suitably glorious hero." Mary shook her head in negation at some of her mumbled thoughts. It was fascinating listening to her. I leaned into Harvey. My husband had been silent throughout Mary Simpson's monologue. We exchanged mutually horrified looks.

"Damn. It's a pity I've already committed us to *Swan Lake*, Bitty. Well, it's too late to change that now." Mary chewed her lower lip in a discreetly ladylike manner. "Next time we really must get together beforehand."

Struck dumb at Mary's audaciousness I could only nod in agreement. It really would be a good idea to get together to discuss things before any more commitments were made.

"The summer season is only a few months off, too," Mary continued. "We must get together before I return to Magdeburg and discuss what you will need for the performance. And that's another thing.

You really should give some thought to moving your company to Magdeburg permanently. Not immediately, of course, but as soon as we can find you some suitable buildings you really must make the move."

This time I actually managed to speak. "*What?* The high school auditorium has some of the best facilities of any theater in the world! Why would I want to move away from first class lighting, acoustics, and sound?"

"Bitty, you need to bring your performers to Magdeburg where they will be properly appreciated. The people in Grantville aren't interested in regularly attending the ballet. Not enough of them, at least, to sustain a professional company. Yes, the high school auditorium has the best facilities in the world. But even the best facilities aren't any good if you can't fill enough seats often enough. You aren't even able to pay your dancers a living wage, are you?"

Embarrassed, I shook my head. That was one of my biggest disappointments. In almost a year of operation my dancers were still dancing for love. The money I had been able to pay them was peanuts, barely enough to cover the costs they incurred training and performing. Even the money they were being paid for the season of *Nutcracker* came down to a measly hourly rate when you counted up all the hours of practice.

"Think about it, Bitty. In Magdeburg you will have the whole imperial court, visiting dignitaries, and various hangers-on as potential audiences. Not to mention what will soon be a little horde of *nouveau riche* merchants and industrialists looking to enhance their social status. They will appreciate your performances—well, attend them, anyway, in the case of some—as the artistic and cultural artifacts they are. And with that potential audience we should be able to afford an Imperial Theater that would be the envy of the world. You owe it to yourself, Bitty! You owe it to your dancers, and to the Art of Dance!"

How she managed to capitalize Art of Dance verbally I'll never know, but she did.

"The Mother of Modern Ballet!" she went on enthusiastically, still capitalizing like mad. Then, frowning with reproval: "But not if you stay buried in this cultural backwater. If not for yourself, think of your dancers. Don't they deserve the opportunities Magdeburg has to offer?"

Harvey saved me from answering. He drew my attention to the time. In only a few hours I was supposed to lead rehearsals for Saturday night's performance. Begging Mary's leave I stumbled out into the night, my arms latched securely to Harvey. Mary had left me a lot to think about. I owed it to my dancers to do the best I could for them. However, Mary was expecting too much. I was just a small-town dance teacher. How could I possibly take on the responsibilities Mary was heaping upon me? All I had wanted when I started out all those months ago was the chance to enjoy a night at the ballet. A chance to watch my Christmas performance of *Nutcracker* again.

I certainly hadn't planned on becoming this universe's Sergei Diaghilev!

Part III: The Trouble in Franconia

So I prophesied as I had been commanded; and as I prophesied, suddenly there was a noise, a rattling, and the bones came together, bone to its bone. I looked, and there were sinews on them, and flesh had come upon them, and skin had covered them; but there was no breath in them.

Ezekiel 37:7-8

Motherhood and Apple Pie, While You're at It

VIRGINIA DEMARCE

December, 1632: Grantville, Thuringia

Arnold Bellamy looked at the assignment that the Congress of the New United States had given the Special Commission on the Establishment of Freedom of Religion in the Franconian Prince-Bishoprics and the Prince-Abbey of Fulda. Its members were to go to the area that King Gustavus Adolphus had assigned to be administered by Grantville the previous autumn. They were to establish a headquarters at Würzburg. There were to be regional offices in Bamberg and Fulda. They were to hold hearings. In the course of these hearings, they were, basically, to explain a number of things to the civil downtime administrative personnel of these regions. The most important were, reduced to their essence:

1) Under the Constitution of the New United States, there is Separation of Church and State;
2) Religious Toleration is a Great Thing;

175

3) Burning Witches is a Bad Idea;

4) We Mean It;

—and, also, added as a rider during a late afternoon committee meeting;

5) Voter Registration is Good for You.

Congress had passed it. Naturally, Congress expected someone else—in this case, as it happened, the Department of International Affairs—to figure out some way of actually doing it. Looking at the three newly appointed commissioners, Ed Piazza grinned. "See if you can instill a proper appreciation of motherhood and apple pie in them, while you're at it. And good luck. I'm going to be busy with other projects for the next few months, so talk to Arnold Bellamy if you run into any problems. This is his baby, now."

Bellamy frowned. He always found the bureaucratic acronym N.U.S. rather unfortunate, since the German word Nuss meant "nut" and could be easily extrapolated to "nuts." Knowing how humans react to any opportunity to put down the enemy, he could see a "laugh at the interlopers" campaign coming. "They're all nuts."

The Special Commission, for all practical purposes, could be interpreted to mean the Grantville Commission to Force the Franconians to Accept the N.U.S.' Laws Establishing Freedom of Religion. It was one of those things Mike Stearns thought needed Ed's personal attention quite a bit more than the upcoming Rudolstadt Colloquy, if only because the administration already established by the N.U.S. probably wouldn't appreciate being gifted with a special commission. Its very existence at least *implied* that they wouldn't be doing their jobs right. Or that something, somehow, was lacking.

"I wish you were going to handle this, not Arnold Bellamy. It's not that he's hard to work with. He's just . . ."

". . . reserved," Ed said. "Reserved and still not entirely comfortable working with you."

"Stiff," Mike said. "*Rigor mortis* and all that."

"It won't get better unless you work with him. Arnold is perfectly competent. He had a different teaching style than I did, sure, but the students never really griped about it." Ed thought a minute, "It's likely, of course, that not even his wife ever calls him by a pet name. But this is no longer a few thousand people with an administration run by an Emergency Committee that you by and large picked because you knew them and—mostly at least, with a few exceptions like Quentin Underwood—liked them. It's a country of nearly a million people. With an administrative staff comprised mainly of down-timers whom you have never met and may never meet face-to-face. Whom you *probably* will never meet face-to-face. The commissioners report to Arnold; Arnold reports to you, at least for as long as I'm otherwise occupied. Welcome to the bureaucracy, Mr. President."

Arnold Bellamy, looking at the congressional resolution, cleared his throat and commented, " 'Civil?' Congress does understand that these were ecclesiastical principalities, don't they? That the rulers of the three biggest ones were two Catholic bishops and a Catholic abbot? That the best one can say about the distinction between 'civil' administrations and 'ecclesiastical' administration over there is that it's pretty vague?"

"Well," Mike Stearns answered, "the down-timer delegates do, at least. On the other hand . . ."

"I know. The Congress has a couple of Catholics among the down-timers. And for Grantville's senator we have Becky, who's Jewish. And if Wilhelm of Hesse-Kassel ever showed up to take his seat in the House of Lords, otherwise known as the Senate, we would have a Calvinist. He, however, is chasing around northern Germany in command of an army unit. For all the rest, we've got Lutherans in the N.U.S. Congress. For the simple reason that Lutherans are what we landed in the middle of—the state church of almost every place that's joined the N.U.S. confederation: Badenburg, Schwarzburg-Rudolstadt, Sommersburg, Sondershausen, Saxe-Weimar, Saxe-Altenburg, Saxe-Coburg, Saxe-Eisenach, Saxe-Everyplace Else, you name it. Except for the transients, the refugees who've come in from outside because of the war, they've all been Lutheran for a century, give or take a couple of decades here and there."

Mike Stearns sighed. "You know perfectly well what they *thought* they were voting for. They *thought*, no matter that it's officially titled a Commission for the Establishment of Religious Freedom, that it's really a Commission to Make Catholic Franconia Safe for Lutherans."

"So does Gustavus Adolphus, for that matter, according to the letter he sent down. Our captain-general thinks that it's a grand idea. So does his chancellor, Oxenstierna."

"What other frame of reference do they have?" Mike was directing the question more to the air than to Bellamy, but Arnold answered.

"At least, since they *think* they know what we're doing, Duke Johann Casimir of Saxe-Coburg has loaned us this Meyfarth guy to help. He wrote the original set of German words to that awful tune that won the N.U.S. national anthem contest. And we're going to need all the help we can get. Trust me on that. Here's a summary of the reports I wrote last fall when I went down to scope out the situation."

"Give me a rundown on Meyfarth."

"Johann Matthaeus Meyfarth. Matz to his friends. Middle-aged, more or less; in his early forties. He's a Lutheran pastor. That's a priest, if you're Catholic; a minister, if you're a run-of-the-mill American Protestant. And he's a musician, as if seventeenth-century Germany isn't overrun with them. I expect any day now to find out that the garbage collector on our route plays the flute between pickups."

Bellamy shook his head. He didn't like thinking about witchcraft persecutions, and found that his mind would take any side direction to avoid focusing on them. Pushing himself back to the topic, he continued. "But Meyfarth also, for years, has been Duke Johann Casimir's point man for squelching witchcraft persecutions. As you've probably noticed, you pretty much have to get south of the ridge of the Thuringian Forest, down toward Suhl and beyond, to find a lot of witchcraft hysteria. Or more precisely, before you find anybody taking a lot of action about witchcraft hysteria. Around here there's been some, sure. People believe that witchcraft exists. Villagers accuse old ladies of souring the milk of nursing mothers; or the herdsman's assistant of maliciously drying up someone's cow. But it hasn't escalated into major investigations, examinations under torture, court cases by the dozen, and smoke going up from the stakes. On the map of Dead German Witches, this area right around Grantville is a fairly nice, white, hole among the black dots. Barely speckled, so to speak."

"So Meyfarth is off to Franconia with the commission to work his magic on the second point." Mike raised his eyebrows. "Do I even dare to ask how they managed this?"

"I *believe* that they bribed him with the offer of a tenured professorship at the University of Erfurt. If he survives the experience."

"What I meant was how they managed to create a 'barely speckled' spot on the map amid the polka dots and the black splotches."

"Oh," Bellamy answered, "it's simple enough. Johann Casimir is an old man, close to seventy, and not at all well. He's been childless in two marriages, so he has focused on projects rather than accumulating bits and pieces of the Wettin family's properties for his heirs. He

has been at this for decades. A long time ago, it occurred to him that these organized antiwitch campaigns don't happen without money: money to pay the investigators, money to hold the hearings, money to pay the torturers, money to pay the executioner. They are not lynchings, by and large. They are perfectly legal judicial proceedings. Exercising their right to administer high justice, to have jurisdiction in capital cases, is one of those perks that the various rulers protect very zealously. That means that persecutions will not happen if there's no money forthcoming to pay all that staff. Therefore, if the ruler refuses to allocate money to pay for witchcraft persecutions—"

"—We won't have witchcraft persecutions," Mike finished for him. "Or, at least, no more than an occasional random case. Not these systematic witch hunts that lead to chains of accusations and hundreds of burnings. Charming. Beautiful. Elegant, even. I think that I have to admire this technique."

"Just keep in mind," Bellamy warned, "that we have a democracy now. One duke can take a notion that he doesn't want to spend money on this, lobby his fellow-rulers, who are also his cousins, and make some progress toward stamping it out, at least in his own region. But if we end up with a majority in Congress who believe that witches should be burned, they may well vote to throw money at the problem. We've been moving awfully fast. If we ever forget that not all our citizens share up-time values, it could turn into something like letting the inmates run the asylum to suit themselves."

Mike grunted. "That's always the problem with top-down solutions to social and political problems. The ideal way to handle a problem like this is for some mass movement to do it. From the bottom up. That's why I usually try to have the Committees of Correspondence tackle something like this, whenever it's possible."

Bellamy didn't entirely share Mike Stearns' enthusiasm for the revolutionary Committees of Correspondence which had, by now, sprouted up like mushrooms all over Thuringia and were beginning to do the same in and around Magdeburg. But it was all a moot point here, anyway.

"The CoCs don't amount to much, in Franconia," he pointed out.

"I know," Mike sighed. "So we'll have to try a top-down approach. Dammit."

Common Sense

Virginia DeMarce

December, 1632: Frankenwinheim, Franconia

"Of course no one is happy. Why would anyone be happy?"

Old Kaethe sniffed as she poured some very thin beer for her husband, Rudolph Vulpius. The wife of the head of Frankenwinheim's village council doubling in her role as the wife of Frankenwinheim's tavern keeper.

Kaethe gave her husband a toothless smile. He had been a good catch forty years before, when they married. Even the fact that his family had at some point Latinized the name from Fuchs to Vulpius indicated that Rudolph had some pretensions to social standing in the village. All things considered, he'd stayed a good catch throughout the four decades that followed the wedding.

"It will be hard for these 'up-timers' to be worse than the Swedes were last winter." He smacked his stein down on the table with a thump.

That seemed to be the only consensus the village had reached so far.

Constantin Ableidinger, the school teacher, tipped back

precariously on his three-legged stool. He was a stocky man, bull-necked, broad shouldered, with straight black hair, brown eyes, and a dark olive complexion. "When do you expect Tobias to get back from Bamberg?"

"Today, perhaps. He's a reliable boy." The mayor was justifiably proud of his oldest grandson.

"If we're lucky, he'll bring more information. I sent some money with him, to buy pamphlets and newspapers for sale. We shouldn't just read the free things that the up-timers are handing out."

The mayor frowned. "*Das Erfolgreiche Dorf*," he snorted. "Why do we need foreigners to tell us how to make a village successful? We could make our village successful without their advice. Which, I would like to point out, we never asked for. We know what we need. In fact, before the damned war, we had most of it. A bell in our church tower. Now melted down by the soldiers. A bridge across the creek. Now with its timbers taken for firewood by the soldiers. A stone-lined ditch from the spring on the hill, so we had water here and the boys and girls didn't have to spend half the day going up the hill to fetch a pail of water. Which we can probably have again, once we get the ditch cleared out. They ruined that just for the meanness of it."

"At least we have the free pamphlets," Ableidinger pointed out. "When the Swedes burned the schoolhouse last winter, they burned most of the books we had with it. The ones that weren't in my cottage, anyway. So I'm using these 'hand-outs' for the children to read. Some of them are pretty good. The one they call *Die Wochentliche Bauernzeitung* is the best, I think. Apparently these up-timers have an organization called a 'grange' that's been publishing this weekly newspaper for farmers for almost a year up in Thuringia. We've only gotten a few issues, so far. Mostly old ones. It has articles on farming, of course, but also woodcuts and jokes. Stories for fathers to read to their families in the evenings."

The village pastor frowned. "Very few of them are edifying." Otto Schaeffer didn't find many things to be edifying, once the members of his flock had completed their perusal of Luther's *Shorter Catechism*. Which, he thought, they should peruse much more regularly than most of them did.

Ableidinger shook his head. "They aren't biblical or classical. But some of them are really funny. Especially the woodcuts, the 'cartoons.' One of the issues introduced 'Peter Baufaellig.' He makes me think that maybe we'll be able to understand these up-timers after all. The introduction said that there were woodcuts about him in a newspaper about farming up-time. The head of this 'grange' read about this 'Peter Tumbledown' when he was a child. Every village has a man like that now. I guess every village still had one then. The one who doesn't oil his harness, who lets his hinges rust, who doesn't fix the leak before something inside is ruined."

"Materialistic," the pastor proclaimed.

"Fixing things that need fixing fits into 'render unto Caesar the things that are Caesar's,'" Ableidinger said stubbornly.

Kaethe frowned. She, along with most of the women, thought the village was lucky to have Ableidinger as its teacher, even if he wasn't local. His family had been Lutheran refugees out of Austria who had settled up around Coburg. He wasn't an easy man, but he kept the children disciplined and, most of the time, interested. That wasn't easy. Energetic and vigorous, at least when the melancholy didn't seize him. Moody, when it did. In that case, there wasn't much to be done except wait it out. And feed the boy, of course, if his father forgot to. Matthias was a good boy, well worth a few bowls of soup or porridge.

Kaethe knew that Pastor Schaeffer wasn't as pleased as Frankenwinheim's mothers and grandmothers were. She also knew one main reason why. It wasn't just that the teacher—who was, of course, also the organist back before the soldiers had smashed the organ, as well as the sexton and the clerk for the village council, since no one could reasonably expect a man to survive on what a village schoolteacher earned, much less feed a family—had lived in the village for years before the new pastor came and knew the people better. It was that he had been to the university at Jena, just like the pastor. He had finished the arts curriculum and started to study law before he was thrown out for getting a baker's daughter pregnant and marrying her.

She shook her head. Rudolph kept saying mildly that this was the young pastor's first job and he was still full of himself and all of his book-learning. Rudolph argued that Pastor Schaeffer would season all right if they just put up with him for a while.

She sort of doubted it. Ableidinger, who was fifteen years older than his new supervisor, was sure that he knew just as much and probably more. He didn't hesitate to say so in public, either. She moved over to the window, pulling back one of the wooden shutters that kept out the winter air, hoping to find a distraction in what was left of the winter daylight that would head off another dispute between God's representatives on earth—or, at least, between God's representatives in Frankenwinheim.

It didn't help that Pastor Schaeffer so strongly disapproved of Ableidinger's marriage. The pastor was still unmarried. He had heard all about the scandal when he was studying in Jena—a Professor Lenz had told him all about it. He still disapproved strongly, even though the poor woman had been dead for five years now.

Kaethe shook her head. Maybe the pastor had skipped over, "Let the dead bury their dead."

Today, she was lucky. "Tobias is coming," she said. "And it looks like his rucksack is full."

"It's a new one." Vulpius picked up *Die Moderne Landwirtschaft*, which Tobias had shaken out onto the table in front of his grandfather. "*Modern Agriculture*, no less. Our new governors must be setting out to make every printing press in Bamberg profitable."

Ableidinger moved over to stand at the shutter Kaethe had opened, sorting through a package of pamphlets that he had ordered from Würzburg. That was where the new governors of Franconia had set up the center of their administration, so he thought that the most important publications were likely to be printed there—not in Bamberg, which was just a regional center, if he understood the newspaper right.

The stack wasn't as big as he would have liked it to be. It was going to be another grim winter. If food was scarce and prices went up, he had to keep some kind of a reserve if he was going to feed his son and himself. He could afford a few short items and broadsides, but he could not risk buying expensive books. Not this year, no matter how glum it made him. Winter was a glum time in the best of years, with the days so short. Glum. Grim. The only comfort was having something to read.

So the small size of the package that Tobias had been able to buy was discouraging. He picked up the first. *Der Gesunde Menschenverstand*. Below, the subtitle read, *Thomas Paine's "Common Sense" Translated into German, with an Explanation of Unfamiliar Terms.*

He frowned. The first unfamiliar term was "common sense." He had never heard of something called *gesunder Menschenverstand*. "Healthy human understanding?" He thumbed through the foreword. The translator had considered using *schlichte Vernunft* as an alternative translation before settling on the one he chose.

"Simple reason?"

He had just begun to lose himself in reading the pamphlet when Rudolph Vulpius started to laugh. "Here, Pastor Schaeffer. You being named a shepherd, here's one for you." Vulpius tossed an issue of *Die Wochentliche Bauernzeitung*, one that hadn't previously reached Frankenwinheim, across the rough boards of the table.

Schaeffer read the page, the expression on his face becoming grimmer with each line.

Stuffing *Common Sense* into his belt, Ableidinger came back to the table, looking over the pastor's shoulder. It was the entertainment page. At the top, large type proclaimed, *The Latest from Grantville.* Just below, on the left, was a woodcut of a scruffy but very well-endowed ram. The title was *Schade, Brillo! Schade!* "Shame on you, Brillo! Shame!"

"What's a Brillo?" Old Kaethe asked. She was looking over the pastor's other shoulder with no more deference to his status than Ableidinger showed.

"Maybe it explains it somewhere in the story," Vulpius said.

Pastor Schaeffer was turning red and starting to sputter.

"For the sake of your health," Ableidinger said, reaching over and taking the newspaper. "It's a fable, like Aesop. That's classical enough." He started to read it out loud for everyone in the tavern. His booming voice, trained in rhetoric and debate, caught the attention of even the people who didn't pay much attention to the politics of the village or the region. "The English title of the story was *Bad, Ba-a-a-ad, Brillo!*"

Everyone knew animal fables. Nobody had trouble figuring out that Brillo, whatever a Brillo might be, stood for the sturdy German farmer. Nor that the merino ram stood for the rulers who made their lives difficult.

Ableidinger was no more than half way through when Pastor Schaeffer got up and left the tavern.

None of the rest of the audience paid any attention to his disapproval. Frankenwinheim provided him with an unruly flock.

Kaethe pulled the shutter closed and brought in an oil lamp. "Read it again," she ordered. "Maybe there's something to be happy about, after all."

Rudolph blinked up at her. "What?"

"The up-timers printed it, didn't they? The plain old ordinary ram was clever enough to outwit the highly bred one. This wasn't smuggled in. Our new rulers—they printed a fable in which this Brillo triumphed."

Ableidinger grinned. "Not edifying, of course. To be properly edifying, I'm sure Pastor Schaeffer would insist that Brillo should have come to a proper insight that God the Father had established the merino ram as the representative of His secular sword on earth and deferred to the gentleram, giving him proper precedence."

"Teacher." Old Kaethe rapped him on the top of the head. "That's not respectful."

Ableidinger nodded. "I know." His voice rumbled as he started reading through the fable again.

He had to read *Schade, Brillo! Schade!* a half-dozen times. Not that the rest of the villagers couldn't read, but they only had one copy of the story. In any case, most people would rather hear something read out loud, with feeling and emphasis in the reader's voice. By the time they got out of the tavern, it was full dark. Old Kaethe had given them a crock of hot broth to dunk their bread. Matthias was sleeping on his cot. The comfort in his stomach had put him right to sleep.

The oil in the lamp wouldn't last much longer.

Ableidinger hadn't been that surprised by the fable. In other issues of the weekly newspaper for farmers, the up-timers had published paragraphs of political philosophy. Sayings. Maxims. He had copied out some of them, from John Locke, from Benjamin Franklin, from Thomas Jefferson.

But those authors were Englishmen, and they had written then, not now. If he understood properly what this Grantville city signified, they had written in a "then" that now would never happen. In a future that never would be.

The Bible provided comfort for all tribulations. "With God, all things are possible."

Thus, a city from the future, too, was possible.

Not that Pastor Schaeffer would be likely to see it that way.

Ableidinger had been a little surprised by the fable. The other authors had written "then." Not to mention "there." Brillo was, most certainly, here and now. An ordinary German ram.

Ableidinger opened *Common Sense.* He would make the most of this evening's ration of oil. He didn't have much time for reading in the daylight in winter. That was when most of his pupils spent most of their days at school, so he had to teach the lessons.

That was his job. Teaching. Not thinking about political philosophy.

Then and now. There and here. Thomas Paine. "The cause of America is in a great measure the cause of all mankind." How local circumstances could give rise to universal principles. "The laying a Country desolate with Fire and Sword, declaring War against the natural rights of all Mankind, and extirpating the Defenders thereof from the Face of the Earth, is the Concern of every Man to whom Nature hath given the Power of feeling; . . ."

Ableidinger frowned to himself. Looking up, he frowned at his pupils, directing the older ones back to doing simple addition on their slates.

Did the up-timers who would be administering Franconia agree with Paine?

If so, why were they working for the king of Sweden?

If not, why had they published this pamphlet in German?

He continued reading, fascinated by the distinction that Paine made between society and government, the first produced by men's wants and promoting their happiness; the second produced by men's wickedness and restraining their vices. Society was a blessing; government a necessary evil. "The one encourages intercourse, the other creates distinctions. The first is a patron, the last a punisher."

Hey, this was a good one! ". . . The palaces of kings are built upon the ruins of the bowers of paradise."

> For were the impulses of conscience clear, uniform and irresistibly obeyed, man would need no other lawgiver; but that not being the case, he finds it necessary to surrender up a part of his property to furnish means for the protection of the rest; and this he is induced to do by the same prudence which in every other case advises him, out of two evils to choose the least. Wherefore, security being the true design and end of government, it unanswerably follows that whatever form thereof appears most likely to ensure it to us, with the least expense and greatest benefit, is preferable to all others.

Ableidinger was very happy to discover that the new administration—or, at least, the men who had founded the country from which the new administrators came—had a clear and distinct picture in their minds of the way a village *ought* to work. Whether or not it did, of course, was another question.

Looking up at the children, he told them to stop working and listen while he read to them.

None of them objected.

He read through Paine's description of a small number of persons, settling a new land and, in a condition of "natural liberty," establishing a society by cooperating with one another.

"A thousand motives will excite them thereto . . ."

He assigned the older children the task of thinking of just ten of those motives for establishing a society in the wilderness. Each of them should talk with his or her parents and bring the list to school the next day. They would combine all the lists and then compare them to the reasons that Thomas Paine gave for this action.

They did combine the lists. Then he had each child copy Paine's reasons and take them home to their parents.

The pastor, when he heard about this assignment, was not pleased. He said so to the mayor.

"Surely," Old Kaethe asked, "you would not deny that God's children should endeavor to assist one another? Charity is a virtue."

"When you put it that way . . ." Schaeffer turned and went back to his house.

At the school, Ableidinger was still proceeding through *Common Sense*. Once Paine's hypothetical emigrants had established a society, because they began to "relax in their duty and attachment to each other," they reached a point at which "this remissness will point out the necessity of establishing some form of government to supply the defect of moral virtue."

Ah. How remarkable! A lot of what Paine wrote was specific to the circumstances of England and England's handling of its colonies in America. That was specific to time and place. Ableidinger skipped over this in school. It wasn't something the children really needed to learn, and he did have to find time for the regular lessons. England was far away and every educated man in the Germanies knew that the place was terribly backwards. Besides, if Thomas Paine had believed that the "English constitution" was complex, one could only assume that he had never made a study of the Holy Roman Empire.

Some things, though, were worth emphasizing. Paine even knew of the ancient custom of the villages in many parts of the Germanies according to which the council met under a tree.

*   *   *

> *Some convenient tree will afford them a State House, under the branches of which the whole Colony may assemble to deliberate on public matters. It is more than probable that their first laws will have the title only of Regulations and be enforced by no other penalty than public disesteem. In this first parliament every man by natural right will have a seat.*

Paine didn't seem to realize that it ought to be a linden tree. But then, there was a limit to what one could expect of foreigners. Perhaps there were no lindens in England or this far-away America.

As Ableidinger taught Paine to his students, he started sending out circular letters to the teachers in other villages in the vicinity urging them to obtain their own copies of the pamphlet and helpfully enclosing the lesson plans he was developing for teaching it.

The most complicated one dealt with the increase in size of the imaginary colony, which required that village-style government be supplemented by a system of elected representatives.

> *Here then is the origin and rise of government; namely, a mode rendered necessary by the inability of moral virtue to govern the world; here too is the design and end of government, viz. Freedom and security. And however our eyes may be dazzled with show, or our ears deceived by sound; however prejudice may warp our wills, or interest darken our understanding, the simple voice of nature and reason will say, 'tis right.*

The "simple voice of nature and reason."

Der gesunde Menschenverstand. Common Sense.

Even in those sections specific to England, there were some good diagnoses of the general problems and occasional sentences from which general principles could be derived.

Ableidinger found Paine's analysis of scriptural principles to be not only excellent, but also quite in keeping with many of the assertions made at the time of the Peasant War in 1525—the one in which the farmers' hope for liberty had been so betrayed by the leaders of the new Reformation. He looked at the piece of paper on the table in front of him. Yes, Lutheran though he was himself, he would write it. In this matter, Luther had betrayed the Germans' hopes for greater liberty.

> *Government by kings was first introduced into the world by the Heathens, from whom the children of Israel copied the custom. It was the most prosperous invention the Devil ever set on foot for the promotion of idolatry. The Heathens paid divine honours to their deceased kings, and the Christian World hath improved on the plan by doing the same to their living ones. How impious is the title of sacred Majesty applied to a worm, who in the midst of his splendor is crumbling into dust!*

Ableidinger laughed out loud. After what Franconia had suffered from the invasion of the Swede and his allies, he could only agree with Paine's statement that, "Absolute governments, (tho' the disgrace of human nature) have this advantage with them, they are simple; if the people suffer, they know the head from which their suffering springs; know likewise the remedy; and are not bewildered by a variety of causes and cures."

January, 1633: Frankenwinheim, Franconia

The agricultural newspapers and pamphlets kept coming. Almost every weekly edition of *Die Wochentliche Bauernzeitung* had a new Brillo story. It was worth sending Tobias to get the new issue every week.

Ableidinger read every Brillo story out loud in the tavern. According to what Tobias heard, there were many villages in Franconia in which someone read the Brillo story out loud every week. He was getting a lot of replies to his circular letters. It was breaking his budget to pay the postage when they arrived.

Other villages were also reading *Common Sense*. A printer in Bamberg sent a letter requesting the right to print an edition of a thousand copies of Ableidinger's abbreviated version with annotations for teaching its principles in village schools.

"There's time," he said to Rudolph Vulpius. "It won't hurt the children to miss school for just a few days, no matter what Pastor Schaeffer says. I need to go to Bamberg."

"Need?" Vulpius gave him the kind of look Ableidinger was accustomed to giving his own pupils.

"Well . . . I want to meet the printer who will be publishing my pamphlet. That's important. I want to get some idea of how many other pamphlets and books are being published, better than I can from here. I can walk down with Tobias, if you will just put on your other hat as the head of the parish's board of elders and get me permission to go."

"That's important," Old Kaethe said, "but it's not the most important thing. Rudolph should go with you. A couple of other men with him, and a few men from other villages around. We're on the edge of things, here. We need to just look at these up-timers, these men from Grantville."

"We?" the mayor asked.

"I did think," she said, "that I might come along. See what kind of Germans they have surrounded themselves with. See how they are doing things in more important towns and places."

Vulpius nodded. "Watch them. For the time will come, perhaps, when we have to test them. You read their words, Constantin. Think, though. It's going to be more important for us to find out if their actions match their words."

So, not long after Christmas, they went to Bamberg, to the press of Frau Else Kronacher. She did, as promised, pay Ableidinger for his manuscript. Not that she had any obligation to pay him, she pointed out, but the convenience of working from it all at once rather than chasing around Franconia after copies of his various circular letters and piecing them together in the proper order for her daughter Martha to set in type made it worth her while.

Of course, the woman hadn't lost much. Ableidinger turned around and spent half of the money on other books and pamphlets that her press had published. He spent most of the rest of it on warm clothing for Matthias and treats to give his pupils on the festival of Three Kings. Some, however, he reserved for future postage.

"What did you think?" Old Kaethe stomped her cold feet on the ground. The weather was worse on the way home than it had been when they left Frankenwinheim.

Ableidinger pulled the collar of his cloak up. "Paine was certainly an optimist when he wrote, 'I draw my idea of the form of government from a principle in nature which no art can overturn, viz. that the more simple any thing is, the less liable it is to be disordered, and

the easier repaired when disordered.' Still . . . If the up-timers can simplify the system under which we poor Germans have to live . . ."

Kaethe frowned. "Why do the up-timers have to do it? Why can't
the Germans do it themselves? Like the ram?"

Ableidinger smiled. In spite of the weather, he had never been so
happy in midwinter. Most years, he spent hours praying for the sol-
stice to come, that the turn of the season might start to bring more
light to his day. But he had been so busy that he scarcely noticed the
passing of the shortest day of the year.

"According to their principles, if the people of Franconia set out
to simplify their government, the up-timers should be obliged to refrain
from interfering with the process."

Vulpius nodded. "It would, after all, be expensive for them to interfere. Interference means soldiers. Soldiers cost money."

"They certainly cost a lot more money than circular letters and
pamphlets," Tobias said.

Ableidinger agreed. Not that postage was cheap. Common sense
all by itself reminded a person of that.

The Suhl Incident

ERIC FLINT AND JOHN ZEEK

January 13, 1633

Warrant Officer Hatfield was using a lever to hold the engine steady while Private First Class Cooper bolted it to the motor mounts when he saw Captain Pitre walk into the shop. Turning to Cooper's assistant, who was nearby, he said, "Filss, take over here and hold this steady. It looks like the captain wants to talk to me."

"Good morning, ma'am," he said, as he walked to meet the captain. "The second locomotive is looking good. All we have left to do is set up the controls and fit the wheels and it'll be ready to test. Close to one hundred horse power and a ton heavier, it should out-pull number one by a goodly margin. Private Cooper here is a wonder as a mechanic. He does good work, and is just full of ideas."

"That's great, Mr. Hatfield. Your engine shop boys are doing an excellent job." Captain Pitre responded loudly enough so that the entire shop could hear. Then in a lower voice she added, "But the reason I stopped by was because General Kagg sent word he wants to see you and me this morning."

The New United States was now part of the Confederated Principalities of Europe, with the Swedish king, Gustavus Adolphus, recognized as its official military leader under his title of captain general. After lengthy negotiations, President Stearns had agreed that Gustavus Adolphus could station one regiment—one, no more—in or near Grantville. The regiment he sent was one of his oldest "first guard regiments." It was known as the Yellow Regiment, and while most of its soldiers and officers were mercenaries, usually Germans— as was true of the Swedish king's army as a whole—the commanding officer was a Swedish general, Lars Kagg.

As the two trudged through the snow, Hatfield wondered what Kagg wanted. He decided it couldn't be about anything the train crew had done wrong. They all, even Jochen Rau, had been on their best behavior lately. And Kagg had been very polite at the reception for his arrival last month.

Then the thought hit him that it might be about what Henry Johnson told him only this morning. General Jackson had wanted Pat, Anse's brother-in-law, to watch for any movement of guns out of Suhl to people who were unfriendly to the CPE. Maybe a letter from Pat had arrived.

"Ma'am, did the general say why he wanted to see us?"

"No, but he did ask if you were doing anything really vital. I told him your crew could probably keep working for a while without you. You've done a good job of training them."

"Thank you for the compliment. You're right, ma'am. Benno and Jochen can run the train without me and I would bet Cooper can finish this new engine. Bringing in Bill Frank as an advisor was a great idea. But I hope General Kagg doesn't want you to send me anywhere. The company might get called for active duty shortly, and I sure don't want it to go without me. You'll need me for that."

Captain Pitre gave her surroundings a somewhat sour examination. "Mr. Hatfield, from the look of things, we're not going anywhere until winter's over. Except to the regimental headquarters, and here we are."

Through the closed door of the office Anse could hear the rumble of the general's voice. That was no surprise. Kagg seemed to have only one volume setting: loud. Anse looked out the window to the outside. "Ma'am, was anyone else going to be at our meeting with the general?"

"Not that I know of. Why? Does it make a difference?"

"Not to me, but, stay calm. Your friend and mine, Captain von Dantz, is walking across the parade ground. And it looks like he's coming here."

Anse could sense the sudden stiffness in Captain Pitre. That von Dantz was both arrogant and incompetent was an opinion, he was sure, the two shared. The fact that von Dantz refused to accept the idea of women in the army, much less a woman officer, automatically insured there were going to be problems between him and Captain Elizabeth Pitre. Anse's problems with the Pomeranian mercenary captain were more personal and had arisen out of a dispute over the captain's baggage being crushed on the train Anse had commanded.

Luckily the door to Kagg's office opened just as von Dantz entered the building. As the general's clerk came out the door they could see Kagg himself, who was walking toward the door, waving his hand for them to come in.

"Captain Pitre, Herr Hatfield, come in. It is good of you to make time to see me."

Kagg's English, though heavily accented, was fluent. Anse was pretty sure that was one of the reasons he'd been sent to Grantville. The Swedish general also seemed to be punctilious about courtesy. Whether that was because of his own personality or blunt orders from Gustavus Adolphus, Anse didn't know. Probably both, he suspected.

The general spotted von Dantz coming through the outer office. "Come in, all of you. Captain von Dantz, you know Captain Pitre and Warrant Officer Hatfield. Captain Pitre, Herr Hatfield, I know you have met Captain von Dantz."

"*Ja*, I have met Fräulein Pitre and Hatfield, General."

"That is *Captain* Pitre," Kagg said curtly. "You should remember that you and she are the same rank and use proper military courtesy at all times. And Warrant Officer Hatfield should be addressed as Mister or Herr Hatfield. You should think of him the same as one of our master gunners. You do not address them by their bare last name, I hope."

Von Dantz turned red. "Captain, Herr Hatfield."

Anse thought that was as close to an apology as they were going to get. It was not an invariable rule, by any means, but he'd found that lots of Germans who enjoyed the "von" business seemed to find it well-nigh impossible to be courteous to those they considered their social inferiors.

Once they entered the general's office, Kagg said: "Now everyone sit down, and I can tell you why you are all here."

As the three found seats and the general moved behind his desk, Anse realized there was another man in the room, leaning against a side wall. It was the big Swedish lieutenant whom Anse had seen with Kagg several times. They'd arrived together, Anse thought. He was a bit older than Kagg, but had the same hard-as-nails look of a professional soldier.

If the seventeenth-century Swedish army worked about the same way the up-time American army of Hatfield's experience did—always an uncertain proposition—then this unnamed lieutenant would serve General Kagg as one of his staff officers. It was hard to tell, however, just exactly what authority he possessed. No down-time army that Anse was familiar with used the same tight and clear system of ranks that up-time armies did. Generals and colonels commanded specific units, as a rule. But down-timers used the terms "captain" and "lieutenant" very loosely. It was not uncommon for "lieutenants" to command "captains," for instance, since the term "lieutenant" might really signify *direct subordinate to the big cheese*, rather than *very junior officer*. But exactly how and when the authority of a staff officer superseded that of a line commander was something Anse still hadn't been able to figure out.

Once everyone was seated, Kagg spoke. "Captain Pitre, Captain von Dantz, Herr Hatfield, we have a problem. General Jackson has received reports that the gun-makers of Suhl are continuing to sell their products to anyone who will buy them, including the enemies of our king. He arranged for Patrick Johnson to look into it. Just this morning his report arrived and it looks like the earlier reports were true. He tells us that large shipments of weapons are leaving Suhl, going by way of Schleusingen. Toward the south. And I can assure you they are not being sent to General Banér in the Upper Palatinate."

"What do you expect? They are Franconians," Captain von Dantz interrupted. "Catholics. We should send troops to hang the traitors. Suhl is in the territory given to the Americans, and all have sworn allegiance to King Gustavus Adolphus. In Pomerania we know how to deal with people like that."

"Not exactly." Elizabeth Pitre's voice was mild and calm. "True, its citizens have sworn allegiance. But that is because Suhl—the city— like Badenburg, became a state in the N.U.S. by its own free will. That

was months before the captain general's agreement with President Stearns concerning Franconia."

She raised one eyebrow. "Not to mention that you, as a Pomeranian, surely misspoke in saying that the town is Catholic when it is in fact Lutheran." Her implication was that if she herself, as a lapsed Catholic, knew this much, surely the other captain should know more.

Von Dantz took the bait. "Suhl's city council became a 'state' of your N.U.S. under false pretenses. It is not an imperial city. The council had no legal right to declare itself independent from the Saxon administrators of the Henneberg inheritance." His disapproval of "do-it-yourself" politics was plain.

Kagg frowned. "Captain von Dantz, if you would let me finish, I will tell you what has been decided. Your job is to carry out the orders you receive. And I do not want to have to remind you again that you are serving with American troops and the New United States is *not*—directly—part of our king's territory. Neither, since last fall, is Franconia. So politeness toward our hosts is the order of the day."

Anse decided he liked the Swedish general. But he could see where this was headed, and started a mental packing list.

"Now, before I was interrupted, I was about to tell you I have been in contact with General Jackson and President Stearns. They both agree that we need to send some people to Suhl. A small investigative party, however, not a large military force. There is already an American administration set up for Franconia proper. It is headquartered in Würzburg. But since Suhl is a state of the N.U.S. rather than part of Catholic Franconia, Stearns' people in Würzburg have no authority there. In any event, our group will be only looking for evidence of gun trafficking with the CPE's enemies."

Kagg turned to Pitre. "Because of Suhl's status, I do not want to send a large expedition, or a purely Swedish one, or even one under Swedish command, although"—he nodded toward von Dantz—"there will be someone along from our army. There is already a garrison in the town, should more troops prove necessary. The king placed it there before Suhl chose to join the N.U.S."

His expression became very bland. "Negotiations between the Swedes and Suhl's city council in regard to its removal have been . . . protracted. Thus far, President Stearns has not seen fit to make its removal a priority. But we all feel that an American soldier should be officially in command, for political reasons. General Jackson specifically recommended Warrant Officer Hatfield. Captain Pitre, I would appreciate it if you would release him temporarily from his duties with your unit and loan him to me."

Captain Pitre frowned. "Well, certainly, if General Jackson says so. Although I'm not quite sure why he'd want someone from TacRail."

Kagg shrugged. "Nor am I. From what I understand, there is no early prospect of creating a rail line to Suhl. Not over that part of the *Thueringerwald*, certainly! But that was his suggestion." He turned to Anse. "Mr. Hatfield, do you have any objection? If nothing else, you can visit your brother-in-law who is already residing in Suhl."

Anse was surprised, as well as impressed, that Kagg already knew that much in the way of the personal details of the American soldiers he'd be working with. "Of course, General Kagg. Captain Pitre, I'd like to take a couple of my own men with me."

"Let me guess. You want Private Schultz and Corporal Rau?"

"Yes, ma'am. Jochen Rau is the best man around for finding out what's going on. And if we have to open any locked doors he has a lot of experience. Wili Schultz could help be a cover story, too, if we need one. His sister is going to marry Pat. He could be going to check out the wedding arrangements and to see Pat's business. I know that would leave you with only Toeffel as a trained driver, but Jim Cooper can drive an engine. Toeffel and he have worked together before. And in a pinch Chief Schwartz could drive short hauls."

"All right, Mr. Hatfield. But only those two, no more, and I'd like you back before the first of March."

Kagg nodded. "Better still, if you can send three of your own soldiers. In that case, I will only send Nils"—he waved at the lieutenant—"with Captain von Dantz. As I said, I'd rather avoid any larger Swedish presence in Suhl than we need, given the garrison that's already there." For a moment—a very brief moment—he seemed slightly embarrassed. "I'm afraid there's something of a history of ill-will in Franconia toward the Swedish army.

"That will make a party of five," the general continued. "That is a perfect number; enough to frighten off most bandits and not enough to attract attention. Nils, step over here and meet Herr Hatfield." The last statement was to the big lieutenant who was holding up the office wall.

"Herr Hatfield, I would like to introduce Lieutenant Nils Ivarsson. He has been with me since I became a soldier."

Hatfield measured the Swede with his eyes, as he extended his hand. Ivarsson was a little taller than six feet and looked strong as a bull. "Pleased to meet you."

"*Ja*, I am happy to meet you also. Captain von Dantz has spoken of you often." There might have been a twinkle in Ivarsson's eyes. Anse had a feeling the big Swede was not a member of the captain's fan club.

January 14, 1633

Anse looked up in surprise. It was early in the morning for one of the young Germans whom Ed Piazza had started assembling as part of his staff to be hand-delivering him a note. Or for anyone to be delivering a note at all. Ed's staff were no slouches. The secretary of state had several up-timers working with him also, of course, but he'd made it a point to incorporate down-timers as soon and as extensively as possible.

Anse didn't know this one by name, although he recognized him. A former student at the university at Jena, he thought. Eddie Junker—that was his name. Piazza tended to favor recruits from there, partly because Jena was not much more than fifteen miles away, and partly because Grantville had made it a point to develop relations with Jena that were as close as their relations with Badenburg.

Anse wasn't privy to the discussions in the inner circles, but he knew the general plan was to develop Jena into central Germany's premier educational and medical center. It made sense. Given the nature of its West Virginian topography, there simply wasn't room in Grantville—in the whole Ring of Fire, for that matter—to expand all that much. The town was already jammed with immigrants, and people were starting to build on hillside areas that Anse himself thought were questionable at best.

As he opened the note, Anse couldn't help grinning. However much the down-timers in the area were adapting to American custom, in many ways, the reverse was also happening. The note was just a three-way folded piece of paper, but the embossed wax seal keeping it closed was as ornate and fancy as you could ask for.

The message was short, to the point—and surprising.

> Dear Mr. Hatfield:
> The Secretary of State requests that you consult with him regarding your upcoming expedition to Suhl. Today at 14:00, if possible.

Jamie Lee Swisher
for Ed Piazza

Anse folded the note back up and nodded to the courier. "Tell him I'll be there, as requested." A moment later the young man was gone.

In some ways, of course, Ed Piazza was not adapting. The secretary of state could just as easily have *required* Anse to show up when he wanted to see him, and no "if possible" about it. But one of the reasons Piazza had made such a successful and popular high school principal for so many years was his meticulous attention to simple courtesy.

Anse himself was too old to know personally, but rumor had it that even when Piazza had been chewing out some wayward student, he'd been as polite as possible. Which Anse himself certainly wouldn't have been. *Do as I tell you, you little snot, or I'll whup your ass* was more his style in such affairs.

"Wonder what it's about?" he mused.

He found himself wondering a lot more, after he was ushered into Piazza's private office that afternoon. In fact, it was all he could do to keep his eyebrows from crawling onto his scalp.

Piazza wasn't there alone. Also in the office—a bit crammed, in fact, since it wasn't all that big—were President Stearns, General Jackson, and Rebecca Abrabanel. Mike Stearns was smiling blandly; Jackson was frowning. The solemn look on Becky's face made it clear that she was here in her official capacity as the national security adviser, not Mike's wife.

"Have a seat, Anse," said Piazza. As soon as he'd done so, the secretary of state nodded at Stearns.

"As you've probably figured out, my invitation was something of a subterfuge. It's really Mike who wants to talk to you."

"Sure is," Anse heard Jackson mutter. Becky shot him a look that seemed to combine reproof with exasperation.

Stearns chuckled softly. "As you'll soon discover, there is dissension and dispute in the top ranks of what passes for our august government. Here's the thing, Anse." Mike nodded toward Jackson. "Frank here thinks what von Dantz suggested that Kagg ought to do in Suhl is just fine. Go down there and hammer any bastards who are selling guns to our enemies. But Becky has strong reservations about the project. So does Melissa Mailey, for what it's worth. Between the two of them, they've convinced me that the situation is a lot more complicated than it looks."

"What's 'complicated' about it?" demanded Jackson. "Treason is treason."

Anse was surprised to see Becky almost snarling at him. The young Sephardic woman, in his experience, was usually imperturbable and serene.

"Idiot words that mean nothing!" she snapped. "What does 'treason'—or 'loyalty'—mean in Germanies that are not a nation and never have been? And loyalty to a *Swedish* king? Are we speaking of the same Swedes who conquered the area and behaved every bit as abominably as Tilly's army or Wallenstein's in the territories they occupied?"

Jackson looked mulish. "Loyalty to *us*. Suhl is a state in the N.U.S. One of our own states. By choice. It should be living under our laws and making everyone in the town do the same."

But Becky wasn't about to let up on him. "So what if there were no great massacres like Magdeburg? There were massacres enough carried out by Gustavus' army south of the *Thueringerwald*, on a smaller scale, be sure of it. And all the rest! Rapes, arson, plundering. Name the crime and they committed it. Especially in the Catholic areas, of course, but the Swedes were none too gentle in Protestant areas either."

"Enough already," said Mike calmly. Becky subsided, still glaring at Frank Jackson.

Mike looked at Anse. "Here's the point, Warrant Officer Hatfield."

The formality was unusual, coming from Mike Stearns. He was making clear that he was speaking as the President, now. Anse sat up a little straighter. What was coming, he knew, amounted to his marching orders—and, push came to shove, Mike was the boss here, not Frank Jackson.

"The people in Suhl have been making guns and other weapons for centuries. And, for centuries, they've been selling them to anyone who was willing to pay. It's the local custom—hallowed tradition, if you will. Not to mention that it's perfectly legal under the laws they've lived with all their lives, and we've scarcely had enough time to undertake extensive reeducation in regard to American statutory definitions. If nothing else, Becky and Melissa have convinced me that we can't just go charging in there like a bull in a china shop, expecting that anyone who lives there will see the situation in terms of concepts like 'loyalty' and 'treason.'"

Seeming a bit exasperated, he ran fingers through his thick hair. "The truth is, Anse, not even Kagg thinks the issue is really a matter of loyalty or treason. What's really involved, from his point of view, is a simple matter of power politics. The Swedes conquered the region, and so now the Swedes have dibs on Suhl's guns. 'To the victor belong the spoils' and all that stuff. Whether they are N.U.S. citizens or not. Further south, whether he's assigned the Franconians to N.U.S. administration, or not. We're damned lucky that Kagg is being more reasonable than von Dantz."

He gave Jackson a look that was not as unfriendly as Becky's, but wasn't any too admiring, either. "Why this fella—who did a tour of duty in Vietnam, just like you did—has so much trouble understanding that, I'm not sure. But what I do know is this: *I don't intend for Grantville to run roughshod over another N.U.S. state.* Suhl's people are our citizens, even if they still have a lot to learn about the differences between up-time and down-time ideas of citizenship and national loyalty."

Mike raised his hand and brought it down firmly on his desk. That was a variation on one of his most familiar gestures, which could range from a gentle tap of the fingers to a resounding slam. This one was about midway between.

"What's more," he said firmly, "I'm not going to let troubles develop in Suhl that could spill over into our Franconian territories. Whatever Gustavus had in mind when he handed over Franconia for us to administer, I do *not* intend our rule there to be one of conquerors. I can't see any point in it. If for no other reason, because with a war likely to break out between us and the French, we won't have the soldiers to spare to occupy Franconia with more than a few small garrisons in some of the major towns. If we don't get the cooperation of the people who live there—and get it pretty soon—we're going to have a nightmare on our hands. There's no law of geography or geology that I know of that says that 'quagmires' are restricted to Asia."

His eyes came back to Anse. "That's why I specifically instructed Frank to recommend you for this assignment when Kagg raised it with us. First, because I think you're levelheaded. And, second, because I'm hoping that since you're assigned to TacRail you won't seem as threatening a figure as some other type of soldier might be, once you get there. You're essentially a military engineer, not one of the guys who specializes in hitting people over the head."

Again, he ran fingers through his hair. "Ah, hell, Anse, I know I'm handing you a mess on a plate. Just do the best you can with it—and don't assume the Swedes know what they're doing. When it comes right down to it, remember, *we* are the people in charge in Suhl. Not Gustavus Adolphus' mercenaries."

Seeing the look on Anse's face, Mike chuckled. "Yeah, I know. Easier said than done—when they've got most of the muscle. Especially muscle like von Dantz, a good chunk of which seems to reside between his ears and who isn't likely to respond well to having you in charge. I'm sending along someone to help, though. Noelle Murphy."

Seeing the look that now came to Anse's face, Mike and Becky laughed out loud. Even Frank Jackson grinned.

"She's an accountant—and she's planning to become a nun!" Anse protested.

Becky waggled her hand. "Maybe yes, maybe no, as to the last part. She hasn't decided, I don't believe. But she's very smart, and"— again, that sharp look at Jackson—"unlike *some* people, she's actually studied the situation."

Orders were orders. Anse made only one last minimal objection. "What's her cover story? I mean, I can't very well . . ."

Finally, Becky's usually serene countenance made its appearance. "Do not be concerned. I have managed the thing."

On his way back—none too cheerfully—Anse contemplated his new assignment.

There were too many damn layers involved, was the main thought that came to him.

Gustavus Adolphus, Mike, Kagg, Noelle, von Dantz, the garrison commander, the Suhl city council, their militia captain.

And him.

Years ago, his wife Jo had taken him to a party where the hostess served something called an "eight layer chocolate dessert." He'd only taken a sliver, but even so. Cake layers, tied together with chocolate whipped cream, with some kind of chocolate-raspberry jelly, with some kind of chocolate-and-cream-cheese spread. One layer oozing into the next. Worst heartburn of his life. He'd never run into anything like it again.

At least, not until he had started to try to figure out who was in charge of what in these New United States. The overlapping layers of authority for this project gave him a mental indigestion at least as bad as the physical indigestion that incredible cake had caused.

It had some kind of a German name, too, now that he thought about it.

January 16, 1633

Anse looked over the party gathered in Henry Johnson's living room. Jochen Rau was seated near the door with his pack by his feet. Benno Toeffel had stopped by for any final instructions and was standing talking quietly with Rau. Henry himself and Ursula Eckhardt, Pat's fiancée, were bustling around carrying packs of food for the trip from the kitchen. The combined Schultz and Eckhardt children were carrying the food out to the wagon. The only one missing was Wili Schultz. He and his wife Dora had wandered upstairs to say goodbye.

"Uncle Anse," Suse Eckhardt called from the door. "There are two women outside and they're asking for you."

Going out on the porch, Anse found a woman in her late thirties standing with another woman, somewhere in her early or mid-twenties. Behind them was a handcart being pushed by a man Anse didn't know, but thought was a down-timer. The handcart seemed full of what looked like luggage.

Anse recognized the younger woman. She was Noelle Murphy.

"Are you Anse Hatfield?" asked the older woman.

When he admitted he was, she continued. "I'm Gaylynn Reardon. I heard you were going to Suhl and since my husband Gary works for Pat Johnson I'd like to tag along. My friend Noelle here agreed to come along with me. So, Mr. Hatfield, have you got room in your wagon?"

Normally, Anse would have been inclined to refuse. But. whether or not Gaylynn Reardon's reason for traveling to Suhl made any sense—or was even genuine—he knew perfectly well that Becky Stearns was using it as an excuse to quietly insert Noelle Murphy into the expedition.

"We're ready to pull out as soon as we finish loading the wagon. I hope you've packed properly, Mrs. Reardon. It's a pretty rough road once we get past Badenburg, until we hit the trade route, and we're traveling in winter."

"I'm already packed, and so's Noelle." She jerked her thumb over her shoulder, pointing to the handcart. "Our stuff's in there, ready to go. Everyone knows you're leaving today. I spent four years in the

West Virginia National Guard and winter maneuvers were no challenge."

She glanced at her younger friend, and smiled. "As for Noelle, she's a lot tougher than she looks."

Anse did his best not to let his skepticism show. Leaving aside Noelle Murphy's maybe-aspirations to become a nun, there was nothing about the young woman's appearance to suggest she was any sort of sturdy frontier type. Noelle wasn't frail. But she was of average height, rather slender, and her sandy blonde hair and moderately good looks fit a lady accountant a lot better than they did a reincarnation of Calamity Jane.

But it was a done deal, so Anse didn't argue the matter. "Come on into the house, then," he said, "and get something hot to drink. We'll leave within the hour."

He turned to Wili's older son, who was tending the horses. "Wendel, help these ladies pack their stuff on the wagon."

Going back inside, he found that Wili and his wife had rejoined the group. Dora Schultz came over and, taking his collar in her hands, pulled him down to look him straight in the eye. "I want your promise. You will take care of Wili, and stay out of trouble."

"Sure, Dora. We're just going to look over Pat's shop and make some wedding arrangements."

"Ha, you are a terrible liar. You think Wili can hide anything from me. You just be sure I get him back in one piece. And you better come back whole, too. Men all act like little boys, sometimes."

"Speaking of coming back whole," Henry Johnson interjected. "I have a couple of things that might help to that end. Jochen, here, I want you to have this."

Henry held a revolver out to Rau. "That's a 1917 Smith and Wesson. It shoots the same ammo as Anse and Wili's pistols. I packed five-hundred rounds of .45ACP in the wagon and some half-moon clips so you can practice along the way. And because you need a long gun, I want you to have this Browning 'Sweet-Sixteen.' I packed three hundred rounds of 16-gauge buckshot in the wagon, too. Those are gifts, Corporal Rau. They are yours to keep."

"Ha, just going to see Pat's shop," sniffed Dora. "Come, Ursula. We go to the kitchen und let the boys play with the toys." Dora led Ursula out of the room.

Just then Gaylynn Reardon and Noelle Murphy came through the door. "Hello, Mr. Johnson. Are you about ready to put these fellows on the road, Mr. Hatfield? The sooner we get started, the sooner we get to Suhl."

Whether or not the woman was really that eager to be reunited with her husband, she was certainly playing the part.

"Yes, they're all ready to go," interjected Henry. "Except for waiting for Captain von Dantz and Lieutenant Ivarsson. So you have time for a cup of coffee."

"Mr. Johnson, that's the best offer I've had all day. A cup of coffee would be fine. Oh, Mr. Hatfield, in case you were wondering, my .30-30 is on the wagon and I've taken a deer with it every winter since I was thirteen years old, so I can hold my own if we have to fight."

He noticed that she didn't make any mention of *Noelle*'s proficiency with firearms. Anse knew that Noelle had grown up in West Virginia, but he had a strong suspicion she did not and never had shared any of Gaylynn's tomboy proclivities.

After handing Gaylynn a mug of coffee, Henry waved Anse to the side for a private word. "Remember what I told you last night. Pat needs a contract to make rifles for the army. This business I hear about the people in Suhl selling guns outside the CPE is bound to make some of the big mucky-mucks in the government look to other places to buy guns."

"I'm sure Pat would have nothing to do with trading guns with the French. Hell, Hank. It might have been a reason to deny contracts, up-time. Here it seems to be standard practice. No one mucky-muckier than Frank Jackson would even wince, anyway."

Hank shook his head. "Look around. The French aren't our only enemies. Ferdinand II, the Holy Roman Emperor, will have another go at us as soon as he can. So will Maximilian of Bavaria. I agree Pat is smart enough to avoid shipping guns to any of them, but if other gun makers in Suhl are shipping to our enemies it's going to make it hard to get a contract for any factory in Suhl. You're going to have to find out where the source is and make sure the government stops this trade as quick as possible. Shoot the treacherous bastards, if you have to."

"Sure, Hank."

Anse saw no point in getting into the complexities. He wouldn't be at all surprised to find that most up-timers shared Hank's opinion. It had been fairly obvious in the course of his interview with Stearns that General Jackson did, after all. Truth be told, Anse was rather inclined that way himself. But the cautions given him by Mike and Becky Stearns made him unwilling to come to any conclusions until he got down there himself. He had a bad feeling that the situation in Suhl was going to be the political equivalent of "some assembly required."

The party pulled out an hour and a half later. Captain von Dantz had been a bit late. Henry's old farm wagon, with its rubber shod car wheels, was driven by Wili, with Mrs. Reardon riding beside him. Wili had his pump shotgun propped against the seat beside him and Gaylynn had her rifle lying in her lap. Jochen Rau was riding on the back with his new shotgun across his knees. Rau, who was a bit of a conservative about his weapons, still had his long knife and wheel-lock pistol hanging from his belt, but the big Smith and Wesson revolver was now holstered on his right hip.

Ivarsson was riding a large horse beside the wagon and talking to Rau. He had tied the two baggage horses he and the captain had arrived with to the rear of the wagon, for remounts if needed. Anse noted that the Swedish lieutenant looked like an arsenal. He had two pistols in his sash, two more in his boot tops and another pair in saddle hol-sters. In addition he had a long heavy saber and a brand-new SRG carbine hanging from the back of his saddle.

Captain von Dantz, who was riding a bit ahead of the wagon, was the lightest armed of the group. With only a saber and a single pistol, he looked almost unarmed compared to Ivarsson.

Anse reviewed his own armament. The Remington auto loading shotgun was riding nicely in the saddle scabbard, and the Colt auto-matic on his belt was balanced by two double ammo pouches and the belt knife on his left side. The small dagger in his right boot was riding comfortably, but might be a problem if he had to walk any distance.

To his surprise, Noelle Murphy had dredged up a horse some-where and was riding it, adequately if with no great expertise. He wouldn't have thought the woman had ever been on a horse in her life. To all appearances, she was completely unarmed. But the heavy winter clothing she was wearing could have easily concealed a small handgun, and Anse was beginning to suspect that Noelle Murphy was someone who was often full of surprises. So who knew?

The road was well maintained and heavily traveled, so the group made good time. Twice they were passed by trucks from Grantville on their way to Badenburg, and once by one returning.

Captain von Dantz rode up to a position just in front of Anse. He was scowling as he watched one of the trucks receding into the distance.

"If we had taken one of the army trucks as far as Badenburg, we would already be on the road to Suhl, Herr Hatfield. This waste of time is poor planning on your part."

Anse kept his tone of voice even and level. "Captain, this leg of our little jaunt is just to settle the load in. We can check and see how everything is riding when we get to Badenburg and stop and fix anything that goes wrong. If we had started from Badenburg we'd be stopping in the forest."

That caused von Dantz's scowl to darken. "I am also not happy with you letting those women come along. They are going to slow us down. I am sure General Kagg did not authorize that."

Anse was tempted to point out that the expedition was happening under the auspices of the New United States, not the Swedish garrison that the N.U.S. had *permitted* to be stationed on N.U.S. soil. So it didn't really matter whether Kagg approved or not.

But, for better or worse, he was still trying to keep the peace. So he simply said, "To tell you the truth, I'm not too happy with them coming along myself. But Mrs. Reardon was determined to rejoin her husband and her friend Ms. Murphy insisted on accompanying her. It was either take them with us or find their bodies along the road some place."

"How would that have been a great loss? Herr Hatfield, you are going to have to learn to weigh the value of people." He spurred his horse forward into a trot.

"She's worth about ten of you, I figure," Anse muttered to himself, as he watched the captain tiring his horse needlessly.

"You should not insult ladies," came an unexpected, heavily accented voice from behind him.

Anse twisted in the saddle and saw that Lieutenant Ivarsson had ridden up while he was watching the captain. Unlike Anse himself, the Swedish officer was obviously an expert horseman. Anse had never heard him coming. He raised his eyebrows.

"Ten times nothing is nothing, Herr Hatfield. Simple mathematics."

Anse chuckled. "I like your arithmetic, Lieutenant. May I take it you are no more impressed with Captain von Dantz than I am?"

Ivarsson shrugged. "An army makes do with what it has." He seemed on the verge of adding something, but didn't do so. Instead he changed the subject. "Since you are in charge of our little caravan, were you planning to stop in Badenburg or push on until nightfall?"

"I thought we'd only stop if we needed to adjust the loads. We have—what?—forty-five or fifty miles to Suhl? I was figuring three or four days."

"That sounds about right. I would recommend we keep a sharp watch when we camp for the night. Our horses will be tempting to any local thieves. I will stand a watch."

"Well, I wasn't planning on asking the captain. So with five of us we can switch off every two hours. Or do you think we should double up?"

"Five? Oh, you want the older woman to stand a watch. She does seem competent, but I think we should double up, as you say, once we get well into the *Thueringerwald*. There have been reports of bandits in the area between here and Suhl. Or it could simply be disgruntled residents, acting like bandits. There were undoubtedly some people not too happy about turning into part of the New United States when you 'slid' the Wettins' duchy out from under them."

Anse chuckled. He liked that way of describing it. "What about tonight we split the watch five ways, and the next two nights you and Rau take the first watch and Wili and I do the second?"

"Yes, that will work and we can let the lady rest. Oh, I was talking to Rau. Was he really a house breaker before he became a soldier?"

Anse laughed. "Breaking into houses is the least of Jochen's skills. He's a better tracker than I am, and can sneak up on a cat. The man is amazing."

The big lieutenant shook his head. "And you trained him to run that little thing, the locomotive. Seems a waste. He should be scouting for the army. Is that the right name, 'locomotive,' the thing that pulls the carts on the rails?"

"Yes, that's what it's called. You'd be surprised what that little thing can pull."

The conversation soon meandered into a technical discussion on the advantages of rail traffic over wagon transport, and how the railroad would make an army less dependent on foraging.

January 17, 1633

They stopped for the night a few miles past Badenburg. There were no incidents, as Anse expected given their proximity to the town. The worst problem they faced was the bitter cold, with such a clear sky. The temperature was well below freezing. Fortunately, they'd all dressed properly for the climate.

Less than an hour after they started forward again the next morning, Noelle Murphy brought her horse alongside Anse's. He was pretty sure she'd timed her arrival so that Captain von Dantz was up ahead a ways, well out of hearing range.

May as well get started, Anse thought.

"Okay, Ms. Murphy. Since I gather you're my expert adviser, please advise."

Noelle winced. "Insofar as jury-rigged cram courses in 'N.U.S. Constitution' and 'Franconian affairs' make me an expert—which they don't, not hardly. But I'll do the best I can."

She took a long, slow breath, exhaling a visible cloud of moisture into the clear, freezing air.

"We might as well start by being honest about the situation, Mr. Hatfield. When Gustavus Adolphus reached a deal with Mike Stearns that the New United States would assume responsibility for the administration of Franconia, there wasn't anybody at all in Grantville who knew much about it. Truth be told, there weren't a half-dozen people in town who had ever even been to anyplace in Franconia, and those had mostly been there in the military and lived on American bases. Those people thought it was the northern part of Bavaria—Upper Franconia, Middle Franconia, and Lower Franconia. Which it was, up-time. But which it is not, down-time. Bavaria hasn't expanded to include it yet. It wouldn't for a long time yet to come in our original time line and may never in this universe. The rest of the Grantvillers had not even heard of Franconia. That includes me."

Anse grinned. "Me, too."

She gave him a quick, flickering smile. "My training's as an accountant, not a combination historian-sociologist and, I guess, Superspy Juniorette."

That made Anse laugh. Up ahead, he saw Captain von Dantz glance back at the sound.

Frowning disapprovingly, of course. As if there were any danger of drawing the attention of bandits this close to Badenburg! Anywhere within two days' ride of Grantville, for that matter. By now, bandits had learned to steer well clear of the Ring of Fire, where just a few months earlier a large expedition of Wallenstein's Croat raiders had gotten torn to pieces.

Noelle continued. "I've seen some of the correspondence that's gone back and forth between Mr. Salatto and Mr. Piazza. The first headache Mr. Salatto and his team faced, as soon as they got to Würzberg, was figuring out what 'Franconia' meant in the first place. It turns out it's a loose and slippery geographical term—especially when you have to factor in what the Swedes think about the issue. One of the first things Mr. Salatto and Mr. Piazza agreed on—President Stearns, too, I imagine—was that from the context of the deal reached with Gustavus Adolphus it was pretty clear that the king of Sweden did *not* mean for Grantville to mess around in the territories of his influential Protestant allies, even though they were clearly in Franconia, geographically speaking. That meant we had to steer clear of the imperial city of Nürnberg; the margraves of Ansbach and Bayreuth, et cetera and so forth."

Anse grunted. "In short, what 'Franconia' means to Gustavus Adolphus is really 'the parts of Franconia that were ruled by Catholic church officials before I conquered them.' "

"Exactly. What the king of Sweden wanted us to handle were the dioceses of Würzburg and Bamberg and the abbey of Fulda—even though, to a fussy geographer, Fulda is only sort of marginally Franconian. But since it was definitely Catholic and sort of between Franconia and Hesse-Kassel, President Stearns decided that Gustavus Adolphus intended the N.U.S. to take over there. So we did. By last November, the N.U.S. picked out its administrative teams, with Steve Salatto in overall charge, and President Stearns and Secretary of State Piazza sent them on their way."

He sighed, took off his cap, and scratched his scalp. "This is going to be a mess, isn't it?"

"Sure is. Like I said, Mr. Piazza showed me some of the reports Steve Salatto sent in. Our administration teams found out very soon that there weren't many people who had been living in Franconia during the winter of 1631-1632 who were likely to ever join a King Gustavus Adolphus fan club. It didn't seem to matter at all whether they were Catholic or Protestant, or whether they lived in the villages or the big towns. At a rough guess, at least ninety percent of the population of Franconia hate the Swedes. They were every bit as rough on people when they came through as any of Tilly or Wallenstein's armies."

Anse hissed. "Rough on people" was a euphemism for what, up-time, would be a roster of every major felony on the books, starting with murder, rape and arson and working your way down. "*That* bad?"

Noelle started to reply but had to break off to calm down her horse. The beast had gotten a little jittery about something. God knows what. Anse Hatfield wasn't really much more experienced with horses than the young Catholic woman.

"Well, I guess not quite," she said, finally, once the horse settled down. "At least, so far as we know there were no major massacres. Certainly nothing on the scale of what Tilly's army did at Magdeburg. But it was plenty bad enough—and nobody down there has forgotten, or stopped holding a grudge. Real, serious, personal grudges, too. Not just the usual 'they made me convert to somebody else's religion' grudges. There were the 'they burned my Ma as a witch' grudges; the 'somebody's army stole all our horses' grudges; 'the Swedes devastated our property when they passed through in 1631-1632 on their way to crossing the Lech' grudges."

"In Suhl, too? They're mostly Lutherans themselves, I thought. Just like the Swedes."

"Yes, they are. For that matter, you can argue till the cows come home whether Suhl is really part of Franconia or Thuringia in the first place. But it doesn't matter, Mr. Hatfield."

"Call me Anse, please."

"Okay. Look, Anse, here's what I've finally figured out about this so-called 'war of religion.' Almost every army involved in this war is mostly made up of mercenaries, including Gustavus Adolphus' army. The truth is, you'll find plenty of Protestant soldiers serving in 'Catholic' armies, and vice versa. As often as not, religion is just an excuse for a mercenary army to do what it would have done anyway, once it enters territory it considers conquered from the enemy—and their definition of 'enemy' is going to be just as sloppy as everything else. From what I can tell, most of this war is just one plundering expedition after another. I think Gustavus Adolphus keeps a tighter rein on his soldiers than most commanders do. But that isn't saying much, and even that gets really frayed when he's just marching through a territory on his way somewhere else."

This, at least, was an area that Anse felt more familiar with. "Well, yeah, that's a given. Not a one of these armies has a 'logistics train' that isn't made up of spit, baling wire and chewing gum. In fact, that's the problem us TacRail people are trying to solve. To a point, anyway. Without a good logistics train, an army on the march has no choice but to do what they call 'foraging.' "

Noelle's expression got very tight, almost pinched. "What a fancy, antiseptic term."

"Ain't it?" replied Anse, grinning coldly. "Anybody up-time tried to engage in such-like 'foraging' at home, they'd be looking at a minimum twenty-year sentence at hard labor. A fair number would be on death row, if West Virginia still had a death penalty."

Noelle shook her head. "I've always been glad West Virginia gave up the death penalty, back in 1976. But sometimes . . ."

Anse shrugged, being careful to keep the motion minimal. Truth be told, he wasn't any too sure how good a control he had over his own horse, especially traveling across snow-covered dirt roads. "It's a moot point, here. I know Mike's just fighting right now to get all the down-timers in the N.U.S. to agree to restrict the death penalty to murder."

Noelle got that pinched look on her face again. At such times, Anse didn't have any trouble at all picturing her as a nun. That might just be his own prejudices at work, though. Unlike most West Virginians, Anse didn't belong to any church. But his background was old-time Protestant, and he tended to share the image of nuns as pale-faced, tight-lipped, mean-spirited old crones who disapproved of anything and everything.

Which wasn't fair, certainly not applied to Noelle. She might have the goofiest mother in creation, by all accounts, but at least so far she'd struck Anse as a pleasant and levelheaded young woman. She was rather pretty, too.

"Keep talking," he said softly. "This is a help."

"Well, the gist of what Mr. Salatto told Mr. Piazza in his reports was that there doesn't appear to be any reason why the Franconians should like the Swedes any more than they do any of the other armies that have gone trampling through Franconia during the past fifteen years. Fortunately, we—the up-timers, I mean—do have some legacy of goodwill in the Suhl area, because it was our people who defeated that expedition Wallenstein sent into the area a while back. That doesn't extend into Franconia itself, however. So the N.U.S. administrators have to take this into account in their policies, which they are doing. They don't talk about Gustavus Adolphus very much. Just sort of leave him on a back burner, so to speak."

Anse grimaced a little. "I can understand the logic, but . . . That might backfire, you know. When you come right down to it, 'guv'mint' means 'we're the guys with the big guns' and the truth is the N.U.S. has hardly any guns at all down there in Franconia, big, small or medium-sized. If the crap hits the fan—pardon my language—we're going to have to call on Gustavus Adolphus to bail us out."

"Let's hope it doesn't come to that." Noelle shook her head. "It might, though. To make things worse, when the N.U.S. took over the administration of Franconia, the economy was shot. Conditions were a lot worse than in southern Thuringia, where things were bad enough. The only industry that was still doing well on the south slope of the Thuringenwald was munitions, in places like Suhl, Schmalkalden, and Schleusingen. Which aren't exactly Franconia, I remind you. And even there, although Suhl itself is one of our states now, most of the arms manufacturers—maybe all of them—just don't see this as an 'us against them' business. They'll sell to anyone who has the money to buy, even if the guy is likely to use the stuff to invade the N.U.S. the next year. They seem to think that since somebody is probably going to invade the region no matter what they do, and they can't really predict in advance which side it'll be, they might as well make as much as they can from the war. Especially since it's pretty much the only good business going."

Again, she shook her head. "And that's not all. There are also a lot of people who *weren't* in Franconia during the winter of 1631-1632. That is, there are those Protestants who had gone into exile, mostly into Ansbach or Bayreuth or Nürnberg, after the Bishop of Würzburg started his re-Catholicization campaign, and who came tumbling back after the Swedes drove the bishop out. Some of them are demanding their own back—and some of them are demanding not only their own, but more, as compensation for all the pain and suffering they experienced. It's sort of like letting all the Cuban exiles in Miami go home and then trying to manage all the property claims that pop up in Cuba.

"Most of them hire lawyers. The lawyers have clerks. The clerks have apprentices. The N.U.S. administrators don't have three dozen up-timers total, counting the military attachés. At that—being honest—we're pretty much scraping the bottom of the barrel. Small towns of thirty-five hundred people like Grantville just aren't prime material for all of a sudden running a government for nearly a million people, counting southern Thuringia as well as Franconia, especially when it wasn't even the county seat in the first place. And *somebody* has to stay home and keep things running there. Franconia is a sideshow, really. Anybody who takes a look at the comparative budgets for running Thuringia and running Franconia can figure that out."

Anse nodded. "Yeah, same old story. All the members of the N.U.S. Congress are from Thuringia, and like politicians anywhere, they think that their main job is to take care of their own constituents first. And, generally speaking, their constituents see eye-to-eye with them on the matter. Which means, until things in Franconia can settle down enough to hold elections—and figure out how Franconia fits in terms of Thuringia—they'll keep getting the short end of the stick. So how are Steve and his people handling it?"

"The first problem that Mr. Salatto and his teams have is to try to sort out which of the down-time Franconian administrators will be willing to work with them. Not support them, necessarily, but at least carry out orders and not deliberately undermine what they are trying to accomplish. That takes time, and they're still working at it. The main problem with finding local administrators to work with, of course, is that any Franconian official who does agree to work with them is in serious danger of being denounced as a collaborator and taken out by his enemies if, in a couple more years, it turns out that Gustavus Adolphus can't hold on to his conquests in Germany and the Habsburgs or Bavarians come back with a different slant on who should be running things."

"Can't really blame 'em, I guess," said Anse. "Self-preservation's about the most basic instinct there is. And it's not likely to be just them if things go *pfffttt*! It'll be their wives and children, elderly parents." He sighed. "The way things seem to work in this day and age, probably even their servants would suffer for the decisions they take, if it all goes sour."

"It's helped a lot that the other Thuringian states that have joined the N.U.S. sent along a fair number of down-time lawyers and clerks to help out. It doesn't help at all that the Franconians consider Thuringians to be just as much 'foreigners' as up-timers and Swedes and, overall, consider the N.U.S. to be just one more occupation force."

"Well, honest to God, what are we? Noelle, we *are* just one more occupation force. We may have better intentions than the others, but that's what we are."

He broke off, watching Captain von Dantz trotting his horse past them toward the front of the party. "Well. *Some* of us have better intentions."

The pinched look came back on Noelle's face. So strongly, in fact, that Anse involuntarily looked down at her hands, holding the reins. He was a little surprised to see that they were the smooth-skinned, rather delicate hands of a slender and attractive young woman. He'd been expecting to see heavy, gnarled fists. The sort that, arthritis be damned, hold and wield a great big ruler.

*   *   *

At noon, not far east of the town of Ilmenau, Anse called a halt to rest and water the horses and to have a quick lunch. As everyone else loosened the tack on the horses, Wili passed out the rations: dried hard sausage, cheese and bread, with a small apple for dessert.

"Hey this sausage is good," Gaylynn said at her first bite. "Wili, I want the recipe. Will you ask Mrs. Schultz to send it to me?"

"*Ja*, Dora loves it when people ask how she made food."

"You know that's mixed meat sausage, Gaylynn," Anse teased. "Bit of this and a bit of that. Venison, pork, beef—and horse, if I remember correctly."

"*Nein, nicht* beef. Und it is just a little horse."

"Well, whatever, it's good." Gaylynn answered. Anse noticed that the captain, however, put down his portion and ate only the cheese.

"Herr Hatfield, how long are we going to wait here?" von Dantz demanded. "We should be moving."

"I thought we would rest the horses for an hour." Anse pulled out his pocket watch. "We're about thirty minutes short of that."

"Remember, the general wants a report *this* year," said von Dantz sarcastically.

"Captain, the report will be a lot later if we have to walk to Suhl because our horses gave out."

"You should have brought a change of horses for the wagon, or left the wagon."

Anse restrained his temper. "And was the Swedish garrison in Grantville going to provide them? Look, my family has only three horses, these. Wili and I had to kill the former owners to get them. You might be used to traveling on other people's money, but we ain't. And the wagon is going because I want to bring something back from Suhl."

The captain got up and went to tend his horse, his shoulders stiff with anger.

That afternoon, traveling was much like it had been in the morning. The road wasn't up to the quality that was becoming standard around Grantville. But it was well marked, and the cold weather combined with plenty of travel close to Ilmenau had packed the snow into a hard surface.

Captain von Dantz was continually riding ahead. Anse, who had walked point a few times in Vietnam, was happy to leave the scouting to him. So it came as no surprise, in the late afternoon, to find von Dantz waiting, when the little convoy rounded a curve. "Herr Hatfield, there is a small village up ahead. We will spend the night there."

Anse studied the sky for a minute, then pulled out his watch. "Captain, I figure we still have a couple of hours traveling time. But if you don't want to sleep in a tent, we can stop."

Clearly the captain was primed for an argument. "You think we should press on?"

"No, in this case I think you're right. We should stop and get the horses under shelter. I'm not all that good at judging the weather, but it sure looks like we're going to get some more snow tonight. A barn to sleep in would be mighty welcome."

When they arrived at the village, though, Anse was surprised to find there were no separate barns. In a village of six houses, there was only one that had two stories, with the lower floor being a stable. All the rest were one-story with an attached lean-to providing shelter for what few animals the owners had. While four of the one-story houses had smoke coming from their chimneys, one was obviously unoccupied.

Someone in the village must have been keeping watch. As the travelers stopped, the door of the largest house opened and a prosperous looking man came out.

"Ah, *Amerikaner*," he said, after seeing the rubber tires on the wagon. "*Ich bin der Schultheiss des Dorfs, Horst Stoltz. Sie möchten die Nacht bleiben, ja.*"

Anse, whose German had improved under Wili's tutoring, realized this was the head man of the village and he was asking if they needed a place to spend the night. A bit of bargaining and only mentioning the tents on the wagon twice got the party the use of the empty house for the night in exchange for five old silver dimes.

After the seven horses were crowded into the lean-to and most of the supplies were transferred from the wagon to the house, Lieutenant Ivarsson commented to Anse. "We actually made a good distance today, better than twenty of your miles, I think. I was impressed by the wheels on the wagon. They do make it travel better. How does it work?"

"The tires are solid rubber and give a wider area on the ground. It makes them roll easier. The real secret is the bearings in the wheel hubs."

Captain von Dantz called from the door of the house. "We need to get settled in for the night. If we cover as much ground tomorrow, we can be in Suhl before nightfall."

As the captain vanished into the dark interior, Anse noticed Rau waving from the back of the house.

When Anse and Ivarsson joined him, Rau said softly: "I talked to the *Schultheiss* like you asked. He says nothing unusual is going on to the south, but I noticed the villagers are keeping their animals closer than normal. Then I talked to the boy who keeps the village pigs. He said that there have been a lot of people on the road. All traveling north—well, toward Grantville. That's actually east from where we are now. And all carrying all they own."

Ivarsson looked thoughtful. "Now, that is odd. There have been no reports of any army moving down that way. What else could put people on the road, this time of the year?"

"The pig boy didn't think it was an army. He just said people were moving. I did a run through the woods close to the village. Just off the road to the south there are a couple of families camped. Three men, four women and eight *Kinder*. One of the boys is man tall. They are keeping a sharp watch and a cold camp, no fire."

"They didn't see you, I take it?" Anse asked. Rau just grinned.

Anse thought a bit. It was not likely at all that an army could have penetrated Franconia and reached as far as the Thuringenwald without news coming to Grantville. There was a radio in Suhl, after all. Besides, armies rarely moved in the winter, here and now, unless they had to.

He turned and looked at the house they were using. "Okay, change of plans. We keep two people on watch all night. Jochen, I want you to knock a couple of tiles loose on the roof to make a firing point in the loft on the side that overlooks the road. Lieutenant Ivarsson, I want you and Mrs. Reardon up there with your rifles, if anything happens. Jochen, you and me can cover the windows and door on the ground floor. Wili can cover the lean-to, through the door that connects it to the house. I don't think anyone is going to jump us, but it doesn't hurt to plan ahead."

"What about the captain?" Rau asked.

Anse shook his head. He didn't trust von Dantz to be an alert sentry, with his arrogant attitudes. "We'll let him sleep. Hopefully nothing will happen. If it does, he stays with us on the ground floor. Now go make that loophole. I'll bring Wili up to speed. Anything you want to add, Lieutenant Ivarsson?"

"No, your plan seems good. But I think we need Corporal Rau mounted tomorrow. Can you ride?"

Rau nodded, but had a disgusted look on his face as he went toward the door. Anse had to smile, because he knew Rau hated horses.

After a quick supper, cooked by Wili and Gaylynn at the fireplace, the party spread out their bed rolls. Gaylynn walked over to where Anse was sitting near the door. "Which shift do you want me to take?"

"Well, Jochen and Nils are going to take the first watch and they'll wake Wili and me for the second. So you and the captain can have a full night's sleep. Speaking of which, if you want you and Noelle can have the loft to sleep in. That'll give you a little privacy."

Gaylynn looked around the single room of the ground floor and nodded. "Thank you, but I don't want you thinking you have to look out for me. I can take care of myself if it comes to a fight, so none of this 'take care of the helpless woman business.' And tomorrow night I'll take a turn on watch."

"Gaylynn, the loft is where I'd want you and your rifle anyway, if something goes down. You'll have a better field of fire, especially after Jochen makes a firing point up there."

It was five hours later, by Anse's watch, when he was awakened by Jochen Rau shaking his shoulder. He looked around the room by the dim light thrown out by the fireplace and saw that everything seemed normal.

"Anything happen?"

"No one has come near the house, but there has been a lot of traffic on the road. People moving quietly in the night, all heading to the north. Ivarsson is out by the wagon keeping watch, waiting for you. We have been taking turns outside."

"Fine, I'll go relieve him. You wake Wili and get some sleep."

When Anse went outside, he discovered he had been right in his weather prediction. There was a light snow falling, blanketing the area with pleasant noiselessness.

He found Nils Ivarsson huddled near the wagon, wrapped in a blanket. "I got it. Go on in and get some sleep."

The Swedish officer rose to his feet. "If Rau didn't tell you, there have been people on the road all night. A couple started to walk over to the wagon, but when they saw we were keeping watch they went on. They were mostly family groups, as near as I can tell."

Ivarsson gathered his blanket about himself and headed for the house.

Anse stood there asking himself why on earth people would be moving at night this far into the N.U.S. It was miles from the border. They hadn't even crossed the ridge of the Thuringenwald yet. Actually, they were barely into the mountains. Tomorrow they would be traveling along the main trade route between Erfurt and Nürnburg, which had had quite a bit of ordinary commercial traffic. There was just no obvious reason for people to be traveling by stealth here in Thuringia. Why weren't Rau and Ivarsson questioning what they saw? Or had they just become so inured to moving refugees that they didn't ask any more?

He and Wili split the next few hours of standing watch, taking turns ducking into the house to warm up. An hour into their watch, the snowfall ended and the sky cleared. There was now a half-moon in the sky to give them better visibility.

Three times, they saw parties passing on the road. None of them seemed hostile. Only once did it look like anyone took an interest in the village he was passing through, and that was one man walking alone leading an ox cart. He looked over the wagon, but moved on when he saw the gleam of Anse and Wili's weapons in the moonlight.

January 18, 1633

Just before dawn, as he stood watching the road, Anse could hear the village waking up. The sounds of people preparing for the coming day were emanating from all the other houses. From the house the party had rented, he could hear muffled conversation as the expedition members were starting to fix breakfast. When he heard the door open behind him, he glanced back and saw Captain von Dantz emerging into the winter morning.

"*Morgen*, Herr Hatfield. I see there was no trouble during the night. Your fears of attack seem to have been groundless."

The captain's tone practically oozed self-satisfaction. "Tonight, though, if we don't reach Suhl, we will have to keep a better watch. We will be in the heart of the *Thueringerwald*."

Anse was tempted to just let it go, but von Dantz was really getting on his nerves. He pointed to the tracks in the snow. "It wasn't as quiet as you think. Quite a few people came by here in the night. When they saw we were on the alert, they passed on."

"What? There were people on the road last night? Who were they? Soldiers? Bandits? Who?"

"Mostly they seemed to be in family groups, and I didn't see a lot of weaponry. So my best guess is they were refugees."

The captain grunted. "That is no problem. There are always people running away from war."

"Makes you wonder, though. Just what it is that they're running away *from*, Captain? What ever it is, we're heading straight for it."

"Nonsense! There is no enemy army in this region. These peasants are fleeing phantoms and rumors. Or seeking fabled streets of gold in wonderful Grantville, perhaps." He snorted. "Still, it will not hurt to be cautious until we get to Suhl. You should send your Corporal Rau to scout the road ahead, and I will stay closer to the wagon to help guard it."

"I agree, Captain—but Rau needs a horse. I'll have to put him on one of your remounts."

"*Ja, ja*, he can use Lieutenant Ivarsson's spare horse. Now we should get the others moving and load this wagon."

After breakfast, the party was once more on its way. Rau had left while they were still packing the final load on the wagon, and was out of sight ahead. Anse took position beside the wagon, with von Dantz a dozen or so yards ahead and Ivarsson bringing up the rear.

Twenty minutes later, Anse saw the captain waving for him to move up and join him. As he rode forward, the captain rode ahead about a hundred yards to where Rau had dismounted and was standing by his horse waiting for them. When the two arrived Rau said in a low voice, "Just around the next curve there is a group of people. It looks like four families, men, women and *Kinder*. I couldn't get close enough to get a good count, but there are at least twenty-five. Four ox carts, but I only saw three oxen. I saw a couple of long guns and one spear, not a pike but a hunting spear. They had a man walking ahead and I was spotted before I saw them."

Anse could hear the real disgust in his voice. Jochen was proud of his ability to go unnoticed.

Before Anse could speak the captain stated: "Herr Hatfield, we should ride down the road as a group surrounding your wagon. It is not likely that a gaggle of farmers will attack armed soldiers. You and I will lead, riding ahead of the wagon. Corporal Rau, you will join

Sergeant Ivarsson and bring up the rear."

"I'll give the orders, Captain, if you don't mind," Anse said, mildly but firmly.

Von Dantz's jaws tightened, but he accepted the reproof without open argument. Now that Anse had established his authority, he thought about the problem itself. He decided the captain's plan was as good as any.

"We'll do it that way," he pronounced. "Everyone should have a weapon in hand, though. Nothing says a bandit doesn't have a wife and kids or these couldn't be stragglers from someone's army with camp followers."

As they rounded the curve in the road and rode toward the unknown group it became clear enough that these were simply refugees. The three carts with oxen were being pulled off the road. The people seemed to be trying to hide them in the trees that bordered the road, not that they had any chance of doing so in the time given. The one remaining cart, apparently pulled by two men, was still on the road, but four men were unloading its contents. As the wagon approached the cart the men stopped, and stood in silence around it.

Anse called softly, "Wili, you look the most like a farmer. Talk to them and find out what's going on."

Wili stopped the wagon beside the cart and leaned over to talk to the men. Anse couldn't catch more than about one word in five, but he understood enough to know that Wili started with comments on the weather and proceeded to ask about the road conditions to the south. It wasn't until the men started looking a bit relaxed that Wili asked them why they were on the road in the first place.

After they finished, Wili passed them a bag, which Anse knew contained a couple of dozen apples from Henry Johnson's trees. He then snapped the reins and put the wagon in motion.

"Did I get that right, Wili? They are Franconians? Their neighbors forced them out?"

"*Ja*, they are chust farmers. They ver pushed out of their villages for saying they like the idea of a single *Deutsch* nation. Their neighbors do not like being ruled from Grantville because it is in Thuringia. They come from more than one village, too."

That meant the hostile attitudes were not confined to a single locality. Anse felt sorry for the people sent into Franconia to "administer" the area, without—from a military standpoint, anyway—having a pot to piss in.

A few miles after they had passed the refugee party, Anse saw Rau once again stopped ahead waiting for them. When they had joined him, he said: "Crossroads village up ahead. They have the road blocked and are making people go around. Looks like they have had some trouble lately. I saw a couple of burnt houses."

"Same positions, Herr Hatfield?" Wili asked.

"Yes, and we'll ride directly to the road block. We have to find out what's going on."

Von Dantz came up in time to hear the last couple of sentences. "General Kagg must be told. I am thinking we should send a message back to him about what the peasants said, also."

"There's a radio in Suhl, Captain," Anse pointed out. "It will be quicker to send the message from there. Besides, with only five of us, who would we send?"

The captain looked perplexed for a minute, "Ah. Radio. *Ja*, we will send a message from Suhl."

As they approached the village, Anse could see the villagers had blocked the four roads into it by the simple method of parking carts full of rocks side by side in the road. With two or three armed men beside each cart, it was a block no one was going to move before the rest of the village could gather to stop them. Not very effective against an army, but it was good enough to stop refugees. What the merchants and other legitimate business travelers who used the road during the day would make of it was another problem, Anse thought.

Riding closer, it became obvious there was a watch being kept on the road also. Anse could hear voices calling from the trees alongside the road, and people were gathering at the road block.

"Let's keep it low-key, Captain," Anse said to Captain von Dantz, who was riding beside him. "They have men in the woods and we're flanked." Only after he spoke did it occur to him that von Dantz might not understand the American colloquialism.

But, apparently, he did—or at least the gist of it. Von Dantz nodded and said softly, "And there are men on the roofs, too. Someone in this village has experience."

"*Halt! Stehenbleiben! Wer sind Sie?*" a voice called out from the village. Anse's German was good enough to translate that last word into an demand to know who they were.

While Rau called out that they were a party of the New U.S. Army escorting two civilians to Suhl, Anse eased back until he was beside the wagon.

"Gaylynn, don't touch your rifle, but see the guys on the roofs?" Gaylynn nodded. "They're yours if any shooting starts."

Before anything could happen, a new voice called out from behind the roadblock. "Gaylynn Reardon? Is that you?"

Gaylynn almost jumped out of her seat. "Yes! Who wants to know?"

"It's me, Pete Chehab." A young man walked from behind the cart roadblock.

As the man approached, Anse could see he was a N.U.S. sergeant in his early twenties. He was dressed in the tie-dyed camouflage that was replacing the up-time hunting outfits as they wore out.

"Relax, everyone," Gaylynn said. "I know him. That's Pete Chehab. He's from Grantville and used to ask Gary for advice when he was in tech school."

After introductions were made, Chehab continued. "Me and Hans Koeppler were bringing some dispatches from the garrison at Suhl to General Kagg in Grantville."

For a moment, he looked disgruntled. "Why the hell they didn't just use the radio is a mystery to me. Probably because the garrison commander is an old-fashioned down-timer and his up-time 'military liaison'—that's that jer . . . —ah, Lieutenant Horton—seems to think the radio's some kinda virgin, can't get its cherry popped."

Noelle Murphy laughed. No little titter, either, but not so loud as to attract attention. Anse himself had to fight to keep from grinning, in the interests of military protocol. Since Chehab hadn't quite come out and publicly insulted his superior officer, he decided he could let it pass.

Besides, *jerk* was a pretty good depiction of Lieutenant Johnny Lee Horton. If anything, it was on the mild side.

"We just got here a couple of hours ago," Chehab continued, "and we found the village like you see it now. They had some trouble with bandits a few days ago. They ended up with two houses burnt so the've blocked off the little roads up into the hills and they're forting up at night. They move a couple of carts off the trade route during the day to let the traffic through. Once they check their documents. All these refugees on the road are making them even more nervous. I was just getting ready to go on to Grantville when you showed up. Do you have any idea what's going on? Some of these guys act like we just shot their dog."

Anse shook his head. "Last time we heard, everything was calm clear to Nürnberg. How was Suhl when you left?"

"Suhl was quiet. Well, as quiet as a town where every other house is hammering out gun barrels can be. But there was nothing like this. No refugees coming through. They must have been taking back paths around the city."

"Sergeant," Captain von Dantz broke in, "can you delay your departure until I write a message to the general?"

"Sure, Captain. We're a regular pony express."

The captain walked to the wagon, shaking his head. Anse had to smile. The captain spoke good English, but now he was learning American.

As they passed through the village after seeing Sergeant Chehab and his party depart, Anse saw that most of the home owners had painted red and white stripes on their doors to show their allegiance to the government in Grantville. In the middle of the crossroads, they had planted a flagpole and were flying the flag many of the Committees of Correspondence had adopted. The thirteen red and white stripes were the same as the American flag, but the snake painted across them was not the semifamiliar timber rattler. Instead, it was an adder.

Just south of the village, the normal commercial traffic became heavier. They were passing parties every mile, and Rau was reduced to riding only a hundred yards in front of the wagon.

"Herr Hatfield, we are going too slow," von Dantz complained. "At this rate, we will never make it to Suhl before nightfall."

"Captain, we were figuring three or four days when we started. So even if we don't make Suhl tonight, we're still ahead of schedule. I packed tents and enough sleeping bags for everyone. Wili made sure there was hay and feed for the horses. So we should be okay if we have to camp again."

"I want—"

Anse never did find out what the captain wanted, because just then Gaylynn yelled from the wagon seat. "Wili, stop the wagon! Look over there!"

Gaylynn was down from the wagon and striding across the road before anyone realized what she was talking about. Near the road were the huddled forms of two children. They were sitting together, wrapped in a blanket that was mostly holes. Wili tied the reins to the brake lever and dismounted to help her with the translation. The American woman's German was passable, but probably not good enough to decipher what frightened children might be saying

Captain von Dantz rode back to see what the delay was. "What are you doing, woman? We have to keep moving."

"I'm tending to these children!" Gaylynn snapped back. "What do you want to do? Just leave them here to freeze?"

The captain shrugged irritably. "We can load them on the wagon and take them with us, if you insist. Quickly—we have only two hours of daylight left."

Now that he was closer, Anse could see the children were both boys, about five or six years old. He called to Rau, who was still mounted. "Jochen, ride ahead and see if there are any refugees on the road. These boys have gotten lost from their family."

"*Nein*," Wili called, "they live over there." He pointed toward a path that could barely be seen joining the road, about a half mile down. "They say men come and hurt their *Grossvater* this morning. They ran off."

"Jochen, check it out quietly," Anse ordered. Rau dismounted and headed for the woods beside the road.

Wili and Gaylynn had managed to get the boys to the wagon when Rau returned. "It looks like there are eight of them, all on foot, in a charcoal burner's cabin. They left the old man tied to a tree outside. He looks dead. They have two men keeping watch in front of the house and the rest are in the house."

Before Anse could say anything, von Dantz spoke up. "If you will permit me to make a suggestion"—the words practically dripped sarcasm—"I think we should leave Frau Reardon and *Fräulein* Murphy here to watch the boys and the wagon. Private Schultz will take my spare horse, and we will ride to the house and demand to know what these men are doing."

Anse was not surprised by the captain's "plan." He didn't doubt the man's courage, but he had about as few brains as a rabbit.

"Well, that might work, but Wili doesn't ride. And if the bandits decide to make a fight of it, we'll be out in the open with no cover."

"Herr Hatfield, these are bandits, not trained troops."

In Anse's experience, the distinction in the seventeenth century between "bandits" and "trained troops" was a lot fuzzier than von Dantz made it out to be. "It never hurts to have an edge, Captain. Jochen, Wili and I will sneak up on the house through the woods. Then you and Lieutenant Ivarsson ride in with the wagon, with Gaylynn driving, to where the path from the house comes to the road before you ride up to the house. Noelle and the boys can stay in the wagon bed, where they'll have some shelter if the stuff hits the fan. Gaylynn can cover the front of the house and give you some support. The three of us in hiding can give the bandits a nasty surprise if they try to attack you. And it gives us six guns instead of four."

After a moment, von Dantz nodded. "Do not fire until we arrive."

"Give us ten minutes to get in position." Anse handed the captain his pocket watch.

Rau went to the rear of the wagon and started digging in his pack. Anse was not surprised to see him pull out two hand grenades. Rau had developed a positive love for grenades since he discovered you could fish with them.

As the three entered the woods, Anse asked, "How are you going to light those?"

Rau held up a Zippo lighter. "Chief Schwartz gave it to me. He likes fish."

When they arrived at the house, it was much like Rau had described it: a simple one-room structure with one door and only two windows, one on each side. Not much more than a big hut, really. Definitely a charcoal-burner's place, from the nature of the tools scattered around.

The window panes appeared to be made from thin leather and were partially open. There were two outbuildings: a simple privy and a small shed. The shed, which was open on the front, was the home of a large donkey, which was inside. The privy was on the opposite side of the house from the shed and looked in need of repair. From the woods they could see the body of an old man tied to a tree close to the shed. Two bandits were standing guard outside the front door to the house.

While they were still some distance away, Anse laid out his plan. "Jochen, work your way up to the far side of the house. If they start shooting, toss a grenade through the window. Wili, you and me will crawl up on the near side. You take the window and after the grenade goes off, bust open the window and cover the inside of the house. I'll move on to the corner and take the two men out front. Understood?"

When the two others nodded, Anse continued. "Now don't do anything until someone takes a shot at the captain. They might surrender." From the looks on Wili and Jochen's faces, they doubted that as much as Anse did.

Everything went as planned, up to a point. Anse and Wili had just gotten into position on either side of the window when they heard a shot from the other side of the house. That shot was followed by two more, and then some shouting.

"Wili, watch the window. Don't fire until I do."

Anse stepped to the corner of the house. A quick glance around it made immediately clear what had happened. Of the two men who had been watching the front of the house, one had gone to the privy. Either going to or coming back, he had seen Jochen near the house and taken a shot at him. He'd missed, Jochen hadn't, and the man was down near the privy. His partner was kneeling by the door of the house readying his match lock and yelling at the top of his lungs.

Anse stepped out and called, "Throw down your gun. *Geben oben.*" Either the man didn't want to give up or Anse's German wasn't understandable, because he turned and raised his weapon. Before he could get it halfway up, he took two twenty-gauge slugs in the chest. He was wearing a breast plate, but at a range of less than six feet it made very little difference.

As Anse shifted his aim to cover the door he heard the familiar clackity-boom that told him Wili was unloading his shotgun through the window. Jochen's warning call of "Grenade!" was almost covered up by the sound of Anse's shotgun taking out a man trying to flee the pocket hell that Wili had made of the inside of the house.

After the grenade exploded, there was nothing but silence.

When his ears quit ringing, Anse called out, "Wili, Jochen! Are you all right?"

"*Ja,*" the two responded, almost in unison.

Captain von Dantz and Lieutenant Ivarsson were coming at a gallop. The two were just turning off the road. Gaylynn was close behind, driving the wagon.

"Herr Hatfield, I told you to wait!" were the first words out of the captain's mouth, as he slid from his horse. "We needed prisoners to question, not just bodies."

Just then a shot rang out from inside the house. The bullet made a wheeting sound as it passed between Anse and the captain. Anse and the captain both turned and fired at almost the same time. The wounded man standing in the doorway of the house, trying to reload his pistol, was driven back inside by the force of both shots hitting him dead center.

"Sorry, Captain, but I don't think they want to surrender."

"It seems not. So be it, then." He drew his sword and stepped toward the house.

Seeing the captain about to enter with only his sword as a weapon, Anse said. "Wait a second, Captain. Take my shotgun. Just point it and pull the trigger. There's still two shells in it."

Von Dantz took the shotgun. Anse drew his pistol and the two moved to the door. Once they looked through the door, however, it was obvious that the shooting was over. The bodies of the bandits were scattered around the one room of the house. Wili and Jochen were looking through the two windows of the house, their guns pointing inside, but nothing was moving.

"Lieutenant Ivarsson," the captain called. "If you and Herr Hatfield's men can clean the bodies out of the house, we can get the women and the boys out of the weather. We will have to camp here tonight."

Anse rolled his eyes. It was typical of the captain, that he didn't give a thought to the reaction of the two boys or the women—or the men, for that matter—at the prospect of spending the night in a cabin that was splattered all over with blood and gore. Jochen's grenade had practically shredded at least one of the bandits.

"I think not, Captain," he said firmly. "As I told you, we have perfectly serviceable tents with us." Jabbing a finger at the inside of the cabin, he added: "That's a charnel house in there. Even in winter, the stench will be unbearable."

Fortunately, von Dantz didn't argue the matter. He simply stalked off, in a huff.

Lieutenant Ivarsson came up.

"Herr Hatfield, I think we should dig a grave for the old man. But what do you want to do with the bandits?"

Anse made a face. "Well, I'm damned if I feel like digging any bigger hole than we need to, in this frozen ground."

The big Swedish lieutenant smiled coldly. "Why bother?" He nodded toward the privy. "There is already a big hole dug under that. For such as these, a fitting resting place."

Anse smiled back, just as coldly. The idea was certainly tempting, but . . .

Leaving aside everything else, a poor charcoal-burner's privy in the rocky soil of the Thuringenwald probably wouldn't be big enough to hold all the corpses.

"No, we'll give them a grave."

Wili and Jochen took turns and soon had the shallow graves dug, while Anse and Ivarsson gathered some rocks to cover them. Once they realized that the bedrock was less than a foot below the surface, they ended up piling the rocks into cairns. A respectable one, near the house, over the old man's body; a make-shift one, a bit farther off, for the corpses of the bandits. Meanwhile, in a small clearing a quarter of a mile down the road, Gaylynn and Noelle set up the tents.

Once the old man's grave was ready, Anse went over to the campsite. "Gaylynn, do you want to bring the boys out to say goodbye to their grandfather?"

Somewhat dubiously, she looked at the tent where Noelle was keeping the children.

"Yes, I suppose we should. It might make the boys feel better."

Von Dantz, by then, had settled himself into another tent. Anse pulled back the flap and asked: "Would you happen to have a Bible, Captain?"

"*Ja*, a New Testament, but it is in German. Do you read German?"

It'd be in *Fraktur* script, too, the Gothic style, which Anse still had a lot of trouble with. "Not too well, no. But Wili does. Wili's a Catholic, but he'll be willing to say a few words to send any Christian home."

The captain looked a little surprised, but got his New Testament out of his pack.

Later, after the burial and a quick supper, Captain von Dantz approached Anse. "I think we should all stand watch tonight. Three on, three off. You, me and Private Schultz on the first watch and Sergeant Ivarsson, Rau and Frau Reardon on the second. Since the Murphy woman is unarmed and seems not very familiar with weapons, I see no point in including her. Besides, she is tending the children."

"Sounds good, Captain."

January 19, 1633

The night was quiet. Early the next morning as they were repacking the wagon, Anse asked, "Noelle, what do you think we should do with the boys? We can't leave them here."

"You should stop referring to them as 'the boys,' for starters," she said, a little crossly. "You make them sound like luggage. They are Hans Felix Polheimer and Hans Ulrich Moser. They're first cousins. Hans Felix is the older. As to what we're going to do with them, we're taking them to Suhl. Obviously."

Anse couldn't help smiling at her frosty tone. He'd heard that Noelle

Murphy didn't suffer fools gladly—and, admittedly, his question had been a little foolish.

"Load Hans and Hans on the wagon, then. We're almost ready to pull out. Von Dantz will have kittens if they're are any more delays."

"I'd say let him, except I'd pity the poor kittens."

That turned Anse's smile into a real grin.

When they arrived in Suhl, a little after noon, Anse was surprised by the size of the city. It was a lot smaller than he'd expected from Pat's letters. That must be caused by the wall crowding everyone inside, he thought.

Then he noticed the people themselves. Over the past year and a half, he'd gotten used to the mix of up-time and down-time clothing worn around Grantville, and—though to a lesser extent—in nearby Badenburg and Jena. Now, having crossed the Thuringenwald, he was in a strictly German city.

Not only was there no mix of clothing, but many of the people on the streets of Suhl were casting unfriendly looks at the party. Whatever was causing trouble in the countryside had spread to the city, apparently. Anse was getting a weird feeling of *deja vu*. This was all strange, but all too familiar.

Then it hit him. The last time he'd felt this way was almost forty years earlier. In Saigon, in 1969, just before the Tet Offensive.

There were no overt signs of hostility, however. That was presumably because of the tough-looking mercenaries who were guarding the city gates and, now and then, patrolling the streets in small squads. The Swedish garrison wasn't very big, true, but it was big enough to keep the peace in a town the size of Suhl. The problem was that the Swedish garrison shouldn't be patrolling in a N.U.S. state, in the first place. The city council should be keeping the peace with constables or militia.

Anse scowled. He let the wagon pass him and rode close to the tailgate so he could talk to Rau without shouting.

"Can you pass for a local, Jochen?"

When Rau nodded, Anse continued: "Pass me your shotgun and get your revolver out of sight. I want you to do a little walk around here in Suhl. Drop off the wagon when no one can see you. Find out what's going on and meet me at Pat's house. You have the address?"

"*Nein*. But how many U.S. *WaffenFabrik* can there be in Suhl?" Jochen grinned as he handed Anse the shotgun. "I will find you."

Anse rode forward to the front of the wagon. When he turned to look, Jochen was already gone. "Slippery as an eel," he said to himself.

They only had to ask directions three times before they pulled on to the street that promised to hold Pat's factory. Then Anse spotted it, immediately. Pat had marked his shop with a huge sign made like an up-time Kentucky rifle that reached most of the way across the narrow street. Across the front of the building was printed in two foot high letters, U.S. *WaffenFabrik.*

"Anse Hatfield! What are you doing in Suhl?" Anse was disoriented for a moment, until he saw that what he had at first glance taken for a prosperous looking down-timer was actually his brother-in-law. Pat Johnson was dressed entirely in down-time clothing.

"Hi, Bubba. We came to see you, partly."

" 'Allo, Wili." Pat nodded to Schultz, sitting on the wagon seat. "Hi, Gaylynn. Gary didn't tell me you were coming to Suhl."

"That's because Gary didn't know. I wanted to surprise him. Now where is he?"

"Well, he's either in the office, right through that door, or on the shop floor on the other side."

Gaylynn was off the wagon quick as a flash and headed for the door. Then she stopped and turned to the wagon. "Felix, Ulrich, *kommen mit* me. I want you to meet Gary."

Her mixture of German and English might not have been understood by the boys. But Noelle's nudge was clear enough. The two young cousins jumped from the wagon and followed Gaylynn through the door. Noelle went with them, after exchanging a brief greeting with Pat.

After watching the little procession pass through the door, Pat turned back to Anse and Wili. "Does someone want to tell me who those two boys are and what's going on?"

Anse chuckled. "Well, it looks as if Noelle has convinced Gaylynn that her family just got a little bigger."

"*Ja,*" Wili added. "Gary chust become the father of two boys named Hans."

Pat waved his hand. "Tell me over lunch. Come on. We'll put the horses, the donkey and the wagon in the factory yard and I'll buy your lunch. There's a good tavern nearby."

"No Freedom Arches? I make it a point to patronize them."

Pat seemed to grimace a little. "In Suhl? Not yet. And if those boys don't . . . ah, never mind."

*   *   *

Over a lunch of stew, cheese, and rye bread, the two travelers explained where the boys came from. After that they got down to the reason for the trip.

When they were done, Pat Johnson nodded and pursed his lips thoughtfully. "I'd guess about fifteen hundred guns a week are leaving Suhl. Small arms, that is. Not more than one or two field pieces. Most are going north, either to princes who are members of the CPE or friendly to it. But at least five hundred a week are going to someone else. As far as I know, none of my rifles have gone to unfriendly people, although I can't be sure. I suppose I should have put the factory in Jena, but . . ."

He shrugged. "Property values in Jena are getting almost as high as in Grantville—and there were so many trained and experienced gunsmiths here."

"Nobody's faulting you, Pat," Anse responded. "Have you talked to the head of the city militia? Or the Swedish garrison commander? Or the N.U.S. military liaison?"

Pat's grimace, this time, wasn't subtle at all.

"Not much, still less, and none at all. The garrison commander is Captain Bruno Felder, and I can't tell if he's dumb or lazy or both. Either way, he's made it plain he's not interested. As for the N.U.S. military liaison, what idiot sent Johnny Horton down here in *that* capacity? He's dumber than Felder, and I only wish he were as lazy. What he is, is a hothead. Seems like every other day, he's quarreling with one of the locals. Especially with the Suhl militia captain. Usually over some petty bullshit."

Anse rubbed his face. He didn't know the German captain in command of the Swedish garrison, but he did know Johnny Horton. *Stupid* and *quarrelsome* were pretty fair descriptions of the man. He'd been perhaps the least popular teacher at Grantville's high school.

"The whole army's stretched tight as a drum, Pat," he said, by way of an explanation-excuse.

"Sure, I know. Just like I know that it probably looked like a smart idea, back up there in Grantville, to shuffle him off to Suhl. But I can tell you it was one terrible idea. There's enough trouble here as it is, without us stirring up more of it. And why the hell do we need a 'military liaison' in the first place? The whole damn

Swedish garrison isn't more than maybe forty men."

Anse didn't bother answering the question, since it was obviously rhetorical. The answer was the same, anyway: *Somebody in headquarters thought it would be a bright idea to get rid of Horton by saddling Suhl with him.*

"What about that 'trouble'?" he asked, instead. "We told you what we saw on the way here. Are you seeing any of that here?"

"Anse, I've lived here now for over a year, and I've made a lot of friends among the local gunmakers. Masters and their journeymen, both. As you can see, I dress and live just like my neighbors, but no one is talking to me about politics. There's less than a dozen of us up-timers here, and none of us know what's going on. We know there's a lot of bad feeling about Gustavus Adolphus giving Franconia to Grantville to govern, but it doesn't seem directed at us, so much. Not personally, I mean. It's just that I doubt you could find three people anywhere in the area who'd give you two cents for Gustavus Adolphus and his Swedes."

He sipped from his beer. "The truth is that there's really nobody in charge this close to Franconia, beyond the limits of the major towns. We're now officially the top honchos, sure—but we don't have anybody south of the Thuringenwald except a handful of people scattered in the big towns and a 'military force' that's just barely this side of a joke. The Swedes have small garrisons here and there, but since everybody hates them, nobody ever turns to them for help. I doubt they'd be any help, anyway. Truth us, I don't have a much higher opinion of the mercenaries working for Gustavus Adolphus here than the locals do."

He dipped into his beer again, this time for a full swallow. "All that adds up to Franconia and the mountains of the Thuringenwald outside of the walled cities and fortified villages becoming a magnet for every gang of robbers and thieves around—of which they're are plenty, after fifteen years of this madhouse war. The difference between 'army deserter' and 'bandit' is the difference between Monday and Tuesday. And on Wednesday, often enough—maybe Thursday—you'll find them reenrolled in somebody's army. Here, it's likely to be the Swedish army, which makes everybody trust them even less."

"Have you talked to the CoC leaders?"

Pat issued a sarcastic snort. "Leaders? Anse, get real. The Committees of Correspondence here in Suhl—everywhere in Franconia, so far as I can tell—don't amount to more than handful of kids. The

CoCs are not popular even here in Suhl, the way they are further north in Thuringia. Not anywhere in Franconia, so far as I know."

He paused to take a bite of his stew, and washed it down with some more beer. Then, continued:

"The attitude of people here toward the CoCs is pretty much the same as their attitude toward us. Up-timers, I mean. They don't have anything against us personally—not yet, anyway—but since we're associated with the Swedes they figure we can't be worth much, either. They certainly don't trust us, as a group, with the exception of some individuals here and there. Some of the villages in the Thuringenwald, too, like the one you ran across. They've had longstanding ties with Thuringia, many of them. But those people don't carry much weight in Suhl or any of the other major towns, once you get over the mountains."

Anse nodded. "Gotcha. Now, on another subject, I need to talk to you about something other than those guns going south. How many rifles, smooth bores and pistols do you have on hand right now?"

Pat looked thoughtful for a moment. "Finished . . . maybe ten pistols, ten to twelve rifles and at least thirty smooth bores. Wait a couple of days and we can add a dozen more pistols, four rifles, and maybe ten more smooth bores. Rifling takes time, but we can make three pistols for every rifle. Most of our guns are shipped as soon as we finish them. Ruben might have another dozen pistols, and ten to fifteen rifles in his shop. I know he's sold out of smooth bores. He was by last night wanting more."

"Ruben?" Anse asked.

"Ruben Blumroder. He's one of the major gunmakers here—owns some of the stock in our company, too, plus being involved in the same trade in Schleusingen. That's about ten or twelve miles farther down the road. Maybe in some other towns, too. He has a lot of connections all through this region. He's friendly and has been a big help to us. In fact, without him I don't think Joe and I could have got our factory started as fast as we did. The man knows everyone in town, and was able to recommend some good gunsmiths looking for work. He speaks something like eight languages, including English. But why are you asking about what guns I have on hand?"

"It's simple. It looks like the TacRail company is going to war. And we're getting the littlest pig's share when it comes to weapons. What I want to do is to fill the wagon with anything that will shoot, and haul it back for the boys and girls. Think of it as a late Christmas present."

"Okay. We'll write it off against the debt the factory owes you and save you some money. I take it this is not official."

"No, it's not official, although eventually I'll finagle some kind of reimbursement. But I'll pay cash money. Gold, in fact." Anse grinned. "You can handle Krugerrands, can't you?"

Pat chuckled. "Hell, yes. They'd be a lot better than most of the coins floating around."

They'd finished eating. Pat pushed back his chair and rose to his feet. "Let's go down to Ruben's shop and see what he has in stock. I'll introduce the two of you and make sure he gives you a discount."

"It's convenient that his shop is so close to the factory," Anse commented as the two walked along.

"Ruben found the location for the factory, so it's not surprising it's close to his shop. It works out fine. The gunmaking companies in Suhl are competitors, I suppose, technically speaking. But it's really more of a cooperative relationship, in the real world. Kinda like, back home, a bunch of furniture stores would set up right next to each other. Whatever sales one of them might lose to a guy next door, they all gained from the fact that, bunched up like that, they drew a lot more customers to begin with."

He pulled up before a sign and pointed at it. "Here we are. You should notice that Ruben changed his sign. Before, it was two crossed wheel-lock pistols. Now look at it."

Anse looked up. The sign on the gunshop featured two crossed flintlock pistols, just like those that were the output of *U.S. WaffenFabrik.*

Anse liked the shop, the minute he walked through the door. Its walls were covered with all kinds of weapons. Wheel locks, the old Dutch-style flintlocks and the modern flintlocks introduced by Pat were in the places of pride, but there were guns of every description on the walls. The floor was crowded with racks that were also loaded with guns. Those spaces in the floor racks that did not have firearms were filled with crossbows, spears or swords. And in between the guns on the walls there were accoutrements, powder flasks, bullet pouches and tools.

It was so much like his favorite gunshop back in West Virginia, that Anse felt almost at home. *If you added a couple of stuffed deer heads and a girly calendar this place would be just like Jimmy's Gun and Pawn.*

"Herr Blumroder, come on out!" Pat called, waving the sales clerk aside. "I want you to meet Anse Hatfield. I know I told you about him."

When Blumroder came out of the back of the shop Anse saw a tall man somewhere in his late fifties, slightly older than himself. Blumroder had the confident air of a successful businessman. "Ah, Herr Hatfield! I have wanted to meet you. Patrick has said so much about you."

His English was fluent, and less heavily accented than Anse would have expected.

"And he has written a lot about you, sir. I'm glad he had your good advice to help him set up here in Suhl."

"Nonsense. Patrick is a wise young man. My major contribution was to make it easier for him to meet people. As you Americans say, I introduced him around."

"And one of those people must be your tailor. Pat was always in jeans and a sweat shirt, before. Now I find him in the latest styles."

Blumroder smiled. "Of course. A successful man must look successful, or no one will take him seriously. But I doubt you are here to ask for my advice on clothing. What can I do for you, Herr Hatfield?"

"Herr Blumroder, I need all the flintlock rifles and smooth bores in your shop and probably most of the pistols."

Before Ruben could react. Pat said: "He's paying in gold, Ruben, and I promised him a discount. What he can't cover right now we can write off against the debt the company owes him. Besides, it's good business. With a major war looking to be in the works, Anse's railroad outfit is bound to expand. And even after the war, the railroads will keep going. If we get in on the ground floor now, we'll be sitting pretty."

Blumroder considered Anse carefully. "Railroads, ha? When you have time later, Herr Hatfield, I would appreciate a detailed explanation of how these things are constructed and operate. From what I've heard from Patrick, it strikes me that there might be a profitable sideline for us there. Not making rails, of course. That's the sort of heavy iron work we don't do. But if those machines are as complicated as they sound . . ."

He shook his head. "But, that is for later. For now, in terms of your immediate business, I will be glad to give you a discount. You are, after all, one of Patrick's partners—and I hold stock in the company myself. I'll have Horst prepare all of my modern guns for shipping. We'll talk about price and discounts when I know what we have."

"Herr Blumroder," Anse responded, "I have a team and a wagon at the factory. We can pick up the weapons and save you any shipping costs."

"*Ja,* even better." Ruben turned and called to his clerk. "*Horst, wieviele moderne Waffen haben wir im Geschäft?*"

Horst's immediately started making a count of the modern flint-locks. After a short time, he handed a list to Blumroder.

"It seems we have twenty-one rifles and twelve pistols on hand. Will that be enough for your needs? I will personally add a powder flask and bullet pouch for each weapon to the order at no charge."

Anse did his own calculations. "With the ten rifles and thirty smoothbore Pat has at the factory, that makes sixty-one long guns and twenty-two pistols. Yes, Herr Blumroder, that will make a proper wagon load. Gold on delivery, when I leave Suhl. Will that be acceptable?"

"*Ach,* pay the money to Patrick," Blumroder said, waving his hand. "I trust him to give me my share. It is not safe to walk around with that much money."

January 21, 1633

When Anse walked into the factory office two days later, early in the morning, Jochen Rau was waiting for him, along with another man.

"Herr Hatfield, I would like to introduce Jorg Hennel, one of the members of CoC here in Suhl. Herr Hennel, this is Warrant Officer Anse Hatfield of the N.U.S. Army."

Anse studied the man with Rau. He was a bit younger than Rau, in his early twenties at a guess, and a bit shorter. But, all in all, the two looked enough alike to be cousins. Given odds, Anse would have bet that a couple of years earlier Jorg had been in the same business as Rau. He had that look about him.

Anse stuck out his hand. "I am pleased to meet you, Herr Hennel," he said in German.

Hennel replied in English, after shaking the hand. "*Ich bin*—I am— Jorg. You are Anse." His smile was a brash sort of thing, the kind of smile a young man puts on when he's trying to probe an older one. "Jochen was trying to impress me with how important you are."

Anse smiled back. "I'm not much given to formalities, myself. I assume you have some of the information I asked Jochen to find out."

"Yes. He asked for my help in finding who is selling weapons to those Bavarian and Austrian pigs. But perhaps you do not need my help."

Anse frowned. "Why do you say that? We still don't know who's shipping guns or how much they're shipping."

Hennel shook his head. "You just visited—just yesterday again—the man who is the worst offender."

"*Blumroder?* Ruben Blumroder? *He's* shipping guns to unfriendly princes?"

"You didn't know?"

Anse shook his head. "No. Are you sure?"

Rau interjected. "Not only his own guns, either, Anse. It seems that Blumroder is something in the way of a general factor for all the gunmakers in Suhl. He puts together gun shipments from many shops and every two weeks he sends out a pack train loaded with guns to Nürnberg. But only part of the pack train arrives there."

"The rest is split off," said young Hennel. "At Schleusingen, we think. What is your American expression?—'peeled away,' I think—before it gets there. That part goes south to Bavaria, we think, probably Munich. From there . . ."

He shrugged. "The Bavarians and Austrians are close. 'Thick as thieves,' I think you say."

"You've seen this?"

For the first time, Jorg Hennel didn't look brash. Indeed, he seemed a bit embarrassed. "Well . . . no. We know it's true, but we are not woodsmen. Certainly not *Jaeger*—and Blumroder always has some *Jaeger* to guard his pack trains. If we tried to follow, they would surely spot us."

And might very well shoot you, Anse thought to himself.

The *Jaeger* were nobody to fool with. They were seventeenth-century Germany's equivalent to forest rangers, game wardens, and professional hunters, essentially. The best-positioned worked on a salaried basis for a national authority. Well, for a principality, at least. For a duke or count. Younger men, or those less well-connected, worked on what amounted to a contract basis for local employers until someone retired or was injured or died and a cousin or brother-in-law put in a good word so he could get a permanent slot when it opened. There were *Jaeger* family trees almost as complex as noble dynasties, and stretching over as many local borders and political boundaries as those of specialty guilds such as the glassmakers.

The *Jaeger* were crack shots, using rifled muskets instead of the normal smoothbores-and they were perfectly prepared to be ruthless. Even large bandit gangs generally stayed away from them.

At the same time . . .

Anse couldn't help but wince. At the same time, the *Jaeger* were not rootless mercenaries, like the men who filled most of Europe's armies, including the Swedish army. They almost always had close ties to their local communities. In that sense, they were more like the mountain guides of left-behind modern Europe—or their equivalent, along with bush pilots, in up-time Alaska. Which meant that if they were willing to work for Blumroder, the man—and his activities— had the tacit support of the inhabitants of the area.

In short, a delicate situation just got a lot more delicate—and potentially even more explosive. If the N.U.S. really pissed off the *Jaeger*, the Thuringenwald would become impassable for any but large military units.

"Shoot, and I like the man," Anse muttered. "So does Pat."

"That's not all, Anse," said Rau gloomily. "It gets worse. Tell him, Jorg."

What brashness had been in the young man earlier was gone now. Hennel took a deep breath and almost blurted out: "Some of the other CoC members—well, all of them, except me—have been talking to your officer, that Horton *Scheissk*—ah, up-timer fellow. And just last night, they and Horton met with the German officer you brought with you. Captain von Dantz. I think the commander of the Swedish garrison was there, too. I am not sure about that, though." He shrugged. "I was not invited. Things have been strained between me and the rest of the CoC the past few weeks."

Anse had a bad feeling he could guess what the meeting had been about.

"These other CoC members . . . They are, ah . . ."

"What you call 'hotheads,' " Hennel replied, scowling. "Or—what I think—simply lazy. They do not have the stomach for patient work. For . . . I forget the English word."

"Organizing?"

"Yes, that one. Always they think of what they like to call 'the bold move.' "

Bold move. Anse was pretty sure the difference between that, in these circumstances, and *terrorism* . . . was just about nil. But it was the sort of notion that would appeal to impatient, inexperienced and angry youngsters. All the more so with someone like Horton to give it the blessing of "up-timer approval" and an arrogant ass like von Dantz to egg them on.

For that matter, von Dantz might do more than simply egg them on. If he'd gotten the ear of the garrison commander . . .

"Christ," Anse muttered. "This is *way* over my pay grade."

He took a deep breath. "Well, I guess it's time to find out if Mike Stearns is right."

Hennel cocked his head quizzically. Rau just said: "Eh?"

Anse turned and started back into the shop, gesturing with his head for the others to follow. "Never mind. It's too complicated to explain, and you'll see for yourselves anyway."

***

Noelle Murphy was in her room, thankfully. She listened carefully to everything Anse had to tell her, with Rau and Hennel standing against a nearby wall. Throughout, her expression was simply attentive, and her slim hands were folded neatly in her lap.

When Anse was finished, through, an expression came to her face. And she uttered a number of phrases that didn't fit well—not at all, in fact—with her reported ambitions to become a nun.

Admittedly, she did not take the name of the Lord in vain. Didn't mention Him at all, even if there was no act involving procreation or the elimination of bodily wastes that was overlooked.

". . . *Wrong with those fucking morons?*" she concluded. Eventually.

She brought her angry gaze to bear on Anse. "Wha—*exactly*—is your authority here, Warrant Officer Hatfield?"

Anse shrugged. "I'm not sure, really. But it doesn't extend as far as handling this."

Noelle rose abruptly to her feet and stalked over to her handbag, perched on a shelf under the window. "Stalked" was the word for it, too. For those few moments, she bore no resemblance at all to a slender young woman. Anse was reminded of an eagle, shifting its talons on a limb to get a better perch for swooping.

She hauled out a fancy looking envelope and handed it to Anse.

"Read that, please."

It had a fancy seal and everything—except this one was embossed by the insignia of the President, not the secretary of state. And when Anse opened it up, he recognized the handwriting. No assistant had drafted this. Mike Stearns' handwriting was pretty unmistakable. Large, looping letters. Not the world's best penmanship, by a country mile—but it was legible, and the handwriting was about as forceful as the contents.

When he was finished, Anse folded the letter back up and returned it to Noelle.

"Okay, Ms. Murphy." He smiled, slyly. "Or should I say Ms. Envoy Extraordinaire?"

For the first time since he'd come in, that characteristically quick smile flitted across her face. " 'Envoyette Junior' is the way I actually feel." The smile vanished. "Is it good enough for you?"

"Sure, Ms. Murphy. I have no idea if the President's orders are legal, mind you. What I do know for sure is that I could care less. The way I figure it, he's my ultimate boss and he pretty clearly put you in charge if, in your estimation, the situation called for your direct intervention."

Noelle stared at him for a moment. Then, seemed to swallow.

"Well . . . It's not so much that, Warrant Officer. The fact is, what I'm really doing is putting *you* in charge. But I guess I do provide you with the official cover."

"That you do," Anse mused, thinking about it. "We're both agreed, I take it, that any attempt to threaten or attack Ruben Blumroder—or any other gunmaker in Suhl—needs to be cut off at the knees?"

"Yes." She waved her hand impatiently. "For now, anyway. Later on, if and when our authority here gets put on a solid basis, and clear laws are passed, things might be different. But for now, yes."

She took a slow breath and let it out in something that was very like a sigh.

"I've spent months studying the down-time laws that apply to this stuff, Warrant Officer. And the fact is that Blumroder is doing nothing illegal. It might be unethical, depending on how you look at it. But he's breaking no actual laws. Nobody in this time and place ties himself in knots over 'trading with the enemy.' We can't change that in a few months. Even the Swedes really just want all the weapons without having to outbid the other guys, if you ask me."

Anse must have looked a little surprised, because Noelle sniffed. "Please, Mr. Hatfield! The dictates of a conqueror—and that's really all Gustavus Adolphus is, here—are not 'laws.' Not in any sense of the term that our own Founding Fathers would have accepted, anyway. What Blumroder's doing is possibly immoral, if you think in terms of 'us the good guys' and 'them the bad guys.' And it's certainly dangerous for him, if the Swedes find out and get their backs up. But it is neither illegal nor, given the history of the area and its customs, is it even unpopular."

She ran slim fingers down her dress. It was a seventeenth-century garment, although more severely cut than the norm. "So. The way I see it, our responsibility—for the moment, at least—is to forestall an explosion. Hopefully, down the road, we can persuade Blumroder and the others to cease and desist. But, in the short term, what we have to see to is that his rights are respected."

She barked a little laugh. "It might be better to say, establish that he has rights to begin with."

Now, and for the first time, she seemed uncertain. "I admit, I'm not sure where to start or what to do."

But Anse had already figured it out. Most of it, at least. He rose from his own chair and turned to Hennel.

"Do you know how to get to Grantville, Jorg?"

Uncertainly, young Hennel shook his head. "Not really."

Anse nodded, and turned to Rau. "Jochen, tell Wili to guide him. I want them on the road as soon as possible. I wish we had a radio, but we don't—and under the circumstances, we sure as hell can't ask Horton to borrow his."

"And they are to . . . ?"

"Wili is to report—personally, and tell him not to take any crap—to Mike Stearns. Not Jackson, not Piazza—Stearns himself." He turned back at Hennel. "As soon as you arrive, I want you to meet with Gretchen Richter. Tell her everything you know."

"Very well. And what do you want her to do?"

Anse smiled, very thinly. "Plain to see, you've never met the woman. First, it doesn't matter what I want, since—as she'd be the first to tell you—she doesn't take orders from me. She doesn't take orders from anybody. Second, it doesn't matter. She'll figure out what to do, all on her own. Unless I miss my guess, she'll come right down here herself, like a . . ."

His smile widened. "You may as well get acquainted with another American expression. 'Bat out of Hell.' "

He turned back to Rau. "Jochen, do you have any idea if we'd have any influence on the garrison?"

Jochen shook his head. "Not a bit, Mr. Hatfield. They're bought and paid for, and they work for Captain Bruno Felder."

Anse wasn't surprised. Most mercenaries in the seventeenth century didn't hire on as individuals, paid directly by their ultimate employer—who, in this case, was the king of Sweden. They hired on as companies or regiments, and they got their money directly from their own commanders.

"That means they won't pay much attention to Ivarsson, either. If they pay any at all."

"You think . . . ?"

Anse spread his hands. "Who knows? But I'm going to find out. Ivarsson struck me as a levelheaded fellow. I'm hoping he'll see it our way. Whether he does or not, though . . ."

He made for the door. "First thing we do, we make clear to all parties involved that if anyone wants a fight, they'll have it. Follow me, everybody—except you, Jochen and Jorg. Round up Wili, right off, and get on the road. When you're done with that, Jochen, meet me at Blumroder's shop. Or I might be at Pat's, next door."

About halfway down the corridor, he heard Noelle snicker.

"What's so funny?" he asked, a bit crossly.

"You are," came the reply. Her tone thickened, mimicking that of a man. "Follow me, all three of you—except two of you." She snickered again. "That leaves me, the sole follower. Or should I say, fig leaf trailing in the wind?"

Anse couldn't help but chuckle. "You're okay, Ms. Murphy. My strength is as the strength of ten, because my fig leaf is pure."

That brought an actual, down-home laugh. The first one he'd ever heard coming from her.

Anse found Ivarsson in a tavern on the next street. Oddly enough, given the reputation of Swedish soldiers in the area, having what seemed to be a convivial—even jovial—conversation with several other patrons of the place.

All of them, in fact, including the tavern-keeper: some dozen men, all told.

When the Swedish lieutenant spotted Anse entering the tavern, his tough-looking middle-aged face was split by a grin that belonged to a teenager.

"You see?" Ivarsson demanded, lifting his tankard. "Did I not tell you all?"

Everyone else in the tavern swiveled to study Anse, as he approached the big table in the center.

"We still don't know . . ." murmured one of the patrons.

"Skeptic! For shame!" Ivarsson bellowed. He took a slug from his tankard, plunked it down on the table, and wiped his mouth with a sleeve. "Does anyone care to make another wager?"

No one did, apparently. Whatever the bet involved.

Anse drew Ivarsson away from the table, toward the doorway where Noelle waited, so they could talk privately.

"Lieutenant Ivarsson, it has come to my attention that certain persons, it seems, plan to attack Herr Blumroder. I believe Captain von Dantz is involved in the business, along with the military liaison from the N.U.S., Lieutenant Johnny Horton. Probably Captain Felder and his garrison, also. Some other persons."

Ivarsson belched. "To be precise, six out of the seven members of the local Committee of Correspondence."

Ivarsson, clearly enough, had his own sources of inside information in Suhl. Anse wondered who they were, but decided this was not the time to try to find out. Most likely, members of the garrison who had their doubts about the whole thing.

"Uh, yes. I need to know what you propose—"

"*I* propose?" Ivarsson's expression was a comically exaggerated version of surprise and indignation. "Warrant Officer Hatfield, *I* am simply here as a representative of the staff of General Kagg. It has been clearly established—your President Stearns was most insistent—that *you* are the people in charge, here in Suhl. Not us." He waved his hand airily. "So I have nothing to do with it. Other than to wish you the best, of course. Whatever you decide to do."

Anse studied him. Beneath the jovial, almost buffoonish exterior, he didn't miss the keen gaze Ivarsson was giving him. The Swede was perhaps not completely sober, but he was very far from being drunk.

So.

Anse fought off a strong wish that he had been able to down a couple of tankards of beer, himself.

So.

He cleared his throat. "May I assume, then, that neither General Kagg—nor the king of Sweden—have in any way authorized these activities?"

"You may."

"And will stand aside, whatever is done."

Ivarsson smiled. "Oh, yes."

"Will not criticize after the fact?"

The Swedish officer's smile widened. "Wouldn't think of it."

So.

Anse nodded curtly. Ivarsson headed straight back to the crowded table in the middle of the tavern, where he picked up his temporarily abandoned stein.

"Heinrich and Wolfgang, you each owe me a beer," he announced. "Kiefer, by now you owe me the whole tavern. But I'll settle for a pork *Schnitzel*. No gristle, you understand!"

"Well?" Noelle asked, after they left the tavern.

Anse shook his head. "It's weird. What I can't figure out is whether Ivarsson is acting on his own, or whether Kagg gave him instructions."

"Probably both," Noelle said shrewdly. "One thing I found out before we left is that Ivarsson's been Kagg's right-hand man since forever. Runs in the whole family—both families—it seems. Kind of like old feudal retainers, updated some."

"Um. So what you're saying is that Kagg would have given him some general guidelines, and would then rely on Ivarsson to figure out the footwork."

"Pretty much. I think what's happening is that Gustavus Adolphus told Kagg to see if we could handle the situation—and give us the leeway to do so."

Anse sighed, took off his cap, and ran fingers through his hair. Wishing there wasn't so much gray up there.

I'm too damn old for this—and it's still *way over my pay grade.*

But . . . there it was.

"Or the rope to hang ourselves with. Okay, so be it. Let's head over to Blumroder's."

Once they were within sight of Blumroder's shop, it was clear as day that Ivarsson wasn't the only one with his own inside sources of information. Two very hard-looking men—*Jaeger*, from their clothing—were standing guard outside the door. And all the windows had been shuttered.

Just to make things perfect, the shutters all had firing slits—and Anse could see musket barrels poking out of two of them.

In fact . . .

He scanned the whole street, up and down. *All* of the gun shops were shuttered—and he could see musket barrels in at least four of the windows. Even his brother-in-law Pat had the shutters up.

"Swell," he muttered. "One gunfight at the Suhl corral, coming up."

He headed for the entrance to Blumroder's shop. Anse didn't see any point in talking to Pat until he knew where things stood with the central figure in the situation. Noelle followed, a few steps behind.

He wasn't sure the *Jaeger* standing guard at the door would even let him in. But, as he approached, that problem became a moot point. Blumroder himself emerged from the shop, carrying a flintlock rifle, and with a grim expression on his face.

Out of the corners of his eyes, Anse could see several of the shuttered windows of the shops on the street opening a little wider and, he was pretty sure, two more musket barrels peeking out. Fortunately, none of the weapons seemed to be pointed at him. So far. Directly, at least. But it wouldn't take more than a second for that situation to change.

"Yes, Herr Hatfield?" asked Blumroder. Despite the expression on his face, his tone was courteous.

Anse didn't see any point in beating around the bush. He stuck his thumb over his shoulder, more-or-less pointing backward.

"First, I'm pretty sure an attack is going to be launched on you. The Swedish garrison will probably be involved."

"An attack has already been launched. Three shots were fired into my shop last night, through an open window in the rear. They barely missed me—and they did injure one of my apprentices. Fortunately, the wound was minor."

Anse had heard the shots himself, as it happened. He simply hadn't thought much of it, because there were often shots being fired on that street. Just about every gunmaker had a firing range as part of his establishment.

A firing range of sorts, at least. For Anse, accustomed to up-time firing ranges, the distances involved were ridiculously short—not more than ten feet, usually. The purpose of the ranges was simply to check a new gun's reliability, not its accuracy. Even with the new flintlock muskets, accuracy still ranked at the bottom of the list, when it came to the qualities looked for in seventeenth-century weapons.

"That would have probably been some of the people in the Committee of Correspondence," he guessed.

"Almost certainly," replied Blumroder. "Not even the drunken swine in the Swedish garrison would have missed, so closely did the would-be murderers stand to the window."

He jerked his head toward the *Jaeger* at the door. "You can be quite certain they will *not* miss, once they track down the culprits," he said coldly. "The training we get as members of the Suhl militia is not bad, either."

"There's not going to be any 'tracking down of culprits,' Blumroder." Anse's tone was every bit as cold. He turned and motioned Noelle forward. "Ms. Murphy is now in charge, here in Suhl. She has the documents from our President to verify that. And she's placed me in military command. So I'm declaring martial law. Which includes assuming authority over the city militia, by the way."

Anse was pretty sure he was wildly exceeding any formal authority either he or Noelle had, in doing so. "Martial law," to down-timers, was indistinguishable from "conqueror's fiat." And Anse remembered enough of the sketchy legal training he'd gotten to know that up-time American notions were tightly circumscribed by law.

But he didn't care, at the moment.

Blumroder started to say something, but Anse waved him down.

"Be quiet, Blumroder—and don't act as if you're just an innocent party in the business. You've been selling guns to the Bavarians—probably the Austrians, too. You know damn good and well such business is bound to stir up trouble."

"The *Swedes*," Blumroder hissed. "Why are they supposed to be any different from—"

"*Be quiet*, I said." Anse stepped forward, ignoring the rifles in the hands of the *Jaeger*—which were now definitely being pointed at him.

"You're not dealing with Swedes, any longer. You're dealing with the New United States, which happens to be the sovereign authority in the city of Suhl. Since your actions aren't technically illegal—yet—I don't propose to do anything about it. Other than give you a private warning, I guess, that you're playing with fire. But I'm not going to tolerate any 'private justice,' either. Not from you or anyone else."

Blumroder was now visibly angry. Anse forestalled the explosion by adding, a bit hurriedly: " 'Private justice' also includes any unauthorized actions on the part of the garrison here, or any of its officers or men."

Blumroder snorted sarcastically. "As if they will listen to you!"

Anse shook his head. "It doesn't matter whether they'll listen to me or not. If they don't, they are legally nothing but mutineers—and I will deal with them accordingly."

Another sarcastic snort came from the gunmaker. "You? And who else?" The musket still being in his hands, he pointed with his chin at Noelle Murphy. "The estimable *Fräulein?*"

Blumroder's eyes seemed to widen a bit. Turning, Anse saw that Noelle had pulled out a pistol from somewhere in her garment. An up-time weapon, at that—but at a glance, he thought it was just a .32 caliber automatic. A "lady's gun," suitable for fending off a mugger—and damn near useless for real military action.

Still, she seemed quite determined. Particularly when she looked at Blumroder and announced that she would provide the mayor and council with official copies of her letter of authorization from President Stearns. Properly sealed.

Then, over her shoulder, Anse saw that Jochen Rau had entered the street, carrying an up-time weapon that was quite suited for military action—a twelve-gauge pump-action shotgun, that he'd have loaded with slugs.

"My entire force," he said, smiling humorlessly. "Along with the Suhl militia. Except for the posse, of course."

He turned back to Blumroder, who was now frowning. "What is a 'posse'?" the German gunmaker asked.

"You are," Anse replied bluntly. "You and every able-bodied man in this area—and any *Jaeger* who work for you."

Hearing a little commotion, he glanced to the side and saw that Gaylynn Reardon had emerged from Pat's shop, holding her rifle.

"Able-bodied person, I guess I should say."

Blumroder was still frowning. Before Anse could say anything further, Noelle spoke up.

"Warrant Officer Hatfield has the authority to deputize anyone he chooses, to serve in the posse. Under our laws, Herr Blumroder, a 'posse' is a band of persons temporarily enrolled in the officially authorized police force, to suppress criminal activity."

She cleared her throat. "Mutiny is a criminal activity."

Blumroder and his *Jaeger* stared at her. Clearly enough, not knowing quite what to make of her words—or of her, for that matter.

It was time to settle this. Anse cleared his throat.

"That's the way it is, Blumroder. Do it my way, and you might get out of this alive. Might even keep your shops intact. Do it any other way, and the Swedes will be convinced that we can't maintain order here. The consequences of *that* are nothing you want to think about. Unless you're crazy enough to think you and your *Jaeger* can defeat Gustavus Adolphus—where Tilly and Wallenstein's armies couldn't."

After a moment, Blumroder looked away. "There is also an up-timer involved, on the other side. That Horton *Scheisskopf.*"

Anse shrugged. "So? Grantvillers are just citizens of the N.U.S. They don't enjoy any special privileges."

Honesty forced him to add: "Not legally, at any rate. If I tell Johnny Horton to stand down, and he doesn't, then he's just another mutineer."

Blumroder cocked his head, in a gesture that was quizzical as much as it was skeptical. "He is a lieutenant. I believe that outranks you, Warrant Officer."

"He doesn't outrank *me*," Noelle interrupted. "And I turned full authority over to Mr. Hatfield. Legally, that's good enough."

Anse could almost hear the next two words, that she must have been thinking but—thankfully—didn't speak out loud.

I think. Noelle Murphy was jerry-rigging just as fast as Anse was.

What the hell. Anse had seen plenty of jerry-rigged machines work well enough, and long enough, in his fifty-four years of life. Maybe this one would, too.

"That's it, then," he said.

"I swear to God, Anse, I had no idea . . ."

"Shut up, Pat," Anse growled. "Don't give me that bullshit. I'll accept that you didn't *know*. But don't tell me you had no suspicions that Blumroder—your own partner, fer chrissake—wasn't involved in the business."

After a moment, Anse's brother-in-law looked away, then sighed. "Well, okay. But, look . . ."

When his eyes came back to Anse, there was as much anger in them as shame and embarrassment.

"I *live* here, damn you. These people are my neighbors."

They were standing inside Pat's shop. Pat used the rifle in his hands to point to the western wall. "Just three shops down, there's a mother and her daughter who were gang-raped by mercenaries in Gustavus Adolphus's army. The girl was only fourteen. When the mother tried to protest that they were Lutherans, too, the stinking bastards just laughed at her. Two of them were members—still are, goddamit—of the Swedish garrison here. When she tried to register a complaint with the garrison commander afterward—yeah, the same Bruno Felder asshole who's still in command—he laughed at her, too."

Anse set his jaws. "I'm not arguing about that, Pat. I don't like mercenary soldiers any more than you do. It still doesn't change the fact that, within a year, we'll most likely have fought a war—and some of *our* soldiers will have gotten killed with guns from here. And they're going to be pissed as all hell, especially if they find out the gun trade with our enemies is still going on. You know that as well as I do."

Pat looked away again. "Yeah. Well. Look, I didn't know what to do. But I did report the problem to Grantville, at least."

Anse took a deep breath, and let it out. There was no point in staying angry with Pat. If he'd been in the same circumstances, Anse wasn't sure what he'd have done, either. Pat was a civilian. No fig leaf. No backup. Should he somehow have gone for the kind of private justice—vigilante justice—Anse was denying to both Blumroder and the CoC? Somewhere, in his own mind, was there still a sneaking feeling that it would be all right for an American to handle things that way, just because he was an American, but not for Germans who were N.U.S. citizens to do the same?

"All right, forget it. Water under the bridge, and all that. But for the moment, you're a member of my posse also. Got any problems with that?"

Finally, Pat smiled. "Not any, Anse. Not any at all."

"Good. In that case—don't get squirrelly on me, Pat—I want every up-time weapon you've got in the hands of the *Jaeger*. They're probably better shots than you are."

"Not mine," said Gaylynn Reardon sharply. "Not Gary's, neither." Her husband, standing next to her, looked just as stubborn as she did.

Anse shook his head. "Fine, fine. In the interest of maintaining American pride and morale—not to mention keeping peace in the family—you and Gary and Pat can each keep a modern rifle. But I want the rest in the hands of those who can do the most with them."

"I can shoot as well any damn *Jaeger*," she insisted. "Got nothing to with pride."

"Who cares how well you *shoot*, Mrs. Reardon?" he demanded harshly. "How well can you *kill*? Not dark outlines against the snow or distant figures on a roof that you'd have had in your scope if we'd run into trouble on the trip down here. Men standing right in front of you?"

She didn't look away. But she did swallow.

"Yeah. What I thought. We're not deer hunting, here. I want those guns in the hands of the *Jaeger*. If there are any left over, let Blumroder decide who gets them. Understood?"

After a moment, they all nodded.

"Do you really think it'll come to that, Anse?" asked Pat.

"Hell, who knows. But . . . yeah, it probably will." He glanced at the shuttered windows. "Felder's thugs aren't just rapists. They're also killers—and they've been the top dogs here, so far. I don't think they're just going to roll over and wave their paws in the air."

Noelle Murphy cleared her throat. "Still . . . Mr. Hatfield, you *can't* simply wait until there's an armed confrontation in the street. You have to send word to Captain Felder—to von Dantz and Horton, too—that you're now in charge."

Anse made a face. "Ms. Murphy, meaning no disrespect, but it's just a cold fact of life that if I march over to the garrison and start throwing orders around, I'll be lucky if I don't get shot. For sure, I'll get arrested. And then where are we?"

He took off his cap, laid it on a table, and scratched his head. "Look, face it. This so-called 'posse' of ours is shaky enough as it is. Take me out of the picture . . ."

Noelle shook her head. "Yes, I understand. But I wasn't suggesting that *you* do it, personally. Simply that you needed to send word."

"And who . . . ?"

Her face was pale but composed. "I think it's quite obvious. Since I have the documents from President Stearns, I will do it. After I give copies to the city's authorities."

That odd, lightning-quick little smile came and went. "I'm really not what anyone in their right mind would call a 'soldier,' Mr. Hatfield. The only reason I carry that little pistol is because my boss insisted. I'm not sure I could hit anything with it, beyond a few yards."

Abruptly, she rose to her feet. "I'm just a fig leaf here, really—and, once the job is done, a fig leaf is disposable."

Pat looked alarmed. "Hey, wait a minute! Didn't you hear what I said earlier? Felder's guys—probably Felder himself—are a bunch of rapists. You go over there . . . I mean, you're young, you're pretty . . ."

She issued that same insta-smile. "I thank you for the compliment, Mr. Johnson. But the same would be true for almost any woman you sent over there. And Mr. Hatfield is right. Any man would probably just get shot."

"But—"

"I *am* officially in charge, Mr. Johnson. Mr. Hatfield. So there won't be any further discussion of the matter."

And, with that, she marched to the door. At her imperious nod, one of Pat's apprentices opened it for her. A moment later, she was gone.

"Oh, hell's bells," said Pat.

*   *   *

Jochen Rau walked up to Anse. "Wili and Hennel are on their way to Grantville. We couldn't get a truck. Horton has one, but he's got it in the garrison compound. That's where the radio is, too."

"Damn." Anse shook his head.

"So Wili and Hennel they took the best horses we had." Rau grinned. "One of them was von Dantz's."

Anse chuckled. "So we're adding horse theft to the bargain, huh? Well, why not?"

He sent Jochen over to the tavern where he'd found Lieutenant Ivarsson. "See what he's up to—and, if you can, try to get him to come here."

Rau returned less than half an hour later. "Ivarsson's gone," he said. "Nobody seems to know where he went."

Anse muttered a curse under his breath. "What the hell is he playing at?"

Rau just shrugged.

An hour later, it started snowing. By nightfall, three inches of fresh snow had covered the town.

January 22, 1633

The business started not long after daybreak. The sky had cleared and the air was very crisp. The snow covering the streets muffled the sounds of moving men, but mercenary soldiers—this garrison, for sure—were usually not given to maintaining silence. So Anse could hear them coming a good two minutes before the first ranks came around the corner and started down the street.

By then, Anse had shifted his headquarters from Pat's factory to Blumroder's shop. He'd done that, partly, because Blumroder would be the immediate target; partly, because Blumroder's *Jaeger* were the men he relied on the most, outside of himself and Rau. But, mostly, simply to keep driving home the basic political point he was making.

Blumroder might be a conniving double-dealer—depending on how you looked at it—but he still had rights, until and unless they were removed from him legally. So, Anse would make his defense of those rights as visible and obvious as possible.

Von Dantz, surprisingly, was in the lead. Anse had expected to see Bruno Felder, since almost all of the soldiers following von Dantz were part of the Suhl garrison.

"You think von Dantz carried out a little mutiny of his own?" Anse wondered.

Standing next to him, looking through the same slit in the shutters, Blumroder shook his head. "I doubt it. Felder controls the paychest, and I don't think von Dantz is rich enough to buy a garrison."

Rau was at the next window. "Even if he is, he didn't bring enough money with him," he pointed out.

Anse decided they were right. Which meant . . .

His headshake was simply one of disgust. "Felder must have decided to straddle the fence. He let von Dantz—Oh, that son-of-a-bitch."

Anse had just spotted Johnny Horton, following von Dantz. "He let von Dantz *and* Horton call the shots. Let 'em have his garrison, but didn't come out himself. Stinking bastard."

Blumroder shrugged. As well he might. "Mercenary captain" and "man of principle" were not terms that were too often associated with each other, in the here and now. Often enough, mercenary captains were really more in the way of what could be called military contractors rather than what Anse thought of as "soldiers." Petty politics came naturally to them.

On the street outside, von Dantz halted his men when they were still forty yards from Pat Johnson's factory—more than fifty yards from Blumroder's shop next door. Apparently, he'd finally noticed that the shops on the street were shuttered and that the residents in the gunmakers' quarter looked to be willing to fight it out.

Von Dantz was close enough that Anse could see his face. For once, the arrogant captain's expression had some hesitation and uncertainty in it. Anse wondered what combination of emotions had led him to follow this course of action. By now, even a man as obtuse as von Dantz should have figured out that he was treading on very thin ice, politically speaking.

Ambition, of course. If he could demonstrate to his superiors that he had a flair for decisive action, he might get promoted. Anse had the feeling that General Kagg was far too intelligent a commander to be much impressed by simple "decisiveness." But Kagg had only recently come into command here, and von Dantz had no experience serving under him. If Anse remembered correctly, von Dantz had done most of his service under the Swedish general Banér—who had a reputation for being mule headed and was not much given to subtlety.

Still, there had to be more to it than that. Anse couldn't really know, of course, but he suspected that a lot of what was involved was simply festering resentment, finally boiling to the surface.

The up-timers grated on von Dantz, pure and simple. And if, here in Suhl, there was an up-timer even more hot-headed than he was, von Dantz would use him as a cover to vent his built-up frustration.

John Horton. Anse despised Johnny Horton. But why hadn't the army just detailed him off to go back to teaching math at the high school? Now—nearly a sure thing by the time this day was over—they'd be permanently down one more teacher that Grantville couldn't really afford to lose.

But his personal attitude toward Horton was neither here nor there. What really mattered, under the circumstances, Anse thought—was pretty critical, in fact—was that whatever happened there could be no accusation made afterward of favoritism based on origin.

He crooked a finger, summoning the *Jaeger* he'd already guessed was the best shot among them. If nothing else, from the easy way he held the rifle Pat had lent him, the hunter was apparently familiar with up-time weapons.

When the man came to the window and stooped to look through the slit, Anse pointed at the distant figure of Horton.

"You see him? The one in the camouflage outfit standing maybe five feet to von Dantz's left?"

The *Jaeger* nodded.

"If any shooting starts," Anse said harshly, "I want him dead."

The *Jaeger* studied him for a moment, then smiled thinly and nodded again.

Von Dantz's men were now starting to push forward around him, losing any semblance of a disciplined formation. There were perhaps three dozen of them, Anse estimated, which would be most of the entire garrison.

He took a slow, deep breath.

"Okay. I guess I oughta give them a formal warning."

"Why?" asked Rau, smiling even more thinly than the *Jaeger* had. "Just shoot them."

Anse didn't bother arguing the point. It'd be useless anyway, given Jochen's attitudes. The man was *in* the N.U.S. army—in fact, most of the time he was a very good soldier—but he did not and never had looked at the world from what Anse would consider a "proper military viewpoint."

There was no point delaying the matter, much as Anse was tempted to. He went to the front door of Blumroder's shop. After he passed through—making sure to leave it open behind him-he stepped forward three paces.

"Captain von Dantz!" he shouted. "Lieutenant Horton! I am now in command here in Suhl, and I order you—"

"Get fucked, Hatfield!" John Horton hollered back. His beefy face was almost bright red, either from anger or the cold, or both. "You're nothing but a warrant officer! As the ranking American here—"

"There's no such thing as a 'ranking American,' Horton," Anse snarled. Under the circumstances, he saw no point in maintaining military protocol. "All there is, is legal authority under the laws of the New United States. Which I have, and you don't. Ms. Murphy would have showed you the documents."

"Fuck her, too!" came the answering shout. "Some bullshit papers, supposedly from Stearns. For all I know, you forged them. Means nothing!"

Horton stepped forward, pushing past von Dantz. He had his rifle in his left hand, and was pointing his finger angrily at Anse.

"I'm warning you, Hatfield! We're here to arrest a traitor. Dead or alive, it don't matter to me at all. You've got ten seconds to get out of the way or—"

A shot was fired, by one of the garrison mercenaries. Anse never saw where it went. He didn't think it was even aimed at anything. Just someone too nervous, in a situation that was too tense.

Immediately, a fusillade of shots rang out from the shuttered gunmaker shops. Four of the garrison soldiers fell, and several others were sent reeling.

Horton started to bring his rifle up to his shoulder. A bullet caught him in the ribs. He half-spun, dropping the rifle. His face turned toward Anse.

"Hey, what—" he started to say. Another bullet struck him in the jaw. There wasn't much left of his face by the time it fell into a snow-drift.

But Anse wasn't paying attention to Horton, any longer. Von Dantz raised his pistol and fired at him. Astonishingly, the down-time weapon was accurate enough for the bullet to knock Anse's cap right off his head. Anse was sure he'd—literally—felt the bullet parting his hair.

That was frightening. Anse sprawled into the snow, hurriedly bringing up his rifle for a prone shot. Once he got von Dantz in the sights, he saw that the German captain had drawn out another pistol.

Von Dantz fired again. The bullet grazed the back of Anse's boot and tore off the heel.

Jesus! Given the kind of guns he was using, von Dantz was turning out to be a goddam John Wesley Harding.

Then again, Harding got killed. With a modern rifle, at a range of less than fifty yards, Anse couldn't possibly miss.

He fired.

He missed.

A garrison soldier standing just behind von Dantz stumbled backward, flinging aside his musket. He'd been struck in the shoulder by Anse's shot.

Von Dantz was pulling out *another* pistol. If he'd been using a revolver instead of wheel locks, Anse would have been dead already.

Settle down, you idiot!

He jacked another round into the chamber, and forced himself to draw a real bead instead of just jerking the trigger.

Von Dantz was bringing up the pistol. Anse fired.

This time, the bullet hit von Dantz squarely, right in the chest. He was dead before he hit the ground.

By now, the gunfire in the street was almost deafening. The garrison soldiers were grouped in the center, shooting back at the shops from whose windows they were being fired upon.

Anse glanced back at the still-open door to Blumroder's shop. He decided he'd be safer lying prone in several inches of snow than trying to crawl back into the shop. The mercenaries were paying no attention to him, since he wasn't moving and they were taking a murderous fire from the shops.

As inconspicuously as he could, he jacked another round into the chamber.

There was no lack of targets for him, of course. On the other hand . . .

Right now, the enemy was ignoring him. Most of them probably thought he was dead. If he fired, on the other hand, they *would* notice him—and lying in the open, right out on the street, he was a sitting duck. More precisely, a prone duck.

He didn't think they were going to last much longer, anyway. Somewhere around a dozen of them had already been killed or wounded. Von Dantz and Horton had been idiots, leading their men straight into the street the way they had. The gunmakers and their apprentices and *Jaeger* were shooting from behind shelter—good shelter, too; the thick, sturdy walls of seventeenth-century German manufacturing shops—and they had an open field of fire. As battles went, it was completely one-sided.

So . . .

True, it was inglorious. Even ignominious. On the other hand, youth and its excess of testosterone were several decades behind him.

Anse laid his head down, and played dead. The situation wasn't critical and he wasn't Alvin York, anyway—as he'd just proved, by missing his first shot at von Dantz at point-blank range.

Besides, he consoled himself, he'd read once that after the battle of New Orleans was over, several hundred "dead" British soldiers had risen from Chalmette Field. Most of them completely uninjured. Veteran soldiers all—elite soldiers, even—they'd quickly realized that their commanders had led them into a bloodbath that they didn't have a chance of winning.

He was pretty sure the same thing had happened on just about every battlefield in history, at least since the invention of gunpowder.

Tradition, as it were. Inglorious as it might be.

He still felt like a damned fool.

Fortunately, it was all over within thirty seconds. The garrison soldiers broke, and began running away. They didn't slow down any, either, as they neared the safety of the next street over. The gunmakers of Suhl were in a fine fury, and kept firing on them the whole way.

Anse peeked up, then rose.

Blumroder came out of the door, smiling.

"You are a brave man, Herr Hatfield. And what is better, a very sensible one."

Anse gave him a look that was none too friendly. "I guess you've proved you're brave enough, yourself. We'll just have to see how sensible you are."

Blumroder's smile faded. Some, at least, if not enough to suit Anse.

A woman, followed by a man, came out of one of the shops farther up the street, carrying a musket. She marched over to one of the corpses lying in the snow, aimed the musket, and fired. Brains that had already been spilled were scattered still further.

The man with her went to another corpse. Aimed, fired. A dead man died again.

That both men had already been dead wasn't in question. In fact, it looked as if they'd each taken several bullets during the fighting. Those had already been the most shot-up corpses on the street.

"Hey!" said Anse. He didn't approve of mutilating corpses, and if this got out of hand . . .

Blumroder put a hand on his arm. "It is a personal matter, Herr Hatfield. The people in that shop were looking for two men in particular. It seems they found them."

"Oh." After a moment, Anse shrugged. It was a pretty crude form of justice, but . . .

What the hell. If he didn't feel any particular guilt over playing dead in the snow—which he didn't—he had no business getting all huffy and puffy about proper judicial procedure. As long as it didn't get out of hand, at least.

The woman and the man, methodically and stoically, reloaded their weapons. Then, fired again.

"That's enough!" he called out. "*Genug!*"

The couple raised their heads and looked at him. After a moment, the man nodded. The woman took a bit longer to make her decision. But she, too, turned and went back into their shop.

"Okay," Anse said. He looked up the street, in the direction of the garrison's compound. It was out of sight, but it wasn't more than a quarter of a mile away.

"Okay," he repeated. "I guess we'd better finish it."

Blumroder began shouting orders. Within a minute, dozens of gunmakers, apprentices and *Jaeger* were out in the street, lining up in a remarkably good military formation.

Perhaps not that remarkable, really. One of the things Anse had learned in the twenty months since the Ring of Fire was that a lot of his preconceptions of "law-abiding, orderly Germans" were myths. Or, maybe not myths so much as transposing the reality of a much later Germany onto the seventeenth century.

The truth was that, in a lot of ways, Anse felt quite at home among Germans of this day and age. Germany—"the Germanies," rather— was often a raucous and freewheeling sort of place. Just like good and proper West Virginians, most Germans who weren't dirt poor owned guns and knew how to use them. Most towns and many villages had a militia, just as surely—and with just as much civic pride—as they had their own printing presses.

True, there were differences. Already, Germans had a devotion to bureaucratic regulations and legal fussiness that precious few up-time Americans ever did. Outside of Washington, D.C., at any rate. Still, Germans of the seventeenth century had a lot more in common with the frontiersmen of pre-Civil War America, in terms of their basic attitudes, than they did with the regimented populace of a much later Prussia. The *Jaeger* would have found the old Mountain Men sadly rootless, but other than that, they wouldn't have had much trouble understanding them.

Anse led the way. Thankfully, nobody made any wisecracks about dead men lying in the snow being miraculously resurrected. After a while, he realized that very few of them had even noticed.

Rau had, of course.

"Very nice—what is that English word?—'dive,' I think."

"And what would *you* have done?" asked Anse crossly.

"Diven, of course. Only an idiot wouldn't."

"Dove," Anse corrected. "Or maybe it's 'dived.' "

"Amazing that you aren't all idiots. Speaking the language the idiot way you do."

To Anse's relief, no further battle was necessary. As they neared the compound—a wooden fortress, basically, much like the forts put up by the nineteenth-century American army—he discovered that the routed garrison had already been intercepted by the city's militia before they could reach the shelter of their compound.

What must have happened, clearly enough, was that after Noelle gave the city authorities copies of her documents and explained the situation, they'd called out the militia. The militia would have mustered behind the city hall and had managed to get between the fleeing mercenaries and the entrance to the garrison compound.

Just as clearly, the garrison hadn't put up any resistance. After the bloodbath on the gunmakers' street, all the fight had been knocked out of them. They'd simply submitted to arrest.

The militia officers were standing there with their men. Those would be the ones who hadn't been in the gunmakers' street, and Anse hadn't already enrolled in his impromptu posse. Someone would have to sort that little problem out later, Anse thought. But, for the moment, the officers clearly had that look which proclaimed: *awaiting further orders.*

Lieutenant Ivarsson emerged from the compound's gates. Smiling very cheerfully.

"Good day, Herr Hatfield. How delightful to see that the new garrison commander has come to pay a visit."

Anse frowned at him. "Meaning no offense, but where have *you* been?"

Ivarsson jerked a thumb over his thick shoulder. "Inside, of course. Once von Dantz and Horton took out most of the garrison, that is. I thought it would be imprudent to make an appearance earlier."

Anse looked up at the walls of the compound. A couple of very nervous-looking soldiers were stationed up there. Holding their weapons, but carefully not pointing them at the militia outside the gates.

"Where's Felder? And what's more important—where is Noelle Murphy?"

Ivarsson's smile seemed as cheerful as ever. "The former commander of the garrison is sitting in his office. Waiting—eagerly, I assure you—to be relieved of his command. *Fräulein* Murphy is there with him. She is quite unharmed."

There was something very suspicious about that smile.

"I wouldn't think Felder—"

"Oh, certainly!" Ivarsson made an expansive gesture with his big hands. "At least, after I explained to him that he might—just barely—be able to persuade General Kagg that he simply couldn't stifle the mutiny led by the dastardly Captain von Dantz. If I put in a word for him."

Dastardly, no less. Ivarsson's English was really quite good.

"I believe he was also helped in seeing his proper course of conduct by Fräulein Murphy's presence. Although she is unharmed, she is rather furious, in her quiet sort of way. There were threats made, it seems, of a most lascivious variety. Once I removed the guards placed over her, I returned her pistol. She assures me that in the close quarters of Captain Felder's office, she can't possibly miss."

Anse laughed. "This, I want to see. All right, Lieutenant Ivarsson, please lead me there."

Noelle did, indeed, seem irate. At least, in her rather prim-and-proper manner of expressing most emotions. Her face was pale, and the pistol leveled at Felder didn't seem to waver at all.

"You okay?" he asked.

Her face got pinched. "Well. Yes. I suppose. They were very insulting. Well. That's not quite the right word, I guess. *Filthy motherfuckers!*"

The pistol did waver a bit, then. Quiver, rather, from the restrained fury of the slender hand that held it.

Felder's face was at least as pale as hers. His eyes had never once left the barrel of the gun, not even when Anse and Ivarsson came into the room.

"Felder?" Anse asked.

"No, not him," Noelle hissed. "Although he's still responsible. Some of his men. The two he had guarding me."

Anse turned to Rau, who was standing just beyond the door to the captain's office. "Track 'em down, Jochen."

"Shoot them?"

"No, that'd be illegal. Just see to their discipline."

Rau made something that might charitably be called a salute, and left. Anse turned back to Felder.

"You, asshole, are leaving here tonight. Under armed guard." He jerked his head toward the door. "Corporal Rau's guard, to be exact. I strongly recommend you behave yourself. I'll have Ms. Murphy write a letter to General Kagg and President Stearns. If you're lucky, you might keep your commission. I hope not, but I'm used to being disappointed in life."

Now, he turned to Ivarsson. "The big problem—"

Ivarsson was shaking his head before Anse even started talking. "That will not work, Herr Hatfield. You will need Corporal Rau in Suhl, to serve as your adjutant while you assemble a new garrison. The existing garrison is now useless, here. I will lead them out— perhaps I should say, what is left of them—and take them to Grantville."

He nodded toward Felder. "I will take him with me, also. Under armed guard, since that is your wish."

He gave Felder that same cheerful smile. "I do not believe Captain Felder will object. That would disappoint me, and, alas, I do not share your stoical attitude toward disappointment."

Ivarsson looked all of his size, that moment. Felder seemed to shrink still further in his chair.

Anse thought about it. With the entire garrison gone . . .

In the real world, that meant the new "garrison" would just be the existing Suhl militia—the master craftsmen and their adult sons, those journeymen and apprentices who were from Suhl's citizen families. Not most of the *Jaeger*, since few of them would be citizens of the town.

Granted, the militia would make a far better force to maintain order than Felder's mercenaries had been. But they'd be completely unreliable if it ever became necessary to crack down on the town's gunmakers. Most of them *were* the town's gunmakers.

Not to mention that over half of the city council consisted of master gunsmiths.

A return remembrance of that long-ago, overly-rich, eight-layer chocolate dessert attacked his stomach.

But all he said was: "All right. That's how we'll do it."

January 27, 1633

Gretchen Richter came into Suhl five days later, early in the evening, through the middle of a snowstorm. Not quite a blizzard, but awfully close. When she marched into Anse's headquarters—Felder's old office—she looked like a walking snowball.

Insofar, at least, as a snowball could resemble a very large and good-looking bat, coldly furious at having been summoned from a much warmer clime.

"Where are they?" were the first words out of her mouth, as she started brushing the snow off of her heavy parka. She seemed entirely unconcerned with the mess she was leaving on the floor of Anse's office.

Anse didn't try to play dumb. "We've got two of them under guard, here in the stockade. We're pretty sure the other four scampered back to their villages."

"Two will be enough. Where is Blumroder's shop?"

Anse cocked his head, eyeing her skeptically.

"Don't be stupid, Herr Hatfield." Gretchen edged aside, allowing Anse a view of the doorway. Jeff Higgins was standing there. Just behind him, Anse could see the dark figures of several other men. One of them was Jorg Hennel; the others he didn't recognize.

"I brought my husband with me, as you can see. Surely you don't think he would be a party to any illegal violence."

The look Anse gave Jeff Higgins was almost as skeptical as the one he'd given Gretchen. There wasn't much left of the shy geek Anse could vaguely remember from the days before the Ring of Fire. A lot of the fat had been lost, replaced by muscle—and Higgins was a big man. What was more important was that his mental attitudes had been largely transformed over the past twenty months. By reality, by combat—and, probably most of all, by being married to Gretchen.

It didn't help any that Higgins was carrying a shotgun. It might very well be the same shotgun he'd used, not so long ago, to gun down a number of Croat cavalrymen in close-range fighting.

Suddenly, Jeff grinned. And if it wasn't what you could call a shy grin, much less a geeky one, there wasn't any menace in it, either.

"C'mon, Anse, lighten up," he said. "Gretchen's mission here is purely educational."

Anse grunted. "Educational," under the circumstances, was not entirely reassuring. Just a few days earlier, with the help of half a dozen *Jaeger*, Jochen Rau had "educated" the two soldiers who'd subjected Noelle Murphy to their leering attentions. Both of them had been so badly beaten they'd had to be taken out of Suhl on litters.

Fell down the stairs, Rau claimed.

Still . . .

"Okay," he said. "As long as there's no violence. I'll have Corporal Rau release the two CoC prisoners. Then he can guide you to Blumroder's shop."

He rose to his feet. "No, hell with that. I'll do it myself."

By the time they arrived at Blumroder's shop, night had fallen. Blumroder himself ushered them into the main room of his living quarters. His wife and children—two sons and a daughter, all of them in their late teens or early twenties—were present, along with all four of his apprentices and the two *Jaeger* he still kept around as guards.

Once Gretchen, Jeff, Anse and the three CoC members came into the room, it seemed as packed tight as a shipping crate. It didn't help any that Gretchen forced the two CoC culprits—Hennel was the third one—to come to the center of the room.

She got right down to business. Turning to the two chastened CoC members, she pointed a finger at Blumroder.

"You will apologize to Herr Blumroder for trying to kill him."

Apologies babbled forth like a bubbling brook.

Gretchen now faced Blumroder.

"You will accept the apology."

She still looked like a half-frozen bat out of hell, and just as pissed.

Blumroder didn't babble, but he did nod his head. He didn't even hesitate, for more than a second.

"That's the end of it, then," Gretchen pronounced. Turning back to the CoC miscreants, she jerked her head toward the door.

"Now, get out. Remember what I told you. From now on, you will *listen* to Jorg. And I'm leaving two other members of the CoC here also. One from Jena, one from Rudolstadt. Both are experienced, and good organizers. You will listen to them also."

Hastily—eagerly—the two youngsters made for the door.

"*Moment*," Gretchen growled. "You will also tell those other four idiots to come into Suhl and apologize personally to Herr Blumroder. If they don't, I will come back. You do not want me to come back."

They gave her a nervous nod, and vanished.

Gretchen swiveled to face Blumroder again. "I will leave now, Herr Blumroder. There will be no further misbehavior on the part of the CoC here."

He nodded again. "I accept your reassurance."

"Accept this also, then," she said coldly. "Within a few months, we are likely to be at war again. Many of our soldiers will die. One of them might be my husband. Some of them are certain to be my comrades in the Committees. If it is discovered that their deaths were due to the enemy having weapons that should never have been sold to them, there will be consequences."

Her icy gaze move away from Blumroder to fix on the two *Jaeger*. "Do not think you are the only ones who know how to shoot," she told them. "Or gut a carcass. And the *Thueringerwald* is not that big. Never think so."

The gaze came back to Blumroder. "You do not want me to return to Suhl, either."

She straightened a little, jerked the lapels of the parka to shed more snow on the floor, and was gone.

Her husband followed. At the threshhold, he paused, looked at Blumroder over his shoulder, and smiled cheerfully.

"You really don't, Herr Blumroder. Trust me on this one."

There was silence in the room, for a while, after the door was closed. Then Blumroder cleared his throat.

"Herr Hatfield, perhaps we should resume our interrupted conversation. The one concerning railroad work, and its prospects for Suhl."

"What a good idea," Anse said.

Bypass Surgery

VIRGINIA DEMARCE

Bamberg, January 1633

Vince Marcantonio looked at the latest communication from head-quarters. Grantville, that was; not from Steve Salatto in Würzburg, who was his immediate boss. From Vince's viewpoint, his lot as the N.U.S. administrator in Bamberg was not a happy one. Steve was his formal boss and had been since Grantville sent its teams into Franconia a couple of months before. He sometimes wondered, though, if his real boss wasn't his deputy, Wade Jackson, who was a member of the UMWA. The United Mine Workers of America were still, in a lot of ways, the real backbone of Mike Stearns' administration. Until it was clearer that Stearns would back him if he went against Wade—for that matter, until it was clearer that Stearns would back Steve Salatto if he went against Saunders Wendell, who was the UMWA man in Würzburg—he took the precaution of clearing everything with his deputy.

He shook his head. A "Special Commission on the Establishment of Freedom of Religion in the Franconian Prince-Bishoprics and the

267

Prince-Abbey of Fulda." Which they wanted Walt Miller and Matt Trelli to do, here in Bamberg.

Not that Bamberg couldn't benefit from the activities of such a commission, given the string of six hundred or so witch-burnings that the bishop had enthusiastically fostered during the second half of the 1620s.

Vince shuddered. He was Catholic, and he was glad that Johann Georg Fuchs von Dornheim, the bishop of Bamberg, had fled to Austria. Vince wouldn't have wanted to be the guy who presided over his trial. He was even gladder that Dornheim's suffragan bishop, Friedrich Foerner, had died in 1630. Same reason. The up-time encyclopedias said that the bishop wouldn't die until this upcoming March 19. Vince didn't know whether he was dead yet or not, in this world. When and if he did die, he figured, it would be in the newspapers. And he would be stuck with dealing with all of the political problems surrounding the picking of a new bishop.

So here he sat in Bamberg. Taken by the Swedes on February 11, 1632. Taken back by Tilly on March 9, 1632. Taken again by the Swedes . . . Well, the up-time encyclopedias said on February 9, 1633, by Bernhard of Saxe-Weimar. But in this world, Bernhard was a traitor to Gustavus Adolphus and February 9 hadn't quite rolled around yet. In this world, the Swedes had taken Bamberg back again last fall, right after the battle at Nürnberg's Alte Veste.

But if Grantville had found the money to send special commissioners to Würzburg, why not to Bamberg? As if Cliff Priest and his guys didn't have enough on their plates already.

"Yeah, that's the way it looks." Walt Miller looked at Cliff Priest.

"You're telling me that there were a hundred seventy separate and individual fortified castles in this region? In the triangle of land between Bamberg, Nürnberg, and Bayreuth? Not counting the ones in the triangle between Bamberg, Würzburg, and the northern border?" Captain Priest's voice was disbelieving.

"More or less. That's the best that Matt and I can figure it," Walt said. "From the information that Janie Kacere has picked up so far from the down-timers who are helping her figure out the land tenures, they're thicker on the land here than anywhere else in Germany. That's the number we've come up with as a starter, keeping in mind that we've only been here for a few months. Of course, not all of them are really in our jurisdiction, I think. Some of them belong to the margrave of Bayreuth and a whole batch of them belong to local independent petty nobles, *Freiherren*, or to imperial knights, *Reichsritter*. Think 'robber barons' for a lot of those. But some, like the lords of Aufsess or Egloffstein, have a fair amount of clout. Some of them—in fact, a whole batch of them—are Protestant. So Vince thinks they aren't included in what Gustavus Adolphus turned over to us."

Walt looked at the coach—at the captain, rather. He still tended to think of Cliff as his coach, if he wasn't careful.

"I sort of thought that we ought to talk to Vince again. Find out what he wants us to do about it. Or try to do about it. Plus a bunch of other castles that belong to the bishop and are local administrative headquarters. Pottenstein, for example. And Goessweinstein, though that's a sort of ex-castle as castles go. Most of it burned down way back when. The Swedes took Veldestein at Neuhaus and turned it over to us, so we have that one. But they pulled out the fifty men they had left in it as a garrison, so all by itself, now, it's a place where we have to leave more of our not-very-large batch of soldiers than we really want to.

"Maybe we should talk to the Kaceres as well as to Vince. A lot of the castles have been used for grain storage, recently—when the bishop's officials collected the rents and tithes and taxes in kind rather than in money. See whether they want us to try to sell it. If so, does the money come to the administration here in Bamberg or do we have to send it to Grantville and wait for the Congress to appropriate it back for us to use? Things like that."

"There is one bright spot," Matt Trelli interrupted. "Like Goessweinstein, a whole bunch of them aren't in usable shape for anything military. Some of them not even for anything else. There was a big feud through here about seventy-five or eighty years ago, between the margrave of Bayreuth and the bishop of Bamberg, and some of the castles have been in ruins ever since then. Their owners couldn't afford to build them back.

"More recently, there was a big castle at Ebermannstadt, but it's been burned down by the Swedes. So has the one at Waischenfeld. It seems to be the preferred method of getting rid of them. The people of Waischenfeld were so pissed by having the local castle fired by the Swedes that after the captain general pulled his troops back, they went out and burned down Rabenstein, which belongs to one of Gustavus Adolphus' Protestant allies. Some imperials and some troops from Forchheim burned down the Streitberg last June. The Croats burned the castle at Muggendorf four weeks after that. So some of the ground has been cleared for us, so to speak. But there are plenty more. The Herren von Streitberg, the one who held that castle from the bishop, have another big one, called Greifenstein, that's still standing. There's no way to predict right now if they'll play nice and decide that Vince is the bishop's legal successor."

Cliff Priest looked back at his two lieutenants. Special assistants. Ex-students. Whatever you wanted to call them. He had coached both of them when they were in high school and he was a brand-new hire. All three of them had gone into Grantville's military when Mike Stearns called for volunteers right after the Ring of Fire. Cliff had a B.S. in physical education. The closest he had ever been to a military organization before that was the Grantville Volunteer Fire Department. Walt Miller and Matt Trelli were both in their mid-twenties, ten years or so younger than himself. They had never been in the military before the Ring of Fire, either. Walt had been working at the waste water treatment plant, a job he got courtesy of his grandfather who had retired from the staff there, trying to save money for college now that he had gotten engaged to Amy Jo Prickett and finally made up his mind to settle down. Matt had been in his second year of college at Fairmont State, going part time and working part time for Dave Marcantonio. He was dating Julie Anne Abruzzo; they had graduated the same year but she had gotten a year ahead of him at State by taking more classes. She'd been going part time, too, though; full-time college cost more than most Grantville kids could think about. Cliff spared a thought for his wife Sarah and their three children back in Grantville. She was working as office manager for the Congress of the fragile innovation they called the New United States. Then he brought his mind back to the matter immediately at hand.

From the viewpoint of a professional army, they were babes in the woods, all three of them, even now, eighteen months after they first volunteered. But he was a military administrator, the other two were officers, and the three of them had to think about how to handle one hundred seventy fortified castles. Give or take a few.

Matt cleared his throat. "There's something else. Something that the king of Sweden, Gustavus Adolphus—that is, the Captain General—apparently sort of forgot to mention to Mike Stearns when he wished this job off on us."

Cliff raised his eyebrows.

Matt continued. "When the Swedes came through here, they did a kind of *Blitzkrieg*. If they ran into a town they could take, they took it. That's why we're sitting here in Bamberg. It's the capital of the prince-bishopric, but it isn't fortified. The city council takes the precaution of surrendering to every army that comes along, in hopes that they'll be able to come up with a high enough payment to minimize the destruction and plundering that go with being conquered in this wonderful century. The Swedes simply sort of gave it to us."

And then, Cliff thought, pulled their army back north. So that Grantville was trying to police what used to be the prince-bishopric of Bamberg with a couple of hundred soldiers. Five of them up-timers, which included the medic, a newly trained EMT. Who had, luckily, Bennett Norris' wife Marion to help him full-time, even though she wasn't officially on the payroll. She'd gone back to school after the Ring of Fire and qualified as a certified nursing assistant, a CNA. The rest of the N.U.S. military in Bamberg were down-timers, cobbled together from the various mercenary troops who had surrendered to Grantville since the spring of 1631.

"But," he said. "Something else what."

"It apparently slipped his mind that the bishop had two honking big fortresses that the Swedes didn't bother to take. One of them's north of here, called Kronach. The other one's south, called Forchheim. Forchheim has an imperial garrison in it, still. They haven't tried to come out; waiting to see what happens next, I expect. Kronach is something else again."

"How?"

"The fortress there is called the Rosenberg and it's defended by its own people. The city militia. Two thousand or so of them. Stubborn as hell. It's never, ever, been taken—not by anybody who attacked it. They have a history of making war, sort of independently, on the independent Protestant noblemen in the region."

"Well," Cliff said. "Charmed, I'm sure. It occurs to me that it would be nice, really nice, if Grantville would send us just one up-timer who has some actual military training. Too bad they put Guy Hinshaw on some kind of detached duty. He was actually stationed here when he was in. He might have had some ideas for us."

Matt frowned. "Ask them for Tom O'Brien. He was in the National Guard, at least. And before the Ring of Fire, he worked for a construction company." He grinned suddenly. "In the demolition end of things. Clearing out old stuff to make room to build new stuff. In lower management, not doing the demolition on the sites, but still . . . he's probably the best that we have. If we can get him."

"I don't want to give it to you second-hand, Vince," Cliff Priest said. "I've brought Walt and Matt along with me. They're out in the reception room and I'd rather have them run through it themselves."

Which they did, after Vince invited them into his office. Although they had learned a few more things in the past three days.

"There used to be even more castles," Walt said. "A hundred years or so ago, the farmers had a big revolt and burned almost *all* of them down. One of the biggest penalties that was put on them was that after the lords put the revolution down, the farmers had to pay for building them back. Or a lot of them; some never were rebuilt."

"You know," Vince said musingly. "If they burn them down again . . . I don't think we'll do that, guys. I'm not sure that we could prohibit the owners from rebuilding. But at least for the ones under our jurisdiction, we can keep them from making anyone else pay the bill."

"One thing we could *try*," John Kacere suggested, "is putting our regional administration for the northern sector in Teuschnitz. The castle there was burned last year, so we can get in. There's a good-sized city hall. When the militant inhabitants of Kronach see that they're missing out on the money that comes with people coming to do business at the courthouse, they might—might, mind you—open their gates."

"And if they don't?" Vince Marcantonio asked.

"We'll think again."

"We could try publicizing voter registration, too," Bennett Norris added. "If staying locked up inside the walls means that they don't get to vote . . . Yeah, okay guys, I know it's a bit lame, but we might as well try anything in a pinch."

"Is there any way we can do the same to Forchheim? Appoint some other town as the regional administration headquarters, that is?"

"Yeah. Let me think which one," Vince answered. "The real problem, though, is that it's sitting right square across the main road from Nürnberg to Leipzig—the trade route. It was a big problem for Gustavus Adolphus last year, when he was trying to get supplies down to Nürnberg for the battle at the Alte Veste."

"Move the road." That was John Kacere's suggestion again. He was the economic liaison, after all. "If there's anything that the U.S. in the twentieth century figured out, it was how to make a town wither and die. Think how many small towns up-time were ruined economically when an interstate went in a few miles away and took the traffic off the old highway that went along the main street. Advertise to the residents what we're doing. They may be less enthusiastic about supporting the remains of the imperial garrison, once they hear the news."

Eggolsheim, March, 1633

The mayor of Eggolsheim was not certain that he was happy. The mayor of Neuses was certain that he was unhappy. This idea was going to mean nothing but trouble. Just because there was a ferry across the Regnitz at Neuses, the administration installed in Bamberg by the king of Sweden had decided that their little villages were to be combined, turned into a town and administrative headquarters for all of southern Bamberg, and outfitted with the appropriate amenities.

This was going to upset accustomed routine. Not, of course, that accustomed routine had not been upset for most of the past several years.

However. The Forchheimer were not going to like this idea. And the people of Forchheim, when they did not like things, had a tendency to march out in force and burn down neighboring towns.

Of which Eggolsheim and Neuses were two.

The up-timer, a man named Walter Miller, said that they would be protected.

For what it was worth. There was an imperial garrison in Forchheim.

Forchheim, April, 1633

Colonel Fritz von Schletz, Imperial-Bavarian forces, commander of the garrison, stood on the parapet walk that went around the walls of Forchheim. Nice, strong, walls. The bishops of Bamberg had started rebuilding the citadel about eighty years ago, after the feud with the margrave of Bayreuth. It wasn't finished yet, but it was good enough, in his professional judgment, to withstand any attack that the Swedes could likely bring against it. The two Italian-style bastions that protected the prince-bishop's palace were in particularly good shape. The walls varied from ten to fourteen yards high; the moat was up to thirty yards wide and had an iron barrier across the river on the north side of town so enemies could not enter through the waterway. On the outside of the moat, there were four-foot walls and a glacis. There were inner walls inside the citadel, with earthworks. The casements were pretty good. It would be a tough nut to crack. Overall, he was glad that he was on the inside looking out.

The mayor stood next to him, pointing out in detail that things had been bad enough, this past year, without *this*. Namely, in December of 1631 the bishop had fled from Bamberg to Forchheim, bringing along the cathedral treasure. Then in February a Swedish colonel named Hastver who had been besieging Höchstadt an der Aisch came down with a detachment, drove away the imperials who were camped along the Regnitz, and burned the wooden supports out from under the bridge across the Regnitz. Then in March, Field Marshall Tilly had come along, marching toward Bamberg with twenty thousand men. He had stopped at Forchheim to negotiate with the bishop. While he was at it, he had requisitioned almost all of the city's reserve supplies. His army, of course, had brought disease with it. Since then, hundreds of people in Forchheim had died of hunger and typhus.

Then, in May, Duke Maximilian of Bavaria had sent the colonel and the troops he commanded to reinforce the garrison. To "help" the bishop; Duke Maximilian had said frankly that Forchheim was too valuable to let the bishop manage its defense. Just barely in time, considering that the Swedes and the Nürnbergs had attacked again not two weeks later. And again in July. Beaten back both times, of course, for which the city fathers were duly grateful.

After the Alte Veste, Wallenstein's retreating army had come through, taking more food and leaving more disease.

Then, when the bishop fled again in the fall of 1632 after Wallenstein's defeat at the Alte Veste, he had left the treasure behind. That meant that the town—which meant the colonel—was now responsible for its safety. But rations were running out. Fast. While the mayor understood, of course, that the soldiers of the garrison naturally had first claim on what food remained, nonetheless . . .

The mayor's voice trailed off.

Colonel von Schletz grunted. It wasn't as if he had not heard the whole lament before.

But what he was seeing now was something new. Not a siege. Most of what was happening outside Forchheim was in sight, but out of cannon shot. At least, out of shot of any artillery he had available in the city, which weren't bad. He could shoot as far as the Regnitz bridge or the Keller Forest. Forchheim had the only powder mill in the prince-bishopric of Bamberg. He could keep the cannon supplied with powder until they ran out of supplies to manufacture it. Which they would, soon. But, at present, he did not have anything to shoot at.

The up-timers ought to be sending a challenge. Something dramatic on the order of: "We will burn Forchheim to ashes!" That would allow him to reply something on the order of: "The city still has enough beer and wine to put out the fire without resorting to water."

It was a ritual. It wasn't for nothing that the Forchheimer had picked up the nickname of *Mauerscheisser* because of their mode of demonstrating that that there was still food inside the walls, too. After all, that which went in must come out. They figured that it might as well come out in a location that made a point.

At that stage, the besiegers should start to burn down the surrounding villages, forcing the farmers to take refuge in the woods, hunting them down like animals. But he had a feeling that it was not likely. Instead, the farmers who were still around were planting undisturbed. The up-timers were, apparently, even attempting to provide them with draft animals.

And they were undertaking some kind of construction.

If it were an effort to divert the stream of the Wiesent, depriving Forchheim of its water supply, he could understand it. It could be done, he thought, if they started up around Gosberg. But there was no sign of that.

The motto of von Schletz was: "I will hold this place." Which he intended to do, no matter how hardly he had to treat the townspeople.

For that matter, no matter how hardly he had to treat the gentleman canons of the Bamberg cathedral chapter. They had also fled to Forchheim and had not, most of them, managed to get out of town when the bishop did.

For most of the past year, Colonel von Schletz had managed to do more than hold Forchheim. He had responded to every attack with night-and-day cannon shots, no matter what the weather, so they got no rest. They had taken away more losses than his own men. Then, when Tilly fell, he had become *de facto* the imperial commander for the entire region. Well, *episcopal* commander, of course, if one wanted to be technical about it. Through the summer of 1632, when he wasn't dealing with the occasional besiegers, he had sent out dragoons and foraging parties, near and far, raiding through the area to deny its resources to the enemy. And, of course, bring in as much as possible, so it would be there when the next siege party came along.

The farmers complained, of course, just like the townspeople. It couldn't be helped. That was the nature of war. This summer, though, he couldn't get out to raid because of the way these allies of the Swedes had burned clear every inch of land between Forchheim's walls and their own perimeter. Every time he tried a sally, he was turned back. No matter which gate he came out of. He had no idea how the up-timers did it.

But what in hell were the Swedes doing now? Or, more precisely, the up-timers? He knew that the forces outside Forchheim were no longer really Swedes, but he continued to think of them that way.

One up-timer. Walter Miller, the visitors said his name was. He was living in Eggolsheim-Neuses and setting up the outlines of the local administration. Plus, there were five hundred or so soldiers. Not more, von Schletz thought. And a lot of laborers. Really a lot of laborers. But they were not building siege works.

Forchheim, July, 1633

The mayor pointed out in detail that Forchheim's economy was in ruins. The owners of the inns, the Ox, Moonlight, Lion, Crown, Apple, Seven Towers, Old Post, many others, had no commercial customers. The up-timers allowed people to come into the city. But only people. No goods. No money. They stopped all wagons and pack animals at the distant perimeter and diverted them away from Forchheim. Its citizens could stand on the parapets and see them go. Somewhere. Elsewhere. The people who had come and gone more than once reported that their purses were held by the soldiers watching the perimeter, but actually returned to them again when they left. No outsider was to purchase goods or services in Forchheim.

The mill owners, too. They still had water power, but they had no supplies. Not just the flour mills, but the hammermills, the wire mills, the sawmills. They were all standing idle. There was no one around to buy their products, even if they had raw material.

Many of the citizens wanted to leave. Not, however, at the price of having all their property confiscated. Von Schletz had told them that if they walked out, it would be barefoot in their shirts and shifts.

Outside the perimeter, now, no road led to Forchheim. According to the visitors, the "heavy equipment" brought upon the order of the up-timer, plus just ordinary men and women with wagons and shovels, had dug up the trade route that had led through Forchheim for as long as documents existed. Dug it up. Covered it with topsoil. Plowed the soil and sowed it.

There was a new road, the visitors all said. From Baiersdorf to Poxdorf to Pinzberg. From there to Wiesenthau and Kirchehrenbach. Then across the Wiesent to Mittlerweilersbach and then to the new town of Eggolsheim-Neuses. Another bridge, a beautiful, permanent, bridge, at Neuses.

A beautiful road. Graded, ditched, and graveled. Smoothed and rolled, with ditches and culverts, bridges and security guards. A road that no rational traveler would abandon, even if the political scene should change again. Just far enough away from Forchheim that few travelers would bother to detour to the town. Especially not given the new inns that were being built near the new bridges.

The permanent residents of Forchheim prayed very hard to their favorite saints. The three holy virgins:

> "Barbara mit dem Turm
> Margaretha mit dem Wurm
> Katharina mit dem Rädlein
> das sind die drei Mägdlein."

At present, it did not seem probable that even Barbara with her tower, Margaret with her dragon, and Catherine with her wheel, all combined, could save the town. They promised a pilgrimage. If and when they were allowed to make one.

Colonel von Schletz approved. Prayer was a good thing for civilians.

The people of Forchheim appeared to be praying a great deal these days. There were regular processions through the streets, to St. Martin's church, to the chapel dedicated to the Virgin Mary. The number of deaths, the priest told him, was almost twice as high as usual.

Of course, his men were bored from such a long spell of forced inaction. They tended to take it out upon the members of the households where they were quartered. Sieges were difficult for soldiers.

Bamberg, July, 1633

"I hope that you realize," Vince Marcantonio said to John Kacere, "that the money that Walt Miller is spending on your brain child, on this wonderful new road around Forchheim, has eaten up the entire budget for road improvements in the prince-bishopric of Bamberg. We're getting one luxury road for about fifteen miles. Nobody else is getting so much as a street sign this year."

"Don't think of it as a road," John said.

"What should we think of it as, in your opinion?" Wade Jackson asked.

"Alternative medicine," John answered. "Believe me, a full-scale siege would cost a lot more."

Vince sighed. "True. But a regular siege would come out of the military budget. Not out of the road budget."

Forchheim, August, 1633

Colonel von Schletz decided to try one more sally. The largest of the summer. He gathered his men and led them out in an effort to break through the perimeter that the Swedes had set. Idly, he noted that every woman in Forchheim had apparently decided to do her laundry this morning.

With a final prayer for protection to Saints Barbara, Margaret, and Catherine, the mayor of Forchheim gave his orders. The gates closed behind the majority of the imperial garrison. And stayed closed, when the Swede's soldiers drove them back toward the city's walls. Held by men who had nothing left to lose. Men whose wives and daughters were on the parapets, pouring buckets of boiling water down on von Schletz's dragoons.

***

"I don't know," Walt Miller said to the mayor of Forchheim. "You've still got the river. And a fair bit of infrastructure. But what's done is done. The road is there and it's going to stay. The administration is going to stay put, too. I expect that a fair number of your people can find work in Eggolsheim-Neuses. The laws we've put into effect there establish open citizenship. All they have to do is register to vote."

Walt was feeling a little apologetic, to tell the truth.

"I'm afraid that your town has turned into a historical monument. On the bright side, though, in a couple of hundred years you'll probably start picking up some tourist trade. Tom O'Brien's on his way down to make sure that no imperial or Bavarian troops can ever fort up in the place again, but I'll ask him to leave you enough of the walls to look scenic here and there. That's about the best I can do."

Eggolsheim-Neuses, September, 1633

The company of riders who delivered the month's payroll also brought the news about what had happened to Willard Thornton and Johnnie F. in Bamberg.

Walt Miller barely knew Willard, but he liked Johnnie F. He didn't have anything against Willard, either—a nice enough guy, the few times he had ever talked to him at the Home Center, back in Grantville.

The riders also provided a synopsis of the generally prevailing opinion that the Bamberg officials had dared to try it, the fixed court and the flogging, because the Bamberg staff assigned to the Special Commission on the Establishment of Religious Freedom hadn't been spending much time on the project, so they thought they could get away with it.

"Damn," Walt said to himself. "Talk about blowing it."

Then he went out for the day's work. The formal ribbon-cutting for the opening of the Forchheim Bypass.

In the Night, All Hats Are Gray

VIRGINIA DeMARCE

Bamberg, January, 1633

"Hi, Janie, what's up?"

Stewart Hawker wandered into the back room of the land tenures office in what had once been the official residence of the prince-bishop of Bamberg. He would have thrown himself into a chair, except that there weren't any extras.

Janie Kacere smiled. "Repenting my sins. Not any recent ones. The ones I committed when I was twelve and thirteen that inspired my parents, even though they were far, far, from prosperous, to decide that I belonged in a girls' boarding school run by nuns until I graduated from high school. Nuns who thought everyone should take Latin."

She hopped off her stool, wondering where the down-timers had gotten the idea that a desk was a slanted board set on a pedestal. Up-time, they only showed up as dictionary stands in libraries and in the annual TV show about Scrooge and Tiny Tim.

"I don't really think that the School Sisters of Notre Dame were the model for the famous PNDR who haunt so many 'back when I

281

went to parochial school stories' for my generation, but they came close. Which means that I'm sitting here, freezing my feet and trying to figure out German land tenures instead of being back home in Grantville with central heating." She picked up the brick that had been under her feet, carried it over to the fireplace, grabbed a pair of tongs, and substituted a hot brick at the base of her stool.

Stew raised his eyebrows. "What's a PNDR? Plain old Presbyterian, here, Janie. Not one of the initiated."

She laughed. "Purple Nuns of Divine Retribution. An imaginary teaching order. Heroines of many a legendary saga of chalk and rulers. We firmly believed that having eyes installed in the backs of their heads was part of the ceremony in which they took final vows."

"Gotcha. Why are you repenting your sins?"

"Kleuckheim. Seventy-nine pieces of property divided among nine different owners. The law court belongs to *Hochstift* Bamberg, which means that we, now, have to adjudicate all the local squabbles or find some lawyer who will do it as one of our employees. But they pay taxes split between the collection office in Lichtenfels and a 'canton' of imperial knights. At least, I think that's what the word means, but I thought that there were only cantons in Switzerland."

"Welcome to Franconia. May I borrow one of your hot bricks? I've brought you a list."

"What now?"

"Independent lordships and imperial knights to be found in a triangle between here, Bayreuth, and Kronach, more or less. Mostly Protestant. Lots of people I sure would have never met if the Ring of Fire hadn't happened. There's a feud between families named von Künßberg und von Giech. They both want to tell us their troubles. Regular Hatfield and McCoy stuff."

He moved over closer to the fireplace. "Fascinating places I would never have visited if I had stayed up-time: Schney. Plankenfels. Thurnau. Schmeilsdorf. Burglesau. Mitwitz. Nagel. Teuschnitz. Schmölz. Veitlahm. Wildenberg.

"With castles. I never dreamed there were so many castles in the world. I read a *National Geographic* article about castles on the Rhine, once upon a time, for a school report. Those weren't a patch on the ones around here. Big things, some of them, but more of them are about the size of that absentee owner's house back home in Grantville—the one where they found the elephant gun. Or the one that the Clarks from New York built. Even the High Street mansion where we have the government offices now."

He tossed an envelope on Janie's pedestal. "That's the list. Right in the middle of the other guys, there's a little place called Marktgraitz that belongs to Bamberg, so we're going to have to think about getting the rights-of-way renewed. Plus, from the other direction, there's a report on the legal status of the Benedictine Abbey of Banz. Würzburg says it's subject to their bishop, the guys here say it's subject to the bishop of Bamberg, Fulda asserts some kind of a claim going back to the early middle ages, and the monks say that they don't owe nobody nothin.'"

He paused. "Um. By the way. The couple of monks I found there, rattling around in the buildings, said that Gustavus Adolphus, or some division of the Swedish army, at least, took the abbot prisoner last summer. They'd appreciate it if we would try to locate him and send him back home. There's a note about that on the back of the report, if you would pass it on to Vince Marcantonio. Or to whomever-is-in-charge of locating misplaced abbots."

"Thank you Stew. I think. What next?"

"Next trip will be Kronach and up beyond it, if I have my itinerary straight. Further north. From what I've heard about Kronach so far, I'm not expecting a red carpet. It's a big fortress. On the main trade route from Nürnberg to Leipzig. In a pinch, I'll do what the Swedes did."

"What was that?"

"Go around it. At least, for this time."

"Good luck."

"I'll probably need it."

After Stewart Hawker sat through the next day's staff meeting, he was even more convinced that he would need luck. After he had listened to Matt Trelli's report on Kronach. On what, as Matt said, Gustavus Adolphus "apparently sort of forgot to mention to Mike Stearns" before Grantville sent its administrative team down to Franconia. That the Swedes hadn't actually taken Kronach. That it was still sitting there, unconquered and closed up, a fortress defended mainly by its own residents. The city militia.

When Matt got to the part about, "they have a history of making war, sort of independently, on the independent Protestant noblemen in the region," Stew waved for attention. As soon as Matt finished, Vince Marcantonio recognized him.

"I was working out of Lichtenfels, the last survey trip I made. It's not really 'sort of independently' I think, from what I learned when I was going through the independent lordships up that way last week. There's a little town called Burgkunstadt this side of Wildenburg. It belongs to us—it's part of Bamberg, I mean. The *Freiherren* and the imperial knights that I talked to say that the people there and the people from Kronach actually do organized, cooperative raiding on the lands of the Protestant nobles in between them. And on their subjects, of course."

"It would be a good idea," Vince said, "if we got the other side of the picture."

"It would be a great idea," Stew agreed. "If the Kronacher didn't start shooting at anyone who approaches their city walls. Which includes us. They haven't been conquered and they aren't about to be."

"Who is likely to know something about Kronach?" Wade Jackson, the UMWA man, asked.

After a while, a silent while, Stew realized that he was going to have to say something. "Ah, Meyfarth maybe. Steve Salatto's adviser over in Würzburg. He worked for the duke of Saxe-Coburg before he died. People say that it was probably Coburg troops, fighting for the Swedes, who skinned five Kronach guys alive last summer. Guys who sneaked out of the the city while the Coburgers were besieging it, to try to spike their cannon."

"Oh," Vince said.

"Sort of like scalping," Stew added. "But all over their bodies."

"Ugggh," Janie Kacere said.

"Wasn't the duke of Coburg the one who disapproved of burning witches?" Wade Jackson asked.

"Yeah," Stew answered, "but that was because he didn't believe that witches really exist or do the things that their accusers claim that they do. He knew for sure that these guys were trying to spike his guns. Or, at least, his commander on the scene did. The old guy probably wasn't with them—he was nearly seventy and already pretty sick last year. What was there was what was called the Coburg *Ausschuss*. That, as far as I can tell, is the part of a local militia that actually gets good enough at it to do some fighting beyond trying to keep foragers out of a village or throwing rocks down from the town walls. Compared to the local militia as a whole, who don't usually. When *Ausschusse* get involved, the fighting tends to get sort of up close and personal, so to speak. Old grudges."

Stew seconded Cliff Priest's motion to request that Tom O'Brien be sent from Grantville down to Bamberg to shore up the local military contingent. And he asked that Matt Trelli be assigned to go with him when he rode up toward Kronach and points north.

Bamberg, February, 1633

"The thing to keep in mind is that it didn't start last year," Johannes Mattheus Meyfarth was saying. Steve Salatto had sent him up to Bamberg to give the staff there a rapid seminar on Kronach.

"Most of the Franconian imperial knights became Lutheran during the Reformation. No matter how small their territories are—no matter how ridiculous they look to you—they still were covered by the Peace of Augsburg in 1555. By the *cuius regio* provisions. They had the right to determine their own religion and that of their subjects. Which didn't cause too much trouble until 1624, when the prince-bishop of Bamberg decided to try to force the knights to return to Catholicism. Part of what you call the Counter-Reformation in your history books. Kronach lay on the border, of course, between the Catholic and Protestant princes. And was a strong point. So there have been armed conflicts ever since. With Coburg, with Bayreuth. Even though the independent knights don't want to be absorbed by the Lutheran princes any more than they want to be absorbed by a Catholic bishop, to tell the truth."

John Kacere asked, a vaguely hopeful tone in his voice, whether there was any prospect of reconciliation.

Meyfarth looked doubtful. "It's been years now. And both sides have been equally brutal. Catholic soldiers and militias invade Protestant territories; Protestant soldiers and militias invade Catholic territories; each side retaliates against the other. The forces from Kronach have raided through the whole territory around Kulmbach. That belongs to the margrave of Bayreuth. Also through Coburg. They plunder travelers. They rustle cattle and drive them back to the city. The farmers call them a 'nest of robbers.'

"The soldiers, at least, are professionals. For them, the brutality is part of the job. It doesn't really make much difference to them which side they are on. The militias, though, the people who are trained for civil defense—for them, it is more. The Protestants don't have the slightest qualms about torturing the prince-bishop's subjects. The Catholic militia from Kronach does things just as horrible in the villages subject to the prince-bishop's Protestant neighbors. Nobody has any idea how to stop it. I most certainly do not, if that is what you were hoping for."

"Hell," Tom O'Brien said emphatically. "I did not, ever, not once in my worst nightmares, expect to have a reenactment of Northern Ireland on my back porch, so to speak."

"Northern Ireland?" Meyfarth asked politely.

Tom explained, as briefly as possible.

"Did the people of Northern Ireland try to burn witches?" Meyfarth asked.

Tom said that he didn't think so.

"The Kronacher have been, for the past fifty years or so. The citizens complained. Not because of the absurdity of the accusations but because of the location of the spot chosen for the executions. Prevailing winds, you see. They did not care for the smell."

Janie Kacere swallowed rather hard.

Bamberg, March, 1633

When Tom O'Brien came down to Bamberg, he brought his wife Stacey and his daughter Amanda. Except for John and Janie Kacere, and Bennett and Marion Norris, whose kids were grown and who had come as working couples, Tom was the only up-timer in Bamberg who had his wife with him. Vince's wife, Cliff's, Wade's—they had all stayed in Grantville, because they had jobs to do. They couldn't drop them and come to Bamberg any time soon.

Stew Hawker was thinking. His wife Lesley was helping his parents run the farm; Barbara Marcantonio and Summer Jackson were both practical nurses; Summer was also in the fire department. Maybe, once Grantville managed to get a few more women through the LPN classes and train some more down-timers as fire fighters, they could be spared.

Maybe.

After all, Bamberg could use a couple of LPNs, too. Stew Hawker, now assigned to the new "Hearts and Minds" team, was drafting an argument that explained how very helpful they would be on his and the EMT Matewski's projects. That would be great for Vince and Wade, if it worked. If some miracle didn't happen that let them go back home themselves. If some disaster didn't happen that meant they would never go back home at all.

Whether Stew could talk his father into doing what the other farmers inside the Ring of Fire had done and hire a couple of down-time hands was another question. Stew's dad was one stubborn old man.

Stew filed his proposal until it would be the right time to bring it out. He would really like to have Lesley here, he thought, if he had to stay much longer. But he couldn't exactly make his father do something.

Maybe, though, if Lesley just up and left for Bamberg, Willie Ray Hudson could make him hire someone. It was a thought, anyhow.

"You know, Janie," Stacey O'Brien was saying, "I never had the slightest idea that you could speak Latin. And I've known you ever since I married Tom."

"It's not exactly the sort of thing that comes up in conversation. Not even the church services use it any more. The funniest thing is that when I was filling out Ed Piazza and Melissa Mailey's questionnaire on 'what skills do you have,' I almost didn't put it down. Just like Roberta Sutter didn't put down that she could read the handwriting that they have down-time. I thought they meant useful things, like nursing and such. After all, when the census up-time had a line that asked if I spoke any foreign languages, I always said no. 'Cause I don't speak it, really. I just read and write it."

Kronach, April, 1633

Carl Neustetter, who was also called by the name Stürmer, stood on the walls of Kronach. Watching a young man with binoculars watch him. There were some things for which the farsightedness of an old man was no problem.

He was no longer as young as he used to be. He didn't deny that. He had, after all, been military commander of the city and fortress of Kronach, of the entire Kronach *Amt*, for more than twenty years. So when the war moved into Franconia in 1631, first the Swedes and then the imperials, the bishop of Bamberg had sent him some reinforcements. A "military adviser," the Bavarian officer Francesco de Melon. Really, given that any practical assistance was far more likely to come from Maximilian of Bavaria than from the Austrians, his boss now. And one of the bishop's relatives, a canon in the Bamberg cathedral chapter: Wolf Philipp Fuchs von Dornheim.

The three men had been through a lot together, already. He had developed a grudging respect for de Melon. For the bishop's cousin . . . He shook his head.

The first major enemy attack on Kronach had come in May, 1632. The inhabitants of the neighboring Protestant territories had not needed much encouragement to attack Kronach. They hated the Kronacher already. A Swedish commander, Colonel Claus Hastver, brought the Coburg militia, the *Ausschuss*, to attack. Kronach beat them back. Then Margrave Christian of Bayreuth tried it with troops from Kulmbach. They didn't have any more success with a direct attack, so he moved to a siege. It had been during that period, on June 13, 1632, that the death registers of the Kronach parish recorded the deaths of the five volunteers from the city's own *Ausschuss*—the skinned men.

Thank God for the militia, he thought. He looked at the banners moving below him. One with the walled tower and three roses of the Rosenberg. One with the arms of the bishop of Bamberg. One with his own arms and colors. Or those of his house, at least. Armed, armored, drilled regularly on the muster place. The city was very short on regular troops. So far, the skills of the militia had been the deciding factor in repelling attacks by the Swedes and their allies. And the city did, at least, have a resident gunsmith. Guns that broke could be repaired and put back into use.

If he only knew what these new allies of Gustavus Adolphus intended to do. He had heard stories of the Wartburg. Probably every imperial and Bavarian garrison commander had heard stories of what they did to the Spanish at the Wartburg.

So far, they had shown none of the war machines outside the walls of Kronach. He would wait. There was nothing to be gained by impetuousness.

He wondered who was going to pay for it all, now that the bishop had fled and the up-timers were collecting the taxes. There were some possibilities, if the imperial troops came back. The previous year, Ernst von Wildenstein at Weissenbrunn had declared for the Protestant side. Wallenstein had declared him guilty of high treason and transferred his possessions to Kronach. Which did not mean, penned up as they were, that they actually had possession of his estates. There were some other possibilities, as well. Maybe the properties of Veit von Redwitz at Theisenort. He had declared for the Protestants also, so if the imperials came back, there would be estates available at Stockheim; others in the Haßlach valley.

He continued to think about the realities of financing war as the militia drilled in the cramped space of the market square. When they weren't under siege, the city maintained its own shooting range and muster place outside of the walls. When it was under siege, then they just had to make do.

Kronach, May, 1633

Matt Trelli had spent a lot of time studying the walls and towers of Kronach—more specifically, of the *Festung* Rosenberg as well as the city itself—with the best binoculars that Grantville had been able to provide to Cliff Priest. Partly by himself; some of the time with Tom O'Brien; and finally with both Tom and Cliff. Then, by the end of the month, all three of them with Scott Blackwell, Cliff's boss from Würzburg.

He was sort of glad—well, more than sort of glad—that the rest of them agreed with him. There was no way that Grantville could take that fortress. Not with the resources they had available in Bamberg. Not with any resources they were likely to have in Bamberg any time soon.

At least, he thought to himself, with some relief, he wasn't just a gloom-and-doom-sayer. It wasn't helping that Gustavus Adolphus' allies in the region were nagging them incessantly to do something. In the bloodiest of terms. At a minimum, they thought that the up-timers should be bombarding the city. In their view, the Kronacher were "like the devil, and their women nine times worse."

Getting across the point that the up-timers were here to govern Bamberg for the benefit of its inhabitants, including specifically the Catholic ones, wasn't easy to get across to a Franconian Lutheran. It sure wasn't what the allies wanted to hear, Matt realized. The folks around here functioned on the basis of "an eye for an eye and a tooth for a tooth." Or, more accurately, he remembered from CDC class, what Mr. Piazza had told them that the "eye for an eye" had been supposed to control.

The villages that belonged to Kronach—its "hinterland" was the technical term that Janie Kacere had given him—were a different matter from the city itself. They weren't fortified. The dearest wish of the local allies was to destroy them all, level them to the ground, drive out their inhabitants, and generally do unto the villagers what the Kronach militia had done to them. After all, each village had contributed its portion of men to the Kronach *Ausschuss* over the years. Not that any of them had a choice.

So far, Matt had kept saying no.

Stewart Hawker explained patiently, over and over, that that was not what Grantville's regency here in Franconia was all about. His "Hearts and Minds" team, almost all of them down-timers, started working in the villages.

That didn't keep raiders out of Thunau from burning one village. Most of the villagers. And two of Stew's guys with it. The raiders just went back into the Protestant *Freiherr*'s territories. When Matt went over to deliver Vince Marcantonio's formal protest, the guy who had led the raid stood right next to his lord and said that as far as he was concerned, he would not spare an unborn child in the mother's body if it came from Kronach or was one of its subjects.

Matt had opened his mouth and said, "You didn't, did you? I was there when they buried the bodies."

The man didn't even look away.

Bamberg, June, 1633

Matt had come down to help Stew explain what they were finding out about the status of the villages in Kronach's hinterland.

"Subjects," Stew was saying, "is exactly the right word for it. Back in the middle ages, they were the city corporation's serfs. They still owe it rents and dues. Just like to any human person who holds jurisdictional rights.

"And talk about officially second-class! The mayor of one of the villages, Dörfles it's called, has a copy of the city ordinances. They go to church in Kronach, when the gates aren't locked up tight, that is, but they have to sit in a balcony, cordoned off from the city people. When raiders come through they can take refuge inside the walls—if, that is, the city council decides that there is room and enough food on hand. On market day, for the first three hours after the market opens, only the town's citizens can shop. They have first right to buy anything that the vendors display. The farmers from the villages that belong to Kronach are only allowed to shop after the citizens have taken their pick. Finally, after they've had an hour to look at things and buy what they want, foreigners and noncitizens are graciously permitted to spend their money."

Wade Jackson was looking at Vince Marcantonio. "Have we," he asked, "checked to see what the laws in the other cities here have to say about this?"

Vince shook his head. "It hadn't even occurred to me," he said honestly.

As political appointees went, Jackson wasn't a bad guy, Matt figured. "Me either," he admitted.

Bamberg, July, 1633

By July, five-year-old Amanda O'Brien seemed likely to become the most spoiled kid in Bamberg. Honorary grandparents and uncles were in competition. Until Stacey, taking a hard look at what was happening, brought home Gerhard and Emilia Kirchhof; orphans aged five and three, and gave Tom this melting look. She told him that she was pregnant again *after* the adoption went through.

John and Janie Kacere had acquired a couple of boys as foster children, but they were basically too old to be spoiled, both in their early teens. Both had been recommended by a Jesuit at the church the Kaceres attended as brilliant but poor and without known relatives. Farmers' sons, from rural villages that had been burned out. One from Weissenbrunn; one from Hummendorf. One burned by the Catholics from Kronach; one burned by the Protestants in revenge. Equal opportunity mayhem. Both villages had been confessionally mixed; neither set of raiders had bothered to stop and ascertain the confessional affiliation of their victims.

For the time being, they were attending the Latin school in Bamberg, with tutors to help them catch up, while John and Janie taught them English. In a couple of years, the Kaceres thought, they would be able to take them back to Grantville, to go to the high school there.

*   *   *

Reece Ellis, from the Special Commission on the Establishment of Religious Freedom, came up from Würzburg to see what Walt Miller and Matt Trelli had been doing. When he found out that Walt was down by Forchheim building a road and Matt was up by Kronach trying to figure out what, if anything, Vince Marcantonio and Cliff Priest could do next about the stalemate there, he was less than happy.

A lot of the things that Reece said made Matt feel awfully guilty. He knew that he *should* have been working on the commission stuff. It was assigned to him. But . . . he just didn't have time.

Vince Marcantonio handed Matt a handful of pamphlets. From Jenny Hinshaw, back in Grantville, he said.

The letter in the package explained things. Her husband, Guy, had just been sent off on some kind of special detached duty. She knew that he had written a briefing paper for the Bamberg team earlier, since he had been stationed in Bamberg up-time and had explored a lot of Franconia while he was there. Picking up tourist brochures, which he had squirreled away. She had stumbled across them the week before while she was looking through some boxes in the closet. There might be something useful; maybe not. In any case, they were welcome to use them, but she would like them back, please, when they were done. They were, after all, Guy's souvenirs. But she thought she would send the originals. Who knew? Maybe even the photos might be of some help.

One term caught Matt's eye. And one name. War of religion. You would think that even when people changed jobs, they would at least stay on the side of the same religion. Sometimes, it seemed, it was just a matter of personal advantage. Or ambition. One guy, an artillery general, Count Johann Philipp Cratz von Scharffenstein, had been in and out of Kronach in 1632 in his capacity as Emperor Ferdinand II's artillery general.

Back then, up-time, in 1633, he had been commander at Ingolstadt, took offense at something Duke Maximilian of Bavaria did or didn't do—the pamphlet wasn't very clear on that—and conspired to turn the Bavarian fortress over to Bernhard of Saxe-Weimar. Who, up-time, had still been fighting for the Swedes. The whole thing got extremely confusing. Scharffenstein's plot didn't succeed, but he managed to get away. The upshot had been that in 1634, Scharffenstein, who had helped set up Kronach's defenses when he was on the "Catholic" side had switched sides and turned up as a commander in the "Protestant" army that put the city under siege.

More and more, these days, Matt had a bad taste in his mouth.

Kronach, August, 1633

Carl Neustetter did not know where the plague had come from. It had started the month before. Plague, certainly. Over a hundred people had died, already. If the observers outside the walls were keeping track, they should be counting the funerals.

It certainly did not help that there was no place to bury the dead except inside the walls.

Unless, of course, they wanted to open the gates.

The besiegers had offered a parley. They had not, naturally enough, offered to allow the city to send out its dead for burial. Or to allow the living to leave. The standard way to handle plague was to quarantine it as far as possible.

Neustetter wanted to open the gates. Wolf Philip von Dornheim did not. But, then, he was no longer the bishop's relative. The bishop was dead in his exile. Neustetter had not received any news by way of a human being for nearly three months, but he had always kept a loft of carrier pigeons, as did one of his old friends in Bamberg.

So Dornheim could not veto. It would come down to de Melon. To surrender now, while possibly most of the city's people could be saved by the up-timers' possibly legendary medicines. Or to open the gates after they were dead.

Plague was plague. A fact of life. De Melon was not anxious to open the gates. Not yet.

Kronach, September, 1633

Stewart Hawker came up himself, to tell Matt the news about how the Bamberg city council had ordered the flogging of Wilbur Thornton and Johnnie F. And the rest of it.

It wasn't Matt's fault. He had to be told that that. Vince Marcantonio agreed. Matt was having a hard time of it, watching people die inside Kronach. Cliff Priest hadn't given him the easiest job going, this year. How did the folks back in Grantville expect him to do the Special

Commission on Religious Freedom work on top of it?

Well, he'd tried. Both of them had, in a way, working with the Catholics and Protestants up here in the north. But up here in the north wasn't Bamberg city, and nobody could be in two places at once.

Vince and Cliff needed Matt here.

"You know, Stew," Matt Trelli said. "I just wish that I could figure out the hat colors."

"What the hell does that mean?"

"Like in westerns. The good guys always wore the white hats. The bad guys always wore the black hats. These guys . . ." He shook his head.

Stew nodded.

What really hurt was that in a lot of ways, the people forted up in Kronach were the kind that a West Virginian would want to admire. Even if they were subjects of a prince-bishop, they were at least commoners. Tradesmen and workers, mostly; that was how they made their livings. They'd had a shooting club for nearly two centuries, already, in the town. The citizens were armed. Those were good things. Grantvillers knew in their bones that they were good things.

And, in a lot of ways, their opponents were the kind of people a West Virginian would want to loathe. Noblemen. Petty rulers who extracted the last penny out of the peasants who were their subjects.

"I think," Matt said, finally "that maybe the right words are 'tormented and afflicted.' For what they do to each other, I mean. The words are in a lot of hymns."

Who's Calling This Race?

VIRGINIA DEMARCE

April, 1633: Würzburg, Franconia

Anita Masaniello—who had kept her maiden name when she married and had some decidedly feminist views otherwise, as well—looked at the group gathered around the conference table. A Grantville girl in origin, she had worked in the Baltimore county public library system before the Ring of Fire; she and her family had been caught up in it because they were attending her parents' fortieth wedding anniversary party that Sunday afternoon. In Würzburg, she was in charge of figuring out the land tenure system.

Steve Salatto, her husband, was not a happy camper. "Is this religious freedom commission on top of us, under us, or flying somewhere out at a lateral? Just when we were, sort of, starting to figure out what we're doing."

Anita wasn't surprised at his grumpy tone. Her husband had been appointed "Chief N.U.S. Administrator for Franconia" in overall charge of the administration of Franconia, right after the Swedish king Gustavus Adolphus had turned it over to the New United States in the fall of 1632. They had come to Würzburg scarcely a month later, that October, six months ago now. Despite being a bureaucrat by training and background, Steve wasn't much given to petty fussiness and turf wars. Still, no administrator likes to discover that he's been saddled with a "special commission" which stands outside of the clearly delineated chain of command.

"Lateral, I think," Scott Blackwell said. "But we'll end up having our feet held to the fire for whatever they do."

If Scott Blackwell had a family motto, Anita thought, it would have been: *Cynicism is the best alternative.* Several months as the chief N.U.S. military administrator in Franconia hadn't helped his mood.

"Who's coming?" That question came from David Petrini, the economic liaison. Most of the Franconian cities didn't have an economic liaison, but in so far as Grantville had been able to muster a cadre of high-powered administrators, it had blessed Würzburg with them.

Steve Salatto grimaced. "Well, we—Würzburg, that is—are being endowed with three would-be but not-yet-quite-hatched lawyers, a legal clerk and three security guys. Specifically, for the commission members: Reece Ellis, Paul Calagna, and Phil Longhi. With Jon Villareal as clerk. And Lowry Eckerlin, Jim Genucci, and Hugh McAndrew for security."

"Oh," Petrini said. "Joy."

"Hey, wait. Those three security guys have decent MP training. Them we can use." Scott's mood had actually brightened a little. "If only they would send us some staff . . ."

"Yeah," Steve said. "Really, I could use all four of the guys that they're sending to be this commission. If, of course, Congress had been so kind as to appropriate enough money into our budget that Mike could have sent them to work for me. But, at least, they're sending them. For Bamberg, they're just piling the commission function on top of what Walt Miller and Matt Trelli are already doing. In Fulda, Mark Early gets the job and they're sending Joel Matowski out from Grantville to help him, as soon as they can get him detached from what he's doing now."

"Joel Matowski is what? Twenty-four years old?"

"Can it, David," Anita said. "All of us were twenty-four, once upon a time. People can't help it. But—why Reece Ellis?"

They all looked at one another.

It was a good question. The sections of Franconia that Gustavus Adolphus had assigned to Grantville for administrative purposes were almost entirely Catholic. Somehow, most of the administrators sent there by Grantville had turned out to be Catholic, with just a large enough salting of Protestants to indicate that these assignments were not entirely based on religion.

There had been a vague hope that sending Catholics would be a conciliatory gesture, perhaps. Or that it would make more of an impression upon the residents of Franconia if the news about changes in the wind was brought to them by their fellow religionists. Or ... who knew? In any case, Anita thought, most of the people sitting around the table had known one another for a long time at St. Mary's. The people in the commission seem to follow pretty much the same pattern. Except for Reece.

Scott Blackwell wasn't Catholic, true, but he had recently gotten engaged to a down-time woman who was. Steve's deputy, Saunders Wendell, was Presbyterian—but his wife Jessica was Catholic. Saunders was not in the meeting because he was out arbitrating a dispute between two claimants to a mill pond. The stream of water in question formed the boundary between two *Aemter*. The *Amtmann*, the local administrator, in each of them had issued a decision that favored the man from his own district; the dispute had been appealed to higher authority. Saunders, armed with a sheaf of paper from Anita's down-time clerks that laid out the course of the claims for the past three generations, had set out in the sure knowledge that no matter what he decided, at least half of the people involved would be unhappy and resentful at the end of it.

Reece Ellis. Well, aaah. He'd married Anne Marie Robinson, who was a member of the parish. No one knew quite why, except for the obvious, of course. For Anne Marie, the Rite of Holy Matrimony was also the Only Path to Sex. Anita sometimes wondered whether Anne Marie ever regretted having walked down that path with Reece, but if so, she had never admitted it.

Reece hadn't converted. He took outspoken pride in not having converted. He seemed to mention at every opportunity that he hadn't converted.

Why Reece? Why to Franconia?

"Maybe," Scott suggested, "they've run out of baby lawyers."

It seemed as good an explanation as any. The morning staff meeting moved on to the next agenda item.

*   *   *

"You what?" Reece Ellis asked Johnnie F. "You fucking *what*?"

Johnnie F., more formally named John Frederic Haun, had come down to Würzburg the previous fall with the first set of military administrators that Grantville sent. It had rapidly dawned upon Steve Salatto and Scott Blackwell that all was not rosy in Franconia. A significant proportion of its inhabitants loathed the king of Sweden, did not appreciate that he had assigned them to be governed by a batch of foreigners and Thuringians (which amounted to the same thing, in their eyes) who were almost all heretics to boot, and considered that, in general, they had been perfectly happy in their "loved Egyptian night." So Johnnie F. had been appointed to head a "hearts and minds" program. At which point, he had brought his wife Tania and their adopted Korean son, Dakota, to Würzburg. They had moved into a comfortable down-time house, with no more in the way of twentieth-century amenities than that of any other master craftsman or minor bureaucrat in the city of Würzburg.

"I joined the Catholic church," Johnnie F. repeated.

"We are damn well supposed to be here establishing religious freedom. Not caving in to what these guys believe."

"Religious freedom includes joining the Catholic Church," Johnnie F. pointed out cheerfully. "Now, I admit we mainly did it at first to make it easier to adopt those kids. Tania just fell in love with all four of them at the orphanage where she was volunteering, and it's run by nuns. But it's done more for getting the people down here with the program than anything else I could have done. I didn't expect that, really. But here I am. Trophy convert in person. Hauled out of a variety of heresy that hadn't even been invented in this day and age into the light of True Faith. Nobody around here is impressed by the fact that Steve or David is Catholic. For heavens sake, they all *expect* Italians to be Catholic. There's nothing exciting about it; dog bites man rather than man bites dog and all that; it would only be interesting if one of them wasn't. But me, I'm on show at all public occasions. Which almost always gives me a chance to say how well it worked the American way. Don't knock it till you've tried it, I always say."

Johnnie F. sauntered off. He wished the commissioners well, but he had his own agenda. That, for today, involved vermin control in stored grain and the seventy-eight rerun of his elementary school program. He was also arranging to import alfalfa seed from southern Italy. He'd have done that already if it hadn't taken him six months just to find out that in this day and age the *English* word for it, or some close relative of it, was "lucerne." Once he figured that out, finding the German and Italian words for it had been a snap, so to speak.

When Johnnie F. looked back on his military service since the Ring of Fire, he admitted to himself that he'd made a pretty poor soldier. Not that he hadn't tried. He still did, but he just couldn't seem to get focused on destroying large chunks of men and materiel. He made a pretty good agricultural extension agent, though, now that he had the chance. *Weird that he'd had to end up in the army to get it.* He'd always wanted to be one, but by the time he graduated, the state office was downsizing. His pre-Ring of Fire job in the Clarksburg office of a big timber firm had just been a way to use his degree in agriculture to earn a living not too far from home.

He speeded up a bit once he was around the corner, trotting off to collect his helpers. He didn't have time to fret about Reece Ellis.

June, 1633: Würzburg, Franconia

The Special Commission on the Establishment of Freedom of Religion in the Franconian Prince-Bishoprics and the Prince-Abbey of Fulda certainly had accumulated a lot of paper. Paul Calagna looked around the storeroom with a certain amount of wonder.

"Are we expected to cart all this home with us when we finish up?" he asked Phil Longhi.

"I think so. The Federal Archivist's Full Employment Act of 1633. That's us."

"We've not even *bought* this much paper. I should know; I authorize the payment vouchers."

"What do we spend our days doing?" Phil asked. "Either going out and meeting with local authorities or calling local authorities in to meet with us here. What happens, either way? They *give* us a stack of paper, that's what. Or, more precisely, they give Jon Villareal a stack of paper. Which he files. Here. Say, by the time we're done, a ream of paper every work day for four or five months . . . That's in addition to what we use ourselves."

"I guess I'd better plan to hire a wagon and team, then. One more item for our poor overstressed budget."

July, 1633: Bamberg, Franconia

By July, the commissioners in Würzburg were to the point that they could check up on what was happening in the other parts of Franconia. Phil and Jon held the fort; Paul went up to Fulda; Lowry, Jim, and Hugh went off with three of Scott Blackwell's men to the little enclave of a pugnacious imperial knight. The knight's enclave was entirely surrounded by Würzburg, but for all of a half-mile was itself located on both sides of one of the main roads from here to there. They hoped he would see reason on the topic of transit tolls.

Reece Ellis, meanwhile, went to Bamberg. Where, belligerent as usual, he decided that the local commissioners just weren't up to snuff. Instead of making the commission work their first priority, Walt and Matt had continued to do their regular assignments first. They'd disseminated information on the Establishment of Religious Freedom only as an afterthought and during those small portions of the day when they weren't thinking about their main jobs with the military. Vince Marcantonio, the N.U.S. administrator, and the rest of the civilian staff hadn't paid much attention to the project either. They'd somehow gotten the impression, when two army men were assigned to do it, that this was a military initiative. They had continued to think about tax revenues, public sanitation, and the like.

Reece had to admit that Bennett Norris had picked up the voter registration part of it and was carrying that through, but that was only a postscript to the Special Commission's real job, as far as he was concerned.

If Reece had only expressed his opinion to Walt and Matt, or to Cliff Priest, who was the military administrator and their boss, or even to Vince and to his deputy Wade Jackson, he wouldn't have done that much damage. It would have been, after all, only among the up-timers. But Reece expressed it in public. He expressed it during a formal speech to the Bamberg city council. He expressed his strong conviction that Bamberg's delegation from the Special Commission didn't really give a damn about the establishment of religious freedom to anyone else who might be listening. He made his view very plain—that, in fact, the special commissioners were bootlickers for Vince Marcantonio, who would let the Bamberg Catholics get away with anything they tried.

Any number of the residents of Bamberg filed this interesting datum away for future consideration.

Early August, 1633: Würzburg, Franconia

"So where do we stand?" Arnold Bellamy asked. The reports he had been receiving from Franconia had disturbed him enough that he had climbed on a horse and come down to take a look in person. "Who's calling this race?"

"Paul is," Steve Salatto answered immediately. Anything to head off Reece Ellis.

"Well, then," Paul Calagna said. "If it's a race, overall, I think, thanks to Tania and Johnnie F., who adopted four children from the local orphanage, not to mention Joseph Matewski, who is volunteering at the hospitals when he isn't bandaging up our own people, showing the ladies new ways to cope with cradle cap and other infant ills, motherhood and apple pie appear to be considerably ahead of the rest of the Special Commission's horses. *Apple Pie* has found a down-time business partner in *Zwetschgenkuechen* and the two of them are showing up together on the bakery shelves. Those damson tarts are yummy."

"Be serious, blast it!" Reece snorted.

"I am serious," Paul protested. "*Motherhood* and *Apple Pie* are far in the lead. *Voter Registration* is running a strong third, though. Let's get Dave Stannard's input on that part of it."

Stannard was the inspector of elections for all of Franconia. Of all Grantville's regular rather than special staff, he was probably happiest with what the commission had been doing.

"Yes, it's been going great," he said. "This is one thing that the down-time district administrators understand. If you tell these *Amtmaenner* and their staffs to go out and make a list of all people in their district who are eighteen and over, arranged by town and village *Gemeinde*, they will by golly march out and make a list of all people in their district aged eighteen and over arranged by town and village. Pretty promptly and pretty thoroughly, too. If you tell them to contact each of those people, male and female, read them a page about the responsibility of voters under the N.U.S. Constitution, and register them to vote—at least for the election to decide whether or not their jurisdiction is going to join us; we can't do much about the qualifications for voting in local elections at the moment—the *Amtmaenner* will do that, too. These guys are really, really, good with lists. They send us tax assessment lists; lists of how many draft animals each village has; lists of who owes rents and dues to whom. Believe me; these guys have lists down pat."

Paul took up the narrative. "I don't know if we've persuaded them that voter registration is good for them, or if the existing elites will want to let all the people vote, when push finally comes to shove, but they've thrown themselves into getting it done. If you let them loose with personal computers, they'd put every single egg that a village chicken lays into a cross-indexed data base that assigned it a unique identification number. With provision for transferring the number to the proper chicken, if the egg hatched somewhere along the line."

"Tell me about it," Arnold answered. He had been subjected to the *Joy of Statistics* as represented by an Abrabanel with a laptop, more than once. "Thanks, Dave." He looked at their faces. "The other horses aren't doing so well, I take it."

"*Forget about the Witches* is hanging in there, thanks to Matz." Paul nodded toward Meyfarth, who was sitting on the other side of the table. "The people aren't really going to forget about them, of course. But we have managed to make the point to just about every town council and to the judicial officers of all three of the big jurisdictions, here in Würzburg, over in Fulda, and in Bamberg, that is, that we are *not* going to cough up government funding. So they are, for the time being, just stashing their grievances and biding their time, hoping that the fortunes of war will remove us and they can go back to pursuing their delightful hobby of witch-burning. Of course, we can't do anything about the parts of Franconia that aren't Catholic, and therefore aren't ours to administer. But most of them are Lutheran and Matz's boss is putting on the pressure there. We ought to send him a letter of appreciation."

Bellamy duly made a note about an appropriately flowery commendation to be sent to Duke Johann Casimir. Better, two: one from Gustavus Adolphus and one from Mike Stearns.

"Then we get to *Separation of Church and State* and the other horse in that team, *Religious Toleration*."

"Not so good?"

"*Religious Toleration* is pretty much running neck-to-neck with *Forget about the Witches*. Considering that we've managed to hitch them both to *We Mean It*, who has been lumbering along steadily, like a big old Clydesdale. We've been able to make the point that they have to do it—yeah, we've done that. Protestants can settle in Catholic Franconia. We've imposed that law as part of the occupation rules. The towns can't exclude Jews from trading privileges on the grounds of religion. We've imposed that law as part of the occupation rules. That won't stop them from trying to find sixteen other grounds for exclusion that accomplish the same purpose. We'll have to watch every town council very closely. What we haven't managed is to persuade them that it's a great thing, which is sort of what Congress assigned us to do. If enforcing it was our whole job, *Toleration* would be running pretty well. But the real kicker is that Congress told us to make them like it. Fat chance. On that, we're in possession of a thoroughly deceased equine."

Reece Ellis cleared his throat; Paul continued.

"*Separation of Church and State* is running okay, I guess. At least, as a matter of principle. And it is also hitched up with *We Mean It*. We've told them that that's the way it is. We've told them that we're going to make them do it. The N.U.S. has just imposed separation of church and state. That's what Congress ordered. Beyond principle, when we get into practice, things get more complicated. Let me turn this over to Steve Salatto. That part of it is his game."

Steve had a whole report, with appendices for Bamberg and Fulda. "It's harder to manage in practice, when so much of what we think of as civil government was run by the church here, because the ruler was a bishop. Plus, we've been ordered only to confiscate the property that actually belonged to the bishops and abbot *as rulers*. Not to take the church stuff that was in their names—the buildings where they have the altars and crosses, the stained glass and candles. We've got the bishop's palace, the one he lived in, and are using it for office space. But not the convents and the monasteries and the hospitals and the old folks' homes and the schools and the orphanages . . . We've got taxes coming in from a whole batch of rural real estate, and beyond taxes, the N.U.S. is now the direct holder of a lot of agricultural and residential leases on which it collects the rent, which means that we can pay the *Amtmaenner* and their staffs. That's a good thing. Paying your employees on time is a thoroughly sound idea, from a public administration perspective. It really cuts down on the temptation to graft."

He paused. "That reminds me. We could use a couple of auditors down this way, when you have them available."

Arnold Bellamy duly made a note.

"Back to what we've been doing. I'm just sitting in the place of the bishop, so to speak, for that kind of thing. I'm the State, and I'm trying to figure out what's properly Church and hand it off officially to this guy called the suffragan. Who's the equivalent of a deputy sheriff for a bishop, the bishop himself having run off to the Habsburgs rather than staying here to do his duty."

Steve frowned. Misbehaving bishops offended his up-time sensibilities. "In some ways, that's lucky. The bishop was a Habsburg crony named Hatzfeld from up around Cologne rather than a local, and hadn't been on the job for long. He was only elected in August of1631 and the pope didn't confirm him until January of 1632. After Alte Veste, he scrammed. People weren't attached to him personally, so to speak. The bishop of Bamberg just died last March and they haven't replaced him yet. He was off in exile with the Habsburgs, too, living in Carinthia. Back in our world, the crony also grabbed that diocese. These guys don't seem to pay a lot of attention to the rules about not holding multiple benefices."

"I hear a 'but' in your voice."

"But a lot of them, *Amtmaenner* whom we're paying and all, don't like the idea of separation of church and state, any more than they like our laws on witches or toleration. And, I think, a fair number of them are just doing a 'wait and see' for the time being. They're just biding their time on this too, hoping that old Ferdinand of Austria will work some kind of a military miracle, restore the bishops, and they can go back to the way things used to be."

Arnold pushed his hair back nervously. "That's the thing. That's why I really came down from Grantville. I haven't been able to get any kind of real handle, from anybody's reports, from anywhere in Franconia, on how many people have that attitude and how many think that we're doing at least sort of okay. Not just from you, Steve. I'm not pointing a finger. What I mean is, not from anybody. I'm really surprised that we aren't seeing more popular response. Not just official comments from the city councils and such, but from the ordinary people. It's not that you haven't tried, I know. Press releases. Pamphlets. Broadsides. Handouts in the marketplaces. It's like it's all falling into a pit."

"It's the wrong season," Meyfarth commented cautiously. "You started this commission in the spring. That is planting time; then haying; then harvest. Farmers are starting at dawn and working until it is too dark to see; carters are hauling; farriers are shoeing; harness makers are repairing. By evening, they are too tired to think about all the propaganda that the commission is putting out or to express their opinions about the measures it is taking. Just about the only up-timers they see are your 'hearts and minds' men."

"When can we reasonably expect to hear from them, then?" Arnold Bellamy interrupted.

"It has been too many years since they could work without interruptions and raids, confiscations from friend and enemy. Under the N.U.S., the taxes are still high, but at least they are clear about what they will owe and how it is apportioned. The armies, friend and foe alike, are not just 'taking' or extorting ransoms on pain of burning the village down. There hasn't been a *Brandschatzung* anywhere in Franconia since last fall. It may be a good year. In spite of the problems with the weather."

It sounded to Bellamy as if Meyfarth were doing his analysis as he was speaking. "So what do we expect?" he repeated.

"About October, everything ought to be inside from this year's harvest, and the fall plowing and sowing done. Threshing they can do gradually, indoors. From November through February, farmers gather wood and do chores, but the work is not so heavy. They can go to the village tavern. They will start reading all those newspapers and pamphlets, broadsides and handouts, that have been piling up all summer in a stack on the corner bench. Then they will start asking themselves the real question: 'What does this mean for Unteroberbach? What does this mean for Obermittelfeld? What does this mean for Mittelunterberg?' That's when you will start to hear from them. Or, more likely, to see evidence of what they have decided among themselves, in each individual village. The majority will try to exclude those members of the *Gemeinde* or citizens of the town who disagree with them. You will see people, whole families perhaps, on the move."

Meyfarth smiled calmly at the commissioners. "After all, you up-timers have a saying that describes it perfectly."

"And what," Reece Ellis grumped, "is that?'

" 'All politics is local.' And that, Mr. Bellamy, is why I have advised you not to set your elections on whether the Franconian territories will join the N.U.S. until next spring. Late spring, or early summer; between planting and haying. This is my advice. Do not hold them until each village has had time to think about all of this and about what it might mean for them. They can't know what it will mean. No man can predict the future with such certainty. But to think about what it might mean—that is possible. On this, the commissioners agree with me." Reece, Paul, and Phil nodded.

"The longer we wait to hold elections," Saunders Wendell complained, "the longer the pro-bishop and pro-Habsburg and anti-us, or anti-N.U.S, people have to get themselves organized."

"And the more they will pick, pick, pick. File a complaint here; submit a petition there; write a letter to the king of Sweden; yada, yada, yada." Scott Blackwell had minimal patience with the multiple avenues of political process.

Arnold had an eerie sense that this was just about the point, back when he had been reading the diplomatic correspondence, that he had decided to come down to Würzburg. "Look guys," he said, drawing a deep breath. This was going to be a long, long, meeting. . . .

A Nightmare Upon the Present

VIRGINIA DEMARCE

July, 1633: Near the Coburg border, Franconia

Constantin Ableidinger looked up from the table at which he was working. The breeze was welcome, but strong enough to disturb the various piles of paper on which he was working. He had pressed almost every heavy item in the room into service as a paperweight. A small pewter plate, a candlestick, a small telescope.

He had a housekeeper, too. She was glaring at him from behind his back. He could see her wavering reflection in the glass goblet of cold coffee that stood by his right hand. Undoubtedly, he had committed yet another infraction against her rigid housekeeping standards and she was planning to bring it to his attention. Respectfully, but without yielding.

If he had been paying her wages, she would not be here any more. However, the ram was paying her wages. The ram had determined, some months ago, that his time was too valuable for him to spend it pulling up the featherbed.

Or drinking in the Frankenwinheim tavern with Rudolph Vulpius.

Or planting cabbages in his garden.

His wife Sara had never complained that he was a slob. She had been agreeable and compliant, even when he walked in from the garden with his boots covered thickly in mud. Even on days when she had just swept the floor boards down with sand.

Of course, his late wife's pliancy had also led her to agree that he could bed her right there in the alley behind her father's bakery in Jena. Which had led to his expulsion from the law school.

And to his son, who was standing at the door in front of him. Who had, in this year and a half since the up-timers came to Franconia, stopped being a child. How had Matthias gotten to be fourteen? When would he have time to finish tutoring him so he could enter the university? Was that something else for which his own time was now "too valuable"?

What university should he attend?

"What is it, Matthias?" he asked aloud.

"It's Herr Schulte, again."

Ableidinger thought for the hundredth time that he had never properly appreciated Rudolph Vulpius. Heading a village council took a lot of work. That was obvious to anyone who had ever sat on a village council. But a teacher did not sit on the village council. He worked for it and for the consistory. For years, when he was teaching in Frankenwinheim, he had kept the council's records, so he knew as an observer how much business the council did. Still, he had never understood how much maneuvering it took, before each meeting, to bring the contentious parties in a controversy to the point that when they came before the council, they were either willing to reach a solution between themselves or accept whatever solution the council proposed with reasonably good grace. He had never realized how hard it was to recruit "volunteers" for each of the necessary offices, from fire bucket patrol to bridge and ford inspector to vermin warden.

He wished he had a suitable "volunteer" to listen to Schulte right now.

Herr Schulte was in a feud. Not a formally declared feud, as had existed among the imperial knights long ago in the past, but a normal one, stemming from a brawl over property rights. The recently deceased duke of Saxe-Coburg had, some twenty years before, leased property that crossed the boundary line between Coburg and Franconia to a family of Protestant exiles who came from Austria by way of Bayreuth. The duke had done this because the son of the prior leaseholder, Schulte's father, had abandoned the property, having found a more advantageous situation further south, in the Steigerwald part of Franconia.

So it had remained. But in the awful winter of 1631-1632, Schulte and his family had been pushed out of the Steigerwald when the army of Gustavus Adolphus passed through. Like so many other farmers, he had been dislocated by the Thirty Years War. He was a refugee. So he had returned to his grandfather's old village and was now suing the current leaseholder for return of his family's "traditional" holding.

Of course, one way to explain his actions would be to attribute them to avarice. The Bible itself said that the love of money was the root of all evil.

But at least he had learned to distinguish between avarice and political power. Thomas Paine pointed out that,

> *MANKIND being originally equals in the order of creation, the equality could only be destroyed by some subsequent circumstance: the distinctions of rich and poor may in a great measure be accounted for, and that without having recourse to the harsh ill-sounding names of oppression and avarice. Oppression is often the CONSEQUENCE, but seldom or never the MEANS of riches; and tho' avarice will preserve a man from being necessitously poor, it generally makes him too timorous to be wealthy.*

Constantin Ableidinger now knew more about lease grants than anyone except a territorial ruler or a lawyer ought to know. It was certainly more than he had ever wanted to know about them.

Traditional.

Schulte was, of course, appealing to the Franconian administration run by the up-timers from Grantville—or, more accurately, managed as far as principle went by the up-timers from Grantville and run on their behalf by a gaggle of German bureaucrats—for redress of his wrongs. Ultimately, if they did not settle it to his satisfaction, he would undoubtedly be appealing to the supreme court of the CPE, the Swede having occupied the city where the supreme court of the Holy Roman Empire held its sessions and annexed its personnel. If that court did not satisfy him, he would, if he survived so long, appeal ultimately to Gustavus Adolphus in person as the symbolic "good ruler."

What was the Swede likely to know about it?

Nothing, of course. *Der gesunde Menschenverstand. Schlichte Vernunft.* Common sense. Thomas Paine, in the first American pamphlet Ableidinger had read, a year and a half ago now, had written:

> *There is something exceedingly ridiculous in the composition of Monarchy; it first excludes a man from the means of information, yet empowers him to act in cases where the highest judgment is required. The state of a king shuts him from the World, yet the business of a king requires him to know it thoroughly; wherefore the different parts, by unnaturally opposing and destroying each other, prove the whole character to be absurd and useless.*

Paine was as refreshing as cold spring water on a hot summer day. As Schulte talked, Ableidinger wondered idly if anyone in this famous Grantville had introduced the king of Sweden to Thomas Paine's views on hereditary succession.

> *To the evil of monarchy we have added that of hereditary succession; and as the first is a degradation and lessening of ourselves, so the second, claimed as a matter of right, is an insult and imposition on posterity. For all men being originally equals, no one by birth could have a right to set up his own family in perpetual preference to all others for ever, and tho' himself might deserve some decent degree of honours of his contemporaries, yet his descendants might be far too unworthy to inherit them.*

If not, perhaps he should send him a copy of *Common Sense*. It's views on religious toleration were important.

> *As to religion, I hold it to be the indispensable duty of government to protect all conscientious professors thereof, and I know of no other business which government hath to do therewith. Let a man throw aside that narrowness of soul, that selfishness of principle, which the niggards of all professions are so unwilling to part with, and he will be at once delivered of his fears on that head. Suspicion is the companion of mean souls, and the bane of all good society. For myself, I fully and conscientiously believe that it is the will of the Almighty that there should be a diversity of religious opinions among us. It*

affords a larger field for our Christian kindness; were we all of one way of thinking, our religious dispositions would want matter for probation; and on this liberal principle I look on the various denominations among us to be like children of the same family, differing only in what is called their Christian names.

But perhaps not. Paine had written other things. There was, for example, "One of the strongest natural proofs of the folly of hereditary right in Kings, is that nature disapproves it, otherwise she would not so frequently turn it into ridicule, by giving mankind an ASS FOR A LION."

Considering that Gustavus Adolphus was called "The Lion of the North" and what that would imply about the king, maybe he shouldn't send him the pamphlet.

A year and a half ago, he would have sent it.

Today, he had to stop and think. He had responsibilities.

Powerful people forgave some things more easily than others. They tended to find ridicule very hard to forgive.

Prudence had to be among the more disgusting of the cardinal virtues.

Perhaps the Swede's officials would not be unduly influenced by Schulte's appeal to tradition. Even in this matter, there was some comfort to be drawn from Thomas Paine, who had written: "... A long habit of not thinking a thing WRONG, gives it a superficial appearance of being RIGHT, and raises at first a formidable outcry in defense of custom. But the tumult soon subsides. Time makes more converts than reason."

He only wished that he had time.

Not only in the matter of Herr Schulte's claims.

There was scarcely a farmer in Franconia against whom some claimant did not have some ghost of a reason to file a lawsuit.

It was a situation that made men nervous. The majority of villagers were not primarily worried about the actions of their landlords, or even about the actions of their lords. With the war, landlords were happy to have tenants. Like a barren cow, untenanted farms did not provide milk—or rents, dues, and tithes. With the war, lords were happy to have their subjects within their own territories. Refugees, run into some safer jurisdiction, did not pay taxes.

But an avaricious man, greedy for property, was very often willing to file a suit against the current lessee and the lessor, both.

Claiming "tradition."

Tradition be damned. With any luck, the administrators sent by the thrice-damned king of Sweden might understand that also.

A century before, in the Great Peasant War, *der grosse Bauernkrieg*, Germany's farmers had based their demands upon tradition, upon a return to long-established ways of doing things.

It had made sense, back then, when the landlords were trying to abolish the long-established communal rights over pasture and woodlands. That was oversimplified. But in the Germanies, if one did not oversimplify, the forest definitely got lost in the thickets of individual trees. One reached the point that one could not find a general rule because there were so many thousand exceptions to it.

Simplify, Thomas Paine had written. "I draw my idea of the form of government from a principle in nature which no art can overturn, viz. that the more simple any thing is, the less liable it is to be disordered, and the easier repaired when disordered; . . . ."

The man had been a dreamer. Or, at least, simplicity was not to be found in Franconia. Not in this summer of 1633.

Even the up-timers had learned that. They spent a lot of their time trying to understand land tenure. They spent even more of their time trying to adjudicate disputes among and between various claimants to property rights.

Mostly near the larger cities, where they had their headquarters. Where their writ ran with some effectiveness.

Up here, in a village near the border with Coburg, their writ had not yet made much impact. No villager in this region had ever seen any of the up-timers except the "Hearts and Minds" team. Who were, for them, the bringers of free newspapers and pamphlets. Newspapers, in particular, with Brillo stories.

Which meant that both parties to the Schulte suit, rather than hiring expensive lawyers in Bamberg, had appealed to the ram to decide the issue.

So Schulte's appeal was on his table, under the pewter plate.

And Herr Schulte was standing in the door of the room, expressing the opinion that Constantin Ableidinger could not reach an impartial judgment in the matter because he, like the other party to the suit, descended from Austrian exiles.

Paine had covered a lot in that little pamphlet called *Common Sense*.

*   *   *

In the following sheets, the author hath studiously avoided every thing which is personal among ourselves. Compliments as well as censure to individuals make no part thereof. The wise, and the worthy, need not the triumph of a pamphlet; and those whose sentiments are injudicious, or unfriendly, will cease of themselves unless too much pains are bestowed upon their conversion.

Ableidinger tried to follow the same principle in everything he wrote. For now, he kept his face impassive while he listened to Schulte rant.

Dreaming of simplification.

There was no need for the ram to make his call for restoration of "old, established" usages and rights. Even if, when one read it carefully, that was largely the way the American Declaration of Independence was couched.

That was the path to a continuing nightmare. The more he thought about it, the surer he became.

Thomas Jefferson's logic was not the same as that of Thomas Paine. Jefferson had tried to graft natural rights onto the tree trunk of precedent.

Paine had not. As he put it, "He who takes nature for his guide, is not easily beaten out of his argument . . ."

Simplify.

Alexander the Great had solved the Gordian knot by cutting it.

Why couldn't the farmers of Franconia do the same? Get rid of these thickets of traditional claims and cross-claims? Draw a line and start over? No more one-half of a village under one customary law, the other half under a second and different set, which let the lords constantly dispute over whose law applied to which lands and which tenants. Much less having the lordship fragmented into a dozen or more fractions, and the only recourse the farmers had some city lawyer whose main goal was to maximize the profits for the shareholders, the *Ganerben*.

His mind wandered to his next pamphlet. Benefits for the current lessor. No more disputes over the possible dower rights of the lessor's grandfather's cousin's widow's second husband.

Benefits for the current lessee. No more lawsuits over whether or not a century-past transfer from one party to another had been properly carried out and recorded. No more allegations that a lease for three lives had already expired because some lawyer's clerk had searched the church books and found that the father of the current holder had begotten an older son who was recorded as having been born and died on the same day. Since the long-dead priest had not specified that the child was stillborn, the pile of papers under the candlestick had been generated by the lessor's claim that the child had possibly breathed, and thus extinguished the third life on the lease when it died.

Somewhere. He had read it somewhere, in something published by the up-timers. He had no recollection where it had been or where he had read it. He would paraphrase the quotation from memory, as closely as he could. "The tradition of all dead generations weighs like a nightmare upon the minds of the living." "The past lies as a nightmare upon the present."

The second way was better. Shorter. Pithier.

The first version sounded too much like something that merino would say.

The Franconians' ram was Brillo.

Schulte finished his presentation.

Matthias indicated by a signal that he had gotten it all down in shorthand.

Ableidinger rose and escorted Schulte to the door.

He stood there for a moment, looking up at the ram banner waving from a flagpole at the edge of the village.

He wished he could go out and enjoy the breeze. He wished he could go out into the glorious long day of autumn sunlight. The days were already getting shorter. Soon they would be in the grim, glum, winter again.

But poor Matthias was obliged to stay in the office, transcribing everything that idiot Schulte had to say.

Not to mention that there was still the pile of papers weighted down by the telescope.

The young pastor Otto Schaeffer had left Frankenwinheim and taken a position in a parish under the patronage of one of the most intransigent imperial knights in Bayreuch. Fuchs von Bimbach, the name was. From that perch of safety, he was peppering Franconia with pamphlets asserting that Christianity required that believers who had been offended turn the other cheek and forgive seventy times seven. So. Back to *Common Sense.*

> *But if you say, you can still pass the violations over, then I ask, hath your house been burnt? Hath your property been destroyed before your face? Are your wife and children destitute of a bed to lie on, or bread to live on? Have you lost a parent or a child by their hands, and yourself the ruined and wretched survivor? If you have not, then are you not a judge of those who have. But if you have, and can still shake hands with the murderers, then are you unworthy the name of husband, father, friend or lover, and whatever may be your rank or title in life, you have the heart of a coward, and the spirit of a sycophant.*

Yet another pamphlet to write and send to Else Kronacher in Bamberg. He wouldn't even be violating his principle against personal recriminations in political controversy. Paine had been writing in another future, nearly a century and a half from now. He had never heard of Otto Schaeffer, so certainly could not have called him a coward and a sycophant.

Could he? No, of course not. It was just an academic quotation. Schaeffer couldn't possibly take offense at the ram for including it.

Else Kronacher. She was the only woman he could think of who was more intransigent than his housekeeper. She was writing pamphlets herself now. The ram had its ewe. Ewegenia, she used as her pseudonym. The last pamphlet she wrote, he thought, had been deliberately meant to tweak his own fondness for Paine. Frau Kronacher had started with a quotation from *Common Sense* in regard to kingship:

> *But there is another and great distinction for which no truly natural or religious reason can be assigned, and that is the distinction of men into KINGS and SUBJECTS. Male and female are the distinctions of nature, good and bad the distinctions of Heaven; but how a race of men came into the world so exalted above the rest, and distinguished like some new species, is worth inquiring into, and whether they are the means of happiness or of misery to mankind.*

Else Kronacher did not care for the political implications of the statement that male and female were distinctions of nature.

Perhaps he could get rid of his housekeeper by proposing to Frau Kronacher's daughter Martha? He probably should remarry one of these days. The house would be very empty when Matthias left for the university.

What university should the boy attend?

He didn't have time to think about that right now. He had a pamphlet to write. A speech to give. Or several of each.

His time was too valuable now. So they said. Worse, they were right. Paine's words belonged in Franconia this year:

> *The Sun never shined on a cause of greater worth. 'Tis not the affair of a City, a County, a Province, or a Kingdom; but of a Continent—of at least one-eighth part of the habitable Globe. 'Tis not the concern of a day, a year, or an age; posterity are virtually involved in the contest, and will be more or less affected even to the end of time, by the proceedings now.*

A different continent, but it was nonetheless true.

So, for now, his time was too valuable for him to step out into the breeze. He turned back to the table and picked up his pen. Placing the first sheet of paper over one printed with heavy black lines to provide guidance in keeping the lines of his handwriting straight, he entered the heading.

The Past Lies as a Nightmare upon the Present.

At least, he still knew better than to think his efforts were indispensable. If he were not writing pamphlets, somebody else would write pamphlets. Not precisely the same ones, saying precisely the same things, but close enough.

If he ever forgot that, the ram might as well be a king.

On Ye Saints

EVA MUSCH

April 1633: Grantville, Thuringia

"Dem bones, dem bones, dem *dry* bones; dem bones dem bones dem *dry bones* . . ." Willard Thornton's perpetually off-key humming was starting to get on his wife Emma's nerves.

"Willard," she lamented, "I have papers to grade. I honestly do. I am trying to grade these papers. Honestly I am. Please, Honey, please. Take the dry bones out and spade the garden, or something."

"I'll be good," he swore, hand on his heart. "I promise, Teacher. Please let me stay inside. If you look up from those papers and out the window you will see that . . ."

"It's raining." Emma leaned over and kissed him on the back of the neck, then returned to the stack of senior English literature essays.

"*Dem dry bones* would be getting very wet." Willard returned to hunting and pecking on the old manual typewriter that he had gotten back when he was in high school. "The toe bone's connected to the *foot* bone, and the foot bone's connected to the *ankle bone* . . ."

Emma got up. After checking to see that each kid was about his or her assigned chores, she went into the kitchen to make meatloaf. Whatever it was, Willard would tell her about it when he got good and ready, but not one instant before.

Good and ready came on Monday evening.

"I never did my missionary service," Willard said, after he had led the family in their devotions. "Because, well, you know."

Emma knew. In 1980, Willard and Emma ran off and got married the night of their high school graduation, believing (quite rightly, in regard to Emma's side) that both sets of parents would be profoundly opposed to their marriage. Immediate marriage meant that he would not do his stint as an LDS missionary as his parents thought he should; and her parents, whether the marriage might be now or later, considered LDS to be a cult. They were both eighteen, with no more sense than the average run of teenagers. Willard had really been afraid that if he left for two years, Emma's parents would manage to change her mind. So they ran.

They hadn't taken their first baby on the honeymoon, if you could call three nights in a strip motel in Charleston a honeymoon, but they had certainly brought her back with them. She was born dead, barely seven months into the pregnancy. Emma, sobbing, had said that she looked like a little bird without feathers that had fallen out of the nest too soon.

Then Emma had gone through a crisis, believing that this was some kind of divine punishment for the elopement—a punishment which she associated with not having honored her parents. Willard worked at the Home Center, sent her to college, and hung in there with great determination, studying LDS materials on his own. When Emma discovered that she was pregnant again, the same week that she received her M.Ed. degree and seven years to the day after the first baby's death, she had interpreted this as a sign of divine forgiveness and joined the LDS. In which, she admitted to herself, she often still felt rather like a fish out of water, even after more than a dozen years of membership.

Willard was drawing a deep breath. She knew that he had always hated the parts of school that involved standing up in front of the class and saying something.

"You know how we've talked and prayed about how the events in the Book of Mormon are unlikely to happen that way in this timeline.

And we've agreed they were inspired by God, and are as relevant to this timeline as to the old. We're ready. The German version of the *Book of Mormon* is at the printer's. We were certainly blessed that Howard Carstairs was stationed in Germany and kept all his materials after he came home. We're ordering more of the little pamphlets we've been handing out to the refugees here, inside the RoF. The branch has to start its missionary program here, down-time, some time. It looks like the time is now. And, well, Howard wants me to be the one. It's going to be one, to start with. Full time. There's no one else who can go with me, to make a pair. But I'm not an eighteen-year-old kid, either. They can count on me to be responsible. Howard said that once I've sort of, well, pioneered the thing. Tested the water. After that, he said, they can send the boys out. We should pray about it."

Emma looked at her husband. In her heart, she thought that she knew what Howard Carstairs must be thinking. The Church of Jesus Christ of Latter Day Saints in Grantville—LDS, as it was generally called—had served a much wider geographical area than the Ring of Fire. It had come back in time with all of its buildings, but with only a small portion of its members.

Howard was into conservation. He was going to change the way they do things. He wasn't going to risk the young unmarried guys until they'd had a chance to marry; not until after they'd had their families. Willard . . .

Was expendable.

No, that's mean, Emma chided herself. But Howard knew that she could support the kids and that Harold and Arthur, Willard's father and brother, would give her backup if the boys got out of hand. He could spare Willard. Everyone on Emma's side of the family would say: "I told you so." And Willard knew that never, in front of the children, would she break the united parental front.

Oh, damn, damn, damn!

"Well," she said. "If you've been called to your missionary service, then you should do it . . . We'll all miss you while you're gone."

While, not *when*. Never *when*. Furiously, she stamped down the remembrance of Benny Pierce's voice, as it lived in her mind, rendering, "Will You Miss Me When I'm Gone?" at the fairgrounds last fall.

While you're gone. While. Willard Thornton, if you do not come back to me in Time, you're going to regret it for every moment of the Eternity for which they sealed me to you. While.

May, 1633: Fulda

Willard thought that, at least from a distance, Fulda was a pretty place. Getting there had been a pretty decent hike, though, for a guy who wasn't as young as he used to be. At least, the branch had bought him one of Steve Jennings' down-time bicycles. He couldn't ride it a lot of the time, though it did surprisingly well on these plain dirt roads when they were dry and packed. Mud and ruts were different problems, but even then, it was a lot easier to push the thing than it would have been to carry everything he had brought with him on his back.

Willard was transporting a hundred copies of the *Book of Mormon*. Plus quite a lot more paper, all carefully wrapped in waxed canvas. He didn't have much more than that, but it was enough. Especially on the up-hill grades. *If I had all this in a backpack*, he thought to himself, *I'd have had a heart attack at least twenty-five miles ago.*

The bicycle was good. But a grocery cart would have been even better. Willard could be trundling all his worldly goods with him, like some homeless person in the streets of Charleston.

He headed for the city gate.

The bicycle proved to be the focus of considerable popular interest. Willard had to admit that people of Fulda showed far more curiosity about it than they did about any message he tried to share with them.

Wesley Jenkins, the N.U.S. civil administrator in Fulda, observed this with profound relief. Derek Utt, the military administrator, as a kind of precaution, tried to make sure that there was at least one up-time soldier in sight whenever Willard was out door-to-dooring.

By the time Willard left at the end of the month, he had distributed a lot of the one-page flyers and two-page brochures. He didn't know whether the families had kept them. No one at all had accepted a copy of the *Book of Mormon* or invited him for a follow-up visit. He believed that his missionary efforts had probably inspired only the placement of eleven orders at Jennings' bicycle factory in Grantville.

Oh, well.

He dropped his letters for home off at the post office pickup station in the administration building, remembering Howard's announcement that if they were going to be using mature men with families as permanent missionaries, then the rules about limiting contact with their families were out. That had been all right for young men just out of high school who needed to grow up in a hurry, but in this new universe it would be counterproductive.

Wes Jenkins had seemed a little worried about bandits and the bicycle, the whole time Willard was in Fulda. About the middle of May, he had suggested that since he was sending Denver Caldwell down to headquarters to deliver some reports, Willard should leave when the kid did. Willard wasn't finished yet, then. About a week later, Wes had suggested that he should to along with a group of down-time traders. Willard still wasn't finished yet. When he finally decided that he had accomplished as much in Fulda as he probably could, Wes had given him a map the same afternoon.

Shaking the dust of Fulda from his feet, Willard headed off toward the southeast.

June-July, 1633: Würzburg, Franconia

Wes' directions on how to get from Fulda to Würzburg were pretty good. Willard hadn't gotten lost, but there weren't any good-sized towns along the route for him to visit, either. He picked up a packet of letters and newspapers that were waiting for him at the post office, caught up on the news from home, and went back to missionizing.

A month later, Willard felt that Würzburg had gone well. After four weeks of work, covering a city with twelve thousand or so residents nearly door-to-door, he was leaving behind not only another batch of flyers and brochures, but numerous small pamphlets and three copies of the *Book of Mormon*. That did mean, of course, if you reckoned it another way, that he would still be pushing ninety-seven copies of the *Book of Mormon* on the bicycle when he left. He leaned the bicycle against a tree and sat down to rest his feet.

He was also leaving behind one young man, an orphaned journeyman baker from Silesia who had been washed up in Franconia by the fortunes of war, who was setting out to make an informative visit to Grantville. Franzi would be carrying letters from Willard to the branch, to his family, and to the *Grantville Times*.

Of course, there were a lot more people in the territory of Würzburg than just in the town itself—about a hundred and eighty thousand of them, Dave Stannard had estimated. But they were scattered in little villages all over the place, maybe a couple hundred people each, on the average.

Willard had already discovered, much to his dismay, that Grantville's attachment to the installation of signposts and route numbers had not been extended to Franconia. Or maybe the attachment had been extended, but not the actual signposts.

He didn't fool himself about the reason for his plan of visiting first the big towns; then the smaller towns; then do follow-up visits in the big towns. He was afraid that if he left the main roads, he would get lost. Johnnie F. claimed that he wouldn't, but Willard wasn't so sure. Johnnie F. was like a homing pigeon—always had been, even when he was a kid. He was one of those people who just never took a wrong turn. Lesser people appreciated sign posts a lot. Willard hoped that the Franconian economy would pick up enough that the administration could start to install sign posts pretty soon.

August, 1633: Bamberg, Franconia

Willard made it to Bamberg even without signposts, checked in with N.U.S. administration headquarters, said "Hi," to a couple of old friends he knew from his years of working at the Home Center, and found a place to stay that had a shed in which he could lock up his bicycle.

A copyist who was extracting land title registries for Janie Kacere noted that the American *Schwarmgeist*, the heretical religious enthusiast of whom they had heard so much, was in town. He did nothing unusual until he finished his shift. Then he went and reported to Councilman Färber.

Willard had expected to do his work here just as he had before; to go from one house to the next. During his first week in Bamberg, that was what he had done. This evening, he was looking a little doubtfully at his visitor and saying, "I'm really no good at public speaking. I'm not sure that putting up a booth at the weekly market would be the best thing, either . . ."

About public speaking, he was sure. About the booth at the market though . . . After all, the stake in Fairmont had always had a booth at the Grantville Fair, with volunteers to hand out literature and talk to the visitors. A booth in the marketplace might be a way to reach the villagers, too. *A booth might work. . . .*

The next market day, Willard's booth, so kindly furnished to him by Councilman Färber, went well. He handed out a lot of material. He was pleased.

Councilman Färber was pleased, also. If he had known that as a token of his gratitude, Willard had given a copy of the *Book of Mormon* to his wife, the Frau *Stadtraetin*, and to each of his three adult daughters, his satisfaction would have been notably diminished. Frau Färber found the book quite fascinating. Sufficiently so that she tucked it safely away beneath her handkerchiefs and collars and advised her married daughters to take the same precaution with their copies.

The second market day, there was more muttering and unrest around the booth. Stewart Hawker, Bamberg's "hearts and minds" man, was picking up some worrisome rumors. Not bad enough to bother Vince about, of course. But he sent a worried note off to Johnnie F. in Würzburg. Johnnie F. read it, took the morning to clear a few urgent items off his desk, and told Scott he was running up to Bamberg for a few days. In the nature of Johnnie F.'s work, he spent a lot of time running all over Franconia. Down-time transportation had eradicated the concept of "tight schedules." A few days would be a few days, more or less. Scott didn't give it a second thought.

One of the ongoing problems that plagued Franconia's senior administrators, both military and civilian, was that their subordinates who hadn't had up-time military service had been, by and large, brought up on the principle that if you saw a problem, you took care of it yourself, as inconspicuously as possible, without *bothering* anybody. Scott had said to Steve more than once, "I wish that just occasionally one of them would buck it up the chain. I'd have a lot fewer interesting surprises in the morning briefings if they could just bring themselves to do that. Now and then."

Johnnie F. wasn't worried about wasting his time in Bamberg. He and Stewart had plenty to do, even if the Willard problem didn't turn out to amount to anything. Still, on the third market day, he was in the square. So he got to see it all: the arrival of the mendicant friar who attacked the booth; Willard's defense of his supplies; the arrival of the city watch; the arrest. He noticed that a lot of people who wouldn't take Willard's literature when he was handing it out for free scooped it up eagerly after it had been scattered around on the cobblestones.

The court had to have been fixed in advance, Johnnie F. thought. Otherwise, why would it have been so conveniently in session, fully staffed, with no case before it, waiting for the accused and accusers to arrive? He wrote a note, gave it to Stewart, and sent him off on their best horse.

Stewart had only ridden this route once, the other direction, when he came up to Bamberg from Würzburg. An hour and a half later, he bore left when the road forked. There weren't any signposts. The left fork looked to be more traveled. It was. But it didn't lead to Würzburg. That accounted for six hours, right there.

Early September, 1633: Bamberg, Franconia

No N.U.S. cavalry had come to Bamberg in the nick of time. Johnnie F. guessed that his message hadn't gotten to Würzburg—or, at least, not soon enough for Grantville to Save the Day. Again. The show was going to go on.

They weren't going to burn Willard. Or hang him. Or behead him. Or anything else that was directly lethal. That far, at least, the N.U.S. had managed to impose its will. Heresy was no longer a civil crime in Franconia. Although the local church authorities, at the friar's behest, had duly declared him a heretic, the valid statues no longer authorized the civil judges to take action. Willard could believe what he pleased. He was not exactly *welcome* to believe what he pleased, but he had the system's grudging assent that the law guaranteed him the right to do so.

However, the civil authorities of Bamberg had drawn a sharp distinction between privately holding a belief and publicly advocating it. Since the persecutions of the late 1620s they were almost all Catholics, the city's well-to-do Protestants having almost all either fled or been executed as witches.

The Commission's going to have to do something about that, Johnnie F. reflected as he watched. Willard had been duly tried and condemned for inciting to riot, inflaming public opinion, and a half dozen other charges. They were going to flog him, in public. Everything was ready.

The bailiffs hauled him out of the cart, stripped him to the waist, folded him over the block of wood, and tied his wrists to the manacles that would hold him in place.

Johnnie F. left the platform. He walked into the center of the square, taking off his shirt as he went. He knelt next to Willard, on the side where the executioner was standing, and as close as he could put himself. He leaned forward, his arms across the block. There was no way that the executioner could flog Willard without hitting Johnnie F. at the same time.

The executioner looked at the VIP stand. The chief judge raised his hand; then brought it down. The executioner brought the knotted lash down. Again. Again. Until the spectators who had been standing around the square dragged him down to the ground. Along with the VIP stand.

"Why in hell did you do it?" Saunders Wendell asked.

"I went to six o'clock mass in the morning," Johnnie F. explained. "I mean, I've figured that if I was going to join this church, I was going to do it right. I'd actually go; take the kids; things like that. So I went to mass that day, before they were going to have the whipping. And it came to me, there in church. While I was looking at the big painting behind the altar."

"What came to you?"

"We're going about this wrong. Okay, we've all been brought up to think that the proper thing is that when the saved damsel thanks the hero, he blushes, scrapes the toe of his shoe in the dust, and says, 'Oh, shucks, Ma'am, t'warn't nothin.' We were brought up on cowboy movies. Somewhere inside, we know it's the proper answer."

Johnnie F. shifted on the cot. He had a suspicion that even if his heart and mind had no regrets, his body was going to be registering protests about the events in Bamberg's market square for a long time to come. Not to mention those that Tania was sure to file, once she'd made sure that he was going to live.

"It was the picture. Everything in it was, well, flashy, you know. Showy. All the saints and the angels were really strutting their stuff. Doing miracles. Like the Old Testament prophets, calling down lightnings against the priests of Baal. No hiding your light under a bushel, for these guys. They're really into 'show and tell.' And it's mostly the 'show.' They've got to *see* it. Mumbling about it isn't going to work."

He looked around the room. "Hey. Where am I, anyway? And where's Willard? Is he okay?"

"It's Sunday morning. You're in the infirmary at a convent—the local branch nunnery, or maybe a chapter of the organization, if you can call it that, of the ladies that you adopted the kids from in Würzburg. The nuns patched you back together. And Willard. He's in the room next door. The ladies patched him and salved him and bandaged him just like they did you. That was all done before we got here. But we've still put a guard on his door, just in case."

"When *did* you two get here?"

"About an hour after your friends and admirers, whoever they are—and that's a little mysterious, right there, by the way—had tackled the local judiciary and pretty well swamped them. The city government seems to be having a revolution, from what we can tell. Unless it gets too bloody, we're staying out of it until things shake down. I've sent to Würzburg for some more soldiers, just in case, but the truth is we don't have enough N.U.S. soldiers to garrison a city. Not even one, if we were all together, and we're spread out over nearly twenty-five thousand square miles. We borrowed a company of Swedes who were just passing through."

Scott Blackwell laughed. "So they're standing out in the courtyard, whatever, of this convent, singing Swedish hymns. That's the racket you're hearing, if you noticed it. The nurse nun said that the music was *maechtig schön*. Who would have thought that people said 'mighty purty' so long ago and far away? It was cute. I'll tell the story more than once. But running Franconia on sweetness and light, charm and persuasion, isn't going to cut it. What we really need is a regiment. Or two."

"What we need," said Johnnie F., "is a hero. A big *heroic* hero. Us ordinary guys are all well and good for most purposes, but if we're going to get away with this, if we're going to get away with everything that Mike Stearns is trying for these folks, that is. We need a hero. A huge, dramatic, bigger-than-life, grab the imagination, honest-to-God, *hero*! Ask Arnold Bellamy to tell Mike that, will ya? When he gets back home."

Suits

Eric Flint

After Arnold Bellamy finished his report, Mike Stearns leaned back in his chair and folded his hands, fingers interlaced, across his belly.

"Thanks, Arnold. I'll need to think this over and talk to Ed"—he nodded in the direction of Ed Piazza, sitting in another chair—"and then I'll get back to you on it."

Recognizing a polite dismissal, Arnold rose from his own chair. "Thank you, Mr. President. I realize you're very busy, but I'd appreciate a response from you as soon as possible. I'm afraid things are going to start blowing wide open in Franconia pretty soon."

After Bellamy had left the room, Mike got a slight grimace on his face. "Let's hope so."

He swiveled his chair and looked out the window. "Suits," he muttered.

He hadn't intended to, but he'd spoken loudly enough for Ed to overhear the last word.

"He's not a bad guy, Mike," Piazza said mildly. "In fact, I think Arnold's doing as well as possible, under the circumstances."

327

"No, he isn't," Mike replied forcefully. He unlaced his fingers and held up a hand, forestalling a protest. "Oh, sure, he's doing his *job* well enough. Like you say, probably as well as anyone could. The problem is that it's the wrong job in the first place."

Ed cocked his head, just a little, and raised his eyebrows, just a little. It was a familiar expression, that translated more-or-less into: *And now will you clarify that quintessentially Stearnsish cryptic comment?*

" 'I'm afraid things are going to start blowing wide open,' " Mike quoted. "For Pete's sake, Ed, that's what we're *supposed* to be doing over there in Franconia. Blowing the setup wide open, so we can piece it back together again the way we want it. More or less, anyway. Arnold's like an engineer assigned to cut a road through a mountain who's now explaining to me that he's afraid the dynamite's about to go off. Well, hey, no kidding. If I wanted to be churlish about it, I could add: 'It's about time.' "

He slapped the table, half-angrily. "The single most important thing about that whole incident down in Bamberg was the fact that the crowd stopped Willard and Johnnie F.'s beating. Not only stopped it, but tore down the reviewing stand and made real clear to the so-called 'authorities' what was what. For the first goddam time since we started administering Franconia, we've finally got what amounts to a revolution starting—in one town, anyway. A *real* revolution, mind you. Not something we 'administered,' but something the *people themselves* did. And how does Arnold deal with it? He barely mentions it at all in his report, and then as—God help us—a 'problem.' "

Once again he mimicked: " 'I'm afraid things are starting to blow wide open.' " This time, the sarcasm in his tone was right at the surface.

Ed's expression got a tinge of exasperation in it. "If that's what you wanted, Mike, you never should have sent that crew down there in the first place. None of them are really what you'd call demolitions specialists—well, except maybe Johnnie F., and that's more by temperament than training. They're civil servants, and you know it. What did you expect? If you wanted rabble-rousers, you should have sent some of your UMWA guys."

"Couldn't," Mike grunted. "First off, because despite our reputation, there aren't really all that many coal miners who are natural agitators and organizers. Most of your UMWA guys are just regular working stiffs. Ask them to tear down and rebuild a car or just about any kind of machine, and they'll do it. Ask 'em to tear down and rebuild a society, and they wouldn't even know where to start."

He laced his fingers back together. "If I could clone Red Sybolt, and a handful of other guys like him, I'd have hundreds of them scattered all over Europe. Unfortunately, there aren't all that many Red Sybolts at our disposal—and we needed him in Bohemia more than we did in Franconia."

"So, fine. You never hesitate to ask the Committees of Correspondence to give some an informal helping hand, do you? Why not approach them?"

"They're not ready for it. Not yet. Most of them are just youngsters, still. The CoCs are just starting to get their feet solidly on the ground and firmly planted on hospitable soil like Thuringia and Magdeburg. Ask them to go to Franconia at this point, with their lack of experience, and they'll most likely just screw up. You saw what happened in Suhl, before Gretchen put a stop to it. If Noelle Murphy and Anse Hatfield hadn't been there, we'd have wound up with a complete mess on our hands.

Mike shook his head. "So," he concluded, "I just went with the best alternative I had available. I sent what's probably our top team of civil servants over there to do a job they can't do—but can probably manage okay once somebody else blows up the joint. Might even manage *very* well, actually. Those are some pretty sharp pencils in that box."

Ed got a wry smile. "What's this? Am I actually hearing praise from Mike Stearns being ladled—okay, spooned—onto a bunch of suits?"

Mike smiled back. "I don't recommend calling Anita Masaniello a 'suit.' The sneer at her class wouldn't piss her off, but the implied sexism would. With that caveat, I never said they were *incompetent* suits, Ed. They're very good at what they do, from what I can tell. But, as you said yourself, they're civil servants—whose qualifications have never once in the history of the world included 'talent at fomenting revolution and unrest' as part of the job description. Still—"

He sat up straight, unlaced his fingers and planted his big hands on the desk in front of him. "If somebody or something *else* blows it all up, I'm pretty confident they can put the pieces back together properly. Better still, they might even manage to control the explosion and channel it constructively from the getgo. That's what I'm hoping, anyway."

Piazza winced. "Let me see if I've got this straight. You basically sent Steve Salatto and Vince Marcantonio and all the rest of them down there in order to act as a shaped charge—once somebody else sets off the explosion?" His eyes got a vacant look, as if he was dredging his memory. "Odd, though. I don't recall you ever putting it that way to them, in the briefings they got before you sent them off."

"Well, of course not. If I'd warned a bunch of suits ahead of time that their suits would most likely be blown off, they'd have spent all their time since then designing explosion-proof suits instead of getting on with the job of setting themselves up for the charge." He grinned. "Which, I've got to say—damn good people, did I mention that?—they seem to have done extremely well."

Ed's humor faded. "That's awfully cold-blooded. You're gambling with people's lives here, you know that."

"Sure, it's cold-blooded. And so what?" Mike's own expression got very grim, for a moment. "I've been gambling with *everybody*'s lives—my own included, if that matters—ever since we arrived in this benighted century. I don't see where I've got much choice."

Piazza sighed. "Well, neither do I. But . . . what are you going to do if it all blows the wrong way?"

"Tell Gustavus Adolphus that in the middle of a war he's got to peel off a good chunk of his army and send them down to Franconia to suppress anarchy—that we sorta fostered but couldn't control." Mike matched the sigh with a heavier one of his own. "Have you noticed that our beloved captain general has one hell of a ferocious temper, when he gets riled?"

"He hollers right good," Ed allowed. After a moment, he added:

"So. Who's this 'something or someone else' you're counting on to blow everything up?"

"Hell, how should I know? That's a real nice start, what those people in Bamberg did. The core of it, though, will be a farmers' rebellion. Got to be, with that setup in Franconia. But there's no way of telling what or who might set it off. Or—more properly—what combination of someones or somethings might do the trick."

Once again, he leaned back in the chair and laced his fingers together. "There's only one thing I can tell you for sure, Ed. Whoever it is, or whatever it's about, you won't find a suit anywhere in sight."

Part IV: The Ram Rebellion

Eric Flint and Virginia DeMarce

Then he said to me, "Prophesy to the breath, prophesy, mortal, and say to the breath: Thus says the Lord GOD: Come from the four winds, O breath, and breathe upon these slain, that they may live." I prophesied as he commanded me, and the breath came into them, and they lived, and stood on their feet, a vast multitude.

Ezekiel 37:8-10

Chapter 1: "Not the Three Graces"

Würzburg, Late August, 1633

Johann Matthaeus Meyfarth had, somehow, managed to appoint himself as office dragon. He wasn't officially Steve Salatto's chief of staff, but he had his desk in the outer office in Würzburg's episcopal palace and fiercely defended the time of the New United States' chief administrator in Franconia from those who would waste it. Or even might do so.

He looked at the latest arrivals with some surprise. Three up-time women. They scarcely qualified as the Three Graces. Not one of them had ever been as attractive as—say—Fräulein Murphy, who was no more than moderately pretty herself. They were accompanied by a down-time man about thirty. He had to be a down-timer, Meyfarth thought, because no up-timer would ever look quite so at ease in a bureaucrat's formal robe. The man's forehead was practically inscribed with the words: *treasury official*. Each of the four was trailed by a quite young man, in his late teens or early twenties, all of whom appeared to be down-timers, even though two of them were dressed in up-time style clothing. Each of them was carrying a load of ledgers and papers.

The largest of the women announced, "We're here."

Meyfarth cleared his throat. "And you are?"

Not one of the Saxe-Something dukes for whom Meyfarth had worked over many years had a duchess who could have matched the arrogance of her answer. "The Auditors." The capital letters were inherent in her tone.

It had slipped his mind that when Herr Bellamy, the deputy secretary of state of the New United States, made his visit to Würzburg earlier in the summer, Herr Salatto had, in passing, mentioned that it would be a good thing for the administration of Franconia to have auditors. Apparently, it now had them. Forcing to his face the kind of smile with which people almost universally greet the announcement of an investigation by the General Accounting Office, Meyfarth rose, invited them to take chairs, and went into Herr Salatto's office.

Steve was pushing papers. At the announcement of auditors, he asked, "Who?" and pushed another piece, this time right across the desk and onto the floor.

Meyfarth retrieved it. "They announced themselves by function, not by name. As in, 'the bishop' or 'the baron.' They seem to think that you expect them and know all about it."

"Let me take a look through the peephole." One of the first amenities that Meyfarth had added to the inner office was a small aperture, screened in the outer office by a large vase of dried flowers, through which Steve could look out and get a preview of the people to whom he would shortly be speaking.

Twenty seconds later, Steve said, "Holy smoke," and sank down on the hard bench on which his visitors sat. Then: "Coffee. Have one of the kids make a whole pot of coffee. Smile, tell them you're ordering coffee, and that I'll be right with them. Then come back in here through the rear door before you go into the reception room again."

Meyfarth left. Steve headed toward the back offices where his wife Anita and several other Grantville natives worked. This was beyond an old Baltimore boy. "Anita," he beckoned. "I need a fast low-down."

Among the things for which Meyfarth admired his up-time boss was that he was so fast with a summary. By the time he had ordered coffee, Anita Masaniello—she had kept her maiden name—and Fräulein Murphy, who was in the back room with her, had scribbled down the following for him to read on his way back to the outer office.

Estelle McIntire. The skinny one. About forty-five. She was born Estelle Colburn; she's Huddy Colburn's cousin; he's a big muck-a-muck in real estate in Grantville. Married to Crawford McIntire. One grown son. Methodist; she got her husband to change over from Presbyterian when they married.

Willa Fodor. The short one. About the same age as Estelle, maybe a year or so older. Born Willa Voytek; she's Cyril Fodor's wife. One married daughter—that's Lynelle, married to Paul Calagna who is here in Würzburg with the Special Commission. You've met Lynelle—she wasn't about to be left behind in Grantville for who-knows-how-long; she packed up the kids and came along. Willa is Catholic, as you can guess. Cyril and Willa had a couple more kids, lots younger than Lynelle, left up-time, one in college and one in the army. Willa finished high school after she had Lynelle; then started college and had finished two years, going part-time, when she got pregnant again. About then, Cyril and his brother decided to start their own business, an auto repair and body shop. She quit school for a while to help manage bookkeeping end of it; then the next kid came along and she never got around to going back to college.

Maydene Utt. The big one. Born McIntire. Also a year or two older than Estelle. She's Crawford's sister, so she's Estelle's sister-in-law. Also switched from Presbyterian to Methodist when she got married. Bit of hard feelings in the McIntire family there. Belva, the third sibling, has gone off to Geneva with her husband so he can be trained as a super-deacon to help Enoch McDow at the Presbyterian church. Two grown sons; one of them, Farley, has a down-time wife.

All three of the gals are corkers. Estelle and Maydene have some college, too. They worked outside of Grantville as commuters before the Ring of Fire. In offices, somewhere. I don't know exactly what they did. Some early meeting after it happened, one of the less perceptive of the Civil War reenactors got up and started spouting off about how, now that we were back in the past, the ladies would go back to their proper roles and stay home drying vegetables and keeping house. Estelle, Willa, and Maydene stood and started yelling about the stupidity of expecting Grantville to waste half of its talent. Things got pretty lively from there.

Terry Sterling saw the right temperament and grabbed all three of them right away as auditor trainees for his accounting firm.

Added at the bottom, in Steve's handwriting, were a few more sentences. "One of Arnold Bellamy's letters must have gone astray in the mail. Check whether they are here as NUS employees or contractors. Don't have the vaguest idea who the down-timers are. Find out tactfully."

Meyfarth read through it hurriedly on his way back to the reception room. What was a "corker"? The essence was clear, however.

"Not the Three Graces," he murmured to himself. Probably the Three Furies. He shoved the note into the side pocket he had had a tailor add to his robe and returned to the outer office wearing a professional smile. "Ah, Mrs. Utt, Mrs. Fodor, Mrs. McIntire. We are so pleased that you have made the trip successfully. Would you be so kind as to present me to your associates?"

The obvious treasury official was one Johann Friedrich Krausold. He was indeed a former Saxe-Weimar and now New United States *Kammerverwalter* assigned to Jena. The four young men were the next generation of trainees. Johannes Elias Fischer, from Arnstadt; Michael Heubel, from Stadtilm; Samuel Ebert, from Saalfeld; Ambrosius Wachler, from Weimar.

Meyfarth smiled at the young men quite genuinely. Not so much in greeting as because he recognized the eternal verities. Having brought astonishingly few bureaucrats from the future, the up-timers were now growing a supply. Government would go on. He led them into Steve's office.

"The books and encyclopedias in Grantville that told those of us in the administrative teams that got sent to Franconia about such general concepts as *cuius regio* as deciding a principality's religious allegiance and the requirement that subjects accept the religion of the ruler . . ."

Steve Salatto placed his hands on the desk, leaned forward, and gave the three lady auditors sitting in front of him a smile. "I won't go so far as to say they were junk. But they were at least as misleading as they were useful. Or maybe the problem's been with us, and our assumptions, coming to it out of an American background. We thought there would be one piece of ground here and all of its residents would be Catholic; then there would be a border; then another piece of ground over here and all of its residents would be Protestant."

He shook his head ruefully. "When it came to Franconia—dream on!"

He gestured toward the window. "For instance, the Steigerwald—or Steiger Forest, we'd say—takes up a space roughly twenty-five miles or so from Volkach to Bamberg, west to east, and a little under fifty miles from Knetzgau down to Windsheim, north to south. Or, maybe, five miles or so more in each direction, depending on how you count it. Also, it isn't all forest. There are a lot of clearings in it with villages and agriculture.

"The people who lived there swore their oaths of allegiance to a lord. But they have the right to move, which means that they don't necessarily live within that lord's territories. They might rent a farm somewhere else. Or sometimes what once was a single piece of territory has been split up between two lines of heirs, one Catholic and one Protestant. Or a family of lords who were Catholic died out and their estates escheated to a Protestant overlord. Or *vice versa*. Anyway, what it means in practice is that we've run into villages where eighteen of the families are Catholic and fourteen of them are Protestant, depending on who is their lord. It might be the count of Castell on one side of the street and the bishop of Würzburg on the other side. Or, sometimes, if people have moved into houses across the street, all intermixed.

"For every rule, there are a half-dozen exceptions."

"How long has that been true?" Estelle McIntire asked. "The part about everything being mixed up, I mean."

Salatto considered the question, for a moment. "Well . . . say a century or so. Since the beginning of the Reformation, in lots of places. In the Steigerwald area, for sure. There was a very famous lady named Argula von Grumbach—yes, that was her name, believe it or not— who corresponded with Martin Luther and brought Lutheran preachers onto her estates already in the 1530s. When our team went there the first time, some of the local farmers from a village called Frankenwinheim took us to see the house where she lived, and the pulpit from which the first Lutheran pastor preached."

"In other words," Maydene Utt interrupted, a bit impatiently, " 'Catholic' Franconia has a lot of Protestants in it. Lutherans, like in Thuringia?"

Salatto nodded. "Most of them. But a few are Calvinists—and some others are Anabaptists or Jews. They're not supposed to be there at all, in theory. But there they are, anyway."

For the first time, one of the auditors smiled. Willa Fodor, that was, whom Steve had already tentatively pegged as the most easygoing of the trio.

"Sort of like illegal aliens back in the USA up-time," she said.

Steve returned the smile. "Pretty much, yes. Except there's no Immigration and Naturalization Service here to chase after them and get them deported. Not on a national scale, for sure, or even a regional one. Now and then, one of the local authorities carries out a little campaign. But all that does is just mix everything up still further. Franconia's even more of a crazy quilt of principalities than most of the Germanies. If a group gets rousted from one area, all they usually have to do is move a few miles and they're in somebody else's official jurisdiction."

Fodor was still smiling, but Maydene Utt had a frown on her face. "It sounds a lot more . . . I don't know. Tolerant, I guess. Than what I'd expected."

Salatto leaned back in his chair and shrugged. "It is, and it isn't. Depends on the time and place. The Catholic parts of Franconia actually had even more Protestants in them until just shortly before the Ring of Fire. But during the years 1626-1629, the bishop of Würzburg started a big campaign to force the re-Catholicization of the Steigerwald.

"And by 'force,' I mean just that. He sent troops into villages that had become Protestant to drive out the Lutheran clergy, confiscate their rectories and any tithe grain they had in storage, reprogram their churches to be Catholic, and generally pushed pretty hard. In some villages, if there was resistance, the episcopal troops took the adult men as hostages, carried them off to prison in the nearest walled town where they had a garrison, and told the rest of the people in the village, 'either promise to convert or we start shooting your husbands and fathers one by one.' "

All three auditors were frowning, now. Steve continued:

"That's made a lot of the Catholic administrators whom Grantville sent down to Franconia really uncomfortable, as you can imagine. But that's what the bishop was doing, and we can't close our eyes to it. Because of the bishop's campaign, it isn't really surprising that a much higher percentage of the population in the Prince-Diocese of Würzburg was Catholic, officially at least, in 1632 than had been the case five or six years earlier. It also isn't really surprising that a lot of the ex-Protestants are still holding grudges and think that a new administration installed in the episcopal palace ought to be a good time to start getting their own back."

Willa Fodor chuckled. "What a mess. I imagine you weren't all that happy when the NUS administration hit you with the Special Commission on the Establishment of Freedom of Religion."

Steve matched her chuckle. "Well . . . we certainly had mixed feelings about it. Just when we thought we were starting to get a handle on things . . ."

He shrugged again. "But I'm not complaining. The Commission probably helps more than it causes me headaches. Truth be told, I'm a lot more bothered by the ongoing corruption in the area. Government in Franconia—if you can even call it that—has been so screwed up for so long that people have gotten accustomed to cronyism and personal contacts and swapping favors as the way to do things. Can't say I even blame 'em, really. But I'm bound and determined to get that problem turned around, at least, by the time we can think of scheduling a regional election sometime in the spring of next year."

He gave the three women another smile. "That's why I asked for auditors to be sent down here. Whatever else, I've got to see to it that those ingrained habits don't start infecting our administration."

"What are you mostly concerned about?" McIntire asked.

"Contracting problems," Steve replied immediately. "Every time we put out a contract, I know blasted well that most of them wind up getting steered to somebody's friend or relative. People here don't even think about it, really. Cronyism has gotten so ingrained in their habits that they take it as a law of nature."

Maydene Utt's frown deepened. "We can fix that."

Steve thought she was overoptimistic. Wildly overoptimistic, in fact. But he figured Utt and the other two auditors could at least make clear to everybody that from now on they'd have to *hide* their corruption.

That was progress of a sort, he supposed. He thought ruefully—and not for the first time—of those innocent days when he'd been an administrator for Baltimore County, Maryland. Not that Maryland, or West Virginia for that matter, had ever been anyone's ideal of "clean government," he'd admit. A high percentage of the state's politicians, including governors, had wound up in prison, after all. Still, by the standards of down-time Franconia, even the most sticky-fingered West Virginia politician had been a veritable paragon of public virtue. Arch Moore excepted, probably.

Willa Fodor interrupted his musings. "We'd best get started, then."

"I'd say so!" That, from Maydene Utt. Very firmly.

Estelle McIntire didn't say anything. She just nodded. Very firmly.

Steve ushered them out of his office, smiling all the way.

Chapter 2: *"Helmut, speaking for the Ram"*

September, 1633

"And just who are you?" demanded the head of Bamberg's city council, after he and the rest of the council had been ushered into the room at the back of the Ratskeller. The man's name was Seifert. He was big, beefy, and had a bluff personality that he was doing his best to summon.

Under the circumstances.

Which were . . . not good for bluff and beefy Bamberg city officials.

Not good at all. Herr Seifert had only to consider the fact that the Ratskeller in the basement of his own city hall was now filled with men—some of them considerably beefier than he was, and not a few obviously *Jaeger*—who were in no sense under his control.

Quite the opposite. He had no doubt at all that the three men who had escorted him and his fellow council members into the back room were *Jaeger*. Seeing as how their method of "escorting" consisted mostly of prodding the council members forward with the butt of their rifles.

It didn't help that Seifert's expensive clothing was torn and dirty from being slammed to the cobblestones of the square where the American heretic was being flogged, when the mob erupted. Or that he sported several visible bruises, and was certain that he had several

341

others under the clothing that were worse yet.

Especially the one on his right leg. He'd had to limp into the meeting room at the back of the Ratskeller.

Still, proprieties had to be maintained. So, again, he demanded: "And just who are you?"

Constantin Ableidinger considered the question, and how he should answer it.

Stupid of him, really, not to have given any thought to it before. Sooner or later, after all, it was bound to come up. He ascribed the stupidity to a momentary lapse; the product of the constant activity he'd been engaged in since he arrived in Bamberg after being hastily summoned from the Coburg border.

To use his own name would be foolish, he decided, on a practical level. The rebellion might very well fail, as most farmers' rebellions did. In that case, he'd be on the run—if he wasn't already dead—and he saw no point in providing his enemies with an easy way to track him down, much less to track his son Matthias down.

But what was more important was that it would be inaccurate, in a much broader sense. In a manner that still puzzled him, whenever he thought about it, Ableidinger had somehow emerged as the effective leader of this new rebellion. One of a handful, at least. Hardly what a schoolteacher from a small provincial town would have expected!

But that was the key, perhaps. The great *Bauernkrieg* of the past century had been led in large part by theologians and knights. Thomas Muentzer. Goetz von Berlichingen. Impractically and flamboyantly, as theologians and knights did things.

And the *Bauernkrieg* had been defeated, in the end. Disastrously defeated. The number of dead, when it was all over, was estimated to have been as high as one hundred thousand people. Most of them farmers, of course.

Ableidinger was determined to avoid that, this time—the great casualties as well as the defeat. He thought they had a good chance of doing so, basically for two reasons.

First, official authority in Franconia was now in the hands of the American up-timers. Who, obviously, had no good idea how to wield that authority—but who, just as obviously, were not going to serve as a center for organizing a counter-revolution. In fact, if the Suhl incident was any guide, were far more likely to give a rebellion their blessing. Tacitly, if not openly.

Secondly, there was no Martin Luther to stab the farmers in the back. Even if a theologian of his stature were around—thankfully, there wasn't—Ableidinger had been very careful not to give the new rebellion a theological content of any kind. Well, at least nothing that wasn't directly quoted from the Bible by way of Thomas Paine. And only pertaining to the proper powers of the secular authorities. There'd be no convenient Anabaptist extremists, this time, to provide the reactionaries with an easy way to muddle the issue

Keep it simple, uncomplicated—and, most of all, purely political and civil.

Ableidinger grinned. The Americans would like that. It would appeal to their *common sense.*

So, grinning, he gave his answer:

"You may think of me as Helmut, speaking for the Ram."

Some Americans might even appreciate the joke. He'd gotten the idea, after all, from one of their up-time books—a copy of it, rather—that had, in the circuitous way these things happened, somehow worked its way into the house of the printer in Bamberg. Else Kronacher's daughter Martha had lent it to him, one of the times he'd visited and had had to spend a few days in the city.

Galactic Patrol, the title. One of those bizarre, feverish fantasies that some Americans seemed to dote on. Ableidinger had found the book enjoyable enough, despite the overwrought prose and the preposterous plot. If nothing else, he'd gotten a new joke out of it.

"The Ram?" blustered Seifert. "What 'ram'?"

Unlike the other councilmen, who had by now slouched into the chairs provided for them in the center of the room, he had remained standing. An attempt, obviously, to retain what little semblance of authority he still had.

One of the *Jaeger* stepped forward and put a stop to that. A quick thrust of a rifle butt into the large stomach collapsed Seifert onto the chair behind him. More from the continuing series of shocks, Ableidinger thought, than the actual force of the stroke. The *Jaeger* who'd done it was Gerhardt Jost, a man so strong that if he'd delivered the sort of blow he was capable of, Seifert would have been on the floor, gasping for breath.

"Don't waste my time," Ableidinger said. "What difference does it make—to you—what ram it is? Accept that it is, and that it is a ram. Or you will continue to be afflicted by head-butts."

Constantin leaned back in his own chair, and waved his hand toward the windows high on the wall of the room that looked out over the square. "Do we need to make another demonstration? You thought you were in control, here in Bamberg, and would have the American flogged in order to prove it. We showed you otherwise."

Finally, one of the other councilmen spoke. His name was Färber, if Ableidinger remembered Frau Kronacher's briefing properly. The description fit, anyway.

"You *planned* this?" he asked. His jaw seemed a bit loose.

Ableidinger wagged a scolding finger. "For shame! Was it the ram who plotted to inflict injury on the American? Was it the ram who schemed with monks to humiliate him?"

"He's a *heretic*," Seifert hissed.

Such a stubborn man.

Foolish, too. Jost came forward to deliver another butt-thrust, but Ableidinger waved him back.

"Yes, he is. A most flagrant heretic. " 'Latter-day saints,' no less. And so what? Haven't you read the new legal decrees, Herr Seifert?"

Seifert set his jaws and half-muttered, "We did not charge him with heresy."

"No, you didn't. Instead you trumped up civil charges. Do you think everyone is as stupid as you are?"

"You can't—"

Jost was still standing there. He lifted his rifle and gave Seifert a tap on the head. Not enough to injure the man, although it couldn't have been enjoyable.

"Yes, he can," the *Jaeger* growled.

"Do you want us shoot him, Const—ah, Helmut?" asked one of the other men in the room.

Seifert's eyes widened and his red face got redder still. The man who'd asked the question was Hermann Ackers, one of the ensigns of the city's militia. No outsider, he; no rural bumpkin.

"Ackers, you can't—"

Jost tapped him again; harder.

"Yes, he can," the *Jaeger* repeated.

Ableidinger decided to elaborate. "Unfortunately—for you, not Bamberg—Herr Fassbinder is no longer in command of the militia." He pointed a finger at Ackers. "He is."

Stubborn to the point of mindlessness. "You can't—"

"Hit him," Ableidinger commanded.

Jost came around the chair and sent Seifert sprawling to the floor of the cellar, his mouth a ruin.

Ableidinger glanced at a tooth skittering across the stones until it came to a stop against the leg of the chair where another city council-man was sitting. The man—Reimers, he thought the name was—lifted his foot in automatic reflex. Pale-faced, he stared down at the bloody tooth.

"So foolish of you, Herr Seifert," Ableidinger mused. "The only good dentists are in Grantville, you know. Although I am told a German has opened a practice in Jena. The Americans have started a dental school in the university there."

But Seifert was in no condition for repartee. Not that he ever was, of course, being so thick-witted. All that came out through the hand covering his mouth was a groan.

"So it is," Ableidinger pronounced, his eyes leaving Seifert to scan the faces of the rest of the city council.

He was pleased to see that all the faces were pale. That boded well for the future.

"For the moment, you may keep your offices. At least, those of you who did not directly instigate the flogging of Herr Thornton. Until such time as the city can replace you in an orderly manner. Do not, however, make the mistake of thinking your titles have any significance. They have none, any longer. They are merely figures of speech."

His finger lifted and swept across the line of men standing to one side of the room. "That is the new city council in all but name, just as Herr Ackers is the new commander of the town militia, in all but name. Private elections were held, and they were the ones selected."

One of the councilman still had a bit of spirit left, apparently. "But . . . selected by *whom*?"

"By the ram, of course. Who else?"

Ableidinger rose. "Remember. Figures of speech. Or we will have you flogged in the same square you flogged the Americans. And—be assured of this—there will be no one to intervene this time."

A smile came to his face. "Certainly not the Americans. Who are, I remind you, officially in charge."

Within a week after he got out of the infirmary, Johnnie F. had pieced together most of the truth. All of it, really, except the identity of the mysterious man who'd come into Bamberg for two or three weeks and somehow engineered what amounted to a political revolution in the city.

Noelle Murphy arrived just a day after Johnnie F. finished his inquiries. She'd been sent there as soon as Ed Piazza got word of the incident in Bamberg. By Mike Stearns himself, Johnnie F. was pretty sure.

"So, who was he?" she asked.

Johnnie F. shook his head. "I think the name he used was a fake. Even if it wasn't, it doesn't tell us much. 'Helmut, speaking for the Ram.' "

Noelle burst into laughter. "You're kidding!"

"No, I'm not." He cocked his head, looking at her. "And what's so funny, anyway?"

She covered her mouth with a hand, stifling the laughter. "It's a joke. Germans don't even use 'Helmut' as a given name in this time and place. It's almost *got* to be a joke. 'Helmut, speaking for Boskone' was the villain in one of the Lensman books."

"The . . . what?"

She shook her head. "Never mind. If you've managed to reach this stage of your life without having your mind rotted by science fiction potboilers, far be it from me to seduce you to the Dark Side."

They'd been talking in one of the cramped offices in the American headquarters in Bamberg. "Can we get some air?"

"Sure." Johnnie F. led the way out. "I want to show you something, anyway."

Once they reached the street outside, Johnnie F. kept walking.

"What does the joke mean, d'you think?" He waved his hand. "I don't mean the arcane stuff. Like you said, I don't need my brain rotted. Any more than it is already. I mean politically."

Noelle pursed her lips. "Well, at a guess, it's a subtle hint to us."

"That he's a villain?"

"No, no. Just . . ."

But Johnnie F. had already figured it out for himself. "Never mind. Yeah, I can see it. His way of saying he's been studying us. But that seems like an awfully cryptic way of doing it. I mean . . . how many people in Grantville could he assume had read that book? Whatever it's called."

"*Galactic Patrol,* if I remember right."

They'd reached the big town square where the flogging had happened.

"Who knows, Johnnie? Maybe it was just his own private joke. I've been piecing together what I can about this guy, from the reports that have come into Grantville. Not all of them, by the way—not even most of them—are from our administrative staff here. Ever since the incident in Suhl, we've been on good terms with the *Jaeger* in the Thuringenwald and they pass bits and pieces on to us. Mostly, I'm pretty sure, whatever they're told to tell us."

"Told by who?"

Noelle shrugged. "This 'Helmut,' at a guess. Or maybe it's the gunmakers at Suhl, especially Ruben Blumroder. Pat Johnson—he's Anse Hatfield's brother-in-law, the one with a gun shop in Suhl—tells us the Suhl gun-makers aren't sending guns south to the Bavarians any more. But he says they're still making more guns than he can account for. He's pretty sure they're selling them—at cost, he thinks—to somebody in Franconia."

Johnnie F. took a deep breath. "Oh, boy."

" 'Oh, boy' is right. What *I* think—so does Mr. Stearns—is that there's a rebellion brewing here. And one that's already got what amounts to its own armament industry."

"That's got to be worrying Mike."

Noelle seemed to choke a little. "Uh, Johnnie, when I told him my conclusions—just before he sent me here—I thought he'd split his face. Grinning."

Johnnie F. rolled his eyes. "I keep thinking because his title is 'President' that we're still back up-time. And he's entertaining dignitaries in the Rose Garden. All of them wearing expensive suits."

A smile flicked across Noelle's face. "There's an image for you."

The smile was gone almost as soon as it came. "This is the first time I've heard the name 'Helmut,' but 'the Ram' is all over those reports. Something's coming to the surface here in Franconia—something big—but it's still mostly invisible. Whoever this 'Helmut' is, I think he's one shrewd cookie."

Johnnie F. thought about it. "A little on the whimsical side, too, it would appear. But don't kid yourself." He made a little nodding gesture with his head, indicating the square in front of them. "Take a look. Take a close, careful look."

Noelle did so. After about a minute she said, "This town's under martial law, isn't it? Not ours."

"Not . . . quite." Johnnie F. studied several of the men who were sitting at a small table outside the entrance to the town hall's Ratskeller.

To all outward appearances, they were simply workmen enjoying a lunch. But the beers in front of them were only being sipped, and there was too much keen observation in the way they kept an eye on the square.

"Not quite," he repeated. "Not 'martial law' so much as civil law. But it's a very hard hand, and it's very much in control. That's become obvious to me over the last week. And the city council's essentially disappeared. The official one, I mean."

Again, he gestured with his head. This time, toward the town hall. "There are still men meeting in there. Every evening, in fact. But none of them are on the council."

"Who are they?"

"Most of them, from what I've been able to find out, are from the guilds." He grinned. "Not a single member of the printers' guild, which I'll explain to you later. A lot of men from guilds with ties to the rural areas—fishers, boatmen, carters. More from the craft guilds than you would normally expect to see on the inner council; fewer merchants, but some. The real difference is that they aren't all masters. It includes some journeymen who never could afford to start their own shops. And a few members of the old Protestant patrician families who were thrown out in the 1620s. Vasold, Dittmayer. Steiner, I think. Getting some of their own back, even if they have to support a revolution to do it."

"In a word, it's authoritative."

"Very. Don't kid yourself, Noelle. For all practical purposes, Bamberg is already under the control of this 'Ram' we keep hearing about. Even if we ordered out the small Swedish garrison we have in Bamberg, I think we'd get flattened. Worse than Suhl, if we were dumb enough to do what Horton did instead of Anse."

"But they're taking pains—considerable pains—to avoid clashing with us."

"Yes. I think it's more than that, in fact. I think they're using us as their figurehead. Well, not that, exactly. Brillo is their figurehead. We're sorta their fig leaf. Official cover, so to speak."

Noelle was now studying the men sitting at the table. They returned her gaze. Not in an unfriendly way, just . . .

Impassively. As if they were simply waiting.

"Winter's coming," she said abruptly. "The Ram will use those slow months to keep building support. It'll all come to the surface in the spring and summer of next year."

"You think?"

"Yes. Is this what you wanted to show me?"

"Part of it. But we're going somewhere else."

A few minutes later, they entered a street that seemed to be Bamberg's "Printers' Row."

"Where are we going?"

"I want to introduce you to somebody. One of the printshop owners. Frau Else Kronacher."

Noelle raised an eyebrow. "A woman? Heading up a printshop?"

Johnnie F. grinned. "She's having a battle royal with the guild. As you can imagine. Although that seems to have settled down, this past week. As you can also imagine."

Both of Noelle's eyebrows were up, now.

"Oh, yeah," said Johnnie F. "I'm not sure yet, but I think she's real close to the 'Ram.' Helmut himself, unless I miss my guess."

They'd reached the entrance to one of the shops. Johnnie F. turned to face Noelle squarely, his face very solemn.

Johnnie F. was never solemn.

Noelle rolled her eyes. "Let me guess."

"Yup. Your mission, should you decide to accept it . . ."

"Cut it out, Johnnie!"

"Mindrot comes in lots of flavors. I loved that show. Should you decide to accept it . . ."

Chapter 3: *"The natives are restless"*

Würzburg, Early October, 1633

Meyfarth stood watching. He had furnished the auditors with temporary quarters the day that they arrived. Now they were standing impatiently outside the doors of considerably more spacious ones. The Special Commission on the Establishment of Freedom of Religion in the Franconian Prince-Bishoprics and the Prince-Abbey of Fulda was preparing to wind up its work and return to Grantville with its wagon load of accumulated paper.

Well, two wagon loads. The commissioners should have left the first week of September. However, Phil Longhi's prediction of the need for a wagon and team to transport paper had turned out to be inadequate. Paul Calagna had only budgeted for one wagon. When they started to load, they had to scrounge around for a second wagon and team to transport the paperwork that their efforts had generated. Finally, however, the teamsters were bringing out the last crates and barrels.

Relations between the two sets of officials would have been more strained if the special commissioner who provided inadequately for its transport needs hadn't been Willa's son-in-law. As it was, Estelle and Maydene had bowed to the need to be understanding about the delay.

It was Meyfarth's opinion that the up-timers' theories about administration and the way it really worked among them in practice were far from the same. Ties of blood appeared to be as effectual for them as for the down-timers.

The three women were talking in English about what happened to Willard and Johnnie F. in Bamberg the month before. The five men were talking in German about what happened to Herr Thornton and Herr Haun in Bamberg. It seemed as though everybody in Würzburg was talking about Bamberg.

Meyfarth had to do some serious thinking about Bamberg. And some serious praying. He would schedule it into his daily routine.

After Willard Thornton recovered from the flogging, he went home to Grantville. Not permanently, but the bigwigs in the LDS church there wanted to hear from his own mouth what had led up to it.

Johnnie F. Haun, after introducing Noelle Murphy to Frau Kronacher, just went back to work. Harvest time was not the right season for an ag extension agent to be lollygagging around as an invalid. He pulled his "hearts and minds" team together and sent them out into the villages to demonstrate improved techniques in hand thresh-ing. He would love to have them demonstrate threshing machines, but there weren't going to be any threshing machines in Franconia for a long time yet. There were, however, easier and faster ways to sepa-rate the grain from the chaff than beating it with a flail.

Johann Friedrich Krausold found it difficult to work with these up-time women. He had a clear vision of the duty of an auditor. It was to make sure that the government received every *Pfennig* in dues, taxes, and labor services that was coming to it, while preventing local administrators from siphoning any of it off into a project of making their private fortunes.

The women had no objection to that. Indeed, Frau McIntire showed an admirable concentration on tracking down graft and cor-ruption, wherever it might be found. She told him that before the Ring of Fire, she had been a "data input clerk" for the Fraud Division of the "IRS." This Internal Revenue Service would be well worth a man's time to learn about. When he advised her where, in a given *Amt*, the si-phoning would most likely be occurring, she burrowed into the records until she found it, documented it, and drew up a report on it. Krausold did not yet clearly grasp what a "data input clerk" might have been, but he found her descriptions of the internal culture of the "IRS" fascinating. Their conversations were most illuminating.

But Frau Fodor! She had another vision in addition to this auditing assignment, apparently formed by her background in her husband's "small business." As she went around from *Amt* to *Amt*, she constantly told merchants and artisans, farmers and landlords, ordinary *subjects*, that they should be careful not to pay the government *one more red cent* than it was entitled to by law.

Frau Utt was, if anything, even worse. It appeared that she had for some years of her life worked for a corporation whose whole purpose was to *minimize* the tax obligations of the government's subjects. With handbooks from this "H&R Block," she conducted seminars, after her regular work day, designed to teach ordinary people to understand the "rights of citizens" under the tax code.

There was no doubt that their ideas were contaminating the four trainees. Krausold couldn't do anything about it. Under the terms that Herr Bellamy had established for this project, he was the auditors' subordinate.

He could, however, collect his grievances and send reports on them to the proper duke of Saxe-Weimar. To Wilhelm Wettin, as he was calling himself now. He also complained a lot to Johann Matthaeus Meyfarth who could, as a fellow down-timer, be expected to understand.

Meyfarth understood, all right. He also summarized every conversation with Krausold and, with Steve's approval, sent the summaries on to Arnold Bellamy and ultimately, he presumed, to Don Francisco Nasi or to Michael Stearns. *His* proper duke had been Johann Casimir of Saxe-Coburg, who had assigned him to these up-timers. The old duke had died just recently, in July. Meyfarth had regretted not being able to attend the funeral. Childless in his body, Johann Casimir had been a true father to his subjects.

Childless. Meyfarth's mind wandered. His own wife and children had died in Coburg the previous year—the summer before the NUS administrators came to Franconia. Plague. Because of that, he had been free to come. No hostages that he had given to fortune. No one, any longer, on whose behalf conscience could make a coward of him. It had been good to have a demanding new task. More than a year now, his family had been gone. *To a better place*, he reminded himself firmly. More than a year . . .

Since the duke's death, however, Meyfarth served no master. He worked for the government of the New United States. It was a strange feeling, in some ways. Naked and unprotected. Liberating.

The two wagons that the Special Commission was using pulled out of Würzburg. There were guards up in front, and a hired driver for the first wagon. The Special Commission's personnel were in the second wagon, which had considerably better springs, with Reece Ellis driving. He let the others ride in peace for a couple of miles. Comparative peace, anyway, since Paul and Lynelle's two-year-old was squalling her little head off. The two older kids were playing a game in the back. Finally, Reece decided that he couldn't put it off any more. Shifting the reins to his left hand, he reached into the inside pocket of his jacket, brought out an envelope, and said, "Guys, I've got news for us. Sealed orders, but I know what's in them, pretty much. We're not going back to Grantville."

Phil Longhi said, "What the hell?"

"Matz Meyfarth brought the idea up. I took it to Steve and he took it to Arnold Bellamy. Whence the orders. It's too good a chance to miss. We're spending the winter in Coburg."

Phil reached out to take the envelope.

"Why?" Paul Calagna sounded only mildly curious.

"Because Matz's duke died." Reece was the only one of them who had gotten on first-name terms with the German clergyman. "He didn't have any children. The heir to the property will be his brother. That's Duke Johann Ernst, the Saxe-Eisenach one. But *he's* sixty-six years old and doesn't have any children either. When he goes, both little duchies will be up for grabs among the other Wettins. If we let them be."

"What do you mean, 'if we let them be'?" Phil asked.

"Matz was explaining about oaths. These German states being what they are, there isn't any of that business about, 'The king is dead; long live the king.' When even the *emperor* dies, for goodness sake, if they haven't already elected an heir, it's up for grabs. Even when the duke or count who died does have a son to inherit, it's not absolutely automatic. The new guy makes a tour all around the county or duchy and his subjects come in and take something called a *Huldigungseid*. I guess the closest thing would be an oath of allegiance. It doesn't have anything to do with knights or fealty or stuff like that. A *Huldigungseid* goes right down to your ordinary farmers and artisans. They come in to a big meeting and promise to obey him; he promises to protect and

shield them; then they all have dinner. Usually, it's a big outdoor picnic, really. Then he goes on to the next *Amt* and does it again."

"So?" Lynelle asked.

"So, at the moment, old Johann Ernst has been too tired and sick
to come over and collect oaths. The people in Saxe-Coburg aren't
oathbound to anyone, right now. We're not going to be messing around
with the Wettins' properties. They keep their money and their estates.
But we're stepping in and taking a *Huldigungseid* from everybody in
Saxe-Coburg, directly to the Constitution of the New United States.
And if it works—okay, I know that's quite a bit of an 'if,' but if it does—
we'll do it again in Saxe-Eisenach when Johann Ernst dies. And,
gradually, beyond. Just like we did for the folks who got themselves
annexed to Grantville because the count of Gleichen had died without heirs. Remember Birdie Newhouse and the people in the village
where he's farming now? If we keep at it, slow but sure, eventually the
NUS won't be this loose confederacy with lords and things. We'll have
something like a country, with every single person owing allegiance
to the Constitution, not to some lordship."

Paul Calagna reached for the squalling kid and said, "Smooth."

"So we're going to Coburg and we'll spend the rest of the fall, maybe
into the winter, collecting these oaths. The wagon up front," Reece
nodded, "actually does have the Special Commission's stuff. You didn't
really miscalculate, Paul. This wagon has stuff for the Coburg project.
We sort of sneaked it into the storeroom. Steve didn't want any leaks.
Lynelle and the kids can go on to Grantville with the first wagon,
and . . ."

Lynelle said, "Over my cold, dead body."

Reece stared at her.

"Look, Reece," she said in a level voice. "There's no more risk of
smallpox in Coburg than in Würzburg; there's no more risk of plague
in Coburg than in Würzburg, there's no more risk of anything in
Coburg than in Würzburg. The kids won't be in a bit more danger in
Coburg than they have been for the last few months while your Special Commission did its thing."

"But what about getting them into school?" Paul asked.

"If I could home-school them in Würzburg, which I did last spring,
I can home-school them in Coburg this fall. And I can do more than
that. You can deputize me and I can take oaths. Show these folks that
a woman can be a citizen as well as a man. Remember what Saunders
Wendell said that Johnnie F. figured out, up in Bamberg. You can't just

tell people something. You have to show them. Show them that we mean it."

"Lynelle," Reece said, "I'm not going to do that."

"Why not?" Over the summer, Lynelle had had a little more of Reece Ellis than she could endure gracefully. "Since when are you the only one who decides things? Do you think I'm too weak? Do you think that you can wrap me up in cotton batting and stick me on a shelf somewhere the way you try to do with Anne Marie when it's not handy for you to have a wife around? Listen to me, Mr. High-and-Mighty-very-old-settler-Protestant-son-of-a-DAR-member-Mr.-Ellis. My grandparents, all four of them, were the first ones born in the U.S. of A. My great-grandparents went through a lot, really a lot, so they could get out of horrible places in the Balkans and come to better places in Pennsylvania and West Virginia so people like you could spend their spare time looking down their noses at them . . ."

"Lynelle!" Paul said faintly.

"Well, somebody ought to say it. We've all thought it often enough."

The subsequent discussion was rather painful. From Coburg, the front wagon went on to Grantville without Lynelle.

Würzburg, Late October, 1633

"If they can do it in Coburg," Johnnie F. asked, "then why *can't* we do it here? At least for the people who are living on lands that used to belong directly to the two bishops and the abbot? We've taken those over. There's never any use in leaving one of your opponents the financial resources to mount an opposition. Since we're here for the NUS, and we're certainly willing to promise, on its behalf, to protect and shield them . . . Hell, that's what we're down here for. Isn't it?"

Steve Salatto looked a little doubtful. "I'm not one hundred percent sure what the legal status is. We're—that is, the NUS—is supposed to be administering Franconia on behalf of Gustavus Adolphus. I'm not so sure that we're supposed to be incorporating the people into the NUS itself by taking oaths of allegiance from them to our Constitution."

"The suggestion came from Arnold Bellamy, himself," Scott Blackwell pointed out. "And it's in writing. We're covered."

"Well, at least it came to us under Arnold's signature." Steve looked

at the letter again. "But there's something sort of, um, mischievous, about this idea. I just don't see it as the sort of thing that Arnold would come up with. Now I could suspect Ed Piazza of it, if he had time. But since last spring, when would he have had the time?"

Johnnie F. grinned. "There's always Noelle Murphy. It's the sort of thing she would think of and sneak into a memo if she had the chance."

Anita tended to tire of the tendency of the guys to analyze the underlying significance of their orders endlessly. Or, at any rate, tediously. "The point is, are we going to do it?"

The men looked at her.

"Or not?" she added.

"Do we have any idea what the response would be, out in the countryside?" Steve looked at Johnnie F.

"I'm not sure. I could ask around. One thing is pretty sure, though. It would make the farmers on the estates of the other little lords, the imperial knights and the petty nobles, just as jealous as could be. Not necessarily because the ex-episcopal farmers will want to take the oath. Not even because the other farmers would want to take the oath, necessarily. But because we would be giving them the chance. The grass is always greener, and suchlike. When it comes to the farmers who are subjects of other lords, it would sort of double, maybe triple, the effect of what we did when we abolished the remaining obligations of serfdom on the ex-episcopal estates."

"What effect?" Anita asked.

"Well, farmers are farmers, pretty much everywhere. We didn't make the ones who hold leases directly from us significantly happier. That's because they never wanted to render the obligations of serfdom anyway, so they just think we've given them what they properly deserved, which isn't something they need to be grateful for. However, on the estates of other lords—which are not different great big plantations, remember; a lot of times, three or four lords have tenants living next door to one another in the same village—the farmers still have to pay up. Which they think is grossly unfair; they think that they are put upon and badly done by. The farmers on the estates we're administering don't love the boss. But the farmers on the other guys' estates are nursing a major grudge against the boss right now, by and large. That's a pretty big difference."

Johnnie F. leaned back, then forward again.

"To be very un-PC, the natives are restless. Personally, I'd recommend that we ought to take advantage of it. That's where we started

this conversation, I think. But I'd be a bit more at ease if Scott or someone else would come out with me and take a look at things."

Chapter 4: "Last time, it was a work shoe"

Franconia, Late October, 1633

"What's with the sheep?" Scott Blackwell asked. The NUS's military administrator for Franconia was frowning down at the village below them. He and Johnnie F. Haun had paused their horses on the crest of a hill, just above a village somewhere out in the back of beyond. Scott had no idea where he was. In spite of his compass, he was utterly lost and quite sure that he would never be able to find his way out of this complex of hills and hollows by himself.

But he was sure he had been to this village before. There was a really odd church tower to confirm his memory. And there had *not*, last spring, been a huge banner with the head of a sheep on it blowing in the wind from a tall pole where the road ran into the central square.

Johnnie F. had been moving along with his usual complete sense of orientation. Now he looked over and said patiently, "It's a ram."

"What's the difference?" Scott asked.

"Look at the horns. It's male."

"It wasn't here when I went around the villages with you last spring." Scott was sure of that.

"None of them were."

"None of what?"

"The rams-head banners. From here on up toward the border, you'll see a lot of them."

Scott might not be able to tell a sheep from a ram, but, unlike Johnnie F., he could spot possible flash points that might require the attention of the military police from a very long distance indeed.

"Nobody reported on these?"

"Well, the guys on 'hearts and minds' have noticed them. They've told me that they're all around. Not just here in Würzburg. Over in Bamberg, too. Actually, they're thicker over there. Not very many in Fulda. But they've showed up really gradually, and nobody's been making a fuss about them. They're just there, on the poles. Nobody's brought them up in conversation."

Scott sighed. "Do me a favor, will you? Try to find out why the sheep are up there on those poles."

As soon as he got back to Würzburg, Scott had a long talk with Saunders Wendell. This was one of those things that the UMWA needed to know about.

Würzburg, November, 1633

Johnnie F. brought back a broadside. He had collected it in a remote village at the utter backside of anywhere, up in the *Fraenkischer Schweiz*.

"Isn't that," Scott asked rather cautiously, "on the letterhead of the Grantville League of Women Voters?"

"It was that letterhead. Once upon a time. Now it is more." Meyfarth leaned over the table. "See, here at the top. There is your Grantville paper. The head of the ram and the slogan:

> " 'Better to be hung
> For a sheep than for a lamb.' "

"That's your League of Women Voters motto. Then, here, the German version. It's pretty much the same:

> " '*Soll man mich denn erhaengen,*
> So für ein' Schaf', nicht für ein Lamm.'

"But," Meyfarth continued, "they have added two new lines:

> " 'Doch Du, brav' deutscher Bauer,
> Wie ein Bock zerbrich den Damm.'

"That is, oh, let me think a minute-something like:

> " 'But you, sturdy German farmer,
> Break down the dam like a ram.'

"This broadside then has a paragraph that explains it. About how these women challenged your government about horse manure in the streets and won. And that the son of the courageous ewe, the leader of the protest, is now the chief justice of the NUS Supreme Court."

"Oh. Nice." Anita grinned at her private vision of the redoubtable Veleda Riddle sprouting a nice crinkled white fleece on her cheeks and neck to match the carefully tended white curls on the top of her head. .

"Then, here," Meyfarth continued, picking up a different broadside that Stewart Hawker had sent over from Bamberg. "This one has the lines not quite the same. I think that means that they aren't all coming from one source. There must be different versions springing up in many markets and villages. The first two lines are the same, but the second two are different.

> "Und Du, gut' deutscher Bauer,
> sei nun der Bock, der brave Ram.'

"That is, more or less . . .

> "But you, good German farmer,
> Now be the buck, the valiant ram.' "

"Look, Herr Meyfarth," Johnnie F. interrupted. "Up there, if I'm following you, you translated 'brave' as 'sturdy.' Here, I think, you translated it as 'valiant.' "

Meyfarth, who had been leaning over the table, stood up straight, once more silently thanking God that he was a poet as well as a pastor and had a feel for languages. "It's both, really, depending on where the author uses it. The German 'brav' isn't quite like the English 'brave'—which, I think, means, 'not cowardly.' It means really one who does not give in. One who stands his ground firmly. He persists. He endures much to defend that which he protects. Stubborn. Sometimes, even, 'worthy.' Or, maybe, more like in the language of English writers of this day. The 'sturdy yeoman.' Not—how would you say it?—not a flash in the pan."

He raised his hand and recited:

" *'By the rude bridge that arched the flood,*
Their flags to April's breeze unfurl'd.
'Twas there th'embattled farmers stood,
And fired the shot heard 'round the world.'

" 'Brav' would work there, too. For 'embattled.' The farmers were standing their ground. That's 'embattled.' But if they were not 'brav,' they would not have stood to fight. So it is implied in the word that the poet used."

"Okay," Johnnie F. answered. "Got it. I think."

The sad state of twentieth-century public education was demonstrated by the fact that of all the NUS administrators in the room, only the seventeenth-century German had committed the "Concord Hymn" to memory. There were at least two up-timers who did not have the vaguest idea what Meyfarth had quoted, which did not keep them from nodding in solemn approval.

"Then," Meyfarth said, "another paragraph in German, with the story of your Brillo and how he overcame the Merino aristocrat."

"Brillo," David Petrini protested, "is not ours."

"He is a down-time ram, that is true. To some extent, that is the point. But you, you up-timers from Grantville, that is, have made him yours. So . . ."

Meyfarth paused. "So he is ours. And he is theirs—he also belongs to the farmers of Franconia, now. This broadsheet—"

Meyfarth pulled another from the stack in front of him. "—has instructions on how to make a Ram banner. With a German motto. Perhaps, from the ram's story, it began as your English, 'Don't fence me in.' But the German, somewhat, is different. *'Mich nicht bedruecken.'* That is, 'Don't hold me down.' "

"Is that the same as 'Don't tread on me?' " Johnnie F. asked.

Meyfarth shook his head. "They're using that on banners up around Suhl. *'Tritt nicht auf mich,'* with a *Schlange,* a serpent. But it hasn't become popular down here in Franconia proper."

Steve Salatto then asked the question that gladdened the heart of any Lutheran pastor. "What does this mean?"

Meyfarth was delighted to explain. From the perspective of tradition, he produced a long lament on the topic of just how rare it was to find anyone at the bottom of the social pyramid who had a due appreciation of the fact that this was where he was properly placed in the Great Chain of Being and this is where he should be happy to remain, performing his duty in the station to which God had called him. He managed to bring in his observation that the Grantvillers, with rare exceptions among those who had up-time military experience, also appeared to have extraordinary difficulty in realizing that God created the world with a hierarchy, in which some give orders and others take them.

"Fine," Scott Blackwell said, "but what's with the sheep?"

Johnnie F. groaned. "It's a ram."

"It is the revolution that your Committees of Correspondence want. It is starting here in Franconia. With these broadsides. Under the banner of this ram. Not the ram for the children, with the little toys for sale. Even Franconian Catholic peasants, as benighted a group as exists within God's creation, appear to have noticed that the people of Grantville do not care for hierarchies. Nor does this ram. Also, while Franconian farmers are certainly most hard-hearted and stubborn, they lack a certain *élan* when it comes to choosing their revolutionary symbols. No torches held high. No swords. No daggers. No chariots of fire. No rattlesnakes."

His mouth twitched into a smile. "They just have no flair. Last time, it was a work shoe."

"Last time?" David Petrini, the economic liaison, had majored in economics, not history.

"During the Great Peasant Revolt," Meyfarth answered.

"I didn't know you had any peasant revolts. I was sort of under the impression that European peasants just sat around being oppressed." That was Saunders Wendell. The political training that the UMWA provided to its members had a rather pro-American chauvinistic tinge, to tell the truth.

Meyfarth stared at him in utter bewilderment. "That was the one just over a hundred years ago. The big one. It was centered in Thuringia and Franconia—well, Swabia also, to some extent. The *Bundschuh*. Thousands of peasants gathered into armies. 'Hordes,' the rulers called them. *Haufen.* They put down the revolt with no pity. But there have been many since then. Many smaller ones. Some quite large, such as the ones in Switzerland and Austria. Do you think the farmers you meet every day are mostly not serfs now because of the goodness of their lords' hearts? They have been so obnoxious during the past century that most lords decided it was just easier to let them lease the fields for rent rather than try to compel the labor services that are required to cultivate a large demesne. It is to the north and east, now, Brandenburg, Mecklenburg, Pomerania, that the nobles have been trying to force the farmers back into servitude, so they can farm the lands the way that the Americans did the 'plantations' before your Civil War."

Meyfarth paused. "It will be very interesting to see how the king of Sweden handles this in Mecklenburg and the two Pomeranias, since he has made himself duke in all three." He turned back to Petrini. "How come Herr Wendell has not seen this? You have been studying the tax structure as it affects the farmers. I have seen the reports."

Petrini, the economic liaison, sighed. "Yeah, I've been trying to get some kind of a general picture. Figure that taxes, to the government, whoever it is, run a man about eight per cent of the value of the harvest. Then the tithes or other church taxes, about the same or a little more—maybe up to twelve per cent if the landlord is a church or abbey or something of the sort. Most of those are paid in kind—in grain or woad or flax or whatever he's growing. The tax people insist on that, because it cushions them quite a bit from inflation. Plus local taxes. Figure about seventy percent of the harvest left for the farmer, after tax. But he's got to set aside at least twenty per cent for the next year's seed and running expenses. That's in an average year. In a bad harvest, the set-aside takes a much bigger chunk of the whole. So figure that maybe the farmer gets fifty percent of his cash-crop production to market. I'm not figuring in the stuff like a vegetable garden that they grow and use for themselves, even though they do have to turn in the 'small tithes' on that. Those are so variable that it would be hopeless to try to track them without a mainframe and an army of data input clerks."

Johnnie F. nodded. He hadn't been collecting statistics, but from the seat of his pants as an ag extension agent, fifty percent sounded about right. "But . . ."

Petrini continued. "Oh, I know. Out of that fifty per cent, he's still got to pay his rent to the landlord. Whoever the landlord is. I know that Grantvillers tend to have nobles on the brain, so to speak, but one thing that's clear to me now is that an awful lot of the landlords are merchants and other fairly rich people in the towns who have picked up rural real estate as an investment. In a lot of places, more than half of the farmers aren't renting from nobles who have estates. They're renting from a cloth manufacturer or a lawyer who has bought up the *Lehen*. Well, he has to pay rent unless the terms of his contract are for a percentage of the harvest in kind and not cash. In that case, it's already gone before he gets his crop to market. That's not the same everywhere, either, not always even from one household to another in the same village. Sometimes, out of a dozen households, five will be sharecropping the rent and the others paying cash."

Petrini leaned forward, his face intent. "Either way, the farmers don't end up with a lot of margin for capital improvements like buying a new team or other equipment. That's going to be a big roadblock to introducing mechanization, even without *Brandschatzungen* leaving the villages burned or the forced contributions for the armies. Something's going to have to give."

Scott Blackwell interrupted. "That's long-range, guys. This is immediate. What are we going to do about the sheep?"

The staff meeting meandered to an inconclusive ending. Steve finally suggested that everybody go home and sleep on it. For his own part, Meyfarth gave him and Saunders Wendell a long tutorial about peasant revolts during and after supper. Partly the where and when of the most recent ones. "Recent" being defined in Meyfarth's mind, apparently, as the past half-century or so. "Current affairs" extended as far back as he himself actually remembered as a kid. For Meyfarth, born in 1590, "history" began some time before the great famine of 1594-1597, which had been followed by the big plague epidemic of 1597-1598.

Meyfarth spent more of his time, though, talking about the ways that things interconnected. How the workers in the towns often supported the peasants—that, in fact, a lot of the "peasant" leaders were often townspeople from guilds like the fishers or coopers who had a lot to do with the farmers. Or village school teachers. How villagers who worked in the towns—and a lot of them did, when they were young, as maids and seasonal laborers, for years before they went home to settle down—contributed to dissatisfaction in the towns themselves. After two hours, revolts in Naples spun dizzyingly in Steve's mind around revolts in Croatia and France, Lithuania and the Ukraine, but above all in Austria. Everywhere in Austria, it appeared, there were or recently had been, masses of unhappy farmers—Upper Austria, Lower Austria, the Steiermark, Carinthia. The last big one had been five years before Grantville was dumped down into the middle of the Thirty Years War.

Meyfarth remembered that one clearly, since the news-sheets and pamphlets had covered it extensively. Ferdinand II had pawned Lower Austria to Duke Maximilian of Bavaria. He'd had to, to pay him back for military aid against the Bohemian Protestants. Maximilian had come down with a hard hand. The revolt had involved a mix of anticlericalism, protests against death duties, objections to foreigners who had been brought in to occupy lands vacated by expelled Protestants, and protests against the excesses of Bavarian soldiers quartered upon the people. It wasn't a few farmers shaking pitchforks; there had been about thirty thousand men under arms. Meyfarth started quoting poetry from the Austrian revolt. It wasn't any better *poetry* than the Brillo rhymes, but it sure did skewer tyranny, graft, corruption, and oppression of the individual conscience. The message was pretty clear: the lords would flee and the peasants would rule in their place.

Meyfarth gestured for emphasis. "We call each of these a *Bauernkrieg*—a peasant 'war' and not a 'protest.' They besieged several towns, including the provincial capital of Linz, and waged campaigns against the Bavarian occupying army. It involved sailors on the Danube barges; several local nobles allied themselves with the peasants; so did some Lutheran clergy. Its leader, Stefan Fadinger, was killed, but he is well on his way to becoming a 'folk hero' just as you say of the Brillo ram. The last time I heard someone sing the whole 'Fadingerlied,' it had fifty-seven verses. By the end, when Duke Maximilian and Ferdinand II managed to put it down, more than twelve thousand farmers had been killed."

Meyfarth paused. Then he suggested cautiously. "Perhaps, if the up-timers are not familiar with this . . . Just in case it has not occurred to Don Francisco Nasi to bring it to the attention of the prime minister . . ."

Meyfarth's hesitancy was a constant irritant to Saunders Wendell. He spit out, "Get to the point, man."

"Ah. Well." Meyfarth continued. "This is one of the reasons that Ferdinand II may not be able to throw his full forces against Wallenstein. You do realize that? If he strips Austria of troops, there will be another uprising among the farmers, as large as that of 1626.

That is not a hypothesis. That is just the truth. If the Austrian farmers think that they have even a hope of support from the king of Sweden and the USE, they will revolt again." He looked up at the ceiling of Würzburg's episcopal palace, with its elaborate, gilded, plaster moldings. "Franconia could put as many peasants into the field as Lower Austria, you know."

Somewhere, maybe in a Monty Python movie, Steve had once heard the line, "The peasants are revolting." It was supposed to be a funny pun, in the movie. According to Meyfarth, it was the literal truth, a lot of the time. Mama Salatto's little boy Stevie had not signed up for a major in public administration expecting to deal with enough revolting peasants to constitute a major army by the standards of the seventeenth century. Dissatisfied civic associations were about his speed. He had spent his pre-Ring of Fire days helping people establish Neighborhood Watch associations in the Baltimore suburbs. If he hadn't given in to Anita's plea to attend her folks' fortieth wedding anniversary party in Grantville, he would still be establishing Neighborhood Watch associations in the suburbs of Baltimore. And he would be a happy man.

He sipped at his wine. Then he asked, "Do you know what the epitaph of a successful civil servant is?"

Meyfarth made his face carefully noncommittal. "No."

"He never did anything that got his name in the paper."

Saunders Wendell guffawed.

Steve said, "Don't laugh. If we manage things right, maybe the damned sheep banners won't make the news at all, except locally. If they make a really big splash in the national news, that means that we failed to manage things right. If your name gets in the paper, you've screwed up. The bigger the headlines, the bigger the screw-up."

On that thought, he went to bed.

Dave Stannard, who had been supervising the NUS voter registration project in Franconia since the fall of 1632, had a word with Steve on the way into staff meeting next morning. So Steve recognized him first.

"I think that Johnnie F. is right. We should do this. It's been hanging fire too long." Dave waved at the letter from Arnold Bellamy, which was back on the table, carefully quarantined in the middle where it couldn't seem to be claiming any one administrator as its patron. "We use the voter registration lists. We've got those. It won't take the

Amtmaenner an hour to cross out anyone who has died and add on anyone who has turned eighteen since last summer. Then we blitz them."

"Why bother blitzing?" Anita asked.

"Because we've left it too long," Dave answered, "so we've made ourselves a problem. We should have started earlier, like the commissioners did in Coburg. If we had, a few teams could have handled it and we'd have been done by now. Or close to done. Leaving it this late, unless we do it all at once, we'll get into bad weather and have to stop. Then the folks in Unterpicklesdorf will start complaining that we valued the folks in Oberrelishhausen more than them, because we took the oaths of all the Relishes before the bad weather and left the Pickles unsworn for a whole season. No point in letting people manufacture grievances. God knows, they have enough real ones that we need to deal with."

Everyone at the table nodded. The Swedes had pretty well devastated this region during their campaign in 1631.

Dave continued, "As Dad always said, 'People don't need an important issue to fight about. They'll take anything available and inflate it to the size they need.' So just do it all at once. Every single one of us, in Bamberg, in Fulda, here in Würzburg. Out into the *Aemter* and take the oaths. Before the Pickles get their feelings hurt."

He grinned. It was a remarkably predatory grin. Dave was another Masaniello cousin from the out-of-town crew who had been at Vince and Carla's wedding anniversary. He'd been a Baltimore County child welfare officer before the Ring of Fire; his father Archie had been a fire department battalion chief. Dave had cut his teeth on Baltimore local politics. "Consider it a preemptive strike on the 'moan and groan' contingent. And invite the guys in the villages who aren't eligible to take the oath to the ceremony. Feed them dinner, too. Let 'em hear all the great speeches about citizenship and patriotism."

"All of us?" Steve asked.

"Yeah, all. I mean the army privates and the copy clerks. The ground is frozen, but we haven't had a lot of snow yet. The roads are passable. If we start tomorrow, we can get it done before Christmas."

There was consensus.

"I suggest," Dave added, "that you radio Fulda and Bamberg tonight, as soon as we get a window of opportunity, and tell them to do it the same way and the same time. Total stand-down for the ordinary routine; everybody out into the field."

"I suggest," Meyfarth interjected in a very soft voice, "that you use the auditor team as well as the permanent staff. I have determined that they are not contractors, but are indeed employees of the NUS. Or of whatever you are going to call it, now. Then your permanent staff will not complain that you have given the auditors special privileges or exempted them from an onerous duty. As you said about not giving people the chance to manufacture grievances . . ."

Chapter 5: *"Prophesy to the breath"*

Bamberg, early November, 1633

There was a ladder leaning against the side wall of Kronacher's print shop. Noelle Murphy tilted her head against the sun, which was, if thin and watery, at least out for a change. Hanna, Else Kronacher's far-from-young maid, was up on the ladder, scrubbing the morning mixture of mud and manure off the wall. The diamond-pane windows were partially open. Through them, the unmelodic sound of Frau Else screaming at her sons came out to join the other noises in the alley.

The screeching was followed by a clatter; then by a crash. Either Melchior, who was seventeen, or Otto, just turned fifteen, had apparently been grabbing type from a bin and throwing it at his brother. Or, possibly, they had been throwing it at one another. That wasn't at all unlikely. The crash was probably one or the other of them upsetting a bin. Or shoving his brother, who fell and upset a bin. In either case, lead type would be scattered all over the floor of the working part of the shop the way up-time kids tended to strew Legos.

Noelle walked around the corner and entered by the front door, wrinkling her nose at the odor of the boiled linseed oil that constituted the base for printer's ink. "Good morning, Martha. Chaos reigns, I take it."

Martha Kronacher pressed the heels of her hands to her temples. "Oh, the boys are fussing again that no other printer will apprentice them because of Mutti's fight with the guild. That no other printer will ever be willing to apprentice them. That even if Mutti succeeds in her fight with the guild and keeps running the shop, they won't have had their proper apprenticeship and journeyman years and therefore the guild won't let them take it over when they are old enough."

"Oh, yecchh! Are they all the way back to casting you in the role of the sacrificial lamb—moaning that they just can't understand why Frau Else wasn't willing for you to marry the guild's candidate because at least that would have kept it in the family more or less?"

"Melchior's position is that it isn't as if I wanted to marry anyone else in particular. Otto's position is that it isn't as if anybody else is ever likely to want to marry me."

"Don't listen. They're just being brothers." Noelle plopped her tote bag down on the sales counter.

"Both of them have decided that Mutti wasn't really doing it for them, but because she's selfish and just didn't want to give the management over to a son-in-law. That if she'd been willing—"

"If she'd been willing, there's not a single guarantee that your husband would have helped either of them to open a shop of his own when the time came. There's also no prospect that either of them could have married into a shop by way of a widow or only daughter. They're daydreaming." Noelle picked up a guide rule and slammed it down. "Honestly, though, if things are that bad between your brothers and your mom, why doesn't she just send them off to help the Ram?"

Frau Else, her ample figure covered by an apron and ink stains on her hands, pushed open the curtain between the shop and the sales room. "Because I can't get any one else to work for me as apprentices or journeymen, that's why! But having my sons at home is insane. Everybody in the world knows that it is insane."

Noelle's eyebrows went up. "What's insane?" A flicker went through her mind of Gretchen Richter's—Gretchen Higgins'—frequent proclamations that this or that Grantville custom was *wahnsinnig, absolut wahnsinnig*.

"To try to deal with your own children at this age. Nobles foster them to the courts of higher-ranking nobles. Then they hire tutors to take them away for a grand tour for two or three years. Merchants and craftsmen apprentice the boys and send the girls to the households of friends. Bureaucrats send them away to live with relatives in other towns and attend a good Latin school. Laborers and peasants put them out into service by the time they are fourteen or fifteen. No parent who has the slightest amount of Herr Thomas Paine's famous 'common sense' keeps them at home during the stage of youth. They are too unruly. Where do you think the term 'unruly apprentices' comes from?"

Frau Else waved her hands in the air. "At the very least, any other master would beat them for the way they are behaving this morning. Even better, Otto and Melchior would be apprenticed to different masters and therefore would not be available to fight with each other. But can I do that? No. No other master will take them. In any case, I can't do without them. If I send them to the Ram, no one else will work for me. Martha and I don't have the strength to handle the presses by ourselves, and someone must be available for the sales room. Someone has to take orders. Someone has to keep the books."

Noelle had heard all this before. And knew that "someone" was Martha. Good, reliable, Martha. When it came to Otto and Melchior, Frau Else was writing her own version of the Book of Lamentations. She shook her head. "Speaking of unruly apprentices, I saw Hanna on the stepladder in the alley. The printers' apprentices are still throwing filth at the shop, I presume?"

"Only in the alley, now. The front to the street is well enough patrolled since the power changed in the city council. There are no more cobblestones. No more open threats. Just noises in the night. Shit in the morning. The guild masters piously say to anyone from the Ram who confronts them that they do their best to control the boys, but what can one expect? With much more of the same." Frau Else picked up an old rag and wiped off her hands.

Noelle pushed aside the curtain and went into the back of the shop. "Melchior, shame. Poor Hanna is not young and yet you let her stand on a ladder while you are wasting time here fighting with your brother. Get out there, right now, and clean the wall if you expect to have food at noon. Otto, I heard you. Turn that bin right side up and sort the type. Don't waste any time. Now, now, now!"

"Didn't I say it?" Frau Else inquired of the ceiling. "Anyone but a mother. Anyone but a mother or father and boys will do what they are told. Anyone else. Anyone at all." When Noelle came back into the sales room, she repeated herself.

"I do have a reason for being here," Noelle said finally.

Frau Else snapped her mouth shut.

"Duplicating machines from Vignelli in Tirol. They started coming on the market in March. He is now producing them in fairly large numbers. I have ordered a dozen. They will be shipped from Bolzano, Bozen you call it, this week; they should arrive here in January. One, you may keep in your shop. It will be useful. The remainder are to go to the Ram for quick reproduction of pamphlets and broadsides in places where the movement doesn't have print shops accessible. And in places where quick mobility is desirable."

"Who is paying for this?" Frau Else was not so revolutionary as to ignore her bottom line. "Not I."

Noelle frowned at her. "They are prepaid. I will give the paperwork to Martha."

Frau Else nodded.

"About the boys . . ." Noelle waved her hand at the curtain. "Once things settle down a bit, why don't you send them to Grantville to learn the new printing technology? It's not covered by the guild regulations." *Yet*, she thought. There was no real reason to assume that the guilds wouldn't be scrambling to catch up. There was also no real reason to bring that up at this very moment.

"The whole reason for what I have done is to keep *this* business for my sons."

Noelle ran a hand through her sandy blonde hair. The basic truth was that Frau Else didn't really want to overthrow the system. She just wanted to be part of it. "Could you—maybe—just think outside the box for a minute?"

That required quite a bit of explanation.

Ending with a repeat of Frau Else's protest that she couldn't send her sons away because no trained journeyman printer would work for a woman who was not a master. And since she was not a master, she could not accept apprentices even if there were parents who were willing to send their sons to her. Not that any reasonable parent would be willing to waste money paying a master when the boy would not be eligible to enter the guild at the end of not. Not to say . . .

Blast it! Luckily that was inside Noelle's head and not coming out of her mouth.

"Ah. Well, maybe we could kill two birds with one stone. Something to keep Melchior and Otto occupied. Someone to work for you in the shop."

"There's no way."

The world does not end at the borders of Bamberg. Noelle hadn't said that, either. Though she had come close.

"I'll see about having them organize a Committee of Correspondence in Bamberg. Maybe, given their age, a kind of 'junior chapter' with a lot of training involved. They'll need mentors. Something like Boy Scout leaders, I guess."

Martha looked skeptical. "Where would these mentors come from?"

"That's the other end of my idea. I'll see if they"—she left "they" undefined quite deliberately—"can send a couple guys down from Magdeburg. CoC members who are printers and will be willing to work for Frau Else. Create a liaison with Helmut. Organize a junior chapter at the same time."

Frau Else crossed her arms over her ample chest. "I will not turn my shop over to any other master. Not to one from Magdeburg any more than to a guild master from Bamberg."

"Journeymen. Working for *you*. There won't be any masters from Magdeburg who are interested in a project like this, anyhow." Noelle laughed. "It's the nature of revolutions to be rather short on wise old elders. Mike Stearns is seriously frustrated at the shortage of Red Sybolt types."

That required more explanation also.

By the end of the conversation, Noelle wasn't too sure about just how far this fledgling Franconian revolution was going to go. Her mind skipped to the passage in Ezekiel where God told the hapless prophet to "prophesy to the breath." In her limited experience, it just wasn't exactly a snap to put flesh on dry bones. Much less raise the dead.

A second image rose up. She saw herself fanning the flames of a wood fire in an old-fashioned cooking range to make them burn more hotly. Blowing upon them. Someone would have to breathe more life into this revolt before anyone could prophesy to the breath.

Frau Else marched back through the curtain with a firm, "I can't just stand around talking all day. There's work to be done."

For one morning, Noelle thought, she had probably done as much as she could.

Martha rubbed her temples again. "I won't marry one of them, either."

"What on earth?"

"If you bring journeymen from Magdeburg. I won't marry one of them, either. I don't intend to be anyone's sacrificial lamb." She glared at Noelle. "Not for my brothers. Not for anyone else, either."

"Look, honey." Noelle put an arm around Martha's shoulder. Martha was a little older, twenty-five to Noelle's "going to be twenty-three next month." Equal stubbornness was the main foundation of their rapidly growing friendship. "People are just teasing when they call you the 'ewe lamb' and say that since your mom is the Ewe, you're destined to marry Helmut. Whoever he may be in real life. Nobody really expects you to marry him. Or one of these guys, whoever they turn out to be."

"Some of them are serious." Martha circled her shoulders. She had spent most of the morning cleaning display cases. "I've got to be realistic. Mutti has turned into a revolutionary. That's fine, I suppose. We need a revolution. About some things, at least."

Noelle laughed. Martha was far less of a flaming radical than her mother. Whose radicalism also had very sharp limits. "Realistic about what?"

"Well, people do tend to marry inside their own trade. There's some marrying across guild lines, but especially in the highly skilled trades—glass making, printing, lens grinding, and the like—families are a lot more likely to arrange marriages into the same trade, even if it means looking outside of your own town. We—the family, I mean—aren't really printers any more in the sense that we're part of the guild. We're revolutionaries. So it's not that odd that people are thinking that she'll find a revolutionary for me to marry. That someone like Helmut would make a suitable match."

"So what do you have against the idea?"

"He's . . . Well, I don't care whether he's been to the university or not, he's just *crude*," Martha proclaimed. "He can speak Latin, but he's just as crude in Latin as he is in German. Not all the time, but a lot of it. When he's not being a public person. He's been teaching out in that village in the Steigerwald so long that he's practically become a peasant himself. That's . . . I don't want a husband like that. I want one who is just as cultured at home as he is when he's speaking in the city council chamber."

"Cultured?"

"Music," Martha said. "You know. Poetry. Literature. I know that Helmut does lesson plans, and he's smart. Shrewd. He did the annotated version of *Common Sense* that we published."

She elaborated, from her point of view. Helmut was not only crude, but *loud*. If Martha wanted *loud*, all she needed to do was stay home with her mother and brothers, who were loud enough to drive a person mad. Helmut had a voice that boomed. Which was good for giving speeches to large numbers of people in open fields, but would become terribly tiring if it were inside a small house.

Inadvertently, by listing all the reasons she didn't in the least want to marry Helmut, she gave Noelle more information concerning the Ram than any other up-timer had. Everything, practically, but his name and the exact location of his headquarters.

Walking back up the alley, Noelle checked to see that it was Melchior rather than Hanna on the ladder. She wondered if she was legally or morally obliged to share what she had just learned with Vince Marcantonio and Steve Salatto and their various official subordinates. By the time she had reached the episcopal palace which was serving as administrative headquarters, she concluded that she wasn't. What they didn't know, they wouldn't feel obliged to do something— anything—about. After some reflection she decided that she didn't think she would even tell Johnnie F.

The Ram movement needed a little breathing room, was her sense of things. That had certainly been the gist of the private messages she'd gotten from Mike Stearns, when he'd been the President of the NUS. Now that he'd moved up to Magdeburg and become the prime minister of the new United States of Europe, she no longer had any direct contact with him. But the two messages she'd gotten since from the new President of whatever-the-NUS-would-wind-up-calling-itself, Ed Piazza, made it clear that nothing had changed.

Well, some subtleties, perhaps. Stearns had been more prone to relying on the Committees of Correspondence than Piazza seemed to be. But that hardly indicated any new formalization of affairs, as far as she was concerned. Ed Piazza simply substituted working through the Genevan fellow Leopold Cavriani instead. It had been Cavriani who had obtained, no doubt through his usual tortuous means, the duplicating machines.

It was obvious to Noelle that Cavriani often worked closely with the CoCs, in addition to being a revolutionary of some kind in his own right. So, she was still working very much in what, in a now-gone up-time world, would have been called "gray operations."

Steve Salatto wouldn't approve of what she was doing, of course. He'd be especially irate if he found out she was doing it behind his back. But his position made him oblivious to a lot of things, anyway. The real problem was Johnnie F., who wasn't oblivious to much of anything.

On the other hand . . .

Johnnie F. was also a past master at the art of looking the other way, when it suited him. Noelle was pretty sure he'd do it again here, if he found out.

Grantville, Late November, 1633

At first, the LDS church in Grantville had more or less decided that Willard Thornton ought to stay in town for the rest of the winter. It wasn't the best traveling weather. That suited his wife Emma just fine. She would even be glad—delighted, ecstatic, and enthusiastic, she told her friends—to listen to him hum "Dry Bones" just as often as it crossed his mind. Just as long as he was home and safe.

Then the letter came from Bamberg. Frau *Stadtraetin* Färber reported that her husband had been disabled by a stroke. She believed that it was apoplexy, brought on by the events of September. She had saved Herr Thornton's bicycle, with the many copies of the *Book of Mormon* in the saddlebags. She had taken the liberty of giving some of them to her friends, since she knew that Herr Thornton had been giving them away.

The Frau *Stadtraetin* wrote further that she wished that the missionary would return to Bamberg. She and her friends would benefit from further explanation of many passages in the book. If she might be so bold, she advised that, if possible, he should bring his wife, since a woman could go many places that a man could not—at least, that a man could not go without arousing suspicion. She made an offer, and a joke. She would gladly be a Lydia to their Paul, providing them with hospitality in her home.

Howard Carstairs read the letter to the whole congregation. Because of his army service in Germany, he had become sort of Johnny-on-the-Spot for things like this. Reading the letter aloud, he realized that Willard's reports had left the umlaut off her name, and it was not Farber. It was Färber. Dyer. Symbolic.

No one said anything. His father and Willard's father looked at one another. Those two, Levi Carstairs and Harold Thornton, were the senior men in the church. Logically, they should have been making the decisions. More and more, though, it seemed like they looked at one another and then looked at Howard.

They looked at Howard. Monroe Wilson looked at Howard. Amos Sterling looked at Howard. As did Alden Blodger and Leland Nisbet. Ted B. Warren was looking at him. Myles Halvorsen was looking at him. All the other men were out of town.

Howard said, "We should pray about this overnight." Everyone seemed to find that acceptable. He prayed; then he slept.

In the morning, he knew what they should do. That seemed to be happening more and more, too. Henceforth, the LDS missionary standard would not be pairs of young men, but pairs of mature married couples. Even if it was more expensive. The other men agreed; clearly, that was what they should do. It was obvious, now that Howard had mentioned it. The down-timers respected maturity; they would not pay much attention to boys not old enough to have finished their journeyman years.

Over warm broth at her kitchen table, Emma said, "Willard can start out now. I need to finish the semester, I really do. I'll give Victor Saluzzo my resignation Monday, though. He can find someone else for senior lit by the time second semester starts. I'll join Willard after New Year's. I think that I should stay with the kids for Christmas. The kids need to stay here for school. I won't have time to home-school them in Bamberg, if I'm being a missionary. Our two, plus the two German boys who are boarding with us." She looked at Howard expectantly.

"Arthur and Bev will take your two. Joel and Gigi will take the boys."

Howard knew that, too. He just, well, somehow, *knew* things these days. Not things about the business, or whether Liz wanted him to pick up pork chops for dinner. For those, he still had to calculate an estimate or pick up the phone. Things he *needed* to know.

Chapter 6: "I shall nonetheless do this"

Franconia, December, 1633

"Where are we?" Maydene Utt asked. Maydene, the "large one" of the three up-time auditors provided to the Franconian administration by Arnold Bellamy, always had a tendency to take charge of things.

"Somewhere northeast of a town called Gerolzhofen. That was Gerolzhofen, about a mile and a half back. The town that we had to go around. At least, according to Johnnie F.'s map, it should have been. Locked up tighter than a drum behind its walls. 'See us on your way back, after we've verified your credentials.' "

Willa Fodor, the second up-time member of the audit team, brushed the snowflakes off her eyelashes. Willa was navigating. The down-timer sergeant of the guards who had been sent out with them was very efficient in a lot of ways, but he had never learned to read an up-time map. Worse, he was from somewhere in Brunswick, so had no more idea about where he might be in rural Franconia than anyone else in the group.

They had had a professional guide until three days ago, but he had come down with what looked to Maydene like walking pneumonia and she had insisted on leaving him in a place called Volkach, where the group had reserved rooms at the inn for two weeks. They had seen a whole bunch of villages since Volkach. They stopped at the bigger ones, where the *Amtmaenner* or district officers were head-quartered. Most of the places had been willing to provide a boy to lead them to the next town or village on their list. They had collected oaths of allegiance in Schwebheim and Grettstadt, Donnersdorf and Sulzheim, with no problems. But, for some reason, no one in Sulzheim had been willing to guide them to Gerolzhofen. And Gerolzhofen had been locked down. Nobody outside the walls. No people. No pigs. No chickens. Definitely no welcome for the NUS administrators.

"Where are we going?" Estelle McIntire, the third auditor, thought that was the more important question, given the way the flakes were starting to come down.

"Someplace called Dingolshausen. That's the last stop on this route. Michelau is beyond it, but the people from Michelau and Neuhof came up to Donnersdorf and did their oath-taking there. Bless their beauti-ful hides. Then we double back not quite to Gerolzhofen and head south to someplace called Neuses am Sand and then someplace called Prichsenstadt. And from Prichsenstadt, we go back to Gerolzhofen and see if they'll let us in. Charming place, according to Meyfarth. They burned more than two hundred fifty 'witches' about fifteen years ago. We've got to go back by way of Luelsfeld, again, though. Too many people had gone to market in Kitzingen the day we went through there. Then we go back to Volkach and from there we cross to Astheim and go home to Würzburg. The guys gave us an easy run, comparatively speaking. Chivalry and all that, I suppose."

"We'll let the army deal with Gerolzhofen." Maydene's voice was decisive. "The kind of behavior they are showing is Scott Blackwell's problem, not ours."

Willa rubbed her eyes again. "If Johnnie F.'s map is right, the left fork here has to be the one to Dingolshausen. We're lucky that it's cold enough that the snowflakes aren't melting and making the ink run." She shook them off the map.

"It's just delightful that *something* is going right today," Maydene said. "I am duly grateful."

Willa kept on. "The right fork has to go to Neuses am Sand, so the worst thing that can happen is that we take the oaths out of order. We can fib about that, in a pinch. It's a loose-leaf notebook. Let's move *somewhere*. This snow is starting to come down really hard. We need to get inside."

Maydene felt like the strap of her rifle was about to cut through the muscles of her right shoulder. Wrapping her reins around the saddle pommel, she reached up to transfer it over to the left. A sudden gust of wind blew a clear spot amidst the snowflakes, giving her about forty feet more vision than any of them had had for nearly an hour. The rifle came into her hand and she shot. In an instant, the three women were in the center of a circle formed by the guard company. Every hill along the roadside seemed to erupt men out of the snow.

Maydene's shot was hurried. She missed her target, but hit the man next to him in the shoulder. He spun around, striking one of his mates with his own gun and tangling up another.

Watching, Gerhardt Jost was impressed. He wouldn't have thought such a severe-looking middle-aged woman could react that quickly to an ambush. In fact, she'd reacted so well that the bishop's mercenaries were startled. And she was already jacking another bullet into the chamber.

That meant the bishop's men had lost the advantage of surprise. Already, the up-timers' guards were starting to fire. So was one of other American women. The third had fallen off her horse, when the beast started from the gunfire, but Jost didn't think she was badly injured.

None of the guards were shooting very accurately, true. But neither were the bishop's mercenaries. It was enough for them to simply be firing at all.

An ambush had just become a small pitched battle.

"Now?" asked Rudolph Vulpius quietly. The old man seemed to be practically quivering with eagerness.

"Not quite," answered Gerhardt. "Let the responsibility for the bloodshed be clear."

He paused, while another loud and very ragged not-quite-volley was exchanged. And, once again, was impressed. The big American woman was still on her horse, and took down her target with her second shot. No accident, that one. The mercenary was smashed into the snow with a bullet square in his chest, that punched right through his breastplate.

"And we don't want to seem *that* conveniently positioned," he added.

Old Vulpius grunted, but didn't argue the point. Jost waited for perhaps another ten seconds, watching the battle taking place below the ridge. After two of the up-timers' guards had been shot down, he decided everything was well enough established."

"*Shoot!*" he bellowed.

The villagers had been waiting, every bit as impatiently as their council head. An instant later, dozens of shots struck the bishop's men, cutting through them like a scythe. At that range, even with mostly old muskets, the villagers were quite accurate. They didn't have the skill of *Jaegers*, but they were no strangers to firearms.

It helped—a great deal—that Jost's cold-blooded delay had allowed all of the bishop's men to come out of hiding and expose themselves.

That first big volley fired, of course, the villagers were out of action for a time. Their weapons couldn't be reloaded quickly.

Jost was not concerned. The volley had hammered the mercenaries so badly that they were now completely confused. But the up-timers' guards were firing more accurately. And the big American woman, still stubbornly perched on her horse, took down *another* man. Jost took a moment to admire the horse.

The outcome was no longer in doubt at all.

One of the mercenaries tried to flee. Jost brought up his rifle and felled him. Then, smiling thinly, jacked another round into the chamber. He adored his American rifle, that had come to him through circuitous means.

Two more tried to flee. Jost killed them long before they could reach shelter.

By then, the villagers had reloaded. With more discipline that he'd expected, they waited for the command.

"*Shoot!*" he bellowed again.

A few seconds later, it was all over. A wounded mercenary staggered toward the safety of the woods, but Jost put a stop to that.

He rose to a crouch. "Best I vanish now," he murmured to Vulpius. "I certainly don't want to explain exactly how I came in possession of my rifle."

The old man nodded. Big as he was, Jost vanished into the trees like a wraith.

"No," the old man said. "They aren't bandits."

"Then what are they?" Maydene asked with exasperation. Their company had two dead guards, four injured guards, Estelle with a splint on her leg (she had fallen off her horse, but kept hold of her gun), two horses that had to be put down, and six horses that would have to be left behind. The villagers—this was Frankenwinheim, a little spot off the main road—said that they would be happy to nurse the horses back to health. Maydene wondered if they would also "forget" to bring them back to Würzburg until after spring planting, but that wasn't her problem.

"Hatzfeld's men, I think. The bishop. His brother is a general for the Austrians, you know. They don't like it that their move to get a lot of Franconia on grants from Ferdinand II has been blocked. This bunch came in through the woods. Moved into Dingolshausen about a week ago. Don't bother going the rest of the way. There's nobody there to take an oath. So we moved everybody out of the village here, up into temporary shelter in the hills. The people in Gerolzhofen wouldn't let us in. The last couple of years have been so bad that we couldn't afford to pay for the right to take sanctuary inside the walls. This year's harvest is decent enough, but we haven't sold it yet, so we haven't paid. Stinking, greedy, townsmen. We've been watching the road. If it hadn't been for the snow, this wouldn't have happened. We couldn't see well enough to know that you were coming. My apologies, gracious lady."

"No apologies necessary. What's your name?"

"Rudolph Vulpius. I'm the head of our village council." He indicated an old woman sitting on the other side of the room. "This is my wife, Kaethe."

Maydene nodded to her. "How many?" she asked.

"How many what?"

"Hatzfeld's men, I mean."

The old man looked over at a younger one.

"Two dozen, at least. That's how many bodies we have in the granary. Possibly up to a hundred. We have trackers out."

"Your casualties, here in Frankenwinheim?"

The old man cackled. "None to speak of. It helps a lot to shoot the enemy in the back."

Willa did not agree that two babies dead of exposure counted as no casualties. The villagers appeared to take it in stride. Babies died every winter, Hatzfeld's men or not. Innocent babies went to the Lord Jesus in heaven; their lot henceforth was better than that of the families they left behind on earth. Each mother had given God another bud in her nosegay of children. Each mother had another baby angel to pray for her soul. They were quite confident of this, in spite of the fact that for a century, Protestant clergymen had been telling them that they did not need baby angels to pray for their souls. There were just some things about which Mother Knew Best.

"Since we're here anyway," Maydene asked, "should we take your oaths? It's not picnic weather, but we have beef jerky in the saddle-bags."

The old man looked at his wife Kaethe. The totally toothless old woman, who looked like she could as well be his mother as his wife, opened a hidden compartment under the manger of the stall that opened into the cottage. She dragged out a heavy chest and opened it. She pulled out a ram's-head banner.

"Yes," the old man said. "You will take our oaths under the banner. Not just the oaths of the villagers who pay their rents to your government in Würzburg. The oaths of all of us in Frankenwinheim, no matter who our lord may be."

Maydene was not in a mood to argue the point. Whoever the old man's lord might have been, he'd been really delinquent in the "protect and shield" department.

"Okay," she said. "First of all, I hereby absolve everybody in this village from any oath he's ever taken to anybody who didn't send a troop of guards in to root Hatzfeld's men out of Dingolshausen. Second, let's get started. You first."

They took oaths. They ate jerky. Somebody threw another log into the fireplace. The old folks started telling stories about what Grandpa did in the *Bundschuh*. Somebody rolled in a keg of beer. It turned into a long night in Frankenwinheim.

"That pretty well sums it up," Scott said. "And, though I know you don't want me to do it, Steve, I'm going to have to quarter some troops in Gerolzhofen. Some of the mercenaries that Mike and Gustavus are sending down to us. I've been stepping lightly, but that town is just too loyal to the bishop of Würzburg. Just because he's a bishop, no matter who the bishop may be at the moment. It's a lot smaller than Bamberg, but it sure isn't any more of a bastion of liberal enlightenment."

"Where? I don't want them quartered on private citizens." Steve was definite.

"Put them in the *Zehnthof*." That was Meyfarth. "Nobody, not even the most loyal Catholic, enjoys paying the tithes, so they won't be all that protective about the tithe storage barn. There's room for a bunch of soldiers there and the officers can keep better control over them than if they are scattered out in different quarters. It's sort of off to one side and next to the walls. The inner walls. Quarter the officers in the residence that Bishop Echter built for his bailiffs. That's right next to it."

"Actually," Scott said, "I'm sort of glad that we sent the gals on that run. The Gerolzhofen city council apparently thought that it could defy three women. Sort of exposed them to the point where I can deal with them."

"We have had," Meyfarth said, "excellent press coverage of the incident."

"The 'gals' did exceed their authority." Steve Salatto felt obliged to point that out. After Frankenwinheim, Maydene, Willa, and Estelle had cut quite a swath through their assigned section of Franconia. Accompanied by scores of villagers. Waving a ram's head banner. They had taken an extra week to get back to Volkach. They were, as Maydene pointed out after they got back to Würzburg, all three of them, members of the Grantville League of Women Voters. She claimed that they therefore had a perfect right to use the symbol.

"Ah," Meyfarth said. "For my part, I think it went well."

Scott asked, "What about the sheep? Are we going to have farmers marching out under ram's-head banners come spring? And, if so, what do we do about it?"

Johnnie F. said, "You're going to have them marching, I'm pretty sure. Not just here, but in Bamberg and maybe Fulda, too. Stewart Hawker and Orville Beattie agree with me on that." Stewart and Orville were headquartered in Würzburg, but Stewart spent most of his time in Bamberg; Orville was mostly in Fulda.

"People are already on the move," Johnnie F. continued. "Some of the villages are squeezing people out—where the majority are subjects of some lord, folks who weren't eligible to swear to us, the way the law is now. I don't know if the landlords are doing the pushing, or if the other villagers are doing the pushing because they're afraid of the landlords, but we're seeing people on the roads. Heading north into Thuringia, a lot of them, though this isn't the best time of the year to be crossing the Thuringian Forest, now that the snow is accumulating in earnest."

"So they are pushing out the ones who swore allegiance to the Constitution. Are the oath-takers pushing out the ones who didn't?" Saunders Wendell asked.

"We're sort of trying to persuade them not to," Johnnie F. answered. "At least, not if other people's subjects are willing to live peacefully among our citizens, with the banner up. No use in creating grudges where none have to be. No use classifying people as enemies when maybe they're not."

"We might have a clearer idea of where the lines are going to fall out if they did," Scott Blackwell remarked.

"They didn't not take our oath because they love their landlords," Johnnie F. pointed out. "They didn't take it because they've already sworn a *Huldigungseid* to some other guy and we for sure didn't have any authority to tick off lords who are, or might be, allies of Gustavus Adolphus by ripping off their peasants. We just ripped off the peasants of the lords who for sure are his enemies. Well, except for the gals."

"What are my obligations if they do march?" That was Scott again. He was, after all, the military administrator.

Nobody else answered right away. Finally, Meyfarth said, "You can put the revolt down, as lords have always done before. It would contradict many of Herr Stearns' words, but no one would be surprised, Herr Blackwell, if you gathered troops and did so. If that is the course upon which Herr Salatto and this council decide, that will be your obligation. And, as you have observed, Gustavus Adolphus is sending you a couple of regiments."

Scott nodded.

"You could let it run, if that is the course upon which Herr Salatto and this council decide. That will unquestionably bring attacks on the houses and barns of landlords and overseers, the burning of castles, killings, with enough atrocity and ferocity that the margraves of Ansbach and Bayreuth, who are allies of Gustavus Adolphus, will come to fear that it will spill over into their lands. Until enough has happened that they can demand that he put it down. Until he might have to agree to their demands, which would drive a wedge between him and Herr Stearns."

"Or?" Johnnie F. asked. "There's an 'or' in your voice."

"Or, between now and then, you, all of you, here and in Bamberg and in Fulda, can try to harness it and direct it. Control it, as a cavalryman controls a war horse ten times his weight. Get it used to wearing reins. Try to ride a ram."

Finally, Steve asked, "New business?"

Meyfarth pushed a sheet of paper across the table. "My resignation."

They all looked at him, utterly shocked.

"I have done what I can for you. I will not be going back to Grantville or Thuringia. The University of Erfurt will have no lack of takers for its prestigious tenured professorships. Because of the death of Duke Johann Casimir, I am free of obligations to any lord."

"So?" Saunders Wendell was deeply suspicious.

"Herr Wendell, for much of my life, I have been employed as an administrator or in diplomatic matters. But I am a pastor. That was my first oath. I assure you that I have prayed extensively in regard to this decision. I have also consulted with many others—with Dean Gerhard in Jena, with Professor Osiander from Tübingen. Indeed, with your up-time colleague, Herr Lambert. I am going to Bamberg, where I am going to establish a Lutheran congregation in a Catholic city. Although much of the patriciate there was Protestant up into the 1620's, the bishop's campaign and the witch trials broke all organization among the Lutherans and took the property of the Lutheran churches and wealthy Lutherans such as Councilman Junius, whose daughter came into Grantville for refuge. Now, there are only a few who are openly Protestant, those who went into exile and have come back. Many who converted in order to stay are ashamed. We must begin again."

The entire table buzzed with objections.

Meyfarth waited them out; then shook his head. "Herr Ellis was right, you know."

Johnnie F. asked, "How?"

"When he said that what happened to you and Herr Thornton in Bamberg was because your special commissioners there did not take their assignment seriously enough. They paid it only lip service, and did a little around their regular jobs, when they had time. So the Bamberg authorities, such as Councilman Färber, did not believe them when they said, 'We mean it.' They thought that it could be evaded."

Johnnie F. nodded slowly.

"I know that many of you do not like Herr Ellis. You find him to be a harsh, prejudiced, abrasive man. You do not find him to be a colleague with whom you can work easily or well. But sometimes, harsh, prejudiced, unpleasant men are also right. It is my best judgment that in this matter, his opinion was correct. As I said already, I have prayed, a great deal, concerning this matter. So I am going to Bamberg. Without a prince and without a patron, with no consistory to pay me and no building in which any flock that I gather can meet. With no tithes to support me. With only my hope that you will continue to mean it when you say that there will be religious toleration in

Franconia. And though I feel more like a lamb led to the slaughter than a belligerent ram, I shall nonetheless do this."

Franconia, December, 1633

Willard Thornton stood at the unmarked crossroads. He was glad that his bicycle was in Bamberg; it would have been hard to push the thing over the hills in this snow. He wondered which of the two forks would lead him back to his bicycle.

A thin man, huddled into a black cloak, was coming up the road behind him, walking alone. Willard waited. Perhaps he knew which road went to Bamberg.

"Ah, Herr Thornton."

"I'm, ah, afraid you have the advantage of me."

"My name is Meyfarth. I have been working with the NUS administration in Würzburg. I heard a great deal about you, last fall."

"Oh." Willard was still vaguely embarrassed about last fall. "Um, do you happen to know which of these forks leads to Bamberg?"

"It is this one. I am going to Bamberg, myself. We can walk along together. Two men are safer than one alone."

They moved forward.

Some distance behind them, a half dozen game wardens coming from the direction of Coburg noted several other men stepping out of the trees onto the road leading from Würzburg. It was all right, though, upon a closer look. They were *Jaeger*, too; and they wore the ram's head on their sleeves.

"*In Aprils Luft*," one of them said.

"*Entfalten sich die Flaggen*," the others completed the sentence.

The up-timers were manifestly insane to have let either of the men ahead of them go out walking the roads of Franconia alone. Each of them should be guarded by a full company of armed soldiers, at the very least. The *Jaeger* walked on to Bamberg, keeping just out of sight behind the hills and trees, intent on ensuring that the two innocent, good-hearted, oblivious, but inspirational damned fools who had been placed under their protection by the Ram would live to see the banners unfurl in April.

Chapter 7: "Recriminations will get you nowhere"

Würzburg, January 1, 1634

Steve Salatto opened one eye, experimentally, and took stock. He felt pretty good. The "American New Year's Eve" party that he and his wife Anita had hosted for the administrative staff of the New United States in Franconia and the city fathers of Würzburg and their wives—paper hats, paper whistles, confetti, and all—had actually been rather sedate. He was beginning to feel like a traitor to his Italian roots. He had even admitted to one of the city's vintners that he was coming to prefer the dry Franconian white wine to Italian red. It certainly left a guy with less of a head the next morning.

There was light coming in through the window. He ought to get up. Then he remembered that he had declared the up-time New Year's day a holiday for the administrative staff, even though the official calendar change to the year 1634 would not roll around until March 25 for a lot of Germany outside the NUS. The feather bed was nice and warm. He tapped his wife Anita on the shoulder and asked, "Ummn?" She turned over with a smile and they settled in for a nice snuggle.

                    *   *   *

Later on that morning, after they'd begun stirring around, Steve's eyes fell on a newspaper lying on the table where most of the festivities had centered the night before.

"Oh, Lord," he half-moaned. "I forgot about that. It seemed a lot funnier last night than it does today."

"What are you talking about?" Anita asked, coming over.

"This." He held up the newspaper, showing the first page. It was a very recent issue of the main Bamberg newspaper.

Anita leaned over his shoulder and started giggling. "I *still* think it's funny. I like all those Brillo fables."

Glumly, Steve stared down at the thing. Prominently displayed in a box in the lower right-hand quarter of the page was a German headline which read "New Brillo Verses," followed by, in English:

> In a field by the hillside some little ewe-lambs sang
> "Brillo, 'tis Brillo, 'tis Brillo."
>
> And I said to them, "Merinos, why do you stand singing
> 'Brillo, 'tis Brillo, 'tis Brillo'?"
>
> "Is it wild boars come ravaging, my ewes?" I cried,
> "Or a wild cat come nipping at your tender hide?"
> With a kick of their heels, they all baaad then replied,
> "Oh, Brillo, 'tis Brillo, 'tis Brillo."
>
> As a scruffy ram butted against the field's fence
> "Brillo, 'tis Brillo, tis Brillo."
>
> And I saw them leap up and go gamboling thence,
> "Brillo, 'tis Brillo, 'tis Brillo."
>
> As he leaped o'er the fence in a tremendous bound,
> And all the ewes "baaaa'd" in approving resound,
> Oh! My hopes for rich wool were quite dashed to the ground!
> Oh, Brillo, 'tis Brillo, 'tis Brillo.

                    *   *   *

Soon many more lambs in the field could be seen
Brillo, 'tis Brillo, 'tis Brillo

Their coarse kinky wool had no fine silken sheen
Brillo, 'tis Brillo, 'tis Brillo

As they chased off a wolfling with kicks full of fire,
Their great bravery somewhat reduced my sad ire,
"Oh, tell me, brave lambkins, just who is your sire?"
"Brillo, 'tis Brillo, 'tis Brillo!"

At the bottom was an announcement that a German translation would be provided on the third page, along with the announcement of a contest to see who could produce the best German versification of the rhymes. From experience, Steve knew that within a month this new Brillo fable would have transmuted into half a dozen variations— all of which were aimed at the Franconian establishment.

"How in the hell did that stupid scruffy ram of Flo Richards' turn into an endless supply of gasoline poured on the flames?" Steve demanded. "Somebody please tell me."

Anita shrugged. "You might as well ask how in the hell a bunch of stupid tea leaves dumped into a harbor turned into something that's still talked about two hundred years later. Face it, Steve. This place needs a revolution badly—and damn near anything could have served as the channel."

She headed toward the kitchen. "I still think it's cute. A lot cuter than tea leaves, that's for sure—and, for my money, it beats 'one if by land, two if by sea' by a country mile."

"I'm a civil servant!" Steve protested.

"Yup. A veritable Chinese mandarin. In interesting times," came Anita's rejoinder from the kitchen.

Würzburg, early January, 1634

"Guess what, guys?" Saunders Wendell said, "we finally know who we are."

"What do you mean by that?" Scott Blackwell asked.

"They sent down someone to replace Meyfarth, and he brought

along an official notice that the former New United States is no more. Bet Arnold Bellamy's happy to get rid of that NUS acronym! He was sure that everyone in Europe would start referring to us as 'the nuts.' "

"Wonderful," Maydene Utt said. "What are we now?"

"Don't know. Steve's saving it for the meeting, when he introduces the guy."

"Who is he?"

"Don't know that, either. German. But he speaks English. A 'must hire' from Axel Oxenstierna, I understand."

The door opened. Steve came in with a thin man who wore a mustache and a goatee. He had a twinkle in his eye. About fifty; older than the departed Meyfarth, at any rate. After the general exchange of "good mornings," Steve said: "I would like to introduce my new chief of staff to all of you. Ladies and gentlemen, Georg Rodolf Weckherlin, who is going to tell us who we are."

Weckherlin bowed with a flourish.

Scott Blackwell thought that the man would be happy on a stage, playing one of the Three Musketeers. When he opened his mouth, he sounded like he belonged in a Shakespeare play, too.

"Ah," Weckherlin said, "it was my privilege to be in Grantville delivering my letter of recommendation from the king's, ah, emperor's chancellor. Thus, I had a chance to observe this. First, there was a meeting of the cabinet, presided over by your President Mr. Piazza, to receive suggestions. Then there was a full session of the Congress.

"Someone suggested that it should be the Province of Thuringia. Mr. Arnold Bellamy raised most strenuous objections that he did not wish to be a citizen of PoT. An acronym which, by the way, the youngest son of your Mr. Thomas Stone was kind enough to enlighten me about just before he left for Italy."

Weckherlin grinned. Everyone else at the table broke into laughter.

"Ah, so therefore you are not a PoT. The cabinet did not even present the suggestion to the Congress.

"Then it was noted that Gustavus Adolphus himself had suggested 'East Virginia.' This was not received with enthusiasm. An aspect of your prior history, I understand."

Nods all around the table.

"So, subject to a referendum at the next election, they have adopted the name . . ."

Weckherlin paused dramatically.

Twirled the ends of his moustaches.

"State of Thuringia."

"You know," Scott Blackwell commented, "I can't see that SoT is a big improvement on PoT."

"True, true." Weckherlin winked. "That is *precisely* what Mr. Bellamy said."

Laughter again.

Steve watched in admiration. In a few minutes, a man who came into the room as a complete stranger had managed to break the ice and make considerable strides toward being accepted as a member of the working group that it had taken him two years to develop.

"What are *we* in connection to the SoT?" Wendell asked.

"Until the election you are holding this spring, just the Franconian Region. Very dull, alas. Which you will remain if the people here do not vote to become part of the State of Thuringia. If they do vote to become part, there will be yet another discussion and, at least everyone presumes, yet another name."

"What are the parts?" Willa Fodor asked. "That is, all the *Aemter* and *Gemeinden* and *Gerichte* and markets and other little administrative units. Are they doing something to straighten that out and come up with one set of jurisdictions?"

Weckherlin nodded. "Oh, yes, something. Lots of talking. Lots of 'discussion,' that is. Should the new state have counties? If the English word 'county' is also used to translate '*Grafschaft*,' then will it insult the towns, such as Badenburg, or other lords, such as the dukes of Saxe-Weimar, who would not wish to see their former duchy demoted to a county? Would they take umbrage? It became very complicated.

"I did suggest. Just suggested, since I was there at the 'town meeting' where people were talking about it, that they could call them 'shires' and then they could call the state's appointee in each of them a 'sheriff.'

"Woe is me!" Weckherlin's face fell into a parody of grief. "They decided that this was much too 'English.' But they agreed that making everything a county was not good. So every jurisdiction will keep its own name, madam. That is, whether a document is in German or in English, unless the people themselves decide to change the name, a former *Reichstadt* such as Badenburg will remain a *Stadt*, a *Herzogtum* such as Saxe-Weimar will keep that name, a *Grafschaft* such as Schwarzburg-Rudolstadt will keep that name, a *Freiherrschaft* will remain itself also. But each one will have exactly the same governmental rights and responsibilities and be expected to adopt the same administrative structure and offices, none more or less important than the others. For land and taxes and such matters.

"They can change, though, if they wish. Thus, your Grantville and its surrounding land, inside the Ring of Fire and what it has annexed, have voted to become West Virginia County, Thuringia. There was some discussion of 'Ring of Fire County,' but it was decided that because of the annexations, it isn't exactly a circle or a ring any more. More like an 'amoeba,' a man named Mr. Birdie Newhouse said. One of your high school teachers showed me an 'amoeba' through his microscope. Fascinating. Grantville will return to being a city with a charter and there will be a county government established for the remainder of it. Mayor Dreeson said that this was a good thing. But they will not have time to do it right away.

"Much of the region that was once *Grafschaft* Gleichen, but the *Grafen* are extinct, all the parts that were not annexed directly into the Ring of Fire, has voted to become Vasa County, Thuringia. *Graf* August von Sommersburg and his subjects have decided to be Sommersburg County rather than a *Grafschaft*, although nobody else is sure why. Erfurt city wishes to remain a *Stadt* but the hinterland around it has voted to become Erfurt County, Thuringia."

"Shrewd," Steve Salatto commented. "Keep the familiar terms, but remodel the underlying structure. Not a bad idea. Comfort zone thinking."

Willa hadn't given up yet. "What about below the county level? The *Aemter* and such?"

"I am not sure," Weckherlin admitted. "But neither are they. At least, they were still talking when I left."

Grantville, early January, 1634

Emma Thornton was in the outer office of the President of the State of Thuringia. President, not governor. There had been a president of the New United States. There had also been a Congress of the New United States. Neither of them, thus far, had seen any good and clear reason to demote themselves to governor and legislature, just because the NUS had become the SoT. None of the other of the states that now comprised the United States of Europe used any of the four terms, after all. Instead, they featured a wide variety of titles for the heads of state and the general term *Stände*, usually translated into

English as "Estates," for their legislative assemblies.

So, the matter didn't seem to be urgent. What was an occasional "president" among dukes, landgraves, margraves, and counts? Would a "governor" be any less unique when his colleagues were *Herzog, Landgraf, Markgraf,* or *Graf?*

"Okay, Liz, what's the most important thing for me to take?"

Emma was eyeing the president's chief of staff, Liz Carstairs. Ed Piazza had inherited her from Mike Stearns. He would keep her only until she could make arrangements to move to Magdeburg and become the prime minister's chief of staff there. Liz also, of course, happened to be the big sister of Emma's husband, Willard. And president of the LDS Relief Society. And secretary of the Grantville League of Women Voters.

Emma was never entirely certain which of these personages was the one to which she ought to be deferring at any given moment, but . . . the truth was that although Liz only had an associate's degree in administration whereas Emma had a M.Ed. in language arts education, Emma had no doubt at all that Liz was the dominant personality, of which she herself would never manage to be more than the faintest shadow.

Which was ridiculous. She managed her home and her children; she had no trouble controlling her classes—discipline had never been a problem for her.

In spite of that, she was in constant awe of Liz. There was a line, somewhere, between being able to do things and being able to do them superbly. Emma was on one side; Liz on the other.

Even Liz's mother was in awe of her. Which said something.

So here she was. "Not the most important thing for clothes and stuff. That's all sorted out and packed. Your folks are dealing with renting out the house; they're using Huddy Colburn. I've put our things in storage, except for what Willard asked me to bring. I've rented a wagon and hired a driver.

"But I've never done any mission work. This Frau Färber in Bamberg—we'll be staying at her house, at least for the rest of the winter—wants me to be talking to other women, mainly. I think. So what should I take?"

Of all the things that Emma might have predicted an hour before, two hundred copies of an abbreviated German translation of *Robert's Rules of Order* would not have been right at the top. But that was what Liz gave her.

Along with a great big hug.

Bamberg, mid-January, 1634

Noelle Murphy pushed through the front door of Kronacher's print shop. "Hello. I'm back from Grantville. Anybody home?"

Martha came through the curtain and hugged her. "I'm so glad you could spend Christmas with your family. Everyone else is down at the city council meeting, listening to the debate about the missionaries who have come to town. Pastor Meyfarth and the up-timer. Thornton, his name is. After they're done, Mutti will bring them home for dinner. The two missionaries, I mean. Not the city councillors."

Noelle tipped her head to one side. "Is there enough in the pot for a couple more?"

"You and . . ."

"I brought you someone to help keep a lid on Melchior and Otto until I can get some CoC printers for Frau Else. He stopped at a street vendor's grill to get some breakfast, but he should be here . . ."

The door opened again.

". . . right now," Noelle finished. "Martha, this is my friend Egidius Junker. We call him Eddie. He's been studying law at the University of Jena. And economics. He's also spent a lot of time in Grantville, so he can sort of help explain things. Back and forth. Between, oh . . ." She paused. "Between people for whom explanations would come in handy. So I want him to meet your mom and brothers. He'll also get started on a couple of projects for me."

Martha looked doubtful. This Egidius Junker did not appear to be old enough to control her brothers. Though Noelle could make them pay attention and he was, perhaps, about the same age as Noelle.

"Eddie will work for you as an in-house translator," Noelle said to Frau Else between bites of sauerkraut.

"I can't afford . . ." Frau Else began.

"Don't worry about it." Noelle's tone was sharp. "Eddie will work for you as an in-house translator. That's why he's in Bamberg. That's what his letters of introduction say. That's the way it is."

Martha didn't look up, but glanced around the table while keeping her head down. First at Noelle, whose face was suddenly pinched and older than her years. Then at the up-timer, Thornton, who was talking to Pastor Meyfarth. Then at Pastor Meyfarth. Again at Pastor Meyfarth. She had looked at him before. At a break in the theological discussion, she asked, "Will your families be joining you soon?"

Willard Thornton smiled. "My wife Emma is already on her way to Bamberg. She should arrive any day, if the group she is traveling with isn't seriously delayed by this weather."

Meyfarth shook his head. "I am a widower. My wife and children died of the plague in Coburg, nearly two years ago."

Martha extended her sympathy, wondering a little why she didn't feel as sorry as she should and then not wondering. Meyfarth was a very attractive man. Perhaps twenty years older than she was. Mature. She liked that.

"Have you found a place to stay?"

Herr Thornton answered first. "We will be with Frau *Stadtraetin* Färber until we can find something more permanent."

"For the time being, I am at an inn," Meyfarth added. "I can't afford to remain, of course. As soon as I have taken a census of those persons who are likely to become my future parishioners, I will see if one of them is in a position to rent me a room."

At the head of the table, Frau Else looked up. "I know someone," she said. "A very respectable widow and her house is conveniently located. I will be happy to introduce you to her."

Meyfarth thanked her solemnly.

Most of the conversation was political.

"Thanks again for the dinner, Frau Else," Noelle called back as she went out the door.

Martha followed her. "Umm."

Noelle grinned at her. "Everyone in Würzburg says that the pastor is a really nice guy. And he's a poet. Very cultured. Everyone says so."

"We, ah, sort of stopped being Lutherans back when I was a teenager. Because of the bishop, you know."

Noelle raised her eyebrows. "That's one of the beauties of freedom of religion, Martha. There's nothing to say that you can't start being Lutheran again. If you're interested in theology, of course."

"Oh." Martha looked back a little nervously at the door where Pastor Meyfarth and Herr Thornton were still standing, talking to Egidius Junker. "Oh, of course. Theology. Err, Noelle."

"What?"

"That 'respectable widow' Mutti mentioned to Pastor Meyfarth." Martha squirmed a little. "She's the mother of Judith Neideckerin. The woman you asked if I could find some way to put you in touch with. The woman I wrote you about. The one that Helmut mentioned the last time he was here."

"*Freiherr* von Bimbach's mistress, you mean?"

"Yes. Her. Mutti has talked to her mother. The one with the room to rent. She can put you in touch with Judith. If you still want to be, that is."

Noelle thinned her lips, pulling them in between her teeth. "Oh, yes. I would very much like to be put in touch with Judith Neideckerin, if Helmut is willing. His Bimboship presents problems. Judith Neideckerin may offer opportunities."

Würzburg, mid-January, 1634

The rector of the University of Würzburg had come to talk about libraries. Specifically, the wonderful library of the late Bishop of Würzburg, Julius Echter von Mespelbrunn. Before Gustavus Adolphus had assigned the prince-bishopric to the New United States in the fall of 1632, the king of Sweden's troops had managed to pack up the library. The rector had last seen it crated up, on wagons, on its way to improve the cultural ambiance of Stockholm.

The rector's message, Steve Salatto noted ruefully, was quite clear. He wanted the library back. Or, if the up-timers could not get it back, an equivalent library. Which would cost a lot of money. Which he wanted the administration to provide.

Steve's new chief of staff, Georg Rodolf Weckherlin, cleared his throat significantly and started to discuss the removal of the library of the late elector palatine from Heidelberg to Rome at an earlier stage of the Thirty Years War. Weckherlin was the son of a Württemberg bureaucrat. Although he had spent time in England even before the marriage of the luckless Bohemian Winter King whose adventurism had been the trigger that started the Thirty Years War, to Elizabeth Stuart, his ties to the country had been strengthened through that marriage and he had worked for the electress palatine for a while.

The rector brought up the Peace of Augsburg and the fact that the Calvinism of the late elector had made him an outlaw within the Holy Roman Empire in any case, whereas this was a clear case of theft of property from an institution which followed a religion that was legal under the constitution of that empire.

"Recriminations," Steve said, "will get you nowhere. I can't guarantee you any money. You know what the budget looks like just about as well as I do. But there is one thing that I *can* guarantee, which is that if you keep raking up old grievances, there won't even be a budget request."

He looked at Weckherlin. "That goes for you, too. If you want to keep your job."

Weckherlin smiled back quite cheerfully.

Steve thought for a while after Weckherlin left to show the rector out. "Tinker to Evers to Chance." Oxenstierna to Stearns to Piazza, who had sent Weckherlin to Franconia. Steve had not had anything to say about it. He wouldn't have any more to say about getting rid of him.

At least, being a poet like Meyfarth, Weckherlin was more than willing to write propaganda pieces. And Steve couldn't complain that they had stuck him with an incompetent. Weckherlin had studied law and been a low-level diplomat as well as writing poetry. He had married an English girl, the daughter of the Dover city clerk, in 1616; she was here in Würzburg with him and they had a couple of kids. He got full-time employment in the English government in 1626, became an English citizen in 1630. The entry under his name from the 1911 *Encyclopedia Britannica*, kindly provided by Ed Piazza, indicated that up-time, he had joined the Parliamentary forces during the English Civil War, becoming John Milton's predecessor as "Secretary for Foreign Tongues" under the Commonwealth. In this world, he had caught a boat from Dover to the continent in a timely fashion, before the royal troops who had nabbed Oliver Cromwell caught up with him.

Well, a poet. Not a poet like Meyfarth, though. Replacing one man sitting in your outer office, the poet who had written "Jerusalem, Thou City Fair and High," with another man sitting in your outer office, the poet who had written "Seduction in the Garden, or Love Among the Cabbages," took some getting used to; a bit of readjustment, so to speak. Not that Weckherlin had gotten this job because of the cabbages, or the roses, or the girls with too-beautiful eyes who populated most of his verses. He owed this job to his sonnet in praise of Gustavus Adolphus.

The one that addressed him as a "king whose head and fist were alone adequate to conquer the world, a ruler whose heart and great courage were adorned by fear of God, justice, strength, moderation, and wisdom, whose sword was the terror of persecutors and drove lamentation, fear, and danger away from the persecuted." And that was just for a start. Somewhere before "Mars, of divine descent and from the blood of the Savior who was worthy to triumph over pride and tyranny." The more that Steve read, the more he suspected that it would be pretty hard for any propagandist to get to a level at which the USE's current emperor would consider effusive praise to have reached the point of overkill.

Weckherlin was a competent chief of staff, but a very different man from Meyfarth. Steve would just have to adapt, he supposed.

The thing was, for all his tendency to be a poseur, the man did goddamn well believe that there was such a thing as "Germany." A Germany, moreover, that could and should be a decent place for human beings to live in. One without the "anger, arrogance, treachery, disloyalty, servility, injustice, and superstition" that had destroyed "freedom, laws, and divine worship." If Weckherlin really did, for some reason, believe that Gustavus Adolphus could reverse all that, teaching "the enemy to turn his madness and splendor into repentance, the ally to turn his suffering into joy," maybe it was worth putting up with the rest of the poem.

Not, Steve thought, that he was likely to ask his mother-in-law to cross-stitch a copy of it for him to frame and put up over his desk. His mouth quirked then. He reached across his desk for a pen and clean piece of paper and wrote a note. With a copy of a sonnet. Folded them together, sealed the packet, and addressed it to Grantville. Anita's mom could cross-stitch it for Mike Stearns and send it to Magdeburg. It would fit right in with the rest of the decor of his office, from what Steve had heard.

Better that Mike had to put up with all that garbage than himself.

Würzburg, February, 1634

"As far as any leadership that I can see," Scott Blackwell said, "it's still fairly inchoate at this point. I mean, insofar as there is any visible leadership, it's come to be focused on Frankenwinheim. But that's largely because of the publicity stemming from the attack on Maydene,

Estelle, and Willa back in December and our *own* propaganda. I don't have the vaguest idea who the real leader of this ram movement is— or who the leaders are, if they are multiple. Or where they are. And that, believe me, bothers me a lot."

"At least," Johnnie F. Haun said, "we do pretty much know what they're thinking. Or, at least what they're putting out in pamphlets, what they want their followers to think. They have to have access to some pretty good printing press. Which means they, or some of them, at least, have to be somewhere that they can get paper. Somewhere that they can haul the paper in; haul the pamphlets out. The broadsides and placards are one thing, but not all the pamphlets. They have to be using a press in one of the cities. I just can't see some little village up in the hills producing those under the noses of the *Amtmann* and the constable. Not to mention under the nose of the priest. Not, at least, unless some fairly prominent people are in sympathy with the whole thing."

"Is that the way it looks to you?" Scott asked.

"Not here in Würzburg, I'm sure of that," Johnnie F. answered.

Steve Salatto raised his eyebrows. "Somewhere?"

"Over at Fulda, maybe. Orville thinks . . ."

Steve motioned to Weckherlin. "That's Orville Beattie, the Fulda organizer for Johnnie F.'s 'Hearts and Minds' team."

"Thank you." Weckherlin nodded as he took notes.

"Orville thinks, but he can't prove it, that some of the monks from the abbey are backing the farmers. Not the important ones, so much— the nobles who are there because their families put them there. But the guys out in the rural regions, the provosts as they're called, who manage the farms and the estates, and see more of what the people have been put through these last couple of years. The invasion by the Hessians and all. Yeah, I know that the landgrave of Hesse is one of Gustavus Adolphus' allies, but his soldiers aren't any different from all the rest. Some of the provosts, at least, are sort of sympathetic to the desire of the people in the ram organization. To fight back, I mean. Against—well, against anyone who comes along to hassle them again."

Weckherlin was frowning. But still taking notes.

Johnnie F. felt a little guilty for not mentioning Frau Else Kronacher in Bamberg, but he wasn't a hundred percent sure it was her press being used by the ram. Just ninety-nine percent sure. If Scott and Vince had Stew look into it, that would cause trouble for her, and she had problems enough with those two boys. Not to mention that she did a

lot of work for Stew and the rest of the Hearts and Minds team in Bamberg and it would be a nuisance for Stew to have to find another printer. And . . .

He suspected he was just rationalizing his decision to keep quiet. But he figured if there did turn out to be a problem, he'd take care of it himself without bothering Steve and Scott.

Chapter 8: "But you think that we are going to hell"

Bamberg, February 1634

It was a very small flock. Johann Matthaeus Meyfarth looked out at the fruits of his efforts to organize a Lutheran congregation. He proceeded through the liturgy. General prayer for the church. Collect for peace. Prayer for those whom God had placed in authority over his flock. Sacrament of the altar.

In the afternoon, he wrote. Accompanied by more prayers. Propaganda pieces—many organizational in nature, but well salted with the theme of, "This isn't the time to settle your personal scores; hold that until after we have won. Then we can take our complaints through a fair judicial system in which we have a say."

Propaganda for people who were preparing to revolt against those whom God had placed in positions of authority. Propaganda that might, if they heard it, hold the flock back from worse sins than simply demanding justice.

Twelve Points. Twelve because of the echo of the *Bundschuh* that it raised. Shorter, much shorter, than the Twelve Articles of 1524. Some the same. Some different. Printed, circulated.

The ram had asked him to do this. The ram, he had found, was guarding his flock. And himself.

1. There shall be complete separation of church and state, with no imperial knight, free lord, or other ruler, be he count or duke or king or emperor, having the right to dictate the conscience of his subjects;

2. Catholic, Lutheran, and Calvinist parishes request the right to choose their ministers from a list of qualified men provided by the ecclesiastical authorities, which we know that the administration, because of the separation of church and state, cannot make the churches do, yet we ask it; we say that other religious groups tolerated by the civil governments may pick their own leaders by their own rules, however they set up their organization;

3. All lords and imperial knights whose lands are enclaves within Franconia must permit their subjects to vote in the upcoming elections, saying that they themselves should have such a right to vote also;

4. We demand the end of all vestiges of serfdom on private estates of imperial knights and lords as well as on those which escheated from the bishops and abbot to the administration of the New United States; specifically the ending of restrictions on movement, restrictions on the right to marry, death duties of the best beast and best garment, and compulsory labor services on the lord's own land, though we state that we are nonetheless willing to work the corvées when they are needed for the common good, as on the roads, fords and bridges, as is customary;

5. We demand that local custom be respected in regard to inheritance rights of leases on farms and other rural property, with no requirement for partible or impartible inheritance, etc. being imposed from above;

6. All towns in Franconia must open their citizenship to villagers, as long as they are of good repute and not criminals; citizens of Franconia and their families are to have freedom of movement and settlement anywhere within the territory administered by the State of Thuringia, whether city, market town, or village;

7. Guilds in the towns and cities of Franconia must open training in skilled work to rural applicants and not exclude them on the grounds that they are dishonorable because they carry the taint of serfdom, for all vestiges of serfdom are abolished; guilds must permit widows to continue to operate their husband's business until such time as they marry, pass them on to an heir, or sell them, and make free choice of a buyer;

8. Secondary education is to be open to all; Latin schools in the towns must provide recommended scholars from the village schools with Latin lessons and admit them as soon as they qualify to do the work required by a Latin school;

9. Village-born persons must have the right to enter the service of the state and counties and be promoted as their education qualifies them, with no jobs reserved for the nobility or town patriciates;

10. We demand a standardized coinage and currency, resulting in fair tax assessments, and we request the publication of a clear, easy to understand, tax code written in plain language, in order that we need not pay more than we owe because we are simple ignorant men. We also ask for the abolition of the tithes, being willing to pay fair compensation to those who have bought them and submit the adjudication of fair compensation to impartial arbitrators;

11. We demand the end of internal tolls and tariffs, those imposed by the local lords and the imperial knights whose lands are enclaves within Franconia, saying that if such lords and knights are willing to become citizens of Franconia, they shall have all the rights of other men;

12. We demand standardized weights and measures, so that it is less easy for the clever and cunning to cheat the simple and trusting, that a bushel may everywhere be a bushel and a tun everywhere a tun.

Frankenwinheim, Franconia, February, 1634

"It is safe for Pastor Meyfarth, I think," Old Kaethe said. "At least as safe as anything can be in these latter days. I am glad that Frau

Else thought of her. *Die alte Neideckerin."*

Constantin Ableidinger nodded. He tried to get back to Frankenwinheim on a regular basis. The villagers there were the closest thing he had to friends. He had finally, since his obligations to the ram had become so heavy, sent Matthias to the *gymnasium* in Coburg. The boy should be safe there. As safe, as Old Kaethe had said, as anyone could be in these latter days. But he missed his son. Since the remarkable episode of the three auditors, he had returned to Frankenwinheim twice.

"At least, in Bamberg, the ram's men can continue to keep an eye on Meyfarth." He tilted back on two legs of his stool and waved his stein at Old Kaethe.

"What do you think?" She poured his beer.

"I would have preferred, if possible, to keep religion out of it altogether. Since I can't, apparently, it's just as well that the religious points are being pushed by a rational man rather than by some visionary on the model of the 1536 Muensterites. Or by an up-timer such as this Herr Thornton. If he were writing this *propaganda*, as they call it, Fuchs von Bimbach and his followers would rejoice. As it is . . . Well, the radical demands of a century ago seem comparatively conservative in this day and age." He laughed. "Which may represent progress."

Rudolph Vulpius stroked his goatee. "What about von Bimbach? He's the leader of the most intransigent of the knights and little nobles. I think we need to do something about him. What about the request that we have received from this Miss Noelle Murphy through the Hearts and Minds Team? Have you taken my suggestion seriously? That we should contact Judith Neideckerin? It's not the only possibility. I have ties to other people on the estates of various branches of the Fuchs family. Not amicable ties, necessarily, but ties."

The villagers present looked at each other.

Ableidinger, a comparative newcomer to Frankenwinheim, cleared his throat.

"In the days of my grandfather," Vulpius said, "there was a maid serving on their estates here in the Steigerwald. Children for whom the *Freiherr* of that day provided funds for education. A lease on favorable terms for the man the maid eventually married that set him up as one of the village's most prosperous tenants. An appointment as bailiff. The kind of thing that got a boy sent to school to the point he Latinized his name to Vulpius."

Ableidinger grinned.

"Judith owes us," Old Kaethe insisted, refusing to let irrelevant history distract her from more immediate concerns. "We are the ones who took her out of Bamberg in 1628 and saw to it that she reached Bayreuth safely. Now that Pastor Meyfarth is living in her mother's house in Bamberg . . ."

Her voice trailed off until a new grievance crossed her mind. "Not to mention that Pastor Schaeffer is over in Bimbach's castle serving as a chaplain since he left the village. *And* is suing to try to force us to continue paying his stipend on the grounds that he did not leave voluntarily . . ." Old Kaethe snorted. "I can't imagine that Judith Neideckerin likes Pastor Schaeffer. He's probably condemning her as a scarlet woman, sermon after sermon."

Ableidinger chewed on his upper lip. "Did von Bimbach force her to become his mistress? Does she hold a grudge against him?"

"He made it plain that if she wanted him to continue providing her with a refuge from Bamberg's witch-hunters, he expected adequate compensation for the risk. Otherwise, if she valued her virtue too highly, she was quite free to return to her parents' house. That was at the height of the burnings."

"She's good looking."

Everyone jumped a little when Vulpius' grandson Tobias threw his opinion into the conversation.

"I've seen her. Hefty, but good looking. Clear skin and strong teeth."

"Bimbach must feed her well enough, then," Old Kaethe said sourly.

Ableidinger's mind wandered. What looked like "hefty" to a skinny teenager whose standard of comparison was Old Kaethe might look . . . well, "voluptuous" to a thickset middle-aged man like himself.

He called his mind back to order. Clearly, he had remained a widower for too long.

"Her position is privileged, in a way." Vulpius waved his hand. "If it wasn't, there wouldn't be many advantages to contacting her. Not many advantages to us, that is. She has the freedom to go wherever she will in the castle. That doesn't mean that she has any affection for the *Freiherr*."

"Practical of her," Ableidinger said.

"I doubt," Vulpius warned, "that she's given any thought to political theory. Or has any ideals about it."

Frau Lydia Färber, although no longer a Frau *Stadtraetin* since the late councilman's death, was nonetheless still, by the standards of

Bamberg after a decade of war, a well-to-do woman. She found a guide for Willard Thornton and paid him. In spite of the season, Willard alternated his time—a week in Bamberg, talking to the women there to whom Frau Färber had given copies of the *Book of Mormon* and sometimes to their friends; three weeks out in the countryside, distributing not only LDS literature but also Meyfarth's pamphlets.

Both of the Thorntons rather liked Meyfarth. They had gotten to know one another pretty well since he and Willard walked into Bamberg together.

While Willard was out in the villages, his wife Emma, who had to do a lot of studying about LDS history and such when she converted, wrote up a great deal of what she remembered about the church's organizational principles into pamphlets. Willard's friend Meyfarth translated those, adding sections on the best way to incorporate them into the existing structure of village *Gemeinden*, and sent them out into circulation within the ram movement as well.

Meyfarth was a funny guy, Emma thought, so terribly serious and conscientious. He had taken at least an hour to talk about the fact that his personal liking for them did not in any way mean that he was endorsing their teachings, or even that he respected their teachings. "Only," he had insisted, "that I have come to see that if truth is to have a chance to prevail against error, then the civil authorities may not be given the right to suppress any one body of ideas. No, I do not respect your beliefs. If I respected them, I would join your church. I do respect your right to have and teach those beliefs."

So anxious, he had been, as though he had expected them to order him to go away and never come back. "I do not respect your faith," he had continued. "I believe that it is contrary to biblical truth. Utterly contrary, utterly wrong. As Herr Blackwell would say, 'wrong-headed.' But I respect that you honestly hold that faith. And, however reluctantly, I have come to accept that if the law forbids one variety of error, that of the papists, from forbidding us to teach the truth, then the same law must also prohibit us from forbidding the teaching of other errors, such as those of the Calvinists and Anabaptists. And that we, to gain the right of free teaching, must allow it as well. But . . ."

"But you think that we are going to hell." Willard had completed what Meyfarth clearly did not want to say.

"Well, yes. And I also make no claim that everyone else within Lutheranism shares my views. For which reason, if 'We mean it' does not prevail, I may someday lose my head. But until that day . . . I am here."

Emma also talked to Frau Färber's friends, and to other Bamberg women. When the weather was good enough, she handed out literature at the weekly market. Someone had replaced the booth that the friar had torn down the day that Willard was beaten. She winced. She did not like to think of what Willard's back had looked like when he came home after that happened.

She even managed to give away some more copies of the *Book of Mormon*. Not to mention many, many, copies of the abbreviated edition of *Robert's Rules of Order*. Emma had run out of that. Meyfarth had said with great seriousness that the ram would find funds to reprint it. Or, possibly, the ewe.

When he showed her the ram literature, with Brillo, not to mention the caricature of Veleda Riddle as Ewegenia, symbol of the Franconian League of Women Voters, Emma practically went into hysterics.

Until Meyfarth introduced her to some of the men. And said that Willard's guide through the villages was one of them; that others remained here in Bamberg to keep watch over her, and over Frau Färber. And, Meyfarth said with a rather shamed face, over him. Although he was a Lutheran minister and should not, properly, be involved in such matters.

He also introduced her to the ewe. Else Kronacher, a printer's widow. And to Frau Else's daughter Martha, a formidable young woman in her mid-twenties. Meyfarth seemed more than a little in awe of her.

Frau Else, Meyfarth explained, had taught the ram rebellion an object lesson in the importance of careful proof-reading. When the Twelve Points went to the printer, only the first half of the seventh point had been in the text. Frau Färber, however, had taken it to her friend. Being the widow of a printer, Frau Kronacher was currently locked in battle with the guild. She had two sons, Melchior and Otto, seventeen and fifteen, as well as the daughter; she wished to run the business using journeymen as employees until her sons became masters. The guild master insisted that she must marry her daughter off now, to a journeyman ready to become a master and take the shop over immediately, thus excluding the woman's sons for the lifetime of their brother-in-law. Oddly, the guild master had a third son who met the qualifications his father was demanding.

When the bales of broadsides came back from Frau Kronacher, they contained the second part of point seven. No one else—well, no one except Fräulein Martha, who had typeset the lines—had noticed until after they had been distributed.

"And thus," Meyfarth said a little ruefully, "with such great foresight and planning, our revolutions are made."

Würzburg, mid-February, 1634

"It's an odd batch of demands," Saunders Wendell said.

The administration had met to discuss the Twelve Points. Every broadside and brochure they had collected, inside Franconia and out, included them.

"And if you ignore the numbering," he continued, "they've included more than twelve different ones."

"For a down-time piece of writing, though," David Petrini said, "it's amazingly succinct."

They looked at the various versions. Most started with the standard Twelve Points. Some went on and on, to specify local grievances, although mostly those were ones that had been collected "out"—over in Bayreuth, down in Ansbach, in various villages belonging to *Reichsritter* and various independent Protestant lords who were exempt from the administration's control. Even some from Nürnberg's hinterland.

The subjects of the *Freiherr* Fuchs von Bimbach had thought of sixty-three points, some of them very specific, involving the allotment of hay mowed in the upper meadows and the annual worth of the acorns consumed in the *Freiherr*'s forests by his subjects' hogs. All of which they announced themselves quite willing to take all the way to the imperial supreme court for adjudication.

"Fox from Bimbo?" someone asked.

Everyone else pretended not to have heard. The general impression that they drew from the sixty three points was that the subjects of the *Freiherr* von Bimbach were not happy campers this *Anno Domini* 1634. However, he was Protestant, and out of their jurisdiction, having most of his estates as an enclave over to the east of Bamberg, surrounded by those of the margrave of Brandenburg-Bayreuth.

"The emphasis on education in Latin and access to secondary education. Are those really all that important to the farmers?" Estelle Colburn was frowning at her copy.

"It doesn't strike me as quite the ringing revolutionary cry of 'to the barricades' with which Gretchen Richter has been trying to inspire the Committees of Correspondence," Anita agreed. " 'Admit our sons to the civil service' doesn't have quite the same effect in grabbing the reader's attention as, 'Workers of the world, unite! You have nothing to lose but your chains.' "

"But they do go into the civil service, if they can, Anita," her husband Steve pointed out. "I talked to Count Ludwig Guenther's chancellor before we came down here, way back. He's the son of a farmer from one of the count's villages. His father sent him to school because the pastor recommended it; he went into the count's service straight out of the University of Jena and climbed right up the ladder. That's not so unusual. Along with being a priest, it's just about the only path to social mobility around, for a farm family, given how the towns and the guild trades freeze them out."

"Gretchen's grandma, maybe," Maydene Utt said.

Everyone else at the table stared at her. This comment seemed to be coming out of left field.

Maydene persisted. "Ronnie Dreeson has students from Jena talking conversational Latin to the toddlers at the St. Veronica's schools. I think she's got pretty much the same idea."

"Thought I heard a few echoes of what you and Willa were doing last fall, in the tax stuff," David Petrini interjected.

All three of the auditors pointedly ignored him.

"Gretchen Richter isn't writing this stuff. I don't think that anyone involved with the Committees is writing this stuff," Johnnie F. said. "The CoCs really haven't spread much in Franconia, except in some of the industrial towns. There are Committees in Suhl and Schmalkalden and Schleusingen. The honest truth is, though, that they don't have much interest in the farmers. They're focusing on the cities—places where they can get hold of good-sized audiences all at once, not country villages where maybe they get a half-dozen or a dozen."

"It sure isn't what Spartacus is writing. It's not intellectual, analytical stuff. The style is way different, too. They aren't even plagiarizing him," Dave Stannard added. "The Twelve Points aren't like the Brillo Broadsides or the Common Sense pamphlets, either. The author has his own agenda."

"Where is it coming from, then?" Maydene asked.

"Some of the points, from the farmers themselves," Johnnie F. said.

"Like, 'don't try to tell us how to divide our property when we die.' The rest . . ."

"There are two kinds of revolutions," Dave Stannard interrupted. "The 'down with the system' revolutions. Those are really hard to handle. Especially when the people in them don't know for sure what they want to put in place of what they have. Then the 'let us into the system' revolutions. Those are a bit more manageable, generally, and that seems to be, mostly, what we've got here. A lot of the rest of the points, I think, from talking to the *Amtmaenner* and people out in the villages who are working on the voter registration lists, are what our old friend Meyfarth thinks would be good for them."

"Meyfarth!" Scott Blackwell choked on his coffee.

Johnnie F. cleared his throat. "Stew says . . ."

Steve motioned to Weckherlin again. "Stewart Hawker, Johnnie F.'s counterpart over in Bamberg."

Weckherlin nodded.

"Stew says that he's churning out the propaganda pamphlets, apparently spending all night writing with both hands at once, plus songs and poems and talking points and," he grinned, "getting a lot of help from Emma Thornton. So you can put that in your pipe and smoke it."

Steve looked warily at Maydene, Willa, and Estelle. "Don't tell me," he said, "that Emma Thornton is a member of . . ."

The three of them chanted together, "the Grantville League of Women Voters."

Willa added, "So's Liz."

"Liz who?" Weckherlin asked.

"Liz Carstairs. Her sister-in-law. Was Mike Stearns's chief of staff; now Ed Piazza's. You must know her."

Georg Rodolf Weckherlin looked down at his notes to disguise a wince. Were all these up-timers related to one another? How could a person possibly keep track of it? He doubted that he would ever forget his first encounter with that, that . . . creature who sat in the anteroom of the SoT's president. She was not an Araminta. Nor an Ariadne. Nor any of the other nymphs who populated love poems. His job required him to exchange correspondence with her regularly. It was not his favorite activity. No one short of a dowager empress should be so self-confident. Certainly not that woman. She was, really, only the wife of a small town guildsman who belonged to a heterodox religious sect.

At least, he had known enough to treat her with outward respect. He had been warned about her already in Magdeburg, before he took the letter of recommendation to Grantville. Which meant that he owed a big favor to *Graf* August von Sommersburg. A very big one which, undoubtedly, the count realized. And would, someday, call in. Dealing with these up-timers could be a touchy business.

Chapter 9: "Unless it should happen that I am unlucky"

Franconia, February 22, 1634

David Stannard had been quite right the previous fall when he said that down-time *Amtmaenner* really had lists down pat. They had the electoral lists in shape. Every *Amt* had just as many preprinted paper ballots as it had potential voters, with a dozen or so to spare in case someone made a mistake. The spares were sealed. If one was used, two different election officials had to sign an explanation of the circumstances why it was needed, written on the envelope next to the opened seal. With the spoiled ballot, crossed out, put into the envelope.

In a few places, such as the town of Gerolzhofen, the election had to be conducted under military supervision.

The administration had given the ram its point three. Every adult in Franconia got to vote, even the people living in the little independent enclaves, just as long as they were within the general boundaries of Würzburg, Bamberg, and Fulda.

So in quite a few *more* places, the electors had to be conducted under military supervision, so to speak. Conducted from their village of residence, where some sputtering local lord was trying to prohibit voting, to the nearest functioning polling place.

Followed by a visit from the military police to the lord or *Reichsritter* to explain what they planned to do if they received any information in regard to attempted retaliation against legal voters.

"We mean it" did very well in the Franconian election of 1634. "Motherhood" and "Apple Pie" were not on the ballot.

The *Amtmaenner* had counting the votes down pat, too. The results were tallied, certified, and delivered to Würzburg within a week.

With a few exceptions like Bamberg and some of the industrial towns nestled against the Thuringenwald, the towns and cities had not been enthusiastic. The guilds had led a bitter opposition, largely based on the argument that if incorporation passed, the "foreigners" would impose points six, seven, and eight of the "Twelve Points." In most of the towns, incorporation either failed or barely squeaked by.

However, eighty percent or more of Franconia's population did not live in chartered towns.

Some villages were solidly opposed; some few were a hundred percent opposed. Dave Stannard proposed to take a look at possible undue pressure from landlords, here and there, in spite of all the precautions that he and Scott Blackwell had taken in regard to secret ballots. The simple truth was that if a precinct only had a dozen voters, if one of them disagreed with the local boss, the boss could probably find out who it was. Even with a ballot held secret, there were a very limited number of choices about who it might have been.

Overall, however, sixty-three percent of the registered voters cast ballots in favor of the incorporation of Franconia into the State of Thuringia and citizenship for its inhabitants.

Grantville, State of Thuringia

On March 5, 1634, the Congress of the State of Thuringia adopted a formal name change, subject to a future referendum, from the State of Thuringia to the State of Thuringia-Franconia. There had originally been some discussion to the effect that as a courtesy and in the name of welcome, the name of the new region should be placed first. Arnold Bellamy pointed out that this would result in the acronym SoFT, not an image which the USE or its component states wished to present to the League of Ostend just now.

Therefore, it was SoTF. Unpronounceable, of course, but also not evocative of any undesirable associations whatsoever.

Until the next crisis, which occurred very shortly thereafter, Bellamy was in an unusually good mood.

Franconia, mid-March, 1634

Several minor lords, mostly Protestant, whose lands were enclaves within Würzburg and Bamberg, objected vociferously to the incorporation vote. Especially the Fuchs von Bimbach family, which turned out to have not only a Protestant branch centered in Bayreuth but also a Catholic branch with estates intermingled among those formerly belonging to the prince-bishop of Bamberg.

This, Johnnie F. found out from Meyfarth on one of his jaunts up to Bamberg, was not at all unusual in Franconia. A lot of the *Reichsritter, Freiherren,* and lesser local nobility had split into Catholic and Protestant branches, in order to have a foot in each camp and someone among the relatives with an arguable and viable claim to the family's lands whenever the politico-religious situation underwent a minor shift or major earthquake.

Bamberg, mid-March, 1634

"So how are the CoC English lessons going?" Janie Kacere asked.

Eddie Junker sighed. "Apprentices. Unruly apprentices."

" 'Amid gloom and doom' is the normal situation for first-time teachers," she consoled him.

"Most of them are just antsy and energetic. If I tell them to write a sentence using the words pink, green, and yellow, they'll toss paper airplanes at one another—those are quite a fad, these days—but they'll write something like, 'I got out of bed, put on my pink shirt, harnessed up my green wagon, and looked at the yellow sun.' "

"That's not bad," Stew Hawker said.

"Yeah." Eddie sighed deeply. "Then there's Otto. Frau Else's younger son."

"He wrote?"

"The telephone *greened. Green, green.* I *pinked* it up and said, '*yel-low!*'"

"I take it," Janie said, "that he knows better."

"Oh, sure. He's the best student I've got. He's just . . . Well, he knows he's the best student I've got and he takes advantage of it. None of the rest of them are anywhere near to the point of making puns in English."

Noelle shuffled through the mail that had arrived at the Bamberg *Schloss* in the diplomatic pouch and picked out the letter from Ed Piazza to be read first. The one from the administrators in Suhl, second. Arnold Bellamy's went to the bottom of the pile.

Fuchs von Bimbach is going to be the key. That was the gist of Piazza's letter.

Well, she didn't disagree. Here on the ground in Franconia, His Bimboship maybe looked even more key than he did from Grantville. Or from Magdeburg. There was a letter from Don Francisco Nasi's office, too.

"I have to get inside," Noelle said that evening. She rapped her knuckles on the table in front of her.

"I don't like the idea." Eddie Junker was chewing on his lower lip. "*Ja*, Helmut has supporters among the servants there. Bimbach's subjects don't have any love for their lord and master. Frau Else can put you in touch. But if the bosses catch on that you're not just one of the Ram's people but also that you're an up-timer, there would be hell to pay."

"It's not that dangerous. After three years talking mainly to Germans, my German is pretty good. Plus, with all the different dialects, accent isn't that much of a problem. I can avoid the castle authorities. I'll be Downstairs, not Upstairs. Even if His Bimboship's personal staff hear me say something, it won't be fatal. They'll know that I'm not from right around here, but with all the population displacement that the war has caused, they'll just think that I'm from somewhere else."

"Do you actually trust the old Neidecker woman?"

"Not as long as her daughter is in that castle. She lived through the witch trials. It's not like the nun who's helping us."

Eddie nodded. Anna Maria Junius at the Dominican convent in Bamberg was so grateful to Grantville for saving her sister Veronica when those fanatics hauled her into Suhl a couple of years ago that she had really gone out of her way to help the NUS administration.

"Taking Johnnie F. and Willard in and patching them up last fall. Everything. I'd trust Sister Anna Maria with my life." Noelle grinned. "I do trust her with my political maneuvers. That history of Bamberg during the war that she's writing has been a lifesaver when it comes to figuring out the various factions and such. *Die alte Neideckerin*, though. In her heart, I think, she's afraid that we'll be putting Judith in a lot more danger if she helps us deal with von Bimbach. After all, they sent her away in the first place in order to keep her safe."

"If you go," Eddie said, "I'm going too."

Noelle shook her head.

"Yes," Eddie persisted. "I am." He pulled out his own stack of mail. "I bet you put your letter from Arnold Bellamy on the bottom of your stack, didn't you?"

"Umm. Yes."

"Well, I opened mine. He's written to Steve Salatto and Vince Marcantonio. He can't rescind your 'special envoy' status when it comes from Prime Minister Stearns, but he's made it clear to them. If you go in there, I go with you. Down-time muscle. Thick of skull and strong of arm, that's me."

Noelle leaned back, looking at him. Eddie was better known for brains than brawn, even though he was quite big.

"You think they'd let in someone who looks like a huge hulking bodyguard coming with the new maid that Judith Neidecker's mother sent her from Bamberg? Me, they won't even notice."

Noelle pulled out her letter from Arnold Bellamy and read through it before she answered.

"Okay. It looks like you're coming. But I don't like it. You're just a kid."

"I'm as old as you are," Eddie said. "And just as stubborn. I may not be as wrong-headed and snobbish as my father, but I'm just as stubborn as he is. Plus . . ." He flashed her an impudent grin, "I got my mother's smarts, too. The combination is unbeatable."

"Except, maybe, by Otto Kronacher."

"Well, yeah. There's always Otto."

Würzburg, mid-March, 1634

"The person with whom you are meeting this morning," Weckherlin said, "is an agent of the Fuchs von Bimbach family. A lawyer and administrator. His name is Dr. Polycarp Lenz. Nicknamed by almost all who know him, I hear, 'Pestilenz.' Signifying . . ."

"Plague," Steve Salatto interrupted. "Why?"

"Irascible. Irritable. Obnoxious. Obstructionist. Uncooperative. Unreasonable."

"Got it. Enshrines all the worst qualities presupposed in a Libertarian's view of the typical bureaucrat."

"What is a Libertarian?" Weckherlin asked.

"A person who thinks that sort of thing about us—the noble civil servants who give of themselves unstintingly that the citizens of their country may receive their driver's license renewals in a timely fashion."

"What is a driver's license?" Weckherlin had, after all, spent only a week in Grantville and that had mostly been devoted to acquiring a passport from the consular service, a health certificate from the Leahy Medical Center, and other mandatory activities that interfered seriously with getting to know more about life in the twentieth century.

"A permit to drive a motorized vehicle. Did Lenz tell us what he wants?"

"No."

Dr. Lenz delivered a petition, signed by over two hundred of the Protestant imperial knights and petty lords of Franconia. All of Franconia, not just the parts included in the SoTF, but also Bayreuth, Ansbach, and the Nürnberg hinterland. In fact, mainly Bayreuth, Ansbach, and the Nürnberg hinterland, since the majority of those inside Würzburg, Bamberg, and Fulda were Catholic.

The petition was addressed to Gustavus Adolphus. It requested that he annul the election that took place on February 22, revoke its effects, and remove Franconia from the unnatural administration imposed by the foreign up-timers. That he restore it to its rightful lords, the native-born Protestant nobility. Offering, in a spirit of noble self sacrifice, that they, should the emperor see fit to burden them with the onerous task, would be willing to assume the duty of governing the heretical, rebellious, Catholic principalities.

Dr. Lenz announced that this was the third copy of the signed and sealed petition. The first had been sent to the emperor directly; the second, through one of the administration's auditors, Herr Johann Friedrich Krausold, to Duke Wilhelm of Saxe-Weimar, who was now using the name Wilhelm Wettin. Lenz's distaste for the latter version of the name was clear in his voice.

Steve said that he was delighted to hear it.

He didn't know what Dr. Lenz had been expecting, but it clearly wasn't that.

Steve really was delighted to get the full list of signers. It was the first really concrete information he had about which of the knights and lords were not going to budge from their objections to what the administration was doing. Not to mention external confirmation that Krausold had not just been griping to Meyfarth but was actively involved in undermining the administration.

Weckherlin saw Dr. Lenz out.

Steve wished he had a buzzer. But he didn't, so he got up to walk down to the auditors' office, where once the special commissioners had sat. He looked around. The coast was clear.

"Maydene," he said. "You may have a little problem in your bailiwick."

The gals promised to get right on it.

Within a minute after she stopped by to visit Eddie at Frau Kronacher's print shop, Noelle was having to fight down laughter.

She wasn't entirely successful, either—which drew a quick glare at her from Eddie, where he was standing at the front of the little storeroom that served him as an impromptu classroom for the apprentices.

"No, Melchior," he said, "I *know* it's pronounced the same way. But"—here he pointed to a small slate chalkboard propped up against the far wall—"in English, it's actually spelled *women*. W-O-M-E-N. Not wimmin."

"Makes no sense," protested Melchior's brother Otto. "That should be pronounced 'Woe-men.' "

The glare now fell on Otto. "And you think our German doesn't have plenty of quirks, when it comes to spelling?"

"Not as many as English," Otto countered stoutly.

Noelle got the sense this was an old and long-running argument. Eddie shook his head, a bit wearily, and went on.

"Never mind. Let's run through the verses again. Just the first six."

Obediently, the small group of apprentices began chanting in English:

"Once upon a time there were three Brillo Rams Gruff—a little baby ram lamb, a medium-sized ram lamb, and their great big, sturdy, strong, daddy ram.

"Every day they trotted over to the field where there was sweet green grass and all the wimmin. Sometimes there was a fence, but that wasn't much of a problem. The daddy Brillo ram would give the fence such a PINCH, and it would tumble over.

"One day, a bridge and a set of tracks were laid on the way to the field with the sweet green grass and plenty of wimmin. That was no problem, because the three Brillo Rams Gruff just made a nice trit-trot sound on the tracks as they went to the field with the sweet green grass and all the wimmin.

"They went to the field with the sweet green grass and all the wimmin every day. Every afternoon, the Flo lady would take them back to their own place. First she would take the daddy Brillo ram, then the medium-sized Brillo ram lamb, and last of all the little baby Brillo ram lamb.

"One day, a terrible troll blocked the tracks. It puffed and steamed with terrible smoke, and it made a loud chuffing sound, and it rattled its terrible noisy tail. It even made a terrible screeching sound, and had a terrible tinkly bell sound.

"The three Brillo Rams Gruff wouldn't let that troll stop them from going to the field with the sweet green grass and all the wimmin."

Later, as they went out to share lunch at a nearby tavern, Noelle did start laughing. "Why in the world do you use those Brillo fables? Even by English standards, the spelling in them is crazy. Most of that stuff is supposed to be a *joke*."

Eddie sighed. "Yes, I know. But the Brillo fables are the one thing that is always sure to interest them. Especially these new ones, about Brillo and the railroad people."

"Why's that?"

"You need to ask? Ever since the Suhl Incident, Germans in Franconia associate everything involving your American railroad people with things they find favorable about you. Well, the farmers and most of the poorer townspeople, anyway. The guild masters aren't too fond of you, of course."

Noelle thought about it, for a moment. "Still seems odd. In every one of those fables I've heard, Brillo's pretty much at odds with TacRail people."

Eddie shrugged. "Yes? So much the better. They like the interchange, you might say. Yes, Brillo is at odds with the railroad people—but it usually gets sorted out in the end, to everyone's reasonable satisfaction. There's a political lesson there, if you think about it."

They walked on a very more steps. Then, Eddie added:

"Your Anse Hatfield is now quite a hero, for many people here in Franconia. Not so much because they think he is one of them, you understand. Just . . . that he is someone strong, whom they can deal with without fear."

Noelle laughed again.

"What's so funny?"

"Without fear! You *do* know who Anse was named after, don't you?"

Eddie shook his head.

"Ah, wonderful. A whole new set of American fables you need to learn." They'd arrived at the tavern. "But you'll need to brace yourself, first. A stein of beer and a good sandwich. Then I'll tell you about the Hatfield-McCoy feud. And the man they called 'Devil Anse Hatfield.' "

On their way back to the print shop, Eddie said to her, "I don't think I'll tell the apprentices about Devil Anse."

"What a good idea."

"Do you have time to ride out with me again, Scott?" Johnnie F. asked. "For a few days, not just a short run."

"Why?"

"Sort of like last fall. I'd just feel easier in my mind if somebody brought along another set of eyes to look at what I think I'm seeing."

"What do you think you see?"

"I'd rather not say. That's why I want fresh eyes."

Franconia, mid-March, 1634

Scott recognized that village. They were up in the back of beyond, it had a funny church tower, and the biggest ram banner he had seen anywhere in Franconia.

His nose was cold. His toes were cold.

"We'll be there," Johnnie F. was saying, "in time for the meeting."

"Johnnie F.," Scott said pleadingly, "will you tell me. Where in hell are we?"

"Right up against the border with Coburg. As far as we can go and still be inside our part of Franconia. The border stones march right along the crest of those hills behind the village; half of its fields are in the USE."

Johnnie F. smiled. "I spent one summer while I was in college in Washington, D.C., you know. Of all stupid-seeming places for an ag major to intern, but I was working for the Forestry Service at the USDA—Department of Agriculture, that is.

"There were reports in the paper all the time. Gangs, shooting at one another. Then jumping into another jurisdiction. Out of D.C. and across the street, into Prince George's County in Maryland. Different jurisdiction; cops come to a screeching halt at the border, the perps thumb their noses and disappear. And so forth. There must have been a dozen little jurisdictions around there, in a space no bigger than the Ring of Fire, really."

"So?"

"So, it's a handy kind of place to be, right on a border. If you think that somebody might be coming after you."

Johnnie F. looked down into the valley, at the village strung out along the creek.

"We'll be going to a meeting, tonight, after we eat. If you just keep quiet, I think that maybe you'll get to meet the Ram. The Big Bad Brillo, himself."

"No Ewegenia?"

Johnnie F. didn't even smile. "No. She's in Bamberg."

Scott looked at him. "You know who she is?"

"Sure," Johnnie F. said mildly. "Once it occurred to me that they had a press in one of the larger cities, it wasn't any real trouble to find out."

"Inclined to tell me?"

"Depends. Do you really need to know?"

Scott was constrained to be quiet, but Johnnie F. hadn't told him not to write notes in school. As soon as the pipes struck up the melody, he scribbled, "Isn't that 'America'—you know, 'My Country 'tis of Thee'?"

"It was, once upon a time," Johnnie F. scribbled back. "The tune is the same, but the words go off from the second verse, 'Our fathers' God to Thee, author of liberty, to Thee we sing' and it's real different."

> Gott uns'res Vaterlands,
> der Freiheit, des Verstands,
> Dich loben wir.
> Leih' uns die Moeglichkeit,
> Dein' Liebe, dein Geleit,
> Von Deiner Ewigkeit,
> Justiz von Dir.

Scott sat quietly, trying to translate as he listened. The German seemed like it had sort of been crammed into the tune, by someone writing too fast to make it a good match. The heavy Franconian accented German of the singers wasn't helping, either. A lot of the village dialects didn't bear much resemblance to what was spoken in Würzburg.

"God of our fatherland, of freedom, of reason, we praise you." *Was that right?*

"Give us the possibility." *Did that make sense, or did it mean something else?*

"Your love," then—a "Geleit" for a soldier was a military escort, "from eternity, justice from you."

The singers were well into the second verse, now.

> Gib uns das täglich' Brot,
> Spar' uns des Elends Not,
> Dich ehren wir.
> Wende den Kriege ab,
> Bis wir den Frieden hab'
> Nie mehr des Hochmuts Raub,
> Das beten wir.

"Give us our daily bread, spare us the famine of suffering. We honor you." *Okay.* "Avert war until we have peace, no longer the loot of arrogance. We pray that."

Johnnie F. leaned over and whispered: "There's several more verses in the whole thing, mainly a run through the beatitudes, but they mostly only sing those two to open a meeting. Must be a cinch to write verses in a language where most of the abstract nouns end in either "heit" or "keit" and can be made to rhyme with one another."

"It's sort of . . . calming, as revolutionary songs go."

"I told you all that Meyfarth wasn't writing stuff that cries for vengeance and bloodshed. You can't expect him to be a re-run of Spartacus, either. He's a preacher, for Pete's sake. He's bound to use a lot of religious stuff in what he writes. None of the 'be a revolutionary atheist' gig for him."

"Meyfarth, again?"

"Yeah. Some of the farmers have written other verses that say rude things about tithes and taxes, but this is the 'official' version. As far as Orville and Stew and I know, they, the ram people, are opening all of their meetings with it."

A middle-aged man got up. A quite ordinary man, a person might think, aside from the booming voice that emerged from his thick body. The kind of voice that could be heard by a couple of thousand people gathered in an open field.

He was holding a copy of *Robert's Rules of Order*, and proceeded to conduct the meeting in accordance with it. Starting with a pledge of allegiance to the flag of the State of Thuringia-Franconia. Ending, a couple of hours later . . . something was so familiar. Scott's mind went back to that meeting last fall.

Scott scribbled again. "Did Meyfarth really translate the 'Concord Hymn' into German?"

"Yeah. And they've *all* memorized it. They sing it to the tune of 'From Heav'n Above, To Earth I Come.' That's a children's Christmas song that Martin Luther wrote. Same number of syllables in each line and everybody knows the tune."

"In Aprils Luft entfalten sich die Flaggen."

In the "few days" that Johnnie F. had asked for, they attended several more meetings. The man with the booming voice was speaking at most of them. He was carefully guarded by a dozen *Jaeger* wearing the ram badge on their armbands. They let Johnnie F. and Scott approach him.

"Who am I?" he asked. "Why, who but an actor on this stage that is life? A pupil in the Coburg *Gymnasium* when I was much younger than I am now. A scholarship boy, brought in from a border village by the duke's charity, because the pastor recommended me. A failed university student, once upon a time, a would-be-lawyer who had to leave because he not only got a baker's daughter pregnant, a bad enough scandal, but married her—a far worse one in the academic world. A village schoolmaster in Frankenwinheim, more recently. A thinker of thoughts and a dreamer of dreams."

He looked at the pamphlet in his hand and laughed uproariously. "Now a pupil of inspired fools. A student who takes what they say and shapes it so that the farmers of Franconia understand."

Blackwell looked over the man's shoulder. The man was reading *Common Sense*, by Thomas Paine.

"Will we meet you again?"

"Probably, very probably. Unless it should happen that I am unlucky."

Chapter 10: "Just a truce in a little corner of it"

Würzburg, late March, 1634

"I think they've harnessed it," Scott said to the morning briefing. "This *Common Sense* guy, using Meyfarth and the Thorntons. If they haven't accomplished miracles, then at least near-miracles. I'm not going to try to tell you how deeply it has all sunk in, or how widely. They've had, what, a few months? On top of grievances and grudges that have been building for years. But the stuff is all over the place. It's being read, and sung, repeated in this guy's speeches, talked about. They've made us a harness."

"So now," Scott said, "we get to ride the ram."

"Speaking of which . . ." Johnnie F. tossed a newspaper on the table. It was one of the ones printed in Franconia. "Have you seen 'Brillo's Little Red Rider'? They've got Princess Kristina riding Brillo in that one. You've all got to read it."

"Later," Steve said firmly. "Right now, we need to deal with the petition that the knights and lords have sent to Gustavus Adolphus. This is what I've gotten back from Ed and Arnold in Grantville. And from Mike Stearns."

"They're different?"

"Mike's language is considerably more colorful, and . . ."

"And?" Scott asked.

Steve sighed. "We have an intervention from Margrave Christian of Brandenburg-Bayreuth. Diplomatic, at the moment. Very diplomatic. Just asks us to consider the difficulty in which our policies are placing the Protestant nobility of Franconia. Doesn't say anything about a military action, not even obliquely. Dr. Lenz, however, the agent representing the *Freiherr* Fuchs von Bimbach, claims that the margrave is prepared to undertake an invasion of Franconia in support of the petitioners."

David Petrini interrupted. "Of course, they're trying to take advantage of the fact that Gustav Adolf himself is very busy in the north dealing with the League of Ostend, so they presume that they're really appealing to Oxenstierna. Who, in his heart, believes that the nobles really should rule."

"Aren't they forgetting," Anita asked, "that he's all the way up in Stockholm and unless someone radios the petition to him, he isn't going to get it very soon?"

"Unless it's really meant for Wilhelm Wettin—a stick he can use against Mike," Steve answered.

"Oh, holy shit!" Scott said. "I go out of town for a few days and all hell breaks loose!"

"Brandenburg-Bayreuth?" Johnnie F. asked. "I'd just heard it called Bayreuth before. Brandenburg, I know, turned into Prussia later on. But what are the Hohenzollerns doing down here?"

"The Hohenzollerns *started* 'down here,' " Weckherlin answered. "These men, now, Margrave Christian in Bayreuth and his nephews in Ansbach, are a cadet line of the family represented by Margrave George Wilhelm up in Berlin, who is a brother of Gustavus Adolphus' wife. The Hohenzollern family though, back in the middle ages, began here. As the *Burggrafen* in Nürnberg, holding the big castle there for the Holy Roman Emperors. Acquisitive bunch, overall."

He hesitated a moment; then, added: "This is perhaps more serious than you may assume. By themselves, the knights and small lords will have a difficult time getting organized. They will not hesitate to become violent, but the violence is likely to be disjointed. For a fact, it seems to me, the farmers are much better organized. Better led, too, from what I can determine."

"Who's leading the knights?" Scott asked. "This von Bimbach character?"

Weckherlin waggled his hand. "To a degree, yes; to a degree, not. He is certainly the most prominent figure. But he is not really very popular among the knights. His arrogance and overbearing manner is not something which only the farmers resent. And the nickname of 'Pestilenz' is applied to his agent by knights as often as it is by farmers and townsmen."

"But you're saying it could still get serious?" asked Steve.

"If the Margrave of Brandenburg-Bayreuth chooses to intervene, yes," replied Weckherlin, nodding. "Very serious. He is not a small lord, and his geographic position makes him important to Gustavus Adolphus. The emperor can ignore a pack of unruly knights. He cannot ignore Margrave Christian."

Kulmbach, Bayreuth, late March, 1634

Margrave Christian of Brandenburg-Bayreuth was at the Plassenburg, in Kulmbach. He had moved his official residence to Bayreuth in 1625, but when he needed to think, he still went back to the Plassenburg. He had left Marie and the children in Bayreuth; they were safer there, right now.

He hated war and all that war meant. When he was a child, his tutors had shown him what Margrave Albrecht Alcibiades had done to Bayreuth and the rest of Franconia with his feuds. Not just told him; that madman had died less than thirty years before his own birth. His tutors had been able to show him the scars on the land, the burned villages never rebuilt, the ancient churches sacrificed upon the altar of ambition and greed.

For as long as possible, he had strived to keep this new war out of his lands. For years, he had succeeded. His brother, Margrave Joachim Ernst of Brandenburg-Ansbach, had died in 1625 after a career that involved helping to organize the Protestant Union in 1608, helping to dissolve the Protestant Union, and finally going into imperial service. Christian had become regent for his nephews, Friedrich and Albrecht.

He had tried so hard to keep Bayreuth out of the war. So what if the more belligerent called it hesitancy, passiveness, a "wait and see" policy. Harsher things, some of them: vacillation, pusillanimity, cowardice. For years, though, while the rest of Franconia was burned and stripped, he kept foreign soldiers out of his lands. Away from his subjects.

In 1631, it had become impossible. The bishop of Bamberg, Johann Georg II Fuchs von Dornheim, had been the hardest to deal with, right next door, threatening, declaring that he had to clarify his stance and make a final decision, either for the emperor and the Catholics or for the Protestants, for the Swede who had taken over the leadership of the Protestant cause in Germany.

Even then, he would rather not have done so. But the terms in which Fuchs von Dornheim had put it had made his decision inescapable. He could not abandon the Protestant cause. He and Friedrich had allied with Gustavus Adolphus. Friedrich was in the north now, with the Swedish army.

His people had taken the consequences, just as he had known they would. Bayreuth had suffered severely under the imperial forces. He had read the reports, report after report. In this village, a farmer thought that he had recognized his stolen horse in the nearby camp of some imperial soldiers. He had gone, with some of his fellow villagers, to demand it back. The soldiers had hanged every adult man in the village. In that village . . .

He had tried to keep Ansbach out of the war, too. Not so easy when the mother of his nephews was an aunt of Wilhelm V of Hesse-Kassel and the older boy itched to get into battle. Ansbach had suffered like Bayreuth.

He had sent people to Grantville to learn what they could from the notorious books and encyclopedias from that future universe. In that world, his nephew Friedrich had been killed in September of 1634, this very year, in a terrible battle at Noerdlingen that shattered Germany's Protestants. Albrecht, the younger, had lived to rule Ansbach. Probably because he was still too young to fight in that battle.

In 1634, after Noerdlingen, Ferdinand II had deposed them from their principalities, entrusting the government to an imperial commission. A year later, Ferdinand's son had negotiated a peace, called the Peace of Prague, and restored them. From then until 1648, the armies of both sides had passed back and forth through his lands.

He had sponsored services of joy and thanksgiving in all the churches of Bayreuth when the Peace of Westphalia was signed in 1648. He had tried to heal the wounds of war. The terrible wounds of war. He had not succeeded. It had been a century before Bayreuth began to recover.

He looked at the small piece of paper, the notes that his agent had made in Grantville. All that another world had remembered of him. So little for a long life. For a life that had lasted almost three-quarters of a century. He had built a new building for the Latin school in Bayreuth. He had abolished the laws that forbade peasants to marry or learn a trade without the permission of the lord whose serfs they had once been, or from whom they leased their lands.

He had forbidden the smoking of tobacco.

Almost, he smiled. He hated tobacco. The smell, the grime, everything associated with it. He would still forbid the smoking of tobacco, for all the good it would do. Mankind was afflicted by original sin; determined to drive itself into hell.

As was clearly demonstrated by the present petition that the Protestant nobility of Franconia had sent to Gustavus Adolphus. And which Fuchs von Bimbach was pressing him to support.

Bamberg, early April, 1634

Meyfarth shook his head. "I am no longer a diplomat, Herr Salatto. Nor a functionary of the secular arm. I am now a pastor. Even more, I am afraid that you are trying to recruit me because I am a Lutheran pastor and the margrave is a Lutheran prince. You want me to manipulate his religious scruples, genuine religious scruples, real enough religious scruples, to the advantage of the State of Thuringia-Franconia."

Steve Salatto looked at his former chief of staff. He had used up all his arguments. After everyone he had sent to Bamberg had failed, he had come himself.

Meyfarth continued. "This is something that I cannot do."

Steve nodded. This was it, then. Meyfarth simply refused to come back to work for the Franconian administration, even temporarily; would not serve as emissary to Margrave Christian. Even though he was the only person available who might really understand what the margrave was thinking. He rose.

"Please," Anita said. "Please." She handed Meyfarth a letter. "Please read this. Then listen to us. Please."

Meyfarth read, slowly. Nothing that he expected. The first was a letter from the gracious lady to her daughters in Grantville. A simple letter. She had told him before, when he was in Würzburg, that the hardest thing that she had ever done in her life was to leave her daughters Emily, then four, and Mary Carla, then two, in Grantville with her parents when she and Steve agreed to take this assignment. Now they would be how old? It had been eighteen months since they all, Meyfarth too, came from Grantville to Würzburg in October of 1632, shortly after the Battle of Alte Veste. Still small children. So a simple letter.

What had she said to him then? "It would be different, if I hadn't come here to work. If I could be with them here, they way Tania and Lynelle are with their kids. But the hours we keep, into the office at dawn and reading by a candle until we are exhausted. I wouldn't see them here, either, so it was really a choice of having them grow up there, with family, or here, with a governess. Not much of a choice, really."

Another letter. "Dear Mom." To her mother, then. "I understand, Mom. Really, I do. We waited to have the girls, and that means that since we were older parents, you and Dad are older grandparents. I can understand how they exhaust you, especially after you've managed the day care center at the plant all day. You're right. Since Dominique is taking some time off anyway after the baby, it makes more sense for her to take them. Don't feel bad about it. I know that everyone is doing the best he can. She can. I understand. I love you all."

Meyfarth looked up.

Anita's eyes were full of tears. "All right, maybe it is blackmail. But if you won't go talk to him as a diplomat, then please go and talk to him because you're a pastor. Not a Catholic priest, but a pastor. Because we've got to have some kind of a breakthrough, Herr Meyfarth. For our girls. And for all the rest of the children. My girls are going to live with Dominique and Marcus; by the time we see them again, they won't know us. It was different, somehow, when they were with my parents. Even little children can tell Grandma and Grandpa from Mom and Dad. But now, for every real purpose, Dominique will be their mommy, Marcus will be their daddy, little Mark will be their baby brother, and . . . and I'll be Auntie Anita who lives a long way away and they haven't seen her for so long that they're shy with her."

She put her head down on the table and started to sob. Steve put his hands on her shoulders.

Finally she lifted her head up. "This isn't a good time or place to tell you, Steve. There isn't any good time or place to tell you. Not the way things have been going this spring, since the election. I'm pregnant, again. I'm sure, now. New Year's Day, I guess." She started to cry again; then forced herself to stop.

"Please, Herr Meyfarth. As a pastor. Help us make enough of a peace that we can bring our children to Franconia. Just that much. I'm not asking for eternal peace in the whole world. Just a truce in a little corner of it. Please."

Chapter 11: "Brillo, four feet or not, is a creature of free will"

Bayrcuth, mid-April, 1634

Margrave Christian appeared to be interested in discussing modern literature. If that was where hc wanted to start, Meyfarth was quite willing to let him guide the conversation. Particularly since Weckherlin had come with him to Bayreuth. Eventually, they would get to the point. These things could not be forced.

The margrave and Weckherlin were deep into a discussion of one of Weckherlin's sonnets. "To Germany." Not, Meyfarth thought, really a bad place to start.

Break the yoke beneath which you are bound.

Not a bad first line, if one was really discussing peasants who had defied their lords and what should be done about it. No, not bad at all. Perhaps Margrave Christian had something to contribute to a resolution of this current problem.

> O Germany, wake up; grasp your courage again,
> the usage of your ancient heart. Resist the madness
> which has overcome you and, through you, freedom
> itself.

439

*   *   *

Usage? Was that right in English. Customs, perhaps? The exact word was often hard to find. Germany. *Teutschland.* A concept of the humanists, not of the politicians. Could Germany do anything? No. Could the Germans, the dozens of varieties of them, do something? Perhaps.

> Now punish the tyranny which has utterly shamed you,
> finally wipe out the fire that is consuming you,
> not with your own sweat, but with the foul blood
> flowing from the wounds of your enemy and false
> brothers.

Meyfarth shuddered. He did not share Weckherlin's vision in this. If this was carried through, it would only prolong the war.

> Relying upon God, follow the princes
> whom His right hand will, if you desire it, preserve,
> to the consolation of the faithful and the wreck of the
> faithless.

His just hand, perhaps, rather than His right hand? *Gerecht*, in a way, could mean either.

> So abandon all fear; do not let the time slip by
> and God will reveal to all the world that the enemy's
> treachery and pride are nothing but shame and disgrace.

Meineid. Perjury, perhaps, rather than treachery? But no, Weckherlin's poem was well known, but for the ram's purposes, it was worse than useless. Patriotic gore. Meyfarth examined his fingernails while the margrave and Weckherlin talked.

"The up-timers call it 'sheep stealing,'" Meyfarth said. "You have heard, I am sure, that many different religious groups share the same town."

Margrave Christian nodded.

"They have worked out rules—not laws, but informal understandings, generally shared—that permit them to live in harmony, most of the time. One of these prohibits 'sheep stealing.' One minister is not to raid the flock of another, taking away his members. A kind of 'live and let live.' I am not sure, myself, how it works. It is not, certainly, a universal principle. It is not uncommon, when a man and a woman of two different of these 'denominations' marry, for one to change."

Margrave Christian cocked his head inquiringly. "There are no laws about whether it is the man or woman who changes? There are no laws requiring one of them to change, or prohibiting it?"

"No. It is regarded as a purely personal decision. One often leading to family dissension, to be sure, but still personal. And sometimes leading to odd results. The Catholic priest now has a member of his flock, such a convert, whose given name actually is 'Calvin.' "

Weckherlin snorted his beer up his nose, spraying it on the table; Meyfarth pounded on his back, a little anxiously.

"What," the margrave asked, "does this religious 'sheep stealing' have to do with the oaths that the up-timers are accepting from the Franconians who are subjects of the imperial knights and petty lords, first to the constitution of the New United States and now to their State of Thuringia-Franconia?"

Meyfarth looked a little uncomfortable. "Partly, I think, it was a joke when we started talking about it. The term 'flock.' The peasants' use of the ram, Brillo they call him, as their emblem." He paused. "Have you read the Brillo material that I obtained for you, Your Grace? The up-time Brillo, not the broadsides written in Franconia?"

It was Weckherlin who answered. "With great interest. Remarkable really. An entirely new set of fables such as the ones Aesop collected, developing before our very eyes."

Margrave Christian smiled. "I very much enjoyed the newest one I've seen. *The Three Brillo Rams Gruff*, it's called."

Into the silence that followed, he added: "That one that mentioned railroads. I would be very interested in discussing railroads with someone from Grantville."

"Anse Hatfield," Weckherlin suggested. "The man who was commander in Suhl during the, ah, incident there. Or, perhaps, Captain Pitre herself? I'll see to it."

Margrave Christian nodded his thanks. Meyfarth continued with the topic he'd been discussing. "We thought about it. Decided to do it. Steal some sheep. Not, at first, in Franconia. Originally, as in Coburg, only those who were currently without a shepherd. To make them citizens, not subjects."

"According to the petition," Margrave Christian said, "it would appear that Herr Salatto and his subordinates have gone far beyond that."

"I still say that the administration in Franconia has not rustled the sheep, not poached them, not stolen them from their owners. Unlike sheep with four feet, men do have free will. In secular matters," Meyfarth said precisely, "if not in regard to the salvation of their souls, which is of course entirely dependent upon divine grace."

Weckherlin laughed. "It would appear that this Brillo, four feet or not, is a creature of free will."

"Which is, of course, why the up-timers like him so well. They believe greatly in free will. Often, I suspect, more strongly than they believe in God. So. The followers of the ram made the right of all Franconians to vote in the election one of their Twelve Points. It was their initiative, to which the administration only responded."

"You are arguing, then," Margrave Christian said, "that the issue is, properly, not one between the nobility of Franconia and the USE's administration there, but between the nobility of Franconia and their subjects, who first proposed the action that has become a point of contention."

Neither Meyfarth nor Weckherlin had thought of this approach. They were, however, more than willing to listen to the margrave's idea. A face-saving diplomatic out was a face-saving diplomatic out, no matter who thought of it first.

"Which would mean . . ." The margrave was starting to speculate in the subjunctive. "Would mean that it would not really be a matter in which the emperor should intervene directly, much less something that anyone could rightly interpret as providing sufficient grounds for changing the administration . . . Local, merely local, between each of two hundred minor lords and his subjects."

He smiled. "Not something that I should be expected to do anything about, either."

"No," Weckherlin agreed, "not at all."

Meyfarth nodded solemnly.

"But possibly," Margrave Christian continued, "something that might be applicable in Bayreuth if . . ."

"I don't think," Weckherlin said, "that you were authorized to say those things."

"I was asked," Meyfarth answered, "to see if things could be so arranged that a small truce will ensue in Franconia in our time. I am carrying the margrave's declaration that he will remain neutral in the dispute between the lords and knights of Franconia and its administration. I do not see that I could have been expected to obtain more than that."

"You are also carrying," Weckherlin pointed out, "knowledge of something that neither of us should know."

"Ah. Then we do not know it. Or will soon have forgotten it."

"If neither of us knows it, then how will the ram find out?"

"Somehow, the ram will learn. In Franconia, now, the ram soon knows everything. It is unlikely that he will miss this. Margrave Christian, I am sure, will somehow let it be known that he would be willing to accept oaths of allegiance from sheep belonging to the flocks of the imperial knights and petty lords whose lands lie within Bayreuth and Ansbach. And that he would be willing to grant a substantial number of the Twelve Points if the ram proved cooperative in the project of mediatizing the lower nobility. Should such a project occur, of course."

"Surely, the good Lutheran margrave would never be guilty of stealing sheep," Weckherlin said.

"Perish the very thought," Meyfarth answered. "No more than the good Lutheran dukes of your Wuerttemberg were, once upon a time."

For several minutes, Weckherlin did not reply. Then he asked, "What does the margrave intend to do with these oaths? If he should accept them?"

"Sufficient unto the day is the evil thereof, Herr Weckherlin. Tomorrow will have troubles of its own. Perhaps we should also ask what the farmers intend to do with them."

Bamberg, mid-April, 1634.

"Good morning, Stew," Janie Kacere said. "Sit down and chat."

"No time." He leaned one elbow on her pedestal desk. "The boss arrived in town yesterday evening late."

"I didn't know that Johnnie F. was due."

"He wasn't. I didn't have any notice. He came in with Noelle Murphy trailing along after him. Or maybe he was trailing along with Noelle. Who knows? She was in town a month ago, but went back to Würzburg for a while."

Janie whistled. "Did she ride in 'with rings on her fingers and bells on her toes?' "

" 'She shall have music wherever she goes'?" Stew asked, raising his eyebrows.

"More on the line of, 'She shall cause trouble wherever she goes.' Have you ever noticed that when our little special envoy turns up, even if she does smile and call herself a junior envoyette, things start to pop?"

"Hadn't, really." Stew leaned back. "But now that you mention it . . . yeah."

"Darn right. Every time Little Miss Muffet sits her tush down on a tuffet, something happens to it. Firecrackers fizzle when faced with her mere presence."

"Mother Goose on your mind this morning?" Stew chewed on the splinter he was using as a toothpick.

"I was baby-sitting for Stacey O'Brien's kids last night. Tom's out on patrol somewhere, doing his thing, and Stacey had a meeting of some kind at Else Kronacher's. League of Women Voters, I think."

"Doing his thing," Stew echoed her.

Janie looked up at the elaborate ceiling. She put her right hand over her heart while her face assumed the vacuous expression of a Baroque cherub. "We keep reciting that the administration's policy toward the Ram Rebellion is hands-off. Repeat after me, 'The citizens of Franconia must exercise self-determination' while Tom's out there giving adult education lessons in the safe handling of explosives to 'citizens' who've been hand-picked by Walt Miller and Matt Trelli. Pardon me, please, while some butter doesn't melt in my mouth."

Castle Bimbach, near Bayreuth, late April, 1634

Looking up at Schloss Bimbach as she and Eddie Junker approached it, Noelle didn't think it looked anything like what she imagined a "castle" ought to look like.

Well, okay. It was on top of a hill. It was big.

"Schloss," my ass. Just a huge ugly stone barn, is what it is. A white-washed stone barn.

She'd discovered, since she'd arrived in the seventeenth century in the Ring of Fire, that most German "castles" of the period fell between two stools. As far as her aesthetic sense was concerned, anyway.

Truly medieval castles—or at least ones with a major medieval element—could be pretty impressive, in their own way. She'd visited the Wartburg, after the reconstruction had begun repairing the damage caused by the napalm Mike Stearns had used on it to force the surrender of the Spanish army that had tried to use the castle for a refuge. Even with as much damage as it had sustained, she'd had no trouble understanding why so many Germans considered the Wartburg the archetypical castle of the Germanies.

Granted, the toilet facilities were a joke. But they were still a joke in castles built long after the Wartburg—and at least the Wartburg still had a certain primitive majesty to it.

On the flip side, although she'd never visited it, Noelle had seen plenty of photographs of Versailles, the enormous palace that the French "sun king" Louis XIV had built half a century in the "future." That was impressive in a completely different way, even though she was pretty sure that the toilet facilities hadn't improved much. If any.

But German castles in Thuringia and Franconia were generally what people considered "Renaissance"—using the term incredibly loosely. So far as Noelle was concerned, that meant they had been built after the farmers burned down some genuinely medieval castle a century earlier and combined Baroque with the grandiosity of a would-be miniature Versailles with all the stonepile ugliness of medieval construction.

She had no doubt an architect could explain how wrong she was. She also had no doubt that she didn't care.

"Great ugly stone barn," she muttered. "Not a turret or a moat in sight. All the architectural charm of a state office building."

Walking next to her, Eddie grinned. "Please! You are offending my culture. I believe that is grossly—what is the term that Frau Carstairs explained to me?—ah, yes. 'Politically incorrect.' "

Noelle sniffed. "We're West Virginians, Eddie. Not much given to political correctness."

The grin didn't fade at all. "Indeed. So Frau Carstairs explained to me. In a manner I suspect was deeply incorrect."

"And it's *still* a great ugly stone barn."

She was a little mollified once they reached the top of the hill and passed by the front entrance of the Schloss. That, at least, was fairly impressive.

In a great ugly sort of way. The door was immense, double-doored, and made out of some sort of heavy wood that had been painted dead black. Two black columns flanked it on either side, with some sort of semi-circular white stone carvings along the semi-circular top of the doors. She couldn't remember what that was called. A "frieze," maybe.

It looked as if it would take a team of mules to pull it open. Fortunately, they wouldn't have to find out. The front entrance of a Schloss was not for the likes of them.

They continued past it, walking along the white stone walls toward the rear entrances used by servants and tradesmen. The stables were back there, too, judging from the smell. Far above their heads, she could see grilled windows. Nothing close to ground level, though—which meant there wasn't much chance of any officious persons spotting them.

Even if they did, it probably wouldn't matter. A Schloss like this was the center of local government, as much as it was a personal residence. Von Bimbach would have private apartments in one wing of the castle, but much of the edifice would be devoted to administration and record-keeping. Clerks, bureaucrats, tradesmen, cooks, servants—not to mention people just visiting for some sort of business—would come and go from the Schloss all hours of the day. Noelle and Eddie were dressed inconspicuously and were walking along in broad daylight as if they had every right to be there. As long as they didn't presume to use the front entrance or enter the *Freiherr*'s private rooms, they would remain beneath notice.

To any except the Schloss' staff, of course. But, for that, the Ram had already made arrangements.

She hoped, at least. So the letter she'd gotten from him had claimed.

The letter was accurate. Getting into the Schloss and situated in a small room set aside for them in the servants' quarters went as smoothly as she could have asked for.

"Now what do we do?" asked Eddie, after the maid who had led them to the room departed.

The small, narrow chamber had only two pieces of furniture, a rickety-looking wooden chair and a solidly made if unattractive bed with a straw mattress. Two thick wool blankets were folded on the bed. There were no pillows of any kind.

Noelle sat down on the bed. "I'm not sure," she admitted. "It's already late afternoon, though. So I think the smartest thing to do is just wait until nightfall, and see if the Ram's people here approach us. If not . . . we'll decide tomorrow."

Eddie nodded. Then, none too cheerfully, examined the rough-hewn wood floor.

"Oh, relax," said Noelle. "We can share the bed."

He got a solemn look on his face and placed his hand over his heart. "I vow that I have no intentions on your virtue."

Noelle chuckled. "I wasn't actually worried about it."

She wasn't, in fact. In the time since they'd started working together, her relationship with Eddie Junker had settled into something quite comfortable for her. For Eddie too, she thought. Something of a cross between friends and older sister/younger brother.

There was certainly nothing romantic about it. That might seem odd to someone observing them, since she and Eddie were both reasonably attractive, intelligent, and were almost the same age. But, for whatever reasons these things happened—or didn't—there had simply never been any "chemistry" between them.

True, some of that might be due to Noelle's still-official *I'm thinking about becoming a nun* position. But, she didn't think so. She just wasn't Eddie's "type," whatever type that might be. And he certainly wasn't hers, insofar as she could figure out if there was any type of man who might appeal to her that way. She hadn't met one yet, leaving aside a couple of casual boyfriends in high school and junior college. Those relationships hadn't lasted long, however—and she was the only virgin her age she knew.

"So I feared," groaned Eddie. Noelle chuckled again.

Franconia, late April, 1634

With Margrave Christian's declaration of neutrality on behalf of himself and his nephews, the Franconian Protestant knights and lords took arms against the USE/SoTF administration, under the leadership of *Freiherr* Fuchs von Bimbach.

Which, of course, made the newspapers. Banner headlines, in fact.

Steve Salatto was very unhappy.

Arnold Bellamy was even unhappier, mainly because he had no additional resources whatsoever with which to assist the SoTF administration in Franconia. Nor was the SoTF Congress meeting. He spoke urgently with Ed Piazza about the need for a special session.

Mike Stearns was more than profoundly annoyed. Not with Steve Salatto or the Franconian farmers, however, but with Wilhelm Wettin—who was viewing the situation in Franconia with alarm. Great alarm. Quite frequently. Wilhelm thought that something should be done.

Scott Blackwell was not as unhappy as Steve. The knights and lords, collectively, could not put many men into the field. Few of them had the financial resources to hire more than a couple dozen professionals. Most were dependent upon calling out a levy of their own subjects, who largely refused to cooperate on the grounds that they had already sworn oaths of allegiance to the State of Thuringia-Franconia, against which their lords were rebelling.

"They'll get hammered," he said confidently. "You watch. My money's on the farmers."

Steve eyed him quizzically. "I take it you don't propose to intervene militarily?"

Blackwell shrugged. "Oh, at some point, I imagine I will—here and there, anyway. But I think it's all to the good to let those arrogant knights get the shit beat out of them. Better still, if it's done by the local farmers instead of us."

Steve understood the logic. He didn't even disagree with it, although it rubbed all his well-honed civil servant instincts the wrong way. But, still . . .

Unhappily, he gazed down at the newspaper on his desk.

"Big headlines, huh?" said Scott cheerfully.

"You are not joking?" asked Captain Boetinger.

"No," replied the lieutenant. "The city council invited a peasant delegation to come into the city. The delegation included a couple of the ram movement's prominent leaders, including two men from the *Gemeinde* at Frankenwinheim. And then, no sooner were the gates closed, than they arrested the entire delegation."

"They say they are going to deliver them, as rebellious and insubordinate subjects, each to his own lord, for a fitting and suitable punishment," added the sergeant who had come into the headquarters with the lieutenant.

The captain of the USE/SoTF garrison at Gerolzhofen shook his head. "Amazing. Some people seem incapable of learning anything.

Ah, well, so be it. Order out the garrison, Lieutenant Neidhart. We shall continue the educational process, as the Americans call it."

His second-in-command nodded. "Vigorously?"

"Oh, very vigorously."

The lieutenant hesitated a moment. "We *did* promise not to intervene in the city's domestic affairs."

"Indeed so. And we have kept the promise. But since the city council took it upon themselves to arrest people who were not citizens of Gerolzhofen, it is no longer a domestic matter."

He bestowed a grin upon the lieutenant that did not bode well for someone. "I was given most explicit instructions by Colonel Blackwell, should such an event come to pass. Summon the garrison, Lieutenant."

Less than a quarter of an hour later, the garrison marched out of the Zehnthof and headed for the Rathaus. The streets were noticeably deserted. The captain had expected some sort of opposition, given the intransigent nature of the city's citizens. But, apparently, even the residents of Gerolzhofen had enough sense to realize that their city council had finally crossed a line.

The entire city council emerged from the Rathaus to meet the garrison, once it entered the city square. They looked nervous, but stubborn.

They had good reason to be nervous, the captain thought. And the stubbornness was handy. There would be no need to track them down.

"You are violating our agreement!" shouted once of the councilmen.

Captain Boetinger's reply came in a tone of voice that was almost conversational.

"Shoot them," he commanded.

"No," said Scott Blackwell, "you *can't* leave the bodies on display."

Sourly, he stared up at the corpses of the city councilmen, suspended by ropes from the windows of the Rathaus. "You shouldn't have done that in the first place. I don't mean the shooting. That was okay, if maybe a little on the extreme side. But this . . ."

He grimaced. "Dammit, Friedrich, it's uncivilized."

Captain Boetinger shrugged. "Yes, true. But what part of *We mean it* did you think was ever going to remain civilized?"

Scott had no ready answer for that. "Still," he insisted. "It'll cause bad public relations. Have them taken down and their bodies delivered to their families."

"As you wish," said Boetinger. He walked off, mentally shaking his head. He rather liked the Americans, all things considered. If for no other reason, because they met the payroll on time. But there was no denying they were not sane, about many things.

Bad public relations. As if shooting dead the entire city council with no warning was likely to be popular!

And what difference did it make, in any event? Every citizen in Gerolzhofen might hate the USE and the State of Thuringia-Franconia with a passion. So what? Gerolzhofen's days of being a thorn in everyone's side had just come to a complete, total . . .

What was that American expression? Boetinger was charmed by the things.

Ah, yes. Screeching halt. He'd been particularly charmed by that one, after the up-timer Harry Lefferts had demonstrated it to him once, with an American motor vehicle.

Boetinger smiled thinly, thinking of Harry. He wondered what Harry was up to, these days. Boetinger had spent some time with Lefferts, when he'd visited Grantville. The two of them had gotten along very well.

Now *there* was an American fellow who'd have had no objection at all to stringing up corpses from windows.

The knights carried out several reprisals. In one case, on the estates of the von Bimbach family—the Catholic branch, near Bamberg— quite severe reprisals.

Blackwell did not order out the troops, however. First, because he didn't have all that many. Secondly, because he was quite sure the ram was going to retaliate, and was willing to let the farmers do the dirty work. Finally, because he was compiling a list. At the very top of that list was the name "Fuchs von Bimbach."

Before too long, he thought the list would come in handy. Especially after Noelle Murphy was able to add her findings, now that she'd gotten into the castle. In his own mind, the title of it was *Rope to Hang Themselves By.*

The city council of the imperial city of Nürnberg formally notified everyone it could think of, from Gustavus Adolphus and the Council of Princes down through the chain of command to the district administrators of the *Aemter* of Franconia, that it was seriously concerned about the situation, viewed it with considerable alarm, and would be compelled to take unspecified measures if the imperial knights and petty lords whose lands lay within Nürnberg's hinterland became involved in the contention between those in Franconia and the administration there.

In short, the knights were put on notice. By one of the most important cities in the USE, and—the knights were gloomily certain—one of Gustav Adolf's favorites. His great victory at the Alte Veste had been won within eyesight of Nürnberg, hadn't it? With a great many of the city's citizens in the ranks of his army—and none too many of the knights.

Margrave Christian spoke with representatives of the ram. And started accepting oaths, from market towns as well as from village people. On behalf of his nephews as well. Albrecht, of course, was still very young; Friedrich was in the north with Gustavus Adolphus' army. So it was his responsibility.

The form of the oath was carefully negotiated between them. Quite carefully.

Several of the Protestant knights and lords whose lands lay primarily in Ansbach and Bayreuth, led by *Freiherr* Fuchs von Bimbach, came to the assistance of the branches of their families whose lands lay primarily in Bamberg and Würzburg.

April had arrived. Indeed, it was almost May.
Across Franconia, the ram banners unfurled.

Chapter 12: "I'm sick to death of these swaggering little lords"

Bamberg, May, 1634

"Looks like you have the current hot spot, Vince," Steve Salatto remarked. "Or, at least, the hottest one."

Vince Marcantonio stretched. "Spots."

"Plural? I rode up because of a report of threats to the lives of priests, nuns, and monks by ravening hordes of perverted and monstrous peasants."

"Threats," his chief of staff Georg Rodolf Weckherlin added, "which are being reported in numerous illustrated pamphlets, but which nobody around Würzburg has been able to confirm."

Vince yawned. "I've no doubt that there have been threats. Mostly made in taverns by people who are drunk and who don't have any force to back them up." He stretched again. "Sometimes I wish that I could just lie down and sleep for a week.

"Anyway, there was one threat that Stew Hawker thought was credible, but it was being made by a merchant in Nürnberg against a little convent with six old nuns in it. He has some kind of reversionary right when the last of them dies. He—the merchant, that is—bought it up about twenty years ago. It's based on an agreement that was made sixty or more years ago between the convent and some noble who was secularizing church property in his lands after he turned Protestant, that they wouldn't accept any new novices and he got the land after the last one died. The ones who were already in it have been frustrating the merchant by living on and on and on. I think all six are well over eighty now. Stew thought that he was planning to hire a batch of bullies, burn them out, and blame it on the ram rebellion."

Vince stretched again. "I've brought the little old ladies into Bamberg and parked them with the nuns who patched up Johnnie F. and Willard after the beating last fall. If the rapacious mercantile bandit tries anything, he'll find the convent occupied by several guys who are willing to shoot back."

"If that's under control," Steve asked, "what are your other hot spots?"

"Well, there's the city council election here in Bamberg. After their little revolution last fall, the new council threw out all the guys who were convicted of being in on the conspiracy to try Willard Thornton. But they didn't replace them. It's just been running short-staffed, so to speak. Now election time has rolled around. We've already been through the question of 'who gets to vote' and settled on 'all adult citizens of Bamberg.' That doesn't get us very far, though, because a lot of the residents aren't citizens. They're citizens of Franconia in general, but not of the city, for purposes of local elections. So we have some candidates running on a platform of broadening out citizenship and others running on keeping the current laws. We have . . ." He paused.

"The ewe?" Weckherlin asked.

Vince nodded. "Frau Else Kronacher, herself, one embattled printer's widow amid the embattled farmers of the ram rebellion, running for the Bamberg city council. If nothing else, the guilds are so focused on fighting her that, I suspect, two or three other candidates they might otherwise be opposing will get elected. Which, if I read that daughter of hers right, may actually be the reason that Frau Kronacher is running."

"How old is she? The Kronacher girl, I mean?" Steve asked.

"Not a girl, quite," Vince answered. "There were two or three kids who died between her and the older boy. In her mid-twenties, I would guess. Maybe a little more."

"Well, then," Steve said, "back to the 'ravening hordes of peasants.'

If they aren't threatening the defenseless clergy, what are they *actually* doing? From your perspective."

"Cliff Priest, the military administrator in Bamberg, has ridden up to Lauenstein to talk to Margrave Christian of Bayreuth's *Amtmann* there. We've got to decide what to do about a castle at Mitwitz. Big old thing, with a moat. Belongs to a *Freiherr*—one of the ones who has taken up arms against the SoTF."

"Just what," Steve asked, "is the question?"

"Do we and the margrave want to try to bring it down, between us? Or do we let the ram's people do it?"

"Are there advantages, either way?" Weckherlin asked.

"If we take it, it should be a kinder, gentler, sort of conquest. For one thing, Margrave Christian has some cannon, which the ram rebellion doesn't. So he could set up a siege and tell everyone to come out. If he wanted to ally with us publicly. Which he doesn't, yet, no matter what his *Amtmann* at Lauenstein is trying to talk him into doing.

"Otherwise. The ram's people at Teuschnitz have some kind of major difference of opinion with the *Freiherr* at Mitwitz, who has a *Halsgericht*—the right to impose capital punishment. He seems to have used it rather freely and not always against people who fit the ordinary definition of 'criminal.' If we, the SoTF or Margrave Christian, don't occupy the castle at Mitwitz, the ram will level it. Some way."

"Would it be a great loss to society if the ram did?" Steve asked.

"Not that I can tell," Vince answered. "But burning to death isn't a nice way to die. Not that there are many."

Steve sighed. "Scott thinks we ought to let the farmers do the dirty work."

"Scott would. He thinks like a military man. My deputy Wade Jackson thinks the same way. He's UMWA, and they've always been a hard-fisted bunch. You and I, on the other hand, are proper civil servants. Bureaucrats, when you come right down to it. Honest and capable ones, sure, but we're still pencil-pushers."

He looked out the window onto the streets of Bamberg. "The truth, Steve? At least in the here and now, I agree with them. I'm sick to death of these swaggering little lords. Let the farmers make a weenie roast of that knightly prick at Mitwitz. Maybe it'll encourage the others to learn some manners."

Melchior Kronacher was watching his sister, instead of listening to the sermon. Mutti wouldn't come to church any more. They had become Catholic under the bishop's pressure in the late 1620s. Mutti said that enough was enough. She said that she had been to church enough to last any reasonable person a lifetime and she wasn't going back again. Ever. To any church. Of any kind. Now that the up-timers said she didn't have to.

Martha, though, shortly after Pastor Meyfarth had brought things in to be printed last spring, started going to the Lutheran services. Mutti said that either Melchior or Otto had to go with her because the streets were not as safe as they should be. Mutti blamed that on the guilds.

This week was Melchior's turn to go to church with Martha. He wiggled.

Martha was paying close attention to the sermon. Or, more likely, to the sermonizer. Melchior couldn't think of anything in a learned disquisition on John 3:16 that would bring such a calculating expression to Martha's face. Sort of like she was bargaining with God.

Melchior shuddered. He thought that bargaining with God was probably a bad idea. He was pretty sure of it, in fact. Especially when Martha was doing the bargaining. God might end up with the short end of the stick.

"So," Eddie asked, "how's it going?" He looked out of the small room they were sitting in—just a very big pantry, really, with two stools—into the large kitchen beyond, to make sure that no one could overhear them.

Seeing his somewhat shifty-eyed glance, Noelle sniffed. "Stop acting like a B-movie spy, Eddie. There's nobody here, won't be for at least a half an hour—and even if there was, it wouldn't matter anyway." A bit smugly: "The whole kitchen staff is with the ram. By now, I'm sure of that."

Eddie's eyes widened. "*All* of them?"

Noelle gave him a level gaze. "Yes, all of them. Along with maybe one-third of the rest of the Schloss' staff. The ram is especially strong in the smithy and the stables. The maids . . . well, that's harder. They come and go a lot, since most of them don't have my status."

"I'm impressed."

Noelle's face got a little pinched. "It wasn't hard. Even by the standards of Franconian *Freiherr,* Fuchs von Bimbach is a pure son of a bitch." She nodded toward the kitchen. "He hung one of the cook's sons two years ago. Along with three other boys. None of them was older than nineteen."

Eddie grimaced. "Why?"

"Apparently the four of them got drunk one night in a local tavern and started mimicking his Bimboship. Just teenagers being disrespectful, the way teenagers will. But somebody reported them to von Bimbach, and he charged them with 'petty treason.' That's a hanging offense, and he's got the legal right on his lands to apply capital punishment. *Halsgericht* they call it—the 'neck court.' "

"What a bastard."

"Yup, he sure is. Two years before that, he had one of the blacksmith's apprentices hung for stealing some copper. His Bimboship jacked up the value of the stolen goods high enough to make it a capital offense, even though it didn't really come to much. The guy's mother was sick and he was just trying to get her some medicine. What passes for it, anyway, in the here and now."

Eddie wiped a thick hand over his face.

"The year before that—"

"Never mind. I understand." He dropped his hand and looked out of the narrow door onto the kitchen. This time, though, it was a simple and straightforward gaze.

"You're safe?"

Noelle shrugged. "As safe as you could expect, given that I live in a castle owned by a sociopath."

He grimaced again. Noelle chuckled.

"Relax, Eddie. It's really not that bad." She made a little gesture, indicating her outfit. "It worked just about the way we figured it would. Judith Neideckerin agreed to hire me as one of her maids. His Bimboship doesn't pay any attention to me at all, when he comes to visit her. Which he doesn't do all that often, anyway. I get the feeling he forced her to become his mistress more for the bragging rights among his *Freiherr* buddies, than anything else. Judith's good-looking, in a *zaftig* sort of way."

Eddie seemed to relax still more. Again, Noelle chuckled. "No, that's not a problem. I'm not having to fend off the lustful advances of the lord of the castle, if that's what you're worried about. He's never spoken so much as a single word to me, in the month I've been here. If you put me in a lineup wearing different clothes, I don't think he'd even recognize me."

She gestured, a bit impatiently. "And that's enough about that. What does the Ram want now?"

"Pretty much the same you've been providing him since you got established here. Information, mostly. The Ram shares your opinion that von Bimbach will probably wind up being the key to the whole thing. I can't say I really understand why the two of you seem so sure of that. From what you've told me—and what I've heard from others—he's too arrogant and cocksure to make a very effective political leader."

"That's neither here nor there, Eddie. First of all, there isn't a one of these little lords and knights that I think could win an election in the smallest county in West Virginia. Not for dog catcher. They're all pretty much cut from the same cloth. The big difference with His Bimboship is pure and simple geography."

She twisted her head, as if indicating the countryside beyond the walls of the Schloss. "His estates are nestled in among the lands controlled by Margrave Christian of Bayreuth. From a strategic point of view, looking at it from the ram's side of things, this is what you might call a safe enclave for the counterrevolution. His Bimboship can organize from here, and there's really not a damn thing the Ram can do about it. Neither can Steve Salatto and his people. If they send any troops in—much less if the Ram mobilized an army of farmers—the margrave would be almost sure to intervene. Just to keep the peace, if nothing else."

Eddie scratched his chin. "Well . . . yes. And he's an important ally of the USE's emperor, too, political speaking. So even if Margrave Christian couldn't handle it, he'd squawk to Gustavus Adolphus loudly enough that the Swedish army would come in. And wouldn't that be a mess, as unpopular as they are in Franconia?"

"A stinking mess," Noelle agreed. "Let's make sure it doesn't come to that. All right, Eddie, fire up that near-perfect memory of yours. Here's the latest . . ."

Chapter 13: "This is simply more than we can tolerate"

Bamberg, June, 1634

"The Ram will come today."

Martha Kronacher looked at the *Jaeger* who made that comment while paying for a copy of the latest broadside. He was smirking.

"Thank you." She did not feel called upon to say one word more than that to the man. Checking to see that there were no more customers, she went quickly into the back and notified her mother, not bothering with the codes. She loathed the fact that she was called the "ewe lamb" by the rebellion. She particularly loathed the little jokes and snide comments that came from those who thought that it was clever to pair her up with the Ram.

"Mutti," she said plainly, "Herr Ableidinger will be coming today."

Martha kept her voice even. She did not like the school teacher from Frankenwinheim. She appreciated, she hoped, his organizational ability. His ability to take a set of diffused grievances and turn the people who held them into an orderly group which might accomplish something.

She was glad that he was going to be talking to the Bamberg apprentices, whose increasing unruliness was part of the reason that

459

Mama would no longer let her walk the streets, even go to market, unless she had one of her brothers to accompany her.

But she didn't like him. She thought that he was too loud; she thought that his speaking style was bombastic. She especially didn't like the fact that he was a widower, which tended to bring that *speculative* gleam into her mother's eye. Mutti was beginning to think that Martha was old enough to get married. Herr Ableidinger taught not far from where Papa had grown up, in the *Frankenwald*. The school furnished him with a residence. From Mutti's perspective, he was eligible.

Martha, however, had no desire to spend the rest of her life with a man who made that much noise; just by existing, Constantin Ableidinger made a lot of noise. Whatever Mutti thought, and however much anyone smirked about the ram and the ewe lamb.

Message delivered, she went back into the front shop.

Frau Else Kronacher sent a couple of apprentices out to deliver messages, then picked up her latest campaign speech. She wanted Herr Ableidinger to review it. She just could not understand why Martha did not like him. He was such an *invigorating* man.

There weren't any customers in the print shop at the moment. Martha started singing to herself. "Jerusalem, Thou City Fair and High." No, she did not want to marry the Ram, no more than she wanted to marry the third son of the master of the Bamberg printer's guild. The world held a better husband for her than either of them. She was quite sure of it.

Hasslach Valley, Franconia, late June, 1634

"Vince," Johnnie F. said, "I don't think that you've been up here before."

"I haven't, no. My duties keep me pretty locked in to Bamberg most of the time. Stew Hawker has mentioned the place. So did Scott Blackwell, once, when he was up to Bamberg for a briefing, but . . ."

"But he wasn't sure where it was. I don't think I've ever," Johnnie F. grinned, "seen a man who was so in love with having a piece of paper with a map on it in front of his nose. This is the Hasslachtal. That is, the little stream we're riding next to is the Hasslach, so this is the valley of the Hasslach. You'll note that most of these paths and little roads are well up away from the stream bed, even though that makes it more up-and-down over the hills. It floods in the spring. Most of these creeks do."

"So where does it come from and go to?"

"Basically, it starts not much south of Kamsdorf—you know, where USE Steel has its mines and plant—and runs south. We're north of Stockheim, now; almost to Rothenkirchen, which is licensed to hold a market. That last little village was Pressig. This is a sort of little peninsula of Franconia, if you want to think of it that way, sticking up into Thuringia. That's why its called the *Frankenwald*, the Franconian Forest, rather than the *Thueringerwald*, the Thuringian Forest. Same forest, if you look at it from the viewpoint of the trees, I expect."

Johnnie F. grinned. "It was a regular little checkerboard of feuding minor lordships until we oathed most of them to the NUS Catholic and Lutheran all mixed together. Now it's a regular little checkerboard of feuding small towns and villages, Catholic and Lutheran, all mixed together. No big change on the ground, Stew says. Same feuds, same cast of characters, pretty much. When we get up to the north end, where Margrave Christian of Bayreuth's Lauenstein castle is, near Ludwigsstadt, we'll only be about forty miles from home. From Grantville, I mean."

Vince frowned. "Why don't we come this way, then? Instead of going all the way over to the west, through Suhl."

"Because there aren't any decent roads, not even by down-time standards. The country is pretty rugged, as you can see for yourself. If we could get a railroad through here . . ."

"I can see that. I can't believe that there has been more coal, all along, as close as Stockheim, and nobody told us about it."

"Well, even though it's been mined for fifty years or at Reitsch, on the other side of the creek, they mostly just dig it out of little dogholes and use it locally," Johnnie F. answered. "There's no transportation for moving it any distance. They take some down to Lichtenfels on little rafts and skiffs. They aren't mining commercially, if you call what Reitsch is doing commercial, right around Stockheim, yet. It was the Frankenwinheim mayor who mentioned it to me when I was up there a couple of weeks ago to check on what the ram rebellion was doing over that way. He said that their school teacher, a guy named Constantin Ableidinger, told him that we'd probably be interested. I don't think that I've met Ableidinger. Not to be introduced to. I can't put a face to the name.

"I did think that we ought to bring it to your attention, though. And mention it to Saunders Wendell, since he's the UMWA man in Würzburg. Maybe Grantville could even send somebody from the geology survey down here. Anything to bolster up the Franconian economy. Even just a little."

Vince Marcantonio added a hearty "amen."

Mitwitz, Early July, 1634

"They're doing pretty damn well, wouldn't you say?" Scott Blackwell remarked. "Given that they don't have any napalm."

Sitting on a horse next to the USE's military administrator in Franconia, Johnnie F. considered the irony of the situation. He was normally far more inclined toward what you might call "revolutionary activity" than Scott was. Here, though, where the farmers were quite literally running amok, it was Scott who was observing the scene with something approaching equanimity—and Johnnie F. who was doing his best not to shudder.

The castle at Mitwitz was an inferno, by now. Lacking napalm or not, the thousand or so farmers who were besieging the Schloss hadn't had much trouble overwhelming the *Freiherr*'s few dozen mercenary troops. Those of his soldiers who hadn't run away as soon as the mass of farmers appeared, that is, which had been most of them. Once the farmers got into the castle—helped inside by the servants, often enough—they'd set fire to it in at least a dozen places.

Stone walls wouldn't burn, true. But any Schloss was full of incendiary materials. By the time the raging fires died out, hours from now, the castle would be a gutted ruin. Parts of it were already starting to collapse, where the stone work had depended on wooden supports.

There was no opposition, any longer, except from a knot of soldiers at the front gate. The only reason they hadn't surrendered, Johnnie F was quite sure, was simply because they couldn't. The farmers were taking no prisoners.

For a moment, Johnnie F.'s gaze drifted to the left, before he forcibly took his eyes away. He had a bad feeling he'd remember that pile of butchered corpses for the rest of his life. After killing every soldier they'd dragged out of the castle, the ram's people had stacked their bodies in one place. More or less. He didn't think a single one of those bodies was still intact. The farmers had used their tools-turned-into-weapons with a vengeance.

There was a sudden flurry of motion at the front gate. A body of horsemen was emerging, with four mercenaries in the lead.

Horse-*people*, rather. There was a woman in the center of the group, riding alongside a well-dressed man.

"That'll be the *Freiherr* and his family, trying to escape," Blackwell said, calmly. "He's got one kid, if I remember right. A boy, somewhere around eight years old."

The soldiers in the lead were trying to cut their way through the mob at the gate. One of them fired a wheel-lock pistol. A farmer stumbled to the ground, spilling a weapon that looked like a scythe blade attached to a long pole.

A big man stepped out from behind a tree, to their right. A *Jaeger*, from his clothing. He was perhaps sixty yards from the battle raging at the front gate. His rifle came up

Johnnie F. hissed. That was no—

Crack!

The soldier who'd fired the wheel lock was swept from his saddle. "That's an up-time gun," Johnnie F. muttered.

"Sure is," agreed Scott. He leaned over his saddle and spit on the ground. "Don't think we'll ask where he got it, neither."

Easily, fluidly, the big *Jaeger* worked the bolt on the rifle and brought it back up to his shoulder.

The *Freiherr* had now broken away from the soldiers and was driving his horse toward the road.

Crack! Down he went. Within seconds, half a dozen farmers had surrounded his body and were hacking him into pieces with axes and those ungainly looking scythe-weapons.

Johnnie F. heard a woman scream. Several of the ram's people had seized the reins of the *Freiherr*'s wife's horse and were dragging the mount to a halt. He saw another farmer stab her in the side with a long spear. The woman screamed again and slid off the saddle.

Johnnie F. saw that she'd had her son perched on the saddle in front of her. The boy landed on the ground along with her. But, scampering like mad, he evaded the axes and scythes that were already butchering his mother and made his escape under the horse's belly.

Once clear of the knot of farmers around his mother, he raced for the nearby woods.

Eight or nine years old, sure enough. His face was pale, his eyes wide, his mouth open in a soundless scream.

Johnnie F. saw the big *Jaeger* tracking the boy with the rifle.

"Oh, Jesus."

Crack! Then, after jacking another round into the chamber, he fired again. His first shot had probably killed the boy already. The second one, striking the prone little body, was just to make sure.

"Ever read much about peasant rebellions?" asked Scott, almost idly.

Unable to speak, Johnnie just shook his head.

"Well, I did." Blackwell pulled out a small notepad and gestured with it to the burning castle. "This is pretty much SOP. Burn down the nobleman's castle—making damn sure to eliminate all the tax and other records—and kill him and his entire family. Women, children, babies and all. Don't leave a single one of them alive, who can inherit. If somebody does, it'll have to be a cousin. Somebody who doesn't really know much about the area or the people in it."

Johnnie F.'s stomach heaved, but he managed to fight it down.

Scott started writing in the notepad. "Okay, scratch Mitwitz," he said. "I have a feeling this is going to make my job a lot easier. You watch, Johnnie. Once the word spreads, you'll see most of the other *Freiherren* pulling in their horns. Right quick."

He chuckled harshly. "Some of them'll probably come racing into Würzburg and Bamberg, to put themselves and their families under our protection. Which we'll be glad to give them, of course. But we won't lift a finger to stop the farmers from torching their abandoned castles. As far as I'm concerned—speaking as a military man—the only good Schloss is a dead Schloss."

Then, glancing over at Johnnie F., he shook his head. "Yeah, it's ugly as all hell. On the other hand, when it's over and done, I don't expect the casualties to come to more than a few hundred people. You know how many people these stinking worthless knights and nobles massacred a century ago, when they put down the last big farmers' rebellion?"

"Somewhere around a hundred thousand, people say."

"Yeah. The number might be exaggerated, of course. But even it is, so what? Call it fifty thousand. That's still a slaughter about two orders of magnitude greater than anything the ram will do."

Blackwell's tone of voice was cold. He pointed with the notepad to the small corpse in the distance. "Do you think the knights gave any more mercy to farmers' kids? Dream on."

Johnnie F. didn't argue the matter. He agreed with Scott, in the abstract. He just didn't, personally, have the stomach for it.

Looking away from the corpse, his eyes came to the boy's killer. The big *Jaeger* had his up-time rifle slung back over his shoulder, and was returning Johnnie's gaze with a level stare of his own.

It was not a threatening stare. But there was no give in it, at all. Not a trace of an apology in those eyes.

"Maybe this will end it, once and for all," Johnnie F. said. Hoping.

"That's what I figure. Let's go. One Schloss down, and good riddance."

Franconia, July, 1634

Freiherr Fuchs von Bimbach looked at his chancellor. Dr. Lenz hoped that he wasn't about to kill the messenger.

"Intolerable," Bimbach said. "The idea that this upstart 'State of Thuringia-Franconia' as it calls itself made no attempt whatsoever to protect the castle at Mitwitz is an outrage."

Lenz cleared his throat. "The *Freiherr* there," he felt obliged to say, "is allied with you. Is actively in arms against their administration."

He was fudging the tenses, here. But given Bimbach's furious mood, Dr. Lenz thought it would be unwise to dwell on the fact that the *Freiherr* at Mitwitz was no longer an ally and was certainly no longer actively in arms. The *Freiherr* was, in fact, a corpse. More precisely, several pieces of a corpse.

"Nonetheless," Fuchs von Bimbach orated, "the castle itself is a symbol of duly constituted legal authority. Which, basically, they simply gave over to these peasant hordes. Made no effort at all to turn them away from it. It appears from this report that their so-called 'military administrator' actually observed the destruction. Took notes on it, even."

He got up from his chair and paced around the table. "This is simply more than we can tolerate. There has to be a way to bring these up-timers to their heels. And the ram along with them, since they are tolerating its depredations. Openly tolerating them. Some way to bring down both at once, Lenz! Both at once!"

Chapter 14: "Call off the ram, or they die"

Bamberg, late July, 1634

"Herr Meyfarth." He looked up from the pedestal desk at which he was preparing the Sunday sermon.

"Herr Meyfarth." The knock at his door was repeated; from the voice, it was his landlady.

"Yes, yes. I'm coming." He tried to keep the impatience out of his voice. It was one of the worst things about him, he knew. When he was working, he hated to be interrupted. Yet the nature of the work of a parish pastor was that it was full of interruptions.

"Someone is here to speak with you."

"Thank you," he said absentmindedly. "I'm coming now." He wiped his pen, but left the book open.

He did not recognize the men, but they appeared to know him. Scarcely surprising in itself; a pastor was naturally noticed when he went through the streets. "Good afternoon, gentlemen. What is it?"

"If you could come? A difficult birth."

He did not recall that any of those women who had been attending his sermons was expecting a child right now. Possibly, always possibly, someone from one of the families who had fallen away under persecution and were ashamed to come back. In any case, an innocent child in need of baptism.

"Just let me get my case." He hurried back up the stairs for the small case in which he kept his manual and small Bible, the host and wine for the mother, just in case; a little vial of water.

"Frau Thornton."

Emma looked up. The woman standing at the other side of the booth counter looked very upset.

"Please, excuse me many times. I am the landlady for Herr Pastor Meyfarth. I know that your husband is his friend. This is true, isn't it?"

"Why, yes. Willard is out of town this week, though. Can I help you?"

"Men came for the Herr Pastor, yesterday. To bring comfort to a difficult birth, they said. They did not give their names. He went with them, naturally. But he has not returned."

"Couldn't members of his church help you more than I can?"

The woman looked even more distressed. "I have already been to them. They know of no one who would have had need of him, no one expecting a child. We have checked with the two families they know of who expect God to bless them soon with the gift of a child. Both mothers are well; neither sent for the pastor. No one knows."

"Why come to me?"

"It is said that you know the Ram."

Emma smiled. So much for discretion. Gathering up the literature she had on display, she packed it into the tightly woven basket at the rear of the booth; then picked up the basket and put it on top of the three-legged stool on which she sat when no inquirer was there. Just in case of rain; it should stay dry until she got back.

Drat, she had missed a couple. Rather than open the balky catch on the basket again, she dropped them into the big pocket on her work apron. It was a Grantville Home Center special; the pockets were big, and the motto was an attention-getter when she worked the booth.

"Come with me, please."

Constantin Ableidinger sighed. He had had men from the ram watching them for so long. There had been, as far as they could tell, no attempts against them. With everything else that was going on, he needed every reliable, trained man he had at his side. He called the *Jaeger* back, to be in other places, to do other things.

Now, both Herr Meyfarth and Frau Thornton, gone. And a note on his desk.

Call off the ram, or they die.

As if he could call off the ram, now! What kind of fools could these men be, to think that anyone, even the Ram himself, with a word or gesture, could call back a flood? Find the men who were in Bamberg last spring. Where would they be, now? Thousands in the field. Start asking. Where were they, the *Jaeger* who had guarded them?

Herr Thornton. He was out of the city. Where was he? Did Ottheinrich leave a list, of the villages they were to visit? Was he safe? The itinerary was here; quickly, he sent out a runner to follow the route.

What tie could there be between Meyfarth and the Thorntons, other than the ram?

"You are sure that you saw this?" Martha Kronacher asked anxiously. "Sure?"

The ewe's little flock of apprentices, Martha's younger brothers and their friends, had been talking to people all over Bamberg for two days.

Her brother Melchior had been pushing them hard. He did not like the look that had come over Martha's face when she heard that Pastor Meyfarth was gone. She was sincerely concerned about Frau Thornton, to be sure, but with Pastor Meyfarth, she appeared to take it personally, so to speak.

"Yes, I am sure," the fishmonger said, in response to a question asked by Stew Hawker. "In the market, speaking to Frau Thornton. At the booth where she has the books and pamphlets. It was Herr Pastor Meyfarth's landlady. I am sure that I recognized her. I don't know her name, but she's a widow who keeps a small boarding house, for working men. Has for several years. Respectable, very respectable. The rooms are cheap."

"Has anyone checked there?" Ableidinger asked.

"The other boarders are coming and going," the *Jaeger* in the room answered. He was the biggest of the ones whom Ableidinger had brought with him into Bamberg. The scariest one, too, Martha thought. "Complaining that this morning there was no breakfast. The woman is gone."

"Is she a Lutheran that he was boarding with her?" Wade Jackson took up where Stew had left off.

Martha frowned suddenly. She did not recall having seen *die alte Neideckerin* at any of the pastor's sermons.

Her mother came into the room.

"Neighbors say that the family was Protestant, Constantin," the *Jaeger* continued. "Before, you know. Before 1628. She welcomed the Herr Pastor when he let people know that he was coming."

"Family?"

"None," the fishmonger answered. "None that anyone knows of. Not any more. There was a husband, but he died. A daughter. I don't know what became of her."

Else Kronacher spoke up. "I do." She turned to Ableidinger. "Constantin, I recommended the boarding house because Rudolph Vulpius and old Kaethe thought that Pastor Meyfarth would be safe there. As safe as anywhere. *Die alte Neideckerin* is a relative of Frau Anna Hansen, who was burned as a witch in 1629. Or, possibly, her husband was the relative. In any case, they came under suspicion. They sent Judith, the daughter, away, to safety."

"Where?"

"She was not a native of Bamberg, you know. The old woman. She married into the city. Vulpius took Judith to the lands of the *Freiherr* Fuchs von Bimbach, over by Bayreuth."

"Hell and damnation!" Wade Jackson exploded out of his chair. "We've got to call Vince. Notify Steve and Scott. Right away."

He looked for the big *Jaeger*. The man had already left the room.

"You're certain?" Noelle asked.

The cook nodded. "Yes. I recognized *die alte Neideckerin* and Pastor Meyfarth. The other woman with them, I don't know. But the blacksmith's son says she's one of the up-timer heretics. The wife of the one who was flogged in Bamberg, before the ram put a stop to it."

Her hands folded on her lap, Noelle stared at the wall in her tiny living quarters. As if, somehow, the blankness of the wall could dispel the blankness in her mind.

"What in the name of . . . What is von Bimbach *doing*? That's insane!"

"He's a madman," the cook said, shrugging. "He always has been, even when he was a boy. When he loses his temper, he's capable of anything. Even at the age of six, he was that way. I remember him."

She might, at that, Noelle thought. The cook had to be close to sixty years old, and she'd worked in the von Bimbach Schloss most of her adult life.

"Still . . ."

She shook off the disbelief. Lunatic act or not, Fuchs von Bimbach's kidnapping of the three people from Bamberg might finally provide the handle to topple him. The fulcrum, rather, for the lever she already had more or less in her hands. By now, well over half of the castle's staff was either working for the ram or sympathetic.

Even the soldiers didn't seem attached to their lord. And they were obviously very nervous about the situation. Everyone, by now, knew what had happened at Mitwitz. The only ones of that *Freiherr's* mercenaries who had survived has been the ones who ran away, and did it quickly.

She rose to her feet, abruptly, filled with determination.

"Right. Three things. First, find out exactly where they're being kept. Second, send word for Eddie Junker. Tell him to come to the Schloss immediately. And tell him to bring my Browning with him."

That required a moment to clarify the term. *Brow-ning. Never mind what it is. Eddie knows.*

Third—"

She eyed the cook, wondering if there'd be an argument. "I want you to pretend that he's a new servant in the kitchens. He needs to be here all the time, from now on."

There was no argument. The cook simply nodded. "No one will ask."

She left. After a minute or so, Noelle followed her into the corridor. Then, headed for Judith Neideckerin's chambers.

When she arrived, she found von Bimbach's mistress staring bleakly out of the window.

"He has had my mother imprisoned also," she said, after glancing over her shoulder to see who had entered. Still staring out the window, she added: "Tell the Ram to send me an icepick. I'll drive it into the bastard's ear tonight."

Noelle shook her head. "No. We have to let this unfold for a bit."

Angrily, Neideckerin spun around. "What if he hurts my mother?"

Noelle took a deep breath. "He won't do that right away. We have time to organize. And your plan with an icepick won't work, anyhow. He probably won't come to see you—he's not *that* stupid—and if he does, he'll search you for weapons first."

Still angry, Neideckerin's eyes swept her chambers. "There's some-where I could hide it. Must be."

"He'll have soldiers search your quarters. If he comes at all. Which he most likely won't."

After a few seconds, Judith's shoulders slumped. "Please, Noelle. She's my mother."

Wishing she felt as much confidence as she was projecting in her tone of voice, Noelle said: "I'll take care of it."

Würzburg, August 1634

"So most of it is under control," said Scott Blackwell. "Since Mitwitz burned, more than half of the imperial knights and petty lords have caved in and formally withdrawn their support for the petition. A number of them have come into Bamberg or Würzburg for the sake of the military protection we give them, even though that sort of amounts to house arrest. Well, call it 'city arrest.' Most of the rest are sulking on their own lands. Under siege by the ram's men. Usually by far more of the ram's men than their own lands could possibly account for, but I've avoided examining that too closely. Only six more burn-outs, and those of lords who promised something and then reneged."

He came to the end of his notes. "The real problems that I still have, from a military standpoint, are the ones who have retreated into other lands they hold that are outside our jurisdiction. Those lands that are surrounded by Ansbach, Nürnberg, or Bayreuth. I can't chase them down there, myself, and I can't let the ram's people get ram-bunctious either. Too much danger of offending some of Gustavus Adolphus' important allies."

His report finished, Scott closed the notebook and looked up.

"Hearts and Minds?" Steve Salatto asked.

"Self-government in Franconia is proceeding normally," said Johnnie F. "That is, things are messy, disorganized, imperfect, and squabbly. Tithe compensation committees are disputing with water rights committees, neither of which have much in common with the weights and measures people, none of whom can seem to get a firm answer out of Magdeburg, because the parliament up there is passing things without appropriating the funds to implement them. Lord, how I hate unfunded mandates."

He bestowed a cheerful grin on everyone at the table. "All of which is just fine with me. I prefer any amount of mess and imperfection to a slick authoritarian regime any day."

"Does anyone have an update on what's happening at the Fulda end of things? I'm afraid that we've pretty much been leaving Wes Jenkins to his own devices." Steve Salatto was moving through the morning's agenda fairly briskly.

Weckherlin looked up from his note-taking, annoyed that young Samuel Ebert, whom he had left in his place at the desk in the outer office, was interrupting the meeting.

"My apologies, but he says that it is very important." Ebert came around the table and handed a note to Salatto.

"Who is Constantin Ableidinger?" Steve asked, after scanning it.

"I am not familiar with the name, Herr Salatto," Weckherlin answered.

Ebert opened his mouth, looked at Maydene Utt, then closed it again. The senior auditors were not particularly happy that their juniors had been drafted for other jobs in the administration during this summer's crisis—particularly not after the Krausold debacle. Ebert, Heubel, and Fischer spent a lot of their time keeping their mouths closed and trying to look inconspicuous.

"Why does he want to see me?"

"Since I don't know who he is, I don't have the slightest idea." Weckherlin again.

Ebert opened his mouth. "Excuse me, Herr Salatto. But I believe that Herr Haun may know him. And Herr Blackwell."

Steve looked at them. Both shook their heads. "I've heard the name," Johnnie F. said, "but I've never met him."

"Put him off." Steve waved Ebert out of the room.

He didn't move. Looked at Herr Haun and Herr Blackwell. "Sirs, forgive me. He gave me this to show you."

Scott reached out his hand. Ebert was handing him a well-read copy of *Common Sense*.

"Well, I will be goddamned." He passed it over to Johnnie F. "Remember him, now? He told us we'd likely meet again, if he wasn't unlucky."

Johnnie F. stared down at the book in his hands. "Him? *He's* Ableidinger?"

"Come on, Scott, what's going on?" Steve was becoming impatient.

"You've got Big Bad Brillo himself standing in your outer office. And now we've finally put a name to him. Not just that 'Helmut' alias, or whatever you'd call it. What in hell is he doing here? Did he just walk in?"

"Yes sir," Ebert said. "Like anyone else with business in the palace."

Steve was looking at young Ebert. "How come you thought that Johnnie F. and Scott would know him?"

"Well, they've been up there. To where he has his headquarters now, on the Coburg border, since they decided Frankenwinheim wasn't safe enough. Several times. I just assumed that they would. And Herr Hawker in Bamberg has the Hearts and Minds team's printing done by Frau Else Kronacher. I know that from checking the invoices."

"You've known his name all along?"

"Not his name, no, Herr Salatto. But I recognized him certainly, when he walked in. No one who has ever heard the Ram speak is likely to forget him. I've heard him. So have Fischer and Heubel."

Ebert paused. "Herr Krausold did, too. Before, ah . . . We're, well, we're down-timers, you know. People don't notice us, the way they do you. And we're young, the three of us. Like most of the people who go to his speeches. They don't turn anyone away."

Anita raised her eyebrows. "Frau Kronacher?"

"The woman who is called 'the ewe.'" From Ebert's tone of voice, it was clear he assumed that everyone knew that. "She prints all the pamphlets coming out of Bamberg."

Everyone was staring at him. Nervously, the young German intern looked to Johnnie F. for support.

"But—Herr Haun. Surely you knew this? You visit her shop every time you're in Bamberg."

All stares shifted to Johnnie F. He cleared his throat.

"Well. Ah."

Steve Salatto rolled his eyes. "Jesus H. Christ. The idea, Johnnie, is that we're supposed to win over their hearts and minds. Not—goddamit—the other way around."

"Well," Johnnie F. repeated. "Ah."

Castle Bimbach, near Bayreuth, August, 1634

Emma Thornton still couldn't quite believe this was really happening. It all seemed like something out of a bad movie.

Desperately, she looked over at Meyfarth, as if he might reassure her. But the Lutheran pastor's face, though stiffly composed, was also as pale as a sheet.

Guess not.

Both of them were tied to chairs in the dungeon. Well, not exactly a "dungeon." The big chamber was a half-basement, with narrow windows up on the walls, allowing some light into the room.

"Torture chamber," she'd call it, except it really had more of a resemblance to a very primitive dentist's office. Which didn't make her feel any better at all. Especially given the "dentist" and his assistant.

The "dentist" wasn't so bad, maybe. If he'd actually been a dentist. Just a man in late middle-age, round-shouldered and with something of a stoop, wearing a nondescript cloth coat.

The problem was that Emma knew his actual position. He was *Freiherr* von Bimbach's official gaol-keeper and executioner—a post which, in this time and place, doubled as "official torturer."

His much younger journeyman assistant was even worse. No unobtrusive cloth coat for *him*. He was wearing the sort of outfit that blacksmiths wore while working in their shops. And he was just about as big and bulky as any blacksmith Emma had ever seen.

There was even a brazier glowing in a corner. With tongs being heated in it!

Unbelievably, things got worse. The door to the chamber was opened by a soldier, who ushered in the lord of the castle. He was holding something in his hand, but Emma was too preoccupied with the *Freiherr* himself to notice what it was.

Emma stared at him. This was the first good, up-close look she'd had of *Freiherr* Fuchs von Bimbach since her kidnapping.

His appearance was . . . not promising. Bimbach was in his forties, stocky to the point of being overweight, and with a hard and heavy face. Clean-shaven, which made his jowls prominent.

He came right over to her and held up the object in his hand. Now, she saw that it was one of the pieces of Mormon literature she'd hastily stuck into her pocket when she'd been lured away from her stand in Bamberg.

"You are a heretic," von Bimbach stated. "Here is the proof of it. Heresy is a capital crime, and I am charged with enforcing the law. And I have the *Halsgericht*."

Emma rallied her will. "Not the new laws. You can't—"

Von Bimbach slapped her across the face with the booklet.

"You do not have permission to speak."

He moved over to Meyfarth and held the booklet under his nose. "And you! A man who claims to be a Lutheran pastor, no less. You have tolerated this—no, have conspired with her."

Meyfarth said nothing. But he returned the *Freiherr*'s glare without flinching.

After a moment, von Bimbach turned away. The soldier who had ushered him in was still standing at the open door. The *Freiherr* beckoned and the man brought him over a packet. Apparently he'd been carrying it with him.

Von Bimbach went over to a nearby table and spread open the packet. Emma could now see that it contain paper and writing material.

"You will compose a letter to your authorities," von Bimbach stated. "To abuse the term. Both of you. And you will sign it."

"I will not!" Emma hissed. Meyfarth shook his head.

Von Bimbach gave them a long, heavy stare. "Yes, you will."

By now, Emma's fear has been replaced by sheer outrage. "I will not! Go ahead and torture me, if you want to. I still won't!"

The *Freiherr*'s sneer was something out of a lousy movie, too. "Not you, witch. For my negotiations—unfortunately—I shall probably need you and the so-called pastor intact. Still, you will the compose the letter."

He swiveled his head to the soldier again. "Bring in the old woman."

"You promised me they wouldn't hurt her!" Judith Neideckerin shrieked at Noelle, half-rising from the chair in her chambers.

Noelle couldn't meet her eyes, yet. All she could do was stare out of the window.

Another shriek. "Let's kill him! Now!"

"We *can't*," Noelle hissed.

"You have a gun! An up-time gun! Don't lie to me, I know you have it!"

That was finally enough to break Noelle's paralysis. She spun around and faced Judith squarely.

"Yes, I do." She reached into the pocket of her heavy skirt and drew out the Browning automatic. "Here it is. I've got it loaded, too. But does it look like a magic wand to you? It's got less than ten rounds. And they're not very powerful. What we call a .32 caliber."

Hissing, again: "A so-called 'lady's gun,' that Dan Frost thought I could handle better. As slender as I am. Damn him!"

She stuffed the pistol back into the pocket. "But it doesn't matter, Judith. Even if I had a .44 Magnum—and assuming I could handle the great thing—it wouldn't matter. The soldiers are on alert, all over the Schloss."

"The staff—"

Noelle shook her head. "Not now. Not yet. They're not ready to take on the *Freiherr*'s mercenaries, all by themselves. And if they did, they'd probably be beaten down, anyway. Except for the blacksmith and his apprentices—maybe some of the stable hands—they're mostly just clerks and servants."

Judith slumped back into her chair and lowered her head into her hands. Then, started sobbing.

Noelle went over and placed an arm around her shoulder. "I don't think he's planning to kill your mother."

"He's *hurting* her," came the words between the sobs. Then, Judith lowered her hands and stared at the floor through tear-filled eyes.

"For the first time—ever—I wish the swine had sired a child on me. So I could strangle it."

Noelle tightened the arm. "No, Judith. You wouldn't."

After a while, she added: "Just wait. There'll be a time. Soon, I think."

The torturer and his assistant had the old woman strapped into the contrivance that had reminded Emma at first of a very primitive dentist's chair. Except now she could see that it was more like the equipment that hospitals used for women in labor. The pastor's landlady was secured to the wooden base of the horrible thing with a heavy leather belt across her waist. Her hands were immobilized by other straps and her feet had been locked into stirrups.

Her legs were half-spread and bent upward, removing any support. The torturer pushed back the woman's skirt, exposing her left shin.

"Now."

His beefy assistant raised the iron bar in his hands and brought it down. The sound of the breaking bone was quite audible all through the chamber.

"I'll write it! I'll write it!" Emma shouted, her voice so loud it almost drowned the old woman's cry of pain.

Von Bimbach looked at the pastor. Meyfarth swallowed.

"The other leg," the *Freiherr* commanded.

The torturer and his assistant had already moved to the opposite side of the apparatus. Again, the torturer shoved aside the skirt; again, the iron bar came down.

"I'll write it," said Meyfarth. His voice sounded like a croak. Emma could barely hear the words, beneath the screams.

Chapter 15: *"The ram has taken Halsgericht now"*

Bamberg, early September, 1634

"This has to be," Anita Masaniello said, "one of the slimiest letters I have ever read."

"Ah," Constantin Ableidinger answered, "it was written, of course, by Dr. Lenz. 'Pestilenz.' Who delivered it in person."

"At least, apparently, Emma and Meyfarth are alive. And still in fairly good shape, if we can rely on their notes. But I simply cannot believe the sheer *idiocy* of this."

"The *Freiherr* believes, of course, that the location of his Schloss, well within the borders of Bayreuth, immunizes him from all serious danger."

Anita, since coming up to Bamberg the previous month to take charge of connecting the dots between the Thorntons, Meyfarth, the Neidecker woman who had been his landlady, the *Freiherr*, the printer's widow who was the ewe—though not bearing any actual resemblance to the logo of Ewegenia—and who was still, following the city council elections, locked into a battle with the local guild on the topic of forced marriage of said daughter to a candidate of its choice, and anything else she could put through her analytical techniques, had gotten pretty good at parsing Ableidinger's conversation.

"Believes?"

"Margrave Christian has accepted oaths of allegiance from many of the farmers and townsmen who were previously considered to be the subjects of the lesser nobility within his territories."

"Nice way to put it." She shifted uncomfortably. The theory had been that last month, already, she would be on her way back to Grantville to have the baby at Leahy Medical Center with an up-time doctor doing the honors for the Salatto blessed event. Then Ableidinger showed up in Würzburg. Plus a sudden SOS from the Fulda people that drew off a half dozen of the Würzburg staff.

She looked down at her stomach. If they didn't make progress about getting Emma and Meyfarth back pretty soon, she was going to have the baby in the Bamberg headquarters of the Franconian administration. Probably behind her desk; then pick herself up like a pioneer woman and go back to negotiating. Von Bimbach was demanding that they barbecue the ram. Not just Brillo. He wanted to fill Franconia with roast mutton.

"So he wants to parley."

"The *Freiherr* says that he is willing to return them unharmed. On reasonable terms. Reasonable from his perspective. And parley only under the conditions that he set."

Anita picked up the letter again. By one corner, carefully, between thumb and forefinger. "Why me? Why not you, Vince?

The question was reasonable enough. Vince Marcantonio was the Franconian administration's head in Bamberg. He should have been prestigious enough for any *Freiherr* to meet with.

Vince Marcantonio looked a little abashed. "Previous intemperate statements about what I would do to the certain parts of the man's anatomy if I ever caught him, I'm afraid. Wade Jackson said worse. We were more than a little pissed that he plucked them out right from under our noses. And a reporter overheard us."

"Curses. I suppose that Cliff Priest can't possibly get back here, and then up to Bayreuth, by the deadline this guy has set?"

"Not a prayer."

"Okay, go back to Lenz. Say that I'll go up and talk to the *Freiherr*. Not in his Schloss. No way am I going inside the man's walls, not if I could bring the whole USE army with me, which I can't. Outside. In a field. With a big enough batch of troops along to make a difference.

Tom O'Brien and his pick of the crop. As many as von Bimbach will let him bring."

"And," Constantin Ableidinger said, "stipulate that people have the right to come and watch. Ordinary people. Standing around the edges of the field. Witnesses to make sure that Fuchs von Bimbach attempts no treacherous undertaking. He can hardly object to that."

Enclave within Bayreuth, September, 1634

The negotiations were going well, *Freiherr* von Bimbach thought. The fact that Salatto's heavily pregnant wife had actually appeared reinforced his convictions about the importance of his hostages. Which meant that his strategy was going well. Once she acceded to the demands that Lenz was presenting, he would have humiliated the man, Salatto, doubly by doing it through the woman. Much more effective than dealing with the administrator directly.

Yes, he could afford to be quite intransigent. Require them to give him the ram and the ewe to get the hostages back; send out propaganda proclaiming that this showed how little the USE cared for the Franconians by comparison to his own people, while hanging the rebels. Demonstrate to the Swedes that only he was capable of bringing sanity back to the region.

Lenz thought that he was doing well on the *Freiherr*'s behalf. He had not conceded a single point. All they had to do now was wait for the up-timers to admit that he had won.

Breaking into the torture chamber proved to be as simple as opening the door and walking in. There had been no soldier standing guard, as Noelle had feared there might be. That wasn't really surprising, though. Most if not all of the soldiers still in the Schloss were at the windows on the upper floors, watching the parley taking place on the field beyond the castle.

She took three steps into the room, with Eddie following her.

"Where are they, do you think?" She looked around the large empty room. There was nothing here that even vaguely resembled "cells." In fact, to her surprise, the chamber had very little resemblance to what she'd thought a "dungeon" would look like. It was more like a half-basement a man might devote to a workshop.

It was not gloomy at all. There was a bright sun outside, and plenty of light came through the windows near the ceiling.

Before Eddie could reply, Noelle got her answer. The door opposite the one she and Eddie had entered swung open. A middle-aged man came though, followed by a very big younger one.

"What are you doing here?" the man demanded. "Get out!"

Noelle pulled out her pistol. "I want the prisoners. Now."

The man gaped at her, for a moment. Then shouted: "Seize her, Johannes!"

The big assistant came around and moved toward her. Noelle brought up the gun. Before she could aim it, Eddie grabbed her by the shoulders and swung her aside. Then, lunged at the assistant.

A moment later, the two men were grappling. Noelle stepped to the side. The older man—the castle's executioner and torturer, she assumed—was just staring at her. He was not more than fifteen feet away.

Weeks of tightly repressed fury boiled to the surface. She raised the gun, grabbed it with both hands as Dan Frost had taught her, and fired.

Four times. Ricochets zinged from the stone walls, causing her to duck frantically.

When she looked up, she saw the executioner running out the door he'd come in through.

She'd missed. All four shots!

A heavy weight hammered into her, knocking her down. On her knees, gasping from the shock, Noelle looked up and saw that she'd been accidentally slammed into by Eddie and his opponent, as they wrestled fiercely.

Eddie was losing the match. Pretty badly. He was a big enough young man, and stronger than he looked. But he was simply overmatched by his opponent.

As she watched, the torturer's assistant swung Eddie around and slammed him against some sort of huge, horrid-looking chair. The impact caused Eddie to lose his grip on the man's arms. A moment later, the torturer had him by the throat and was starting to choke him. Bent backward over the chair the way he was, Eddie had little leverage. His hands scrabbled helplessly at his strangler's thick arms.

Noelle lunged to her feet and strode over.

She couldn't afford to miss again, and she certainly didn't trust her marksmanship. But how—

She saw an opening and thrust the pistol under the torturer's right arm. Under, and up against his chin, below the jaw. As soon as she felt the heavy flesh yielding beneath the barrel, she fired.

The torturer flung his arms aside, and stumbled back from Eddie. Blood was gushing everywhere. He smashed against a wall and collapsed to the floor, his back propped against the stonework and his head hanging loosely.

Noelle thought he was already dead. He certainly looked like it. But as big and strong as he was, she didn't dare take a chance. She stepped forward and shoved the barrel against the top of his head. Pulled the trigger.

Click.

Nothing. The gun had misfired.

It wasn't supposed to do that!

As much angry as confused, she stared down at the weapon in her hand. Then, hearing a grunt, turned her head.

Eddie had straightened up from the chair and was rubbing his throat with his hands. There were already bruises forming there. His eyes were wide open. He tried to speak, but couldn't. Just swallowed, before removing one hand and pointing to something on the floor.

Noelle looked down and saw the magazine of a pistol lying on the floor; one cartridge was sticking straight up from the lips. Startled, she looked down at the gun in her hand. Sure enough, the magazine was missing.

What—

Belatedly, she remembered. Dan Frost had warned her once against firing the gun pressed directly against a body. That might produce too much pressure in the chamber, he'd said. The bullet would fire, but it might damage the gun.

Apparently, it had blown out the whole magazine.

She stooped, picked it up, and looked at it. It *seemed* undamaged, at least; she thumbed the top cartridge back in place.

But would the gun still work?

There was only one way to find out. Which she needed to, since she might very well need to use the gun again. She shoved the magazine back into the pistol and pulled the slide. Then, looked around for a suitable target.

There wasn't any, that didn't risk another ricochet. Except . . .

The body of the torturer slid from wall. The sound drew her eyes. She saw that from a half-sitting position, it had gone to being sprawled across the floor. The man's eyes were half-open, staring emptily. There was still blood spilling out from the gaping wound, but it was no longer spurting. The man's heart had stopped.

Not surprisingly, she realized. Even with a .32 caliber, that shot must have scrambled half his brains.

She looked over at Eddie. He shrugged.

Noelle turned, raised the gun, aimed it carefully with both hands at the center mass of the torturer's body. The target wasn't more than six or seven feet away. She pulled the trigger.

The gun worked, sure enough. But she missed again. Another ricochet zinging all over the stonewalled chamber had her and Eddie down on the floor.

When she looked up, Eddie even managed a laugh.

"Okay, fine," she snarled. "So I'm not Annie Oakley."

Eddie had read a lot of up-time books, in the three years since the Ring of Fire. "Sure aren't," he croaked. "But you do a pretty good imitation of Calamity Jane."

Anita asked herself whether Lenz was actually insane? Or his master was insane? There was no way that Gustavus Adolphus would ever place *Freiherr* von Bimbach in charge of Franconia!

No sooner had Noelle and Eddie gotten to their feet than a small group of men came into the chamber from the main entrance she'd used to enter. She was relieved to see that it was the blacksmith and three of his journeymen.

"You are not hurt?" he asked. She shook her head.

He looked over at the body of the torturer's assistant. "Saved us some work, I see. Very good. Where is the swine himself? And the prisoners?"

She shook her head again. "I don't know where the prisoners are." She pointed at the still-open door through which the torturer had fled. "He ran through there."

The blacksmith headed for the door.

"Be careful," Noelle cautioned. "I missed, when I shot at him."

The blacksmith's answering grunt made it crystal clear that he was not especially worried. Given his own size, and that of the three journeymen following him, that wasn't perhaps surprising. Especially since all four of them were carrying heavy hammers.

A few seconds later, she heard him call out. "In here, Fräulein Murphy!"

When she passed through the door, with Eddie on her heels, she found herself in a corridor. Several heavy doors lined it on the left. Finally, something that looked like it was supposed to! Those were cell doors, she was quite sure. Leaving aside their heavy look, the hinges faced into the corridor.

But she didn't give them more than a glance. Her eyes were drawn to the figure sitting against the far wall, over whom the blacksmith and his journeymen were hovering.

It was the torturer. He was moaning, and had his hands clasped over the ribs on his right side.

"Apparently you did not miss with one of the bullets, Fräulein," the blacksmith said cheerfully.

He reached down, seized the torturer by the scruff of his coat, and jerked him roughly to his feet.

"Up, swine. I have business with you."

The torturer shrieked. The blacksmith ignored him, turning instead to one of his journeymen. "Start prying the hinges off the doors, Hans. Easier than trying to break the locks."

The younger blacksmith nodded.

"You have a chisel with you? If not, you can use mine. When I'm done with it."

The journeyman reached into the big pouch on his work belt and drew forth a heavy chisel.

"Good," the blacksmith said. "Mine might be a bit slippery."

He moved toward Noelle, hauling the torturer with him. "Come with me, Dieter and Axel. You can help Hans in a moment. Please be so good as to stand aside, Fräulein."

She and Eddie stepped away from the door. After the blacksmith and his two assistants passed through, they followed.

"This will do," the blacksmith said. He slammed the torturer against the heavy chair. The man groaned again.

"Grab his hair, Dieter. Axel, press his head against the wood. I want the neck braced."

Before Noelle could quite grasp what they were doing, the two journeymen had the torturer's head and neck pinned against one of the thick wooden legs of the chair. The blacksmith drew out a chisel. It was very big, perhaps an inch and half across the blade.

He placed the chisel firmly against the man's neck. Right against the spine. Then, lifted his hammer.

"Jesus," Noelle whispered.

The blow was hard, sure, craftsmanlike. The torturer jerked once. Then his body became slack. The unmistakable stench of urine and feces filled the air.

The two journeymen let the body slide to the floor. The blacksmith stooped and took the time to wipe off the chisel blade on the dead man's coat, before rising to his feet.

The look he gave Noelle seemed as hard and solid as the metal he worked with. "The ram has taken *Halsgericht* now. This swine"—he gestured with the hammer—"once executed one of my apprentices. For a theft so petty he should not have been more than flogged."

All Noelle could do was nod. Looking down, she saw that she still had the pistol in her hand. She'd forgotten all about the gun, and the fact that it was still armed and cocked.

Dan Frost would have words to say about that, if he ever found out. Carefully, Noelle disarmed the weapon.

By the time she was done, she heard familiar voices in the corridor. Then Emma and Meyfarth were coming through, and she was able to shake off the horror of the past minutes.

"You're all right?"

Emma nodded, as did the pastor.

Noelle turned back to the blacksmith. "What's happening in the rest of the castle?"

The blacksmith grinned. "*Die Neideckerin* has everything well in hand. The Schloss now belongs to the ram."

"The soldiers?"

Amazingly, the grin widened. "*Die Neideckerin* reminded them of what happened at Mitwitz. At some length. I do not foresee any problems."

Fuchs von Bimbach noticed that at the edges of the field, some of the people in the crowd were beginning to move, turn their heads.

No danger, though, he was sure. There couldn't be. Margrave Christian's troops were here—a guarantor that the up-timers would not be sending any more men through Bayreuth than the number to which von Bimbach had agreed. In any case, people were looking toward the Schloss, not away from it. Pride prevented him from turning his head around.

The captain of von Bimbach's mercenaries did look around. There was chaos at the castle gate. Not people trying to force their way in.

People trying to force their way out, it looked like. He was dismounted; someone had led his horse back to the paddock area. He started to run, clumsy in his high-heeled riding boots on the dry hummocks of sheep-grazed grass.

Ableidinger smiled. The gawkers and onlookers at that end of the field were breaking toward the castle gate, far faster than the captain was moving. Meeting the party that was forcing it way out. Fifteen to twenty people there, if they hadn't lost anyone when the servants and staff seized the castle. Not experienced fighters, any of them; mostly women. But it hardly mattered, as Ableidinger had known it wouldn't— especially with that somewhat peculiar but very capable and determined young American woman set loose in their midst.

It could not have been that hard, really. The *Freiherr* was not the world's most popular employer. Sixty-three points still held the record for specific grievances from any Franconian lord's subjects, as far as he was aware.

Ableidinger would have liked to run toward the castle also, but he had to be a model of discipline. He held himself steady. Wearing up-time clothing, hair short, closely shaved, inconspicuous within the small knot of officials behind Anita Masaniello's chair.

There was a ring of his people, now, around those who had come out of the castle.

About half the onlookers were running away. Uninvolved. Real spectators. Prudent people. The rest, his own, were starting to turn toward the end of the field behind him.

Yes. The right livery. Margrave Christian's men. Reinforcing the few troops of the Franconian administrators; interposing themselves between von Bimbach's mercenaries and the up-timers; ringing the party coming out from the castle, a second defensive perimeter around the people in the center.

Von Bimbach had risen from his camp chair, drawn his sword; one of the margrave's men was on him, too, holding a pistol, telling him to sit back down; two more of the margrave's men there, standing at that side of the table.

No shots, so far. No blood.

The party from the castle reached the table. Frau Thornton and Herr Pastor Meyfarth, on their own feet. Frau Masaniello, Salatto's wife, running to embrace them. Herr Thornton following her. Two menservants, liveried, their hands crossed to make a chair, carrying an old woman. *Die Neideckerin*. Both of her legs splinted. The up-time EMT, the *medic* they called him, running to her.

A well-dressed woman; far too well-dressed to be a servant. The *Freiherr*'s mistress, then. Sent from Bamberg to his estates, six years ago, for safety. The old woman's daughter. Von Bimbach's leverage against *die Neideckerin*. Holding a copy of *Robert's Rules of Order* in one hand; a book in the other. *The Book of Mormon*. Judith Neidecker had not been so cowed as to accept her mother's abduction and torture meekly. With Fräulein Murphy, she had organized the servants; even, according to the Fräulein, had said that if the ram would send her an ice pick, she would save them all a lot of trouble by putting it through the *Freiherr*'s eardrum and into his brain while he snored.

Ableidinger shivered. The female of the species. Martha Kronacher, who now seemed to consider Pastor Meyfarth to be her property. Ableidinger smiled to himself; Meyfarth had not noticed yet. His own deceased wife. Every man would do well to remember that his wife was one of them. Judith Neideckerin. Judith with the head of Holofernes.

The medic, Matewski was his name, put *die Neideckerin* on the table; Anita Masaniello sat down again.

The captain of the *Freiherr*'s mercenaries, still running towards the castle, caught his spur in one of the hummocks of sheep-gnawed grass, stumbled, fell on his face.

Ableidinger laughed, a booming laugh heard all across the field. Tensions dropped a notch. Except for Dr. Lenz, who jerked up from his chair. He had been sitting, frozen, through it all. Two of the margrave's troops grasped his arms, held him down.

Anita stood up.

"What should we do with him?" one of the troopers asked her. "Hand him over to you up-timers?"

"Not," Ableidinger said, moving out from the knot of officials. "Not quite yet. There is something that I need to do. Or want to do." He stood there, as if thinking.

Anita sat back down.

Ableidinger beckoned. "Bring him here."

The margrave's men handed the lawyer over to two *Jaeger* who were wearing the ram badge on their armbands. One of them was Gerhardt Jost.

*   *   *

Tom O'Brien, in charge of the USE/SoTF troops on the field, held his breath.

Ableidinger laughed again. It didn't seem to make Lenz feel any better.

Ableidinger's voice. That booming voice, everyone could hear it. "Ladies and gentlemen!"

O'Brien let his breath out.

"I shouldn't do this, I suppose. But then, I am not a gentleman, anymore than Brillo is a gentleman. Am I?"

The onlookers roared their approval from the edges of the field.

"I present to you! The man who chaired the commission that expelled me from the law school at the University of Jena. Because I had married my late wife rather than leaving her to have our son by herself." Ableidinger put his arm around a boy who had run to him from among the spectators.

Another roar.

"I have wanted to do this ever since." Ableidinger walked up to Lenz, paused an arm's length away, reached out, and twisted his nose. Very hard. It started to bleed.

The crowd loved it.

The voice again. "I probably shouldn't do this, bad for my dignity and prestige you know, and not suitable to a leader. But I've wanted to do it for so long. And I'm a scroungy down-time ram you know, no aristocrat."

Ableidinger turned around, dropped his pants, and mooned Lenz. Including an audible fart.

"All right. Now they can have him. Due process and all that. Give him to the proper authorities."

The crowd went wild.

Tom O'Brien's shoulders sagged a little with relief. Too soon. Anita was saying something.

"Matewski, if you're about finished with Frau Neidecker's legs? Could you scour off the table? This isn't going to take very long, I think. It's my third. And no way am I going inside that castle."

Chapter 16: *"Now you're scaring me to death"*

Würzburg, September, 1634

Steve Salatto would have liked to hang them all from the nearest tree. Friends as well as foes. However, he had Anita back safe; baby Diana, too. She had fuzzy hair.

The commander of the regiment that Gustavus Adolphus had sent down to Franconia had offered to blast von Bimbach's castle into rubble and eradicate the whole family. Steve had thanked him kindly, but said that it wouldn't be necessary.

It wasn't. Margrave Christian had already taken care of the "blasting into rubble" bit and had escheated the *Freiherr*'s Bayreuth estates to himself. The *Freiherr*'s relatives had run off to Saxony. As for the lands in Bamberg, Steve told Cliff Priest just to occupy the administration building—it wasn't a fortified castle—and told Vince Marcantonio to escheat the estates to the SoTF and have Stewart Hawker and his folks arrange some equitable lease arrangements for von Bimbach's tenants and submit them for approval.

"As for the final disposition of the individuals involved, leave it up to the courts." It hurt to say it, when he would have liked to squash the *Freiherr* like a cockroach, but he managed.

Scott Blackwell had some difficulty in getting the mercenary commander to swallow those orders. But he managed, too.

491

*   *   *

Ed Piazza and Arnold Bellamy looked at Steve's final—or, if not final, at least most recent—report on Franconia.

" 'Sorry about all the publicity'!" Ed exploded. "*Sorry about it?* It's some of the best we've had all year!"

"Professional civil servants don't see things quite the same way you do," Arnold said apologetically. "They're temperamentally inclined to work behind the scenes. And it *was* his wife who had a baby in the presence of a couple of thousand spectators. I can understand how he feels. I would have been very embarrassed if Natalie had ever done such a thing."

He pointed to the rest of the papers on Ed's desk. "You'll find a draft of our proposal to Congress enclosed. In brief, our recommendation is that the SoTF Congress just scoop up all of the little *Reichsritterschaften* and petty lordships in Franconia and incorporate them. Not confiscate the property from the owners, mind you; just end their jurisdictional authority over their so-called subjects who are now our citizens. The people in general voted for incorporation. If you want to, I suppose, we could do an individual referendum in each of them, but I don't think it's necessary."

Ed looked up. "Will the Congress go for that? Especially the House of Lords?"

Arnold nodded. "I think so. Most of the lower house of the Congress consists of commoners who have been angry at these petty lordships for centuries. And the larger rulers in the House of Lords, the counts and such, have been annoyed by them for just as long. It's one of the few topics on which the commoners and upper nobility are in harmonious agreement. Both of them think that the quasi-independent lower nobility are big pests and a plague on the landscape. It goes right back to the days when the Swabian League went on a campaign to wipe out as many of the robber barons as it could lay hands on. That's more than a century ago. Plus, it also fits well into the national project of abolishing internal tolls and tariffs. I think it will be safe to present it. Especially if you go on to the next item."

Ed read on.

"If the SoTF congress agrees to this, just incorporating them as we propose without any further fuss and feathers, then Margrave Christian of Bayreuth, upon behalf of himself and his nephews, will petition for admission into the State of Thuringia-Franconia on the same terms as the other of its counties and with a seat for each of the principalities in the SoTF House of Lords. The only special point he will be making is that he wants the approval of Congress to do unto the *Reichsritter* and petty lords who have enclaves within his and his nephews' territories just what we are proposing to do unto them in Würzburg, Bamberg, and Fulda."

Ed frowned. "Does the margrave actually mean this?"

"I think so. Informally, apparently, he has already taken oaths of allegiance from a lot of their subjects. Backed up by the ram. Given the geography of Franconia, he'll be a lot stronger if he can manage that. He'll have us as a buffer between him and Gustavus Adolphus when the crowd of the dispossessed start spewing petitions and law-suits like a volcano. For that matter, he will have our military to back up his if they go into revolt. Not that that's very likely, given what happened to Mitwitz and von Bimbach. Apparently, he's willing to accept being, for all practical purposes, a constitutional monarch within Bayreuth County, Thuringia-Franconia, as a reasonable trade-off."

"Is Gustavus Adolphus going to like it? The arrangement he made with Mike, whatever it was, didn't include having us swallow his allies." Ed was sure of that.

"The king, ah, emperor, can't do much about it. Margrave Christian is volunteering. His politics are local; his main interest has always been keeping the war out of Bayreuth. Right now, he sees us as his best bet for doing that. No guarantees that he would continue his allegiance if we fall flat on our faces at some future date, of course. But for right now, I think, our honorable captain general will just have to live with it."

"I'll put the best face on it that I can. Mike should love it, even if he has to keep his own face poker-stiff. Next?"

"All right. Steve's final point. The Nürnberg city council is increas-ingly worried about the quasi-independent status of Nürnberg as an imperial city and an independent state within the USE, separate from Thuringia-Franconia."

Ed raised his eyebrows. "Do they have reason to be?"

Arnold looked at him. "Not right now. After all, Rhode Island managed to survive. It will depend, in the long run, if they're good enough politicians to hang on. If they aren't . . ."

"Speaking of politicians, what's Big Bad Brillo doing at the moment?"

Arnold smiled. It was a rather thin smile. "Running for Congress. He *was* thrown out of law school, you know. What else is left for him, when he isn't organizing a revolution?"

Magdeburg, October, 1634

"I still don't like capital punishment," Mike Stearns said softly, in a tone of voice that was more thoughtful than accusatory. He was standing at the window of the USE prime minister's office, looking out over the Elbe river, his hands clasped behind his back.

"Yes, Michael, I know you don't," came Francisco Nasi's voice from behind him. "But—be honest—that's not so much a moral or religious stance on your part, as it is a matter of . . . I'm not sure what to call it. Class antagonism, perhaps."

Mike considered his words. "I guess that's fair enough. The one thing I always noticed, back in the up-time U.S. of A, starting from when I was a teenager, is that you never saw a rich man on Death Row. Never. Didn't even see 'em serving life sentences that often. So I concluded by the time I was twenty that, once you stripped away all the bullshit, the death penalty was just another way for rich people to kill poor people—and I figured they already had enough ways to do that."

"You can hardly object to this one, then."

Mike turned away from the window and sat back down at his desk. "Well, sure, there's that savage and primitive part of me that's practically howling with glee. Especially since they hung Dr. Lenz along with von Bimbach. Yes, sir. Too bad they didn't shove one of Pestilenz's pamphlets down his throat—the one he wrote about Becky, I mean— before they yanked open the trapdoor."

For a flashing instant, a very fierce grin came and went on his face. Among the many reports that had come to Magdeburg after the Ram Rebellion—as it was now universally being called, across Europe—had been the results of the thorough investigation the authorities of the State of Thuringia-Franconia had made of Dr. Lenz's papers. One of things that had been discovered was that Lenz had been the author of the notorious political pamphlet *Pestis Pontifica, Pestis Judaica*, that had circulated widely in Franconia in the course of 1633. Included in the pamphlet's anti-Semitic and anti-NUS rantings had been some very vile accusations leveled at Mike's wife Rebecca, involving grotesque sexual acts between her and Cardinal Richelieu.

Nasi matched the grin "Indeed. Of course, he was not the only such pamphleteer. And, unfortunately, there was no direct reference in his papers to whichever up-timer fed him the *Protocols of the Elders of Zion*. So that's still to be determined, if it ever is. Nonetheless. He's dead. Along with von Bimbach. And both of them as a result of scrupulously legal—if very quick—judicial proceedings."

"Sure was quick," Mike drawled. "But I imagine the SoTF authorities in charge saw no point in dawdling. Bad idea, that would have been. Might have stirred up the ram again. Speaking of which . . ."

He leaned forward, sifting through the papers. "Remind me. I know it's in here somewhere. Your assessment of Constantin Ableidinger's election chances."

"The details hardly matter." For a moment, Nasi's face held a peculiar expression. *Longing,* you might call it. Mike had seen it several times before. The first time after he'd explained to Francisco the up-time methods of polling voters. Alas, the preconditions for that didn't exist in the seventeenth century. Not yet, at least.

Mike was just as glad, actually. He thought it was a *lot* more interesting to have to use your brains. But it wasn't surprising that Francisco, who doubled as his unofficial political adviser as well as his chief of intelligence, didn't see things the same way.

Nasi sighed, and the look faded from his face. "Never mind the details," he repeated. "Constantin Ableidinger's chances for election range from 'guaranteed' to 'landslide victory.' Probably the latter."

Mike grunted. "Good. Better news, really—much better, in the long run—than His Bimboship and Pestilenz hanging from the neck. I'll be looking forward to meeting him, when he comes to Magdeburg."

Nasi cocked his head a little. "Ah . . . Michael. The general elections for the United States of Europe won't be held until *next* year. Ableidinger is running for one of the new Franconian seats in the congress of the SoTF. He'll be in Grantville, not Magdeburg."

Mike's grin, this time, stayed on his face. "Don't be silly. A man that smart? It's called 'stepping stone,' Francisco. You watch. He'll run in the nationwide election, come next year. And he'll win handily, I bet. I'm expecting Wilhelm Wettin's party to win in the USE as a whole, but I'll be very surprised if Thuringia—and now Franconia, too— doesn't remain one of our bastions."

He rose to his feet and went back to the window. "That means Ableidinger will be here, sometime next year. Like I said, I'm looking forward to meeting him."

Without turning around to see, he added: "You aren't rolling your eyes, I trust?"

"I was thinking about it," Nasi admitted. "The thought of you . . . and Ableidinger . . . A bit frightening, actually."

"Oh, don't be silly. I'll sure we'll get along just fine."

"Yes. As I said. A bit frightening."

Mike laughed. "One thing more. Send Ableidinger a letter asking him to have a tailor take his measurements. He'll need a proper suit, now, and I doubt very much if he owns one. I also doubt if he's got much in the way of money. Leading a revolution's not generally a well-paying proposition."

He swiveled his head, and laughed again. Now, Nasi *was* rolling his eyes.

"Don't tell me," Francisco stated.

"Of course I'm going to tell you. We'll have the suit made here, by my own tailor, and send it to him with my compliments. Best tailor in Magdeburg, probably the whole USE. Make sure you pay for it out of my personal account, though. I wouldn't want any accusations of pilfering official funds for partisan purposes."

Nasi was still staring at the ceiling. "God forbid."

"The ceiling's not that interesting."

"Only because you have—so far—failed to have it plastered with one of those grotesque political paintings."

But he did lower his gaze. "I will say that being in your service is never dull. 'A bit frightening' just went to 'a bit more frightening.' "

"You're being silly, again. But enough on that. Does Noelle Murphy have some free time? I'd like her to come up here again, as soon as possible."

"Now you're scaring me to death."